OF LAVENDER AND ASH

THE ASCENSION RISING SERIES
BOOK 2

K. R. RAINBOLT

Of Lavender and Ash

Book 2 of THE ASCENSION RISING SERIES

Cover design by *Artscandare Book Cover Design*

Editing and Proofing by *Ashley Oliver at Enchanted Author Co.*

ISBN (paperback): 979-8-9863026-2-1

ISBN (ebook): 979-8-9863026-3-8

ASIN: B0BC52XT2M

To my momma. Thank you for always having my back and believing in me when I didn't believe in myself. I love you.

To all the readers out there who just need a second away from the real world, I hope you can find that here.

Authors Note

Hey, all you tortured souls. I'm happy to have you here, and I have a few things to note before you dive in. This is a slow-burn, dark-themed, paranormal, 'why choose' novel. This book and the others in this series contain content that may be triggering to some people. If you think you may need a bit more information on the cautions/triggers of this book, please check my website or Linktree.

Said website: https://krrainbolt.com

Or my Linktree: https://linktr.ee/k.r.rainboltauthor

If you're ever confused about something or just want to know what something means, I've included all translations and general information at the end of the novel. I've also added a list of important characters that were mentioned in book one after this note, so if you're looking for a reminder on who's who, give that a read.

That's all from me! Kick back, relax, and enjoy the read.

Important Characters

Aaliyah — The main character.

Prince — Aaliyah's best friend/first love, also a ghost.

The Vivas Crypt — The main MCs. Vampires from different eras.

Osiris — Also called: Rex interfectorem (Kingslayer).

Eirik — Also called: The Emperor's Shadow.

Adrian — Also called the following: The Collector.

Fallon — No additional nicknames.

Nero — The Vivas Crypt's lost brother.

Eliza Barlow — Aaliyah's friend, the one who is trying to help her figure out who/what she is before Aaliyah meets the boys. She's a Siren.

Dezen Lal — Eliza's husband. He's a Hemomancer.

Carter Halsen — Eliza's husband V2. He's a Dragonkin, and one of the many sons of Eternal Teviticus.

Grigen Barlow — Eliza, Dezen and Carter's young son. Assumed to be a Dragonkin.

Curtis Hadfall — The one who stole Ali off the street to sell her at auction. Also, one of the *many* sons of Teviticus.

Darius Verslini — The owner of *The Devil's Details*. He's a Vampire and the one who officially sold Ali.

Axandre (Xander) — Also called the Keeper; he's a hoarder of information and a Dryad.

Magelav — A Chronomancer that the Vivas Crypt is considering going to for information. Also called The Bog Sorceri.

Archon Sewire — The Djinn Eternal; also speculated to be the one who tipped off Curtis when Ali and Eliza would be going through Century Side.

Ilenia Barlow — The Siren Eternal and grandmother/matriarch to Eliza. Also called baba, and The Red Witch of the Atlantic.

Teviticus Halsen — The Dragonkin Eternal.

Avedal — The Basilisk Eternal, and ally to the Vivas Crypt.

Audric — A Venomcaller tailor, and an ally to the Vivas Crypt.

Sebek Ra — The Vampire Eternal, and Maker of everyone in the Vivas Crypt.

Ascension Rising — Not a person, but the foundation/group that held Aaliyah captive before she escaped.

CHAPTER 1

OSIRIS

He may have turned you, Osiris, but you'll always be mine. Even Sebek knows you make a better pet than a man.

That day, and those abhorrently cruel words, were permanently etched into my memory, trapped in the cracked parts of my mind that I couldn't get rid of. I remembered it so clearly, even now, thousands of years later. Kali, with her disgusted gaze—pointed and cold—to the snarled expression that had twisted her red lips. The way she'd pouted as though someone had stolen her favorite toy.

That *was* what Sebek had done when he'd turned me, wasn't it? Stolen me from them, from Kali and Darius the Great. In a twisted way, despite all the wrongdoing Sebek had done since, I still saw him as my savior for that.

I slid into the house that my brothers and I had made a home with a soundless poise. I kept my head high and eyes forward, never daring to glance toward the red oak kitchen table where I knew Kali to be. The tense slogging weight of a teleportation spell still lingered, telling me she'd likely taken shape from thin air right in the middle of the room. Her power ebbed and breathed, testing the boundaries of our home, smelling of crumbling limestone and potent, ancient magic, a combination that made me ill. I risked grabbing my exposed wrist if only to garner some control and push away the dread that followed her appearance.

"Ah, Osiris. I was wondering when you'd get back. I've been entertaining our *guest*," Adrian said, the strained words drawing my gaze to him.

His eyes weren't on me, the deepened amber never leaving the dining room table. The tenseness in my shoulders dropped a degree when I noted he was shaken but unharmed. I could only imagine how shocked he'd been when she appeared. His smooth smile clashed with the blistering fury in his eyes, but to his credit, he marvelously played calm and well-collected.

He leaned against the island in the middle of the kitchen with his back to the cold black marble and his arms crossed curtly over his chest. His loose white dress shirt was wrinkled and worn, much like his white-speckled black slacks.

He'd obviously been in the middle of making something before Kali's surprise appearance. His confusion, above all else, was what I focused on.

He didn't know the monster that sat at our table, wasn't aware of who she was or what she'd done. That was a mistake that now sat on my shoulders, like the rest. Because why would he need to know about her? She *was* the Sorceri Eternal, but she resided in England, as far from us as possible. I hadn't told them of her threat to us nor shared the details of a past I'd sought to reduce to ashes to even Nero, the brother I'd held closest to my chest before he, too, died of a mistake I made. I'd hidden my human life from my brothers, hid it even from myself, and now it was back from the grave to haunt us.

A shiver shot down my spine as Kali made herself known with a mocking click of her tongue.

"My, *my*. You've really grown into your immortality, Osiris. It looks delectable on you," she hummed, her sweet tone drowning out the echo of our front door closing.

Fallon stalked in, his arms flexed and his hands falling into easy fists that were still marred with blood from whatever bout he had found in Oakridge. Though that splatter didn't reach the crisp white of his suit, he wouldn't have allowed it to. If Fallon was anything, he was particular, and being put together was a form of armor. He stood strong, the endless green of his eyes cold and angry, never losing that tension. It was when he looked at me that the guilt became overwhelming, ripping my insides apart. *I'd* done this, and now I needed to handle it.

I took a settling breath and faced the monster that had taken root in our home. Kali looked exactly as I remembered from all those years ago: blonde hair pulled into a tight ponytail and secured with a thin white bone, flawless porcelain skin, and devious gray eyes that grew ever so entertained when I reached for my wrist again. She wore a tight-fitting lascivious black dress. It drew the eyes exactly as she'd meant it to, its purpose to distract much like her full lips and pointed nails. She'd painted them a rich maroon that reeked of iron, and she flared them like talons, tapping her chin in a way that flashed the savage color.

It took everything in me not to rush forward and rip out her throat, to paint our walls red with her blood and hope it was enough to kill the vile wretch. Instead, after she finished her appraisal, I walked to the table, taking a seat like I was talking to an old friend and not a tormenter. Yet I had to thank whatever brought her here, be it my rotten deeds or merely bad luck ... because at least it wasn't Darius sitting before me.

I could deal with Kali and her twisted smile, her taunts and jeers, but I couldn't handle *Darius the Great* when I was right in the mind, let alone how I was now. For everything Kali did, it was nothing compared to his methods. Darius made sure I understood *he* was in control.

And the thought of his eyes on me? His *hands*?

A tremor worked its way down my spine, and disgust trickled over my nerves as I forced myself to stay still.

"You know, I always did like you in suits; they bring out the *lovely* blues of your eyes," she mused, coyly leaning back in the chair.

My jaw clenched, hating her play on words because she had always found my eyes distasteful. It was *Darius* who loved them, and who grew obsessed with them. He'd killed over them once, when a handmaiden had watched me a little too long, her touch growing just as insistent as his had, her eyes never leaving mine. His hypocrisy was like the dying cry from her lips.

No, Kali had other uses for me, but at the end of the day, I was Darius's. I warmed his bed, as well as any bed he sought fit to loan me to. *Kali* made sure I was broken enough to stay there.

She grinned then, white teeth on full display, and gave a push of magic. It danced along my skin, along my breath and into my lungs. It lured my gifts to the surface, and she clicked her tongue again. "Though, your magic feels rather strained. Have you been ignoring my teachings again?"

Mocking, always mocking. Like she hadn't said the same thing at the last Eternium and the one before that. I'd spent over two thousand years crushing those same gifts under my heel and it still hurt, still scorched me to my core to even hold her gaze.

Ten years. That was all it took. *Ten* years in that prison Darius called a castle, and she had stained my entire existence.

Even thinking of the nights trapped between their sheets, the running leers of those they'd bring to join them. Every touch, every breath, and every rotten word made my skin ache. Made it hard to breathe.

"Quite a surprise to see you here, Kali," I finally said, ignoring her statement altogether, my hands shaking despite my best attempt at keeping my voice even. I didn't take my eyes off her, even as she smirked. "To what do we owe the pleasure?"

She leaned back, watching me for a moment. Each second dragged on, and on, and *on*. She assessed me with the same calculating gaze she had when she'd realized I was gifted with the magic she also wielded. Another toy for her to play with and mold as she saw fit, to distract her from her long life. Toys she could gift to Darius to abuse and molest.

"What, aren't you going to offer me a drink first, before we talk business?" she asked suddenly, with an indignant huff, one that was followed by a flashy flip of her hair as she raised an eyebrow. "I've had quite a long trip, coming all this way to see you, Osiris. You aren't being a very accommodating host."

Kali knew exactly where to hit to make rage bubble up in my stomach. It clashed so headily with the panic that came with her arrival that I struggled to find the proper words to say. They caught in my throat, drowned out by the thought of punishment that I would no longer receive. My hand went to my shirt cuff on instinct.

She saw the move, eyes widening with sickening glee.

"I'm in no mood for games. Talk," I said through clenched teeth. Another mistake.

She grinned and turned her gaze to Adrian, then Fallon. My brothers, the family that I'd sworn to protect, now stood firm in the face of a threat they couldn't begin to understand. The slow drag of her wandering gaze was pointed and meaningful, eyeing them like they were nothing more than meat.

"You must be the newest members of the Vivas Crypt. Adrian and Fallon, wasn't it? You haven't had a proper introduction at an Eternium yet, but I've heard quite wonderful things about you," she said, twirling a stray piece of hair over her thin finger, not bothering to hide the way she licked her lips. "Why don't you tell me about yourselves, or better yet, go get Eirik? Haven't seen him in *ages*."

Soft words that sounded ever so pleasant. To most, they would have seemed polite, even kind. I knew better. One glance, and I knew she had something else up her sleeve. She was well aware I didn't want to speak with her and had to know that whatever she had to say would be denied. She and

Darius had lost their power over me when I became a spawn of Sebek Ra. It was one of the few good things I had gained from my death: immunity from *them*.

I tensed when she glanced at the stairs again, a mocking smirk taking over her expression ...

No.

I snapped to my feet, barely biting back my snarl as she spoke. "And also that little thing he has with him."

Aaliyah. Her soft heartbeat echoed in my ears, suddenly drowning out everything else. *Aaliyah* was upstairs, the woman we'd taken into our home, the one who made it *feel* like home again. The one person on this entire rotten planet that I wanted to touch ... and Kali knew about her.

Sought to threaten the little *lux* to get her way.

With my hands clenched onto the table, I leaned forward, sparks of fire bouncing along my skin as the *Flame* roared to life in my blood. I jolted at the power of it, flinching even though it wasn't the magic of my human life. It didn't matter that it was a gift I had made mine long ago; it was magic all the same. The *Flame* was unbearably cold compared to the burn that was my human power. Wrong, in some ways. Our line had always held the gift of fire, Sebek's own Maker having passed it to him before it eventually came to us. Just like my gift of the Echomancer lived in me after my turn.

I hated it, hated the reminder like I loathed Kali's twisted red *fucking* lips.

"Enough, Kali," I said through clenched teeth.

Adrian sank into the counter, my *Charm* unraveling around us with enough force to knock most off their feet. *Most.*

Kali leaned over the table, unperturbed as she set her chin in her open palm, trailing a pointed nail over the polished red wood of our table. I jerked again, eyes on the small indent she caused in the sturdy red oak.

"I can practically feel her around your home, you know. If I hadn't known any better, I would have sworn *he* turned her," she said.

The tap of her nails against the table, Adrian's harsh inhale, and Fallon taking a step forward with the creak of old floorboards under his feet. Even the dual heartbeats that fluttered wildly above us. It was all too much, and my hands twitched against the table, the strain in every inch of my body burrowed in my bones. I didn't break under her continual gaze, refusing to give her another reaction even as every atom in me begged me to fall to my knees. She didn't allow me a reprieve, barely sparing me a moment to breathe before she continued to speak.

"But your Maker has never been one for turning women, has he, Osiris? Does he know about her then?" Her tone, coated in a black sludge of deceit and wicked cruelty, was the final straw.

I slammed my mouth closed, the crack of my teeth echoing in my ears. No. *No.* He didn't know about Aaliyah. He would *never* know about her. Sebek wasn't one to let his name be sullied; to show weakness was to be already as good as dead. And that was exactly what he'd see in Aaliyah. *Weakness.*

Kali's eyes shimmered, and she showed her cards without care because she knew she had me. She could tell Sebek about Aaliyah, and who knew how the beast would react?

I'd been a fool and forgotten so much over the last few weeks that I was sickened by myself. But it was worse than that. I had forgotten so much over the past *decades* since Nero's death. I should have stopped this, should have known to up our wards, increase security and make sure something like this couldn't happen. I knew the risks and had blindly trusted the strength I'd gained in my centuries of life.

I'd thought myself impervious. Untouchable. Yet here I was, staring at the monster of my human years without Nero by my side to help guide me, as Fallon and Adrian looked at me to fix the problem, fearful gazes wavering. *I* should have protected us better ...

But I didn't. I'd let this monster into our home, and I failed us, just like Nero all over again.

A red sheen covered my eyes, and my fangs dropped, piercing my lip as I snarled. *Another* mistake. But I couldn't hold it back. How fucking *dare* she threaten those in my home, those *I* protected?

And how dare I let her?

"You will not speak of her, Kali. Of them!" My *Charm* ate at the air, coating it like a thick fog, and Kali's eyes widened as the weight of my age sank through some of her senses. She was older than most, nearing even Sebek, but I had garnered enough power to make her question herself. A flare of magic, one that wasn't the *Flame* ... It twisted at my insides, making me feel far more human than I was comfortable with. It scattered across my nerves like I had set my hand on a live wire. "You'd do well to remember whose home you're in."

Adrian became rigid, taking a step back to get further away from me as my *Charm* truly spiraled out of control. Fallon sank into the seat to my left, a strangled breath the only sign that he endured the weight of it.

As quickly as the fear had sparked over her eyes, it faded, and Kali purred.

"Oh, so protective." She reached her hand up, unbothered by the unintended *Charm* that still toppled my brothers.

Her hand skimmed across my cheek, and I couldn't stop the shiver of revulsion. The lust that crawled through her eyes confirmed what I already knew: that she liked watching me squirm. I froze as her pointed nails traveled across my skin, leaving loathing in their wake.

"Now come, Osiris. We taught you better manners than this. I was just asking, making conversation," Kali drawled admonishingly, walking her fingers along my arm, pulling back the white undershirt that I had left in tatters, exposing that harsh black tattoo that Darius had commissioned shortly after my introduction to his harem. "I thought we culled that temper of yours, so volatile."

She touched it gently, reverently. It was wrapped around my wrist, beautiful in its design to all those who didn't know of Darius or his brand.

"I have no words for you, Kali," I seethed, my jaw set. "Stop your games and tell me why you're here."

A delighted expression lit up her face, and she laid her hand palm down against my wrist. I flinched away from her, suddenly the feeling of her skin making me so sick I nearly lost what little I had in my stomach. The need to flee suffocated me, and the room appeared to shrink, everything getting louder, more *jarring*. My mind focused on the shuffle above us, the beat of dual heartbeats, and the subtle scent of lavender.

It reminded me of what was at stake, of the lives that depended on my response.

I pushed past the disgust as I grabbed Kali's wrist, a surprised noise falling from her lips as I squeezed it roughly, my ungloved hand trembling but unrelenting as I spoke.

"Either tell me why you're here or don't. I don't particularly care which," I hissed, narrowly keeping a spark of my *Charm* from slithering out with the words.

Her expression fell for only a moment, a blip that most wouldn't catch as her jaw tightened in anger when I didn't fall before her as she expected. I squeezed again, watching her face twist in pain and surprise before I dropped her hand like hot coals, the sound of it hitting the table echoing.

"Then get out of my house."

She rolled her eyes, agitation slowly building in the gray depths. I didn't miss the sharpening of her face, her beautiful façade falling away as her mood soured.

"Temper, temper. I've come to give you *good* news, Osiris," she said, laughing coldly when I twitched. "Darius, in all his wisdom, has graciously backed your Challenge at the Eternium when you pose one. I will as well, of course."

Challenge? She stormed my home, broke our wards, and threatened my family ... over a *Challenge* I'd never intended to make? The Eternium was a lawless place filled with people that would tell you they knew the law. And the Eternals were nothing more than spoiled, ageless beasts who thought they were better than the rest of us. Brought to power because they thought they possessed power.

If I thought for even a second that Sebek wouldn't punish us for not making an appearance, then we wouldn't be going at all. Sebek could gut me where I stood without so much as a sneer. Challenging him for the title of Vampire Eternal was a last resort and a *death wish*. She knew this.

Yet she believed she could push me to do it anyway.

"I have no wish to be the Vampire Eternal," I seethed, raising my head to meet her eyes. "You have overstayed your welcome. *Leave.*"

I pushed as much *Charm* into the words as I could muster. Even then, the power of my voice lurched and hesitated. And the switch in Kali was instant, gray eyes going completely white as her face shifted the rest of the way, mouth becoming too large, teeth extending and sharpening into fine points. She'd never taken well to being disobeyed, and I knew the signs of her encroaching punishments. She was an Echomancer, someone who dealt in dark magic, with the ability to dip her hands in each differing pool. Hemomancy, Chronomancy, Forgemancy. I knew its pull well because I felt it too, but before I could react and stop whatever she had planned, she reached out, snapping her fingers.

A cry, one that was choked and broken as Adrian fell to the floor. I jerked, the noise so visceral and raw that it sounded more like a wounded animal than my brother. A chill, one that I was intimately familiar with, stuck to the air like tar and sank bone deep as Kali's binding spell held me in place. I could only stare at where Adrian had crumpled, curled into a ball, pain keeping even his voice silent.

No. *No.*

"Adrian!" Fallon screamed, rushing to his side just as Kali tsked, shaking her head.

She stood, the tap of pointed heels against the ground making familiar clicks. She took small steps as she walked around the table; slow, measured.

The room faded away, even as I screamed at myself, even as I tried to force Adrian to stay in my line of sight. The home that I took comfort in slipped away from me, cracking until all I saw was Kali in that cursed room that haunted my nightmares. Red walls, concrete floor, and the horrendous *click* of her fucking heels.

"You've forgotten much, Osiris," Kali admonished, the crack of her teeth clashing breaking up each syllable.

"You raging bitch!" The snarled words, so sharply said, were coated in ice as Fallon shot to his feet. "What the fuck did you do to Adrian?"

How long have I been tied to the bed? Why is Fallon here?

"Pity." Another snap, one that shattered the red walls.

I blinked lazily as the numbness truly sank in. This time it was Fallon, *Fallon* who fell to the floor with surprised horror sparking in his eyes as the crack of blood magic forced him to his knees. It showed in his veins as they flared to the surface of his skin, a streak of red sliding from his nose.

Kali clicked her tongue again, "You are an insolent pet, Osiris. You may have garnered temporary freedom being a turned of *Death's Butcher*, but you've *never* stopped being mine."

I snapped my jaw shut, forcing a snarl even as the movement sent waves of pain down my spine. Then the fire came like someone had replaced my blood with gasoline and lit a match inside me. She rolled her eyes, shrugging her shoulders like I was an impudent child.

"*I'll kill you for this.*" Fallon's words cut through the air, twisting and garbled as agony ravaged his body.

He spoke Nimanburru, the tongue of his childhood, likely the only one he could manage as his eyes fell closed and his body convulsed. From the surprise in her eyes, I doubted she was expecting him to be able to speak.

It surprised me he could. I couldn't even *think* of speaking. The burn was so thorough I knew I'd feel it for weeks. But Fallon had always been strong in ways that I wasn't. He was brave in the face of any fight.

But he didn't *know*.

None of them knew what had happened before my turn. Not Eirik. Even Nero only got bits. Kali tapped her finger again, the sound reverberating in my skull, reminding me of the sickening sensation of skin against mine.

Be a good pet.

I was going to be sick.

"You know, I thought you'd be warmer after all the fun we had, Osiris." She let loose a disappointed sigh, like it was *my* fault. "And I was so excited when Darius asked me to pay you a visit."

Her narrowed eyes told me this was exactly what she wanted. To see me like this, again torn low. Kali smirked at me, picking apart the panic that she saw creeping below the surface of my skin.

And I hated her all the more for it.

"Let." Her eyebrow rose as the word struggled past my aching vocal cords. "Them." Another push. "Go."

She leaned in, so close her breath brushed across my cheek.

"Not if you can't ask nicely." She picked at her nails, flicking a disinterested leer at Fallon and Adrian. When I didn't respond, she lifted her hand, pressing her palm slowly down through the air like she was forcing it through oil. Adrian and Fallon choked, strangled cries becoming louder. Louder and *louder*. "Apologize, pet. And I'll consider your request."

My breathing stopped, and saliva flooded my mouth as I grew sick to my stomach in a way that overshadowed even the pain. Pet ... I wasn't hers anymore. So why did one word burrow deeper than any blade?

How did this go so wrong?

"Please." The word burned in my throat.

Kali shook her head just before a cold tongue trailed its way across my cheek.

"What was that? I didn't hear you?" she whispered into my ear, and the dreadful realization of what she wanted broke down what had been left of my will.

My eyes jerked to the stairs, past her. She left them visible for a reason. She was showing her power, showing what else she could do.

Showing who else she could hurt.

Even Sebek knows you make a better pet than a man.

"Please," I said again, looking at the ground. The crack in my chest grew into a chasm, and my soul spilled onto the floor around me. "Master Kali."

My wrists burned, but it was no surprise. The ache there hurt even worse than the shredding of my veins as her magic turned my blood against me, boiling me from the inside out.

She nodded affectionately before pulling back. I hated that the pain faded, leaving me feeling alone in a room full of people. Fallon and Adrian slumped to the floor, gasping for breath as I fought to stay standing.

"Was that so hard?" she asked, patting me on the cheek in a goading manner. I still couldn't move, not that I had any desire to. "Now, before you so rudely cut me off. I've come to *warn* you, Osiris. Your Maker has gone bloodthirsty. Even more so than usual. There's reason to believe he's taken part in the recent deaths of the Titan and Gargoyle Eternals. And there's been talk of your Challenge, talk of you. *All of you.* You need to take him out before he becomes even more of a problem."

I froze where I stood, hating that hearing her words had such an effect on me. We'd heard of the recent deaths before we'd gone to the auction that had led us to Aaliyah. But for *him* to be the reason for it? It didn't make any sense; it wasn't strategic in the way that I knew Sebek to be.

But I knew the fear in Kali's eyes, and that worried me. We knew it was likely that he had been monitoring us, but from the way she spoke ...

No. He wouldn't actually cull all of us. We were his blood, and as broken and jagged as our bond was ... we were *his.* Not even Sebek would kill his entire line. Me, maybe. But the rest?

There was no way he had gone that mad.

"Darius heard it himself, Osiris. *He* hopes to rid his throne of competitors, and soon."

Silence followed, the creeping kind, the kind that ate at your nerves before Kali flicked her hair back and hummed.

"You *will* Challenge him. You have to, Darius has demanded it," she said, shrugging her shoulders and moving forward with a seductive sway. "Well, that's all I had."

She pressed her hand to my chest, wanting a reaction out of me, but there was none left to give as the numbness sank past even the disgust.

"I will want to be meeting the others at the ball, properly. So make sure you all live long enough to be there. The fresh blood..."—she looked at Fallon over her shoulder, that same crawling, scheming look that she had given me—"excites me."

Fallon's newly healed knuckles shook as he bared his teeth at her, fangs already down. Even his patience was gone, his mask of ice cracking in the face of Kali.

Cracking in the face of me.

"Oh, and don't forget to bring that lovely little thing that Eirik's wrapped around." Kali's eyes cleared just as I reached her, and her magic spiked in the air, the tugging pull of Chronomancy as she picked through the memories that our home held. "Aaliyah."

The name was a whisper as she slipped from my hold, and whatever spell she'd uttered made my hands go right through her. She flowed past me like an invasive parasite, the ghost of her lips against my cheek. I swung out, meeting only air, and the caress of words that still made me sick. "Goodbye, pet."

I trembled, and she was gone, the last traces of her magic hovering in the air.

Sulfur and limestone.

Out of our home, leaving only my brothers and I to deal with the carnage.

I may have lost the physical shackles, but the ones she held the reins to, the ones that *Darius the Great* had forged, were still defiantly unbroken. The tension in me snapped, and what started as a snarl morphed into a scream, one that ripped through me like her words.

Fucking. Pet.

"What. The. *Fuck,* was that? Wait, wait. I'd like to change my question," Adrian said, breaking the silence and flinching with his hand to his head. He let out a low groan, his face still twisted in a grimace. "*Who* the fuck was that?"

Adrian pulled himself up to a sitting position, leaning against the black cabinet doors that were under the sink. He huffed a breath, clutching his middle with both arms.

Betrayal. It was clear in his eyes. He was the record keeper, the informant, and the valued Collector. While he may know the general gist of most things in our territory, nothing would have tipped him to investigate Kali.

"I'm not used to being the one out of the loop, Osiris. I need an explanation *now.*"

But it was an explanation I didn't *have.*

"For once, I agree with Adrian," Fallon replied, gripping his throat, his eyes opening.

I didn't miss the way they shut down; mistrust buried so deep that it made my soul ache. It was understandable, a reaction I warranted. I *hadn't* shared Kali, Darius, or anything that happened before Nero. Not even *to* Nero, and I doubted I'd be able to start now, even with the furious accusal in Fallon's eyes. Even with the burn that still lingered in my blood. I couldn't force the words past my lips, their intent trapped in my soul. They hurt too much, and I worried that if I let them out, I'd never seal up the wound they'd leave behind.

"This isn't something you keep in the dark, Osiris." He ground the words out as he walked toward the island, stepping over Adrian's outstretched legs. He crouched down, grabbed a random bottle of blood wine, and poured himself a drink.

"Kali Rourovic is an Echomancer I've known since my human years." Since before them, thousands of years before them. Fallon's head jerked in a nod, and I knew there was no avoiding the truth. "She's the current Sorceri Eternal."

The sound of shattering was hardly surprising. Fallon stood like a stone wall as his face contorted in a rage. Even his eyes flashed red as blood and wine trickled down the wall where his glass had hit, staining the gray a deep ruby.

"An *Eternal*?" he asked, his voice so low and acidic I almost didn't hear it. "I thought we knew of the Eternals to avoid, knew what we needed to do to keep them away from us. Do you mean to tell me that a fucking Eternal that you *knew* was a threat, just strolled into our house? And we're only just learning that this was a possibility now?"

I knew his rage. *Deserved* it, in fact. Kali was an Eternal, one with allies. And not having a discussed plan in place to keep her away was a mistake. I thought the wards were enough, foolishly thinking she'd leave us be because of our Maker.

But now it was too late. She'd been here, threatened us, threatened Aaliyah ... and we couldn't even fight back against her without fear of Retaliation from another Eternal.

From Darius the Great.

Because just like we had the power Challenge them, they could strike back for the senseless killing of their rank. Call for vengeance, *Retaliation*, and force us into a fight we wouldn't win, and Darius the Great wasn't a man you wanted to face in battle. I'd trapped us in this bind, leaving the only one with true power here to be Kali.

Fallon *flitted* toward me, obviously tired of my silence. His closeness, the rage on his face, was too much. I took a step back, grabbing my wrist, unable to silence the words that burned in my skull.

You're mine, pet.

Power, something I had cultivated, grown, and aged over the years of my life, sought to reduce us all to ash. The *Flame* licked along my skin, as it did Fallon's, his own gift reacting to his volatile emotions. My *Charm* was at my vocal cords, and the press of old magic from my years as a human settled in my stomach like lead.

"What the fuck, Osiris? We were completely blind there! Our lives are at stake, and you didn't think this was important enough for us all to know? And now you mean to tell me I can't even kill the bitch for *boiling my fucking blood?*" Fallon screamed the words like I wouldn't hear them, and I nearly didn't.

I gripped my tattered shirt, the frigidness of my skin aching like a roaring inferno. Fallon didn't wait for me to say anything, instead grabbing my suit coat, and I went rigid as his fingers brushed against my skin. Power pulsed again, spreading, consuming. I closed my eyes, fighting the feeling of bloodlust and the fangs that pressed against my gums.

I was frozen, unable to move away. It was my brother in front of me, a member of my family for decades, and it wasn't the first time we had fought. So why couldn't I move?

Weakness, Usire. You have to purge it out. Sebek's warning. The same one he'd given me the night he'd taken my hand for wearing gloves to hide my skin. I hadn't even known if it would grow back then, and I was left staring at the nub in shock as Sebek stalked away, mumbling under his breath about 'insolent children.'

"Say something! For all the meticulous plans you have, how did this somehow slide by?" The pulsing in my mind and the ache in my throat dulled Fallon's screams. "Fucking *say* something. Give me a reason why you didn't tell us!"

That cursed magic dragged up inside me, surging across my vocal cords, blending with my *Charm* and catching me by surprise. It burned, and it nearly tore me apart to hold it back. I tried to focus on Fallon's face. It wasn't Kali in front of me; it wasn't Darius. But the magic didn't realize that. I tried to back up, but the wall behind me was unyielding.

"Calm down, Fally—" Adrian tried, and Fallon flipped his furious face toward him.

His eyes were now fully red in an instant, matching his already dropped fangs.

"No, I will *not* calm down. An Eternal just walked into our house and dropped us like we were nothing but humans. And she threatened us, threatened *Aaliyah*! I have every right to be pissed right now!" Fallon's grip on my suit coat tightened until his hands grew nearly translucent under the pressure. "People who are threats to our Crypt are *need-to-know people*. You risked our safety, our *lives*, by keeping this a secret, Osiris!"

I hated the truth in his words, and the searing pain of my magic became too much to bear.

"You do not know—" I started, and he *screamed*.

It was desperate, hollow, and devastating. I had only heard that sound twice before. Once on the night Nero died. Once the night we'd found him sitting in a pool of blood after his turn.

"Of course, I don't! You don't tell us anything. When we ask you to share your burden, you push us away. You mope, and you wallow, and you *run*. You're a fucking *coward*, Osiris!"

For five hundred years I was alone, five hundred years I tried to forget my human life. It was only when Nero came along that I even thought I might bury it.

And now I risked losing them all.

Coward. Coward. *Coward*.

"That's enough!" A voice, airy but filled with resolve, echoed in the buzzing air.

A warm hand hovered over my chest, and the sweet aroma of lavender grounded me. Aaliyah wedged herself between us, pushing Fallon away with a gentle but insistent hand. She stood there, between two Vampires, with her head held high and not an ounce of fear on her face.

I blinked once, twice. The dimness of the room finally registered, and the soft spark of exposed wires rang in my ears. The air was heavy with the stench of potent magic, *my* magic.

"That's enough." A whisper this time, one that had me sluggishly looking down at the wisp that held us apart. "Look at yourselves! Now isn't the time to fight."

Violet eyes narrowed in stark worry as she glanced between me, Fallon, and Adrian. It was impossible to miss the way her hands shook.

"You're brothers. Family. And the last thing we need right now is for you to rip into each other." There wasn't another moment where I remembered Aaliyah speaking so clearly, so loud. She was soft-spoken but brave, always a guiding hand. To see her stand so unyielding ...

We were monsters. *I* was a monster. And in Fallon's never-short words, a coward. So why did Aaliyah look at me like that? With *light* in her eyes? And why in the hell had she thrown herself between two raging beasts?

She pulled back, just slightly, so her hand was even further from my chest. Her eyes narrowed as she searched my face for any hints of discomfort still buried there. The flowing white of her hair glowed, disheveled from her day. She looked so fragile, tiny between us, and I so desperately wanted to reach out like I had that day at the auction house, to make sure I still marveled at the softness of her skin. But I didn't dare risk it now.

"Osiris?" she whispered, keeping her hand up in its subdued position.

Compassion radiated off of her, the kind that came from knowing about pain. I grabbed my wrist, wishing that the ink there would fade from my skin, that it would stop burning so I could reach forward and grab her hand. I wanted to feel the touch that I didn't deserve yet craved anyway. Right now, even Aaliyah's touch was too much to bear.

Aaliyah's eyes scrunched, and she bit her lip, but her gaze never left mine. I didn't have the words to answer her, nor the affirmation that she was looking for. That I was anything but a shattered man, pretending to be in control. It was a joke, a sham. Kali's appearance proved as much.

I couldn't lie, and I couldn't seem to speak the truth either.

Weakness, Usire. You have to purge it out.

It seemed weakness was all that I was anymore.

CHAPTER 2

AALIYAH

Had I been in this position a few weeks ago—standing between two snarling Vampires with fangs on display and eyes a violent red, with only my hands to hold them back—I would've run away screaming.

But I guess sometime between that fateful day when I'd crawled out of my shallow grave, barely knowing my name, and right now, I stopped being the woman who ran.

Osiris watched me cautiously, and I was struck silent by his deeply soulful eyes: that stunning royal blue and rolling aqua. I recalled how feral they'd been when he'd ripped the heart out of a man for me, how the terror had matched my memories of the compound that had been my childhood. They were eyes I'd once thought to be void and angry ... but now, I wondered how I ever saw them as anything but warm.

Now they were clouded with a numbness with which I was intimately familiar. One that spoke of trauma and pain that never left you. I was lucky, in that way, not remembering bits of my confinement. I could pretend it wasn't *me* strapped to that cold metal table.

I could pretend I didn't feel the phantom ache of broken bones or needles sliding beneath my skin. The blows of hammers and the way my vocal cords would tear when I screamed. Castillion and his *ruthless* words. I was lucky because for *me*, my time at Ascension Rising was little more than a terrible nightmare I got to wake up from. Osiris didn't have the luxury of forgetting, and that was something I saw now more than ever.

After what I'd just heard, I'd never *fail* to remember it. The coarseness of words that were too heavy for one person to bear, the same ones that had bled directly into my ears after the presence that I now knew as Kali had spawned in our home.

She'd *wanted* me to hear, and based on the desolate hollow in Osiris's eyes, I'd guess it was to further his torment. I hated seeing it and knowing I couldn't do anything to help.

He didn't answer me, and I didn't expect him to. The way he trembled with his hand tightly covering that old ink on his wrist and the devastation in his eyes told me enough. That he thought this was his fault, that he placed every ounce of the world on his shoulders and was buckling beneath the weight.

I didn't touch him, didn't want to burn another bad memory into his soul, though I wasn't given much time to.

He was out of the room between one breath and the next, the front door clicking shut before silence reigned. I *hated* that he was hurting, that he didn't ask for help, that he couldn't find the words to.

I rolled my neck, shaking off the leftover ache from whatever spell that crazed woman had cast on Eirik and I. We hadn't been hurt, not like the others had, but we'd heard every word, every pained groan and aching whimper. The mocking taunts from Kali, and the crushed responses that had come from Osiris. Even thinking of them now, remembering the sharp intakes of breath from Osiris, made me sick.

There'd been some pain, like we'd been compressed, but nothing like the others had gone through. The headache that'd come once the spell lifted was another story, my fingers still tingling with the lingering heat of my blood, a soft thud behind my nose like building pressure. I shook from it, and I couldn't find the will to meet Fallon or Adrian's gaze.

I didn't want them to see how much it had affected me, didn't need them worrying about me when they were the ones that were hurting.

There was a huff behind me just as a large, warm hand curled around my wrist, pulling me gently but with determination toward an equally warm body. My cheek brushed Eirik's abdomen, the violent thunder of his heart beating against my ear. The way his arms tightened was nearly constricting, and it was a touch that would have sent me spiraling a few weeks ago, horrified by the sheer size of the man that now encircled me. Just like I'd been when I'd first woken up here, after our nerve-wracking first meeting at the auction house. But this was a different day, and I trusted the men in this room as much as I trusted myself.

I'd half stumbled, half bolted out of the room just after the spell had lifted, the ache in my bones nothing but an afterthought as I sprinted down the stairs, Eirik's voice following me.

A rumble, one that my brain automatically associated with safety, vibrated down my spine, and the coarseness of his thick beard against my temple made goosebumps pop up on my neck.

"I thought I said to wait," Eirik grumbled, his words a hoarse whisper.

I was unrepentant despite his chastising words, but I was also sorry for worrying him. I couldn't stay in that room a second longer, not after what I'd heard.

I ran a hand down his shirt-covered chest in an effort to comfort us both. I wasn't afraid to touch him, not after he'd carried me out of the training room and rooted me to the ground again. The connection that I already thought to be there glowed, and I fell headfirst into the warmth in my chest.

I still needed to talk to them about it, and I would ... I just needed time to process everything and figure out what all of this meant in the meantime. What it meant for me *and* them. And with everything else going on, that thought could wait.

"Sorry, Eirik," I murmured as I tipped my head back, catching Eirik's stubborn gaze. His eyes were a swirling blue, like a turbulent ocean in an unforgiving storm. I traced the savage twist of his thin lips, the charcoal black ink against his tan skin, and the worried way his brows tilted toward one another. "I needed to make sure they were okay."

He huffed, his jaw clenching as he held me slightly tighter.

I moved my gaze away, inching until Fallon slid into view. He glared at where Osiris had been. It was a look that ripped and tore, and even with it not directed at me, I shivered. Rage wasn't something that I liked, especially not on Fallon's face. He had too caring of a spirit for that, even if he rarely showed it.

Adrian didn't appear much better where he was, pressed against the floor cabinets by the stove with his head in his hands, a soft wheezing being the only sound coming from him. I ached to go to him, but Eirik's arms were bands of steel. The rolling flex of his muscles and his hoarse breathing told me he needed me as much as the others did, his beast crawling just below the surface of his skin.

Eirik huffed again, his heated breath rolling over my chin, then my cheek, before he settled on the top of my head. He was silent for a moment, obviously also checking the others. "I can't believe I have to say this, but you shouldn't *ever* throw yourself between Vampires. **And *don't* run from a *Úlfhéðinn*.**"

The last part was growled, the sound hollow in his chest as his teeth clashed over the words. The familiar tone, deep and gritty, gave away his beast.

I frowned. "They weren't going to hurt me, Eirik."

His arms tightened, the rumble that was the melody of his wolf beginning again.

"They wouldn't have *meant* to hurt you, *smár Valkyrja*. That doesn't mean they couldn't." His endearment warmed the ache in my bones, and the gentle way he said it made my face flush.

It was so easy to see the power he held, the strength, and now that I knew him, it was even easier to smile as he scowled. Such a savage man held me like I was nothing short of precious.

"You're right, they could have hurt me. But I trusted they wouldn't. I couldn't just let them fight like that. I'll apologize for leaving without you ... but I won't apologize for trying to help."

Eirik frowned, going to say more when Adrian let out a wheezing breath. Silence followed by smooth laughter that felt like sitting by a cozy fireplace, or sipping on hot tea, echoed by Adrian. He coughed just as that beautiful laugh finished. I looked toward him just as he flinched, his head tipping to the side as a grimace stole his tender expression, and my heart sank.

"Best not go there, Eri. You lost that fight." He gave me a crooked grin, wincing as he brought his hand to the floor, and struggled to stand. Fallon *flitted* to his side and held Adrian up as the other man pressed a hand to his head. "Man, I could use a hot bath and a nap."

I grimaced, tapping at Eirik's arm to see if he'd let me go. His face now lacked the sharpness that I'd grown accustomed to seeing when his wolf was closer to the surface, though I knew it still prowled behind his murky blue eyes.

He nodded just as a sudden pressure built behind my nose, and the clouding smell of iron flooded around me. I reached up, pressing a finger beneath the steady stream of blood, tilting back.

Arctic hands found their way to my face before I could really recognize the bloody nose for what it was, likely an effect of the power that Kali'd wielded. When Fallon tipped my head forward gently, his green eyes came into focus. Worry had replaced the rage in those emerald depths, and even with the tinge of guilt that came when I realized the worry was for me, I felt better knowing that at least he was no longer as angry.

Fallon's eyes flashed red, settling on the blood that slid over my fingers and down my lip. For a brief second, panic took root in my heart, and memories of his *Call* had me freezing in Eirik's arms.

My hand flexed, and I almost lifted it to clutch the small lavender gem that sat around my neck that stopped them from biting me. But just as soon as the red had shown up, it was gone, and Fallon was pulling me gently out of Eirik's grip. Eirik protested with a huff but let me go to check what he could no doubt smell.

"Were you hurt? Fuck, did she cast that spell on you, too?" The *tinking* of shards of glass hitting the hardwood echoed, and Fallon had me sitting on the now-cleared counter before the last of them hit the ground.

The room finally settled, and that trickle of power that still lingered made me shiver. The spell that kept us frozen had been gone when the second flare had knocked all the lights in the house out, so I *knew* it was Osiris. It was like the makeup of it was ingrained in my DNA, the feel of him. The carnage of the room slowly came into view, my tunnel vision lessening as I took in the damage. Pitch-black gouges in the shape of lightning spread out from where Osiris had been standing, and every light flickered with sparks above us.

The room was charged, filled to the brim with heady magic. It made me dizzy, and I pressed my other hand to my head as I glanced around us.

Prince's transparent form quickly came into view as he took in the wreckage with a worried glower. He eyed the scorch marks on the floor and turned his gaze to the closed front door just as Fallon swiped his finger across my cheek. He cupped my face, gently tipping my head back again.

I'd nearly forgotten what he'd asked until his lips curled back in a snarl. "I swear to god I'll kill her."

I pinched my nose with one hand, keeping my head back as I pressed my clean hand to Fallon's, which was still on my cheek.

"We weren't under the same spell as you guys, and I'm *not* the one you should be worried about," I said firmly, frowning when Fallon looked shocked.

The familiar sensation of my nose clotting and the blood flow stopping had me dropping my head forward. Dizziness and the growing headache were the least of my worries as I moved to get down and was met with an incredulous look from Fallon once again.

I grimaced. "You guys were the ones that were hurt, Fallon. The spell she put on Eirik and I made it so we couldn't move. But we heard everything. *Everything.*"

Closing my eyes, my fingers tightened around his as I tried to push back the penetrating sound of agony that had come from Adrian, or the groan that had caught behind closed teeth as Fallon tried to keep it from coming out.

Pet.

I shivered, goosebumps rising on my arms as I tried to rub them away. Even that hint of a phrase, the way she'd said it with such cruel confidence. She'd pressed and played on the emotions she knew would sting.

It was taunting, evil ... and so familiar.

Pressure built behind my nose again, this time moving to my temples for only a moment before fading, and I wondered if I might *Rend*. Be forced out of my body, to crawl another step toward death whether or not I wanted it. But the pressure faded like it normally did around the members of the Vivas Crypt. I took a deep breath, reaching my hand from the top of Fallon's to cup his cheek. He jolted at the warm contact but didn't pull away.

"So, with the risk of sounding like a broken record, are you okay?" I asked gently, and Fallon flicked his gaze away, landing it on the door with a bitter glare.

His forced nod did little to pacify me, his hands still trembling slightly against my cheek. I didn't know exactly what they'd gone through, although I'd heard enough to know it hurt, but if it was enough to bring *Fallon* down ...

"Fine now, love," Adrian broke in with a more chipper tone than I was expecting. But I supposed that wasn't too shocking for him. He always did try to raise the mood where he could.

He pushed Fallon out of the way with a comical prance, taking his place in front of me. Even with everything that had happened, I was glad to see his typical playfulness, even if the slight limp and somber rings under his eyes muddled it. It helped center me when all I wanted to do was cry.

He had a rag in his hand, one damp with warm water. He pressed it to my nose, wiping away the quickly drying blood. His gentle touch had me leaning toward him, my eyes unwittingly dropping to his lips. The copper hints in amber his eyes sparkled when he realized where my gaze had wandered. I reached up, clutching my necklace. It was warm against my palm, as it had been since Osiris put it on me at the bonfire. Again, my chest ached.

I rubbed the gemstone, closing my eyes and even as I tried not to, it was my own torment I saw. It was Castillion with his cruel sneer and twisting laugh. His *words*.

"Will he be okay?" I asked.

They knew who I was talking about. Fallon said as much when his jaw snapped closed loud enough for the sound of his teeth clashing to echo in the room. Adrian's face contorted, and it was hard to miss the spark of betrayal in his eyes as he looked at the scorch marks on the ground.

No one spoke for a moment before Eirik sighed.

"Kali is ..." The name rolled envenomed from Eirik's thin lips. Of all of them, Eirik seemed least affected by the appearance of the cruel woman. "Complicated."

"We should have fucking known about her. We should have known. If he's okay, he won't be when I get to him!" Fallon sneered as his hand slammed down so hard on the dining table that Eirik snarled. The red oak piece groaned under the force.

Fallon, seeming to realize what he'd done, cursed before spitting words in a language I didn't recognize as he pulled his hand to his chest like he'd been burned.

Then he turned his cutting glare to Eirik. "Do you know her, Eirik? Fuck, why didn't *you* tell us?"

Eirik glanced away, his body tensing as if remembering something he'd rather forget. His hand reached for his neck and the scar that cut across the skin there.

"I've only seen her a handful of times, at each Eternium we've been forced to go to. I know as much as you do about her past with Osiris." Eirik's words came through gritted teeth and rapidly thinning lips. His eyes slid closed, and he took a few deep breaths before they opened again. "You made your point, Fallon. But there are things older than you and I at play between those two. I'm not saying it's right, just that—"

He didn't finish, his jaw clenching like he was searching for the words.

"This shouldn't be only on him," I supplied, recalling the shattered look in Osiris's eyes. He hadn't told them of Kali, and that was on him. He would need to apologize and rebuild their trust. But ... "He needs help. He needs *your* help. I just don't think he knows how to ask for it."

Eirik grunted his affirmation just as Fallon barked out a sharp, fake laugh.

"Understatement of the millennia. Damned bastard." Fallon pinched the bridge of his nose, shaking his head. "Been telling him to lean on us for decades, but no. Why listen to me?"

Fallon cursed something else with a scowl on his lips.

A warmth spread into my chest, and the natural way of Fallon's worry helped to settle the sting I still sensed in my bones.

"He worries about you too, you know. I think that's why he's kept what happened to him a secret, even though he shouldn't have. He thought it would keep you guys safe."

It was a secret he still held close to his chest. His past was a muddied one, and in the few short weeks I'd known him, it seemed like I'd learned as much about Osiris as they had. They spoke of him in whispers, mentioning all the things he'd done, the power he held.

But it didn't feel like they knew him, and that was weighing on them now.

"I'm not worried, I'm *furious*," Fallon roared, his head snapping away, his anger dying when I couldn't hide my flinch at the abrupt outburst.

He took a settling breath, grabbing at his tie and jerking it loose like the constraining fabric choked him.

Osiris needed help; help he wasn't willing to ask for as he drowned in a past that no one shared. Fallon had the communication of a brick wall and was more inclined to settle things with a fight than with words, and it often caused tension. Eirik constantly battled his beast and the scars that seemed so familiar to my own. He tried so hard to be the mediator that they seemed to lack but could never find the right thing to say. Adrian hid demons in his eyes, behind the amused smile he kept so easily on his lips. He fought arguments with distractions and jokes.

None of them knew how to *talk*, and I wasn't exactly better. We needed to work on it, or else we'd never fully trust each other.

An icy breeze teased the air, morphing randomly before Prince flashed in my peripheral. My best friend, in all his astral glory, tipped his head to the side in question when he saw me.

It was easy to catch the subtle changes in his face, the way his grin turned grave, the crease of his brow. He was mostly transparent, beyond the light gray which defined him and his threadbare clothing. I didn't know what color his clothes were, nor his eyes or hair ... I didn't know what his voice sounded like, but in this case, I didn't need to. I saw the confusion and worry mixed with the caring he tried to hide behind his tilted grin. I saw the shake in his hands as he leaned down and traced the lightning-like patterns on the ground.

I knew how to read people, and my memories told me it was often the only way to pass the time at the compound. If it were anyone else in my position, I doubted they would see what I did about Prince or the Vivas Crypt. It wasn't much that gave them away: ticks here, the way they moved there.

Over the last few weeks, I realized that these men who had seemed so in control, so *powerful*, needed someone to lean on. This event, this tipping point, only proved as much. Everyone was teetering on the edge of something ... and we saw Osiris's edge today.

Heard it.

It made me even more sure that I was exactly where I needed to be. These men had saved me, had brought me hope, and maybe ... maybe I could be there for them to confide in, to help them as they helped me. Give them someone they could trust with themselves. Protect them as they did me. I took a deep breath, just as a thought came crashing down on me.

"What Kali said about your Maker. What did she mean?" I asked, fiddling with my thumbs, legs swaying in the open air, heels tapping the island beneath me. "Would he really—"

"Kill us? It's hard to say." Eirik barely hesitated. I liked that he didn't mince his words, although they did sting. "He's a terrible man, a broken one. But even with all that, he's always been an estranged kind of family, in his own fucked up way."

"Crazy uncle with a cannon in his upstairs bedroom and a freezer full of questionable meat would be a better way to put him," Adrian added with a sigh and a coarse, bitter laugh. His thumb ran over my cheek. "He hasn't killed us because he didn't see us as a threat. With talk of Osiris Challenging, that's likely changed. He'll come for us. And soon, I'd bet."

Adrian pulled back, wheezing as his eyes seemed to go far away.

"And he has fantastic timing, mind you. With everything else going to shit, now would be a perfect time for him to crash our party. But ... there has to be something we can do," Adrian mumbled, his hands pulling away from me completely, going to his temples. He flinched, and I hopped to the ground again before he could protest, narrowly dodging broken glass.

I grabbed Adrian's hand, pulling him toward the table and directing him to a chair. The stare he gave me was one of amusement, but he did as I instructed, sinking into the seat with a sigh after I brushed it off. I looked over at Fallon next, raising an eyebrow when his eyes widened. He sighed but did the same as Adrian and sat.

Satisfied that they were at least off their feet, I walked back over to the island, where I knew their blood fridge was tucked underneath. I reached in, pulling out a random bottle as I looked at the others, motioning for them to keep talking.

Eirik huffed, heated eyes never leaving me as he rumbled out a response.

"The Eternals have wanted our Maker gone since they were founded, but they've always been too chickenshit to go through with it. So something had to have made Kali come here. It's never been bad enough for the others to turn against him. They're too scared." Eirik scratched his stubbled jaw. "But what?"

I set three glasses on the counter after a moment of deliberation, eyeing the door where Prince still stood. Osiris should be here, as he deserved to hear this, but I doubted he was in the right mind to. I was barely holding it together myself, and I'd just been reminded of Castillion. What if I were to come face-to-face with him again?

I didn't know what I'd do. But I wouldn't take it well, and I would take the isolation I'd put myself in afterward even worse. I'd need to find Osiris soon, but I'd give him a while first to sort through whatever he was feeling.

Then he needed to know he wasn't alone here.

"Well, he's behind the deaths of the other Eternals, if the bitch's words are to be trusted," Fallon chimed in, head tipped back, tension draining from his shoulders. His white suit creased where his arms crossed over his chest, but he didn't seem to notice. "She offered the help of two Eternals, ones with more allies than us. Support like that at the Eternium would be invaluable if we ended up at odds with *him*. We have to consider them."

I froze, hand gripping the bottle so tightly I worried it might shatter.

Oh, Aaliyah ... the only help you'll be getting is from me.

Master Kali.

The words blended together, striking like a knife as they twisted inside my chest.

"No." I set the bottle on the counter, shaking my head. Each of them looked at me, questions burning in their gazes.

I rocked my head from side to side, trying to dislodge Castillion's maddening voice. *No,* we didn't need their help, didn't want it. I refused to side with the people who caused that misery in Osiris's eyes. I steeled my gaze as I tried to find the right words.

"Someone like her can't be trusted." I bit my lip as I poured three glasses of the odd-smelling blood wine. The alcohol hit first, iron second. It shocked me, even though it shouldn't have. I shook off the feeling and walked the drinks over to Fallon and Adrian, just as Eirik helped himself to the last one. "Help from her ... from someone who enjoys hurting people, is going to have a price that isn't worth what she's offering."

It was quiet before Eirik sighed.

"This is a cluster fuck," he muttered, running a hand down his face. "We have two Eternals breathing down our necks, Osiris in shambles, and none of us are much better. And *him* to contend with." No one responded, and Eirik snarled, his eyes flashing so deep a blue that they almost went black. "We're in over our heads. Kali just blatantly threatened our Crypt. If we don't accept her and Darius's backing, they'll go after us. Go after *Aaliyah* now that they know of her. And this is all forgetting that we still have her *Rends* to deal with."

The ever-pressing knowledge of my imminent death bled into the room, and even Prince stopped his pacing by the door.

Death. It was what led me to them and what was slowly leading me back to my shallow grave. Death, as fickle as it was, couldn't be ignored. I tried to remind myself that I'd felt good here, that I wasn't *Rending* anymore. I wanted to hope that maybe it didn't need to be dealt with, that I was fine now ...

But I always remembered the pressure, and the small hints that it was still there, just waiting to throw me over the edge. To take me once and for all, back to that grave. I rubbed my temples, swallowing hard as I tried to remind myself that the headache I currently had wasn't from them. That it was from Kali.

It had to be because of her.

"Her *Rends* come first. I don't care what Kali said; the Eternium is still weeks away," Fallon broke in, his sharp jaw clenching tightly, as he motioned at each word with a solid point of his hand. "We get Ali better first. Everything else can fucking wait."

I rubbed my arm at that, overwhelmed at Fallon's staunch words and sure eyes. I worried about what it might mean for us.

The Eternium wasn't something that waited.

"I agree. I doubt we need to call a vote for that. Ali comes first," Adrian said, sipping his drink with a disgusted grimace, the taste making his nose curl. "But if we can't accept Kali and Darius's deal, we definitely can't accept their threat. And that means there are only two real options that I see."

It was deathly quiet for a long moment before Eirik finally shook his head. Some kind of silent communication passed between them, the years of their bond showing as Eirik downed his glass in one go and said, "Osiris will never agree to a Challenge."

And he was the only one who could if I understood the rules correctly. Eternal candidacy was based entirely on how long they lived, and with Vampires, you had to be at least twenty-five hundred years old to pose a Challenge.

Osiris was the only Vampire to live long enough to reach that limit.

"Which is why we *don't* Challenge. That's not the only way to remove an Eternal, Eri. If *his* tantrum is enough to pull the other Eternals out of their shells, then we've as good as won," Adrian responded.

"Are you implying we use that to our advantage?" Eirik asked with a raised brow.

"I am, you glorious tactician. The best way to deal with a raging beast—"

Adrian didn't get to finish, as Eirik's eyes filled with an emotion I couldn't place, and he said, "Is to not deal with them at all. It's a coward's plan."

"Maybe. But if the other Eternals were to vote on it, *he* would face Exilium, *The Honored Death*. He'd be stripped of his status and executed for his crimes. For the good of all Naturals."

I'd never heard that term before, hadn't known it existed, and from the look of it the others weren't sure what to make of it either.

The *Honored Death*. I leaned in, a spark of hope building in my chest.

"We'd need eighty percent of the Eternals to agree. It's never happened before, Adrian." Eirik sighed as he spoke, shaking his head.

"No, it hasn't, but as you said, something changed. Now might be the only chance we have to quell his threat without bloodshed."

"We don't have the numbers. It might work if we had enough Eternals behind us, but many see us as nothing more than *his* spawn. They'll want us gone with him," Eirik said, muttering to himself.

"We already have a few. Ilenia, for one. Possibly Avedal if I can sweet talk him into it. And Xander, I'm sure. Even though he isn't an Eternal, you know he has sway," Adrian added, spewing off names faster than I could keep track.

Ilenia, the Siren Eternal, was the grandmother of one of my best friends, Eliza. Xander I only knew by name as the 'last hope' for finding out what I was. The only one I wasn't sure about was Avedal, but I didn't have time to ask as Adrian continued.

"And ... you're going to hate this idea, Eirik. Osiris even more when he hears of it, but what about asking Magelav for help? They might spare us some time. They've stayed neutral through every major event, even forgoing the Eternium, but if we show we have a Chronomancer on our side, it might tip things in our favor."

Fallon scoffed before coughing.

"Crazy Mags? Really, Adrian?" Fallon asked like Adrian had just grown a second head.

"Do you have any better ideas? Or are you just getting a hard on from giving me shit right now?" Adrian bit back. "My blood just spent a wonderful day at the spa getting boiled. That's all I've got."

I stiffened, and Adrian snarked out another response I didn't listen to. I'd heard them suffer at the hands of Kali and had to listen to their cries ... but I didn't know what she'd done to them. And until that moment, I'd hoped it wasn't something too horrible. But was that what happened? Did she boil their blood?

Indignant rage sparked in my soul. I clenched my teeth, eyes flicking between Fallon, Adrian, and Prince by the door. The kitchen wobbled, and the shadows around the room seemed to flex.

I squinted, surprise suddenly overwhelming me, and as quickly as it had built up, the extra darkness faded from view. Fear crept into my chest, and my thoughts quickly wandered to the training room incident only hours ago. When meditating with Eirik sent me to Void without having to die.

Bog.

The word came back to me, like a soft echo. With everything that had happened, I'd forgotten about it, but it sounded significant, and I struggled to find how to say it out loud.

I looked around, taking in the sunken faces and the pained looks, and found I couldn't speak. Placing more on their shoulders right now just seemed cruel.

So I said nothing, and Eirik began speaking again.

"Adrian, see if you can find anything or anyone else that might side with us. If Kali and Darius were desperate enough to come for us, then we might get the rest under our palm as well," Eirik mused.

"On it," Adrian quipped back, saluting Eirik with a cheeky simper. "I have been meaning to pay Audric a visit. Needed to get a new suit, anyway, and the snappy Venomcaller makes the best tea."

Eirik nodded, looking at the door.

"I'll talk to Osiris. He might listen to reason about Magelav," he said finally, pushing off from the island and walking toward the door. "And I'll make sure he's been in touch with Xander. The sooner we can meet with him about Aaliyah, the better."

"This is all assuming *he* doesn't come here first. We're really going to do this." Fallon's eyes glazed, horror filling them. "Start a war with *him*?"

Eirik stopped, glancing over his shoulder as he shook his head. A savage pride built in his eyes, and his posture screamed warrior. He looked every bit like the Vikings I'd heard about in my studies after I woke from the grave.

Proud. Strong. *Handsome.*

"No. Osiris is going to start the war. I'm in the business of finishing them."

Adrian scoffed but didn't seem at all surprised. "This isn't the fourteen hundreds, Eri. You can't just whisper a few words and *boom*, start a war anymore."

A low, hoarse rumble echoed from Eirik. It was unlike anything I'd heard, and it took me a second to realize that he was laughing. It was sinful and *dangerous*, and more than a little attractive as it traced its way down my spine.

"You've still got a lot to learn, Adrian," Eirik said, shaking his head. "If anyone can start a war right now and turn the Eternals against themselves, it's Osiris ... *Rex interfectorem.*"

There was a pause like neither Adrian nor Fallon knew the words before a light sparked behind Adrian's eyes, and he laughed. It was a startled sound that had me looking his way.

"Kingslayer? Seems a bit cliché, doesn't it?" Adrian asked, leaning back in the chair again. "How many nicknames do you beasts have?"

Eirik shook his head, lifetimes passing over his eyes, and I got the impression there were more than any of us could imagine.

"More than I can count. But that one? Well, there's a good reason for it. So let's hear you say that in six weeks, Adrian. That's how long we have until the Eternium, and that's assuming our Maker doesn't pay us a visit before that."

Silence met us, and an unseen determination lit up the air.

"You have to convince Osiris to act first," Fallon said, and Eirik nodded.

"I will. We'll call a vote on whether to push for Exilium once I've talked with him." With those final words, he was gone.

Their speed still shocked me sometimes. Most things about them did. They seemed so *normal*, so human most of the time. But they weren't. They were strong, terrifyingly strong.

They were Vampires.

And I'd never felt safer than when I was with them, not even with Eliza. The woman I'd spent six months with, someone I considered as a sister. She'd meant so much to me, and yet somehow, in this room that still reeked of magic ... I was more content than I'd been in months.

"Right," I said, clicking my tongue as I looked at Adrian and Fallon. "Now, you guys need to rest."

Fallon blew air from his nose. Not a snort, but not quite a laugh either. I raised my eyebrow, crossing my arms.

"But—" Fallon didn't get to finish, as Adrian pulled himself, then Fallon, to his feet.

He flashed me a wink, mischievously cackling when Fallon's eyes narrowed.

"As the lady wishes," he said with a mock bow, walking over to me with significantly less limping. He stretched his arm out, and I took it without thinking. The sharp jolt of energy from touching him warmed me to my core. "Want to sit with me awhile, love? I'm rather cold and traumatized, and I could really use a comforting shoulder to lie on. Between you and me, Fally's too pointy for that."

I blushed, heat burning my cheeks, but even then, I beamed. I nodded, surprising Adrian more than he surprised me, but I would do anything to keep seeing that burning grin on his face, the one that lit up rooms and set my soul ablaze.

Fallon was quiet. Then he was gone, and I knew I would need to address this feeling with him soon. With *all* of them soon ... but for now, this was enough.

Chapter 3

Adrian

God, I *hated* our armory.

Luckily, I hadn't had to spend much time in the dreadful place, not after we'd moved everything to our cellar some decades back. Which meant my time around all the creepy things in it was down to a bare minimum. Except for today, of course.

Because today, I needed the big guns.

Ali was still sick, and that didn't fly with me. Well, she'd been sick since I'd met her, but yesterday's clusterfuck with Kali hadn't exactly helped the matter. Between her nosebleeds and the constant threat of her *Rends* ... well, I wasn't quite in the mood to wait for Xander to get back to us. Which meant I had to take matters into my own hands, and that started with who'd imprisoned her, the people that killed her. *Ascension Rising*.

It was time to figure out who the fuck hurt my girl.

This wasn't my first time looking, nor my second or *tenth*. I'd been searching relentlessly for a group that was practically a ghost. And as much as I hated myself for it, I was running out of people to ask. Which meant I had to dig a little deeper, a little harder. Because if we found them, maybe they'd know how to fix this. Make Ali stop *Rending*.

And if not, we could still gut them like pigs. Win-win.

The Vivas household had gained many treasures over the years, most of them older than me by several centuries, and a certain Venomcaller I knew had a love for fine gems. Audric would talk if he knew anything about it, as he always did for us, but it was never a bad idea to butter him up first.

If I could find the damned chest the sparkly little bastards were in, that was.

I pressed my hand to the side of our house, the siding cool to the touch as I moved my hand over the door habitually before saying the pass phrase. *Et in domum suam in solem.* The house of the sun, Nero's name for our humble abode. It was only fitting.

The wall flexed and moved, fluttering under my fingertips before it faded away to show a long, stretching staircase that disappeared far down below.

I slid my way down the narrowed passageway, the illusion that hid the door from trespassers fading away behind me. I could touch both walls from the center of the stairs, and my claustrophobia only grew worse now that I couldn't see beyond the steps. I lifted my hand, snapping my fingers as the *Flame* trailed along my bloodstream, lighting the small candles that lined the walls and bathing me in light.

I shivered from the feel of it, the ache it left hauntingly familiar to the spell Kali had placed on us. I shook it off. All too soon, I was staring at a seemingly endless room, with only those dimly lit candles to guide me.

I sneezed as I kicked up dust, forgetting to not breathe as I looked around, dismay keeping me plastered to the stone floor. Rows upon rows of endless bullshit greeted me, with absolutely *zero* order.

It was sad how obvious it was that Eirik had been the one in charge of moving things down here.

I sighed, throwing my head back with a groan as I started down the first row, past armor, trinkets, weapons, and the sort, none being what I wanted. You'd think I'd get smarter about it and put these gems somewhere easier to find, considering this wasn't the first time I'd traveled down here for them.

But where was the fun in that?

"Damn it, where was it?" I grumbled, glancing up and down the stray bobbles, hoping the little chest of wonders would jump out and bite me.

It was only fair. I didn't want to spend any more time down here than was *absolutely* necessary. Not when Aaliyah was just upstairs, likely reading another novel Osiris had translated. I could practically see her now, nose buried in the pages with her knees pulled to her chest, covered in a blanket like it might protect her from plot twists.

I grinned, looking like a fool for all the dusty relics to see. I was smitten, that much was easy for me to admit.

First, it had been the blood at the auction that drew me in, then that beautifully tender demeanor she always had, like she'd never grow tired of the wonders of the world. Her unrelenting fortitude and the way she stood tall in the face of everything the world threw at her. Trivial things, the touch of her hand, the way she worried, and the ease at which we laughed together. The way she stuck her tongue out when baking, or the little dance she would do around the kitchen when she thought I wasn't looking. The serenity that came with sitting with her, even in silence.

They built up, day after day, and after our kiss in the pool house, a moment that still had me reaching up to touch my lips, I found myself craving her presence even more. I craved that soft smile and the smooth press of her skin, the way her cheeks flushed when I kissed her.

I'd imagined that kiss every spare second since it'd happened, and I was quickly failing at my attempts to keep things slow for her. But I would. I would hold back until she was comfortable and ready for the step that kept me up at night.

For breathless groans and the dance of heated flesh.

I shivered, so caught up in my fantasies that I nearly missed what I'd been looking for. The chest was placed neatly in the middle row, tucked between a ratty cape and an old mace that looked to still have blood on it. It was made of dried oak, the deep red wood making the sapphires that lined the edges and cracks glow. I popped it open, and sure enough, sitting inside was a pile of gems. I didn't pay much mind to which ones I grabbed, pulling out three and shoving them into my pocket. They'd do nicely.

A brittle cold brushed over me, and I shivered, glancing around before closing the chest and placing it back where it had been, so I'd get the joy of walking through this clusterfuck again.

I turned toward the staircase, intent on leaving as quickly as possible when a clink sounded a few rows away. I looked over the stack, past an old gladiator helmet that was lacking even a single speck of dust and saw a glint on the ground.

"Well, that wasn't creepy at all," I mumbled, contemplating just leaving it be when my curiosity got the better of me. I *flitted* to the item, a shock of surprise sliding down my spine as I reached down and picked it up.

It was diamond-shaped, with a liquid that resembled gold sloshing inside of it. I eyed it wearily, checking for cracks in the old glass. It was one of Osiris's many ancient treasures, one he'd obtained through a bet long before even Nero'd been turned ... It was older than me, than Eirik, even Osiris. I had only seen it once before when we first moved it down here.

Distilled High Fae Mana. A truth serum.

It ... might be useful.

We were planning to take on Sebek eventually, the beast himself, currently with no *real* plan much to my dismay. And while in terms of this shitshow, that was a ways off, I still wanted to check all our bases. Which meant it was up to me to figure out what to do and *who* we could use to do it. This might just be our ticket to freedom.

I chuckled to myself, looking around the room, feeling prickly and cold. Sweat pooled at my neck, and I clutched the vial.

"Prince? That you?" I asked, again laughing as unease settled in my stomach.

Well, this was fucking awkward. I was afraid of a ghost—and Aaliyah's best friend, at that. I shook my head at the absurdity, just as another object fluttered to the ground in my peripheral vision, and I jumped, a manly squeal on my lips.

The manliest, really.

I didn't check to see what the object was as I shoved the vial in my pocket, hearing it clicking against the gems, and rushed toward the stairs, resisting the urge to flit.

Didn't need Prince thinking I was scared of him. That would be silly.

He is a ghost, after all.

"You know, if I didn't know any better, I'd assume you were playing with me." I grinned as I reached the bottom of the staircase that led back up to the main level, shaking my head at the fact that I was talking to a *ghost.* "But thank you. You've been a great help. I'd kiss you if I could."

Then I was gone, leaving the damned cellar and that mischievous ghost behind me. No doubt Aaliyah would have a laugh when she heard what her friend had been up to, and I was more than happy to share a story at my expense if it meant I got to hear it.

I brushed off the dirt as I strolled out of the little cellar door, its illusion falling back into place just as I stepped past it. In a blink, the only thing in that spot was a few potted daisies and the side of our house. I shook my head and left it at that, hand tucked against the small diamond-shaped vial that rested in my pocket. It was warm in my palm, an artificial heat.

I walked with a joyous hop to my step, given the circumstances. I ached from the encounter with Kali yesterday, and if I moved wrong, I could still feel the rush of my blood as it burst in my veins. But it was easy enough to push it back and forget it happened. I was rather used to that, and what better way to cope than to push things down until they came bursting out?

Such was the Osiris way.

I *flitted* through the front door, the rest of the dust following in a trail behind me, but surprise kept me just past the entrance when my eyes landed on what should have been an empty kitchen. I hadn't been expecting to see Aaliyah standing in front of the stove.

I'd designed the space myself, from the mixed marble counters and shiny black oak floors. We'd even got most of the shock marks out of it, from where Osiris's magic had gone haywire. I loved this room and had claimed it as my own from the moment we'd started building our home. I knew every nook and cranny, and seeing Aaliyah in it always brought butterflies to my stomach.

The subtle, small action of her simply being here? *Perfection*. It made it all worth it.

"Love, so good to see you," I said, hiding my mirthful grin when she jumped, flipping around with a blush. It differed from how she used to move when she'd first gotten here. It lacked the sharpness of someone expecting a blow, and that made my chest a little lighter after my stint in the armory. "What are you doing?"

She looked at me with wide eyes, glancing between me and the stove. She wore a plain gray t-shirt, one that was covered in specs of white dust, her pale cheeks partially flushed from more than just my sudden arrival. I looked over her head—not that it was hard with how short she was—and down at what she was hiding behind her as I realized now that something ... smelled. Not pleasant or unpleasant, really. It was just there.

"Adrian! Sorry, I didn't think you'd be back so soon! Fallon and Eirik went out to scout the perimeter of the ward now that it's back up and Osiris isn't in, and—" She crossed her arms behind her back, stuttering over the last bit as she took me in. "Well, I was ..."

I didn't miss the way her eyes traveled over me, lingering across my hips and at the arch of my jaw. But I was too stunned to speak, glancing around her again at the stove. It was a shock to see it used when I wasn't the one preparing something. But I knew almost immediately what she was doing. My eyes landed on the open cookbook on the counter, the page flipped open to a difficult risotto.

Joy ... wasn't quite what I experienced. Elation. Surprise. Ease. Nothing fit the encompassing emotions that rushed through me. I felt everything, and for a second, I was taken back to a wintry day in London, to the warm aroma of dinner on my grandmother's cast iron stove. This woman in front of me, *my* Aaliyah, had rendered me breathless.

"You were making us dinner?" I asked, and it made my entire heart sing when she blushed again, glancing around before her eyes landed on the air beside me.

Her lips twisted into an irritated pout, and I realized all too easily that Prince must have been helping her before he came down and assisted me.

"I—" She struggled to find words as she pushed her hands behind her back, that red blush extending down her neck. She sighed, looking almost guilty, and I frowned at the sight of admonishment on her face. "Yeah, I was trying to, anyway. I really wanted to do something nice for everyone, to bring us all together after what happened. Unfortunately, Prince knows as much about cooking as I do, so he was no help. Then, it was too salty, and he pointed at the sugar, so I added that and, well."

She glanced back at the risotto, then to the space next to me again, and I paused, hand again going to that vial in my pocket. A shiver had me peering back at the front door. Something had knocked this off the shelf, had known I was down there.

Something that wasn't Prince?

An almost irrational fear had me swallowing, searching the room for Kali as if she would slink through the shadows. A cold sweat pooled at my neck.

"Prince was with you the whole time?" I asked, and Aaliyah's face narrowed in worry as my mood shifted.

"Yeah, he hasn't left my side," she affirmed, fidgeting as she reached for her arm, hugging herself.

She hunched, the familiar way she stood now seeming so wrong. She'd grown into her skin here, and I hated seeing her so afraid again, like a blow might come from the shadows.

"Strange, I could have sworn he helped me out down in the armory," I mused easily, forcing the fear off my face with my smile that felt too wide, even as my arms ached, and the phantom pain of my blood boiling seized me again. It wasn't unlike the *Call*.

Aaliyah's shoulders softened a bit, as she stood with straighter shoulders and looked at Prince again. She didn't speak for a moment, her eyes focused, and her lip between her teeth. That look, so simple and determined, cooled my blood, and just as quickly, my attention was back on her. She centered me.

It was adorable.

"He ... he's going to go check. I think he's telling me to tell you to 'behave'." Aaliyah just covered her mouth, hiding a laugh behind her hand.

I took another breath, letting the strain wash over my shoulders. If something was wrong, we'd know about it, and I wasn't about to let this time with Ali go to waste over some wind in the cellar.

"Not sure he can get there. It's behind a magical door," I said, only partially joking, but Aaliyah merely shook her head with a rueful expression.

"Oh, he just went through the floor," she replied, rubbing the back of her hand as she glanced back at the stove again, reminding me of her dinner attempt as her face again twisted in dismay at the sorry state of the rice. "I don't suppose you'd want to help me fix this?"

Everything else melted away, and I grinned at her as I took another step forward.

Being this close to her, just out of reach, was torture, and remembering that she had done this for us? That she'd thought to make us dinner? Well, it made me all kinds of giddy.

"Sure, love. We'll get it right as rain," I promised, watching every little move she made. I reached out, grabbed the wooden spatula, and tried the risotto. It ... tasted. Well, nothing a little seasoning couldn't fix.

Ali watched me closely, inching ever closer as I reached above my head to grab some things.

I cleared my throat, asking, "What made you decide on risotto?"

This was my favorite recipe, and I'd flipped through the weathered pages so many times that I'd lost count. I loved the way she reached her hands out in front of her, her thumbs twiddling as she bit her lip. She didn't take her eyes off my hands as I sprinkled some dried herbs over the rice. I'd have cut it fresh if we had any, but I knew in this case we didn't. We were far overdue for a grocery run.

She shrugged. "I'm not really sure. The page was pretty worn, so I assumed you all liked it. I just didn't think it was going to be this hard." Each word extended her blush, and when she finally looked up at me, lavender eyes wide and attentive ...

It was too much to bear, and the sensible gentleman in me snapped. I just stared at her, this wonder of a woman who was in my kitchen. The one who wanted to mend what had cracked with the appearance of Kali. She was like glue, here to bring us back together. I glimpsed her efforts on her hands, across her clothes, and on the counters. The determination in her gaze. It all clattered down on me, and all I could think about, all I could see, was *her*.

"Is that it then?" she asked, shuffling on her feet, eyes back on the rice. "Did you fix it?"

I took another breath, needing to ground myself before I made another mistake and scared her again. But the bastard part of my mind wasn't with that idea. I moved, angling us so she had her back to the counter with my arms on either side of her. I reach out, twisting off the stovetop, before reaching that hand up to her face.

I'd thought I'd grown used to the spark that came with touching her, but just like always, it stunned me to my core, sending every nerve I had into overdrive. I shivered, my body urging me forward, arousal spiking in the air, and I realized with all too much euphoria that it wasn't just my own.

"It was never broken, love. You did so good, and I was so excited to savor every bite of your dish. Even before what I added." She sucked in a breath to protest, her head angling to glance back at the stovetop and the burned rice. I stopped her with a gentle hand, keeping those distant eyes on me. "But I've been wanting to try something else again first. Something far ..."

I leaned in, just enough to feel her breath against my lips. I gripped the counter as she shivered against me, her pupils blowing wide as she swallowed hard, and when her tongue shot out against her pink lips, I nearly groaned.

"Sweeter." I could barely distinguish that the word came from me, the hoarseness of it making her breath catch. My heart thundered, and my fangs pressed against my gums, making my mouth water.

"Adrian—" she started, her eyes blown wide with innocent desire, but I didn't give her the time to finish.

Kissing her was like basking in the rich rays of the sun. Her lips were as soft as I remembered, seeping heat into my skin, making every inch of me flare to life. She tasted like ambrosia, like warm cookies and sunlight. I held my arms steady by her side, not moving, waiting to see if she'd pull away. For the longest few seconds of my life, I was worried I'd pushed too far again, like our night by the pool.

Until she slid her arms up, gentle fingers caressing my chest and neck, sending a delicious zing down my spine, before circling my shoulders in a light embrace.

Fuck me.

My hands fell to her hips, and I lifted her without effort, keeping our mouths sealed together as I set her on the countertop. She sighed into the kiss, only giving me the chance to deepen it. I slid my tongue along her pouty lips, pressing and playing, tempting her to join in. The tentative press of her tongue was enough to steal my soul as I settled myself between her ivory thighs.

I needed to get closer, to feel more of her. A strangled gasp fell from her lips, breaking our kiss as her legs tightened around my hips, accidentally grinding me against her core. She made another startled noise; the sound strangled and confused as her head tipped back.

When she didn't pull away, I slipped back just enough to stare into her eyes. Then I inched my hips forward, just a touch, just enough to elicit another of those breathy moans. Her hands tightened around my shoulders, and I was nearly leaning back to seal myself to her lips again when she whispered my name.

"Adrian?" The question was clear in her eyes, a stark worry blending with lust. It took all I had to focus on her and not on the way her heels dug into the backs of my thighs.

"Hmmm?" I hummed out, pressing my nose to hers, holding myself still against her.

"Do you like me?"

I froze, confused by her words. I pulled back, just a touch, startled by the worry in her eyes. "What do you mean?" I asked.

I was expecting another shy answer, but always carrying surprises, Aaliyah held her head high. It was fucking beautiful, the defiant tilt to her nose, and the way she stood her ground even as it scared her.

"I like you, Adrian. A lot. I really enjoyed kissing you before, and now ... and I'd like to do it again, sometime. I—" Her sentence tapered off, just as her hands shook. "I just wanted to make sure you feel the same. That you actually like me and that I'm not—that I don't—"

As adorable as her rambling was, I finally understood, and I didn't even realize I was leaning back in, pressing a soft kiss to her lips. There wasn't an incessant hunt for pleasure behind it; it was just a kiss. Soft and lingering, neither of us wanted to pull away, and that made it even sweeter. It stunned me as much as it did her, but the action of holding her close was natural.

"Deep breath, love," I encouraged, moving both hands up to her face. I held her lovingly, brushing my thumbs over her high cheekbones and under her eyes. "Do you think I don't?"

Aaliyah blushed and tried to look away, her eyes trailing down the front of me.

"Not exactly ..." was her soft reply. Hesitation, even fear, clouded that word, and I warmed considerably. "I just don't have a lot of experience like this, Adrian. I really don't want to mess it up."

I almost didn't know what to say, too stunned by her confession to move. I'd suspected and hoped that she had feelings for me. I'd been playing myself a fool all this time, worrying about saying something wrong, when I should have been saying *anything* at all to ease her fears. Seeing her now made me realize I was quite a fool, not making it clearer that I felt the same.

That she made my days better. Sweeter.

"I'm sorry, love, I'm realizing I needed to be clearer with you ... I was trying to take things slow," I whispered, achingly gentle as I moved up, pressing a kiss to her forehead. She let out a small breath, her hands moving to settle softly against my chest. "I fancy you, Aaliyah. I love your smile and the way you laugh. I love your kindness, your warmth, and the way you can brighten any room you walk into."

Spilling my soul had never been so hard, never seemed so daunting. But I did anyway, because I knew that if anyone deserved to hear it ... deserved the world? It was Aaliyah. My sweet little love, the one who made this home bright again.

"When I think of home, I see you there," I breathed, just as tears filled her eyes and a small smile spread over her lips.

She looked like a weight had been lifted, tension leaving her body in waves. Watching her made my chest hurt, realizing that she had been agonizing over this. I vowed at that moment that I would do everything in my power to make sure she never looked that way because of me again.

"Oh," she said, the word slipping out on a hiccup.

Her fingers tightened around my shirt like she was trying to keep me anchored to her, and I was all too happy to oblige. I slid back, keeping her at arm's length but still wanting to be as clear as possible with my next words.

I wanted her to be mine, to be *ours* hopefully one day, and I needed to say it in no uncertain terms. No more dancing around it, like the idiot I hadn't realized I'd been.

"I'd like to court you, Aaliyah." Her face twisted in confusion, head tilting to the side.

"Court?" she asked, and I chuckled a bit, brushing my thumb along her cheek again.

"Date is the term now, I believe." I grinned when her face again flushed crimson. "Hopefully more in the future."

Dazed and looking like she wasn't sure if this was real, she nodded. "You ... really?" she murmured, sliding her own hands up to my face, as I had done with hers.

Her touch, the way her eyes crinkled at the corners, and the color flushed across her cheeks. Gods.

"Above all else, love," I said, meaning it with every fiber of my soul. She'd brought joy to me that I'd thought I'd never get to experience. Brought happiness to my family, and no matter where this ended, I would always treasure her for that.

Some part of me ached, would always ache, from the horror of my turn. From the bloody dreams that haunted me and the eyes of those I'd never be able to apologize to. It was a toxin I intended to purge out, one day at a time.

Today, I pushed it away, finding no place for it. Not here, not with this.

"Yes. I'd really like that," she said finally, gifting me one of her breath-taking, tender smiles. It was normally reserved for Prince, one that now looked like *mine,* too. She loved Prince. It was so easy to see in how she spoke of him. So for her to peek at me with the same tender expression ... damned if I wasn't already hers. "Is this real?"

She stole the words right out of my mouth, and I laughed. Too over-joyed not to lean down and seal her lips to mine again and again. I'd chase this joy forever and never grow tired of the twist of her thin pouty lips as they curved up at the corners. I was *entirely* smitten, lost in Aaliyah, and goddamn if it wasn't my piece of heaven. I'd found my happiness, and I would do anything in this world to keep it.

Now I just had to convince my brothers to do the same.

Ali leaned back in, and I nearly jumped out of my clothes. More than happy to continue our little make-out session.

Until the scent of iron hit.

My fangs fell hard, startling us both as Ali snapped away from me, and I pulled back as my eyes-tinged red. Blood. It slid down her nose, over her lip, and her hand shot up to rub it away.

She shook as I *flitted* off, wetting a rag only to *flit* back and press the cloth under her nose. I waited, holding my breath, for the dreaded pull of the *Call* to steal my mind away like it had so many times. Sebek's demand for blood was the price I had to pay for disobeying him after my turn. I waited for it to twist up my insides, to make me feral and *hungry.* To turn me into a monster again. The tang of blood lingered in the air, scented with lavender and tea, smelling so delectable that I couldn't force my fangs back up.

"Sorry," Aaliyah said, her lips now pulled taut as she tipped her head up. Her eyes flared wide, and she bit her lip, flinching as I followed her, keeping the rag under her nose. "I'm not sure what that was."

We were both shaken, Aaliyah still trembling in my arms as I stepped back to allow her some room. She gripped her forearms and jumped down from the counter, looking around the room with startled jerks.

"Are you alright? Any pressure?" I asked softly, dreading that the answer might be yes.

Aaliyah paused, and I stood rooted to the ground for seconds that dragged like hours before she shook her head.

"No, not right now. I think I just need to rest. After what happened yesterday—" She didn't need to finish; I understood well enough.

But I couldn't just let her leave like this, not when the moment suddenly felt so raw. I reached out, easily pulling her into my arms, earning a squeak out of her as I did. I tried and failed to find the words to apologize.

"Come on then, what do you say to a warm shower? You relax, and I'll get dinner finished," I suggested, and her shoulders dropped in appreciation as she leaned her way into my arms. Her nod was all I needed.

She was safe, she was alright ... but she was also still dying. And Fallon was right: The Eternium could fucking wait.

We needed to fix Aaliyah first.

CHAPTER 4

PRINCE

This was *not* how I wanted to spend my day. Of all the places I wanted to be, this was dead last, or second to last, on the list. I should be upstairs, making Aaliyah blush and laugh. I *should* be enjoying her company, helping her ruin a risotto, because Goddess Edesia knows I was never much of a cook.

Instead, I was here, staring at shit even older than I was, and the only flutter of emotion I got was that of irritation. So fuck whatever entity took root in this stupid, unorganized, and dreadfully *dull* room. Fuck it, and fuck Adrian for taking what little alone time I had with Aaliyah. He could hold her, goddammit. Got to feel her skin, and—that lucky bastard—her lips. That meant that *I* should get a minimum of an hour a day with her by myself. It was only fair since I couldn't do much else.

I shook my head, disgruntled as I floated down to the dank cellar floor and glanced around the shit stain of an armory. It was entirely too caliginous, even with the few candles lit along the walls. The rows went on and on endlessly, farther than I could see. And, speaking of what I could see, there were no other ghosts to be found. Just my luck.

Leave it to Adrian to be scared of his own damned shadow, or *gasp*, a nefarious gust of wind! Now he was up there, swooning our girl, while I was stuck here on guard duty.

Bastard.

I floated around, intent on at least checking, although expecting to find little. Rows upon rows of familiar bullshit greeted me, and nothing was placed with any care or order. I huffed a silent snort, rolling my eyes at the clutter. I skipped it all, lingering over only a few pieces. Still no chill.

Ghosts had a way of searching for Aaliyah, and if there really had been one, it wouldn't have been here fucking with Adrian. And honestly, I was *glad* that I didn't feel one. Aaliyah didn't need to stress about sending some poor soul on right now. She had enough to deal with.

And I'd be damned if some cocksure ghost made her sad today.

Each aisle led to the same thing: emptiness and a desire to smack Adrian upside the head. Until I turned around, my hand brushing along a copper-painted gold helm, and I *felt* it. It wasn't quite a chill—no; it was more like an annoying itch I'd never scratch. It pricked at the back of my head, and for a second it *almost* seemed like a touch. I glanced over my shoulder, scanning the space and observing nothing out of the ordinary.

But that interaction didn't leave, growing instead like a persistent mold. I gnashed my teeth, wishing to grind them if only to feel it. I couldn't speak, not even to the other dead, but I flashed a bit of energy, searching for a reply. It was a lot like someone with a physical form waving and screaming into an empty room.

To my endless surprise, I got one back. It was weak, so weak that it barely seemed real. But it happened.

Well, fuck me. Adrian wasn't kidding. That's a ghost.

I'd never met another spirit this low on energy before, and to my knowledge I was one of the older specters. The dead faded away, after enough time without finding Aaliyah or someone like Aaliyah to send them on. I had no idea what happened to them, whether they went to the Void or just disappeared, and I tried not to think about it.

Not when my energy was waning, too. Over a hundred years I'd been dead, and in the last ten, that slow sap of power had gotten stronger, more insistent. Maybe this would be me one day, bothering poor souls in shitty cellars and making things move in hopes of garnering some attention.

Or maybe one day, I'd let Aaliyah send me on. The thought made my entire body ache, like someone had doused me in gasoline and set me on fire, but it was a thought I forced myself to consider. I knew having me around hurt her, probably as much as it helped, but now that we were out of the compound, my leaving might give her time to heal. She could learn how to love someone who would give her what she deserved, who could love her as she deserved.

Someone who could touch her, hold her. Whisper how much she

meant to them. And say her name. *God*, I would trade every spare second I had if it meant I could just say her name just one time.

And she'd watch over everyone for me, and I knew they'd do the same for her. I wouldn't trust anyone else to and hadn't ever thought the paths of my past and the road of my future would collide like this. I was as thankful for it as much as I was devastated. Because it wasn't my joy to have.

I may love Aaliyah, and she may love me, but I'd never be enough as I currently existed. Which is why, begrudgingly, I was glad Adrian was upstairs to keep her company.

I was content with that, or much as I could be. It was a thought, one that I doubted I'd ever go through with. I would always hold her needs above my own, but gods, if I weren't a selfish man, too. As long as she'd have me, I'd stay by her side, even if it meant that was the only place I'd ever be.

Another small brush of power stopped my brooding. It was non-oppressive and settled, which was good enough for me. Whatever, or whoever was down here, wasn't intending to hurt us, and it didn't seem like it wanted to slink to the Void either.

I waved nonchalantly, flipping around.

If it wanted to stay, then I wasn't going to say no seeing as it wasn't a threat. I ambled down the row, the feeling slowly fading as the newest ghost on the block slinked back to whatever it was doing. I ignored the room, intent on getting back to Aaliyah when I spotted it. A fluttering red scarf.

The significance of it was lost to me, but all too soon the obnoxious itching grew again, and the fabric moved as if it had been caressed.

So you're stuck to the cloth. Interesting.

I noted it and floated up, past the floor and the wards that hid this room, moving toward the ever-present pulse that led me to Aaliyah. Stay or go. Those were my options, and I would die a thousand more times to spend even another second by her side.

If the time ever came when I was forced to choose, well ... *I just hope I have the guts to do what's right for her.*

I peeked my head through the floorboards, half hoping Aaliyah and Adrian would still be here so I could spook her. But they were no longer in the kitchen, the room once again empty. There was more clutter spilled about now, spices strewn about the counters, a glass of blood wine sitting on the table. With the moonlight spilling in, the kitchen looked inviting.

Though I did note that the ruined risotto was still on the stove.

Oops.

I brushed it off as I ambled upstairs, toward the pull that was always calling me forward, eventually finding myself in front of the bathroom. The jolt of the Void told me to walk forward, to find peace beyond.

Which meant I'd be coming back later.

I sighed, reaching up and pressing my hand to the door. I couldn't feel the wood, but I knew it was cold, the air of the house wintry, even though it was much less now. It was instinctual to want to find Aaliyah for more reasons than one. I'd spent years, *decades* not leaving her side, and something as simple as modesty wasn't a problem for us anymore.

But it felt wrong to see her in a state of undress now, just like the fake heat that traveled down my spine like a shiver felt wrong. Because now I wasn't going to be eyeing the wounds that Castillion made with disgust and horror, and I wouldn't have to question if she'd make it through the night.

My desire to see her was just that. *Desire.*

And I wasn't selfish enough to use her trust in me to see her when I shouldn't. I sighed again, shrugged, and moved toward the library. Intent on bothering whoever was there if anyone was.

Maybe I can get Eirik to jump. That would make my day.

I was barely a 'step' in when I heard it. A strangled cough that was blocked by a tight palm. It was a broken sound, one that would haunt my every waking nightmare. For a second, I was tossed back to that fucking building, to *Ascension Rising*. Aaliyah and her desperate cries, Castillion and his wicked sneers.

If he wasn't already dead, I'd find a way to come back and kill him.

I didn't hesitate as I moved through the wall and into the bathroom this time, choosing to ask for forgiveness over permission if I stumbled on something I shouldn't have. It wasn't like I could ask, anyway, and I *needed* to make sure she was okay. The moment I saw Aaliyah, I was glad I had.

She was leaning against the pristine white cabinet doors that were under the sinks, sitting on the cold tile. Her hair was damp, and the room still held the steam of a fresh shower. She'd pressed her hands to her head; her face tensing every few seconds. The pain had her so distracted that she didn't even feel me enter the room, or the pulse of energy I sent her way to get her attention. It was only when she opened her eyes to stand that she finally saw me.

She was stunned for a second, face going slack in surprise. Her eyes, the deep lavender, were sunken compared to only a few minutes ago. She shook, and her nose bled, her hand moving up to stop it. My hands flexed at my sides, and I struggled not to reach out to her.

What the *fuck* was happening to my girl?

"I'm okay," she said, her voice showing the agony she tried so desperately to hide.

Even she didn't seem to trust the words, tears flooding her eyes as she *shook*, trembling so hard it made her teeth chatter.

Like I fucking believed that.

I pressed my hands together at the palms before I dragged them apart, our signal for a *Rend*. She reached for her hair, pulling so hard that some strands broke, and she whined. I was desperate to take a step forward and pull her into my arms. I choked on my uselessness as Aaliyah shook her head back and forth relentlessly.

"No, not a *Rend*." I didn't like how her voice cracked on another cry, and an almost irrational rage sucked at my soul and made my chest burn. "I don't know what's happening."

She was supposed to be getting better; she *was* better here with the others, so why was this happening now? What the fuck had she done to deserve this? I hated the unjustness of it, and I hated even more that I couldn't do anything to help.

Why couldn't I pull her into my arms? *Why the fuck did I have to die?*

It had never really bothered me before, even in the years at Ascension Rising, because being close to her, someone that she could lean on, had been enough. But now that she had the Vivas Crypt, it almost burned that I couldn't do the same as them.

The small touches of comfort, the press of fingers against her soft skin, things that I would have taken for granted in my living years now haunted me. And I was so tired of being so fucking *useless* to her.

"What am I doing wrong now?" she asked, hauling me from my pathetic pity party, staring past me, eyes clouded. I straightened and pushed all of my shitty, selfish thoughts behind me. "Was this all just a fluke? I thought I was getting better. I'd hoped—"

She halted her words, her usual strong façade cracking. It was so strange to see genuine fear in her eyes after so many years of her hiding it from me. I'd grown used to picking it out of her, only receiving small bits of what was wearing on her, and the burdens I knew she didn't want me to have to bear with her. I couldn't do anything about it now but float over to her. I sat by her side, always at least an arm's length away. I cracked a smile, one that I knew was shaking, and I knew in an instant that she saw it, too. She sobbed again, no sound finding its way past her lips.

"I'm still dying, Prince," she cried, and those words broke me.

She couldn't die, not yet. She had too much to do, too many things to see, and too many bastards to love. I couldn't bear to see her like me, to *die* like me. I'd give my soul in a heartbeat if it meant this would stop for her; I'd give *anything* for her. So she couldn't die.

I wouldn't let her.

"I know I shouldn't say this. I know it's cruel, but I don't know what I'd do without you, Prince. I know it's selfish to want more ... but I wish you could hold me," she rambled, leaning back, incoherent in her words, as another burst of pain broke past her defenses and she choked on a gasp.

She pressed her thumbs to her temples, and I wondered if she even knew she said those words. Words that I'd been holding so close to my chest that they nearly swallowed me whole. She spoke about the want that had been on my mind for years. So easily breaking apart the barriers I'd kept around them to keep her safe from my desire.

"I'm just so scared," she sobbed, wiping her eyes.

Then I saw them, her walls building back up as she straightened her spine. Before I could even think of a response in our limited vocabulary, her eyes opened, losing some of their shine.

Piece by piece, the bricks were placed until her face was carefully neutral. It was the same method she'd used to block out the experiments. She eased back against the cabinets behind her, her hands settling on the tile as she grounded herself with three steady breaths. She still flinched, still hurt.

"Sorry, I—" she paused, pushing away the pain, covering it, masking it. "Can you tell me what you found in the armory?"

I was caught at a crossroads, and like always, neither option was wanted. I wanted to drag her close to me, into my arms where she wouldn't have to worry, to carry her away and make sure she got better. To tell her that the armory bullshit could wait and that I'd take care of her until she was better. I wanted to feel the press of her lips, the touch of her skin, to breathe her name as the others did. If I could pick even one word to speak, that's what it would be.

Aaliyah.

Instead, I lifted my hands, giving her a false bravado kind of grin, forcing every emotion away but confidence, so I didn't overwhelm her with them. It was what I did because it was all I could do.

I made a wonderful distraction. The damned bastard that I was.

I lifted my hands, pointing my first two fingers at my eyes, before crossing my hands over my chest in an 'X'. Then, I pointed at myself, making a small circling motion with my hand.

It wasn't a perfect sentence—fuck, it was barely a sentence at all. All clear, danger, then the last one, an attempt to note something like me.

Aaliyah contemplated a moment, her eyes furrowing as she tried to decipher my meaning. I waited patiently, admiring the soft slope of her jaw and the adorable tilt of her nose. My eyes caught on the scar there, a small nick right on the tip.

An accident, Castillion had called it, getting too excited with his knife. Rage flared briefly inside me.

"There's another ghost?" she asked finally, and I waved my hand left and right, meaning *kind of.*

Aaliyah nodded again in understanding.

"A ghost that doesn't want to be found?" she amended, and I nodded, having no other way to describe it.

"That's odd. I haven't sensed anything different," she mused, pulling her knees toward her chest and biting her lip as she considered her words. She flinched after a second, bringing her hand up to her head again. "I've never had a ghost not seek me out before. Besides you, that is. Maybe I should go down there and see if I can find anything."

I shook my head, not finding the need for her to do so, especially not in the state she was in now. No offense to the new guy, but I wasn't risking Aaliyah's already unstable soul for him. Whatever bastard was down in the cellar wasn't a danger to us. It just wanted to be left alone with the cloth, and who were we to tell it how to find happiness? It would be hypocritical to make it leave when I'd fought the pull of the Void for years just to stay by Aaliyah's side.

Aaliyah's eyes snapped shut, and my patience for her pain grew unbearably thin. I moved, flashing brightly, until she looked at me again. I made a little symbol for walking, a pointer finger and middle finger over my palm, before pressing my hands together and setting my head on the backside of one of them.

Time for bed.

Aaliyah laughed, and it helped to settle me, though I still kept a close eye on the way she stood and moved with pained grace.

Xander had better get back to Osiris soon; we needed a permanent fix for this *yesterday*. I just hoped the bastard actually knew something. I'd spent far too long getting my hopes up, and it was time we caught a fucking break.

"Okay. I'll lie down for a bit. I'm sure it's just stress." She looked about as convinced as I did, swallowing hard as she tried to shove the fear out of her eyes. But I saw it, I always saw it. "Adrian said he was going to finish dinner. He's fixing up that risotto we tried to put together."

I nodded, bowing like a proper gentleman, all the flair and bullshit making her laugh again.

A gentle expression took over her face, and she lifted her hand like she was going to touch me. The crack in her joy pierced my chest as she pulled her hand back, placing her hand over her heart, ring and pinky finger curled under.

It was a sign I'd take with me to my grave, one that I'd never forget. Because it was a symbol of *us,* of the world we wanted to see. It was our promise to stay by each other's sides *forever*.

"I love you, Prince." Those words would be my downfall, my hopes, and my dreams. I held onto them because those words alone were more of a victory than any battle I'd ever fought. "Forever."

And one day, maybe they'd be my redemption.

Chapter 5

Aaliyah

The near-endless ache that had started in the kitchen didn't lessen after sleep like I'd been begging it to. Everything in me was rioting, and the need to flee, to find a small space to crawl up into, was almost too much to bear.

Everything had been going so well. I was comfortable, safe, and hadn't had any *Rends* ...

What changed? Had Kali's spell really done this? Or was this just me?

I sat in my bed, contemplating it with Prince at my side. Lucky for me, he'd always made a pleasant distraction when my mind was fighting me like this. It was impossible not to notice his broad shoulders and sharp jaw, or the way his transparent eyes crinkled at the corners. He had an energetic expression, one that said more than his hands could. The thick, corded muscle that should have flexed stayed static, but that didn't take away from the sheer size of his arms, his chest ... all of him.

He was so striking, so *strong*. He was beautiful in a brutal way, and just staring at him helped to settle some of my more chaotic thoughts.

His arms moved animatedly, telling a broken story I only half paid attention to. He'd thrown in some new symbols, ones I was adding to our ever-growing list. One of these days, I would write them down, so I didn't forget any. There had to be a stray notebook around here somewhere.

He glanced my way, as if able to feel me staring, his hands freezing in the air and his lips curled into a familiar, foolhardy grin. His hands began moving again, fluid, and even with the ache in my head and the uncertainty I felt, I beamed back at him.

I wished, at that moment, Prince could talk. It wasn't a new wish. In fact, I'd had that same one more times than I could count.

"Maybe Osiris knows sign language," I mumbled, catching as Prince's hands fell completely, his face twisting in a confusing grimace before he nodded.

I furrowed my eyebrows at him, bewildered by his drastic change in emotion, the thickening sense of his hesitation bleeding into the air.

I hadn't really thought of it up to this point, with everything else going on, but seeing Prince so stricken had me wondering why. He knew the Vivas Crypt. That much had been made clear the day they found me at the auction, but *how* did he know them?

Would they know who he was?

As if knowing what I was going to ask before I said it, Prince raised his hand, his eyes falling closed. The pain he couldn't hide seeped into the air, stealing the breath from my lungs. He put his palms together, pulling them apart in a way that was similar to our motion for a *Rend* before he mimed talking.

It took me a second before I understood.

"Long story?" I asked, and Prince nodded.

I knew extraordinarily little about Prince's life before death. I was aware he *knew* things, was aware that he differed from other ghosts in that he didn't want to go to the Void, but that was the extent of it. Curiosity sparked inside of me, and I struggled to keep my questions at bay, even with Prince looking so distraught.

But eventually, his pain won over my questions, and I sighed.

"Will you tell me? One day?" I asked, and Prince grimaced forlornly before nodding.

Letting it go, I moved to stand. The room was beautiful, the gray walls not claustrophobic like my cell had been. It was cozy, with the large plush bed directly in the center. Though, I would admit it was lacking in color. Maybe that was something we could address after all this madness was done with. Regardless, I was tired of staring at the walls. I still ached, but I'd moped enough in this room, and the aroma of food was now beginning to slip past the door. I wanted to go to the library and grab my book, so it was downstairs for me after dinner. I'd been meaning to get a few pages in, and hopefully, this pain would fade between now and then.

So I could pretend I wasn't sick, if only for a moment longer. We had enough going on; me getting worse? That was the last thing we needed. Time was already not on our side. I didn't want to shorten it even more.

I stood on wobbly legs, inching toward the door until I was close enough to swing it open. The hinges creaked, and I was met with an empty hallway. The geometric stones that lined parts of the wall were easy enough to hold and I braced myself against them just as Prince floated through the now closed doorway.

Walking was far harder than it had been just a few hours ago. My head pounded, and every ounce of strength that I'd gained back from my nap sapped out of me. I leaned against the wall, begging my legs to take another step, for the library to be even an inch closer.

I shook, barely holding myself up.

Please.

I forced another step, nausea rolling in my stomach as *pressure* built in my skull. It made me sick all at once, and I struggled to breathe as panic set in. The pressure ebbed and flowed, building until it overwhelmed me. Prince stood strong behind me, urging me to turn around as his worry sank into the air, tasting bitter on my tongue.

I hadn't lied when I said it wasn't a *Rend*. This *was* different. It wasn't like my soul was tearing itself to shreds to get me to remember something with no *Rend* to catalyze it. It was like someone else was digging around, prodding at my mind while I was powerless to stop it.

I ground my teeth, forcing the feeling down, aching to take just one more step when the familiar glass mosaic door that led to the game room and the library slid open. The setting sun that was painstakingly etched into it glowed and then disappeared as a sharp, narrowed face peeked through.

I hadn't seen much of Osiris today, and even now I was surprised that he was in the house. My gaze caught on his aching beauty, with the cruel twist of his high cheekbones and defiant eyebrows. His hair, that inky black that looked so soft, was brushed back. He was in one of his signature pinstripe suits, one that seemed just a bit too tight for his body, as the muscles of his arms and shoulders stretched the fabric. It was the kind of perfection that marble sculptors spent hours desperately trying to mimic.

His face was angled down, another book in his hands, one that I'd been holding the other day. I recalled being drawn to it, and the beautiful, unfamiliar script. It was only a moment later when he looked up, and for a second, I was confused when his eyes grew wide in abject horror. Then I remembered the ache, and the slamming pressure rattled back down my spine.

"Aaliyah?" My name on those thin lips cracked, and electricity charged the air. One moment, Osiris was by the door, and the next he was in front of me. Leaning down so our faces were just inches away. The sound of something clattering to the ground registered before he finished. "What's wrong?"

I opened my mouth to speak, unable to force any words out.

I'm fine.

I wasn't. It hurt so badly that I wanted to scream.

Just tired.

My entire body burned and raged. I recalled memories on the table that were easier to ignore than this.

Just a dream.

It had to be. Because the only other option was that I was still *dying*. Like not even fate could give me a break, that pressure snapped like dead wood, and the scent of iron flooded my nose. A single urging word echoed in my mind, stealing any hope of normalcy from me.

Bog.

By either luck or fate, my legs gave, and Osiris pulled me into his arms. The embrace was familiar, with his hands under my knees and neck, cradling me to him. His face, so twisted with worry, brought unbidden tears to my eyes.

We were downstairs far before I could even try to convince myself of what I already knew was a lie. The tears kept flowing as Osiris set me on the couch in the living room, and Prince came into view. Even his steady presence did little to stop the sobs when they started.

"How many times do I have to tell you to stop—" grumbled Fallon as he walked into the room, my gaze jerking to him. The moment his eyes landed on me, his hand already over his breast pocket, likely reaching for a chocolate, his sentence stopped. "Crying."

He blinked in shock. Once, twice.

"What happened?" he demanded, looking from me to Osiris. His expression twisted into a malice-filled snarl, his hands balling into tight fists. Osiris didn't move from next to me, his face carefully blank. "What the fuck did you do, Osiris?"

The flinch was barely there as Osiris's jaw gripped tight. Demons flashed in his eyes, and Fallon was too lost in his rage to notice it.

"It wasn't him," I promised, my voice sure, even if slightly cracked.

I hated the mistrust in Fallon's gaze and knew that sooner rather than later, this would need to be discussed. There was too much going on to let

Kali and her hateful words and actions continue to hurt everyone. They couldn't keep sitting on what happened, pretending that it didn't exist. It was going to break them.

I looked away, eyes settling on Prince and the way his own eyes flashed with worry. That familiar curiosity from our conversation in the room built.

"Wouldn't be surprised if he *had* done something," Fallon seethed, teeth showing in his sharp glower just as Adrian and Eirik shuffled in.

The small living area barely fit all of us, and the congested room made my skin tight. I brought up a hand, pressing it to my temple, just as a soft growl echoed in the air. Before I opened my eyes again, I was being lifted, my head falling into a warm lap as large, calloused hands gently rubbed at my scalp. The warmth of Eirik's skin, and the rumble that vibrated through me, helped to dull the ache.

"Fally, now you're just being sour." Adrian's words cut through my haze. "What happened, love? Did the shower not help?"

Adrian moved swiftly, crouching down next to the couch, taking my hand in his and swiping away the blood that had slid down to my lip with a damp rag. He practically had to shove Osiris out of the way to do it, though Osiris barely blinked at the offense, his eyes still far away.

Just a dream.

"I'm fine." The lie tasted of bitter regret, the sensation so strong that even Prince shook his head from across the room.

"Don't lie, **never** to this one. Tell us what's wrong." The coarseness of Eirik's words gave the beast away as his hands froze in my hair.

There was a sharpness to his voice that left no room for argument, and even though I considered lying again if only to forget for a second longer, I knew it wouldn't be of any use.

They'd find out either way, and I was happier to have it on my terms. So, even as the thought made me uncomfortably numb, I spoke.

"My head hurts, and it almost feels like I'm going to *Rend*," I said, squeezing Adrian's hand when his eyes shot wide. "Before it happens, there's that pressure in my head, and I've felt that for the past few hours."

Tears sprang again, and I looked away.

"I didn't mean to hide it, I just—" I choked on my words, suddenly finding it hard to breathe. "I didn't want it to be real. I thought I was getting better."

The silence only lasted for a second before Adrian leaned forward, pressing his cool hand to my cheek. He angled my head toward him, gentle but firm, and when he caught my eyes, the weight of what I said lifted. Just a touch.

"We're here for you, little love." The adoration in his words didn't go unnoticed. Eirik stiffened beneath me, and for a terrifying second, I considered what Adrian had to be seeing.

He'd asked to court me, and I agreed. Now I was laying across his brother's lap. I wasn't sure how to navigate this, but he didn't *look* angry.

As if seeing my worry, he gave me an adoring smile, before leaning forward and sealing our lips together. It wasn't a long kiss, barely a brush of icy skin, but it still set my nerves on fire, breaking through my headache enough to make me gasp as Eirik's growl shifted into something heated beneath me. When Adrian pulled back, leaving me flushed and confused, he winked, and I was left wordless as Osiris began speaking like he hadn't just seen Adrian's move.

"If your symptoms are progressing even with our proximity, then we need to hurry." His eyes zoned out on the gray wall and the several trinkets sprawled across it.

Prince flashed across the room, grinning with more joy than I'd ever seen. The smile was so wide it almost appeared false, and my chest clenched as I realized he was happy ... happy for me and devastated at the same time.

"We need to talk to Xander," Fallon said, his voice smoothly flowing over me, clear if not cold.

"He hasn't been responding to my letters," Osiris retorted flatly, tugging at his blue undershirt. "You know how he works. He's like a petulant child. He won't respond until he's ready."

Fallon scoffed, rolling his eyes and never letting go of the glare his face still held. "Then message him again. Threaten him if you have to, Osiris."

"I will," Osiris assured, before turning back to me. "What else can you tell us?"

Bog. It was a whisper this time. I pressed my hand to my temple, lips shaking as I closed my eyes.

"When I went back to the Void in the training room with Eirik, something happened ... something that I can't really explain. I was going to tell you about it, but with everything that happened so soon after..."

Osiris didn't need to hear me say her name, his eyes fluttering as he swallowed harshly.

"A voice told me something. At the time, I was worried they wanted to hurt us, but I heard it again today. It sounded urgent, *panicked.*"

Like I was running out of time.

I tensed my hand around Adrian's, using his presence to ground me.

"Do you know what 'bog' might mean?" I asked, glancing between them. Each of them held an expression between confused and shocked, but it was Osiris I focused on. How his eyes grew slightly wide, his hands shaking as he grabbed his wrist. He held his hand over it, squeezing so tight the skin went white.

"Bog?" he asked, taking a step back, a furious expression taking root in his eyes.

"I can only think of one thing," Adrian said, his own voice trailing off as he once again ran his thumb over the back of my hand, bringing me comfort. "Osiris—"

"The Bog Sorceri," Osiris bit out, cutting off Adrian's words.

"Why would your Void want you to find Magelav?" Adrian asked softly, but I didn't get the chance to answer, as Osiris spoke again.

"Because they're more than just a Sorceri. Magelav is a Rourovic ... and they prefer Chronomancy above all other magic."

My blood went cold, and my mouth suddenly tasted sour as my stomach twisted and rolled. Even my fingers grew numb. Rourovic. *Rourovic.*

The only other person in the room who didn't look surprised was Adrian.

"Wait. You mean to tell me that Crazy Mags—" Fallon started but was again cut off as a spark of power exploded off Osiris, the lights flickering overhead.

"Is the elder sibling of the Sorceri Eternal, *Kali Rourovic.* They must have seen her coming and were trying to warn you," Osiris confirmed, a startled and broken laugh stunning me. "And it sounds like we'll be needing their help after all. My guess is you're hearing their prophecy through your Void." He looked lost at that, like it was something that shouldn't have happened. "Magelav wouldn't physically intervene in something like this if it weren't a calamity in the making. Kali was likely just the start."

Silence, and then Fallon gave a laugh of his own. It was cold, if not slightly cracking. The fury in his gaze could have melted permafrost. "You really do just keep all the fun to yourself, Osiris," he sneered, disgust so clear in his words that even Prince flinched. "Got anything else to share with the class?"

Osiris didn't speak, his eyes closing as he once more took the weight of the world onto his shoulders, and again he pretended like it was only his to carry.

"I'll look into the matter." Was his quiet promise. Then, just like last time, he was out the door before I could find something to say. We were left with only our thoughts.

And the unending tick of time, as I regretfully accepted that death wasn't quite done with me yet.

CHAPTER 6

FALLON

"Eri, you're overreacting."

Those were the words I heard as I made my way down the creaking stairs that lead to the main floor of my home. There was an agitated quality to Adrian's voice that told me it wasn't the first time he'd said that to Eirik, and I doubted it would be the last.

Had I felt better, I would have probably enjoyed watching Eirik's endless stubbornness pitted against anyone but me, but as Adrian's tone echoed in the narrow stairway, it only helped to further foul my mood.

Sick. I was *sick*. My head pounded, and if my stomach twisted any harder, I might puke. I ached like I had when I was just a boy suffering from the flu, with my mother running a cold cloth over my forehead trying to drop my fever. Considering the fight with that bitch Kali two days ago, I shouldn't be surprised that my head *throbbed*.

But I was, and I was *worried*. Worried because I hadn't suffered this kind of sickness in centuries, worried because it had grown so horrible so quickly. And worried because I knew Ali had been feeling much the same and had been sick in more ways than just with her *Rends*. Whatever Kali had done to her had progressed into nosebleeds and an ache she couldn't hide from us. Something I now endured as well and saw on Adrian's face when he flinched, moving wrong in a way that brought back that twisting feeling of boiling blood.

We were all sick, and I was worried that Kali's spell had done something irreparable to us.

"Adrian, going out right now is dangerous. Our wards were torn through, and until Osiris is sure they're back up completely, we have to stay vigilant. Kali might still be in the area, or worse. *Him.*" Eirik didn't back down, and honestly, I couldn't blame him.

He was right this time. Until Osiris—the bastard—could test the wards more thoroughly, leaving the property was a poor play, and even I saw that. Not that I liked the idea of being stuck in this damned house, no matter how much room it had. You'd think with over five thousand square feet and a couple acres to get lost on, I wouldn't feel so stifled here. But I enjoyed going outside, wandering the streets of Oakridge and finding new pieces of art to line my walls.

I loved the culture of the town. The bars and life. The *fights*.

Not to mention, no matter where I went, I'd still bumped into Osiris three times in the past two days, and I was already at my wits' end with him. I was furious and hated how this had all played out. And that he hadn't apologized for not telling us about Kali. Hadn't owned up to it, so we could *fix* this. No, he just ran.

I heard Adrian scoff, "*You* were the one that told me to look around, Eri. Audric isn't a bad guy, and I'm running out of contacts. If he can point us at some allies *and* tell us about Ascension Rising, then it's worth the risk. We can't let an opportunity like this go to waste. I'd prefer we go into the Eternium with that shithole burned to the ground anyway, and hopefully find something that might help with Ali's *Rends* along the way."

He caught my attention with that, some of my split focus narrowing in on him as I made it to the bottom step, the ashy oak board creaking under my weight.

He added, "He's our best bet at finding where they might be or someone who knows. *And* he'll know who'd be inclined to side with us for Exilium. He's just in Oakridge, barely a few miles out. I'll be back before you've even realized I'm gone."

Eirik growled low in his chest, and I turned the corner to find him in a standoff with Adrian by the kitchen island. The shutters covering the floor-length windows were open, shining moonlight into the dim room. They each held a glass in their hands, the thick red liquid smelling like red wine blended with ashes and sea mulch. I covered my mouth, nearly gagging as the swimming in my head blew into even more nausea. This distaste for our blood wine wasn't new. It'd been a growing problem for us for the better part of seventy years, one that only I seemed to notice was getting worse.

It was ten years ago when we realized it no longer tasted like blood wine. Three weeks ago it was bearable, two weeks ago it became rancid, and now I could barely look at it without getting sick. And that was exactly what I didn't need today.

Aaliyah, who had stayed silent through this, cleared her throat. I turned to her, not having realized she was there. She was the object of my ill-omened obsession, one that I couldn't shake no matter how much I tried. Not that I tried hard. She glanced between Adrian and Eirik, chewing on her bottom lip as she worked through her thoughts. There was always such bravery in her eyes, the kind that came from being scared, yet standing firm anyway. I admired it to a fault, and like always, I couldn't look away from her.

"Ascension Rising is a threat to you guys. You *can't* take them lightly. If they ever came looking for me—" Aaliyah's words cut off with a flinch and a breath, and Eirik snarled, the sound furious as he fought himself. "If they ever found out I was here, they'd hurt you to get me back. I *can't* let that happen. If this man, Audric, might know where to find them, then we need to go to him."

Her hair was pulled into a loose ponytail that bounced as she dipped her head, having noticed me. Her eyes were dimmer than normal, and her skin didn't glow. She took another hesitant breath, flinching as she did. I didn't know what to make of that stare, and I knew even less what it made me feel.

Ali was a force to be reckoned with in her own way. She didn't have physical strength, but what she lacked there she made up for in grit and determination. I admired that about her, even possibly adored it. Her will was unlike anything I'd seen, and her ability to keep going even under the worst circumstances struck every chord inside me.

But seeing her looking so frail the other day after Kali had left cracked something in me. My hand shook, and I was reminded of a frighteningly familiar moment in the woods just a while ago. With her splayed against the ground, dead and unmoving after Eliza had teleported her away from our home, and we learned that nothing about Ali was what it seemed.

It was a sight I'd tried to burn out of my mind, and yet every time I saw her it came back, and the need to go to her, to protect her, became overwhelming.

But how could I protect her from death?

How was I supposed to protect myself from the impact I knew it'd have on me if she died *again?*

Aaliyah wasn't aware of my inner turmoil, as her legs swayed in front of her, not quite reaching the ground from the dining chair where she sat. Her eyes were on Adrian and Eirik as she blew at the top of a small steaming coffee mug with a kitten plastered on its side. It smelled of oolong tea and honey, and she sighed as she took a deep drink. She wore a tight pair of jeans and a loose black t-shirt that smelled of Osiris.

"If they come, they *die.* They will not hurt you again, *Elskan,*" Eirik's words were a vow, his eyes deepening to a raging sea blue. His entire body tensed, his skin becoming tighter as his face sharpened to prepare for a shift. **"Ever."**

Aaliyah just gave him a sorrowful look, and Eirik's anger deflated. He shook his head before setting his glass on the table and walking over toward her. He kneeled by her side, taking her hands in his.

Aaliyah murmured, "Eirik. You're strong, *so* strong. But I've seen what they can do to people, to *Vampires.* I don't want them to find me, and I don't really want to find them. But of the two options? I'd rather they be the surprised ones."

And strangely enough, Eirik, *on his knees* by her side, nodded. He brought her hands to his lips and kissed each of her wrists.

"Then we'll find them and show them why fighting with Crypt Vivas was the worst mistake of their lives," he said with a determined furrow to his brow, turning to watch Adrian as he nodded. When he shifted his gaze back to Ali, he stood. "We'll be your shields, *smár Valkyrja,* but I doubt you'd even need them."

Shield didn't hold up if they were going against cannons. And Ascension Rising was a fucking cannon waiting to go off when we least expected it.

"What do you think Audric is going to know about them?" I chimed in, butting into the conversation and catching the attention of my brothers. "He likes to stay neutral in Natural affairs."

I rolled my head from side to side before walking forward. My entire body had ached since I'd woken up, and a dull pulse started behind my eyes. It was absurd—*sick*—something I hadn't been since my human life over two hundred years ago. It almost felt like my blood was still boiling inside of me. The reminder of the Sorceri Eternal made my gums ache and my blood turn in my veins.

I looked at the table that still held an imprint of an elongated talon, as well as the imprint of scorch marks we couldn't get off the ground. I should have killed her when I had the chance. Better yet, she shouldn't have been allowed to harm us to begin with. My ire with Osiris stemmed and grew inside my chest like mold. My heart was a winter storm in my chest, thundering, pushing me forward.

The need to fight, to spill blood ... I craved it, and today I craved Osiris's most of all.

I walked toward Adrian, my eyes never leaving Aaliyah, who was looking at me like I had just walked out of a morgue. I was exposed under her observant gaze, hating and loving at the same time how she so easily made my nerves spike.

"As I was saying to Eri, Audric is a tailor first. People get loose lips in places like that, Fal. Trust me on this. He'll have something to say," Adrian hummed.

"And if he doesn't?" I pressed.

Adrian rolled his eyes, hiding the worry in them with a sarcastic laugh.

"God, that head of yours is thick. Does it get hard to carry it around?" Adrian snorted, finally responding to my remark, barely even looking at me. "There has been no other trace of them, none. Not a whisper, not a breath. The only other place I can think of to check is the only place where *everyone* goes. Audric sees everyone, knows everyone, and he would have heard something about this if there was something to hear. *He had to.*"

Adrian whispered the last bit before clicking his tongue, taking a second to *flit* over to Aaliyah.

It was hard to find a crack in his judgment, but Adrian had always been adept at finding information others desperately wanted to hide. You didn't gain a name like the *Collector* without good reason, and if he was struggling this hard, I wondered if this was our last option.

"At least it's heavy to carry and not empty like yours. I'm worried you might blow away if a light wind comes by," I quipped back, dulling the sharpness of the conversation.

Adrian cracked a wicked grin, shaking his head as he reached out to Aaliyah, and just taking her hand was enough to get his lips to tilt into a genuine smile.

That need, the one to *go* to her like the others, exploded. I hadn't known what to think since Adrian kissed her in the living room. I'd been too shocked to even breathe then, and now it was *all* I thought about. I'd been so careful and done my best to keep my distance, but she was like a raging fire, and I was nothing but dried cotton. Even trading blows with

Eirik hadn't been able to make me forget the way she blushed, and the loving way she beamed at Adrian.

Because it couldn't be mine. I would break my soul if it meant someone else wouldn't have the opportunity to break it for me. All it took was another memory, another burning flash of her dead against the ground, and I turned away.

My head, still throbbing, helped at least to keep my mind off of her, and the way she hesitated to look away from me. Her eyes narrowed, even as Adrian leaned over, placing an easy kiss on the top of her head that she glowed under. He stalked off toward the fridge, likely to start breakfast. Eirik stayed by her side, fiddling with the strands of hair that had come loose from her ponytail. All the while Adrian tapped each cabinet on his way across the kitchen, humming softly.

"You fight like children," Eirik huffed, crossing his arms with a raised brow as he stood fully, still a sentry by her side.

He looked at me too, like there was cause for worry, and maybe there was.

"*But we fuck like champions,* or whatever Eric Northman said," Adrian retorted, deepening his voice and shifting the tone to mock the character he was talking about.

I rolled my eyes again, and Adrian stuck his tongue out at me, mockingly putting his hands on his hips. I couldn't for the life of me remember what show it had come from.

He added, "Oh Eirik, why can't you be more like *that* Viking Vampire hunk, huh?"

Eirik huffed, and Aaliyah wiggled under his arm. He let her slide from his grip easily, head tilting when she stood and took a step toward me. That worry had never left her face, I realized.

"Fallon ... are you okay?" she asked softly.

She stood in front of me with all the grace you'd expect to see from a queen, her head held high, hands crossed loosely in front of her. That will glittered in her eyes again, shocking me into staring as she bit her lip, and I found myself unable to rip my attention away from where her teeth indented the skin.

She can be yours.

"Why?" I snapped, jaw clenching when she flinched.

It wasn't the kind from when she first arrived, the one that reminded me there were still people I had to kill, but one of surprise.

Aaliyah didn't back off like I thought she might. Instead, she took a step closer, until I heard the steady thrum of her blood under her skin. A sickening twist of my insides had my mouth watering, and I couldn't tell if it was the *Call* that was driving me to pull her close or my own thoughts. I held back, holding my breath as her hands reached up. She gave me a moment to pull away if I wanted, and I nearly did.

But I *couldn't*. Like always, I was too weak to do the right thing for my sanity, and when her hands moved to my collar, another chip of my control tumbled away. My fangs slid out, piercing my bottom lip as I held them tightly closed. Lavender, her marker, a scent that would forever be chiseled into my mind as *hers* flooded me with a sharp desire.

Then I heard the distinct snap of my dress shirt falling into place, and as I looked down, I realized it wasn't the only thing that had been in shambles. My shirt was untucked, and my white dress pants were *wrinkled*.

How had I not seen that? I clenched my jaw, my fangs pulling back as my stomach dropped, and my hunger was replaced with a humiliating shame.

"Damn ..." Adrian said, the fight from his words draining out. "*Are* you okay, Fally?"

I didn't look at him as I jerked away from Aaliyah's hands. The worry in her eyes was unfounded, and it wasn't something I needed or wanted.

Yet it hurt to see the way she jolted when I turned toward the island. It cooled the roar of my blood, and all too vividly, the reminder of why she moved that way froze me to the ground. It was so strange to remember sometimes. She carried herself well and was always putting herself after everyone else, even now, as she continued to fuss over my state of dress and worry about what it meant.

I forgot she'd been tortured and *experimented* on. It was so easy to forget that Ascension Rising, the *reason* for her scars and why she still flinched when someone moved too fast, was still out there. For a brief second longer than he deserved, I even experienced that same gnawing pain for Osiris.

The difference was that Aaliyah had trusted us with herself and her secrets. Told us about Castillion, the doctor who used to strap her down and cut her open. About Nox, Nilus, and everyone else who had taken part in her fucked up childhood. Yet Osiris, in all the decades and centuries since we'd known each other, hadn't. It left an empty hollow in my stomach. Like this family we had made was nothing but a falsity. Nero would be disappointed with my thoughts, and that was the only thing that kept me from raging again.

"I'm fine," I bit out, tucking in my shirt and running a haphazard hand through my hair. "I'm going with you to Audric's, Adrian. I need a few extra suits, with the Eternium coming up."

And to monitor Adrian, I didn't like the idea of him going out alone right now. Not with everything going on. He hesitantly nodded, just as Aaliyah stood.

"I am too," she insisted.

And, of course, it was only barely seconds later that a sinister growl echoed across the room. Eirik's eyes flashed red and his face tightened like he was going to shift.

Seemed that the tentative peace Eirik and his beast had made was short-lived.

"Absolutely **not**," Eirik snarled. "It's not safe."

He was a beast of a man as he towered over her, but she didn't fall. Hell, she even raised an eyebrow as if to chastise him, and he had the mind to look regretful of his words.

"Nothing's safe, Eirik. They're still recovering from the other day, and I don't like the idea of them going alone," she insisted, unrelenting as she admonished the man who had made more conquerors tremble than most could dream of remembering. "And ... I have to do this. Ascension Rising held *me* captive. I need to help."

Aaliyah turned her head to face Adrian and I, worry suddenly replacing that spark of fight in her eyes.

"I'm pretty good at picking up when people lie. Prince is too," she said, looking over my shoulder to stare at the ghost in question. "I'd like to help if I can, be there if I can ... if it's alright with you two."

"You're still sick," Eirik said, his teeth still clenched tightly. "They can go talk to him alone. They'll tell you whatever he says."

That hint of his wolf hadn't left his features. The beast was just as worried as Eirik was. Ali, in all her goodness, stepped into his arms easily.

He held her to him like a treasure, his nose running along her hairline. He was so much bigger than her, nearly swallowing her whole as he wrapped himself around her small frame. Yet he held her so gently, moving so slowly and with such intent. It was strange to see it from the outside. I'd seen Eirik *rip* people apart in fights, and yet with her, there was only care. The same hands that had toppled armies now rubbed circles on Aaliyah's back.

"Eirik, I've always been sick. Yesterday was just a reminder of that. I *can* help. So, please, trust me?" she asked, gazing up at him.

It wasn't the look of someone trying to coerce. Like always, she was open about herself, laying bare before him, and Eirik muttered a curse. He reached up, playing with a strand of her hair before nodding.

Adrian *flitted* to her again, stretching a hand out for her to take. When she placed hers in his, he pulled her into a hug that had her laughing.

The effortless way his hands fell on her hips, the doting adoration in his eyes ... It was everything. I wanted to not care about how sick I felt or the Eternium, Ascension Rising, or even *Sebek*; I just wanted Aaliyah to smile at me like that. I wanted the press of her lips, the joy of her laugh.

I wanted her cries of pleasure, and I wanted *her.*

I recalled our vote for our *happiness* the other day. Adrian said we deserved it, that he wanted happiness for all of us, and it was with a bitter taste that spoke of my jealousy that I realized Adrian had found it. Even worse, somewhere in the depths of my soul, I knew I wanted that happiness too. It didn't matter how much I denied it to myself, how I hid behind my own fears.

I wanted her so badly it hurt.

"You've got my vote, love. I've heard what you can do with a bedpost." Adrian looked at Eirik, who reluctantly huffed in agreement. Aaliyah blushed, shuffling when Eirik purred at the reminder of her first night with us. "Besides, Osiris wanted her measurements anyway, remember? Now would be a good time to get them."

I clenched and unclenched my hands. The thought of caring for someone else, someone after my sweet Aislinn ... terrified me. It had been unfathomable for so long, a thought I hadn't even considered beyond a few flings. I didn't want to love someone, only to lose them. To be the reason they were lost. The *Call* had taken Aislinn away from me and turned me against her in a way I'd never be able to forget. I didn't want Ali's blood on my tongue unless she *asked* me for it.

I shook my head, beating down the feeling, choking it with what little strength I could muster.

Aaliyah's sweet laugh echoed in the room, and even Eirik's beast quieted. It was so innocent, so free. It made my chest tight, and I averted my gaze. Eirik's teeth clenched, and the dragon tattoo around his eye flexed as though just as angry as its master.

"I don't like this," Eirik huffed. "Audric is formidable."

"Then come with," I replied, and he turned his sharp stare at me. His lips pulled back, exposing extended teeth that weren't quite fangs.

"I can't. I have to talk to Osiris about Xander and our defenses." Eirik gritted his teeth as he spoke, shaking his head.

Even I couldn't imagine having to have that conversation with Osiris, but if anyone could get through to our eldest ... Well, it was Nero. But Eirik would have to do.

"It'll be fine. We'll take care of each other," Aaliyah assured us, already moving to get our coats from the little closet by the front door. She wouldn't let us leave without them, even knowing the cold didn't affect us as much as it did her.

"Fine," Eirik ground out, shaking his head. "I *do* trust you. No one with half their sense would challenge you, *smár Valkyrja.*"

He turned back to us, the fire in his eyes burning hot. It was almost funny how protective he'd become, and he hadn't even sought her hand as Adrian obviously had. How much worse would he be when he finally broke?

"Keep her safe," he bit out, and I nodded.

"We will," I swore, slightly indignant at his lack of faith in us, though as I looked down at myself again and felt the headache still brimming, I understood. "You could use a fight. Up for one when we get back?"

Eirik didn't say a word, his energy speaking for him as he tore off his shirt and turned toward the door, likely to go for a run and then find Osiris by the graves. He gave one last lingering look at Ali, her cheeks flushing red. It was a sight to see his own eyes soften before he was gone.

"Let's go, love. Before mean, old Eri changes his mind," Adrian said with a grin.

She stepped over to us, coats in hand. Adrian and I dutifully put them on before we walked out the door.

Despite the late evening lull of Oakridge, Audric's shop, The Weathered Needle, was brightly lit. It was an older building, keeping true to the name of *weathered.* These were the buildings that had been around for decades, the wet climate and rot slowly turning the old bricks to dust. Though this place had a charm about it, something that made you want to come back and enjoy the scenery. Birds were still happily trilling in the air, and the soft sound of music echoed a few buildings down the street.

This was one of the few places that still operated past sundown, and while humans didn't know it, it was because every shop in this area had been run by Naturals for nearly as long as the town had existed.

A couple walked by, and Aaliyah watched them curiously as they passed a sweet treat between the two of them, gazing at each other lovingly. They smelled like stone—cold and hardy—and I scoffed when one of them flashed rocky fangs our way.

Gargoyles. Angels, by the looks of them. They didn't have the signature size of a Gargoyle Sentinel but were bigger than Imps. Though it was impossible to tell for sure which class they were without seeing their stone forms.

I paid them no mind, my hand reaching to my breast pocket on instinct, an action that had become ingrained in my day-to-day. I pulled out a small chocolate and handed it to Aaliyah. She murmured a quick thank you, the soft tone airy as she held the foiled sweet close to her chest, a fond expression on her face.

The Aldovin chocolate was something that I rarely ate myself, a last relic of my human life. It was the treat I used to eat on the sandy shores of my home, with Aislinn by my side.

When had I grown so fond of giving them away? When was the last time I'd had a piece and not thought of Aaliyah, instead of my past?

Aaliyah popped the chocolate into her mouth, humming contentedly, before sharing one more glance at the couple that had disappeared down the street. Then she turned back toward the building in front of us.

"This is it?" Aaliyah asked, breaking my thoughts as she took the first step toward *The Weathered Needle*, her pointer finger on her chin. "It's so ... bright."

"That's right, love. Audric's very own shop. In quite the prime location, if he must say so himself," Adrian mused, his eyes trailing the same streets as mine. "He's expecting us."

Though he continued to grin, there was a tension in his eyes, an intensity that only came when he was working. When he was hunting for something, information or otherwise. It seemed even deeper today, as he stayed close to Aaliyah's back, continually glancing down at her as she finally hummed and opened the door. It crept open with a groan, and the scent of fresh cloth and recently made dyes leaked pleasantly outside. Adrian moved to Aaliyah's side, keeping in step with her as they both walked in, with me right behind them.

As expected, Audric was in the main room, hunched over one of his many pieces. He didn't notice us at first, mumbling about the cloth until Adrian knocked softly on the doorframe, causing the weary Venomcaller to jolt up.

Audric was an elder, his age nearing what Nero would have been if he was still alive. He was impeccably dressed in the same way he always was, with a black tailcoat and ruffled white shirt, accented with a blue bow tie. His speckled black hair was tinged with white, and his delicately trimmed beard and mustache were a bit more frayed than normal. Regardless, he relaxed a bit when he realized it was us, his blue eyes wide at the sight of Adrian; polite but reserved.

"Adrian," he greeted, a natural hiss to his words over a thin, tube-like tongue. Though he was in human form, some aspects of his spider crept through. He shuffled, hands idly fraying the stitches of the work in his hands. "So nice of you to stop by. Come, come."

We had dropped this visit haphazardly onto Audric's lap, and the tension only continued to grow as Adrian tipped his head with a calculating expression on his face. Aaliyah was tense next to him, looking between the two with concealed curiosity. Her button nose twisted slightly, and she glanced over the spider's shoulder before the stress she held lessened, and she took a second to examine the space.

The soft red Victorian flare Audric loved seeped into everything in the room. From the maroon carpeted flooring that hadn't been replaced in decades, to the red oak that covered the walls, only to be shadowed by soft velvet curtains. The room was packed with a mix of clothing and odd pieces of furniture, none of which matched. The old, faded black couch was the most comfortable looking piece in the entire room, and it was likely years my senior.

It was a warm building, and even though I wanted to find something wrong with it, it was pleasant. And open. No spare rooms for others to come slinking out of, and no stairs leading to other levels. Which meant no threats that we wouldn't immediately see, and that allowed me some semblance of relief.

"Audric, always a pleasure," Adrian said, pressing his hand over his heart. "Sorry for the abrupt session. I know you're very busy."

Audric did the same in return before he crossed his arms lightly behind his back. It exposed his chest and his throat, a subtle sign of submission that helped to cool my blood.

"You know it's no trouble for you, Collector. You're always welcome in my shop. But ... what's the meaning of your visit, if you don't mind my asking? You were rather vague as to why you needed me so late."

Adrian hummed, stepping toward Audric.

"First, I'd like to apologize for Osiris's call. He was rather upset this last week. I hope you understand." Adrian said the words like they were a question, but I knew there would be no problem with Audric. He'd been loyal to the Vivas Crypt for decades, and he wouldn't risk our wrath over a few terse words.

And from what I'd heard, they'd been *terse*. Osiris had called the tailor for pieces for Aaliyah before Eliza had brought her clothing over, and he'd been furious when the Venomcaller had told him he'd have to wait.

"Of course, with the Eternium coming up, I'd expect no less. No offense taken, of course. But you wouldn't have come all this way to issue an apology in person." Audric's smooth words were poised and said with such precise efficiency that it almost made my skin crawl. Audric was perceptive and always had been, but that didn't mean I wasn't hoping he wouldn't slip up.

I straightened and took a step closer to Aaliyah on instinct. It helped to calm me, knowing she was within arm's reach.

"Quite right," Adrian said easily, as he reached his hand out to Aaliyah, letting her decide if she was going to take it. The rest of her tension drained as she set her palm in his, and Adrian rubbed his thumb over the smooth skin on the back of her hand. "Audric, this is Aaliyah. Ward of the Vivas Crypt. We were hoping you might get her measurements, preferably over some tea."

Audric tensed for a moment, the subtle ask for information not going unnoticed. It was strange seeing Adrian work his magic. He knew what to say to get people to talk, and he was damn good at playing the room.

Audric did a quick glance around us, noting no one else in the building before he nodded once.

"Quite the beauty. I understand the dilemma," he said, keeping his eyes carefully on Adrian, only taking glances at Aaliyah. There was a wary panic to him as he traced her up and down. I struggled not to step closer to her, to snarl like I was Eirik. Audric hummed, finally reaching Adrian's eyes again. "I'll get her measurements, and we can enjoy some tea."

He scuttled away, motioning for us to follow him. He brought us to the back of his shop, the walls a similar maroon to the front. It had an aged look, the wood bowing in some places along the walls, and the floors creaking as we moved. In the middle was a small inclination on the floor, and he motioned for Aaliyah to stand on it as he proceeded to his workstation.

"How many cups?" he asked, turning his back to us as he shuffled through some material on the tabletop.

Another push and another give.

"One, maybe two, depending on how good it is." Adrian weaved his intent into his words. One cup, one question. It was how Adrian operated, and Audric understood, as he closed his eyes and nodded. "Assuming you have tea ready."

"Always, Collector. Please, ask." Audric moved over the wall to pull out a long measuring tape. He rubbed his hand against the well-aged leather.

Ali watched him like a hawk, her fingers twitching as she tried to stay still on her raised platform. She hunched, and her breathing caught. I watched her carefully, probably more carefully than I should, but I wanted to make sure she wasn't overexerting herself. She'd been pallid since the incident with Kali, and from what Adrian said last night, she'd dealt with another nosebleed *before* she'd been brought downstairs by Osiris with another one.

Her breath quickened as Audric took a step toward her, flinching as he reached out for her hand, which she hesitantly offered. I realized all too late the mistake this might have been, as Ali panicked, suddenly breathing heavily. Before I could intervene, Adrian moved.

"Audric, would you mind terribly if I took over?" he asked, stepping forward before Audric could start his measuring. He extended his hand, and Audric looked at him with a narrowed gaze as he hugged his measuring tape to his chest. Aaliyah took a deep breath when the Venomcaller stepped back. Adrian pushed again, "Been feeling rusty with my skills. Figured I could use some practice."

Audric looked stricken but handed Adrian the tape as though it were a piece of himself. But he didn't protest, eyeing Aaliyah as she trembled on the stand. "Of course."

"Thank you," Adrian replied as he walked up to Aaliyah. There was an enraptured expression on his face as he had her stretch out her arms. He'd said once that his mother was a tailor, and it seemed he still knew a few tricks. His hands skimmed her arms, and she sighed. I stamped down the jealous rage the sight brought, and the need to take his place.

"We're looking for information on a group. Presumably Naturals.

They'd likely be in the business of trafficking or purchasing from traffickers. They go by Ascension Rising," Adrian said, extending the tape to begin his measurements. Aaliyah relaxed under his hands, and I settled as well. "What can you tell me about them?"

Audric contemplated that for a moment, leaning onto his cluttered workbench. His face showed nothing.

"Ascension Rising? I don't think I've ever heard that name before. Trafficking happens far more than you'd hope. Such as Darius Verslini, with *The Devil's Details*. Though I told you about him last time."

I didn't sense any kind of deceit in his words, and even the way he stood bled a kind of honesty that you couldn't fake. The hope that we'd find anything here crumbled.

"Are you sure you haven't heard anything? Anything at all, Audric? This is important," Adrian retorted, glancing up from Ali.

I saw the way his hand tightened on the tape, his jaw clenching like he was out of options. He'd been scouring the area, talking to any he trusted to find out about Ascension, and Audric must have been his last hooray.

"All things are, Vivas," Audric mused but shook his head again. "No. I've heard nothing by that name. I'm sure of it."

Adrian wrapped the measuring tape around Ali's waist, reading the number as a means of distraction. He was taking it worse than she was, and she reached out, cupping Adrian's cheeks in her palms.

"He's telling the truth," she whispered, never letting go of his face as he sighed.

He sagged into her hold, his stony mask dropping long enough for him to press a heated kiss to her wrist. So easily she calmed him, lifting his mood even when we were talking about *her life*.

"How do you know, love?" he asked, and she looked over at Audric.

"His voice is honest, and his eyes ... he didn't lie to you. He doesn't know." She studied him for a moment before she leveled her gaze on the space to my left. "Prince agrees."

Adrian sighed but didn't fight it. He merely leaned forward, showing more than he probably should of our interest in Ali as he pressed a gentle kiss to her forehead. Then he turned back to face the Venomcaller.

"Thank you, Audric," was his simple reply.

Another dead end and another bit of hope shot down with it. Now it really was just Xander, and I'd never enjoyed relying on the Dryad. He was shifty, and he had a mean bit of magic in him.

And now Ali's fate was truly in his hands.

"I'll keep my ears open for you, Collector," Audric added, his fiddling becoming more apparent as he picked up a thimble and passed it between his hands. "Would you like another cup?"

He glanced at us and the door, and I realized we were quickly overstaying our welcome. And in that case, might as well stir the shit pot.

"What can you tell us about the current state of affairs for the Eternals?" I chimed in, much to Adrian's disapproval, as he shot me a searing glare.

Audric's eyes widened at that, but he nodded regardless. "They're scared. My clients have been rather loose about their grievances with this Eternium. I'm sure you've heard of the recent deaths?"

We all nodded. It was hard not to know about something as big as the death of an Eternal. And two had been found recently, the Gargoyle and Titan. The Gargoyle Eternal lived somewhere in Spain, and I couldn't even recall his name, but the Titan, Roderick, I knew. He'd been an ally of ours, someone who would have supported us against Sebek.

Figured he'd wind up dead.

"We have," Adrian said carefully. "What have you heard surrounding their deaths?"

Audric paused, tapping at the old oak counter that housed his many needles. He pulled at his collar, the first hints of sweat appearing on his brow as he swallowed. "I wish I knew, but I haven't heard anything." The words tumbled out, a kind of dormant fear clinging to them.

I fucking *hated* lies. I took a deep breath, the threat already primed, when a soft voice echoed in the air.

"Why would you lie about that?" Aaliyah asked, making my eyes shoot to where she stood.

White hair under the cool lights, eyes so vibrant they glowed. So defiant, so unrelenting in her gaze, yet kindness held there, too. Audric let out a shaking breath.

"I beg your pardon?" he asked, curling defensively around himself. It was a tick if I'd ever seen one, something that gave away his deceit, and I wasn't the only one who saw it.

"You're lying this time. I'm asking why." Aaliyah tilted her head, never looking away from Audric as she studied the way he stood. She didn't give, barely even blinked. She commanded the room with grace in her words, and damn if she wasn't the most stunning woman I'd ever seen at that moment.

"Now, Audric. We agreed." Adrian hummed, rolling up the tape before passing it back to him.

Audric gulped, pulling his arms toward his chest and guarding the space where his heart was. We had him there; he agreed to the tea, a truth for a debt. He couldn't refuse, not when Venomcallers always kept their deals.

"It's believed they were murdered, with most others suspecting *him.* Your Maker. The other Eternals are not taking kindly to it, too scared to even speak his name for fear of invoking the wrath of the boogeyman. *Death's Butcher,*" Audric whispered like Sebek might jump from the walls and kill him where he stood. "Me included."

We were all silent for a moment, soaking in what the words meant. Kali had been telling the truth, and Sebek *was* behind the recent Eternals' deaths. Which meant he had truly gone off the rails.

There wasn't a particular law against killing an Eternal, but it had never been a problem before. Those who'd been foolish enough to kill one were often faced with Retaliation and paid for their audacity with their life. But Sebek was too strong to beat in a fight, which meant even the most seasoned Naturals were terrified of it. It was why he was being so bold; I was sure of it. But others would want justice for this. They had to. The question was, was it enough? Exilium had never been called before, not in the entire history of the Eternals.

Even speaking it might cause an uproar.

"Thank you, Audric," Adrian said at last, hand in Aaliyah's as he helped her down from the raised platform. She brushed off her clothes, smoothing the wrinkles of her shirt.

"Might I be so bold as to ask what you intend to do with this information?" Audric's hands shook.

"That depends. How was our tea?" Adrian asked, his eyes flashing red for the barest of seconds.

A press of power, the *Flame* in the air, before it faded. It was a warning, one Audric was smart enough to catch. I knew Adrian would kill Audric in an instant if he told us his loyalty lay elsewhere. And as Audric watched Aaliyah, who had her eyes on the space next to him, he knew it, too.

"Calming, as always," he said, lowering his head in a bow. "We can always share a cup."

There were a few tense seconds of silence before Aaliyah let out a breath.

"He's telling the truth," she affirmed. "Prince trusts him."

Adrian debated it for a second before nodding slowly and turning back to Audric. "We plan to unseat our Maker."

The terror on Audric's face doubled, and he sputtered, "Truly? How?"

Now wasn't that the golden question? It was a toss-up; even the idea was a joke. We planned to overthrow *the* Sebek Ra. The man who'd been the Vampire Eternal since the Eternals were made. We should keep our heads down and hope he doesn't kill us for existing. But we couldn't, because now he wasn't only threatening us.

He was a threat to *Aaliyah.*

"We were hoping to see what other Eternals would be on our side, should a fight come to it," Adrian said, easily leaving our options open, while still offering enough to satiate the Venomcaller's curiosity.

"You mean Exilium? *The Honored Death,* for none other than *Death's Butcher,*" Audric said contemplatively, before he nodded. He was no longer slouching, now standing at his full height as he turned and shuffled at his cluttered table. Once he found what he was looking for, he turned his head back to us. "I was wondering if this day would come in my lifetime. I can get you a list of others that may be inclined to side with you, and perhaps the ones you should be wary of ... should you see fit?"

"That would be wonderful, Audric," Adrian said before he handed Audric a piece of paper I hadn't seen, mixed with the familiar red hue of gemstones.

Audric traded it, handing Adrian a single sheet of crumpled paper, the scrawling script something likely only Adrian would understand. Payment for our questions. I recognized the print on the paper as well. It was Adrian's writing, loose yet flowing.

"Here are the measurements. We don't need anything made up yet, but we'll be in touch."

Adrian bowed slightly, and Audric did the same. He wasn't quite an Eternal. If I recalled correctly, he didn't want the spot. The current Venomcaller was a close friend of his, meaning they were a friend of ours. Still, he was a powerful ally to have.

"As always, thank you for the tea," Adrian said, turning away without another glance.

"My pleasure, Collector. And know that the Venomcallers would have Osiris's back, should it come to a Challenge, or Exilium." His voice followed us out of the shop as we stepped onto the empty street.

People rarely came out past dusk in Oakridge, for good reason. Most blamed the Vampires, and I wasn't going to say the rest of my kind was helping our image, but the other Naturals were just as much to blame.

Curtis showed that only a few weeks ago, when he'd plucked Ali off the street.

"That went pretty well," Adrian said, before whistling softly.

The town was dimmer now, and the gentle melodies that had been bouncing along the near-empty sidewalk had gone dormant. A light wind pushed through the square, blowing dead leaves across the ground.

"I thought he was going to eat us," Aaliyah teased, a joking lilt to her voice.

She brushed her hair back behind her ear as she stepped up to Adrian, easily sliding her hand over his arm, seeming to do so without even realizing it. Adrian's joy reached his eyes as he leaned down and placed a tender kiss on the top of her head.

"No, he's all web, no bite," Adrian joked back, walking us the short distance to Osiris's McLaren.

We were parked on the side of the road, the flashy car looking more than a little out of place on the old cobblestone street. Not that Adrian minded as he quickly opened the door for Aaliyah, winking at her when she blushed.

He added, "And he's an excellent ally to have. But something tells me this is only the beginning. It's going to get worse, especially if *he* hears of what we're doing."

Adrian's words killed the conversation for a moment, as silence drowned out our thoughts. I hadn't seen Sebek since my turn and had only heard stories of the horrors he'd inflicted. But if he was as unhinged as I thought he was—and if he found out we were plotting against him—then our proposed deaths wouldn't be so farfetched.

"All we can do is keep going. We'll get through this," Aaliyah said, a trembling sigh following as she crawled into the car. Adrian was quick to follow, taking the driver's seat even as I protested. He twisted the heat on as Ali blew warm air into her hands. "I know it."

"Find a fix for your problem, dethrone our Maker, eat some fancy hors d'oeuvre at the Eternium, and sail off into the sunset," Adrian mused, pulling out onto the empty street. "It sounds like quite the plan to me."

"Unless Osiris doesn't agree," I noted, and Adrian raised his shoulders as if to say, 'What are we going to do?'

"Maybe he needs a break. In fact, I think we could all use one," he said, tapping his chin. Just as quickly, he lifted his hand, a gleeful smile taking over his lips. "Hot spring trip, anyone?"

The denial was already on my lips when Aaliyah laughed again.

"I'd like that," she said, and I held my words.

Her joy ... I wanted to see it, even if she wasn't mine.

She can be yours.

"Anything for you, love."

She might've been mine ... in another life, or another time. But right now, she wouldn't be, couldn't be. For both our sakes, it had to stay that way.

Chapter 7

Aaliyah

We walked back into the house a few hours before sunrise, the cold of the coming winter months sinking in, and I shivered even through my jacket. I walked slowly, Adrian by my side as I struggled to keep my gait even. After my last bout with this *Rendless* pressure, I was glad I could walk at all.

The kitchen was empty, and the lights were dimmed, casting eerie shadows over the room. But the quiet was soothing tonight, and I relaxed as Adrian draped his arm over my shoulders, easily tipping my head up to look at him with a finger under my chin. As always, I was drawn to the serene expression on his face and the endless sunshine in his eyes.

I didn't see it much anymore, the sun. But I didn't feel the need to. At Ascension, I'd craved it. The heat, the *light*. But now it seemed so trivial. Why would I need the sun when there was something just as bright behind Adrian's eyes?

"You're looking a little worn, love. Everything all right?" Adrian had always been more careful about how he said things, pushed in a way that really hammered home how good he was at conversing. "You handled your-self amazingly, you know. I doubt we would have gotten so much out of Audric without you there. You did well."

But not good enough. I tipped my head down, pulling my lip between my teeth. While we'd gotten some useful information about the Eternium, what I'd been hoping to find there had been a bust. Audric didn't know

80

about Ascension, and we were one more step away from them. I didn't *want* to find them. The idea of coming face-to-face with Castillion had every nerve in my body rioting. But I wanted them to find us even less.

"Thank you, Adrian. For letting me go," I said, and Adrian shook his head.

"Letting you? Oh, no, love. That was all you. You're strong and more than capable. Thank you for trusting us to help." I blushed at his praising words, my hand lifting on instinct to hold my arm and curl into myself. "I'm sorry that my lead was a dead end. I'd hoped ... damn."

Adrian ran a hand through his copper-tinted hair before he rubbed the back of his neck, jaw clenched tightly. I wasn't sure why he felt so guilty about this, like it was his fault. I reached out, cupping his cheeks.

"You did your best, Adrian. That's all I can ever ask for," I assured him.

He didn't smile, but he reached up to grab my hands.

"We'll get them, love. We'll make sure they can never hurt anyone again," he said, uncharacteristically serious as anger flashed across his face. It was almost deranged, manic, but it was gone just as fast. It probably should have scared me ... but that vengeful wrath? I knew it wasn't directed at me, but rather *for* me, and it made me kind of bubbly inside. "Now, you seem tired. Do you want to call it an early night?"

I hummed and looked around the room again. I wasn't tired. At least, my mind wasn't. My body could use a good seven-year nap, but my mind was racing, still stuck on Ascension. Maybe they would have a fix for me. Well, I tried to hope they might. Though, if they knew I was alive, they never would have left me buried. No, the far more likely answer was that they had no idea I was going to come back, and that meant they'd have no idea how to fix me now that I was. It was an unsettling thought, one that stung as I rubbed my temples.

"No, but I'd love some tea. Maybe we can drink some in the library before sunrise?" I asked, turning toward him fully. I sank easily into his arms, the chill of him overridden by the spark that flared as he lifted his hand and skimmed my cheek with his thumb.

"That can be arranged," he whispered as he pressed his forehead to mine, breathing deeply. "For a price, of course."

He grinned jokingly, and I adored it. It was nice to fade away from everything for a moment, and just enjoy him. There wasn't the imminent Eternium—or my death—to deal with. It was just Adrian and I. I'd always wanted something like this, the ability to play and tease, and so I pulled back slightly, unable to hide my excitement.

"Now, what kind of *sensible* price do you have for procuring tea?" I asked, stumbling slightly over the words, blushing through it all.

Adrian stood still for roughly a second before tipping over and laughing so deeply I couldn't help but laugh with him. It was only when we settled, and he reached up and cupped my face again, that he spoke.

"Why, my fine lady, I can think of only one thing," he said, pushing his accent deeper into the words as he leaned in. His breath skimmed my skin, and I shivered as his lip curved up at the corner in a tilted grin. I struggled to stay still as he continued with his teasing movements. "Something soft and sweet. And *addictive.*"

His thumb traveled along my cheek again. His eyes sparkled, so full of mirth that I couldn't stop myself as I reached up, grabbing his shirt, and consequences be damned, did exactly as Eliza had said that day at her *babas*.

I slammed my mouth against his before I could talk myself out of it, throwing caution to the wind. It held much less finesse than his kiss in the kitchen or even the one in the pool house, and it had my hands shaking, my heart thundering so hard in my chest that I struggled to breathe. But Adrian proved I didn't need to as he hoisted me up and wrapped my legs around his waist. It was quickly becoming my favorite place to be, as I held tighter, accidentally grinding into the front of his pants. The move came with a sharp spike of pleasure, one that scared me as much as it excited, and it dragged me away from him.

I looked at him again, hunting for the sun in his eyes and the tousle of his copper hair. He huffed his breaths, grinning widely.

"Price paid?" I asked, resting my forehead against his.

"I suppose I'll accept it for now ... but I'll be expecting the other half of your payment in the library," he said, setting me down with a wink. "Now, I'll go make your tea. Why don't you get comfortable, love?"

I just nodded as he turned and walked off, whistling a jaunty tune, before the sound of tapping echoed from the kitchen. I shook my head at his antics, feeling unusually giddy considering the ache in my head as I walked upstairs. I reached the top step just as Osiris was closing the door to his room.

I hadn't really seen him since the last nosebleed incident, only passing glances as he headed out. He looked ragged in a very put-together kind of way. Though he still wore a suit, the material was frayed and wrinkled, and his hair lacked the clean brush back it typically held, instead flowing wildly around his head. His usually tanned, olive skin had lost much of its vibrance. And ... his eyes were turned down, his mind obviously anywhere but here.

"Osiris?" I said his name quietly, trying not to startle him. "What are you doing?"

Even with my efforts, he jolted, his body unmoving as he angled his head almost unnaturally. That lack of breath and movement made my heart seize, and unneeded fear coursed through me. But just as quickly, Osiris took an exaggerated breath.

"I plan to walk the property and check our wards again," he said, gripping his wrist.

There was tenseness to his moves, a false sense of calm that didn't come close to looking real. His appearance threw me off balance. I had so many things I wanted to say, anything to drive that numbness from his eyes. But nothing came out, and my mind stalled.

There was another spark of worry, another push to ask, but I knew with the delicate way he spoke that if I even tried, he'd run. So I did my best to show him I was *here* when he could find the will to speak.

"Wait—" I said, freezing when he looked over his shoulder at me. "Adrian, Fallon, and I talked about a trip to the hot spring. You'll come, won't you?" I asked, and for a second I assumed he'd say no.

But his eyes cleared just long enough for me to see the life buried behind them, and he nodded. "Of course, I'll accompany you. I'm sure Eirik will be pleased as well. I will make the arrangements."

I nodded, and his gaze lingered on me for a moment longer before he turned away and silently moved down the stairs. I shook my head, staring at where he'd gone for much longer than necessary, hoping that he'd turn back.

Eventually, I left, walking through the vibrant mosaic door and through the game room. I ran my hand along the back of the red couch that sat in the middle of the room as I did before I came to the doors of the library. Thoth sat silently on the wood, the intricate carving watching me as I slid inside, sinking to the couch there with a heavy sigh. I'd only just sat down when the heavy oak doors opened again.

Adrian reappeared with two steaming mugs of tea in his hands. He juggled the cups, grumbling when some of the drink spilled over the side.

"Love? Weren't you going to get changed?" he asked, his head tilting slightly.

Right, I'd completely forgotten.

"Yeah, sorry. I was just talking to Osiris," I said, and Adrian's eyebrows shot up.

He set the cups down before taking his seat next to me. His arm wrapped around my shoulders easily, and I sank into his chest. The touch was calming, and I soaked it in as he hummed a question. "Oh? What did he have to say?"

"Not enough," I mumbled. "He's going to make sure it's safe for us to go to the hot spring."

Adrian hummed, and I stole a glance at his face. He looked into the fireplace, eyes on the dancing flames. He was the easiest to read, at least on the outside, but right now, I wondered what he was thinking. I knew that what had happened with Kali had hurt him, and the fact that his family was split had to drive that painful wedge a little deeper.

"Give him time. He's processing is all," he said like he was trying to convince himself as well. Adrian had been just as hurt by Osiris's lack of trust in them, but his worry had quickly replaced it. He saw what I saw, I thought. "Come on, before the tea gets cold."

Chapter 8

Eirik

There was nothing better than Aaliyah's smile, I decided, as we gathered supplies for our trip to the hot spring. It had been a tense few days since Kali had barged in and thrown everything we knew into chaos. Before that, it'd been a tense few *weeks*, with Aaliyah still sick and the threat of her death never far away. Adrian had suggested that this brief excursion might settle our minds.

With Audric not having any information for us on Ascension Rising, and Aaliyah feeling alright today, I had to agree. We needed a moment to breathe. Then it was time to go back to the board. Hopefully, Xander would meet us before the Eternium, and *hopefully*, he knew anything about Aaliyah.

This extra time making food, as well as getting ready for the small trip to the hot spring that sat just inside our border, allowed Osiris the time he needed to sort out the rest of the deal with the obnoxious Dryad. Xander was nearing five thousand years old, one of the few creatures in the States that beat Osiris's impressive age that wasn't our Maker. And the bastard was undoubtedly going to want something in return for helping us. He always did. Hopefully, it was less intrusive than the last request, one that required less prodding. I never had been a fan of needles, and that day had only made me hate them more.

For now, though, I took in our moment. I couldn't complain, not when Aaliyah lit up with her entire soul on display. She'd been talking about it nonstop since she'd woken up, and even the relentless headaches I knew she was plagued with didn't temper her enthusiasm. She was a whirlwind of excitement, and we were all just as caught up in it. It was adorable, the way her cheeks flushed and her grin arched down on one side.

I huffed, adjusting myself in the loose swim trunks I wore. I couldn't remember the last time I'd used them, swimming being Adrian's hobby. Even with the unfamiliar clothing, I had to admit it was entertaining to watch Osiris and Fallon looking the least pompous I'd ever seen from either of them. Aaliyah was much the same, wearing a spare t-shirt—one of mine—and a pair of boxers. Her clothes from Eliza hadn't included swimwear, so we made do with what we had.

As glad as I was that Eliza had finally delivered on her part of the deal to get us Aaliyah's clothing, I was equally irritated. Aaliyah hadn't been spending as much time in our clothes anymore, understandably. Beyond sleep, I hardly saw her in them at all.

My wolf wasn't as willing to let it slide, as he twisted up my insides with the desire to scent her again, to cover her in us. It gave me a sense of male pride I hadn't experienced in a long time to see her in our clothes and only furthered the need to protect her. It drove my *Úlfhéðinn* as crazy as it excited him.

Mine, he snarled, the sound bouncing around my skull, and as selfish as it was, I wholly agreed. It felt good to think of her like that. As mine, as *ours.* Vikings took what they wanted, and I wanted *her.*

Gods of old, did I want her.

I just needed to get a courting gift for her to make it official. It was old-fashioned, but the thought of my mother scowling at me pushed me to do this right. Because Aaliyah deserved nothing but the best from me. Adrian may have gotten to her first, but I was going to woo her properly.

So there I was, watching Adrian show the little Valkyrie how to make sandwiches the way we all liked. He was patient with her, marveling at her innocent questions the same way I was. She was so serious about it, wanting to make sure she got them all right. She'd just finished mine, a proud glow lighting up her face as she put it in its own Ziplock bag. She even added an 'E' to the front to signify it was mine, showing me with more joy than I thought was possible over something so small.

But it was something she hadn't had the luxury of doing in the past: picnics, walks ... making sandwiches. I wanted to show her all of it, everything that Ascension had stolen from her. And I was going to steal much more than that from them. When we found them—and we would find them—not even the Hallowed Three would be able to save their souls.

For now, we just needed to find a hint of them, a rumor they couldn't quell. And it'd be over. Then Ali could rest easy at night. Hopefully, *Rend* free. That was all I wanted, her happy, healthy, and in my arms.

Aaliyah was packing the last sandwich into the little lunch box when my gaze found her again. She was taking care to make sure none of them were squished against the others, her tongue sitting slightly out between her lips in concentration. It warmed my chest to see her so at ease. After every-thing she had been through, and after that hell with Kali, I was happy to see her smiling at all. She hid it like a master, morphing pain into determina-tion. I admired that about her, her strength.

Aaliyah zipped up the lid to the basket, the sound drawing my atten-tion. She stepped around the counter, walking toward me with a swish of her hips.

"I think we're ready, Eirik," she told me, the tender emotion in her eyes making the lavender pools swirl.

Her voice sang against my skin, and I stopped to take a moment to let her presence sink past the mounting tension from my beast. Her scent washed over me like a calming wave, smelling like lilies in an open field blending with the lavender that had swiftly become my addiction. My fangs ached as they pressed to be released. There was nowhere I would rather she be.

"Got everything?" I asked, and she nodded eagerly.

"I think so. Just need to go grab Fallon and wait for Osiris to finish up his call." I huffed when she looked away, back toward Adrian, her bottom lip bitten between her teeth. "How far is the hot spring again? Will it take long to get there?"

She barely reached my chest. So small, so fragile. I brought my hand up slowly, tucking a piece of her hair behind her left ear when she didn't protest my sudden closeness. My fingers grazed over her skin, sending that sharp bolt of leisurely desire down my spine, and her eyes fluttered closed.

"Not long," I answered. "It's a short walk."

Heat rose under my fingers as a flush took her over. Her eyes glim-mered, and I barely bit back the possessive growl of my *Úlfheðinn* as he beat against the cage of my mind.

He desperately pushed me to drag my lips down to hers, to let her sweet flavor consume us. To pull her into our arms and steal her away, if only for a little while. I was right there with him, but I carefully pulled back. He raged within, furious with me.

I didn't want to push too hard, too fast, not yet. She was still coming to terms with her interaction with Adrian, the lucky bastard, and I didn't want to overwhelm her with *me*. Because she *would* be mine. I'd do whatever I had to convince her of it. Make her come until the one thing she could think of was me. I'd done some terrible things in my life, but loving her would never be one of them. I would be her wall, her strength. Everything and anything she needed, because she had stolen my soul the day I looked into her lavender eyes and she carved a mark into my skin. She was mine, and I was hers.

My beast purred at the thought.

She snapped out of her haze, offering me a small smile before she stalked up the stairs, the same sway to her hips. My dick strained against the front of my swimwear, and I ached to follow her, to worship her and sink into the tight flesh between her thighs. It was a goddamn nightmare.

Adrian's deep chuckle drew my attention to him. He waggled his eyebrows in a taunting manner, his gaze dipping down to my pants. I bared my teeth at him, even knowing it would only egg him on further.

"Down, boy." His voice was condescending, joking.

I was going to fucking strangle him. A growl rumbled in my chest, and my lips split further into a snarl. "Like you're doing any better."

He didn't look down; he didn't have to. All of us were in a perpetual state of turned on, no better than fresh bloods just awakened. Had been for days. Even Osiris, though he wouldn't dare admit it. Adrian's show in the living room had only made it that much worse.

Made me crave her that much fiercer.

Any time her scent hit me, it was like my entire body was engulfed. I wanted her more than anything I'd ever wanted in my long life. I wanted her skin on mine, huddled in my arms, safe from the world. I wanted her blood on my tongue. I want *everything* on my tongue.

My beast forced out a growl as she hopped back down the stairs, and I nearly threw away my thoughts of the gift. Fallon trailed behind her, staying a few steps away. She'd tied up my shirt, bunching it above her hips, leaving the barest slivers of skin poking out above her shorts. She looked comfortable and at home. My gaze softened as I watched her walk back around to the counter to check on the state of her sandwiches, as though they would have fallen over in the space of time it took her to find Fallon.

Silly little thing.

Osiris walked down the stairs just as she replaced the lid, his head held high for once. There wasn't that expected numbness in his eyes, instead replaced by a fury so deep I thought they might bleed red. I only raised my eyebrow. I didn't need words as he gave me a nod, telling me without them that we'd talk about it later, before turning to Aaliyah.

His face must have softened based on her response, as she excitedly told him about the sandwiches she and Adrian had made. The stress dissipated from his shoulders, even as he distanced himself from her.

Being around her was like being in the sun. She ignited warmth along our skin. It was as if, as long as we were next to her, we could face anything.

Adrian pulled her hand into his, and she relaxed into it as she turned to him.

"Let's blow this popsicle stand, love." She beamed at Adrian's words.

"The house isn't a popsicle stand, Adrian." Her nose tilted up cutely, and she couldn't stop the laugh that spilled from her lips. I wanted to listen to it again, to play it on repeat until there was nothing left in my mind.

"No, I suppose it's not," Adrian replied with a smirk.

His laugh matched hers, and the spark in his eyes brought me peace. I had never seen Adrian truly let go. He didn't allow himself to truly feel. Though none of us did, not really. It wasn't something Vampires did if they wanted to survive. But as he held Aaliyah's hand, I had hope. Hope for us all to find peace, to find an anchor in this world.

Hope for most of us, anyway. Nero's face settled in my mind, his self-assured grin proudly on display. I didn't want to think about his charred skin as we pulled him off that pyre in Russia. A war criminal, they'd called him, chained him up outside for the cold to get to him. The sun reached him first. We hadn't been there, and because of that, he died alone, died in pain.

His death would forever haunt me, and not even the deaths of those who had killed him were enough to settle me. I wished he could be here. With her.

With us.

I bit back my guilt, still raw even after all these years, as I turned to grin at Aaliyah.

We wasted no time walking out the door. Aaliyah practically ran, bashfully rubbing the back of her head as she realized we were still coming. We mirrored her joy, *flitting* to keep as she stepped outside. I ignored the pain that still lingered in the hollow of my chest, and even my beast sat silently in mourning.

But for the first time in decades, it was manageable.

Aaliyah walked a few paces ahead of Osiris and I, one hand firmly placed in Adrian's right and the other settled in Fallon's left, a detail I was still shocked by. But when she'd reached out for him, he'd have been a fool to turn her away.

He looked like anything but the frigid asshole we'd known over the past two hundred years. His face held a softness to it as he told Aaliyah all about the trees and plants that we passed, something that he'd been cataloging over the years. He pointed them out as we walked, and she listened with such attention, so honest in her wonder as she asked quiet questions about the flora and fauna.

Adrian would pitch in now and again, mentioning things that reminded him of his homeland. Sometimes something related to his schooling from back then.

Still, hard to believe the little shit had been studying to be a doctor.

Osiris and I stayed back watching for threats and because it was easier to talk about the sensitive information that Osiris had learned from Xander. Or, in our case, the lack of.

"What the fuck do you mean, he wants to meet her?" I kept it quiet, so Aaliyah wouldn't hear me from her spot between Adrian and Fallon.

Though they went rigid at her sides.

"He needs to see her in person to narrow down exactly what she is." His voice was numb, and gone was any hint of my brother in his eyes. I'd have preferred the rage from earlier. But he'd become a shell, emptier than I'd ever seen him, and even my beast worried that he'd tipped past the point of no return. He'd been teetering this edge since Nero's death, and with Kali's appearance, as well as his guilt over the pain he'd caused to Fallon and Adrian, I knew his thoughts were drowning him. "He was adamant about it. Wouldn't falter even under the threat of our wrath. Those are his terms, and we have to abide by them, for her sake."

Her. That one word held a different tone, a different light. It was only when talking about a cure for my *smár Valkyrja* that any kind of life shone there.

At least there was some hope he might bounce back. I longed to see past the numbness that had taken root in his eyes once again, but there was nothing. He watched her, the same obsessive way he had since the auction, but any emotion that used to come with the gesture was so buried that even I couldn't see it. It was fucking worrying, and I damned near took a note from Fallon's book and considered throwing a hit to see if he would react.

"But *why* does she need to be there?" I pressed, getting his attention on me. I didn't like putting her in Xander's sight. He was curious, as people of his age always became, and with that curiosity came a moral decline. And if he even thought to look at her like she was something to learn, an *experiment*. My jaw cracked, and I was halfway through a turn when Osiris shoved his hands in his pockets, looking at me with a sigh that told of his age.

"Calm yourself, Eirik. I wouldn't have agreed to them if I thought he would turn on us," were his simple words, ones that bled power and forced my shift away. "She needs to be there in case he needs a blood sample. It would need to be fresh."

The rage that licked Osiris's words was enough to say that he was *adamantly* against the idea of the Dryad getting her blood.

My *Úlfhéðinn* snarled at the suggestion, his fangs bared. I had to fight not to let the expression take over my face. The possessiveness I had over her only intensified at the Dryad's request. I wanted to tear him apart, split his skull, for even suggesting he draw my female's blood.

"He's going to need a new fucking arm if he thinks he's going to get anywhere near her blood." The sentence came out louder than I wanted, but Aaliyah was so caught up in Adrian's tale that she didn't even notice.

"If he needs it to find out, we may not have a choice." Osiris's words were level. Someone from outside our family would even say calm.

Osiris was many things right now, but calm was not one of them. He looked fractured, like he was one push from falling headfirst into a breakdown, and I knew from experience that would be bad for all of us. Osiris didn't break; he couldn't afford to. Someone with as much power as him had to be careful, or else they'd end up on the wrong side of the line. *Sebek's* side of the line.

We didn't have the strength to deal with another ticking time bomb.

"Her blood isn't his price?" I asked somewhat pacified, eyes on Osiris's blank face.

The fact that the Dryad didn't *need* her blood didn't quell my *Úlfhéðinn's* rage, but it helped me think more clearly. He wouldn't let her be hurt willingly, for any reason. He was foaming at the mouth at the idea of it. The feral beast had a point because I wouldn't either.

"Then what does he want?" The Dryad was no doubt going to take full advantage of our need for help. He always did.

Osiris paused for a moment, focusing on Aaliyah, on the sway of her hair under the fall moon and the shine of her lavender eyes. Then he sighed.

"He wants a vial of Sebek's," he finally confirmed.

The sound of my Maker's name made me physically ill. We hadn't seen Sebek since before Fallon's turn, sometime around the early 1600s. He was already gone by the time we found Fallon—hell, already on a different *continent* by the time we finally tracked Adrian down.

"Of course he does." The fucking Dryad plucked at my nerves and made me want to tear his face off.

Leave it to Xander to want something so impossible for us to get. He had to know about Sebek's recent atrocities and the fact that Osiris was now past the age of Challenge. The bastard was probably worried he wouldn't get another chance to get a vial.

"Do you have any way of getting it?" I asked, keeping my eyes on Aaliyah as she stepped over a fallen tree.

That was going to be a resounding *no*. Sebek only showed himself when he made a new Vampire, turning another poor soul over to us, or when he wanted to flaunt a new project. His presence brought death, and he wasn't exactly known for his kind streak. Sebek had portrayed anyone from Vlad the Impaler to Genghis Khan over the years of his long life, and that was after he stopped being discreet about his meddling with humans.

The tales of the boogeyman didn't appear out of thin air, after all. Sebek had haunted children's dreams for centuries. You didn't gain the name *Death's Butcher* for nothing.

"I still have a few vials from when you were turned, though they are over a millennium old now. I plan to give Xander one of those," Osiris said, and I sufficed a nod.

My turning was problematic. My *Úlfhéðinn* fought hard against the Vampire poison, and it was only through regular consumption of Sebek's blood that I even survived. Blood that Osiris had fought tooth and nail to get. A concession Sebek agreed to if only to be the first to turn a Shifter.

I should have died; every other of my kind that had been forced to change had. But my wolf and I weren't strangers to pain. That was what kept us alive, even when the Vampire poison made us want to die.

"Think he'll accept it?" I asked.

I could scent the heat of the springs in the air now, the subtle lining of sulfur making my nose burn. Aaliyah was telling Adrian and Fallon about how her mother used to make her 'sugar toast' for breakfast. Adrian's eyebrow was upturned as he listened to her recite the 'recipe.' The poor smitten fool promised to make her some tomorrow.

"He won't have a choice. He agreed to the deal. The vial of blood I give him will fulfill our end of the bargain." Osiris was listening to her story as well, his gaze firmly on her as she spoke.

I doubted that tricking the Dryad was in our best interest. Stunts like that seldom went well, especially to one as old as Xander. He was known for his flamboyant personality and his complete *lack* of empathy.

"The deal is in two weeks. That was as soon as he would see us. We need to tell her beforehand. Get her ready for the tricks he will inevitably pull." The tone of his voice told me our conversation was over. I knew not to say more. Besides, we had arrived.

The hot spring was a small pool that bore into a towering limestone boulder, and it smelled softly of sulfur and heat. It would be a tight fit for us all, and I couldn't tell if I was more excited or worried about that. The other part of me wanted her to see me naked, even if only partially. See if it excited her. I wanted to see a blush creep up her cheeks as she marveled at us.

This was going to be interesting.

Aaliyah released Fallon's and Adrian's hands, all but running to the pool. The two in question looked distraught to be separated from the small contact.

Since they were so close in turn, the two had been practically inseparable—Adrian's boyish nature meshing with Fallon's cold disposition in a way no one expected. It was good for them to have someone to lean on like Nero, Osiris, and I had been for each other.

Aaliyah's hand slid into the water, and she giggled as she twirled her hand through the steaming spring, effectively dragging me from my dimming thoughts.

"This is amazing!" She turned to take off the flats that adorned her feet, as well as the winter jacket and sweatpants, before sliding her legs into the steaming water. A throaty groan slid past her lips as she settled all the way down, sitting on the small rim inside of the spring. The water reached right below her chin.

That groan *broke* me. I looked at her through hooded eyes, trying to decide if it would be worth it to just strip naked and walk into the pool like that was expected. My sharpened nails bit into the palms of my hands.

"Are you guys okay?" Aaliyah was glancing between us, her lip back between her teeth.

After looking so calm during our walk, I hated to see that expression on her face. She deserved this moment after everything that had happened. Deserved to enjoy this time, but I could feel the heat boiling beneath my skin, my fangs hanging just below the surface. I forced it down with a vicious snap against my control. My *Úlfhéðinn* growled in protest.

"Yes, *lux mea*, we're fine," Osiris's voice was husky, and I didn't miss his endearment.

My light. It was fitting.

There was careful restraint behind his words as he tried to hold back his tone, but his breathing was ragged, his voice husky. Though I doubted she even noticed from where she sat. As quickly as I had seen that longing in his eyes, it was gone, again clouded in numbness.

"We're going to change real quick, little love. Think you'll be okay by yourself for a moment?" Adrian practically undressed Aaliyah with his gaze as he spoke, the corners of his eyes crinkling when her skin flushed a bright red.

A brief nod followed her hesitant smile, before she dropped her gaze down, focusing on her hands that sat right below the surface of the water. Her eyes shot to my left, no doubt looking at 'Prince.' Small shiver bumps were visible on the skin that wasn't underwater. It was a crisp fifty degrees outside, cold for a night in Pennsylvania, even in September.

Adrian moved forward with easy steps, a carefree sway leading him right to her before he leaned down. He kissed her gently, washing away any worry that had been on her face. Again, my wolf paced.

Tonight. We get the gift tonight, his rumbled voice echoed in my mind.

We *flitted* from the area without another word. Losing sight of her numbed me to my core, but we needed a moment, a second to breathe, to calm the fuck down before we did something we'd regret. My teeth ached, and even my hands shook from remembering the sight of her. She was a fucking addiction, from her soft laugh to her honeyed fragrance.

Fallon was leaning against a rock, his arms crossed tightly over his chest. He struggled to portray his usual grim demeanor, his eyes flashing between green and red furiously.

I pulled my shirt over my head in one swift movement, nearly ripping it with the force I put on it. A growl slipped from my lips as I glanced down at my ... *problem.*

"We walk out there like this, and she's going to lose it." It was Fallon who spoke, his voice clear and crisp.

He didn't turn away from the sky, only stated a fact. One that I was *blatantly* aware of right now.

"Well, we have to do something. If we don't show up soon, she's going to question where we are." Adrian had a wistful sigh on his lips. "And I, for one, would like to spend as much time in that pool with her as possible."

His shirt was the next to go. He folded it deftly in his arms, setting it on the ground next to him.

Osiris moved next, his hands shaking against his buttons, that damned numbness in his eyes making me feral with rage. He moved slower than we had, as if hesitant to expose skin. Flawless, unmarred skin only interrupted by the ink on his arms. Another hint at what his life had been like. He hated to be stripped even partially bare, said it made him feel vulnerable.

It had been normal three weeks ago, before Aaliyah, and I'd grown so used to not seeing it that now that it was back, I realized how much I hated it. He wasn't meant to be this hollow shell, and I'd been almost optimistic that Aaliyah had helped to pull him out of the rut he'd been in.

"Osiris, wait," I said, catching everyone's attention. "We need to talk first."

Dead silence, and a blank stare. But this needed to happen if we wanted to move forward. But Osiris had only opened his mouth to speak when we heard it. The unnerving sound of a gargled scream that was buried behind forcibly closed lips. It ran across my eardrums like shattering glass, and my *Úlfhéðinn* was a snarling fit of rage at the sound, pounding at my skin with vicious intent.

No. It couldn't be her; it couldn't be Aaliyah that was screaming. The wards were still up, a fact that I *knew* because we'd checked them just hours ago. Osiris would have felt something.

But a single whisper from Fallon had me shifting, igniting all of my fears as my skin tore, and my fangs dropped. The change happened in an instant, and my wolf took over.

"Aaliyah."

CHAPTER 9

AALIYAH

The guys left the clearing so fast I didn't even see them move, and I was left staring blankly at where Adrian had been. My lips tingled as I settled into the water, a silly smile taking over my face as I reached up to touch them. Prince shook his head, a knowing look on his face as he sat about a foot away from me, perched on the edge of the spring but not quite in the water. He even dipped his toes in, making an exaggerated face as if to say it was 'too hot'.

The trip to the hot spring had been serene and everything that I didn't know I needed. My head still hurt and worry for what was to come was still there ... but for a moment, I was okay with that. The green earth aroma of the forest, the light of the moon peeking through the trees. It was like a dream. I loved hearing Fallon talk about the flora, his eyes lighting up as he picked me a wildflower. The sound of Adrian's laugh on the cool breeze as we argued over what to have for dinner.

Even just knowing that Eirik and Osiris were behind us, watching over us all. It gave me a glimpse of what life might be like when all of this was over. When I wasn't sick and when Ascension Rising was gone. When the Eternium was over, and their Maker wasn't a threat.

It gave me hope for a future, and my soul flourished.

And when Adrian kissed me like that ...

It was everything.

I needed to call Eliza and tell her, rather begrudgingly, that she was right. She'd seen how Fallon and Eirik had reacted to my *Rend* and even given her approval of Adrian and Fallon after our time at her *babas*. And I'd watched them like she suggested, every spare second I could. Even found out that Adrian felt the same. It was all I could seem to do, watch them like I did Prince ...

The only thing was now I wasn't sure what the next step was. Would the others want the same thing I had with Adrian? Fallon had held my hand, *but was it just to make me happy?* Eirik had brushed my hair off my cheek and smiled, *smiled*. It was just too much, and I knew I needed to ask. It wasn't fair to anyone to keep dancing around this, not when our time together might be limited. So, with a steady breath and an extreme amount of will ...

I decided that was happening tonight.

I sank a little farther into the water, blowing bubbles as my nose dipped under. I couldn't help but think about everything that might go wrong. I should be happy to have Adrian. He was amazing, *perfect*. So why did I want the rest, too? Would he understand that? He hadn't made any indication that he'd be mad about it, but I didn't want to go forward without seeing his feelings about it first.

What if they don't feel the same? What if Adrian didn't want me to love them, too? What if, what if, what if?

All that didn't even account for the fact that I didn't have *any* kind of experience with relationships. Not to mention that the thought of expanding my knowledge in the area, even with them, was *terrifying*.

I hadn't ever been with someone sexually, and as much as it made my thighs clench to recall the heat that had taken over in the kitchen with Adrian ... I also knew I wasn't ready for what came with it. Not yet. Those at Ascension hadn't raped me, at least not that I remembered, but they'd done enough damage with their words to haunt me forever. I didn't want them to stain this, and I knew if I jumped in too fast, that's exactly what they would do.

There was a rustle of bushes behind me, and I sighed as I realized they had returned. I brushed my hair back, the long white strands clumping from the water. I rubbed at my arms, feeling slightly exposed and self-conscious about how many of my scars were showing. It had taken them longer than I was expecting to change, but they were back. It was all okay. Prince moved, standing beside me but took no notice.

I was safe.

"What took you guys so long?" I asked, lifting myself from the water just a touch, making waves ripple around me.

I quickly sank back down, running from the air cold on my wet skin. The shuffling got closer, and fear coiled in my belly on instinct. Why hadn't they said anything yet? I glanced over at Prince and my blood froze at his panicked movements. He had his arms crossed over his chest in a familiar 'X' motion.

Danger.

As I jumped to move forward, a hand settled hard over my mouth, firmly stopping the scream that had been on the tip of my tongue. The grip tightened, and my heart thundered in my ears. I sucked in a terrified breath as the stench of gasoline lit up my nose.

Wrong.

This was all wrong. The wards were up, and someone else couldn't have gotten in. But whoever was behind me wasn't one of my guys, a fact that was only confirmed when a vicious chuckle met my ears. Panic set in as the person's other hand worked around and grabbed me around my torso, dragging me out of the water in one swift movement. The familiarity of it, the sickening bite of a hand on my skin, made my head pulse.

Pressure. That grim, gnawing pressure forced its way into my mind. Nausea rose, and I struggled to stay calm as my vision flashed.

Not again.

"I was wondering when those fangs were going to let you out of their sights. I thought it would take them longer to get tired of you," a wolfish voice said, bubbling over my skin.

A tremble took over my limbs, and I struggled desperately to see who it was that had me in their grasp. The face was vaguely familiar for a moment before a horrid sense of recognition slid over me.

It was one of the men who'd nearly bought me at the auction.

That night was so hazy that it was almost like it had happened before I'd died, and something I'd remembered before coming here. The lights, the smells, the fear ... but I remembered him, picked him out of the crowd from where he stood by the back wall. He'd offered a million for me and had almost *owned* me. Of all things, it was his eyes I remembered. Just like that night, they were furiously bright, his yellow teeth standing against the slimy white of his skin. His wispy white hair was in shambles, and he was in what had to be the remnants of a suit that was now tattered and worn.

"Hope they haven't ruined you yet. I hate loose pussy."

I couldn't move, couldn't breathe. I couldn't even scream, too paralyzed by the instincts of my confinement, choking on my fear until that fear was all that was left.

They get more violent when you make noise.

My instincts screamed at me to stay silent, to relent. And that mantra, that stupid *fucking* mantra, echoed in my mind. How many times had I heard it? How many times had it ruined my life? It always came up, always told me I couldn't do anything.

But I was so tired of that thought. I wasn't weak; I wasn't useless. I was *free*. And this man wasn't going to change that. A snarl built on my lips, though it was muffled by the hand over my mouth.

I dragged my eyes to Prince. His hands were in his hair as he stared at me. His entire body trembled as he screamed. His pain was like it was my own, settling over the clearing like a thick mat in the air.

If the man holding me sensed my rage, he didn't mention it. He pulled me hard against him, his body like a thick mass of mush. I had to fight the gag as he dragged his nose across my neck, his tongue darting out to taste me.

It was the sound of a belt that sent me over the edge. Words from the compound filtered in my ears, what they wanted to do to me but weren't allowed ...

A fire ignited deep in my belly. With my limbs trembling and tears in my eyes, I settled my resolve and bit hard into his hand. My teeth sank into his skin, taking him by surprise as his blood flooded my mouth, tasting like sweat and ashes. He released me slightly to acknowledge the pain before he wrenched me hard against him again.

But it was too late. His move gave me an opening—the only opportunity I needed. The scream bubbled from my lips, sounding like a war cry. I wouldn't be the victim of this man.

I refused.

His hand clamped painfully hard against my face, and claws dug deep into the skin on my hip. I thrashed, scratched, and kicked to get him off me. His growl was low in his throat as he flipped me around. I opened my mouth to scream again before it died in my throat.

His hit was devastating, and he held nothing back from it. His fist landed solidly against my jaw, and I knew it was only because I'd had *worse* that I stayed conscious. He was yelling at me, but I couldn't hear it over the roaring in my ears. My body burst into horrid agony, and my fight left my body as I sank into his arms.

I tried to strike out, to do something, *anything*, but I couldn't force myself to move, so it was a good thing that I didn't have to.

What I could only assume was a *wolf* tore through the clearing, and he landed just shy of us. His eyes were like molten blue lava, boiling ruthlessly. I should have shielded myself away from his sight. I should have been terrified. But I wasn't.

Because he felt like *home*.

The beast moved a step closer, his almond fur shining brightly in the moonlight and a snarl shaping his maw. I tried to reach for him.

"Eirik." His name slipped from out like a prayer, and my eyes locked on him.

The man growled at Eirik, his anger seeping into me. Eirik was huge in wolf form, standing as tall as I did. A calmness slid over me as I looked at him, and as the other three burst through the tree line, I knew I didn't need to be afraid. They looked like avenging angels, with their eyes blood-red and fangs standing proudly against their tight lips. Even Prince took his place by them, looking at home with his lips curled back against his teeth.

I wasn't afraid of them, I found. Even when everything about them said that I should be.

"You would find it is in your best interest to let her go, Crustava." Osiris's voice was more barbarous than I'd ever heard it.

The man at my back pulled me closer, but I didn't miss his flinch at Osiris's warning. One of his hands snaked up to wrap around my neck, his claws extended, and they pierced the soft flesh.

I didn't scream or whimper, and the man behind me seemed mad at that fact as he sent out another growl. He wanted me scared so the others would panic and make a mistake ...

I wouldn't be giving him that.

"She wasn't yours to buy! You stole her from me!" His scream sounded barely human at this point as he jerked viciously behind me.

The men all looked horrified, their eyes trained on me as they tried to decide what to do. Acid boiled in my stomach as they watched his hand tighten.

"This will not end well for you, Crustava," Osiris said, almost too low. "Let her *go*."

The brush of his *Charm* swept over us, drowning the small hot spring clearing in a fog of power that made my legs weak. But Crustava's hand tightened brutally, and I gasped at his stranglehold.

"I don't think so. Did you think I'd come in here without *Charm* protection? No, I've thought of everything," Crustava sneered, manically holding up his hand, and displaying a polished silver ring. "I'm in control here, Vivas. Now, if you don't want to see her die, then get on your fucking knees."

I saw the moment Osiris's eyes cracked, his soul brimming. The emotionless light in his eyes died, and the numbness came crashing back down like the world upon his shoulders. I knew the moment he accepted the defeat and swallowed his pride. He didn't want to back down. But he would, for me.

It was all my fault. My fault he sank to his knees, and my fault that the others followed with their palms held up in surrender.

No.

"That's right, fucking fangs. Men like you don't deserve a prize like this. She's *mine.*" At the sound of Crustava's voice belittling the men who saved me, *my men,* I snapped.

No, it was *his* fault. Heat bled from the air, and my breath frosted in front of me. How dare this man, how *dare* he?

Everything froze, as though time itself had stopped on the other side of the Void, and pain spread through my skull. Words I didn't know but sounded so familiar slipped from my lips, and I let them. I wasn't sure what it was, this sudden brush of savage, vengeful power, but I let it consume me. My eyes never left the men who still kneeled for me.

Each word I spoke was like a curse, my skin splitting open at each sylla-ble, blood stark red against the alabaster white, and that pressure that had all but swallowed me for months exploded. But it didn't matter. *Nothing* mattered compared to my rage.

Crustava's cry echoed in my ears, and he tried to pull away. Tried to escape after he'd said such cruel things, after he'd threatened to defile me.

He dared to *run.*

"Pathetic," someone hissed in my ear, so loud that it echoed in my skull.

The voice was low and acidic, sinking into my skin as my hand jarred up, grabbing hard at Crustava's wrist, holding him in place with a strength I didn't know I had. He was screaming as I turned to face him, his eyes hollow, haunted. I reached up to his neck, his pulse beneath my fingertips. Fire ripped through my veins. I felt powerful.

The pain didn't matter. The blood didn't matter. All that I cared about was his audacity—his cruel intentions—and how he would pay for them.

How he would pay for them all.

"What the fuck are you?!" His voice was shrill, tears streaming down his cheeks as he stared down at me like he hadn't been about to ruin me in ways no other had.

I froze, head tipping in contemplation, that power making my hand shake as adrenaline scoured every inch of me. The answer came easily because of *course* I knew what I was.

Death, something deep whispered inside of me, breathing it, praising it. I grinned, and Crustava struggled harder.

"What the *fuck*? Let me go, you freak!" He was sobbing now, an ugly mess of rot.

Nothing around me dared to move as shadows closed in on me, a rayless sheen of black glass covering my vision. They swallowed up the world around me and let only the hate out.

"Why would I let you go?" a voice asked as my head tilted to one side, my fingers leaving bruises on his neck to match my own. "I haven't even *ruined* you yet."

The wretched voice resounded around the small area again, still echoing, sounding so full of hate and brutally familiar. And I finally realized ...

It was coming from me.

Crustava was back to screaming, and alarm bells rang in my mind as I realized I wasn't in control right now. Not as I stared at him, my hand gripping ever tighter as that devious press of power muddied my brain. Not as blood dripped down my arm, following the newly formed cuts that opened on their own, splitting my skin into an abstract, bloody painting. Not as a burn followed them, as though my limbs were being engulfed in an invisible flame.

I shook my head to clear my thoughts or tried to ... but I didn't move. Bone-wrenching terror should have made me drop him, should have made me stumble back and scream at myself, but I couldn't even do that.

I'd seen enough death and passed enough souls through to the other side to know that I didn't *want* whatever was happening. It was almost like a *Rend*, the same fear suddenly flooding me, drowning me, and I was powerless to stop it.

Crustava's screams refused to end, even as they came out garbled and harsh. Something that sounded like begging reached my ears, but the roar of blood and thundering of my heart muted everything but my own thoughts.

Everything but death.

My other hand, shaking as I tried desperately to stop myself, dug deep into the skin of his chest, *claws* finding purchase, and with a sick rip, the fingers I'd had around his neck went straight through him. The crunch of bone and flesh made my stomach turn and twist as blood splattered across the ground.

Across my face, tasting like ash and guilt. But the screaming—the horrible screaming—finally stopped. That roaring overflow of power engulfed me as much as the fear did, swallowing me whole exactly like the agony that followed it. What I hoped was *my* blood slid down from my nose, settling on my parted lips. A metallic flavor filled my mouth, and red overtook my vision. I half expected to see a head sitting in my bloodied hand as his body hit the ground, lifeless.

But ... Crustava was still there, in my hand. *Still screaming.* Only there was no sound.

Because the dead couldn't scream.

If I could have choked, I would have. Even for all he did, no one deserved this. I ... I didn't want to kill anyone, but he was there, sitting in my palm, his body already cooling on the ground. Even though he couldn't scream, he tried, squirming and seizing until his eyes fell closed while his mouth stayed open in that endless panic. He faded away as my power ate him, sending him to the Void.

Small wisps of deep gray fluttered around my arm, as though part of him still clung to me. My lips stretched into a wicked grin against my will, one too wide for my lips as my cheeks stung. Then I turned, slowly spinning around. My focus never left my arm, or that swirling, twisting mass. It felt alive, condensed. It felt like *Crustava.* Something deep in my bones told me it was him, and as I watched the wild black thing seize around my arm, I grew sick to my stomach. My hands flexed of their own accord, and that wretched part of my brain made my fingers tense, pushing me to crush it, to destroy every ounce of him so even his soul wouldn't know peace.

The black wisps blended with the red that coated my arm before my focus sharply shifted, and the men came into view, shrouded in a black and red film. The horror in their eyes, the *fear,* was enough to break me. I tried to move, to force my hand down, but I only continued to stare.

And then I took a step forward. Another. Each one made me flinch, and each one I tried and failed to stop. Eyes were on me, but my gaze was only on one of them now.

Prince.

I screamed in my head as my body came to a stop directly in front of a frozen Prince. Nothing I did worked to stop me, yet I *knew* exactly what my body was doing. The need to go to him, to touch, to *send on*. He looked bewildered, staring at me as though I wasn't me.

Like I was a monster. A monster I knew I was now, the evidence dead on the ground behind me.

Prince watched that flowing mass on my hand the same way I had, his eyes clinging to the open wounds on my skin that didn't feel like they were closing. My heart stopped in my chest when my hand moved, and I screamed again, begging to stop, or for him to run ... but like watching myself during a *Rend*, everything happened in slow motion.

Prince flinched, not fast enough and too startled to move away. I begged my body to listen to me, prayed to any god that would listen, and cried even as I continued to *smile*.

Why was this happening? *Why?*

My hand settled on his cheek, onto *Prince's* cheek, and the wisps of energy shot out. They wrapped around him, sinking into his astral form and spreading until his body turned a deep gray. He stumbled back, clutching at his chest, his fingers disappearing into himself as pain settled on his face and shot into the air. Panic raged inside of me, breaking through the agony, through the blood.

Clarity came slowly, agonizingly. The ache of his agony in the air hit first, stealing every ounce of breath I had left until I was just a shell. Then ... the depth of my betrayal.

The Void sizzled around us, snapping against my skin as foreign words continued to slip from my lips, and Prince started flickering before falling to one knee. Pain ruptured me, nothing like the typical pull, nothing like the kind embrace that usually greeted me.

Nothing about this was right. It was like he was taking my soul with him. Only once the last word was out did my eyes clear, the black sheen fading until I was left with nothing.

Nothing but blood on my hands. Crustava's and my own. Nothing but crushing panic and a loss of hope.

"No. No, *I didn't mean to*," I whispered, my voice again my own. "Please, no."

I fell to my knees, scrambling toward Prince as his body flickered again. I said something, something unrecognizable even to me as I reached my hands out to him, crying out as they fell straight through him. "*Please* don't leave me. I can't lose you, too."

He tried to offer me comfort, his lips mouthing something I couldn't hope to focus on, before his face contorted in agony as though he was in pain. His hand lifted over his chest, pinky and ring finger down ... before the Void took him. It wasn't flashy, dramatic, or anything that I knew of Prince. His eyes rolled back as he faded away entirely; one second here ...

Then the next, he was gone.

Not Prince, please not Prince.

I dug my fingers into the cold earth where he'd been, my nails scraping against an unyielding frost. I waited for him to appear next to me, to ground me with his roguish grin and endless enthusiasm. I waited until my soul fractured, cracking along the seams as pure agony hollowed out the place in my chest where my heart should have been, and on instinct, I held in my startled gasp.

Never make noise.

That had been my mantra, my devil, and my deepest horror. I'd always hated it, but now it swarmed my mind like Castillion's cruel laugh and the click of Nox's pen. Those three words seemed so *loud* now, and as I stared at the place where Prince had faded from view, I wondered why I'd ever held it in.

It wasn't *worth* it. Every scream, every cry ... I had held them in just to end up here.

My best friend was gone. The man who had been a constant presence in my life, my Knight in Astral Armor, was gone. *Prince was gone.*

"Aaliyah?" A whisper, the broken sound of my name setting off everything else. The forest faded away, and when the brush of a cool hand slid over my shoulder, I lost it.

They get more violent when you make noise.

That mantra shattered with me, something in me snapping as my arms shook and my body gave. That one hand became two, but I barely recognized them for what they were.

The break started as a sob, crawling across the ruins of my heart, as my entire body seized and I curled up where Prince had been. It hurt like nothing I'd ever endured; the pain sinking so deep that it seared itself into my being as I *screamed*, the echo of it loud enough that nothing, not even the mocking jeer of Castillion's cruel words, could keep it inside of me.

The open cuts on my skin, the tear of my vocal cords, none of it compared to the desolation in my chest. I couldn't manage anything else, not even as I choked on a breath, my lungs finally caving in their need for air, only to scream again.

What had I done? *What had I done?*

The trembles rocked through me, and the effects of my actions took full hold of me. Prince was *gone*. I sent away my best friend, my rock, my first love, my *Prince*. He'd been in pain, betrayed as I destroyed him.

Why had I done that?

Why?

Why couldn't I stop? More sobs took over my body as I opened my eyes to find bloodied hands. And a cold, damp chest. I looked up and met the stunned eyes of Adrian. His arms tightened around me, and I almost begged him to squeeze harder, to never let go ... I didn't want to lose them like I'd lost Prince. I *couldn't* lose them too. But how could they want me after this? How could anyone want me after this?

I was broken.

I was a monster.

A breath of a whisper in my mind, one that sang brightly and told me everything I needed to know. Even my screams couldn't block it out.

Death.

I was death.

CHAPTER 10

OSIRIS

I'd thought I'd known what pain sounded like. I'd heard it enough in my years, and been the one to voice it more times than I dared to admit.

But I'd never in my life heard someone scream like Aaliyah did. Her cry shattered me in ways I didn't know I could be broken. The black flames that had hugged her skin slowly faded away, the twisting horns surrounding an obsidian crown on her head shimmering like glass before they, too, disappeared. Even as Adrian held her, trembling as he tried to help, the rest of us were too numb, too shocked by what we'd seen.

But that gut-wrenching agony continued until even her voice gave out. With no sound to hold her, she wrapped around herself, pulling out of Adrian's arms, whispering pleas to the space in front of her. She didn't seem to notice that her skin was split open, that blood dripped from her nose, landing on her lips and the frost-laden ground. It slid out of her eyes, painting her cheeks with vibrant red tears. Her face was narrow, sharper, almost like Eirik's before a turn. She didn't flinch, though she had to be in pain.

I couldn't find the will to move. Or take my eyes off of her. She looked like a goddess awaiting sacrifice, her eyes on her hands.

Empires had risen and fallen to me. I had whispered into the ears of kings and started wars, all for my amusement. I had danced with the Fae, spoke with Nymphs, and made deals with Angels and Demons alike. I had seen wonders no other had. So, seeing something so mind-numbingly new had my entire body buzzing with electricity.

She curled tighter in on herself, sobs ripping through her body. The desolation in her eyes further cemented my destruction.

Prince.

Adrian moved again, his soft words not reaching her.

I was a broken man. I had been since my turn, and since Nero's death I could barely even call myself alive. Then, with Kali ... I knew what it felt like for your soul to ache so deeply you questioned your life. So no amount of my own fracturing was going to stop me from letting her think she wasn't worthy of this life.

I was broken, but I would *never* let her be.

I reached her in three long strides, fell to my knees again, and pulled her into my arms before she could protest. I wrapped her tightly against me, against my bare chest, stunned by the heat of her skin. I didn't give myself time to wonder if her touch was going to burn me, or if the rot I'd let fester where my soul was supposed to be would consume this moment.

There was only her.

The first sob hit violently as she trembled and fell apart in my embrace. Her arms hesitantly wrapped around me, holding me close as she came to terms with what happened, whatever it was that happened. I could wager a guess, based on her cries and the body of Crustava at her back.

There was no doubt she'd lost someone irreplaceable today, the one who had been with her through her hell. It was hard to hold her, not because of her touch, but because of the emotion that it brought. Her body shook, and it made me feel startlingly raw.

Adrian, still at her side, wiped away her blood tears. And Fallon came to his knees beside her, fingers threading through her hair. Anything to convince her we weren't leaving. Eirik had settled his head against her side, his *Úlfheðinn* not ready to give power back to the Viking.

Her eyes were tortured, and before I could speak, she was whispering. "I killed him."

It wasn't a question but a statement, one that came out like broken glass. She was trembling, unable to hold my gaze.

"I'm a monster." Her words fell out like sobs. She curled her arms around herself, too scared to catch my eyes. "I killed him. I *killed* him."

I hated that she would even consider calling herself that. She wasn't the monster here; no one as bright as her could be a monster. I resisted the urge to pull away. The emotion dragged me forward as I gripped her chin, pulling her gaze to mine. She tried to tear away, a whine of protest on her lips. I wouldn't let her.

"You are no such thing." The harshness in my words made her flinch, but I couldn't hold back my rage at hearing her declaration.

"I killed Prince. I killed *Prince*. You didn't see his eyes, Osiris. I ... I destroyed him. I killed my best friend ... and that man—" Her trembling didn't stop, and her brittle words tore me apart.

Crustava ... I wasn't sure what happened there. One moment he was alive. Screaming, rather. The next, dead on the ground. His body was unmoving, and beyond the unhealed claw gouges in his chest, he was unharmed.

I wasn't sure how, nor did I have any idea how to ask. It had to be a gift of her race. I just had no idea what she could *be*. I'd never seen something like it, never heard of someone with a death touch, if that was what it was.

Aaliyah wheezed, collapsing against me. More blood slid down her face, ending in droplets on her chin and sliding down my own arms. Pressure built in my gums, and the scent was getting overwhelming.

Her wounds weren't closing.

"If you hadn't taken Crustava down, we would have. He planned to do terrible things to you, Aaliyah." I had no idea how to reason with her, how to show her she had done the right thing.

I didn't know how to breach the topic of Prince. I wasn't sure why she did that, why she would send him on even in that state.

She obviously didn't know either.

"But I killed him, Osiris. I didn't even mean to do it. But I couldn't stop." Sobs rattled her chest. She was in shock. I pulled her back against me, not knowing what else to do. "Why couldn't I stop?" she begged to know, and I wished I had the answer.

"Whatever that was wasn't you, little love." Adrian's voice was clear as day as he pressed himself into her back, his head resting next to her ear.

Adrian was intimately familiar with being unable to stop. It was months before Sebek's Call had worn off and he came back to reality. By the time we pulled him from the edge of his blood rage, he was a mess, his soul in tatters over what he had done and the lives he'd taken.

Adrian whispered into her ear, something I was too distracted to hear. But she eventually calmed against us, her breathing mellowing.

Slow. Too slow.

"We aren't going to be letting you go, Aaliyah." His voice was finally loud enough to hear. She leaned closer to us as she listened to his words. "It's going to take a lot more than that to get rid of us."

The 'thank you' that slipped through her lips sounded so relieved that I couldn't help but lean down and brush a kiss across her forehead. I avoided the blood, too concerned with control to even attempt a taste.

"Osi, she's lost too much blood." Adrian's gentle voice seemed to be her peace right now.

I doubted she even heard what he said. Her head bobbed slightly, falling to the side. She looked exhausted, her skin wan, and the bags under her eyes more pronounced. Then there was the blood, the blood that coated her.

My breathing hitched. The wounds that had yet to heal.

That *still* weren't healing.

"We need to get her to the house. Now, Osiris."

The panic in Adrian's voice had me standing, Aaliyah still clutched tightly in my arms. She leaned into me, taking in my cold skin. I was surprised that she wasn't freezing, but her skin gave off enough heat to warm both me and her.

Her breathing mellowed until I could barely hear it. But it was when her heart stuttered, falling to a stop before pattering back up, that got me moving.

We didn't have two weeks to spare now.

Aaliyah was dying. She had been for months. But now, we were out of time.

Chapter 11

Adrian

I'd forgotten what genuine fear felt like. This all-consuming horror, like I was being swallowed by an endless ocean, sinking away from the surface with no chance of returning.

I hadn't suffered like this since my turn.

I tried to pull into the moment, to focus on anything that would ground me, because I *needed* to fix this. I didn't have time to break down.

Aaliyah didn't have the time.

Whatever happened in the woods had hurt her badly in far more ways than one. I knew a lot of things and had seen and talked to many people, but I'd never seen a strong, healthy Natural drop to the ground like Crustava had. Never seen one die like that. Though, if anyone deserved to rot on the ground, their heart stopped, it was him.

Blood slid down my arms, dripping off the tips of my elbows, hitting the snow-covered ground with defined splashes. One drop after another— the waterfall of crimson painting the moonlit earth.

I could see her eyes now. The fear as I stalked toward her. I couldn't force myself to stop walking, just like the one before.

I jerked hard, doing everything in my power to keep from releasing what little was in my stomach. The *Call* pressed at my thoughts, strangling me with memories that I couldn't bury deep enough. I hadn't been able to keep much down these last weeks, even less than normal. The blood turned vile in my stomach.

Rage coiled in me as I leaned back into Aaliyah's body, ignoring Eirik's snarl at my movement. The hulking beast moved in jerking motions, Eirik fighting his way to the surface of his mind. The sound of snapping echoed, and the fur that marked Eirik's beast dissolved into dust. Eirik stood on unstable legs, forcing himself to keep up with our speed even as his bones cracked into place.

I pressed a shaking hand to Aaliyah's cheek. It was an ashen white, and it burned like I had dipped my hand into a roaring fire—acid built in my throat again. I all but snarled at myself, forcing the panic down and replacing it with Aaliyah's face. I didn't have the time to be weak right now.

My gaze slid to the red liquid still coating my arms on instinct, the call of it almost overwhelming. It was every bit as terrifying as it was enthralling. Every one of my instincts was clashing as we all but broke down the door to get inside.

"Set her on the table, Osiris."

Osiris didn't hesitate to move at my order. His naturally crisp attitude was at bay as he cradled Aaliyah to his chest before laying her across the table, her white hair now stained red. Even the numbness in his eyes was gone for the moment.

She looked like a fallen goddess, with her face a mirror of serenity. Frozen in time, suspended. Was this what Eirik and Fallon had seen that first time when she died in the forest? I glanced between them, taking in the broken emotion on Eirik's face. How Fallon tore at his hair and clutched his chest like he struggled to breathe.

Her body didn't move. Still. Motionless. Dead just like the last. I couldn't stop as I tore her throat out, as I reveled in her screams. Sebek's Call was destroying me.

Did I do this to her? Had I slipped and fallen once again into the shackles that were Sebek's *Call*? I shook my head violently, clinging to every bit of fear that ate at me as I tried to take a step forward. Then Osiris took a small step back, his face lost. The way he moved was choppy, too choppy. Like he wasn't sure of his movements.

And she was ashen, far too pale and lifeless looking.

Dead. Dead. *Dead.*

My subconscious screamed at me, haunting me. Reminding me of the horrors I had committed. Blood pooled beneath her as I *flitted* to her side. My hand found her pulse point on instinct, searching with my hand rather than my ears. I waited, the seconds excruciating as I ran my trembling fingers across her blood-painted skin. I didn't think I was going to find it. I was too late. Another life on my hands, eyes that would never again see the light of day.

Not Aaliyah, please. Not her, too.

No one moved. No one breathed.

Then the subtle thrum of her heart sounded against my fingers. I had to hold back a cry as it fluttered. Not too late. I could still save her. I *would* save her.

"Get the first aid kit. We have to stop the bleeding." Eirik was moving before I even finished the sentence, dropping the box onto the table next to me seconds later. His hands were shaking, his jaw snapped so tight he should have broken it. His hands clenched and unclenched. Blood slid down his arms, and if he noticed, he didn't pay any attention.

I pulled my eyes back to Aaliyah and her blood-soaked body. She was covered in open wounds, painting her red. It was like we were back from the auction all over again. Except this time, she wasn't healing.

This time, she wasn't *breathing*.

I paused, ice racing through my veins as I all but jumped on the table. The searing of her skin burned me, even through my swim trunks. It was like she was on *fire*. Fallon's voice was an afterthought as I settled my hands on her chest, between her breasts.

"She isn't breathing." The words came out on a choked sob as I started compressions. "Aaliyah isn't breathing!"

Everyone was frozen, watching as Aaliyah's body jerked under the compressions. No one spoke, and the silence was broken only by the creak of the table under us.

This wasn't happening. *This wasn't fucking happening.*

I pressed down harder, trying my best to keep my rhythm steady through the panic in my limbs. Trying not to press down too hard and snap her ribs. I wanted to lean down, to breathe air into her lungs, but it wasn't possible. If her blood hit my tongue, I wasn't sure what would happen. This would be enough.

It *had* to be enough.

"We need to stop the bleeding." I got the words out between sobs as my hands trembled against Aaliyah's scorching skin.

I listened carefully, waiting for her to take a breath, waiting for her eyes to open. As if the spell had been broken, the others shot off. Eirik started at her legs, binding them tightly. Osiris started at her arms, trying to stop the bleeding from there as I continued my compressions.

"It's not stopping. This isn't working." It was Fallon who spoke, his eyes alight with fury.

One, two, three.

Fallon was at her head, his hands reaching out to stop the bleeding around her neck, his fingers flinching against the ring of bruises there. Tears were streaming down his face, and the sight caused me to stutter in my movements.

Fallon didn't cry.

"Not again," he begged, so quietly I almost didn't hear it. It made me stumble and made my rhythm drop.

"She's bleeding out. We need to do something else." Eirik's words were a muck of growls I didn't let stop me. I continued moving.

One, two, three.

Osiris went still next to me, the rest of his bandages slipping from his fingers before his eyes set into hard lines. Numbness replaced his determination, and he was by her head in the next instant, tilting Aaliyah's head back and opening her throat.

"What are you doing?" Fallon demanded, pushing at Osiris's unmoving body.

But Osiris didn't waver, placing his hands on either side of her face. His hands shook as he cupped her still cheeks. There was a lovely quality to the way he held her, his thumbs sliding under her eyelashes as they fluttered.

"You have to live, *lux mea*," he said, opening her mouth.

Fallon realized what Osiris planned a fraction before I did, his eyes going wide as he screamed.

"*No.* Osiris, you'll fucking kill her!" Fallon's words were choked, and his teeth bared as he struggled against Osiris's unmoving body. He tried to move him, but Osiris was unbudging. "You'll kill her!"

Osiris paid no heed as he brought his arm up to his lips and bit down. The tear of skin under teeth echoed in my mind, repeating over and over. My movements faltered again, and I understood. Panic raced down every limb as I sat frozen.

Vampire blood was much like a potion of chance. You might live. There was a chance it'd pass through you, fixing the things you didn't know were wrong. Patching up the broken pieces. Maybe it wouldn't do anything ... just leave you to live your life.

Or it could kill you. Light your organs on fire and boil your blood. If she died, she'd die in agony. She'd die *screaming*.

"No!" It was Eirik who yelled this time, but it was too late. Osiris's blood dripped into Aaliyah's mouth.

Eirik tackled Osiris to the ground, his face partially shifting as he all but tore out Osiris's throat. The low, thrumming growl filled the entire space. Blanking out the silence. Barely a drop had made it in, but it was enough.

"*You've killed her.*" Eirik's voice was guttural, raw as he held Osiris down. Even as he raged, trembles took him over.

"She was dead, regardless. I had to give her a chance," Osiris snarled, the words forced past the gurgle of blood as his wound healed, numbness so firmly in his eyes that I couldn't even find a hint of him there.

But I didn't give a fuck about him right now. Sebek could walk through the door and tear out all of their hearts, and I wouldn't move from this spot. Silence once again filled the room beyond my own movements, and I picked up my pace once again, watching for signs in her unmoving body. Waiting for her to convulse and scream as she died. Everything in me was ready to die with her. There was still so much that we had to do. She had so much life left to live.

I had only just found her, heard her laugh, and enjoyed the brush of her breath against my lips. I hadn't shown her all my favorite recipes yet or made her that damned sugar toast. It couldn't be over, not like this.

"Please, Aaliyah," I pleaded as I clenched my teeth tightly. "Breathe. You have to breathe."

I didn't focus on the sound of Osiris and Eirik standing. Nor the strangling feeling of their auras setting heavily in the air. Instead, I listened carefully, desperate to hear anything. For her to move, to tell me she was okay.

"*Please.*" I pleaded again.

It felt like an eternity, sitting there with her. Her skin boiling under my own, the give of her chest as I gave another compression.

Then, the cuts on her face knitted together. Pulling sealed and eventually closing.

Her first breath broke me.

My hands slid from her chest, and I fell forward over her, holding her as close as I could without further aggravating her closing wounds.

She was breathing. She wasn't dead.

She wasn't dead.

Nothing else mattered. Nothing else would *ever* matter. I thanked whatever god would listen, because if she had left this world?

Then I would have followed.

Fallon hit his knees next to the table, his hands going to his head as he let out a choked, broken noise. Words from the language of his human life spilled out around us as Eirik moved to my side. His fingers threaded through Aaliyah's hair, smoothing it down, touching her even as his hands shook. He growled something so low and deep that I knew it had come from his beast, and it only took one glimpse into his eyes to see that the wolf was just as in control as Eirik was.

Then it was silent, besides the steady breaths she took and the consistent chime of the clock above our heads.

"I think I'm going to be sick," Fallon muttered, standing.

His white suit was stained red, and he brushed his hands over it, trying to wash it away but only managing to sink it further into the fabric. The more he moved, the more it spread, and the deeper the panic found a home in his eyes. Then there was a flash of red, his eyes sparking to the color, as what little flush he held fled from his face.

And then he was gone, leaving to face the *Call* ... Normally, I'd follow him, but I couldn't even find the will to get off of the table, my hand having found its way to Aaliyah's pulse point again. When I felt her heartbeat against my fingertips, and my ears trained on her breathing form, I finally inhaled, letting air wash into my lungs.

She was alive ... but she almost wasn't.

Osiris was the next to gain bearings as he inched over toward us. His neck, still healing from the chunk Eirik had taken out of it, continued to bleed over his suit, dripping down his hand. The closer he got, the more savage Eirik's growl became, his face further shifting.

But that didn't stop Osiris, just like it hadn't when he put his bleeding hand over Aaliyah's mouth. But she wouldn't be here if he hadn't taken the risk. I knew that, but God damn if some part of me wasn't *angry* at him for it.

By the time he was by her head, the growl had gotten so loud that it shook the table, Aaliyah staying contently still as whatever had happened took its toll on her body. I looked down, tracing the fresh scars and the still-closing wounds. The blood had taken care of most of them, the major ones, but others had slowed to a near stop.

Further proof of how close we'd come to losing her.

Osiris lifted his hand, like it was instinct, bringing it just inches from her face when he suddenly stopped, flinching so hard it startled me. I hadn't seen him move like that in weeks, not since we'd found Aaliyah. But the deep-rooted pain had sunk back into his eyes, had taken root in even his skin as he pulled away, gripping his wrist. He squeezed so tightly that the bone *cracked*.

"I ..." he started, uncharacteristically at a loss for what to say. But we all were, none of us able to breathe a word.

It was like watching a puppet as the master let go of his strings, and Osiris's eyes dulled, dropping his wrist like it was made of flaming coals. He stood straight, that crisp flick of power again dirtying the air. Osiris had always been withdrawn and reserved, but it had never felt this wrong to see. We'd made progress; I was sure we had. But Kali had done something irreparable to Osiris, and *this* was the straw that broke the camel's back. I saw the exact moment he fractured.

"I need to find out how Crustava got in," he said, emotionless, as he straightened his blood-stained suit. "There was no disruption to the ward. I would have felt it."

My anger boiled at his words and disregard. Even Eirik let go of Ali's hair to stand rigidly straight, glaring so fiercely at Osiris that I was sure it was going to burn him.

But Osiris didn't blink, barely moved.

"Is that all?" I demanded, watching as Osiris turned his dead gaze to me.

"I have to fix the damage I caused," he said, tilting his head toward the door. "There must have been a weak point. I'd stayed up all those days making it. I must have missed it."

"Are you *kidding* me right now?" He offered no reaction, and it only made my blood boil more. "No one gives a fuck about the ward right now, Osiris! *Look at her.* Crustava doesn't matter, the wards don't fucking matter. They'll still be here in a few minutes."

But the spark that had finally been brought back to Osiris had been snuffed out, with not even the embers glowing through his eyes anymore.

"Take a good fucking look at her, because she is the *only* thing that matters," I begged, pleading with him.

But what I'd hoped would sink some sense into him only served to further the pain there. He covered his wrist, the one with the brand he refused to talk about.

With his eyes never leaving her face, he whispered, "I know."

Then he turned, walking toward the door without a single glance, and even Eirik quieted.

"Then get the fuck back here, you coward. She needs you; she needs us all!" The door slipped open, and my hands shook. "You saw what happened. She—"

I couldn't even say it, couldn't breathe it. It didn't take a genius to deduce what happened, the way she'd screamed ... she'd lost someone that had been a part of her soul; she *needed* us right now.

"You're right. She is the *only* thing that matters." He spoke just as the door closed behind him, and I was left on the table, soaked in blood, still searching for that heartbeat, begging that she continued to breathe. Only Eirik stayed, so throttled by his beast, I doubted he could leave if he wanted to. Fallon showed no signs of returning, and if I knew him at all, he wasn't planning to.

The Vivas name meant 'to live', but all we seemed to be good at was running.

The pain of the night built and simmered in my chest until it grew tight and painful. I let it out with a scream.

"Cowards!"

CHAPTER 12

AALIYAH

A haze covered my thoughts, weighing down on me like a blanket made of lead. It wasn't an unfamiliar feeling. In fact, it was one I remembered all too clearly.

But what I didn't expect was the lack of pain.

Even after the tamest sessions on the table at Ascension, I *always* hurt. But now? I was barely sore. For the first time in weeks, I didn't feel like I was dying. There was no pressure, no ache beyond the stiffness of being bedridden for who knew how long.

So there were only thoughts to greet me, to latch on to. I often slept for days after torture with Castillion, and for a brief, *horrible* moment, before I opened my eyes to face my reality, I hoped it was his sickening green eyes I would see. Because seeing him would mean this was all a bad dream.

It would mean that I hadn't killed Prince. It would mean that whatever hell happened at the hot spring was only a dream ... a *nightmare*.

But when I opened my eyes—that hazy sensation forcing my head to lull to the side—it was my room at the Vivas house I saw. Familiar gray walls and the plush sheets of my bed. My head was heavy, my body too weak to muster a move, so I simply looked around the empty room, searching for a man who would no longer be there.

The world somehow still felt cold, even without Prince in it, my breath showing in front of me.

My mind must be playing tricks on me, trying to fill the void that had

119

been placed in the hollow of my chest. I gripped the shirt there, trying to abate the feeling just as something wet and cold pressed against my arm. I jolted, surprised, and I realized I wasn't alone in the bed.

I'd seen Eirik at the hot spring, the beast half of him, but I hadn't realized just how *big* he was.

Eirik sprawled across the other side of the bed, spanning more space than I did. There was feral intelligence in his eyes, the deep blue of the wolf taking over everything. He huffed, his lightly tanned fur shuffling as he inched even closer to me, pressing his nose under my jaw.

I let out a shaky breath as I accepted the comfort, burying my hands in his thick coat. With everything going on, and the unknown that shattered our little world, it was nice to have someone here to lean on. The chill that had been in the room faded, and the door opened. Adrian ambled in, his face stricken, worry so blatant that it made my chest hurt.

When he saw me, his mouth shot open, and whatever had been in his hands slipped. Soup, if I had to guess, as the steaming liquid hit the cold oak. It splattered everywhere.

"Thank fucking God," he said before he was next to me. His eyes brimmed with tears, and I choked on the absolute desolation that came crashing down on me. I tried to hold it in, to stay strong when he was obviously so distressed.

But there was nothing for me to hold on to. No Prince to remind me I was okay. And like a broken record, he was the only thing I could think of. What happened at the hot spring, what I was, and what I did to a full-grown man didn't matter to me. Not near as much as the loss of Prince. He wasn't here to tell me it was okay.

To tell me we were forever.

The first sob bounced in my chest, the sound broken and savage. Like before, my mind didn't scream at me to keep it silent, the sound a hollow echo in the air.

Adrian's face further crumpled as he pulled himself onto the bed, pressing into my back as I curled around Eirik. He was freezing, but I barely noticed as I struggled to breathe through my tears.

I killed him.

Adrian held me softly, saying nothing as I broke apart. I silently thanked him for it, unable to voice any words through my grief.

Through the loss of my first friend, my *best* friend ...

And the love I'd miss forever.

I opened my eyes and knew that I was fully recovered. It had taken longer than expected, and I'd been in and out of consciousness for the better part of the last few days. But it always happened that way. One day, I'd be at death's door. And the next, there would only be scars. Though this time, it wasn't the physical pain that I was begging to leave; it was the steady numbness that had stuck to me. Like a fog I couldn't shake. But now, that was gone too.

I twisted my arm, instinctively touching the scars that had healed along my skin. They were fresh, the pink of healed skin giving them away from the older, silver scars that had already been there.

There were more than I could count, and it was always at a time like this when I would look up and find my strength in Prince's crooked smile. But I didn't search for him this time, my mind almost deadened to the loss of him, like it was pretending.

If I didn't look, then it wasn't real.

He was just out of view.

I closed my eyes, waiting desperately for his familiar cold. I *almost* felt it, the brush of ice, the tinge of worry in the air that gave him away.

He's okay.

When I opened them again, it was Eliza I saw as she peeked over the bed, her worried aqua eyes seeming far away. Eliza looked as haggard as I did, and I flinched, knowing that it was me who had caused it again. Her red hair, shaved on one side, held soft, frazzled waves, and her clothes appeared a few days worn. She sat next to the bed on one of the dining room chairs. It only took a second to guess that the guys had called her and most likely let her know what happened if they even knew.

I wasn't sure *I* knew. I'd killed Crustava, that much was clear. Ripped the soul right out of him, like it was nothing. And Prince ... I'd killed Prince too, sent him to the Void. I couldn't tell them how, or even understand *why*, I'd been so out of control.

I sat up, flinching so hard my breath caught when Eliza made a choked noise and leaned forward. Her eyes grew wide, and she jolted back. I hadn't been this sensitive to movement in weeks, but it was like my mind had been reset the moment Prince passed through me.

I didn't kill him, my mind soothed, like even my thoughts were begging for it to not be true.

Eliza looked at me like she expected me to cry, and I felt *bad* that I wasn't. It was like there were no more tears left in me, no more emotion left to feel.

"Ali—" Eliza started, and I shook my head, the tremble of my lips the only thing that told me I was feeling anything.

Eliza reached out, grabbing my hand softly, for the first time not pulling away when I flinched. My entire body shook, and I tried to find the right words to say.

Any words to say.

"It's going to be okay, Ali," she whispered, her head dropping, as if in mourning herself. But she couldn't be. "One day, it's going to be okay."

One day. That hurt the most, knowing that even though she tried, she wasn't really mourning for *him.* I was the one who knew Prince. I was the one to speak to him, to bask in the unbelievable presence that he was. I was the only one who knew to watch at the crease between his eyes during games to know if he was pretending to lose. I was the one who knew he snapped his fingers when he was thinking about something that interested him. *I* was the one who *loved* him, and I had taken it for granted that he would always be with me.

He was my forever, and I ...

"I killed him, Liz," I mumbled, the words cracking like they didn't belong. Like they weren't real. "I killed Prince."

Eliza didn't speak for a minute, just holding my hand as I stared blankly ahead. There were still no tears, only the stark feeling of emptiness, and a false cold that kept me clinging to the hope that this was a bad dream.

"He loved you, Ali. I knew that without ever having seen him. He wouldn't want you hurting over this," she said finally.

How could she know that? For some reason I couldn't fathom, that made me angry. So blisteringly angry that I had to bite my tongue to not say something I'd regret. She didn't know that, because she didn't know Prince. No one knew Prince ... and that was horrible.

No one knew him, and I was left to mourn him alone.

"What am I supposed to do now, Liz?" I asked, unable to meet her gaze at my twisted thoughts. "He was everything. And I don't know what to do without him."

It was quiet for a moment, with only the sound of our breathing audible before Eliza spoke.

"You live, Ali." Her soft words sounded far too optimistic. Live? "You take it one day at a time, one step, one breath."

She made it sound so easy, like even breathing didn't make my entire body hurt. I searched the room again, desperate, no longer avoiding corners. I searched every inch, begging for him to fade through the wall and appear.

I needed the joyful twist of his devious lips. I needed his strength.

I needed him.

"You aren't alone, Ali. Not anymore. You have me and your fangy boy toys. And you know Grigen is always there to cheer you up." That startled a choked laugh from me, and Eliza gave me a bittersweet grin. She reached out, pressing her hand to my chest, over my heart. It beat against her hand, telling me that despite what I was feeling, she was right. I was alive. "Even Prince hasn't truly left. He's here."

She pulled her hand away, and I reached up, pressing my fingers down over where hers had been. I lowered my ring and pinky finger on instinct, closing my eyes.

"He'll always be with you, Ali. Forever."

Tears rolled down my cheek, reality sinking past the grief, if only for a moment.

Forever doesn't sound so promising anymore.

"Can you go get me some water?" I asked suddenly, choking on the words but needing a moment to myself. A moment to grieve.

Eliza seemed to understand that, her lips thinning as she stood. She watched me with muddled pity, and it made my stomach hurt. "Of course," she whispered, walking out of the room.

It was the click of the door that finally gave me the break I needed.

I took a deep, shaky breath, rubbing my face, desperate to search the room for him ... It was ingrained in my core. So when I sought out that familiar cold, that presence that would forever be seared into my mind, I wasn't expecting to find it.

But there it was. It *was* cold, the breath of a spirit that for a moment seemed like Prince. But when the familiarity passed, and I couldn't place his distinctive feeling, I knew someone else had joined me. I took another deep breath.

There was only one other spirit it could be. The one that had teased Adrian in the cellar.

"I feel you ... and I know you're not Prince," I said, barely forcing the words out past my constricting throat.

Speaking hurt—hell, the thought of speaking hurt—and the spirit seemed to acknowledge that, a sadness sinking into the air. It wasn't a full emotion, one that had undertones of melancholy or pity, and I couldn't pick out where it was coming from, but it was there. This ghost was hanging on by a thread, so spread thin I couldn't even see him, could *barely* feel him. But he was there, and it was nice to feel less alone.

I searched the room, against every sensible part of my mind, gazing at every hidden corner and shadow.

"But can I pretend? Just for a minute," I whispered, closing my eyes. The ghost brushed against me, comforting me enough that I could *pretend* that he was Prince. "Just a minute."

Just a minute to gain my bearings. A minute to come to terms with everything.

A minute to pick up the shattered remains of the foundation that made me *me*. Because I knew that when I opened my eyes, I would have to accept this. What I'd done ...

And that Prince was gone because of me.

CHAPTER 13

EIRIK

With blood roaring in my ears and the hammer of my heart in my chest, I finally came to a stop at our stairs. I heaved a heavy breath, savoring the burn in my lungs. Running was as close to alive as I could feel.

And I'd felt nothing but dead since Ali almost died on our kitchen table nearly a week and a half ago.

I shook off the adrenaline that came from exercise, thankful that for once my beast lay silent. He hadn't so much as left me a moment alone since the stint at the hot spring, tearing, roaring. Pushing me to mark.

To *claim*.

Seeing Aaliyah fall again had broken something inside of me. I swore to her that her demons would die at my feet, and when I failed again, hearing the flutter of her heart as Osiris placed his torn wrist to her mouth ... I'd *shattered*.

I'd been so worried in the days following the hellish moment that she wouldn't make it. That the blood hadn't made its way through her yet, that it'd end up like that day in the woods when we first learned of her *Rends*. That I'd have to say goodbye again. And as furious as I'd been with Osiris, he'd made the right call in giving her his blood. He'd done what none of us were brave enough to do, and Aaliyah was alive because of it. No, more than alive, she was thriving. At least, her health was.

She seemed brighter, her skin more vibrant, her eyes clear. She hadn't complained of headaches or that dreaded pressure. And that was a silver lining. But her mind had shrouded itself, as grief often did. She'd drawn in, had barely spoken, and it gouged a part of my heart every time I saw it because I had no idea how to fix it.

I was at a loss, not wanting to push her in her grief, and I could do nothing more than stay by her side. And that was something my beast was more than happy to follow. The need to tie her to us, to entwine her so deeply into my soul that her demons became my own, had been a thunderous call in my mind.

Adrian was right: She was ours. She was *mine*.

But now wasn't the time for my own fracturing, nor the manic call of my beast. Aaliyah had been strong her entire life, and right now, she needed someone to be strong for her.

I pushed past the door and traced my way to where the soft scent of lavender and the sea was strongest.

I wasn't surprised to find her curled up on the couch of the library, the ancient furniture creaking even under her slight weight. Osiris had refused to replace it, too taken by its rich red. The library was dimly lit by the soft glow of the fireplace, the warmth of the room soothing. It had been built with warmth in mind, comfort being Nero's primary goal. From the bronze oak floors to the tan walls and rows of endless books. Of all places, I was glad she'd chosen to grieve here.

She'd spent every day since she'd woken up in this room, surrounded by blankets and the books I knew she used to escape. The confinement of the room she slept in was too hard for her to shoulder right now.

I took a step toward her, eyes landing on the book she had in her hand. Osiris's novel. It was a shock to see it, one that stopped my advance. The old tome smelled of magic ... and Nero. It didn't have a name, the cover just a simple piece of pulled leather, but I still remembered the day Osiris had written it, nearly a year after Nero's death. Nero had picked the tome himself, even signed it, having expected to draft his own story in it.

Aaliyah didn't notice me. In fact, she didn't even seem to see the book as I finally realized that pain clouded her soft scent.

She was crying. Aaliyah was *crying*.

It wasn't an unfamiliar sight as of late. She'd been torn down by the loss of Prince, and nothing I or Adrian did seemed to help. Fallon and Osiris sure as fuck weren't helping, either. Slinking off, brooding in their own rot.

It made me sick, and it made my beast anxious. But while I couldn't do anything about them, I could help with this. I was by her side in the next instant, pulling her into my arms without a second thought, a gasp of surprise on her lips. I easily sat us on the couch, holding her steady and grumbling when the old wood made another whine. My wolf snapped, pacing as he tried to sort through her chaotic emotions. I ran my nose against the skin of her temple, taking her in, a low growl bubbling up in my chest at the tainted scent of pain.

I didn't ask; I didn't have to. She simply curled into my chest, balling her fists in my shirt as she sniffled, her body heaving as she took a shaky breath, trying to hide her ache.

"My brave *Valkyrja*," I praised softly, lifting my hands to cup her face. I studied it, finding no hint of injury or wound. I ran my thumbs under her eyes, brushing away the wetness. I hated the sight of tears in her eyes. "Tell me how to help, *Elsken*."

She bit her lip, looking away. Her eyes searched the room, further dulling as they scanned the space. She'd done it a lot, the action instinctual, and my heart broke for her every time she found him missing. She took a hard breath, and I expected the same answer she always gave. The same brave face she put on, but her lip merely trembled, tears sliding down her ivory cheeks.

"I don't know," she lamented, closing her eyes like it might make the room disappear. "I don't *know*. I—" Another choked breath. "I can't *do* this, Eirik. I keep expecting to see him, hoping he'll be there, and I can't live with myself knowing I'm the reason he's not."

It was the most I'd gotten out of her in days, the most she'd spoken since she woke up. It was progress. Broken, painful progress, but progress all the same. I hated it, hated the pain I knew I couldn't stop, and it only pushed my beast to snap at my heels again.

I eyed her neck, hands shaking at the sight of unmarred skin.

I knew of a Claiming Mark, had grown up with a mother and father who had spent centuries together. It was a bonding of souls that connected people in ways that nothing else compared to. I wanted it, craved it. And one day, I hoped she'd let me have it ... but for now, I stood with her in my arms.

She gasped at the movement, clinging to me. My beast stilled, content enough now that she was close, encompassed by us.

Tiny, my beast supplied, always watching her.

I turned and began walking out of the room. We passed by the doorway that led to the library, catching Thoth's watchful, stoic gaze on the carved wood.

"Eirik?" she asked, blushing as she looked around, her feet swinging. I huffed, looking down at her. Her eyes were wide, and her head tipped back, showing her throat in that way that always stilled my beast. "Where are we going?"

"Room," I growled, the word pointed.

I couldn't mark her, not yet. She wasn't in the right state to agree, and I wasn't going to take advantage of that. When she became mine, it would be fully in mind and body. But being in the library, surrounded by the scent of her anguish, only made my beast rage.

I didn't want to be away from her, so I compromised and took her somewhere we could both relax. I moved easily through the game room, down the thin hallway, and finally to my room. I opened the door, selfishly deciding that I needed her scent to sink into my sheets, that I needed the warmth of her against me. I took a quick survey of the space, finding the many trinkets of my life strewn about, as I always had them.

I liked to keep my things close, to admire the gems and jewels that I'd collected. It'd been a hobby since I was human, and even now I recalled my father joking that I seemed more dragon than wolf.

I walked us toward the bed and set her down in the middle, smirking as she sank into the fur comforter, nearly drowning in it.

Jesus, she was tiny.

I crawled next to her, watching as her eyes caught mine and her cheeks flushed. Hesitation shone in her eyes, enough that I stopped, picking up her hand to bring it to my lips.

"Much better," I said through the tightness of my mouth. The shift began again, slowly. It always started with my skin straining against bone and muscle. "Let me hold you?"

Tension drained from her, and she tenderly opened her arms. I huffed again, claiming the spot by her side, our fronts facing each other. I pulled her to my chest, fitting her snuggly against me, my hands finding their way to her hair, and I couldn't stop from rubbing my nose down to her neck, sinking my scent into her skin until my beast was lulled into a happy stupor.

She bit her lip again, her eyes closing as she lost herself in the feeling of my fingers threading through the white silk of her hair. I ran them through it, the smooth strands easy enough to move. It was so bright against the dull tan of my skin, the color blending with the scars across my fingers until I could barely see them at all.

My beast thrashed again, and I steeled myself against his push.

"Roll," I grunted, and Aaliyah looked at me with a confused tilt of her head.

Though she did as I asked, rolling so her back faced me.

My hands moved back to her hair, and I hummed calmly at the feeling of her so close to me, the tune the same one I'd sung for her before. The last time she'd died. Aaliyah relaxed further, sighing as I toyed with the locks, beginning to move on instinct. Before she could ask what I was doing, I finished the braid, reaching out to tighten the loops.

She leaned back further, a small hum telling me she enjoyed the feel of my hands in her hair. Those small sounds, innocent sounds, drove me and the beast mad, but I wasn't going to let it stop me. I pulled her back against me, until she was flush to my chest, no longer even trying to hide the hard length of my erection at her back. She jolted at the feeling of it but didn't protest, before she reached her hand up to touch my work.

"A braid?" she asked, glancing over her shoulder at me, and I nodded against her neck.

"I was right," I said, pressing my lips to her cheek. My beast let out an appreciative purr as we admired my handiwork. "A *Valkyrja.*"

She was stunning with her flushed cheeks and braided hair. And that valiant shine in her eyes.

"You're beautiful, *Elskan*," I said, tracing her jaw with my lips.

Her pulse jumped, and my fangs ached. I was close, so close to her. I wound my way tighter, just as uncertainty flooded the room and she tensed. I frowned and pulled back to find her looking away.

I'd spent enough time around Aaliyah now to know some of her ticks, the way she moved. I was a tactician; it was my job to know the finer details. So seeing her reach up to tap at the scar that nicked her nose, then down to the one over her lip ...

Absolutely *not*.

I flipped her around easily, sitting up fully at the same time. She wrapped her arms around my neck with a gasp at the movement, her legs finding their way around my hips.

I leaned forward, pressing my forehead to hers.

"You're the most stunning woman I've ever met," I said through clenched teeth and a shifting face. Aaliyah's eyes went wide, the vivid lavender so captivating it took my breath away. "Here." I traced her face, the gentle curve of her jaw, the defiant tilt of her nose, and her thin, pouted lips. I didn't miss the scars that she'd just touched, instead leaning in to press my lips to each one before I trailed down until my hand was over her thundering heart. It beat against my palm, fluttering as my thumb moved over the skin at her collarbone. "And here."

Her shock blended with confusion, and her cheeks flushed a deep red. Her lips trembled, and she looked like she was going to disagree ... before she nodded. Her head dropped, and I lifted my hand, trailing it along her arm, across a raised scar there.

"They don't change that, Aaliyah. Your scars do not define you. What happened at the hot spring does *not* define you, and you can't let them," I said, still hovering on those raised lines.

She was silent for a second, and I'd assumed she was going to shut down again. That she was going to turn everything off and hide it away.

"You didn't see his face," she whispered, surprising me as her eyes closed. "He didn't want to go. I took that choice away from him."

Such strength to be found in such a small woman. Such grit it took to talk about this.

I shook my head. "I didn't have to see his face. He wouldn't blame you for this, and he wouldn't want you to blame yourself."

She reached up and grabbed my hand, the one that had still been idly mapping her face, memorizing every detail. She pulled it to her lips, kissing the jagged lines that sat against my knuckles. "They're harder to ignore today. I see them everywhere because they *are*. And Prince ... Prince isn't."

"They always will be," I insisted, leaning in and skimming my nose along her temple. Her legs tightened around my hips, pressing her further into me. "But you aren't alone, my *Valkyrja*. **Never again.**" The second half wasn't meant to come out, my beast's words slipping past my clenched teeth.

She sucked in a breath before it came out in a small laugh.

"Thank you, Eirik," she said, shuffling again, her eyes hazing as she looked at me.

But she didn't cry again, instead only leaned forward, pressing her head to my shoulder. I grunted in response as she closed her eyes. And I held her, for as long as she needed me to, as I fell into a peaceful sleep with her in my arms.

It was hours later when I slipped my way out of Aaliyah's arms, my eyes on her as my beast sought to steal every second with her he could. He rumbled, the sound of him finding its way out as I reached over and brushed my hand against her cheek. She sighed into the contact, mumbling something.

Mine, my beast pressed softly. *My smár Valkyrja.*

I didn't disagree as I turned to walk away. Normally, I'd stay by her side until everything crumbled around us. But right now, I had to do something else, something that was now long past due.

I *flitted* downstairs, barely glancing toward where Adrian stood by the stove, preparing dinner. The kitchen smelled of heavy spices and flour, and the entire room was warmer with the oven going.

"Eirik," Adrian greeted, nodding in my direction as I reached the front door. "Where are you going?"

Adrian's eyes were sunken like he hadn't slept in days, and I knew he likely hadn't. His clothes were a mess, and his hands shook as he turned toward me, setting them firmly on the counter to hold himself up as he rocked his head back and forth. He'd been by Aaliyah's side every spare moment. This was one of the first that he hadn't been and by the looks of it, it was because he was making her something to eat.

"Valen's," I responded, scenting the air and finding us to be the only three in the house.

Not that it was surprising. Fallon and Osiris had barely been in the house at all, each dealing with the events in much the same way. Running. Fallon, because he feared his attraction to her, and Osiris because he feared her attraction to *him*. One was terrified the past would find him again, and the other was worried the past had never left.

Either way, I was just as furious as Adrian with how they'd gone about handling it, and as soon as I got back from Valen's, Osiris was going to hear from me.

"The Gargoyle blacksmith? What do you need from him?" Adrian asked, and I huffed.

I needed something worthy of Aaliyah, a gift to get my beast off my back, to show claim without a bite. I needed her to be mine, and this was the best way to do that without pushing her. Without bringing up old wounds.

"Courting gift. I'll be back soon, so keep an eye on her," I said, and Adrian nodded, stirring whatever was in his pot. It was some kind of sugar mixture.

"You know I will. I think I'm going to see if she wants to spend the day baking, something to keep her mind occupied," Adrian sighed.

He was struggling. I saw it clear as day, but the ability to comfort him got caught in my throat. I'd never been the one to help with words. That'd been Nero's specialty, and I was too lost today to try to be him.

"When I get back, I'm going to talk to Osiris. Our meeting with Xander didn't just go away, and I worry that this burst of good health Aaliyah is having isn't going to last as long as we'd like. We need to make sure we're ready. You got Fallon?" I asked, changing the subject.

I was tired of their cowardice, and by the way Adrian nodded, his eyes hardening as his hands clenched into fists, I knew he was too.

"Yeah, I can take care of him," Adrian said, rolling his head from side to side. It was going to be a fight, one that he might even enjoy. "Though, I'm not looking forward to the broken bones."

I grunted, smirking as I strode out the door. Lucky bastard.

At least he got the easy brother.

CHAPTER 14

ADRIAN

The door slammed as Eirik left, and I heaved a heavy sigh as I leaned over the quickly burning roux that I had on the stove.

My body ached in ways that it hadn't in years—*decades*—not since my time as a human. But at least now, I wasn't surprised by it. I hadn't slept in days, barely fed, barely breathed ... and I still couldn't get Aaliyah's dead face out of my mind, couldn't get the heady scent of blood to leave my nose. Even as I made dinner, it sparked in my stomach and made my mouth water as that familiar twisting feeling of the *Maker's Call* tried to slink through me.

It had been a constant, and it was nearly as draining as fighting my unending ire at Osiris and Fallon. The bloody bastards who ran when things got tough. When Aaliyah needed them.

I clenched the counter so hard it cracked, and my fangs snapped out as fury consumed me. I wasn't the angry one; I didn't fight and rage with fists, but right now, even I saw the benefit of trading blows. Because I needed to get my mind off of this, off of everything.

Off of the sound of Aaliyah's pulse stopping, or the crack in her ribs when I pressed too hard trying to save her. Off of the fact that I hadn't found anything on Ascension Rising, the place that held her captive. In fact, I hadn't found anything at *all*, not that I'd had much time to look the last few days. But it worried me. *Everything* left a trace. Yet Audric hadn't known of it, and he was my ace in the hole, and I wasn't sure if we'd be able to weasel an extra question out of Xander. Everything just felt like too much right now, and I struggled to bear the weight alone.

The creak of a door opening upstairs settled that searing anger just enough for me to mellow until it simmered. I let go of the counter and turned toward the staircase just as Aaliyah wandered down it. She was wearing a long t-shirt, one that dwarfed her to such a degree that I barely glimpsed the shorts she wore under it. One of Eirik's.

It was fucking *adorable*.

"Morning, love. You have a good nap?" I teased, delighted when Aaliyah's cheeks lit in a smooth blush.

She shuffled, her hunched shoulders curling a little tighter, making her seem even smaller than she was. "Yes, I did," she said as she walked over to the table and sat down.

She looked better, and that was enough to make me feel better, too. At least now she wasn't dealing with those rampant headaches. Thankfully, the blood did that much for her, though I wish it would have helped in other ways, like lessening the pain in her mind.

"I bet Eirik makes quite the pillow," I said with a wink, aiming to get some joy out of her, but she merely frowned.

Her cheeks lit up a dashing shade of pink, and she crossed her legs, curling in on herself in a way. It was when she bit her lip that I really worried.

"Are you ... are you mad about that?" she asked softly, twiddling her thumbs while keeping her eyes on the floor.

I *flitted* over to her, easily cupping her face with my hands. She jolted, something that took me by surprise, and I pulled away sharply. She shook as she gripped her hands tighter, searching the kitchen, her eyes bouncing around sporadically.

"Not at all, love. Not at all." I reached out and took her hand. Mad? No. I was *overjoyed*. "I'm glad you found comfort with him."

She traced my face, her eyes intent. Sometimes she was the easiest person in the room to read, and others, like now, I couldn't even pick out one thing I was certain was on her mind. Eventually she nodded, though obviously not fully convinced. But I wasn't going to push it, not now.

Baby steps.

"Thank you," she said, her hands finally relaxing at her sides.

"Don't thank me, love, not yet," I chimed, stepping back and extending my hand in a flourish. "Come on, we have some time to kill. How would you like to do a little baking?"

That got her attention firmly, and I used her sweet tooth against her with glee. Her upper lip twitched in an almost grin. She still searched the room as she took my hand, and that shadow behind her eyes was still present. But she moved, she breathed, and she pushed anyway.

My brave little love.

"I'd like that," she said, standing with me.

And bake we did.

Hours slid by like minutes as we joked and played around the kitchen. She even began humming after we'd pulled out the hand mixers. The room was light, and for the first time in days, I didn't fall under the crushing weight of sorrow. And getting to see Aaliyah smile was worth it. Everything was worth it.

"There you have it!" I exclaimed broadly at Aaliyah, taking a second to marvel at our artistic masterpiece.

It may not be a painting like one of Fallon's, but it was damned art if I had any say in the matter. And now, we were finally going to reap the benefits of our hard work.

In like forty-five minutes, as we'd only just gotten it into the oven.

We'd prepared baklava, an old recipe that my grandmother had taught me so many moons back that I barely remembered it. If I hadn't scribbled it down on that old notepaper, it probably would have been lost to time.

"I didn't realize baking was this hard," she mumbled, flexing her sore hands. Her cheeks were slightly flushed, and she was covered in a variety of powders, the little black apron that she had on speckled with white. It was adorable how she always ended up covered in whatever we were working with. "Eliza didn't like to cook, so we ordered in a lot."

An amused pout played on her thin lips, one that didn't quite reach her lavender eyes. I hadn't seen that spark behind them in days, and no matter what I did, I couldn't seem to get it back. Couldn't get her to stop searching the shadows with a hollow expression. But I knew grief if nothing else. She didn't need me to point it out, she just needed me to be there, so I was.

I leaned over the island, planting my elbows on the marble countertop as I listened to her recount her story.

"Or Dezen and Carter would decide it was time to burn water again. I can't count on both hands how many times Carter almost burned the house down." She shook her head at the memory, rubbing her hands on her little apron. "Eliza even said that Grigen's first word was fire."

That I believed. I'd expect nothing less from the little spitfire of a Dragonkin. Eliza's son was a ball of energy, and I honestly missed that. I'd only gotten to see him once, but anyone willing to put Fallon in his place was good in my book.

"Good thing you have me, then," I said, leaning over and pressing a soft kiss to her forehead. "One of the many reasons that I am your favorite Vivas, no doubt." I winked and flashed my pearly white teeth. It had the desired effect, as Aaliyah's head tipped back and a tinkering laugh fell from her lips, a beautiful pink blossoming on her cheeks.

"I don't know ... Fallon has chocolate," she said without thinking, and as fast as that smile had taken over, it slid away.

I *wasn't* the violent sort; I liked to solve things with words, to get my point across with a joke and some well-baked bread. But this was enough to wear my patience thin. My brothers may already be dead, but that wasn't going to stop me from trying to kill them again.

He and Osiris hadn't made any effort to see Ali in days, too chickenshit to even try. It made my blood boil, to know that they should be here, and instead, they *ran*. She needed us, *all* of us, and they fucking ran. It made me angry, so angry that I had to close my eyes. I'd looked up to my brothers since my turn, and while we all had our faults, we were a family.

And they left Aaliyah to swallow her guilt alone. Leaving *me*.

Before I could further stew, there was a soft brush of something against my jaw, and my eyes shot open in surprise.

Aaliyah had leaned up then, pressing onto her toes. Her hands settled on the counter to keep her steady enough to reach my jaw. Tenderness had taken over her expression, showing in the subtle tilt of her lips all the way into the depths of her lavender eyes. Always, *always,* putting others above herself. She'd seen my discomfort, and her first instinct was to soothe it.

My shoulders dropped, and I leaned down the rest of the way to seal our lips in a tender kiss. She hummed against me before pulling back.

"What was that for?" I whispered, kissing her palm as I slid my hand into hers.

"You're thinking too hard," she replied like it was a secret just for the two of us.

She leaned forward, pressing her ear to my chest, just under my heart.

She stayed there, unmoving as she listened to its beat, humming along to the sound of it, and we slowly swayed back and forth. I was content to hold her like that all day, to never let her leave my arms again, but now I had a better idea.

"What do you say we do something fun while we wait for the baklava to finish?" I asked.

She dipped her head to the side, curiosity in her eyes as she lifted her head from my chest. "Like what?"

I grinned and easily lifted her, holding her like a blushing bride on her wedding day. It made my chest ache. The thought of her in white for us. I'd always been a traditional sort, and I would want a wedding, a flashy cake, and a kiss at the altar. Though, it'd have to be changed for all of us.

If the others ever got their heads out of their ass, anyway. Eirik was on the right track, but fuck if I had any idea what the other two would do. Self-sabotage was the name of the game for them, and they were racing to see who could fuck up the fastest.

I shook my head, *flitting* us up to the library. I set Ali on her feet and surveyed the space.

"Well, now that you've whisked me away, what are we going to do?" Aaliyah asked, looking around the room that had quickly become her favorite place in the house.

It was tight, but it'd have to do. And there was no way I was going to dance with her in the game room.

"I can think of a few things ..." I said, wiggling my eyebrows and making her blush again. "But I *do* have a plan."

I pulled her hand to my lips to give it a kiss before I reached out and snapped. Like always, the gift of *Flame* sparked along my skin, hitting the fireplace. Aaliyah grinned, moving toward the now roaring fire. I took that time to scoot the abomination of a couch out of my way. It wasn't needed today.

Or any other day, but *mostly* not today.

Aaliyah just continued to watch me as I moved the side table next and settled some of the books that had been splayed around safely to the side.

"What are you doing?" she asked curiously.

"Redecorating. Rouge plush was so last century," I said, taking the final side table and doing the same with it, dragging it away. "Mostly just moving some things, though. We can't very well dance with them in the way."

That got her attention, her eyebrows shooting up. "When did you decide we were dancing?"

"Well, mostly on my way up the stairs," I admitted, and she shook her head.

But she moved to stand in the middle of the now slightly open space. She crossed one arm over, holding on to the bicep of the other. The flush of her cheeks grew as she shuffled.

"I've never really danced before," she said, her bottom lip sliding between her teeth as she looked at me wearily.

"Oh come now, everyone's danced," I joked and near instantly regretted it, as she reached up and held a hand over her chest like she was brushing away the heartbreak.

She shuffled again, glancing around the room, looking at anything but me. She pushed a stray strand of hair away from her face, smoothing the braid that Eirik had given her. "I guess ... I remember dancing with Prince once. We swirled around my cell, laughing when he pretended to trip." She traced one scar on her arm, and the joy that had built in my chest sank to my stomach. "We couldn't really dance *together*, since I couldn't touch him. But we danced."

Leave it to me to shove my *entire* foot into my mouth as if I was trying to see if I could taste my ankle. I *flitted* to her, pulling her into my arms and setting my chin on top of her head. I wanted to blame my headache for that stumble, but unfortunately, it was just me and my dumbass mouth.

"Oh, love. I'm sorry, I didn't—" Didn't think, didn't stop my stupid thought. Didn't do a lot of things.

Aaliyah's arms wrapped around me tighter, holding me to her like she expected me to float away. I took that comfort as I curled around her, holding her close.

"It's okay," she mused into my chest. She took a deep breath and looked up at me. There were still smudges of flour on her face, and I reached up to brush one of the blotches away. "So, dancing?"

She traced her hand down my arm before grabbing my hand. It was always okay, and for some reason ... I always believed her. It would be okay one day, even if today hurt.

I kissed her palm and *flitted* away before she could question my mood, flipping a record onto our player. *Dmitri Shostakovich - Waltz No. 2.*

"Yes. Specifically, we're going to waltz!" I sang, likely a bit too enthusiastically.

Aaliyah's eyes narrowed a bit, but she nodded.

"Waltz. What's that?" she asked.

"Only the most elegant dance ever created. My grandmother insisted I learn how to. After all, every woman loves a man with good sway." I proved this by giving her a little twirl.

She laughed a bit as I pulled her back into position, her hand in mine, with my other at her hip.

"Eirik can dance too, you know," she said thoughtfully. "He told me about it, how he used to dance under the stars."

That he could, *barely*. More like a bull in a China shop, really. It was something of an out-of-body experience to watch, and it was something you'd never forget.

"Believe it or not, so can Osiris. And there was no one alive that could out-swing Nero," I said, beginning our movements to the rather upbeat song.

"Really?" she asked, blushing when she stepped on my toes.

I easily redirected her, laughing with her as we stumbled over each other a bit.

"I know, it shocked me, too. I almost burst a blood vessel when he told me," I chuckled, smitten with the way she watched her feet, careful not to step on my toes again. "Osiris learned quite a lot in his time in the high courts, playing with all those stuffy human dignitaries. And Nero had a habit of liking all things physically exerting. But that is a story for another time. For now, we waltz!"

I paused for a moment, stepping back. I should have done this to begin with. I tipped at the waist, offering her my hand. When she took it, I leaned in, pressing my lips to the tender skin.

"My lovely Aaliyah, might I have this dance?" I asked sweetly, and she hummed.

"I'd love to have this dance with you, Adrian," she said, her grin spread wide over her rosy cheeks.

We swayed around the room again, waltzing, stepping on each other's toes as songs continued to play. It was the most fun I'd had in years. In fact, the last time I'd danced like this was when I was human.

It seemed so long ago now, a different lifetime. Though, I'd never waltzed like this, never in the arms of someone I cared for so deeply. That thought slowed me down as I took in Aaliyah's face, her calm and open expression. The way her button nose twisted up when she laughed, her eyes twinkling in the firelight.

"How'd I ever get this lucky?" I murmured, leaning in to run my nose over her shoulder and take in the soft fragrance of lavender that mixed so sweetly with warm black tea. The softness of it reminded me of when I used to drink Earl Grey by the lake my grandmother owned.

There was a tremble in her lips, and I worried whether I'd said the wrong thing. So drawn by her I'd forgotten to take care.

"I could say the same thing, you know," she said, curling into me, and I brought us back into a soft sway. Her heartbeat was steady, and she hummed under her breath to the sound of the record playing. "When did you learn to dance?"

I jumped at her question, missing a beat as I stumbled over our feet again.

When *had* I learned to dance? Was it the summer of my year abroad when I first started my studies? Or was it during one of my grandmother's many lessons for me? I couldn't seem to recall the exact moment, that part of my life muddied by the years that had drifted by after it.

"You know, I don't think I recall the exact time," I said, now a bit melancholic about the matter. Aaliyah paused our steps again, this time reaching up to cup my cheek in her small hand. The spark that came from her touch warmed me to my core. "But I do recall my favorite memory of it."

Aaliyah tilted her head curiously, and the attentiveness in her eyes was enough to keep me speaking. I was so happy to see her wonder again, the wonder that had been dulled so much by the events of the week.

"It was midsummer's day, or possibly the fall. It was at a gala at a local Toff's home, a rich aristocrat with far too much money and a love for boosting his ego," I started. "I remember wanting to go. After all, my studies were almost complete, and that meant I'd be going into the workforce soon. I wouldn't have time for such things if I even stayed in that muddy village outside of London. But you see the host and I ... had a bit of disagreement."

Aaliyah quirked an eyebrow, and I playfully dipped her in our dance. Her eyes shot wide in shock, and I winked as she shook her head.

"Disagreement?" she jokingly asked as I pulled her back up. "What could you have possibly done to upset him?"

With such lightness in her tone, I couldn't help but laugh, and had I the ability to blush, I would have.

"I might have convinced his sister to accompany me occasionally. Nothing sordid, mind you. I see where that dirty mind of yours is going," I teased, tapping her nose as her cheeks flushed crimson. And it wasn't a lie. I never slept with Milliana, though she tried. I'd been saving myself for the wife whom I'd never had.

Nothing quite like a hundred-year-old virgin. But I didn't dare mention that.

"Oh? I didn't see you as the shameless flirt, though I will say you are very charming," Aaliyah mused, and I chuckled.

"Why thank you, my lady. But to tell you the truth, I stopped my flirting years after I was turned," I didn't say why, as the reason nearly choked up my next words. "But that isn't the story we're telling. Don't you want to know how I got in?"

We swayed again, and Aliyah nodded eagerly. "Of course. You can't just stop now."

Ah, *so fucking cute.*

"Oh, but I seem to have grown weary in this storytelling. I think I need a boost to pick me up," I said as innocently as I could muster, leaning in close to her. So close, her breath fanned my cheeks.

She blushed, shaking her head shyly again, before leaning up to kiss me. The teasing brush of her lips had me forgetting what exactly we'd been talking about before and wondering why we hadn't been doing this instead.

"So?" Aaliyah prompted, shifting back enough to look me in the eye.

I shook my head, trying to knock some sense back into myself as I recalled the story. The scene came back to me, and I grinned, leaning in to whisper in her ear. "I impersonated the host, of course."

She pulled back in shock. "And that worked? That doesn't make any sense."

"The man working the front gate was from the States and looked to be newly hired. You can do anything with enough confidence, mind you. I strolled up and told him to step aside, as I wasn't about to be turned away from my house, and then I simply walked in."

And what a grand moment that was. Probably one of my greatest feats up to that point, and worth every cent I'd spent on that frilled tuxedo.

"What was it like? Inside?" Aaliyah said eagerly, her eyes lighting up.

"Striking. Right inside the door was a grand staircase that led to the upper level, and all around it were people dancing and sipping their fine champagne. He even had a bust of himself." It was hard to say that without laughing, especially considering they'd got the worst features of him in it, like his gigantic nose. "Like I said, ego."

I twirled her again, and our little dance around the library continued.

"So what does this have to do with the waltz?"

"Well, I was only a few steps inside when I found his sister, or rather, she found *me*. Milliana was her name, if I recall correctly. She led me to the middle of the floor and told me 'Adrian, you'd better ask me to dance.' So, being the reasonable gentleman that I am, of course I did. I was still new to the waltz then, so I stepped on her toes, and we laughed and joked. At least, until her brother found us and kicked me out into the cold, with Milliana screaming the entire way to the door."

That got that laugh I'd been searching for, stopping our dance dead in its tracks as Aaliyah's head tipped back. She laughed until tears sprang in her eyes, and she had to wipe them away.

"Why am I not surprised that you caused so much trouble?" she asked between heavy breaths.

"What can I say, love? It follows me. No fault of my own, mind you. I'm a *saint*."

She shook her head and leaned back into my chest. There were no more practiced movements, just a sway wrapped in each other's arms. The music had stopped, and only the crackle of the fire sang to us now.

"Do you miss it? Being human?" she suddenly asked me, and it took me by surprise.

I wasn't sure about the answer. My human life seemed forever away now, like it was only a dream. It had been years since I stopped moping over the loss of my life and really started living this one.

"To be honest? I barely remember it. It was over a hundred years ago now," I mused. "I'd forgotten so many things. From my grandmother's baklava,"—like the one that was cooking in our oven, which filled the house with the sweet redolence of my childhood home—"to how much I loved waltzing."

I'd always done things from my human life: cooked, danced, and sewed. But I hadn't thought of them as they were in a long time and hadn't associated them with that life. Had forgotten that I needed to remember more than just things ... but the moments, as well.

"You've reminded me of that. Showed me how nice it is to remember something like this, something so small as a waltz," I said, lifting our joined hands.

I curled my fingers around hers, finding that her much smaller hand was dwarfed in mine.

"Do you ... do you think I'll forget Prince?" she asked suddenly, squeezing my hand like it was a lifeline. Her face scrunched as she looked stricken up at me. "I'm a Natural, or at least I assume I am. That means I'll live for a long time. A hundred years is nothing, right?"

The air shifted, and Aaliyah's hand dropped like she'd just had an epiphany, and it was like watching everything we'd built today, all the progress we'd made, crumble.

"No, love. Never. He's a part of you, and he always will be."

My words met deaf ears, and I saw the guilt begin to tear into her. Loathing filled her eyes, then tears.

"Love—" I started, but she pulled back.

"I'm fine. I'm ... I'm—" she stuttered, her breathing beginning to spiral. Fuck.

"Love, *listen*," I begged, taking a step toward her as she let out a sound that made my insides curl and my heart break. It was a mix between a cry and a gasp, like she was fighting for breath and words at the same time.

"How? What can you say that will make this better, Adrian? I *killed* him. And nothing anyone says or does is going to change that. Prince is gone because of *me*." She gripped her middle, squeezing so tightly that she wheezed. "I'm a *monster*."

I was in front of her, pulling her into my arms so firmly that she couldn't get another word out. "No," I said vehemently.

We'd learn about her, about her past, about Ascension Rising. I wanted her to see that she wasn't alone and that she had someone to lean on.

"What—"

"No, you are *not* a monster, Aaliyah. You are a stunning soul, a gift of kindness to a world that is owed none," I assured her, pulling back so she could see my face.

So she'd understand I meant it. More than anything else in this world. She wasn't a monster. I wasn't sure she even had a nasty bone in her body. This was the same woman who was still so bright, so *kind* after what she'd gone through. The same one who still looked at the world with wonder and joy, when even I barely saw it in color.

"Do you think I am a monster?" I asked, the words spilling out.

I'd spent my days dragging through this life, watching my brothers and trying to bring joy to our lives when the world was desperate to prove there was none. I'd spent my entire immortal life smiling, even when it hurt, *especially* when it hurt ... and right now, that felt like a lie.

Because I hadn't ever been this free, not like I was with Aaliyah in front of me. And if either of us deserved the title of monster, it wasn't her.

"Of course not. Why would I think that?" she asked, still trembling in my arms.

"Because a hundred years ago, I was in much the same position. Regretting actions that weren't my own. I spent *decades* thinking the same thing you are now."

The past wasn't something that those in the Vivas household spoke of. Each of us knew there was damage below the surface, but to *speak* of it?

Unheard of. And the thought made me physically ill, made my stomach turn and my pulse quicken. My fangs ached, and the push of the *Flame* told me that my magic was trying to protect me from something it couldn't see. My panic pushed it, and maybe that was why I started talking, or perhaps it was the way her eyes seemed to strip my soul bare.

I could see her eyes now. The fear as I stalked toward her. I couldn't force myself to stop walking, just like the one before.

I was tired of hiding my past. Tired of watching my little love be so strong when I was too weak to afford her the same luxury. She'd been through hell, and she deserved everything. And I was going to give it to her. Me. *All of me.*

She paused our dance as she leaned into me, engulfing me in her warmth. That curious, worried expression lit up her face. She reached up, rubbing her thumb along my jaw.

"What happened, Adrian?" she murmured.

I let out a breath.

"The night of that dance was the night that I was turned." I stepped back, just enough to peer into her eyes. But then I averted my gaze with a grimace; I couldn't stand to look at her when I said such things. "I didn't want to be this undead thing. I was training to be a doctor. I didn't want to *hurt* people. But our Maker ... *he* didn't like that. Didn't like that his creation was hoping to leave so soon. So he made me do something, forced me to hurt people while trapped in my head. I didn't even know what I'd done until after Osiris pulled me back into the real world. Pulled me back from the *Maker's Call.*"

I swallowed my hatred, my pain. She trusted me not to pull away from her past. Now I needed to trust her to do the same. Show her she wasn't alone.

"It still haunts me." I didn't dare peek up at her, too scared of her reaction.

I took a deep breath, trying to stop the tremor in my voice.

"Jack the Ripper is a name that follows me to this day, and it *always* will." I caught her gaze now, and her understanding washed over me like a wave. I shouldn't have been happy to see understanding in those eyes, but I was. *God*, I was. I'd *always* blamed myself. I'd been studying to be a doctor, and recalling what I'd done ... made me sick.

Aaliyah looked stricken, carefully weighing her words before she spoke, "What your Maker made you do wasn't your fault, Adrian. You know that, right?"

And there was no hatred, no disgust in Aaliyah's eyes. She only saw me, and I fell for her a bit more at that moment.

"And you are no monster for whatever made you send Prince away. That wasn't *you*, love. You'd never do that, and Prince knew that, too. I know he did." I held her as her face cycled through several expressions. It dipped between sorrow and anger, regret and rage, before finally settling on numbness.

"Thank you," she whispered, looking down as she reached up to anchor herself to me again, her hand on my shoulder. Her lips curved up at the corners as tears gathered in her eyes.

She reached her hand out, and I set mine in hers.

"Dance with me, Adrian?" she asked softly, her tears soaking into my shirt.

I leaned in, kissing her head softly. For a moment, I just *was*. I was with her in this room. The grief of loss was enough to bring her to her knees, but she stood anyway. And I wrapped around her, being the strength she needed to stand. Always.

"Of course, love."

CHAPTER 15

FALLON

Hell.

That was the only way to describe this week—unrelenting, unending, torturous *hell*.

The hanging red punching bag gave a sharp jolt as the force of my blow vibrated up my arm when my fist connected to the smooth leather. There was a silent snarl on my lips as I pulled back, waiting for the swinging to stop before I shot off to strike again. I wasn't satisfied with the slight movement, with the lurch. I needed more than just an inanimate object. I wanted something that could fight back.

I needed something that would *bleed*.

It would give me something to think about, the drip of blood against a cold gray floor. Anything but Aaliyah's burning skin or feeling her pulse stuttering against my fingers. Anything but the shake of my hands and the sporadic flush of adrenaline in my veins.

The hit didn't wash the soured ache of panic away, just like none of the others before it. I still saw her, unmoving, unbreathing, and covered in blood. As I had every second of the last week, I fought the gripping realization that I had been less than useless to her.

Twice, Aaliyah had died under my watch. *Twice,* I had to question if the past had finally repeated.

Useless. *I was useless.* I screamed at the bag, swinging low with my leg and reveling in the impact as pain shot up my spine, reminding me I was alive.

And that she had died in my arms *twice*.

It was like Aislinn all over again, a sick joke playing on repeat as I once again failed to stop the death of someone important to me. This was the reason I spent so much time reining in my instincts, staying away from Ali, keeping her at a distance, and for what? So I could pretend it didn't bother me when yet another heart stopped?

Her blood stained the dining room table, and the scent of it still clung to the air.

I was ready to go to town if only to find Crustava's pack and tear them apart, to make them suffer and *bleed*. Even if I knew all it'd do was make Aaliyah feel more guilty. The memory of her heart slowing to a near stop rang hollow in my ears, and my next hit to the bag sent the heavy weight spiraling, the chain above it screeching in protest. All I could hear was Adrian as he screamed, desperately trying to keep her heart beating. His voice had cracked, and tears had sat in his eyes as he begged her to breathe.

There was a crippling desperation in his voice, the kind that told me wherever she went, he would follow.

I ripped my bloodied hand through my hair before setting my bare palm against the rough leather of the bag. It stilled under my touch, and the room fell quiet.

How had everything gone this wrong?

I ground my teeth as I landed another uninterrupted succession of hits on the bag, barely holding back enough to keep it from flying off the chain again. I had no more spares, and my brothers were rarely up to fight this late in the evening. If Nero had been here, he would have likely followed me down the moment I'd walked through the door, eager to let out his own stress.

No ... He would have talked to her, brought her out of her grief. Not hidden like a coward who was unable to face his own demons to help fight hers.

She missed Prince; she *loved* Prince. Then she lost him, and the best we could do was barely keep her alive, then leave her alone to her pain? Nero would have made her laugh and helped her forget her worries, if only for a minute.

But we *weren't* Nero, and he wasn't here to help us through this shitshow.

The room glowed under the light of the full moon, the only thing illuminating it. It lit up the white walls, brushing against the chaotic scramble of equipment that I'd pulled out and used over the past hour. None of it had been enough to hold my attention, and while everything in me screamed I should sleep, I couldn't. I lifted my hands, readying to throw hits again, just as the door to my sanctuary opened.

I half expected Eirik here to spar, even Osiris, not that he'd been around much these days. Not that *I'd* been around much these days. But it was Adrian who walked in, his eyes on the ground and his aura volatile, stressed.

It was easy enough to see in the way he walked, his body strung tight. His copper-tinted brown hair was ruffled, and he wore a wrinkled gray shirt and black jeans that had seen better days.

He looked like shit, not that I fared much better.

He'd had it the worst when Aaliyah was first brought back. He bore the weight of her life as if it was on him alone. Every breath she lost, every ounce of blood she shed, tore at him, breaking him apart bit by bit.

He would follow her.

"Hiding away again, I see?" he asked, finally lifting his head. His amber eyes were dulled with exhaustion and rage, dark bags even more pronounced than they had been in these last few weeks, but it did little to diminish the pent-up energy sizzling under his skin. "Though, I guess I should just be happy you're in the house."

It took one glance to know what he wanted, something that he *never* wanted. A fight. My fangs pressed against my gums, demanding to drop, and I walked silently toward the more accessible area in the room. The soft flooring of our sparing area had give as I rocked between my heels and the tips of my toes, rotating my head back and forth.

"Haughty tone coming from someone who's also hiding here," I retorted as I crossed my arms over my chest.

His eyes flashed red, fangs dropping as the boyish charm that defined Adrian faded away. His face contorted into a sharp grimace, veins popping onto his forehead as he stalked toward me. If he needed an outlet, I wasn't going to deny him.

Hell, I'd beg him for it.

"I'm taking a break from distracting Aaliyah. We just got done dancing upstairs, in case you were wondering. So, rest assured, *Fallon,* the only ones hiding are you and Osiris." His words were piercing, digging into my skin like daggers. Fallon. Using my name was not dissimilar to a blow. For a frigid second, I missed his joking nicknames. The venom in his tone made me flinch.

It poked and prodded at things that had no business being in the light. It made me feel raw under his disappointed gaze.

Adrian took a step forward, rolling his shoulders and flexing his shaking hands.

"We're processing," I said, unable to come up with a better excuse.

Because that was precisely what it was, an excuse.

"No. What's your favorite word again? Oh yes. *Cowards*. You're cowards, Fallon." There was an unfamiliar rage gripping Adrian's words as he said exactly what I'd been thinking. "Hiding away, unable to get over your own petty fucking bullshit to focus on what matters most: her."

There was no joke, no poke or prod. Adrian rarely got mad enough to confront me, to lose that serene expression that seemed so distant now.

I didn't lower my gaze. His care for her was blatant, but I'd known that already. We all did, in our own ways. He fought for her; he fought for her happiness. He'd tasted what her love was like, and he was angry because he almost lost her.

My heart clenched in my chest.

"She has you and Eirik. Isn't that enough?" I asked, trying to ignore the acidic feeling it had left in my throat.

"No, Fallon. It isn't!" Adrian all but screamed. He moved so quickly that I almost didn't register when his fist landed heavily on my cheek, shock keeping me standing.

Heat lit up at the sight of the blow, sending a torrent of sharp pain down my jaw and into my chest. He pulled back, shaking his hand as his fingers mended, his bones having snapped at the force of his hit. I would have been proud, if not for the circumstances.

He snarled, "You can't stand here and truly expect me to believe that you feel *nothing*."

Adrian ripped his shirt over his head, practically tearing the thing in half. He didn't fold it; he didn't even watch it as it struck the wall with a smack. Instead, his eyes were liquid with fury, and I was still too stunned to respond.

"You can't stand here, *like a coward*, and expect me to just leave it be!" He raised his hands, motioning for me to fight. "She lost Prince, and rather than being there, you ran. You all *fucking* ran."

I raised my arms to block his next blow, revealing as pain shot down the length of my bicep as his fist connected with my shoulder, sending shock-waves down my spine.

It was a feeling that the punching bag couldn't replicate. The pain reminded me I was here and told me to ground myself. I traded one back, striking him before he could move to block it. I hit him square in the jaw, and I couldn't tell if the crack in the air came from his face or my hand.

"What does it matter what I feel, Adrian? Her death is inevitable. Maybe not today or tomorrow, but she will *die*. I refuse—" Adrian's laugh was cruel, cutting off my words before I could even finish my sentence, and he didn't hesitate to return my blow, slamming into my ribs, nearly sending me to my knees.

When had Adrian ever been this bloodthirsty?

This was the same man who screamed when he saw a spider, who did everything possible to talk something out. And as he pulled back to swing again, I wondered exactly how hard we'd pushed for him to snap like this.

"You what? Refuse to *feel*? Look how far that's gotten us, Fallon!" He didn't flinch as he tossed another blow toward me, his lips curling into a soundless snarl. "She terrifies me too, but at least I'm brave enough to admit that I would rather face that terror than lose her."

I don't want to lose her, I almost screamed at him. But I held it back, trapped it behind closed lips as I stood up, once again taking a fighting stance.

This was for the best.

"You don't understand—" I started.

His leg shot up and struck me in the arm. The bone caved under his attack. I could have moved and stopped his hit, but I needed it. I held on to the pain, letting it center me.

"No. NO, Fallon." Another scream, another blow.

Aaliyah wasn't breathing.

Everything I'd wanted from this fight came crashing down on me. I was bleeding, and the pain muddied my senses. Its strength pulsed in my blood and echoed the roaring of war drums, yet there she was, still crawling along with my subconscious, taking over my thoughts. Her eyes filled my vision, that soft lavender. Adrian knew what I didn't want to be real. He saw it, even when I didn't want to admit it.

"You understand perfectly well. You asked her to fucking live, you begged her to stay. You *cried* for her, Fallon. Then after she came back to us, you *left*." Adrian's eyes closed, his jaw snapping shut. "We're Vivas," he said, his hands shaking as he flexed his bruised knuckles. "Bound by blood and *brothers* by choice. That used to mean something."

I jolted at his use of our calling. Nero's war cry came back to me, his headstrong optimism, his calming demeanor.

He wouldn't have hidden.

"When one calls, the others follow." Adrian ran his hands across his face.

A tremble worked its way down his shoulders, followed by a gasp. Then I heard it—the breaking sound of a sob, and I realized my mistake all too late. The one who had been ignored in favor of myself and my thoughts about her. We hadn't just left Aaliyah to face her demons.

We'd left Adrian, as well.

"When one fights, we fight with them." I let out a breath as I spoke, the weight of the words almost too much to bear.

"Then why am I the only one fighting, Fallon?" Adrian's voice wasn't one that I was used to hearing so broken, and I didn't have an answer, not one that would make up for my abandonment.

"What do you want from me, Adrian?" I finally asked, as terrified of the question as I was of the answer.

That this was a dream that would never be realized. That my hope for a future died with Aislinn on the dusty beach that I'd called home, under the rays of the last setting sun I'd ever see, and that I was right to back away.

"I want you to admit that you have a fucking soul. That I'm not going crazy." Adrian wiped his eyes, standing straight again.

He lifted his hand into the air, snapping his fingers and lighting some of the candles that were scattered across the room. I'd been so absorbed in our fight that I hadn't noticed clouds had blotted out the light of the moon. The training room was now lit with a dull glow, the gelid air making my breaths frost in front of me.

"That I'm not the only one that can't stand the thought of losing her," Adrian finished, his breathing heavy.

My heart stuttered in my chest, and I fought back everything I wanted to say. I certainly didn't want to say he was right, that he'd stolen the deepest parts of me and splayed them in front of us. I needed it to not be real, and if I just kept quiet, then it wouldn't be.

I shook my head. "I had to leave—"

"That's a shit excuse and you know it, Fal. You didn't have to do anything but be there!" Adrian roared his desperation, the rawness of his voice sinking past the pain of his blows.

I didn't care for Aaliyah the same way he did; I didn't need her; I didn't crave her presence. I didn't seek her out when the days grew long, and I didn't want to hear her laugh. Because if I did ... I wasn't sure what I would do, or what it would mean.

"I couldn't stay, Adrian. I couldn't sit by and watch her struggle to breathe again. I couldn't handle the dread of searching for a pulse and knowing it might not be there!" I hadn't meant to speak, didn't mean to let my words pass through my constricted throat, but it was like they spilled out of my chest. I almost tasted iron, like the words had been nothing but bad blood I needed to expel. "What do you want me to say?"

Adrian didn't respond, merely watched me with that pushing, knowing look. I cracked under it, what was left of my will dying as I recalled watching Ali on the kitchen table. Her eyes closed, blood pooling around us in lavender-scented chaos ... and I *had* begged. Begged that she would open those eyes that captivated me one more time. Begged that she would smile so tenderly again and take my hand so carefully in hers. That we would share chocolate, and I would show her my paintings, or just *sit* with her. Because her presence was enough to ground me in ways nothing had in decades.

"She died, in my *arms*, Adrian." The words came out cracked, the back of my throat burning as tears came to my eyes again. "I didn't think she was coming back, and I thought I'd lost her, too."

Lost her like I had Aislinn. I still heard it, still shook at the thought of Aaliyah's stuttering pulse. I tried to stop there, to keep from breaking past the point of no return. Everything in me seized, and even the *Flame* revolted, turning my resolve to ashes, and the words were already out.

Already damning me with what had been haunting me since that day in Eternal Ilenia's home. A fact that had rotted me to the core in every way I'd tried to stop.

"I fucking *loved* her, and she died," I cried, the spark that was our gift igniting my blood, spreading out and scorching the ground, lighting every candle in the room until it looked like daylight.

I loved Aaliyah, so much more than I could ever express with words. I loved the way she always had something meaningful to say. I loved her grace and kindness, loved the way she looked at the world and *marveled* at it.

Silence took over. The cold kind. The *killing* kind. Only the sound of my haggard breathing echoed, something I couldn't hide from.

I loved her, and she died ...

"Fallon—" Adrian started, but I raised a hand.

It shook, and I gnashed my teeth.

"I can't ... I can't handle her dying again, Adrian. *I can't.*"

She couldn't be mine, because if she was, I wouldn't survive this again. There was only so much I could handle, and I'd hit my limit.

A body slammed into mine, knocking me off balance. Adrian hugged me so tightly I couldn't get any more words out. He had broken the dam that I'd built, torn it down brick by brick. And I hadn't even noticed the icy tracks of tears as they slid down my face.

"She died, Adrian," I said through tears, my voice sounding unfamiliar and cracked. "I loved her, and she died."

It seemed wrong to lift my arms, to hug Adrian. I wasn't the hugging type and never had been. But I held onto him like my life depended on it, and for a moment, it did.

"I know, Fal ... it's not your fault, brother."

No, not this time. But next time wasn't certain. Her life wasn't certain, and so she couldn't be mine ... *Right?*

CHAPTER 16

AALIYAH

It'd been barely a week and a half since *the incident.* A week and a half since I'd seen Prince's brash smile, and I'd not been alone for much of it. Adrian and Eirik had made sure that one of them was pretty much always with me, and I hadn't realized how much their presence had been helping.

Until I was sitting alone in the library.

Adrian had whisked away shortly after our dance when Fallon gotten home, saying he had to talk to him about something. I wanted to tell him to lie down instead, unable to not notice how weary he looked. How tired, how *sick.* He'd been up with me for days, and I knew he'd been missing sleep. It was all too familiar to how he'd looked at me in the pool house the night we'd kissed, and it was like a stark reminder that something was wrong with them, too. And now Adrian wasn't getting any rest, and he wasn't getting any better.

I hadn't forgotten how bad it'd been. The headaches and nosebleeds were just the tips of the iceberg, and I knew that this peace we had right now wasn't going to last. I already felt it, the ache. Whatever Osiris's blood had done for me, it was wearing off. Leaving me waiting for the ticking time bomb that was my soul to come rearing its ugly head.

I walked the length of one of the library stacks, running my fingers along the spines like I typically did, going through the motions so my brain would do *something*. I sighed, eventually stopping, eyeing the book that was likely in a dead language.

The spine was an intricate gold, and normally I'd be inclined to pull it off the shelf, but today, I just didn't have the energy. So I turned away, walking toward the couch that was now in front of the fireplace, where I'd asked Adrian to put it after our impromptu waltzing. The book that I had already pulled out lay across the plush red cushions. I'd been admiring it earlier today, before Eirik found me. It had a bare cover, with just foreign wording on the front, and when I opened it, it was much the same. There was only one thing I recognized.

A signature, in English. It was as devastatingly beautiful as it was roguish. The twisting accents held a flare, matching the person who did it.

Nero Vivas.

I swallowed hard, closing my eyes and trailing the signature. I'd thought about it a lot the last few days, unable to keep my mind off Prince. And the way he'd always seemed to watch the men I lived with, the way he knew their home like it was his own. The way he watched them like he watched me ...

I thought of Prince and couldn't help but compare him to what the others had told me of Nero. Their stories by the bonfire came creeping back, and everything they'd said suddenly hit me.

He was proud, a gladiator.

He was sharp as a whip and had a silver tongue to match it.

There's no one I trusted more to have my back.

Prince had *known* about the Vivas Crypt. Had told me they were safe at the same moment they were watching me with blood-red eyes. I'd thought he was crazy, but he was right. He'd known how to get to the cellar below the house, moving in a way that said he knew exactly where he was going. He'd worried about Osiris after the incident with Kali, that feeling sinking into the air.

I hadn't thought deeper into it at the time, hadn't considered the possibility of Prince being *Nero*, because Prince would have *told* me something like that, something so important, something so raw ... right?

My lip shook as I closed the book, unable to look any longer. He would have told me ... or he would have kept it hidden to save his brothers from the pain of knowing he was still with them. The tears came, they always came, and I sank into the couch, burned by the thought that hadn't left me since the hot spring.

I'd killed Prince ... and deep in my soul, past the denial and the grief, I'd begged that I hadn't killed Nero, too. An ache started in my chest, and a dreadful feeling flooded me.

I didn't have time to ponder it anymore, as a chill brushed down my entire spine. It was familiarly unfamiliar, and I knew that the ghost of the armory had come to say hello again. They'd stopped by a lot the last few days, and I found peace in their presence.

Whoever it was, they'd been around a lot since everything happened, almost like they were trying to comfort me. It was painful, but it was also the only thing I could really hold on to. Adrian and Eirik had been my rocks and had grounded me when I swore I was going to drift away. Fallon and Osiris had been my tether. Strained and distant, I worried that their own pain was overwhelming them.

And this ghost? They'd been filling the gap that had formed endlessly in my chest. Giving me the freezing feeling I constantly sought, and I half wondered if it wasn't just a figment of my imagination.

"Prince ..." I whispered to the empty room, "what would you do?"

The spirit grew incessantly, pushing almost. Like it was telling me to move, and I was too tired to ignore it. I stood on shaking legs, clutching the book to my chest as I followed where it led. I walked, the ache of pressure poking at my mind, hinting that it was there before fading away.

But for now, I could walk, so I did. I took the steps slowly, hands trailing on the gray walls, and I listened to the creak of stairs under my feet. I half expected Adrian to be in the kitchen, or to find Eirik sprawled across the couch in the living room. Or even his beast, with feral eyes tracking me as I moved.

But there was no one, so I simply continued to walk, following the trail outside. I shivered at the freezing air, my pants and t-shirt doing little to stave off the cold. My feet, only covered in thin socks, quickly grew numb.

The Vivas home was extremely well kept, from the crisp hedges that were brown in the winter cold, to the moss yard that seemed to always be perfectly maintained. Even the house, painted a deep black, seemed spotless through wind, rain, and snow. Though it showed its age, with some boards creaking as I followed down the patio steps, trailing my hand along dried bushes until coming to a stop at the side of the house.

I knew enough about the home to know that the entrance to the armory was outside, placed between some potted plants, and I had enough wit to guess that this was where the ghost was taking me. I sighed and shook my head.

"Unless you know how to get in there, this is where I stop," I said, and the push of amusement settled.

Then, softly, like I was imagining it, a hand appeared against the siding. The energy of the ghost strained, wobbling as the hand faded in and out, so I observed as he touched the wall, moving his hand in some set pattering.

I reached out, and the hand moved away. I mimicked the motion, waiting for something to happen.

But nothing did.

"Odd," I mused, doing it again with no success.

The ghost waited patiently, pushing confidence I didn't feel.

"Maybe it needs a code word?" I laughed a little at that, but the energy lifted enough for me to take notice. "Open?"

Nothing.

Not even a hint that it had done something. My cheeks flushed, and I moved my hand to try again.

"Abracadabra?" *Nothing.*

I shook my head, and my hand dropped. The spirit grew restless when I turned away, and I sighed again. This was silly, and if one of the guys found me out here with nothing but my pajamas on, they'd throw a fit. But the ghost was insistent, and I felt bad just leaving it like this. They obviously wanted to show me something.

"Fine, one more." I thought about it, considering what the Vivas brothers would do, and what their code might be before I let out a shaking breath.

There was only one thing that came to mind. That day, in the kitchen when I'd first found Eirik. The fear I'd experienced at that moment, and how he'd so easily calmed me down.

Where am I? I'd asked, and his steady reply still stuck in my mind.

"*Et in domum suam in solem,*" I whispered, and the old stone siding creaked, my chest along with it. "Open."

Sure enough, the wall shimmered before the spell keeping the door to the armory hidden slid open. *The house of the sun,* Nero's name for their home. Part of me felt guilty, looking around like someone was going to jump out and chastise me. But I was too curious now to stop.

The ghost was ecstatic as the air shot down a few degrees, and I shivered again as I followed it down the narrow steps. It was near pitch-black, and I had to keep one hand braced against the wall to maintain my balance. Fortunately, I'd always adapted quickly to dim lighting, so by the time I hit the large room at the bottom, I could see well enough to get around.

The room was enormous, seeming to go on endlessly. It smelled like dust and old magic, and I took a shuddering breath. I waited for the icy brush of energy to direct me and moved with it down the first stack.

"Prince said you were stuck here," I said, watching the items go by, the history that was with them. "Why is that?"

Of course, he couldn't answer, but we came to a stop as the emotions shifted, and reluctant optimism filled the air. On the floor, laid delicately, was red cloth. It looked like it had been part of a shirt, or maybe a scarf, but this was all that was left of it. I reached down, picking it up, and the pure elation that filled the air made me smile.

"You're stuck to the cloth," I said, and I swore I saw someone nod as I searched the gloomy space in front of me.

"So pretty, and so red ..." I said, running a thumb over the coarse fabric.

It was more coarse than anything I'd ever worn, the fraying strands brittle and frail, showing their age in the way they split and turned to dust. I pulled back then, not wanting to harm the beautiful fabric anymore. For as old as it was, that color was so vibrant that it captivated me.

"I need something to call you. How do you like Red?" I asked, and a warmth filled the space, a thanks. I hummed, soaking up his pleasant feelings and enjoying a moment of silence. "Red it is."

I turned back toward the stairs, Red no longer pushing me to go deeper into the armory. And I was glad for it. The pressure in my head had grown, and my legs shook as another instance of my curse came to me. Dread filled me again, more intense this time, more pointed in a way that had me looking around. Something felt *wrong*.

I crawled my way back up the stairs, gasping as I finally hit the top. I didn't let it stop me as I went back inside, only checking over my shoulder to make sure that the gateway to the cellar had faded away. I snuck through the door, noting the still-empty house. Fallon and Osiris had been gone a lot since the incident. I knew that after what happened they needed time. Hell, I needed time. But their disappearance made my chest ache. But Eirik didn't normally leave, and as I looked outside to the subtly lightening moss yard, I couldn't help but worry.

I searched the bottom floor, finding a still empty kitchen. The house was quiet, without Adrian bouncing between the cabinets, cooking. I was shocked to find both Fallon and Adrian in the training room.

They were panting, their eyes tinged red with their fangs down. They were stripped bare from the waist up, and had I not been so intently searching for Eirik, I would have lingered a little longer. Probably blushed a little harder.

But there was still no sign of my Viking.

My chest clenched again, this time that worry becoming near panic as my instincts pushed me to move. To find him. So I marched to the library, hoping, *begging*, to find Eirik and Osiris doing something.

Because if I'd learned anything these last few weeks? It was that I needed to trust my instincts.

Chapter 17

Osiris

"Wait, *please*—" was the plea that reached deaf ears, as I crushed the wolf shifter's throat under my palm.

He stilled, his body not even twitching as I pulled back enough to glare at where my skin had touched his. I brushed the blood off my hand, smearing it onto his shirt. His blood painted the concrete red, and the hollow, abandoned building to our back only held more. He'd been the last I'd caught, the last I'd *chased*.

Crustava's pack was abolished, effective immediately.

It hadn't been hard to hunt them down, to figure out where they'd been staying. After Crustava disappeared, they'd taken refuge outside Oakridge, maybe twenty miles away from town. They were shrouded in the thick Pennsylvania woods, and they'd hired a minor Sorceri to put up a ward, though it didn't do them much good.

It had been a long time since I'd done something without restraint. Since I'd bathed in the blood of my enemies, and even after they had stopped screaming, I still couldn't get it out of my head.

I didn't kill like this anymore ... didn't let my instincts rule me because I knew what happened when they did.

But the numbness blocked out even the guilt. Everything faded away but the sight of Crustava behind the single person on this earth I wanted to touch. His hands were on her, grabbing when he had no right to. Then ... Aaliyah, dead. Like all my worst nightmares were flashing in front of me.

Dead because I missed a hole in my ward that I would have sworn on my life wasn't there. Dead because of my mistake, *again*. And now those around me paid the price for it.

He may have turned you, Osiris, but you'll always be mine.

I shook my head and stalked away from the massacre I was likely going to regret come the Eternium. But I couldn't find the will to care. They deserved it; they *all* deserved it. Covered in blood, rotting against the frozen ground. It was barely a fight with the ten shifters that deemed they needed to defend their leader. The rest had fled or tried to.

They didn't get far.

At least now we wouldn't have to deal with them, and we could focus on what was important. On Aaliyah and getting her better before the Eternium.

I wasn't a fool. My blood would run its course, and we'd be right back to needing help. And though I couldn't stomach the thought of showing myself to her after what I'd let happen, this much I could do. With Crustava and his pack out of the way, we'd be able to prepare for Xander, our meeting with him in just a few days now, and hope that he knew how to fix her. Or there just might end up being more blood on my hands.

"Deary me. You really did a number on them, didn't you, pet?" a voice asked, breaking the silence I'd left behind.

I didn't need to turn around for my magic to swell in my stomach, raring to protect me. My hand twitched, and a spark of flame ignited along my skin against my will.

"Kali," I hissed, looking over my shoulder at her.

Hadn't she done enough? She'd torn my home apart and destroyed what little had been left of my sanity. She'd done what she needed to do, so why the fuck was she *here*?

Exactly when I needed her not to be, exactly when I was feral enough to do something even worse than killing a pack of stray wolves. Killing her was a mistake I didn't think I could stop myself from making tonight.

"Don't look so happy to see me," she whined, walking toward me.

I took a step back, my muscles tensing as a surge of black magic swelled in my blood.

"What are you still doing here? You should be across the country by now," I said coldly.

Kali paused, tilting her head to the side. Her hair was pulled up again, this time waving against a blue dress. Her fair skin glowed under the pale light of the moon and the beginning hints of the sunrise.

"You know, the same can be said about you. I expected a call or even a letter, affirming your gracious acceptance of our support. You should be working your way toward the Eternium yourself." She narrowed her eyes as her magic came forward. "You of all people should know that Darius isn't a very patient man, and he wouldn't take kindly to hearing you were spending your time parading around your land, enjoying the hot spring."

My blood went cold, and Kali smirked. Of course ... of course it was her. The hole in my ward, the one that had let Crustava sneak in. It had been her because of *course it had*.

"You need to come forward, show your Challenge. Stop playing around, Osiris, and *do as you're told*." So that was why her shadow haunted my perfectly good evening, why she had again thrown our home into chaos.

Because of that damned fucking Challenge. That was what it always boiled down to, what everything led to. Kali came to us because of Sebek, because of her fear of him. And just as before, I had no intention of Challenging him. I never had, never wanted to, yet everyone seemed so intent on forcing me into the role.

She was the reason Aaliyah got hurt, and lost Prince ... and that was too far.

"I'm not Challenging Sebek! I'll do nothing for you rotten, savage people. *NOTHING!*" I screamed, facing Kali fully. I swiped my hand through the air, sending blood splattering on the ground around us, even against her sky blue shoes. "You've done your damage, Kali! *Now leave me alone or die where you stand!*"

My fangs dropped so hard I tasted blood, and my eyes flashed red so quickly it made my head spin. My hands shook, and I covered my burning wrist, hiding the ink there as I dug my fingers in.

"You can't kill me, Osiris. You and I both know it's not wise and who knows what would happen to your little family if you did? Darius isn't a forgiving man," Kali chided, unmoved by my derangement. She took a step forward, a sneer playing on her lips. "You get so mad when you're left alone. So violent."

My breathing stopped, and I watched her step again and again. My skin grew slick with a cold sweat until she was right in front of me. She reached out to touch me, only stopping when I snarled, barely better than a wild animal.

Come now, pet, be a good boy and lie back.

"You need me, Osiris. You always have. So come back to me, to Darius. We've missed you so much." She pulled back, brushing her long blonde hair over her shoulder. Darius's name, like a trigger, set me off, and I stumbled away. "Think about it, pet. And ... Claim your Challenge. I won't ask again."

There was a threat in her words, as her gray eyes grew pointed.

"And we both know Darius won't *ask*."

Just as quickly as she'd appeared, she was gone, and I was left alone amid the carnage. I shook so violently I nearly became sick, and when I looked down, it was bloodied hands I saw. I hadn't been this out of control in lifetimes.

Darius the Great wouldn't have me again. *Never again.*

I numbly turned away, *flitting* toward home.

It took barely a minute to get back; the sun beginning to peak, the first rays of morning light hitting the hillside. I shook, trembling so hard I nearly tripped as I reached our front steps. I should head inside to where the others were, clean up before I was seen, and gain back a modicum of control ... but instead, I hopped up to the roof. The blood splattered around me, coating the metal sheets.

The need to go inside nearly broke me down, the need to find *her.* Seek her touch like it was a balm and would fix every problem I had. But as I looked down at my hands, still covered in innocent blood, I knew I couldn't let her see me like this. I didn't want to see the look in her eyes when she realized what it was.

What I'd done.

As if responding to that, magic crawled along my veins. Not the one I had grown to control, not a *Charm*, or the *Flame* ... old magic.

Human magic. It tasted of Kali, and with her sick sulfur scent burned into my nose, it stung all the more. It sparked, simmering, until I closed my fist hard enough for the edge of pain to cull every thought of falling to my selfish desires to seek it out. Because that happiness wasn't mine to have. It never had been. Aaliyah deserved better than what little my shattered soul could provide. My *brothers* deserved better. She deserved someone who didn't put her in harm's way. That wasn't a fool who got his own family killed and refused to learn from that lesson.

She deserved a bold figure that I still sometimes saw wandering through our halls. Nero's rusty brown hair with tinges of red sitting on the aged bench of our piano. Silver eyes lit with mischief as his fingers flew over the keys. I heard his voice even now, prodding me to move, to seek the light in Aaliyah.

But buried, muddled by the sickeningly sweet drawl of Kali.

Even Sebek knows you make a better pet than a man.

For a moment, I considered going toward the gravestones, but even that weighed heavy on me. I couldn't bear the sight of Nero's headstone, nor the reminder of what it meant. The reminder of my failure to this family.

One of several.

It had been several decades since I had found my way up to the roof, mostly because of what it represented. Just another spot where Nero's life had molded into our home. The imprint of his favorite spot, with a shingle slightly askew, called me to sit.

I did, my skin beginning to itch as the blood dried. I fell back, eyes to the sky. The cutting wind in the air barely registered as I watched the stars. Each flickering light phased in and out of view, the sky a mirage of blues and violets, keeping my attention away from the steady heartbeats beneath me.

After everything I'd done in my life, those heartbeats were all that seemed to keep me going. And with each one, I grew more tired.

Tired of facing this world as it was. Just *tired*. This world was broken. It had been since my turn and would continue to be for years after I finally faded away. And all I did was add to that. I killed twenty-three today. *Twenty-three* that had no say in their pack master's deeds. Slaughtered them where they stood.

When they ran.

It wasn't something I did. I took value in life. I always had. It was why I'd picked our name, why we were Vivas. *To live.*

Yet I'd taken them anyway.

I watched those same stars until they faded, and the light of the sun peered over the horizon. For a brief, terrible second, I considered what it would be like to see it one more time. The heat, the light. I almost craved it, craved what it would mean, and wondered if I would be lucky enough to find Nero on the other side.

How had he felt when he realized the sun wasn't going to stop? That I had failed him and hadn't gotten there soon enough to save him? Would he forgive me?

Would I forgive myself?

A heat started as the first bits of rays hit me. No actual sunlight yet, not the intensity needed to kill. It ached almost like pins and needles, or a numb limb. My adrenaline spiked even as I let out a calming breath.

I had never seen another Vampire die in the sun. There hadn't exactly been a lot left, with Sebek and all his madness. But I had heard stories of it.

The skin burning away as though lit under a flame, the almost peaceful way they'd close their eyes.

It would be easy, one breath, two ... and I would free my brothers from Sebek, at least for a while. From the threat of Kali and Darius. Free Aaliyah from me.

The ache was more consistent now, but I barely noticed it as I closed my eyes. I lifted my hand, the sun hitting my skin, seizing my nerves as the scent of ash flooded the air. It was a comforting pain, one that I embraced as the tattoo along that wrist charred.

Come on, Osiris, this isn't you, Nero's voice called, disappointed. But I was tired. So, so tired. I held my hand in a tight fist as the heat of the sun hit my shoes. Even through the material, it burned.

I can set them free.

"Osiris?" a gentle voice came, holding my heart hostage as I clenched my wrist until my hand went numb. "Osiris, are you here?"

Aaliyah.

The door to the game room opened, and my heart stopped for a moment. If I ignored her and stayed where I was, then this would end. They'd be able to live in peace, as they always should have.

But I froze, dragging my hand back to my chest, my heart suddenly thundering. It would only take a few minutes and then they'd never see me again. And I wouldn't see Eirik roam our woods, at peace with his wolf. I wouldn't get to savor Adrian's many dishes, the ones he made for me to try, knowing I hadn't spent much of my immortal life eating human food. I wouldn't fight with Fallon, and sneak peeks at his paintings when he wasn't looking. There would be one less person to remember Nero.

And Aaliyah ... I wouldn't reach for her when everyone else made me sick. I wouldn't crave her touch, and she wouldn't gaze at me like I was worth something.

The light burned now, and the marks of sunlit death creeped up my neck. They wouldn't find my body, and they might finally be at peace.

But she would find my soul.

I was back in the house, the door closing before the shutters fully fell. On the other side of the mosaic, watching as Aaliyah glanced around the empty room with confusion marring her face. Just as quickly, she turned around, jumping when she saw me.

That thought, stacked with the things that I knew I'd miss so dearly ... dragged me kicking and screaming back to them. She'd find my soul and know that I'd died. And I couldn't do that to her, not when it would hurt her, hurt *them,* so much.

The numbness faded enough for me to realize what I'd almost done, and I clenched my still-searing hand over my chest.

Aaliyah's eyes went wide, her face paling as she looked me up and down. I didn't have it in me to breathe for her, to act human. I didn't have words to explain the blood, that I'd done it for her, as cruel and savage as those words were.

Her eyes hinted at fear, even as she swallowed and spoke.

"There you are," she said, in that soft tone that made me question everything I was. Her nose twisted in worry, and her hands clenched in front of her in a defensive position.

It only took one glance behind her to spot Adrian and Fallon as well. Neither so much as breathed, looking at me like I was no more than some feral beast, and as I wiped my hand across my suit coat, I supposed I was. I hid my hands behind my back then, hoping that they healed before they had the chance to question the charring skin.

"I think something's wrong," Aaliyah said, again pulling my thoughts. She shuffled in front of me, glancing at the shutters at my back, biting her lip so hard I wondered if she might break skin. "Eirik's not back yet."

I froze, the burning of my skin fading away as I looked at the fallen shutters. My heart seized in my chest as I searched for the pull of our Viking brother. Bile rose in my throat when I didn't immediately feel it, even knowing that I hadn't sensed the pain of death on our bloodline.

Then it was there, weak, but there.

Guilt. It had always tasted heavy, and I almost missed the simplicity of not feeling at all. A few weeks ago, that had been my life, and as much as I loathed numbness, I think I hated this even more. With Aaliyah, and Kali's appearance, these volatile emotions were all I seemed to have anymore.

He may have turned you, Osiris, but you'll always be mine.

I pressed for that bond that tied Sebek's brood together, feeling for Eirik on the other side. It strained, twitching like a sickness. I clenched my fists, the burning ache of the sun coming back tenfold, as I tried to remember where Eirik had been going.

"He mentioned something about Valen. Said he needed some steelwork done, and that he'd be back," Adrian chimed in.

Valen. A Gargoyle that lived some ways into the woods outside of Oakridge, and the only man that Eirik would trust with steel. It was odd, though. He hadn't asked Valen for anything since he found out about his condition several years back.

"He's alive, but the bond feels strained," I said, watching as Fallon and Adrian shared an uneasy look.

Worry flared in Aaliyah's eyes, the kind that made my guilt that much more potent.

"There's nothing to be done about it now. I'll monitor the bond. It's best if you all rest, we'll head there tomorrow." There would be no sleep for me to find.

"Osiris—" Adrian started, but I cut him off with a raised hand, the one that wasn't burned.

Disappointment flared in his eyes, blending with the distrust that I had placed there after my failure.

"If there is to be a fight, I need you at your best. Go." One second, then two. Then it was just Aaliyah ... *lux mea*. My light in a world that was desperate to be swallowed by night.

"He'll be okay, Osiris," she assured, lifting her hand as if to touch me.

I flinched, jerking away from her, and she dropped it like hot coals. Pain flared in her eyes, the kind that translated to me. I clenched my wrist behind my back as she took a step away.

"It'll all be okay." Then she turned her back to me and left.

Something about her words told me it wasn't just Eirik she was talking about.

Chapter 18

Eirik

When I got to Valen's house, I was beating the damned Gargoyle to death.

I swatted away the sixth spider web I'd walked into, snarling as I ducked, nearly ramming into the low branches of the tree that it'd been on. I didn't want to be out here, slogging through the underbrush, nearly fifty miles from Oakridge. I wanted to be home, near Aaliyah so I could make sure she was safe and protected. Preferably in my arms, where even her demons wouldn't dare harm her.

Instead, I was here, in the fucking *muck,* as my beast snapped and snarled at me to move faster.

Gift, he pressed again, making my head hurt with his insistent yammering. He'd never been this vocal, but now that he seemed so hell-bent on claiming Aaliyah, I couldn't get the bastard to shut up.

He'd made it impossible to breathe, and even being around her made my bones ache and my fangs press against my gums. He wanted the claim, to bite and tie the *smár Valkyrja* to us. And this, offering her an official gift of courting, was the only way to pacify him short of claiming. All so he didn't accidentally slip out and mark her before I was ready. He snapped again, reminding me just how ready he was, how ready he'd been since the hot spring.

She was ours. *Mine,* my brothers'. And he wanted a gift for her, to ask her to be ours, and I knew just what to get.

After yet another low-hanging branch tried my life, the small hut I'd seen a thousand times before came into view. It was shabby but well-kept, with a steady stream of smoke filtering from the chimney on top. It was covered in mosses and mushrooms, so ingrained in the forest you couldn't find it if you didn't know exactly what you were looking for.

I huffed and walked up to the old door, reaching it just as it flew open. Valen's disgruntled, ugly face came into view, and he hunched as he stepped outside, having to duck through the doorway even though it was well above my head, his horns still grazing the frame. His grayed marble skin cracked as he did, a few chips falling to the ground. Besides that, he looked every bit like the man who had become one of my closest friends over the years. Daunting wings peeked over his head and extended down to his knees, while his thin tail that defied the stone it was made of whipped back and forth behind him. He was taller than me by over a foot, with the horns on his head making him about eight and a half feet.

"Well, I'll be damned. I didn't realize it was garbage day, yet here you are, looking like shit on my doorstep," he said mockingly as he crossed his arms.

I grinned, doing the same as we started our usual standoff. Valen was one of the few people who had ever dared to insult me like that, and it had become a game between us. "If I look like shit, then you're actively steaming. I almost forgot where I was until I smelled you six miles back. I'd say you looked good, but even I'm not going to lie to you about that."

It was a tense second before his gray face split into a grin, the sharpened points of his upper fangs peeking over his lip, and he extended his hand out to me. I took it, being careful not to further crush the crumbling stone of his arm as I pulled him into a quick side embrace.

"Good to see you, Eirik. Come in." He motioned to the door, ducking back through the threshold.

I followed him, the scent of heated steel and sweet alcohol blending in the air. I took in his home, one that hadn't changed in the several decades he'd been here, minus a few pieces of furniture that had been replaced. It was mostly barren, with a couch, glassless windows, a place to cook food, and a dimly lit forge. It was all visible from the front door.

"Just finished my mead today. You want a drink?" Valen asked, walking toward his little pit in the ground and pulling out a dusty bottle that appeared freshly sealed. I nodded, and he popped the top off.

I noticed it in the air before I saw it, the spark of Valen's magic. He held the power of a Sorceri, much like Osiris, but rather than the mimic power of an Echomancer, he was a controller of chaos—if I could use the word control. An Entromancer. He got an even worse hand than Osiris had. The blending of his blood made his control weak, and chaos followed the stone bastard wherever he went.

A point that was only further proven as the top of the bottle shot off, bouncing off the walls in a sporadic pattern before smashing into Valen's head and ricocheting off of it into the single mug on the counter, shattering it.

I held my laugh back, barely.

"Fuck!" he screamed, jumping back and nearly dropping the bottle. Had this not been a normal occurrence with Valen, I might have acted surprised. "God dammit, that was my *favorite* mug. Ah, my head!"

He reached up, pressing his hand gingerly to the spot where the cork had hit.

"Oh, Valen, am I making you nervous?" I asked, grinning when Valen shot me a murderous glare.

"Ha-ha. It's almost like you make that joke every time you come over. I'd zap you if I thought I could do it without frying your nervous system."

He rolled his neck, flinching as another small piece of skin fell to the ground before he walked to the far wall and grabbed two glasses. Plastic this time. He quickly poured us each a healthy dose of mead, handing me one. I sipped it, enjoying the smooth sweetness and hint of lemon I'd grown used to expecting with his drinks.

"Now, what brings you this way? Don't tell me you've finally decided to confess your undying love for me. I'm not nearly dressed enough for the occasion." He motioned to his threadbare pants and missing shirt and grinned when I raised an eyebrow. "No, that wouldn't be it. You're too shy for that. Let me guess. You want another sword?"

Like that was a guess at all. I'd been coming to him for his steelwork for nearly as long as I'd been a Vampire. Valen merely shook his head, his expression falling.

"So predictable. Unfortunately for you, I'm out of commission." He reached up, flexing his hand as if to show me why. Another piece of his arm fell to the ground, his skin crumbling. It had been nearly five years since I'd seen Valen, and nearly ten years since his condition first began ...

"You're shutting the forge down?" I asked, although I already knew the answer.

"Yeah. Don't know if you noticed, but my arm's giving out. I likely won't have it by the end of the year, and I don't feel like relearning my forge one-handed." As if to prove his point, another piece of him clinked as it hit the stone floor, and he rolled his eyes.

He'd lost the ability to shift back to his more human form, the one that allowed him to regenerate, and his marble to strengthen. The Gargoyle half of him was deteriorating, an anomaly that hadn't been documented before, and one that no one could seem to cure. The fact that he was a Gargoyle Sentinel didn't help. He was bigger than most, sturdy and built for war, and more likely to crack under the weight of his own form.

"Still no luck on a treatment?"

Valen laughed, shaking his head like I'd made a joke.

"Do you think you'd be looking at this beautiful face if I'd found one?" he asked, eyebrows raised in a taunting manner. Then he swallowed hard, his grin falling. "There isn't a fix for me, Eirik, and I've found my peace for that."

Finding peace in death wasn't a strange thought. When I was young, I'd craved the death of a warrior, the death that would lead me to Valhalla.

But that changed with my turn, with my *death*.

I ran a thumb over the scar on my neck, the one Brazen had carved out with a rusted saw, and had led to my turn. I just as quickly dropped my hand down to the emblem that hung there, the wolf defiant on it. The unyielding willpower in Valen's eyes reminded me of Aaliyah, when she first told us she was dying. My chest ached. I looked to Valen again, taking in the weary way he stood.

"You make shitty steel anyway, so it's not like anyone's missing out," I prodded, my eyebrow rising when Valen flashed me a haughty smirk.

"Just one bastard of a wolf, really. Terrible customer. Never likes my timelines, wants the impossible."

I shook my head but didn't disagree.

"Great friend, though. Stuck around the dysfunctional Gargoyle, even when everyone else sought differently." Valen shook his head, chuckling softly to himself.

It wasn't like I had done anything extraordinary. He made a good friend, regardless of his chaotic magic. Though others weren't so kind. He'd been kicked out of his mother's Coven just days after he came into his magic, and they found his control to be lacking. Likely because of his Gargoyle blood.

He tilted his head inquisitively. "So just for old times' sake, tell me what you want?"

My wolf growled low in my chest, glad to finally be talking about what he had dragged me out here for.

"A courting gift," I responded, and Valen's eyes shot wide.

"You sly *dog*, behind my back, no less? Oh, they must be quite fearsome to have garnered your attention." Despite the prod, genuine excitement was obvious on Valen's face.

He'd always been that way, genuine and kind even when others were not.

"You could say that, landed a blow on me," I said, pride burning hot in my chest. "She's had my wolf enamored since. Had all of us since."

A deep rumbling laugh started in his chest, his tail flicking behind him. The flare of his power lit again, and a stray spark bounced from the forge, landing on his skin. He brushed it off and began speaking like it hadn't happened.

"All of you? Even Osiris?" I nodded without question, even knowing Osiris had yet to fully decide what he wanted. He was a stubborn fuck. Valen just laughed again, shaking his head. "Damn, she has her hands full!"

He looked at the forge, then at his hand. He flexed it, flinching as more marble dust fluttered to the ground before he sighed and turned his gaze back to me. A crushing sadness bled into his eyes, and it made me sick to my stomach to see him this way.

I wished there was something more I could do for him, but he had been to every Natural healer there was to see. He was dying. And there was nothing I, nor anyone else, could do to stop it.

"Well, for something like that, I can probably make it work. Give me two weeks."

I forced a grin, noting when his eye twitched when he saw it.

"I need it tonight."

He groaned, throwing his head back.

"Ha. Hilarious," he said, sipping his drink again as he turned away from me and walked toward the forge. He began picking at barrels around it, tossing things into the fire until it molted, shifting colors.

"When have I ever been the kind to make jokes?" I asked, and he grumbled something as he stood back up, hitting his head on one of the overhanging wooden pillars beside him. "You know that was Nero's thing."

"Listen, you damned stubborn bastard. I can have your blade done in two weeks. *Two weeks* and not a damned day sooner, Eirik." Valen's noticeable frustration sank into his words as he pinched his nose between two chipped fingers and glowered at me from his space by the forge.

I bit my tongue, a snarl building in my chest as my beast frothed at the mouth. Tense didn't even begin to describe the tension of my wolf on my heels, pushing me forward with a single goal in mind, even as I tried to pull it back. Valen wasn't in any condition to deal with my wolf, though he'd likely still fuck me up if we were to fight it out as we had in the past.

Gift, my wolf snarled again, snapping at the chains that held him. He had been pressing to get a courting gift for days now, and now here I was standing in front of the only man I'd ever trust to make a blade for me, let alone Aaliyah.

"Oh, stop your shit, you overgrown furball. Your growling doesn't work on me, you fuck. I'm already losing limbs. You'd have to get more creative with your threats." There was no real worry behind his words, and I huffed. He rolled his shoulders, wincing as he lifted his hand up, inspecting the new cracks that formed along his forearm. He shot me a wary scowl. "If I were younger, maybe. But I'm not. I barely have use of my left arm now, and that makes forging a blade tricky."

His shoulders hunched, and he looked almost defeated at his now roaring forge. I realized now that he'd begun preparation to start it, likely without even knowing what he was doing.

"Sorry, Eirik. I can't do it that soon." His voice cracked, and my beast finally stopped his manic snarling. "Don't even know if I *can* do it."

I could have turned around and let it go there, but the way he kept looking back at the coals ... I knew he needed this. Needed one more go at the task that he'd loved for centuries.

"I have no right to ask, but I trust no one more than you with this. With the safety of my mate. I'm asking you for one more sword, any price, and you'll have it," I said, tipping my head at him in a show of respect.

There was a beat of silence, and I almost expected something profound, or even emotional.

Almost.

"Fancy way of saying that no one can make your steel harder than I can." Valen quipped, and I rolled my eyes as his head tipped back in a laugh. "You really care about this girl, don't you? Never seen you so intense about something, not since ..." His sentence tapered off, not saying Nero's name.

I just nodded, letting the emblem fall against my skin.

"She's everything," I said, my beast agreeing with a content rumble.

Valen flexed his hand again, grimacing in disgust as another chip of his arm fell away. Then he sighed.

"Fine. But *two fucking weeks*. That's as soon as I can get it to you. I'd like to remind you that I'm already working with less than two arms." The melancholy in his words was like a knife to the chest, and that emotion was enough to stop even my beast from complaining.

Fine, I'd wait two more weeks for Ali to be mine, but that didn't mean I was going to be happy about it.

"Anyway. Get the fuck out of my shop," Valen said, interrupting my thoughts. He waved his hands at me in a 'shoo' type motion until I shot him a glower. "What? You stink like a wet dog. I understand this is important to you and all, but maybe try to spend some time with the lady rather than me. Otherwise, she might think you're making this lovely blade for my hand. And while you're quite the strapping man, you've lost your chance with me."

I snorted, shaking my head but heading toward the door, nonetheless. Valen didn't like to be disturbed while he worked, a sentiment I understood. But before I could get even a step down, a blade flew past my head, embedding into the wall.

A grunt sounded in the air, and my blood turned to fire as a body flashed twice where the dagger had struck before sliding to the ground. Valen's blade was sticking out of the intruder's chest.

"Well, it seems we have an uninvited guest," Valen said, his voice no longer holding that teasing tone. "I didn't know I was hosting a party."

It was deep and harsh, and when I glanced back at him, the stone of his body was sharpened, his hands extended with sharp, dagger-like claws at the tips. I was glad to see him shift at all. The more pointed stone of his full Sentinel form was a breath of fresh air, showing there was some chance he may get to shift back one day.

He shot me a worried look, then glanced back at the man on the ground. He was small, maybe only five feet at maximum, with fire-red hair and silvery-blue scaled skin. He smelled of salt brine and arid heat. Some kind of Merfolk.

"Now, people don't make their way out here by accident, friend. So, you here for me, or him?" Valen asked, stalking up to the man. He kneeled low, grabbing the dagger and ripping it out without so much as a breath of hesitation. Blood poured from the wound as the man turned his hatred-filled gaze toward me.

I huffed, almost laughing at his pitiful attempt at intimidation. I flashed my fangs, my wolf rising to the occasion, shifting the bones on my face until I was only a second away from fully shifting.

The man had the good sense to turn his head.

"Looks like you, Eirik. Not that I'm not all for some fun, but want to explain why he'd be here?" Valen asked, tapping the bloody blade against his hand.

The steel made a sharp tinking sound against his stone skin.

"I have a guess," I said. Several. Though, the most likely was the one I wanted it to be the least. There was only one way to find out. "Tell me who sent you."

There was no *Charm* forced into my words, though a growl strangled them.

"Go fuck yourself," the man snarled back, flinching away from Valen as the Sentinel lifted the blade.

"Wrong answer," he said, tapping the length of the cold steel against the man's thigh.

I rolled my eyes but leaned down, making sure he couldn't avoid my glare as I allowed the power of my *Charm* to bleed into my voice.

"Who. Sent. You?" The power nearly rocked the house, and Valen trembled next to me as the man's eyes flared wide.

I hoped he would tell me, but I wasn't stupid enough to think he would. His eyes rolled back in his head, his entire body going taut as the command conflicted with the command of another, until mine *lost*. And he went limp, panting so hard I could feel his heartbeat.

"God damn, what just happened to him?"

"Conflicting Charm. Would have to be Sebek's. He's the only one old enough besides Osiris to beat mine out," I sighed, standing again and hauling the man to his feet as I did.

He screeched, his hands gripping my wrists as the wound on his shoulder no doubt flexed. He wouldn't need to worry about it soon. I had no plans to leave him alive.

"You'll die for this. He knows! He already knows!" he screamed, and I froze, my wolf going silent as I held off just enough to hear the last of his words. "I've seen her, your precious human—"

I slammed him against the wall, his body shaking the aged wood before I sank my teeth into his neck. Blood flooded my mouth, tasting like salt and ash, but I didn't stop drinking until the man stopped moving.

When I pulled away, his eyes rolled back, and his heart ceased to beat.

"God *dammit,* you got blood everywhere!" I rolled my eyes, letting the body drop to the floor. The rancid tang of his blood lingered in my mouth, building until the only thing I could taste was ash. It was almost like blood wine, the empty feeling of a false feed. My head spun just as Valen spoke again. "Fuck me, this is going to take ages to clean up. I just got the stain out of the hardwood from the last time you did this."

I barely heard him, the spinning becoming worse until I couldn't keep my eyes open.

"Eirik?" Valen asked.

I tried to respond, even as my stomach raged against the blood, revolting until I stumbled, leaning against the wall.

"Oh fuck, Eirik!" Valen gasped from behind me, and I knew he was close. But his voice sounded far away as I fell. "Didn't think you'd ever end up in my arms. Fuck, you're heavy. And you owe me a pinky finger, as I think mine just fell off."

My eyes rolled back.

"Don't you dare die, you bastard. Osiris *will* kill me," was the last thing I heard.

Before it all went black.

CHAPTER 19

AALIYAH

I hadn't gotten a single second of sleep.

I'd spent the first part of the day rolling in bed, then pacing in front of my door. I swore I was going to dig paths into the hardwood, but I couldn't stop. What if something happened? What if Osiris was wrong and Eirik was in trouble, or worse? That dread that had followed me from the cellar only grew and festered until I was on the brink of tears.

What if?

I couldn't go through this again, couldn't lose one of them. That panic, creeping and endless, nearly made me sick. The surrounding air fluttered as Red tried to show some support, but in the end, I just kept pacing.

I walked until my feet hurt and my head pounded. I walked until the exhaustion hit so hard that I wobbled more than I paced. It was then that I left the room, faced with a gloomy hallway and house that felt too empty. I walked on instinct, moving down the hall until I came to a stop in front of Adrian's door. It was distinct, covered in little stickers and pins and post-cards that he'd collected over the years. I hesitated outside of it, unsure what to do now that I found myself here.

But I was at a loss. I couldn't do this alone, but my ask for help burned in my throat. Still, I lifted my hand and rapped my knuckles along the cold wood, being careful not to disturb the cards. It was barely seconds later when the door opened, and I was face to face with Adrian.

He didn't wear a shirt, his bare torso on display. His lithe, swimmer body was well-defined, and his boxers hung low on his hips. Normally, it would catch my eye. I would linger on the soft ridges of his abdomen or blush at the thought of touching him. But today was just too much, and I clasped my hands together in front of me as I looked up into his eyes.

He was tired, but not like he'd just woken. The same worry radiated off of him as he ran a hand through his hair. Even just being in front of him helped to calm me down, and now no longer as antsy or close to tears, I took a breath.

"Do you mind if I stay with you?" I asked, dipping my head down, unable to keep eye contact.

We talked about this, *us,* already, but part of me was still worried that it was all a ruse. That one day his adoring smile would twist into a glare and he'd slam the door. Just like I worried that one day I'd wake up and not be here, instead strapped to the metal table of my nightmares. But with each day, those fears grew less pointed, less real.

When Adrian opened his arms to me without hesitation, I slid into them, shivering at his cold skin. The spark of heat that came with his touch quickly brushed it all away, and I molded even closer to him as his lips swept against my hairline.

"Always, love," he cooed, letting me go and inviting me into his space.

His room differed from what I expected, the walls a mute gray. But there were small things that made it perfectly clear this was Adrian's. He had little trinkets, a collection of spoons, and another of coins, all carefully placed on display. While there were no windows, there were several lamps, all glowing a yellow-orange that made the room feel cozy. But the best part, the part that made my eyes droop, was the bed. It was covered in what looked like silky sheets and a blue comforter I'd get lost in.

Adrian moved behind me, wrapping his arms around my shoulders and carefully leading me to the bed. I tensed, if only for a second as he guided me onto it, pulling the sheets and blankets back so I might crawl in. He followed behind me, his breath on my neck and shoulder.

But his arms never moved, like bands of safety as he hugged me to his chest.

"Get some sleep, sweetheart," he whispered, sighing into my hair. "Eirik will be alright. But you know he'll be upset if we find him and you're barely standing."

A grin tipped at my lips, even as I tried to stop it. My eyes drooped as exhaustion finally hit me. I held onto Adrian's arm, and surrounded by his soft warm scent, I fell into a dreamless sleep.

But it was only a few minutes, or a few hours later, when I woke with a start, jolting up as a bite of pain hit me in the chest. I knocked the hand that had been toying at my hip bone off, stumbling out of bed as I tried to wake up enough to figure out what happened. Adrian grumbled, his amber eyes blinking open as he wearily looked around. As soon as he saw me, though, he was on his feet as well.

He *flitted* in front of me, wasting no time in cupping my cheeks in his icy palms and examining me with a critical gaze from my head to the tips of my feet.

"You alright, love? What happened?" Adrian asked, rubbing his eyes and squinting to get a better look at me.

"I don't know," I said, taking a few precious seconds to level my breathing. And it wasn't a lie. Whatever it was, that burst of pain was gone now. There was no pressing dread, at least not related to Eirik. This push that woke me up was something different. I didn't know how I knew that, but I did. *"I don't know."*

Adrian's brows furrowed, and he brushed his thumb against my cheek again, just as a knock rang against the door. I froze, instinctually curling into Adrian as he wrapped his arm around my shoulder.

Fallon's crisp, wintery tone slid through the cracks, and I could finally breathe. "Get ready. We found him."

<hr>

We'd made it to Valen's, a man I now knew to be a good friend of Eirik's, in record time after the sun finally set. Osiris had gotten word, just a touch before we could leave, and that thirty minutes of waiting was the longest I'd ever had to endure. The humble little house was buried in the woods, ingrained in the very soul of the forest. It was built into a swamp-like area, covered in trees and moss, but for some reason, it didn't feel cluttered.

There was a hominess to it, one that spoke of a lifetime of memories, and had the circumstances been different, I knew I would have asked Valen about it. About his life here.

I ran my hands through Eirik's thick blond hair, the unruly strands having come apart from his braid. He was pallid, clammy, and nothing like the man I'd grown to know. His chest heaved in deep, labored breaths that all ended in a rasp. But worse than that was how still he was, unnaturally so, and that look had my hands shaking as I begged for him to open his eyes.

Adrian was pacing by the front door, eyeing the bloodstain on the ground and the way Valen's hands hovered in the air.

He was searching the blood for impurities to see what had caused Eirik to get so sick, as he had been since before we'd all but stormed down through his front door. It was something Gargoyles could do; I learned today. Though it was taking Valen longer than normal, and I had to guess that had something to do with his own problem.

Valen was tall, *very tall,* his horns grazing his roof if he stood his full height, and each time he moved, small pieces of him *chipped away.* Like he was slowly breaking.

"He'll be alright. He's a tough bastard," Valen said, his gruff voice bouncing around the small home. "With someone like you to take care of him, he'll be back on his feet in no time."

There was a gentleness to the words, something I appreciated as I pressed my forehead to Eirik's. Another shuttering rasp and I tensed, waiting impatiently for his next breath, and the next. But it was Osiris who let out a breath from across the room, and I turned to him. His face was ashen, and besides that single intake of air, he didn't move again. There was no attempt at appearing human, and even the numbness that had become him didn't look penetrable.

From here, he *barely* looked alive. He hadn't truly been well for days, but last night just seemed to be another tipping point.

Blood still covered the floor of the game room, and the sight of him drenched in it, looking like an avenging angel—both feral and broken—had been enough to knock even my fear for Eirik to the side. He'd been on edge, more so than the last few days, and that wasn't even counting the dreaded numbness in his eyes ... nor the dark streaks on his hands and neck that he tried to hide. I didn't know what they were, but I knew they hadn't faded.

Fallon slid through the door, breaking my thoughts with the murderous scowl on his lips. He shook off his suit coat and glared at the blood on the ground like it had offended him.

"No sign of any others. He wake up yet?" he asked as he strode toward me.

I didn't answer, not when he could see Eirik's head still in my lap. I hadn't moved since we'd arrived. It seemed wrong to leave him on the ground, and I was terrified that he would wake up in pain or scared. It was irrational, but I'd done it myself too many times and wished that someone would have done the same for me.

My heart clenched, and I ran my fingers through Eirik's hair again. I didn't look up this time, didn't search for Prince like my mind begged me to. Instead, I took comfort in the cloth in my pocket and the cold that lingered on it.

I knew things hadn't changed. Losing Prince didn't mean that everything that had been going wrong was suddenly better, but I'd hoped that just once fate would be on my side. That I could mourn my best friend without everything else going to hell.

But the pressure in my head, and how Eirik was currently splayed across the floor, told me I wasn't going to get that time.

Fallon moved so fast that I didn't see him crouching in front of me until his face was only inches away. It was intimate, and I sank into the feeling of him and the scent of heat and the sea. I'd seen so little of him the last few days that I basked in his presence, having missed him.

"He'll be fine, I promise," he whispered gruffly, gently grabbing my chin and lifting my gaze. "Do I look like I break promises?"

My lips quivered, but I shook my head. Fallon was nothing if not honest, but I didn't think even he could promise me that. His eyes calmed, that roaring heat of rage that burned in them mellowing.

He stayed that way, hesitating before he leaned in and pressed a gentle kiss to my forehead. He moved like a pit viper, striking and pulling back before I had the chance to question what happened. The move shook me so much that I jolted, taken aback by the sharp hit of desire that followed his lips.

Then he stood, crossed his arms, and looked toward Valen.

"Anything in the blood?" he asked, like he hadn't just done that, and Valen shook his head.

His hands fell, whatever spell he'd been casting dropping as he sighed. "Hate to burst your bubble, but no. It's just blood," he said, shaking his hands, some stone bits clanking off the ground. I frowned at the sight, but no one else mentioned it. "Not sure what about it made him sick."

Adrian made a worried noise, stopping his pacing. "This doesn't make any sense. We hadn't had any problems with the vein, only with bottled wine."

I froze at the mumbled words, hands tensing in Eirik's hair.

"What do you mean?" I asked, eyebrows furrowed as Adrian's head dipped to the side.

"Oh, for the last several years, we've grown a tolerance to bottled blood wine. It doesn't do much for us now, and even the flavor is terrible." He made a disgusted face, before looking at the blood on the ground with the same expression. "We've been using donors when we get the chance."

I bit my lip, a dreadful worry spiraling inside me. I knew something was wrong with them, but it'd never been explicitly stated. And something about how Adrian looked away told me it was worse than he'd like to admit.

"When did it start to get worse?" I'd barely finished the sentence before Adrian was in front of me, pushing Fallon out of the way and grabbing my face between his hands.

Fallon seethed while Adrian just winked, exaggerating the movement and making me giggle. He did it so easily, and some of the tension drained.

"It's been getting worse for years, love. *Decades*. I see your mind working. This *wasn't* you. It's been a long time coming." He brushed his thumb over my cheek, the spark of touch sending a shiver down my spine.

"Do you think the blood made him sick, then? Like blood wine?" I asked.

He didn't answer for a second, but the concerned way he looked at the blood told me enough. My hand shook against Eirik's head.

"Yes," Osiris cut in, his first words all evening.

I looked at him again, taking in the numb way his eyes focused on Eirik, then on Adrian, and where his hands were on my face.

"Well, fuck. Guess I'm not the only one fucked up in this house. At least you lot aren't losing limbs," Valen said with a laugh before shaking his head. Fallon shot him a scowl just as the giant man sighed. "Damn, I loved that pinky."

"What are we going to do? We can't go on like this," Fallon said, and I tipped my head away from Adrian's hands.

He said it wasn't my fault, and I really wanted to believe him ... but what if I did this? What if it was spiraling because of my showing up, because of them being drawn to my blood at the auction? I lifted my hand to my neck, clutching the lavender charm that sat heavily against my skin.

"We don't know if it was the blood yet, but I agree," Osiris started, his voice level and monotone. "Our meeting with Xander is in three days. We might get a few more questions out of him if we're lucky. We need to figure this out before the Eternium; we can't risk a fight weakened like this."

Silence met us, besides the creak of Valen as he walked toward the back of his home.

"And if we can't find anything?" Adrian finally asked. "Don't suppose you know anyone who can help?"

Adrian looked at Valen as he spoke, and the Gargoyle shot up, hitting his head on the beam to his right. He grunted, rubbing at the sore spot and flicking off another loose stone. "Hey, don't look at me. I make swords, not miracles. I'd offer you a drink of my own, but your pretty little fangs won't be getting through this stone."

Adrian cracked a laugh, just as the man draped over me groaned. My hands tensed in Eirik's hair, my entire body shifting so I could glance down at him.

"No one wants your sour ass blood, Valen," Eirik protested, his eyes opening.

A softness fell over them, and my hands trembled against his head. Eirik lifted his hand and pressed it to my cheek, the heat from him warming my chest.

Thank God.

"Eirik," I said, just as he looked away from me, his eyes narrowing on Valen with a bored playfulness.

"You probably taste about as good as this place smells. Fuck, did you let rats loose while I was out?"

Valen huffed, shaking his head with a grin. I had to take a second to blink and look down at Eirik, who was still *joking*. Did he hit his head when he fell?

"Just the others of your Crypt, and this lovely thing that's taking care of you," Valen said, winking at Eirik.

It wasn't insulting, and though I didn't feel that same pull to Valen as I did with the rest of my guys, it still made me blush. My hands tensed against Eirik's hair, and I pulled away from the soft strands. Eirik let out a sharp sound, his eyes flooding a deep blue just as his hands shot up, grabbing mine.

Valen laughed, the sound deep and rattling the stone before he mouthed something I couldn't understand. Eirik dropped my hands like they were coals, just as his cheeks tinged pink. Was Eirik blushing?

What the *hell* was happening?

He mumbled something, sitting up, his hand going to his head immediately, a flash of pain flying across his eyes. That one look washed away all my questions, and I helped him, letting him use me to lean on as he gained his bearings.

His nose twisted, and he looked around like someone had let a skunk in while he was out.

"Then why does it reek of charred flesh and ash?" His nose scrunched as he looked around the room before his eyes centered on Osiris. It was quick, the look of panic that passed between them. He averted his gaze just as quickly. "And what the fuck happened?"

I didn't look away from Osiris like Eirik had. I traced his face and the haunted way he stared at the ground. It smelled of ash ... I'd thought the same when Osiris first came out of the library yesterday. He'd been in the library, right? I'd assumed he'd gone there looking for comfort after whatever he did. Dread. It pooled, raged, and sucked at my soul as I finally recognized the emotion in Osiris's eyes, the one that told me he'd been *outside*.

I had endured it many times, but most recently, with the loss of Prince. Hopelessness. Numbness. A wish for peace. The charred marks made sickening sense.

"You ate a rotten meal, a wiggly one at that. Took you right down," Valen said, just as I stood. He didn't pick up on the silence of the rest of us as he chucked a piece of stone at Eirik. It bounced off of his chest and hit the ground. "Oh, and you owe me a fucking pinky."

More silence, then Eirik let out a breath. "Osiris—"

It only took one word for the hopelessness in Osiris's eyes to fully crumble, and his hand shot up, shaking. "No, Eirik."

But Eirik was already standing, his legs not able to really hold him as he wobbled and cursed. Then he stared at the hand Osiris had lifted like it might burst into flames. Adrian and Fallon took notice, and the small sharp lines across his skin became even more apparent. They moved along his fingers and up his arm before disappearing under his suit. The ones at his neck had faded, but hints of them could still be seen as indents in his skin.

Osiris's hands dropped to his side, still trembling, as he reached over and gripped the other. His skin was bruised and healed, only to bruise again. Before he walked stiffly toward the door, too shaken to *flit*.

"Man, that can't be good," Adrian said with resigned pain in his words. Even Fallon looked worried.

"Did you catch his hands?" he asked, deathly quiet. "Ashen scars. Like they touched the sun."

That was all I could handle. I gave Eirik one more look, making sure he could stand. His nod was all I needed, as I followed after Osiris, the door slamming behind.

I had to run to catch him, my legs still partially jelly after my own pacing last night, but he wanted me to catch him ... he was a *Vampire*. If he didn't want to be near me, then he wouldn't. But he needed someone right now, even if he couldn't say it. Osiris was an enigma, an ancient power no one could seem to grasp, and he needed someone to lean on. He finally came into view, stopped in a small clearing just past the trees.

"Osiris?" I asked quietly so as not to startle him.

Even with my efforts, he jumped physically. He looked at me with startled eyes, though his face gave none of that tumultuous emotion away. It was a trait that each of them seemed to have, this ability to put on a façade. Fallon was the best at it, and sometimes even I couldn't tell what he was thinking.

But Osiris was like an open book, especially now. He'd been when I first got here too, but I was too scared to see it. Of all of them, Osiris wore his heart in his *eyes*, and if you didn't take the time to look, you would miss it.

He swallowed hard, as those startling, mismatched blues locked on where I stood like I might disappear.

"Go back inside, Aaliyah," he pleaded, eyebrows scrunching together in the barest movement. I saw the crease from where I stood.

"No. Not this time, Osiris," I whispered. He couldn't run from this, not now. I wouldn't let him ... but I also knew I had to take this slow.

"Where do you always go, out into the woods?" I asked, peeking up at him.

Shock took over his expression, and I marveled at the crisp line of his jaw and the curious tilt of his lips. The murky sky above made his eyes glow, making him seem ethereal in the bitter dusk. He didn't answer me for a moment, but his hands opened, no longer held tightly into fists.

"Nero and the others' graves," he said after a few more breaths of silence.

He didn't tense, but I supposed that wasn't an impressive feat, considering he was *already* tense.

"The others?" I asked, trying to keep his attention as he looked at his hands again.

It worked well enough, as he sighed. "Our Maker turned three before me, and each died before my turn. We didn't want them to be forgotten."

The revelation shocked me, but even more was the way Osiris shut down at the words. That was a good thing, keeping their memory alive. So why did he look so torn about it?

"I'm sure they appreciate you keeping them in your life," I said carefully, taking a step closer.

We were maybe three feet apart now, close enough that I could see the wrinkles in his suit. He looked down at me, catching my gaze. When he didn't back up, I took another step and another.

"Osiris?" I murmured, reaching up slowly. He flinched just before my hand touched his skin, so I waited for him to pull away.

Instead, he reached his own hand up, pressing it to mine and my palm to his cheek. When the chill of his skin sank into mine, I had to hold my breath. The spark of touch roared, and I struggled to keep from pulling him closer. The skin on his hand looked marred, streaks of white not yet fading away, only further solidifying what I'd thought. His eyes fell closed, and he looked calm for the first time in days.

"I am fine," he said like he knew exactly what I was going to say.

"I'm not going to push you, Osiris. I know how hard it is to talk about things that twist you up." He jerked again, his hand tightening on mine. "But I'm here. Adrian, Fallon, and Eirik, *they're* here for you. Whatever you're going through doesn't just have to be on you."

It wasn't good to keep it bottled up. If you did, it would tear you apart from the inside, piece by piece. I knew that because I'd been through it, and with Osiris, it was like looking into a mirror. I hated seeing him hurting, hated him thinking that feeling was a weakness and not something to find strength in.

"You can't keep blaming yourself, Osiris," I said, putting all of my conviction into the words. "Not for Kali showing up. Not for what happened to me."

And not for everything else for the past lifetimes he'd lived. He held it all close to his chest, buried so deeply in his heart that even those closest to him couldn't see how molded he was by it. He saw his failures and struggled under the weight. Buckled, bowed. I wouldn't let him break.

Osiris didn't move, just let his hand slide off of mine as he turned away. It broke a part of my soul that Osiris thought it was his fault that *she* was a terrible person, but I didn't reach for him as he grabbed his wrist. Those black tattoos surrounding it seemed bolder than normal. No matter how beautiful they were, they were scars. They had the same meaning to him as my own did.

They were marks of pain, and he needed space to register them, to come to terms with them. Or at least recognize them for what they were.

Scars. Nothing of his fault.

"I do not matter, *lux mea.* I should have known that Kali would come the first time, and I should have prepared them for it so she couldn't have taken advantage of us the second," he said, not breathing as his eyes clouded over. "I told myself I would never allow my fear of the past to consume me. I have failed that twice now. I was selfish, have *always* been selfish—"

"It wasn't your fault," I broke in, the words the strongest I'd ever spoken.

"I—" he started, but I shook my head.

"No, Osiris. *Look at me.*" I trembled as I took a step closer, reducing what was left of the distance between us until I was as close as I could get without falling into his arms. "Whatever Kali and Darius did to you, *that's not your fault.*"

Osiris didn't step away, merely looked at me with an expression I couldn't place, his hands trembling at his sides.

"You may not have handled Kali showing up right; you could have told us, but don't think for a second that Kali's actions are your fault. That's on her, Osiris. *Her.*"

The forest fell quiet beyond my heavy breathing. I waited for recognition, for acceptance, anything to show in his eyes. I didn't think they could get more numb, more lifeless, until they did.

"Kali ... was the reason there was a hole in the ward," Osiris whispered, the words dropping like a bomb as he continued to stare at the forest floor. "Kali let Crustava in, and she's the reason Prince is no longer here. And she did that because of *me.* To teach me a lesson about defying her."

He didn't give me time to respond as he stopped breathing again, pulling my attention like a magnet as he was suddenly looming over me, moving us until I was against a tree. The rough bark bit into my back, and suddenly my heart sped up.

Something inside tried to warn me ... telling me there was a predator in front of me.

"She told me herself after I finished butchering the rest of Crustava's pack," was Osiris's soft response. He lifted his hand, and the fingers that just yesterday were bloodied red were now toying with a strand of my hair. "Last night wasn't the first time I've had blood on my hands. And there was blood, Aaliyah. Twenty-three lives. I killed them for what *he* did to you."

His lips pulled into a snarl as his eyes flashed red, and he leaned forward. I flinched, unable to keep the reaction quelled, even as Osiris's eyes dimmed further.

"All of them. The ones that fought. And the ones that ran. I am not a good man, *lux mea.* I killed them, and I'd do it again. I *will* do it again. Our safety, our lives, fall on me as they always have. And that was why I atoned for it with their lives. It's why you need to leave me be. I'm not someone who can be saved, Aaliyah. Just like I couldn't save you. Or save Nero."

And that was the break, what really was settling on him. Just saying Nero's name was enough to cause tears to well in his eyes, and his voice to crack. Kali had been a catalyst. *I* had been a catalyst. We'd caused the emotions from his lost brother to finally rear up, and he could no longer hold them back.

Osiris continued to hover over me, and my heart lulled.

"Osiris," I said as I cupped his cheek, even as he bared his teeth. His fangs had dropped, the deadly points shining in the dim light of the moon. "Nero wouldn't have wanted you to put this on yourself. I know it."

"Nero—" his voice shattered on the word; the name of the man I knew meant more to him than anything in the world.

Because he'd meant the world to me, too. Prince and Nero, Nero and Prince. The more I heard about them, the more I was sure. Even if I didn't want it to be, even as I hoped that the connections that had been in the back of my mind weren't leading to that.

Prince wasn't Nero. It would be too much, and it would *hurt* too much.

I couldn't imagine being in Osiris's shoes, but I also couldn't help but think of Prince's sure grin. It was a path that always led to pain and joy, excitement and agony. Prince ...

"Nero, above everything, was your brother. And he would have wanted you happy, Osiris. He would have wanted you to forgive yourself," I said, clenching my hands and bringing them to my chest, the ache of loss hitting me as well. "And me? I'd never be mad at you for avenging me. You did the same with Curtis, remember? I'm not scared of you, Osiris. Not anymore."

Osiris watched me, unblinking before he took a breath, that fearful façade falling as even his fangs receded. I didn't have time to continue contemplating, as Osiris leaned forward, putting his forehead to mine. It lit up my soul, warming me even in the cold, and I sighed.

"How can you be so sure?" he asked, choking on the words as he hunched.

I didn't wait for permission as I moved, wrapping my arms around him. The cold of his body soaked through our clothes, and soon his arms came around me as well. He held me so close, so carefully, even as his face buried into the hollow of my neck and the fan of his breath against the skin there made me shiver.

"Because I can see it in everything you do. You're a powerful man,

Osiris. One who gives far more than he takes. You're worthy of forgiveness. Especially your own," I finished.

He didn't say anything, instead only held me for a few seconds longer before he pulled back. Then, he stared at me, before finally nodding once. Slowly, lightly, like he wasn't sure himself.

But it was something.

I looked around us, taking in the cool woods and near barren trees. My thoughts, as usual, focused on Prince. He would have loved the colors ... I grabbed my arm, closing my eyes.

"Why do I get a pardon for what I've done?" Osiris asked the words like a smooth breeze.

My chest clenched for him and his grief.

"I asked myself the same question, you know?" I said wistfully. And I still wasn't sure if I did either. I'd watched Prince die because of me, and I'd carry that forever. But I know that Prince ... loved me all the same. "And I'll tell you the same thing I realized. Osiris, you're not perfect. And you don't need to be. Your past doesn't define you; you aren't bound by it. You grow, and you learn, and you make mistakes. But you're never alone. So when you stumble, I'll be here for you. We all will."

Osiris turned away from me like my words physically hurt him. He went ramrod straight, the tears that had gathered in his beautiful blue eyes falling.

I'd once seen him as a monster, as someone that would hurt me. He was powerful, dangerous, sinfully beautiful, and ... vulnerable. He was one of the kindest souls I'd ever known, and I would cherish any part of him I could. He may never want me how Adrian did, but he would always hold a place in my heart.

Slowly, his hand lifted, cool fingers brushing against my cheek. Tired eyes traced the skin, the scars that I'd always have.

"I'm not convinced I deserve the peace that you offer, *lux mea*," he said, the words coming out brittle. "You are the sun, and I have no wish to smother that light. I need to fix the broken parts of myself to become someone worthy of it."

I let out a hard breath. He'd *terrified* me when I first met him and had shocked me to the core with his numb eyes and bloodied suit. But there was no place for fear now as I reached up and pressed my hand against his, the same one that had torn out the heart of a man, and I found comfort in his touch, in the scent of rich coffee and a mellow mint.

And like the wind, he was gone.

CHAPTER 20

FALLON

The fucker left. I knew he had, and I was no longer in the mood to let him run. Valen's house was a tiny thing, so getting from one side of it to the door took barely five steps, and I stalked toward it just as Adrian's eyes shot wide and he followed me.

"Wait. Fally, whatever's on your mind—"

I flipped toward him, making him stumble back.

"We need to talk, all of us," I said, and his face settled into a knowing frown. "So get Eirik. We're going home."

He just gave a nod, and Valen sighed from across the room.

The Gargoyle cracked his neck as he walked toward Eirik, who had somehow managed to get back on the ground. With one heaving lift, Eirik was on his feet again. Valen's horns grazed the roof, and a piece from the tip of the one on the left came clattering to the ground, though he didn't pay it any attention as he dusted Eirik off.

"Man, I forgot how damned *angsty* you all were," Valen huffed, shaking his head with a laugh before he looked out of the doorway. Aaliyah came walking in just a second later, and I didn't like that he looked at her, even if there wasn't heat in his gaze. "You've got your hands full, don't you, Aaliyah? Give these boys hell for me." He flashed her a trickster smile before pointing back at Eirik with his clawed thumb. "Especially this one. I'll be collecting on that pinky."

Eirik said something under his breath that had Valen grinning, all teeth.

Eirik turned to the door with a hand over his stomach. He was still wan, but at least he was moving.

"Not on your life, you bastard," Eirik muttered, clapping Valen on the back.

It wasn't hard, but flecks of the Gargoyle's stone still hit the ground. Valen didn't seem to notice or didn't care enough to be upset about it.

"Yeah, yeah, we'll see. Let me know if you need anything else." Valen winked, and from the heated way Eirik's eyes traveled to Aaliyah, I knew that whatever Eirik had come here for was in effect. A courting gift, if I had to guess.

He was traditional like that.

I gritted my teeth, turning to her. Like usual, I couldn't take my eyes off her once she was in sight. I'd spent a long time considering my talk with Adrian, and even as my hands shook as that panicked feeling ate my nerves ... I knew what I had to do.

I would look back at this moment as either my saving grace or when everything finally crumbled beneath me. But I realized as I stared into those magnetic lavender depths that haunted my dreams, that I no longer cared which it was.

I confidently strode up to Aaliyah, making sure she saw me before I reached out and pulled her into my arms, surprising her again with a hug. She gazed up at me, curiosity in her eyes, but I didn't say anything. The words would come soon. For now, this was what I could offer, and she seemed to accept that. Her soft lavender scent calmed some of the rage, and the effortless way she hummed against me had my shoulders dropping.

But she was tense too, still glancing back toward the forest. The vibrancy that her skin had held had faded as well, and the dark circles under her eyes worried me.

"You can't talk me out of it. We need to talk to him," I insisted, and she sighed against me.

"I know." She looked up from my chest, putting her chin between my pectorals. "But for me, please be careful with him. He's lost, Fallon. Depressed. And honestly, we may not be enough help. We need to see if he'll talk to someone about it, if not us."

How the fuck was I supposed to say no to that? I'd do anything she asked, a fact that I was barely coming to terms with. I would scorch the earth, Challenge Sebek, fuck. Give *Adrian* a chocolate.

She deserved the world, and fuck if I wasn't going to give it to her on a silver platter. But this was something I wanted, anyway. Osiris was a bastard, often cold and calculating, *dangerous*. But he was ours, and right now, we needed to get him back. He'd been lost for far too long.

"We will. Come on, Ali. Let's get home," I said, easily hoisting her up.

She let out a squeak of surprise, and I glanced at Adrian and Eirik, only giving them a bare nod before I started on my way out of the forest and toward our home.

The sun was still several hours from rising, but that didn't make my bones any less tired. I needed to feed, just not from those damned bottles we kept in the kitchen island.

I needed the vein, or I hoped I did, and the longer I went without it, the more this ache seemed to grow. Fucking blood wine. I cursed whatever bad luck we had that made us turn against it. Maybe it was years of being desensitized to old blood, and our bodies just grew to not take nourishment from it. Either way, it tasted like ashes now.

Though that didn't explain Eirik today.

"What do you want for dinner, Fally?" Adrian asked as he placed a kiss on Ali's head.

She blushed, taking her bottom lip between her teeth. I didn't miss the confusion in her eyes, nor the indecision, though she didn't push Adrian away. Her eyes lingered on his face, crossing over his lips.

"Linguini with clams," I said eventually, brushing my hair back.

"And the white wine sauce?" Adrian asked, tapping his chin with his pointer finger. He looked at Aaliyah for a moment, as if asking her if that was alright. "What do you think, love?"

"I don't think I've ever had it," she said thoughtfully. There were still shadows in her eyes, ones that would always be there, but at least she didn't look away from us, keeping her head held high. "I'd like to try it."

Her white hair flashed brightly under the glow of the moon, and while her eyes were on Adrian, I studied her. The curves of her thin lips, the crinkle at the corner of her eyes. I sucked in those details like they were the air keeping me alive, focusing on them. She was everywhere, and the longer that I stayed around her, the more my control chipped away.

The Eternium was only weeks away, the first of the year drawing closer, and it was no longer a matter of want.

Our lives depended on the truth.

Chapter 21

Aaliyah

"Easy," I said, walking ahead of Eirik and Fallon.

It had taken much longer to get home than it had to get to Valen's little house in the woods. Eirik moved at a snail's pace, and though Fallon had given me the option to get taken ahead, I chose to walk with them. I didn't want to let Eirik out of my sight and was scared he might disappear if I did.

Said grumpy Viking grunted, looking annoyed at how Fallon currently held him up. And as the house came into view, his pace picked up just a touch.

"I'm fine, *Elskan*. It'd take more than some spoiled blood to get me down." He said the words with confidence, but I still noted the way he limped, the sallow tint to his normally bronzed skin. It made me nervous, and Eirik must have noticed, as he shrugged Fallon's arm off and stalked toward me.

"I'll be fine, my *smár Valkyrja*." I blushed at his gentle tone and the way he lifted his hand to brush his fingers across my cheek. "Just need to sleep it off."

I nodded, unable to keep my worry off my face as he turned away and moved toward the stairs. He was so big, so strong, that seeing him move so gingerly struck up a primal fear in me. I was used to death, to pain, but I hated seeing them in it.

"Come on, love. Leave old Eri alone. His pride's damaged enough as it is," Adrian quipped from beside me, startling me as he slung an arm over my shoulder.

I glanced at him, taking in his simple grin and bright amber eyes as I reached up to grab his hand, giving it a squeeze. I loved it, touching him, the spark that followed as our skin brushed together.

"I worry about him," I said, eyeing the stairs again.

My worry had only grown in the past few weeks. The need to see them healthy and safe was nearly overwhelming. The need to just *see* them. It was something that I'd never take for granted again, as I searched the dim spaces of the room, lingering on the shadows.

Always looking for Prince.

Adrian, as always, knew exactly what to do to distract me as his lips descended on my cheek. He made a silly smack noise when he pulled away, walking us toward the kitchen with sure steps.

"I know. And he's delighted about it, love. What do you say we make him something good to eat for when he wakes up?"

I took a deep breath, stealing one more glance at the stairs before I nodded. Eirik would need something to eat. And maybe the meal would be enough to drag Osiris inside for a few hours, though I doubted it. He likely needed time to himself after our conversation.

"Yeah, I'd like that." Adrian kissed the top of my head as I spoke, before sitting me at the kitchen table and ambling toward the stove.

"Perfect," he hummed, tapping each of the cabinets as he walked. "Fallon, you want to help, or are you just going to stand there and glower?"

I jolted at that, forgetting that Fallon was here, and I turned toward him with a blush.

His eyes were on me, never straying, and while that wasn't completely unusual, the emotion in them was. They burned, they raged, and I couldn't guess what it meant. He'd watched me like that nonstop since I'd found him and Adrian in the training room.

"Where did Osiris go? We could use the extra hands," Adrian said, the sound of clashing dishes sounding in the air.

"The gravestones. He'll be back," I whispered, turning my head to watch the snow fall through the window.

"I take it that conversation went well?" Adrian asked as Fallon moved to join him by the island.

Adrian handed Fallon a cutting board and a sharp knife, one that I recognized. It was the same shining blade that I'd cut Eirik with on my first night here.

"He hurts, Adrian. I'm not sure how to help him," I admitted sadly.

"The first step was letting him know we're here. Now we just have to wait for him to realize that he can actually lean on us. He'll come around," Adrian said, seeming confident enough. "Preferably before the Eternium, and hopefully with less blood next time."

Even though the worry didn't really fade, I trusted him and his judgment. I tried not to think about it. Fallon and Adrian began moving about the kitchen, far more in sync than you'd think, considering that Adrian was the only one who ever really cooked.

"Fallon, if you're going to help, at least chop the onion right," Adrian grumbled, eyeing the mess on Fallon's cutting board with dismay.

Of course, that just made Fallon do everything in his power to make the chopping worse.

"I *am* doing it right. There isn't one right way to cut an onion," Fallon replied, raising an eyebrow while waiting for a rebuke.

Adrian merely rolled his eyes, still exasperated over it, before setting a cup of tea in front of me. I lifted it, taking a sip, just enjoying watching them bicker. It was like a play they went through whenever they did anything together. Adrian would complain about something, and Fallon would try his damnedest to make it even worse. With as straight-faced as Fallon was most of the time, I reveled in the chance to see him like this.

"Oh, there definitely is, and it's not the way that you're doing," Adrian prodded, pushing Fallon until the man laughed. It was a soft baritone, one that rumbled from his chest and brightened even his eyes. His sharp jaw and pointed expression softened, and I was struck breathless by it.

It was a melodic sound, an easy one. One that I'd taken for granted.

Kali, tonight's scare, losing Prince—everything. With every turn, there was another problem, and each day suddenly became infinitely more precious than the last. It scared me to think about what the future might hold. I hadn't feared my death, not *really*, in months. I had crawled my way out of the ground for God's sake, but losing *them*? I feared that.

I looked up again, taken by the mirthful expression on Adrian's face, the hints of light behind his eyes that I could watch forever. And I was just as quickly drawn to Fallon's bemused smirk. It gave me that same sharp feeling deep in my chest and made me grin as much as it terrified me.

"I don't want to lose this," I muttered, setting the teacup down on the table.

This had been on my mind for ages. These feelings for them had bloomed and grown, and losing Prince made me realize how precious time was. I feared how they'd react to my feelings for all of them, and even though he'd seemed okay with it in the past, I still worried about Adrian's response to it. But I was *terrified* at the thought of never having the chance to explore these butterflies in my stomach to begin with.

"Love?" Adrian asked, his head tilting to the side. I looked up, glancing between him and Fallon.

Adrian was in his typical kitchen wear now, a floral apron covering his gray t-shirt and light-colored blue jeans. Fallon was as stoic as ever, in one of his many white suits, his curiosity showing in the green depths of his eyes.

And then the words came tumbling out.

"I don't want to lose this, lose you. I was supposed to talk to you all about this in the hot spring. Before—" I couldn't say it without glancing around the room, searching the shadows. That settled my resolve. "I've been so scared, so worried about how you'd react, and how you'd feel that I've kept everything inside." I started pushing the words out even as they tried to catch. "But then I lost Prince, *almost* lost Eirik ... and I-I can't."

I took a shaking breath, gripping my hands tightly together.

"I can't lose you. *Any* of you. I've never been happier than I am here, and I shouldn't be as selfish as to ask for more than you've already given me." But I was, I *knew* I was. I had Adrian, his beautiful smile and the kisses that made me feel so loved. That should be enough ...

"Love—" Adrian started, but I shook my head, needed to get the words out while my throat still allowed me to.

"Adrian, you're the most kind, amazing person I know. You're like the sun, always the one to make me laugh so hard I wonder why it ever hurt to breathe. You've shown me so many new things. So I *shouldn't* need more. I shouldn't. But I—"

But I needed them too.

"I *can't* choose. You're the sun, but Fallon's my moon. He's always there when I'm lost, and I can't even decide my next step. He grounds me when nothing else can, gives me hope in the form of little chocolates that I know mean more to him than gold."

Fallon jolted at my words, his hand going to his chest pocket, to the chocolates I *knew* he kept there. The same ones that he'd shared with me so many times I'd lost count.

"Eirik's my star, the one that I can sit with for hours without worrying if the silence is going to eat me whole. He's the one whose arms always hold me so tight that even my demons don't fight it," I whispered, thinking of all the times Eirik's arms had scared the nightmares away, how softly he'd held me and kept me safe.

Then I reached up, grabbing the necklace that dangled over my chest, savoring the strength it gave me.

"Osiris is the earth that grounds me. He keeps me sane and reminds me I'm *worth* something. He sits and reads with me, always by my side, even when he's miles away in his own past. The silent guardian that I know will never let me down."

With each word, I grew quieter, the emotions that I'd held onto so tightly spilling out. The next one burned, and I almost didn't say it. Didn't include him, but he deserved to be said.

Because I loved him, and I wished he'd been here to hear it.

"And Prince," I choked, the tears finally finding freedom as they slid down my cheeks, leaving cool tracks behind. "*Prince* is the other half of my soul. My best friend, my confidant, and the man I can *never* get back. He's the one I'll regret losing until the day I die, so I can't choose just one of you. I *can't*. I'm sorry."

The silence was deafening, damning, as that familiar mantra came creeping back into my thoughts.

Never make—

But the saying never finished, as frigid hands slid across my cheeks, holding my face steady. At first, I assumed it was Adrian, but I barely breathed before a pair of icy lips settled on mine, the flash of *Fallon's* green eyes stealing what was left of my breath. The kiss was brutal in a way only Fallon could be, intense as it devoured every thought I'd had and consumed me in ways I'd never thought possible.

The contact ended too soon, and I followed him on instinct as he pulled away, his hands still pressed to my cheek, sending those warm sparks that followed his touch to every nerve ending I possessed.

"Never apologize for saying how you feel. N*ever*," Fallon said, shattering the words, breaking through even my panic. I looked at him, shocked at the fire behind his eyes. "We're here for you, Ali. I'm sorry that I haven't made that clear, that I *ran*. We're not perfect, and we're sure as fuck not used to dealing with things like this. But we're here for you, and you *never* have to shoulder your pain alone again. You don't have to choose. We were never planning on asking you to."

My breath caught. I glanced between Fallon and Adrian, catching Adrian's nod. That elated shine in his eyes was unwavering.

"You want me? You *both* do?" I asked, hesitantly, almost too hopefully. "And you're okay with that?"

Hope had never been something I allowed myself fully, even after the grave. It wasn't built into me. And to feel it creep its way up my chest, settling warmly among my heart and lungs, I worried I'd heard wrong.

But Fallon just leaned in, the deep green of his eyes drawing me so close I could see specs of blue and gold.

"*Want*? Want could never describe my need for you, Ali. You've torn down every wall I've built, then laid my new foundation piece by piece with nothing but your goddamn smile. I don't *want* you. I *crave* you. In this life and *every life*," Fallon confessed so fervently that his grip on my chin turned molten, and I made a choked sound somewhere between a gasp and cry.

But I didn't have time to process, didn't have time to note how close Fallon had gotten, or the way his eyes heated, the pupil nearly swallowing the green. Because I was being pulled to my feet, and Adrian was already behind me, easing his hands around me so he could hug me from behind. He did it so slowly, so carefully, that I didn't even flinch.

"He's not alone in that, love," Adrian breathed, kissing my cheek and making me shiver as heat warmed my skin and sank directly to my core. "I crave you too. Your soft lips."

He tilted my head, and I lost Fallon's gaze as Adrian's came into view. His red-tinged amber eyes enraptured me, lit with fire as he leaned forward, his familiar lips only making my mind hazier. They brushed against my own, the soft caress making me jolt before he pulled back just enough to speak. "And those sweet little noises you make just before I kiss you ..." I sucked in a breath, and his hands tightened. "Just like that."

This was not what I had been expecting when I'd started this, but now with them so close? I couldn't get enough of their soft touches, the way they looked at me.

It was so overwhelming that I almost didn't feel the slippery press of dread. My hands shook, and the men that huddled around me seemed to realize that, as their wandering hands immediately froze and they eyed me with worry.

I didn't like the distance they'd created, even as short as it was, but a part of me was terrified of this. Of this raging heat, this *need* I couldn't find words to describe. I wanted whatever this was to continue, but I wasn't ready for *everything*. Prince still burned fresh in my mind, and even knowing it was them, some part of my mind still clung to Ascension Rising and the mocking jeers and comments I used to receive. I wanted this to be a good memory. For all of us.

"I've never done anything like this," I whispered, managing a glance at Fallon. His eyes, still filled with what I hoped was lust, deepened as his jaw clenched. "But maybe we can start slow?"

Fallon swallowed, rubbing his thumb over my cheek before he leaned in again. The kiss this time was gentle and sweet, tasting like chocolate and dripping in care. This was the side of Fallon that gave me chocolates and laughed deeply when no one was watching. It was like he was confirming this as much as I was.

That he was here. That he was *mine* as much as I was his.

"Of course. How slow, love? We can back off, if you need us to," Adrian hummed easily as he set his head on my shoulder. His hands slipped away, and I jolted, reaching down to hold him to me.

There was an ache in me, one that sank to my core and made even my legs shake. I felt the blush before I spoke, but I knew I needed to say what I was feeling, or I'd regret it.

"No," I said, biting my lip, fighting for the right thing to say. Adrian's hands tightened again. "I mean—"

The words caught in my throat and embarrassment had me looking down, away from their burning gazes. But Adrian didn't let me go that easily, the huff of his breath at my neck as he pressed a tender kiss against the skin there.

"Tell us what you want, love," Adrian purred, putting me out of my misery. "Anything."

One breath, then two ...

I risked a glance at Fallon again. His green eyes, with pupils blown wide, held that familiar warmth. Though, now there was also *heat*. His eyebrow raised when I didn't look away from him, my attention now snared by that devious tilt to his lips.

Oh my God, this is real.

I took one more hesitant breath, weighing my need for touch with the incessant press of panic in my mind, and chose *them*.

"Tell us, Ali," Fallon asked, the deepness of his voice coated in a sinful pleasure that consumed me. "Tell us what you want."

He made it sound so easy, and his voice had taken such a molten quality that it had me nearly melting against them. I burned, I ached, and I *needed* something.

"T-touch me?" I asked, so quietly I wondered if I hadn't thought it instead. "Please."

Adrian groaned behind me, his arms tightening around my midsection, pulling me against him firmly, making me gasp and arch as my hands shot up to Fallon's chest to steady myself.

"Good girl, Ali," Fallon whispered, the pleased, heavy tone making my eyes roll back.

He reached up, easily holding me still, with his hands covering mine over his suit-covered chest. He shifted with a kind of expertise that made me blush, his leg sliding between my thighs, enough to keep me firmly between them and drag along that point between my legs that made me tremble. His eyes flared with heat, surging until it was all I could see. The beat of his heart thundered beneath my hand, and I dove into the feeling.

"*Slow*. We can do that," Adrian said, but the wolfish tone of his voice took me by surprise.

His hand ran across the exposed skin above my shorts as he continued to press against me, pushing me flush against Fallon. It was such a simple move, barely a twitch of his hips, but he did it with such precision that it had to be intentional. He smirked against my neck, his lips pulling back as teeth brushed the sensitive skin there, and I let out a startled gasp and I fully registered the hard length that was straining against my back, paired with the one at my front.

I tilted my hips to gain just a *touch* more friction.

Adrian's wicked grin flashed in my peripheral vision. "Fal?"

Fallon's hands, still firmly holding my own to his chest, tightened, and it was like I was seeing his control snap as he leaned forward. He set his forehead against mine as he grunted before easily lifting me. My legs circled around his narrow waist, and I joined our hips together. Adrian supported my back as he chuckled, easily adapting to the move as one of his hands circled around to my front, settling firmly on my stomach to hold me still as the other let go of my hands to reach and thread his fingers through my hair.

I couldn't breathe without pressure settling against that sweet spot between my legs, unable to stop the sharp groan that tumbled past my lips.

Adrian went so stiff behind me that I wondered if I'd already messed that up before a hoarse noise followed, and his hands grew more insistent, more desperate. Then I heard the drop of fangs at my neck.

There was a hint of fear, a warning that my mind had thrown away weeks ago, but it was just that. Brief. I wasn't scared. The sound that had once terrified me only furthered the thunderous way my heart tried to beat out of my chest. The heat spread throughout my body, and the desperate ache grew until I couldn't handle it. Because I knew it meant he was feeling this as deeply as I was, that he was as out of his mind as I was.

His fangs had dropped, and I *liked* it.

"I hope you know what you're getting into, my sweet Ali," Fallon whispered, leaning down just long enough to see that his eyes were tinted red, and before I could blink, we were upstairs. I giggled, breathless, holding him close, almost delirious with joy. He pushed open a door to an unfamiliar bedroom, striding until we reached a plush-looking bed.

I'd always wondered what Fallon's room would be like, and I was expecting something tidy and uncluttered. Maybe bathed in white walls and crisp furniture. But it couldn't be further from the truth. Fallon's room had paintings scattered around every inch of spare space, and splashes of color I never would have expected lit up the walls as the sun might.

It was beautiful, but I didn't get much time to admire it before my back hit the comforter. I bit my lip as Adrian leaned in, my breathing shortening. He didn't push or try to take anything further, just reached up and pressed his hand to my cheek.

His comfort grounded me, and he chuckled as I turned to stare at him, with his hands guiding me. His soft eyes glittered, and the copper hints of the warm amber bounced like sparks off a fire.

"You alright, love?" he asked, pecking my nose with a kiss as Fallon slid next to me.

I nodded and the body beside me vibrated in a laugh, a *laugh*.

Fallon was laughing.

"Seems we shocked her, Fally. She can't even find words." Adrian beamed, winking at the man behind me.

My emotions were in overdrive, the brush of even his hand igniting a need I'd never encountered before. I nodded, and Fallon grumbled something. He tilted my face toward him, searching my eyes. His face commanded attention, the way he watched me making me understand exactly what he wanted before he said it.

"Say it," he challenged, his thumb brushing my jaw. I turned my head, kissing his hand before he could pull it away.

"Yes," I managed.

The grin that took over his face was feral, controlled, and sinfully gorgeous. Fallon stood then, and I was enraptured with the way he moved as his hands lifted to the buttons on his suit coat. He undid each one, taking his time and dragging out each second as I watched him, mesmerized. His smirk grew as he shrugged it off his shoulders.

He thumbed the soft material of his tie, undoing it in a way that made my thighs clench, and something about how he eyed my wrists made me question if he was planning on tying me up with it.

Confused sensations shot through me, but I didn't have to question that long as he set the tie on his abandoned coat and took his spot next to me.

And suddenly I was encased in them, surrounded by the heady scent of my men.

"Now, little love. I seem to recall you asking us to touch you," Adrian said, the words deep, expressing every bit of arousal he kept under control. His thumb trailed along my neck, and he leaned in to whisper. "Do you want us to make you come?"

Fallon shifted until he was behind me, maneuvering me easily until my back was flush with his front. His own hands lifted the rim of my shirt, placing his hands along the skin above my shorts. The hesitant brush of cool fingers made me tremble as Adrian settled between my legs, his palms pressed to the bed beside my hips. His words confused my already hazy thoughts.

"What do you mean?" I asked, unsure what followed and scared to assume.

Adrian chuckled before he leaned back and lifted my leg. He kissed my ankle, brushing his lips against a scar I hadn't remembered yet. He didn't linger, though, each kiss bringing him closer to my core. I trembled when he reached my hip bone, sure his goal was to melt me where I sat, but he just kept moving. He kissed his way back to my lips, sealing our together with all the softness in the world.

"We want to make you feel good, Ali." Fallon's face fell to the crook of my neck as he spoke, the vibrations of his voice startling me. His soft breath made my head fall back, releasing Adrian's lips. "Let us *show* you what we mean. Trust us to catch you."

I lost my breath, my heart stuttered, and I half wanted to pinch myself to see if this was a dream.

"I trust you," I said without hesitating, distracted by the grin on Fallon's smooth, thin lips. That unruly twist was so enchanting that I didn't see Adrian move.

I wasn't sure what to expect, how to move, or how to even breathe. But luckily for me, I didn't have to.

The touches started slow, achingly, *beautifully* slow. Adrian's lips trailed down my neck as he hummed softly. His hands hadn't strayed far yet, trailing up and down my shirt-covered sides. Fallon pressed into my back, firmly molding me between them, his lips seeking mine like he was as desperate to kiss again as I was.

"You feel so good between us, love." Adrian's voice was heavy, the words a growl on his lips.

I kept expecting them to rip apart my clothes or attack, but they moved with a tender grace. Adrian kissed every inch of me he could reach, his tongue leaving no uncovered part of me untouched. When he reached the hem of my shirt, playing with the band of my pants, I lifted my hips, trembling as he slid the jeans off my legs. Fallon couldn't seem to get enough of the sounds he dragged out of me, as each brush was more fervent, more intense. His hands were harsher, more determined, and sure as he grabbed my ribcage, holding me dominantly against him.

They were two completely unique experiences, and each one had me twisted up in a different, equally pleasurable way. It was overwhelming, all-consuming, and I couldn't get enough of it. By the time Adrian had fully settled between my legs again, his lips against my exposed inner thigh, I was incoherent with a near bone-deep pleasure, unable to do anything but hold them and pant.

"You're doing so good, Ali," Fallon growled as he shared a look with Adrian. His words drove straight to my core, and I whimpered as my toes curled. "You're going to come so hard for us, aren't you, trouble?"

He bit my ear, the small nip of pain surprising me as my hips jolted, only Adrian's hands keeping me steady. I just nodded fervently, not even caring what they were going to do as long as they kept making me feel like this. My legs clenched as Adrian kissed my inner thigh again, the brush of his fangs making me gasp as he engulfed me with sensation.

"Are you ready to fall apart between us?" Fallon asked, pushing until I was putty in their arms. "Do you want to know what his tongue feels like against your pretty pussy? He's going to enjoy every second, and when he's done ... it's *my* turn."

A few weeks ago, I wasn't convinced Fallon even knew English. He'd spoken so little, and so briskly. Where had these words come from?

I moaned again, trying and failing to keep my hips steady as I again jolted in Adrian's hold.

He didn't take offense though, his nose skimming my panty-covered core. The deep groan that came from him was like a drug.

"You smell so sweet, love," Adrian panted, his hand beginning to tremble as he licked his lips. I caught one more glimpse of his pink-tinted eyes, lust-filled and needy. "Hold on to Fallon, just like that."

That was all he got out before his tongue pressed firmly against my still-covered core and I choked out a groan as I held onto Fallon's hands, gripping so tight that I nearly forgot to breathe.

"Oh, you're fucking *perfect*," Adrian snarled, his eyes flushing fully red as he tore my panties off before going at me like a starved man.

He ate me, *devoured* me. He was ruthless, his tongue stroking me until I was twisting and turning between Fallon's legs, the hot length pressed against my back only making me squirm more. Each time he dragged me up to a precipice, before pulling me back down with slow, long licks that had me crying out for more.

It was terrifying; it was euphoric, and when my head fell back against Fallon's shoulder as the pleasure grew to the point of pain, I nearly sobbed. Even then Adrian didn't let up, seeming to be lost in his own world between my thighs as he grinned up at me, looking wicked as he pulled up his hand to wet his finger, and at the same time Fallon's own fingers stretched in front of my mouth.

"Suck," was his *command*, his own eyes now that vibrant red, and I did without question, so lost in pleasure that I hadn't realized Adrian had moved his hand again.

"Easy," he breathed, and there was pressure at my entrance. I tensed as Adrian slid a single finger in, easing it in and out as his tongue circled that bundle of nerves that was currently driving me crazy. I bit down on Fallon's fingers, thighs tensing around Adrian's head as Fallon half growled, half groaned in my ear. It was a strange feeling, having something inside of me, but it was one that only made me feel *emptier*.

"That's it, sweetheart. You're doing so good," Adrian whispered before he leaned in close and licked me again, slowly tilting that finger inside of me until he found the spot that had me whimpering.

"Fuck me, Ali. You're driving me crazy, love," he groaned before diving in again, the added sensation of his finger driving me back up, building that sweet ache inside me.

Fallon pulled his fingers from my mouth, his lips going to my neck as he kissed the pulse point there, the press of his fangs making me gasp again, before he reached down, sliding wet fingers under my shirt, along my bare stomach. Adrian moved in tandem, making me whimper as he moved his attention away from that little bud at the top of my sex that was currently driving me mad.

"Do you see how Adrian is looking at you, Ali?" Fallon asked, not stopping the slow descent of his hand. "Feral. Hungry. Like he's barely holding himself back."

He pressed his fingers against that spot between my legs, him and Adrian working in tandem to destroy me, dragging another cry out as his other hand moved beneath my shirt, sliding over my sensitive nipples, flicking the taut peaks.

His whispers brushed against my ear. "He wants to ravish you, Ali. Worship the ground you stand on, so let's give him some more to explore."

My shirt was over my head in the next moment, faster than he probably intended, and a surprised squeal tumbled from my lips as my hands shot out to cover my chest.

Adrian hummed, kissing my inner thigh as he watched me with rapt attention, his eyes glued to where my hands were. "Please don't hide, love," he said, pausing his ministrations, and the lack of movement was enough to get me to drop my hands.

The response was a wolfish grin as Adrian moved back between my legs.

"You're so beautiful, Ali," Fallon said, his face contorted in a lust-filled haze. My face flushed as he nipped at my ear again. "So responsive. I wonder how red you'll go when Adrian makes you come."

The heat inside of me became unbearable, and I trembled at the feel of it. I waited for Adrian to back off again, to leave me shaking in the face of the pleasure that overwhelmed me. But he didn't. He pressed harder, his fingers going deeper, driving against that spot inside of me I hadn't known existed.

"Please," I begged, not even sure what I was asking for.

Fallon increased the pressure at that sweet spot above my core, molding me against his front just as Adrian increased his pace.

"That's right, trouble. Don't take your eyes off of him." Fallon thrust his hips against my back again.

And just as he said, my eyes never left Adrian's. Not until he pressed his finger so deep I saw stars. My thighs clenched, *everything* clenched so deeply I felt it in my bones. My head dropped back, and I cried out, the sound drowning out whatever wicked words fell from Fallon's devious lips.

"You're so beautiful, Ali, so fucking *perfect.*" Fallon's voice was hoarse with emotion as he ground against me again.

"*Please,*" I begged, tears forming in my eyes.

I tried to arch, to hunt for whatever threatened to boil me from the inside out, but Fallon kept a firm hold, trapping me between them in the most delicious way.

It was overwhelming, so close. I was so *close*.

"Now, Ali. Come on Adrian's fingers. Show me how good you feel," Fallon snarled, his spare hand still holding my jaw, cradling my neck. His fangs brushed my skin again, and I jolted at the feeling.

Fallon's words were my last straw, his crude tongue liquid sex on my ears.

The tightness in me exploded, and I screamed their names, holding onto Adrian and Fallon like my life depended on it, my hands pulling and pushing as I tried to get past the fried sensation of sharp pleasure that boarded on pain.

Adrian continued his even, deep strokes, bringing me down to earth with each one. He gave a few more thrusts of his tongue before he gave one more long lick like he didn't want to move away. When I caught his eyes, they were still that vibrant red, but I was too exhausted to comment on it. I leaned back against Fallon, my eyes falling closed as I continued to shake.

They maneuvered me again, settling me between them and pulling the covers over us. Their hands rubbed up and down my sides, their touch lulling me into a comfortable haze. They spoke in hushed tones to each other, arguing about something before their arms encircled me.

And then I fell into a dreamless sleep.

Chapter 22

Adrian

Aaliyah was asleep before my lips left her forehead, her steady breathing like music to my ears.

There wasn't a single soul on this planet that could tear me away from her arms. The evening played on repeat in my mind, the teasing, the joy. The *taste* of her. How her elation clouded my senses with lavender and heat.

I wanted her everywhere. I *needed* her to fall apart in my arms again and again.

I ran my hand against her forehead, that spark that always built when our skin touched just a simmer. Comforting. My head was less achy, my skin less tight, and the rampant need for blood less pressing, though still there. I wanted to sink my fangs into her, not because of the *Call*, but because I knew how sweet it'd be.

She was perfect.

"She's so small," Fallon muttered, his arms wrapped securely around Aaliyah's front like he was intent on shielding her away from the world.

Sharing a woman had never been a thought we'd discussed before, but that changed with her, just like I knew it would. I wished it hadn't taken Fallon so long to see it, to understand this joy. I would share her gladly with my brothers if it meant that I could keep hearing the breathless whispers of pleasure on her lips. Though, I should have known it would take a fight to get through that thick-ass head of his. Just like it was going to be a *war* to get Osiris on board.

Eirik was already mostly there; I imagined it would only be days before he had made his feelings known and we'd have to get a bigger bed.

Aaliyah huffed, sinking further between us with a content sigh.

"She is," I said, so I wouldn't risk waking her. "But strong. The strongest person I've ever met."

And it was the truth, something I felt down to my core as I traced one of the scars across her neck and thought about every time she'd pushed through her own hurt.

Fallon grunted, his eyes growing dim as he saw where my hand lingered. He leaned forward, kissing the back of her head, even as he shook. "I'm worried, Adrian," he confessed, uncharacteristically vulnerable in the way he spoke. There was no bite to his words, no pressing frustration.

Just emotion, clear and numb.

I nodded but still asked, "About what, Fally?"

"The Eternium is close, and you and I both know even without *his* actions, this was bound to be a bloodbath," he said quietly, and I grimaced. Of course, it was going to be. With someone like Sebek, you couldn't expect anything less. "What if we can't protect her? I can't lose this ... lose her."

I nodded again, feeling the same yet not knowing the words to soothe Fallon. The Eternium wasn't something we could avoid. Now more than ever, we had to take a stand there. Our presence was required. It was our only chance to get rid of Sebek, the only way to do this without having to fight the beast ... and Fallon had lost someone before. Lost Aislinn in the worst way imaginable. I'd *known* it was going to be a challenge to get him to realize his feelings for Aaliyah. It was why I'd gone to him in the training room, why I'd beaten the thought out of him.

And now I had to help settle his nerves when my own were just as frayed.

"We won't, Fallon," I finally whispered. "I promise on my life that she'll make it through this."

Because she was everything, and I'd do anything to keep her safe. I'd throw away my own life in an instant if I knew it would save her. I *loved* her. The revelation sent shivers down my spine. If I'd been with any other person, I would have laughed. Love wasn't an emotion I thought would ever be for me, but Aaliyah was good at proving me wrong.

Fallon said nothing for a long while, merely continuing to hold Ali close. Something flashed across his eyes, an understanding, a promise.

"I'd die for her," he said, chuckling like he was surprised to say it. "I'd rip out my heart and present it to her if she asked. But how do we protect her from someone like *him*? If he found her here ..."

He *wouldn't*. Because the alternative was a nightmare. Sebek didn't let us enjoy happiness, didn't do anything but keep us in line like he did everyone else. If he found out we were harboring someone, it would be a weakness he would be sure to exploit. He'd done it once, done it a thousand times.

Killed Fallon's Aislinn. Sent me on a murder spree through London. Chopped off Osiris's hand. Treated Eirik as nothing more than an experiment to throw away.

He couldn't find out about Ali. Because what he did to us wouldn't even compare to what he'd be willing to do to her to get to us. To get us to fall in line.

"We need a plan, an actual plan. And we need allies," I said. "I've been collecting them slowly, but I wanted to focus on her first. On Ascension Rising and her sickness, but they're a *ghost*. At least she seems to be feeling better. I hope it lasts a few more days."

He sighed, "Me, too. Maybe Xander will have a fix or at least a temporary solution that we can use until the end of the Eternium. And it's easier said than done to get people on our side, Adrian. Naturals fear us, and they follow our lead because of that, nothing more. And they fear *him* more than they fear us."

I cringed at his words but didn't disagree. That was the question, the true crux of our plan. Sure, we could say we would fight for Exilium, but there was only so far that thought would get us if no one else agreed to go against him.

We needed foolproof allies, ones who would stand by us even at the threat of death. And they were harder to come by than painite gemstones.

There was pressure at my nose, and I reached my hand up, pressing it under as something warm and wet slid down and over my finger. That peaceful feeling of *almost alright* faded, and again I felt like I'd been struck by a train. I sighed.

"You alright?" Fallon asked, worried. His face had paled as well, and the reality that we had more problems than just Sebek coming for us sank in.

"Yes, just a nosebleed." I shrugged it off, wiping it away.

"We need a fix for that, too," Fallon said, shaking his head.

"One day at a time, brother. Come on, get some sleep. Everything else can wait until we wake up. Right now, she needs us."

She needed our strength, our presence. I hated to throw our issues back on her so soon after Prince, but we needed to get moving to stay ahead of Sebek.

Of our own sickness, and hers.

"Today, we rest," I said, pulling her close and pushing off our worries for just one more day.

"Tomorrow, we plan," Fallon whispered back, but doing the same.

Though, I didn't quite agree with his wording.

The plan may come, but tomorrow? We waged our silent war.

Chapter 23

Aaliyah

I woke between cold bodies with a sense of contentment that I'd been sorely lacking over the last several days. Adrian and Fallon slept easily; Adrian even slightly snored as he huddled closer to me in his sleep. They held me against them, pressed so close they practically crushed me. Like they never wanted to let go.

I couldn't say that I wanted them to, either. They made me feel less like a monster and more like ...

Me.

A blush spread across my cheeks as Adrian ran a soft touch along my wrist, mumbling something in his sleep-dazed haze. His eyes opened lazily, their bright amber mirthful, and the sight of the subtle grin on his lips only reminded me of where they'd been before.

I rubbed my thighs together as moisture gathered between my legs. I doubted anything could have prepared me for that. Let alone with *both* of them. Part of me was still in emotional overload, my nerves singing at the feeling of mouths on me, the whisper of words I never thought I would hear from *Fallon's* mouth.

Adrian pressed a tender kiss where his hand had been, his eyes filling with that unrelenting heat I'd seen last night as his lips tilted as if knowing exactly what I was thinking about.

My breath quickened, and I tried to calm my pounding heart. I wasn't sure what this all meant yet, but I knew it soothed my soul. It was why I spoke up in the kitchen. I could feel it in the way they held my hands, in their stares, and in the emotions that had graced Fallon and Adrian's faces as they did wicked things to my body.

"If you keep looking at him like that, I'm going to assume you want to go again." Fallon's throaty words settled over me as his lips slid across my neck in a soft caress. "You said slow, and we'll go as slow as you need, Ali. But I didn't get a taste like Adrian did, and I'm still starving for you."

My face flushed crimson, and I ducked my head. He'd taken to calling me that shortened version of my name, and it made my insides turn to liquid, a fluttering joy making me dizzy.

That was something to get used to.

Fallon had been the least touchy of the men up to this point. Even Osiris would reach for me before what had happened with Kali. A brush against my arm, tucking a piece of hair behind an ear. Even when he seemed to avoid contact with everyone else in the house. But Fallon? He seemed to avoid it like touching me physically burned him. The few times he had, I held them close to me, hoarding them like he did his chocolates.

That didn't seem to be the case now as his free hand reached up to cup my cheek, pulling my attention firmly back to him as his other arm pulled me to his chest. I had to fight to keep my eyes down. Fallon was overwhelming, making me *feel* things that made my head spin. I wasn't sure what to say.

Could I say *anything* without blushing at this point?

Adrian's hand squeezed a little tighter on mine, drawing my attention. His eyes shone with a vulnerable light. He looked nervous, and not wanting to add to it, I squeezed his hand back.

"What Fallon meant to say is, are you okay, Aaliyah?" The soft shine of Adrian's eyes dragged me to him.

It was strange to hear him say my name, but he spoke it with such gentleness that I didn't mind. I couldn't let go of Adrian if I tried, so instead, I nodded. "I think so. But I want to talk about all of this." My voice was barely above a whisper. "About what it means to you both."

Without the press of lust that had driven last night's emotions. I wanted to hear it with a clear head, and needed to know where we stood. My eyes slipped down to Adrian's lips, his tongue sliding across them in a slow, smooth motion. Fallon shifted behind me, his hand squeezing tighter on my own. As if jealous that my attention was off of him.

"Of course, love. A conversation would do us good," Adrian said like it was the last thing on his mind as he leaned toward me, his motion slow, controlled. Like he was worried about my reaction.

But my eyes never left his lips. How they parted, the sharp breath that he sucked in as I leaned forward. The kiss was soft, much less rushed than before. I sighed against his lips, a small frown settling on mine as he pulled away far too soon for my liking.

"But you need food and probably water." It was a husky whisper, one that had me clenching my thighs again.

Fallon's lips settled on the back of my head, trailing down my neck, teasing me with little nibbles and swipes of his tongue.

They continued their teasing, swiping hands along my exposed skin, whispering sweet nothings. But it wasn't long before they hoisted me up, my stomach echoing Adrian's words. They dressed me, even as I blushed crimson and mumbled my way through half-hearted protests. Fallon carried me to the living room, a sly smirk on his face as Adrian huffed about wanting to be the one to hold me. Then, of course, there was last night's food to contend with, which had been forgotten entirely. Luckily, Adrian had turned the stove off at least.

Now, we sat at the table, talking softly as Adrian mulled around the kitchen. He set a glass of water in front of me, winking with a mischievous smile, before pressing a soft kiss to my forehead.

"Drink up, love. Don't want you to get dehydrated." The suggestive tilt of his lips, and the heated look in his eyes, were enough to raise my temperature a few degrees.

And the way he wet his lips told me he knew exactly what he was doing.

"For someone so well-versed in conversation, you lack subtlety, Adrian," Fallon said from next to me, his eyebrow raising as he mockingly admonished Adrian.

He held my hand in his, rubbing his thumb against my wrist every few seconds.

"Now, don't be a spoilsport, Fallon. Not even you can ruin my mood right now," Adrian said, waving his hands like a diva on the runway, snapping at Fallon. "Now, I believe we have some things to talk about."

Adrian sat and passed me a small ham and cheese sandwich. It looked delectable, but at his words, I found I couldn't take a bite.

So it was finally time. Well, slightly past time, really.

Probably should have done this *before* what went down in the bedroom, when I might have still been able to walk away with my heart in one piece. Now, I'd never ever forget their kisses, the chill of their hands against my skin, the breathless groans and heady smells.

I shivered, and Adrian and Fallon both shot me suggestive stares that only wound me up more.

But they didn't push or try to make me feel uncomfortable as I sorted through my thoughts. Fallon's hand was laid out on the table in an open invitation, and I set mine in his palm-down.

"I'm not sure what all you know, but Adrian and I already spoke a bit about this. He asked me to court him." The memory made butterflies flutter in my stomach, and my cheeks heated just as Adrian leaned over and placed a soft kiss against my forehead.

I would forever remember that moment and would forever have a piece of Adrian carved into my soul.

"I've never really had any expectations for, well, *this*," I started, unsure of what to say.

Just be natural.

"Being in Ascension didn't really leave room for much beyond the experiments."

Nailed it.

"The only other person I've ever felt like this for—" Fallon's hand clenched on mine. The words caught in my throat, like even his name was too much for me to say. "—was Prince."

I pushed them out, ignoring the way his name cracked in the middle, my voice splitting with emotion.

"And how do you feel, love?" Adrian asked delicately, tapping the plate.

He did it to distract me, ignoring a whole other elephant in the room, and I was thankful for it as I grabbed the sandwich, appeasing him with a nibble.

"Like I said last night. I like you, all of you. You, Fallon," I said, nodding toward them both. "Eirik and Osiris. I want to see what this feeling means."

Neither of them spoke, and I shuffled in my seat.

"I've been trying to find a way to tell you guys. I didn't expect you to feel the same way, or, I hadn't—" I rambled, and my throat ached like it was too tight for air to slide by. "I talked to Eliza about it, and in her words, I should just try."

Fallon's hand physically relaxed, and his sigh told me I wasn't the only person who had been worrying about this.

My hand tightened around Fallon's.

"Aaliyah," Adrian murmured. There was something in his eyes that helped me to settle and calm the furious beat of my heart. "When I first asked you for your attention, I *knew* you felt something for the others. I didn't want to alarm you or push you into something if you weren't ready to face that, so I didn't tell you then."

I let out a breath, all the tension bleeding from my shoulders. It sounded like they had spoken of this before, about me.

About me being with all of them.

"You're all I've been able to think about for weeks. The way you can't hide your poker face to save your life. The kindness you still hold after everything you've gone through, the silly way you can't leave the kitchen without being *covered* in flour. I'd be crazy not to feel something for you," Adrian said, conviction clinging to his words.

They were so bright, so real. I almost didn't believe it.

Is that how he'd seen me? The scarred woman who had literally stumbled into their lives. I didn't have time to process it before Fallon's spare hand landed on my chin, and he pulled me to face him. He took a deep breath.

"I'm not a perfect man. I'll never pretend to be," he said, and Adrian huffed behind him, chuckling about being smooth. "But I want to be one that you can lean on, Ali."

Like at Eliza's, one corner of Fallon's lips tilted up, the unpracticed motion seeming a touch out of place but beautiful on his handsome face. It made his blond hair bob, a strand falling down to wave over his eyes.

"Oh, Fallon. You're going to make me cry. Did you see that, love? He smiled again," Adrian said, gushing. He fanned his face before leaning over the back of his chair. It was comically dramatic, and Fallon's eyes closed, a vein popping on his forehead.

"Adrian, I swear to God," he said through clenched teeth.

And as expected, Adrian laughed, happy to poke fun. It made my heart lighter, and I laughed too. When Fallon looked back at me, the malice in his expression was gone.

"Not now, Fallon, we're expressing love. Just let it happen." Adrian snickered before he leaned in and brushed a piece of hair out of my face, a habit all of them seemed to pick up. "In all seriousness, love, we're here for you, in any way you need us to be. So, let me make it *abundantly* clear. We want you, want a relationship with you in whatever capacity you feel you can give. We want to see how this goes just as much as you do. I hope last night showed as much."

Fallon rolled his eyes but nodded. "This goes as fast or as slow as you want it, Ali. I don't promise we'll always have the right thing to say, or that we'll know what we're doing ourselves," he cut in, and I sank into how his eyes conveyed his truth. "But we want this. I realize we may have pushed a little harder than we meant to—" he started, and I jumped.

"No!" I said, cringing when Fallon's eyes widened. The flush on my cheeks grew unbearable, and I sank back down into my seat, toying with the hem of my shirt. "I mean, I don't regret what happened."

They both stared at me with varying levels of amusement and shock.

"I mean, I really liked it ... it's something I'd want to do again. If you want to, I mean—"

I took a deep breath, covering my face with my hands. Then I blushed a bit more. Well, that wasn't embarrassing at all.

"I'd like to further explore what we did last night. I-I don't know what I'm doing, but I want to learn. Just ... I'd like to wait before going *that* far." I tried to reason my way through the sentence, but they only continued to stare with varying levels of heat in their gazes.

Adrian pulled my hands away, kissing each one as he laughed softly. "Want to hear a secret, love?"

I tipped my head curiously, and Adrian leaned in close. His lips brushed my ear as he whispered, "I'm not very versed, either." He looked around like it was some dastardly secret, covering his mouth to hide his mock shock.

"You-you're not?" I asked, and he shook his head, stretching high.

"Why so surprised? I'm saving myself, remember?" Adrian snickered, but his eyes held a familiar shadow. Pain. "But really, it's never been much on my mind. Since my turn, I've feared being with a woman might bring up some unwanted thoughts."

He gripped his hands tightly, and Fallon reached over, settling his hand on his shoulder in a show of support. I could understand that based on what he'd told me when we waltzed.

"Because of the *Call*?" I hesitantly asked.

Adrian nodded.

"But I want to try it with you. Want to experience it with you. So, we can play it by ear, love. For all our sakes. Nothing has to happen, and if it does, then we're happy with that too," Adrian said, that mischievous glint in his eyes.

Goddamn, how did I get this lucky?

I took a breath, looking between the two with an almost shocked kind of reverence, a sudden feeling of possessiveness taking me by surprise. I wanted to stand, walk over them, and crawl into their laps. Brand them with me so that no one would come too close.

"You can't look at me like that, Ali," Fallon said, his green eyes darkening as his jaw clenched.

"Like what?" I asked, inhaling sharply as he leaned forward.

"Like you want to take a bite out of me," he whispered, his breath against my ear. "It'll get you in trouble."

I jumped, not even realizing that he had gotten that close. When he pulled back, his lips were tilted in an amused grin I found I couldn't get enough of. He crossed his arms over his broad chest, and when I glanced down at the table, trying to get away from that heated gaze, I realized the sandwich was no longer the only thing on my plate.

A small, wrapped chocolate.

Fallon nodded toward it when I glanced at him, shaking his head when Adrian looked at me with begging eyes. I wasn't able to deny him looking so *cute*, so when I opened the chocolate, I handed Adrian half.

Or I tried. He happily leaned down, taking it with his mouth. A look of triumph overtook his face as he turned to Fallon with glee, savoring the sweet mouthful. Fallon just rolled his eyes.

"Come on, let's watch a movie," Adrian started, standing and grabbing my plate as he licked his fingers jokingly. The idea of sitting with them, close enough to touch, was everything I needed right now.

A shock of cold brushed against my back, startling me straight as Adrian and Fallon busied around the kitchen, and the savory aroma of popcorn filled the air. I shivered, and my hand moved to my pants pocket, still finding that little red cloth. I brushed my thumb against it, taking in how I felt.

Exhausted, weary, *happy*. Pressure. I rubbed at the space between my eyes and let out a breath. I'd spent the last few days in mourning, and I knew I'd spend the rest of my life trying to stop searching the shadows ... and as much as it tore at my insides, I knew we had to keep moving.

Our lives depended on it.

"Just one more day," I said, glancing out the tall windows by the dining room table.

Our trip to Xander's was in two days now, and that meant that this lull of mourning I'd been allowed to have was about to fade away. Reality was going to come crashing back into our lives, and I tried to soak up the peace while we still had it. Even as the pressure bloomed and iron flooded my nose. I reached up, stopping it, pinching my nose so the others wouldn't smell it in the air. But I didn't turn away from the windows, not yet.

Snow swirled softly toward the ground, coating the earth white. I let go of my nose and took in the scene, pushing down the headache that grew and ignoring the pressure that didn't fade. Prince would have loved to see it, could have watched it snow for hours. I rubbed that red cloth again as Adrian came up behind me, placing a kiss on my cheek. I waited one moment longer.

Before I turned away from the snow.

Adrian extended his free hand, one that was quickly batted away by Fallon, who scowled until Adrian shrugged and walked toward the living area. I took Fallon's outstretched hand in mine, marveling at the little spark of heat that followed the contact.

This was a life without Prince, and though that still chewed at my insides, and I knew I would never look at empty spaces the same ... I still hoped this was the start of something good and that I might live for him.

And for myself.

We were on the third movie of the night when a bright red logo played, and familiar music rang throughout the room. Adrian had mentioned something about 'Marvel', saying that they had the best superhero flicks. That was all it had taken to start on a binge of some of the movies.

We'd already been through Iron Man and Captain America, and I was just as excited about dipping into the next one.

"Movie time? Got the popcorn?" a voice asked from behind the couch, the deep timbre giving Eirik away. I glanced over my shoulder, finding him *and* Osiris standing there.

I was honestly too shocked to speak. I hadn't expected to see him so soon after our conversation at Valen's, but he looked better, less bogged down. The sight helped clear some of the tension that had festered in my chest.

"Of course, you brute. Already made. Now get in here. It's about to start," Adrian hissed, throwing a piece of popcorn at Eirik that swiftly bounced off his chest.

He still looked wary, like he hadn't spent the last day resting. But at least now, he didn't limp when he rolled his eyes and strolled over to the couch. I pulled my legs in, allowing him to sit where they'd been. But rather than letting me move into a sitting position, he placed my legs over his lap, toying with the hem of my sweatpants.

"How are you feeling, *Elskan*?" he asked, his words tumbling into a purr as his eyes shifted between shades of blue.

I noticed Osiris shuffling before he moved, sinking into the seat closest to the TV. I tried to find something to say, questioning if I should just push it off more.

"Don't lie," Eirik warned, immediately throwing off that thought, and I sighed.

"Tired, but good," I admitted, before glancing between Adrian and Fallon with a blush. Adrian turned to me, winking quickly, before looking away again. "How are you feeling, Eirik?"

Eirik huffed, looking at me like I'd gone crazy for worrying. "I'm fine, my *smár Valkyrja*."

He didn't say more, and I didn't push, even as I watched him out of the corner of my eye. He said that, but just like I knew my headache was there, I could tell something was still bothering him. But he did look better, at least enough for me to pull back and not ask again. Vibrant music stole my attention, just as Adrian made an animated pose.

"This is one of my favorites. Thor," he said, as he leaned forward.

Fallon rolled his eyes and groaned. He sat at my head, his hands playing in my hair absentmindedly. Between him and Eirik, I was practically a puddle of goo, melting under their soft touches.

"We don't need to hear about your obsession with Tom Hiddleston again, Adrian," Osiris said, sighing when Adrian gasped.

He picked up another piece of popcorn, flicking it at Osiris who swatted away the flying treat, scowling when Adrian went to throw another. "You'll listen to me talk about my favorite British heartthrob and you'll like it!"

It was an easy joking atmosphere, one that had been missing for weeks. I sank further into Fallon and Eirik's holds, surrounded by them in the most blissful way. Osiris eventually tuned Adrian out, focusing on the movie again. It was only a couple scenes later when the man I assumed Adrian had been talking about showed up again.

"Come on, love, just look at him? Plays a good villain, doesn't he?" Adrian said, pointing out the sharp-looking man.

His long hair was a deep shade of black, and his green eyes held mischief that I knew well. Adrian winked conspiratorially, wagging his eyebrows as he looked between Eirik and Fallon. I caught on to his joke, hiding my grin the best I could while pretending to contemplate his question.

"He *is* pretty," I said, covering my mouth when Eirik's purr deepened into a growl.

He tipped my head at him, his scowl breaking the dam that had held back my mirth.

"Oh boy, it seems we've made them jealous," Adrian sang in a sing-song voice.

I laughed at that, again lost in Adrian's humor. We watched the movie for a while longer, and when the credits rolled, I yawned. I doubted we'd get another movie in at this rate. I was cozy in my spot, surrounded by people that I cared about so much it hurt sometimes. I reached my hand into my pocket, hovering over the cloth there. This was what Prince would want. He'd want cozy days by a fireplace, movie nights, and making each other laugh. He'd want me to smile, and I knew if he were here now, he'd be doing his best to make me do just that.

My headache, the one that I'd ignored for the better part of the evening, had turned brutal, but I just didn't want to move, to disturb this. But the thought of Prince now was like a weight in my chest. I struggled with the doubt and pain I still felt, and I watched the credits as I tried to find the strength to speak.

"Do you think ..." I started, the thought dying as the air grew frosty, and I choked on the words. I waited for my mantra, but it didn't come.

Everyone turned to me, different phases of contentment and tiredness, but it was Adrian who slipped me an easy grin. He'd eventually moved from his place by the fireplace and now sat in front of the couch, rubbing my hand.

"What is it, love?" he asked.

I opened my eyes, searching the room, checking every crevice, before I focused on him. Pressure pulsed behind my nose, reminding me it had never left.

Just one more day.

"Do you think—" I swallowed hard, tears springing in my eyes, making both Fallon and Eirik freeze. *There were no more days left to lose.* "Do you think there's time for a funeral? For Prince?"

He was gone, *gone.* And the only thing I could do now was try to live on for him. For myself. For them. And in order to live, we needed to move forward. We needed to figure out what I was, why I was dying. Needed to figure out why the guys couldn't drink blood anymore, and how to stop the Eternium from turning into a bloodbath.

I didn't want to think about it, but I needed to do this for myself. And for him. Because he deserved to be sent off right, and it was the least I could do for him, after all he'd done for me.

"I'd like to say goodbye," I added, trying my best to stay strong, to keep my emotions in check.

But Eirik just hoisted me up, startling me as I squeaked. He held me to him like he did that first day, my ear to his chest, hovering over his beating heart. His hand spanned the top of my head as he patted it, still rumbling deep in his chest. I fought my tears for as long as I could before a few slipped by. Everyone else was quiet as Eirik continued.

"Of course, we'll send him off the Viking way," he said, surety clear in his voice. "His spirit will find peace."

I didn't know what that meant, but if I had to guess, it was going to be explosive. Bright ... which was exactly what I needed. To celebrate him as he was, the light in when my life had been surrounded by gray.

Adrian hummed his approval. "Hardly a flashier way to do it. I think Prince would quite like that."

An icy hand settled against my back, rubbing easy circles, and I took a shaky breath. I assumed it had to be Adrian or Fallon, but it was Osiris's smooth voice that echoed in my ears from right behind me.

"I'll make the arrangements tomorrow," he said, his tone cracking before his hand pulled away.

He left, his steps even before they faded entirely.

"Thank you," I whispered, pulling back.

The others didn't stray away from me, keeping close as I took a few settling breaths. I didn't cry this time, holding it in. But I did glance around the room, searching the shadows ...

This was a life *without* Prince.

God, would I ever get used to that thought?

Chapter 24

Eirik

People lived. People died. And either way, the only option anyone ever had was to keep moving. Keep fighting until death claimed them too.

I downed my second bottle of blood wine, finishing the vile drink and setting the glass aside. Valen's uninvited guest was still a pain in my ass, even after his body had already cooled. But at least today, after some rest, and an amount of blood wine that would normally keep me going for weeks, I felt functional.

Functional, but *barely*. It was enough to keep me going and help my *smár Valkyrja* today when she needed me most. That was all that mattered.

Aaliyah sat on her chair in the library, a book in her hand as she stared out the window, eyes on the property. She traced the ornate cover absent-mindedly, the shining bold letters saying more than words could.

Home.

She'd grieved, hurt, and broken these last few days, but she continued to live. Even on a day like this, when everything she was feeling had to be so close to the surface. Today was the day she buried Prince, and I would be damned if she had to face that pain alone.

A purr started low in my chest, the sight of her nearly dragging me to my knees. Such strength, such beauty, such kindness that the world didn't deserve.

She turned, hearing the indistinct sound of my beast as she faced me from where I stood in the doorway. The room was dimly lit, the smoldering embers of the dying fire in the fireplace making her glow. Her lips curved, showing a smile that was as genuine as it was devastated, and I huffed as I marched forward with my beast jumping behind my eyes.

Mine, he called.

He wanted nothing more than to touch her, to see her. To make sure she was safe. The same need pushed me forward until I was standing in front of her. She wore a soft blue dress, moving away from the expected black, and her reason for it was enough for me to do the same. Prince wouldn't want to see her wearing something so dull, something that didn't excite, she'd said. So, that was how I'd ended up in a navy suit of my own, tolerating the constraining fabric if it meant it would help to make this day less painful for her.

She gazed at me, hesitance lighting the deep violet of her eyes, making it seem like her soul was peeking through them.

They were soft and inviting, vulnerable, and I moved behind her on instinct. I didn't think before doing it, just *did* as I reached out, threading my hands through her long white hair. The silky strands gave, and I fluidly braided it for her.

Giving her armor, as my sister Tove used to say.

Pulled back like that, away from her face and exposing her high cheek-bones, she fully matched what I already knew was her soul. My brave Valkyrie. I leaned over her then, wrapping my arms around her from behind, engulfing her. I'd say it was because of the prowling nuisance behind my eyes, but this was all me. I tipped my head, pulling in a lungful of her sweet lavender scent as she leaned in close.

"We can wait," I said, brushing my cheek against hers, burning my scent into her.

If she needed the time, I would get it for her, no matter the consequence. Xander's meeting be damned. She would get *whatever* she needed because I couldn't bear the thought of her in pain like this any longer.

But she just raised her hand, gripping my forearm tightly as she took a few settling breaths.

"No, we can't," she said, tilting her head back enough to catch my gaze. "We've waited too long already to get back to it. Whatever's wrong with me isn't going to wait for me to mourn. Ascension won't wait. The Eternium won't wait ... We have to do this now. Or else I won't get the chance to do it at all."

Such sound logic, and I wanted to deny her, to say we could do whatever the fuck we wanted. But there was wisdom in her eyes, as much as there was pain. And I sucked in another lungful of her scent, noting the paleness to her skin, and how even now she shook, hiding a headache from me with sharp precision.

As much as I wanted to be her savior here, she was right. The blood Osiris had given her hadn't been the miracle cure I'd hoped it would be. Instead, it was a Band-Aid for the problem that was still there.

"I'll be okay," she said, shaking her head.

Her voice cracked, but she didn't lower her eyes, even as they flooded with tears. I held her a little tighter, letting my purr wash over us. I would be by her side for as long as she needed me. Be the rock she could lean on, one that would weather whatever storm came our way.

I didn't say she would, or that she wouldn't. She was sure of herself at that moment, and I stood behind that with her. I rose fully, tightening the loops of her braid.

"Are you ready?" I asked, and she hesitated a moment.

She looked around the room, then back at the book that still sat in her hands. *Home.*

"Can you give me a minute? I just ... need to prepare for this," she whispered, opening the book to the first page.

She traced the ornate words, easing over the ink. I nodded and leaned down to place a chaste kiss on her temple, reveling in the way my lips sizzled against her skin. I didn't linger, already moving to set my forehead to hers. We breathed each other in for a moment, and when I was sure she wasn't going to fall apart, I pulled back.

"Of course. I'll make sure everything is ready. One of us will come get you," I said.

I didn't want to leave her here alone, but I understood it. I'd been much the same after Nero's death. We'd pulled him off the pyre in Russia, but that had been the straightforward part. We'd moved his body to Rome, to our family crypt, before the sun rose on the next day. Then days went by, weeks, most of them I couldn't even remember as I spent most of my time as a beast.

It wasn't until months later that a letter arrived in the mail. Milo King, the Selkie Eternal, and one of Nero's best friends had reached out, asking if he'd be ready for their yearly trip.

It was then that it had hit us, that it really sank in that our brother was gone.

At that moment, faced with a death I didn't believe had happened, my own company was the only thing that had grounded me.

And when the funeral happened, it was my brothers by my side. Lighting an empty boat on fire to send Nero's soul on. It was us, for the first time, silent by the steady waters of the lake on our territory. It was the Vivas Crypt, and the last time it'd truly felt whole. We'd watched that raft burn and burn until it was only embers, and the sun was peeking over the horizon. Only then did we leave, with Milo staying behind through the day and well into the next night until the boat finally sank.

And Nero was put to peace.

"Thank you, Eirik. For remembering him with me," Aaliyah said, drawing me back to her. "For understanding how much this means to me."

I knew more than she realized and had felt it just as deeply. So I would be whatever she needed.

"We're with you, Aaliyah," I promised, my face shifting, contorting into sharp points and jagged teeth as my beast slid forward. There was an ache in my chest, one that grew painful at the partial shift. I hid it as I turned to walk away. "**Always with you.**"

CHAPTER 25

FALLON

The last funeral I'd been to was Nero's, and I'd hoped, naively, that it would be my last. But that was a fool's wish, and even though I didn't know Prince, I mourned him.

I'd mourn anybody who got the chance to experience Ali's light, only to lose it. And Prince deserved it most of all. He'd kept my girl safe, kept her spirits up through the worst time in her life, and for that, I would always thank him.

I walked across the snow-covered ground, through the thick trees that had now all lost their leaves, and toward the gravestones that sat on our property. I felt like shit—walking shit, to be exact. Everything in me hurt, and my stomach twisted, rolled, and raged.

It'd gotten so bad that I'd hunted down some fresh blood from our local clinic. And even that now tasted like ashes.

But I kept walking anyway because today wasn't the day for my bull-shit. Whatever my body had going on would just have to fucking wait. One step, then another, moving slowly toward where the ward that protected our home now sat. To make sure the newest addition had gotten here alright.

It had been a rush order, but the money paid was well worth it. Aaliyah needed it to find peace, and I'd do anything to give that to her. My hand settled over my breast pocket on the chocolates that I had stowed away there. I'd grabbed extra for today and had been more blatant with my placement of them around the house, especially in the library. Even knowing that Adrian would have found a few.

Especially knowing he'd left them alone for Ali.

I walked into the clearing, brushing a light dusting of snow off my suit coat, and to my surprise, it wasn't empty. Eirik was standing guard by the tree line, leaning against a tree. Adrian fidgeted next to a cleanly placed new marble stone slab.

And Osiris ... Osiris was sitting next to Nero's grave.

His appearance shook me to my core in a visceral, *wrong* kind of way.

I was still furious with him about Kali, to the point where I questioned our family. I was still shocked by the sight of him absolutely doused in blood, standing in the middle of our game room. I was furious that he ran after the debacle with Valen three days ago.

Fuck, I was furious that he had decided now of all times to break down when Ali *needed* us.

That hypocritical thought was all that kept me from throwing myself at him and spilling his blood all over these beautiful graves. But that had been me as well after Ali had nearly died at the hot spring. I looked at the man plastered across to the ground, and I knew he carried that guilt.

He appeared broken, borderline feral, and when I caught his gaze, I saw my own in it. The day Aislinn died. Desolation, guilt, acceptance.

And a death wish.

He had a similar expression when Nero passed, but now it was hard to even find Osiris in his opposing blue eyes. As quickly as the anger at seeing him came up, it faded, and I cursed. He sipped his drink, which smelled much stronger than anything I thought we had. Something that would take the edge off even for a Natural.

For a second longer, his guilt followed me.

Aaliyah had said that he was taking everything on his shoulders, and at the time, I hadn't really understood. He was Osiris, our elder, the one we all looked to when we needed help because he *always* knew what to do. He'd spent lifetimes learning and preparing. So he *couldn't* break, not like this. Nothing was too much for him.

Until it was, and we were left staring at a husk that I swore used to be my brother.

"How did we let it come to this?" Adrian asked softly.

"He was like this when I got here," Eirik sighed, the end of his sentence muddled with a melancholy growl that ended with a cough. For how much better he looked, it was obvious whatever happened at Valen's was still affecting him. "I came to make sure everything was ready. Aaliyah needed some time alone."

Which meant we had until then to get this sorted out. Osiris looked like he'd just stumbled out of hell. His suit was torn like he'd been in a fight, his hair pulled and tattered.

"Fucking Christ," I muttered, taking a step toward him. Adrian gave me a look, one of worry and curiosity, though he didn't stop me. "Hey, asshole, wake up."

Adrian choked behind me. "Fallon—" he started, but I ignored it, reminded of a talk with Nero that felt like a lifetime ago.

You know, Fallon, violence is never the answer. He'd worn that typical roguish grin as he prepped for a fight, one I was all too pleased to give him. *But it is a question, and the answer is yes.*

It may not exactly fit here, but I was sure as fuck going to make it. I wasn't good with words, and I wasn't about to pretend to be. But I *was* good at fighting, and Osiris needed a fucking fight.

"I know you hear me, Osiris. Pull yourself out of this shit, and fucking look at me," I ordered, yanking him to his feet. "Aaliyah needs us today. Needs *you,* so wake the fuck up."

Before I promptly head-butted him.

My head throbbed, my nose flooding with blood from the force of the hit, but Osiris did stagger, blinking a few times before he looked at me like I was trash. The anger in his eyes flared, and I was glad to see it over the numbness.

"Good," I said evenly, letting go of his suit. I even brushed it off. "Talk."

There was silence for a moment before Eirik moved, leaning forward but not stopping me.

"Fallon—" Osiris began.

I hissed, snapping in his face. "No, no Fallon. No *brother.* No *not today, I'm being a bitch.*" The harsh words seemed to sink past Osiris's foggy mind as he glanced at each of us. "Talk. You don't have to say everything, but you're giving us something. I'm not watching you fucking die because you don't know how to use your words."

There was another beat of silence, and I wondered if Osiris was going to run. He was still and unbreathing, looking a bit like a corpse.

He glanced down at his hands, flexing them, staring at the tattoo marking his skin and the thin white lines that had yet to fade. The change was instant, his eyes softening as he glanced back toward our home, where Aaliyah still was.

"Cowardice is the making of a weak man, but his strength can be found in his conviction," Osiris said, quoting one of Nero's many sayings.

He closed his eyes, and when he opened them, his pain was pressed firmly behind a wall. He seemed less broken, if only for a moment.

"I will speak of the past. But let me say this first," he said, and I nodded begrudgingly. "I'm sorry. I'm sorry for not telling you of Kali and for getting Nero killed. I'm sorry that I didn't listen, that I *don't* listen. You're my family, the only one I've ever had, and I can't stand the idea of you being hurt. I know I've not gone about it right, but that's all I've ever wanted. Your safety, your happiness."

Silence. I was too shocked to speak. I had never heard Osiris apologize. Not like that.

"The other evening, in the library, I'd just returned from culling the rest of Crustava's pack. Kali had been there, to further push her desire for me to Challenge. She's the reason the ward was torn, why Crustava got in without me realizing it," Osiris said, sitting straight, and for once in his goddamned life *telling* us something that he damned sure would have kept to himself.

"So that was the blood," I said, and he nodded. "Will there be consequences to this?"

"I doubt we'd face Retaliation. He wasn't high enough on the board to have any allies that would seek it, not against us. But it may sway our favor with the other Eternals."

His honesty was a breath of fresh air. God damn, we were having a conversation. Nero would be proud.

"I'm sorry I failed you."

Ah, and there was the part that still needed to be fixed. Fucking dammit. Failed? All he'd ever done was protect us. He'd found us after we'd been turned and dragged us kicking and screaming into this Crypt. Because it was the family we *made.*

"You didn't fucking fail us, Osiris," Eirik snarled, voicing exactly what I'd been thinking. "You led us, you saved us, and you've been there through everything. You stumbled, you bastard, but you did *not* fail. We're alive. So pull your head out of your fucking ass. You're the Kingslayer, *Rex interfectorem,* a man who has made even the most powerful foes tremble."

It was Adrian who coughed next, his expression unusually serious.

"You have spent hundreds of years protecting us, Osiris. It's time for us to do the same. We're just as much to blame for never helping lessen the burden," he said cautiously like he was worried about poking a beast.

I rolled my eyes and glared at Osiris until he turned toward me again. Surprise rolled in his eyes.

"And you're our brother. That means we're here for each other. Got it?" I challenged.

Silence followed for another beat. Then he laughed. Osiris's head tipped back, and a shallow laugh filled the air. I hadn't seen something like that since Nero.

"Never ones to mince words," he said, looking between us all. "Well, what do you want to know?"

He'd locked away what had to be centuries of built-up emotion but didn't cower. His back straightened, and the press of his *Charm* filled the air, something he likely didn't even realize.

"Besides Kali, who else do we need to be worrying about?" I asked.

"Darius The Great," he replied instantly. "He's—"

The words caught, and Osiris's jaw snapped shut.

"Kali mentioned him. The Mythic Eternal, right?" Adrian pressed his lips in a small frown as the Collector came forward.

Mythics were such an odd strand of Naturals. They were the one-offs, races that had so few people they were better off just banding together under one name. I'd only met a few that carried the title. Minotaur, Griffon, and Sphinx. There were others, but none that I recalled off the top of my head, especially not when Osiris trembled, his hand going to his wrist on instinct, covering the ink.

"Yes," Osiris confirmed, swallowing hard.

Osiris didn't cower in the face of gods, yet this one man caused such a reaction. Whatever happened had scarred him so deeply that it had followed him through lifetimes. I'd known his past was an ugly one, a bloody one. But how far that went hadn't really sunk in until now.

"They hurt you badly, didn't they?" I asked abruptly, and Osiris flinched so hard he nearly came out of his skin.

It was so fucking odd to see. In the entire two hundred years I'd known him, Osiris had been nothing if not calm, collected, and fucking *terrifying.* Even for me, and I was family. Seeing him so open and vulnerable was shock-inducing. And part of me realized it was my fault. After Nero died, we each did our own thing to cope, and while Adrian and I were better at it than he and Eirik, Osiris was best at masking. I saw now how his tics got worse the more years we spent without Nero.

"Yes," Osiris said, eyes falling closed. "I spent many of my human years in their company. Death was a pleasant surprise after my time there."

Silence, and then I stood. Osiris's shoulders deflated a bit, his spare hand going to his face like he was reliving torment.

"You're not a pet, Osiris." The words sounded hoarse on my tongue. "You're the best fucking man I know. Now act like it. You're not keeping things bottled up anymore. None of us are."

Eirik's growl grew savage in the background, and I shot him a withering glare.

"We don't have to all share today, you idiots, but we *will* be sharing. We're a family. It's about time we acted like one. You talk to us, and you confide in *us*. Do you want to know why? Because the woman who is currently in our house, who's leaning on us for support right now, told us what happened to her. She had more balls than every single one of us. We never used to have this problem when Nero was around, and if he were here, he'd be smashing fucking heads."

I didn't scowl at the thought of Nero, nor question why this had to happen to us. For the first time since his death, I truly smiled while thinking of him. "But he's not. So we need to do right by him. Need to do right by Ali. And now do right by Prince. Isn't that right, Adrian?"

Adrian blinked once, then twice, before his face split into a grin.

"Right," he agreed, walking over to me. He slung his arm over my shoulders like Nero used to do, crossing his leg slightly. He turned to flash me a grin. "You know, Fallon, I think that was the smartest thing you've ever said."

I rolled my eyes and looked at Osiris again, my withering speech spilling into anger again.

"Don't think this means I forgive you. You still need to earn that," I bit out, and Adrian groaned, pushing away from me.

"And you ruined it. And you were doing so good too, Fally. I almost shed a tear." Adrian brushed his suit off, straightening the fabric. Like the rest of us, he wore a colored suit, a soft brown.

"Now, we go meet Xander tomorrow, and that beast is going to take all we have to beat. So today is for her," I grumbled, glancing again at Prince's gravestone. "Everything else can wait."

I didn't give them any more to say about it, moving toward home. Toward Aaliyah.

I just hoped today didn't weigh too hard on her.

Chapter 26

Osiris

I watched Fallon stalk away, with Adrian following close behind him. I kept my eyes on them as they disappeared into the trees, towards our home. Even after they were out of sight, I listened to the crunch of snow and fallen sticks. Making sure they were safe.

"Come on," Eirik rumbled from my side before he was in front of me. "She'll be here soon."

I nodded, brushing off the cold and the snow that had stuck to my blue suit. I straightened the cuffs of my white undershirt, habitually smoothing the crease. When I'd finished, Eirik looked me up and down before rubbing the space between his eyes.

I worried for him, and even though he hid it, I knew he still felt the effects of the bad blood. But he shook his head as if knowing what I was going to ask.

"I'm fine. Today isn't the day to deal with my shit. If I'm still out of it after Xander's we can worry then," he said stiffly. There was no way I could convince him otherwise, not today. I let it go just as he huffed and looked me up and down. "There, looking more like yourself,"

I hummed. Like *myself*. I looked around the small clearing at the stones that littered the ground.

Like every time, my eyes lingered on Nero's crisp marble grave. The energy of the day, the hint of death in the air. It seemed so close, so familiar, and I supposed that was because it was. Funerals weren't common for

Naturals, but especially for Vampires. The few that were left didn't often need them, as we didn't often die. Not unless Sebek saw us as a threat.

"It's so reminiscent of Nero's—" I started, and Eirik huffed, the indistinct sound cutting me off.

"I know. I feel it too," he said, sighing as he moved to stand next to me.

He eyed the stone as well, something he didn't do often. Of all of us, he spent the least amount of time in this place. I knew he mourned. He'd spent months lost to his beast in his grief, but Eirik had never been one to express it outwardly, the stoic way he handled everything bleeding into even this.

But he looked at the stone now, taking in the ornate lettering that haunted me.

"He'd either be dressed in full gladiator armor right now or that horribly patchy shirt he refused to get rid of," I said, shaking my head at the thought of it. The pinch of pain, the ache that came with talking of him, found me, but I kept talking. "Finding some way to keep our spirits up."

I flexed my hand, my spare fingers tracing the marks on my wrist. Eirik huffed next to me, the sound enough of a laugh to make me look at him. He reached his hand up, brushing the falling snow out of his beard. Though some had already melted and refrozen.

"Or trying to pick a fight with Fallon," he said with a grin.

"Or working with Adrian to *prank* Fallon," I replied, unable not to think of the mischievous smirk he always wore. One of the many tricks he had played over the years. Though, one stuck out in my mind. "Remember the pig blood?" I asked.

At that, Eirik's grin turned feral, and his head tipped back as he laughed, likely remembering the same moment I was.

"Like I could ever forget. It took years to get the stains out of the floorboards," Eirik said, his nose twisting in disgust.

It had taken years to get rid of the *smell*. Eirik's eyes lit with mirth, and I, too, recalled the fallout. The way Fallon had sputtered on the ground, having slipped trying to get to Adrian. And ... it didn't hurt for a moment. Speaking of Nero, remembering him as he was supposed to be remembered. Our brother. Our proud gladiator.

My blood.

"No, he'd be by Aaliyah's side. Doing everything he could to make her laugh."

Yes, that was it. I let out a breath, again thinking of how well he would have meshed with Aaliyah. Nero had been our missing piece, the one who had glued our family together, and I was forced to imagine how beautiful he would have been with her. He would have loved her deeply, as he did everything.

"It's strange. Saying his name had become taboo for us, hadn't it? Saying it hurts worse than any wound I've ever had." Another cause of mine. I couldn't speak his name, and the others had tiptoed around that for years, *decades*. "It's nice to speak of him."

For decades, I had let this hurt destroy me. Had let it tear me down, and by holding onto it, I had let monsters into our home. Nero would be disappointed. He would have already beaten me bloody for holding on so tightly and refusing to accept that he was gone.

This day was for Aaliyah, for the little *lux* to come to terms with her own grief. To understand that we were here. So why did it feel like it was for Nero, too? Why was it so much easier to breathe his name and speak of things that I hadn't been able to voice since his death?

"It is," Eirik finally said before he crouched. His tall frame bent, and his suit strained as he reached out, brushing his hand against the gravestone. "He deserves to be talked about, to be remembered."

I could only nod.

"You're right. He does," I said.

He deserved that and more. He deserved to *live*. But if he couldn't, I needed to find a way to do it for him. Needed to remember him, to let him be remembered.

I swallowed hard, resolved as I crouched as well.

"Are you going to be alright?" Eirik asked, glancing at me warily.

Would I? Could I? I hoped so.

"Eventually, yes," I said, turning my gaze toward the sky as the sound of voices reached my ears. They were a ways away yet, but one stuck out. Aaliyah, her gentle tone betraying the ache I knew she felt. Strength resonated through her barely distinguishable words, and I found my own in them. "One day, I hope to be more."

Eirik looked at me with a strange expression. "More?"

"Someone worthy. Of myself." I stood, looking away from Nero's grave as my hand fell away from my wrist. It burned, it ached, and I longed to cover the skin ... but I didn't. *"And of her."*

I whispered the last words, the old Coptic sliding past my lips easily. Eirik watched me, his stare astonished.

"You were always worthy, Osiris. If Nero were here, he'd tell you as much," he retorted before Aaliyah, Adrian, and Fallon walked through the tree line.

Aaliyah, with her long white hair blowing over her shoulders, her violet eyes pained but resolute. She wore a soft blue dress, and even though she glanced at the stone on the ground with an ache in her eyes that would never leave her, I knew she would be okay. We would make sure of it. Make sure she knew she wasn't alone anymore.

"*Elskan*," Eirik said, stepping toward her.

He was so careful of his size as he reached up, cupping her cheek. Her lips wobbled at his touch, her hands flexing as she took a breath.

Adrian and Fallon surrounded her. To her sides like sentinels, each touching her, providing support.

I relaxed my hand, and the burn on my wrist wavered.

"I'm okay," she said, her eyes falling away before landing on the stone again.

It was beautifully crafted, mirroring the others. We'd spared no expense because the man who had held Aaliyah afloat deserved nothing less than the best. We'd never met him, but he'd known her, and that meant more than any bond we could've had.

"It's beautiful. He'd approve." Her voice cracked before she continued. "Thank you again for doing this."

Adrian wrapped his arm around her shoulders, taking advantage of their closeness and kissing her forehead. She soaked up that strength, even as tears came to her eyes.

"Of course. We're here for you, *lux mea*." Her gaze lingered on the stone as I spoke before she glanced at me. Those same eyes that had pulled me from my agony needed the same from us today. Needed us whole. "You once told me to not shoulder my pain alone."

She nodded, and I stepped forward. Each step mended as much as it shattered until I was directly in front of her. It felt new, exposed as I reached up.

I waited for that sickening feeling of dread to circle in my stomach. Waited for the idea of touch to destroy me, or for Kali's words to eat my resolve. They tried, but I pushed past it, cupping her cheek with a gentleness I didn't think I was capable of. Her skin sparked under mine, warming me.

"We're here to help shoulder yours," I murmured.

She took two steadying breaths, her lips quivering as she leaned into the contact.

"Thank you ..." she said, wiping her eyes, breaking our contact as she shifted her gaze toward the stone again.

Her eyes were molded with pain but sure as she stepped toward it. We let her go, let her process as she crouched as I had only moments ago.

"Just give me a second. Then we can send him off right," she said.

The others joined me, and we stood like guardians over her, as she took in what had taken me years to come to terms with. She eyed the stone, sadness palpable. But that didn't stop her from whispering his name.

"Of course, take all the time you need," I said, glancing at the sky, wondering where we'd be if I'd just been able to do the same.

CHAPTER 27

AALIYAH

It was a calm, peaceful day. There was no wind as the snow fell slowly to the frosty ground and onto the marble slab that now sat next to the four others.

Prince, Nero, and the three brothers the Vivas Crypt had lost before Osiris's turn.

I couldn't take my eyes off Prince's grave, his name neatly engraved with a beautiful flowing script that somehow captured his *exact* personality. Bold yet soft, headstrong but endlessly caring.

It made me laugh as I reached out, running trembling fingers over the ornate letters.

I held back tears as I stood, never taking my eyes off the marble. An icy hand settled on my shoulder, then another. The men that had become my home surrounded me, protecting me as I fought the stinging in my chest and the ache that I knew would never truly fade.

"Is it ready?" I asked, turning to Eirik.

His eyes, today a striking sky blue, said more for his empathy than words could ever hope to. He nodded solemnly before reaching his hand out for me to take. I did, using the moment to study his suit-clad form. They'd all dressed up, their ensembles colorful and bold, making this event grand, and celebrating a life they didn't know. A man they never met. At least, a man I *hoped* they'd never met.

I ran my hand over the stone again, one more time like it was Prince I was touching. That stray thought found its way to me, souring the emptiness of my stomach. Every time it came up, I shoved it back down hard, repressed it more, and begged it not to be true. But when I glanced back at Nero's grave, the similarities threatened to drown me. The way Prince had fought at the end when I asked him to tell me more about his life.

Eirik made a choked kind of growl, pulling me to his chest. My eyes were too tired to cry even as my heart tried to push them out. Eirik just held me like that until I had the strength to pull away.

"You are so brave, *Elskan*," he said, understanding bathing every word in a tone that made it hard for me to breathe. "You will survive this."

I shook my head, gripping his suit so tightly that my fingers went numb. I stood there, caught between freezing and disbelief, before I found words.

"How can you be sure?" I asked, trembling. Just a moment longer; I just had to hold it all back a little longer. Prince deserved a proper sendoff, but that didn't stop the ache. "It hurts, Eirik. It's like my chest's been carved open."

Eirik nodded, his chin settling on the top of my head as his hand rubbed circles on my back.

"He'll always have a part of your heart, my brave *smár Valkyrja*. He will never be gone from *you*. It will always hurt, but this pain will dull. It will fade." He spoke from experience, and when I pulled back and looked into his eyes, I saw tears.

Nero's death had hit them all differently, but Eirik hid it well. Hid it behind silence and grief that wasn't tangible. He swallowed hard, leaning down to rub his nose against mine.

The confession of my guess caught behind my teeth, and as desperately as I wanted to voice it, I held it in. I wouldn't bring them more pain, and if I was right, then I would die with that secret.

My body became numb as a soft pressure built in my head, and I wobbled on unsteady feet. Eirik luckily assumed it was because of the grief, and part of it was. But the pain was there too, and it shook me to my core. I almost told him then that it hurt too badly to move. But I didn't, *couldn't*. This day was for Prince.

"And when you need to feel it again, to remember him? We are here to bring him back for you, to remember him as he was. To *love* him and move on," Eirik whispered, and I barely held on.

"I miss him so much, Eirik," I forced out through the press of tears.

"I know, Aaliyah. I *know*," he said, tenderly kissing my forehead.

He pulled back enough to lift my head, his palm settling against my cheek. I leaned into the touch as he brushed away a tear I hadn't been able to hold back.

"Come. Let's give him peace," he let out a small breath, keeping my eyes on his as he added, "and find your peace as well."

I shut my eyes tightly as I nodded to him, and he searched my face for hesitation before pulling me into his arms.

He *flitted* us a ways away, to a body of water at the edge of their property. He set me on my feet, next to the small boat on the water. Eirik had explained it to me, this Viking funeral, and I agreed. This was exactly how Prince would want to go out.

Each of them watched me, hesitant, but I didn't waver. Not yet. He deserved to be sent off. Then I'd break.

Osiris was the one who stepped forward, pushing the boat into the water. It didn't have a body, but there were other things, small things that I equated with Prince. Shirts of mine, trinkets from Eliza's shop.

And the memories I held.

Eirik spoke low, the twisting curves of his native language lulling me into a peaceful sway. He gave me one more glance, but I didn't take my eyes off the boat. I could only nodded.

His jaw clenched, and the four of them reached out, each snapping in turn. The boat went up in flames.

The burning embers fought the cold of the winter air, dancing defiantly just like Prince would have. There was a brush of cold that I knew to be Red, as even he came to see Prince off ... I covered my mouth with my hand and choked on my breath, on the cry that slipped up my throat. Eirik pulled me to his side, and Fallon grabbed my free hand. Adrian came up behind me, and even Osiris touched me with his hand on my shoulder.

Tears flowed as I sobbed, unable to watch as the flames slowly dwindled. Knowing it fizzled out was like saying goodbye for the last time. I didn't *want* to say goodbye. It was never supposed to be like this.

"I'm sorry, Prince. I'm so sorry," I said, letting everything out, laying myself bare.

But it wasn't enough. It wasn't what I wanted, what I needed. So I placed my hand over my chest, my entire body shaking as I placed my pinky and ring finger down over my thundering heart.

"You're my *forever*," I cried, lips trembling, body revolting as my stomach turned. I watched that boat again, the embers that continued to die out. "*I love you, forever.*"

That was it. I sobbed, I broke, and I desperately sought to rebuild myself in a way Prince would be proud of. Hands continued to reach for me, trying to bring me peace that felt millions of years away as I screamed and *breathed*. Everything spilled out, past the pain and the ache, past every memory I'd regained of him and his beautiful, crooked smile. I took comfort in the touches that grounded me, took comfort in the chill that I knew wasn't Prince, as even Red mourned with me.

Because I would always struggle with this, would always search the shadows for someone who was no longer there. Would always be desperate for the comfort of a man that was no longer mine.

But at least now, one of us was at peace.

CHAPTER 28

FALLON

For the first time since the incident at the hot spring—hell since the incident with Kali—our house finally bled something other than tension. Things were back to tentative peace, at least for now.

It was a peace that was taped back together, holding on by a brittle thread that was still smoldering like the boat on the lake that we'd set aflame yesterday.

Watching Ali fall apart like that had been an experience I never wanted to have again. It was gut-wrenching and knowing that the only thing I could do for her was stay by her side *hurt*. But she'd handled it well, as well as anyone could. Though, I knew at least part of it was a front, a way to push past it. Because today was our meeting with Xander, and today there was no more time for grief. If he didn't know what Ali was, if that didn't help us figure out what was wrong with her and how to fix it, then we were going to have a much bigger problem on our hands.

Because of all the stress surrounding this meeting, and the hellish day yesterday, I'd woken far earlier than normal. The shutters that lined the kitchen walls were still down, blocking out the late evening sun. Something played on the television, the noise muddied and quiet as I walked to the kitchen, hearing the bustle of cookware and the soft undertone of voices.

Adrian was busy at the kitchen stove, with Aaliyah by his side, cutting up some vegetables for whatever he was making. He glanced over his shoulder, continuing to hum a little tune as he saw me.

"Ah, Fally. Just in time. Want to help?" he asked, turning to glance at Aaliyah again.

She beamed tenderly up at him as he leaned down, placing a kiss on her forehead before he went back to his own prep.

I didn't answer, at least not verbally, as I walked over to them. I stood behind Aaliyah, not moving to wrap my arms around her until I was sure she saw me, and even then she still jerked at the contact, before she leaned easily into my arms, against my chest.

"Sure," I said, though I didn't move. "What has you up so early?"

Adrian shrugged noncommittally, glancing at Aaliyah, who grew stiff in my arms.

"Same thing as you, I'd guess. Xander has us all a little stressed," he admitted, shaking his head. Worried eyes traced Aaliyah's now brittle form. She'd stopped chopping, her face narrowed in dread. "Come on, there's still a while before we have to leave. There's no need to have this conversation now."

I leaned down, placing a kiss against the top of her head, not letting her go until she relaxed and began chopping again. I pulled away and slowly began doing as Adrian requested, grabbing plates for the table and picking out a blood wine. The food was done only shortly after, and in that time both Osiris and Eirik had wandered in from opposite ends of the home, with Osiris walking down the steps, and Eirik through the training room door.

"Are we ready?" Eirik asked, looking at Osiris.

I took a second to check both of them. Eirik appeared normal enough, if not exhausted. He'd been that way since Valen's, and though he didn't say it, I knew it was still taking a toll on him. Our issues with the blood wine didn't help, but I didn't know how to bring something like that up. I was, however, pleasantly surprised to see color in Osiris's complexion, his eyes having lost some of that numbness. His suit was pressed, and his hair was tightly in place. Even his eyes looked better as he worriedly glanced between us.

"As ready as we can be. I have the price. Now it's only a matter of getting the information," he said, reaching into his coat pocket. The vial he pulled out was filled with a sloshing, deep red liquid. Sebek's blood, somehow still flowing after all these years. "Assuming he has it."

Silence spread through the room, and Aaliyah hummed, setting down her knife. She turned to face us, her head tilting to the side. "He will. I know it."

I wished I had that confidence, but I could only imagine all the ways this might go wrong. Things hadn't been going our way since she got here. Hell, I couldn't remember the last time we'd managed to have anything akin to good luck.

But Aaliyah believed, and I put my faith in that if only for her sake.

"How are you feeling this evening, *lux mea?*" Osiris asked, his eyes lifting as he covered the deep gouge there from where Kali had dug in her nail with his hand.

Aaliyah noticed as well, humming as she walked toward us, after leaning over to kiss Adrian on the cheek. She sat across from Osiris, and he lifted his eyes.

"I'm alright," she breathed.

Eirik huffed at the end of the table, his lip curling slightly as she chuckled. I frowned as well because even though she said it, it wouldn't be the first time she'd said it and been wrong. The bags under her eyes were troubling, and she sighed.

"I *am* alright. My head hurts, but I'm here, and I'm *alive*. And today?" she whispered, biting her lip as she fiddled with her thumbs. But that confidence never dwindled. "Today, we're going to find out what I am. So we can fix this once and for all."

Fix her *Rends*, and I'd never have to worry about what happened in the woods behind Eliza's house, what happened at the hot spring. I'd only have to worry about others taking her from me, and hopefully soon, even that wouldn't be a problem.

"Love's right, so stop all your moping! Have faith for once, you cynical bastards," Adrian chimed in, walking over to the table with a bowl full of spaghetti.

He set it on the table, a little frilly potholder underneath it so it wouldn't burn the wood. It smelled as good as it looked, and we all reached for it at once, the bickering beginning as it was Eirik who made it there first. Only for him to fill up the plate and pass it to Ali, who blushed, thanking him kindly. I gritted my teeth and glared as the smug bastard leaned back in his chair.

"We've got you, Ali," I assured her, filling my plate and watching as she picked at her noodles.

"I know," she said. "We're going to get through this."

Adrian gasped at the end of the table, shocking Ali enough to jolt as we all turned at him.

"Oh! This reminds me, I wanted to bring this up," he said, pulling his own vial out of his pocket. The diamond-shaped vial wasn't much different from Osiris's, though. The inside sloshed gold. "Forgot I had this. After Xander's, I'm assuming our next plan of action is to find some help for the Eternium and keep looking to see if we can track down Ascension. I found this in the cellar a few weeks ago and thought it might be of some use to us."

Osiris narrowed his eyes at it before reaching his hand out to take it. Adrian happily complied, giving up the vial so he could take another bite of his food, moaning loud enough to earn more than just my eyeroll.

"Distilled High Fae Mana," Osiris remarked, thoughtfully running his finger over the aging glass. "It could be useful."

Hell, I didn't even know we *had* that. Getting something so rare was damned near impossible. A truth serum, one that couldn't be avoided or misled. The ultimate trump card.

"Yeah, with as much of a shitshow as that wreck of a cellar is, I'm not surprised. Not sure how we can use it yet, but it may come in handy. Keep it safe, will you?" Adrian asked, and Osiris nodded, putting it away in one of his many suit pockets. "Good. Now, no more work talk. It's food time."

No one else protested, and the table fell into a peaceful silence, broken up by small talk to keep the air open. Aaliyah didn't like silence, and though before her we used to eat dinner without so much as a word, that wasn't the case now. The bickering started about the next movie night, and what we would watch. Then moved on to the thoughts of a Christmas tree and whether or not we should put one up.

And a gasp, one choked behind a palm.

The sound had us all snapping our heads over to Aaliyah, as her eyes widened. Her hand shot up to stop the bloody nose in its tracks, but it'd already done its damage to the conversation as everyone shot up, scrambling.

I was the only one who stayed seated next to her. I reached out, tilting her head forward gently, trying to keep up a calm façade as my hands shook against her cheeks.

"Are you alright?" I asked, knowing that the answer would be *yes,* even if it wasn't true.

"Yeah, I'm fine," she said, taking a paper towel from Eirik as he fussed over her. She covered her nose, pressing her spare hand to her head.

Her skin had always been light, not unlike ivory, but today it was almost sickly translucent, her eyes harboring shadows. She grabbed her head and tried to force a shaky smile.

"I was really hoping I was wrong—" Another jolt of pain made her gasp, and sharp dread made my stomach turn. I leaned forward to wrap my arms around her. To hold her closer, tighter. She sank into me, shivering. I couldn't lose her, lose *this* after I found it. Why couldn't fate deal us a single good hand, just one? "I think whatever Osiris's blood did wore off."

I just needed *one*.

"I'm sorry, Fallon, I'm sorry," she said, cracking. "I didn't want you guys to worry."

I hauled her into my arms and *flitted* us to her room, leaving the others protesting behind me. I easily slid her onto the bed. She sank into the satin sheets, struggling to keep her eyes open.

Her breathing was labored, her eyes hazing as another wave of pain made her shake. I didn't know what to do, was too panicked to even think of a solution. So I just held her hand, brushing the hair out of her face.

"It's going to be okay," I promised, mostly to myself. "Just get some rest, okay? We have a few hours before we have to leave."

She laughed, reaching out to hold my hand. Her eyes were fully clouded now.

"You know, I really struggled to trust you at first. You were so cold. It *terrified* me," she said, and the confession hurt in the worst way. I tried not to take it to heart, knowing that I'd been cold to her, that I'd deserved that thought. "But if I'd known you were this warm, I don't think I would have lasted even a day in this house without falling for you. I should have trusted Prince to begin with. He knew you all were good. He *knew*."

The way she said it, the broken hollow in her eyes that told me the words were just spilling out, made something inside me twist. It wasn't a lie, but it was something hidden in those words. *He knew.* How did he know?

How could he know we were safe?

I shook as I leaned in, pressing my lips to her forehead. She went about something else, reaching up and pressing her hand against my chest, her pinky and ring finger down. The same way Osiris's hand flexed when he'd cast spells.

"*Forever.* That's what Prince would say," she rambled, rubbing her eyes until they clouded over. It was then that she sighed, lips pulling into an adoring smile. "Love you, Fal."

I was too shocked by her words to move as she continued to mutter. I wasn't sure she even knew she said it. But she had. I'd heard the words and breathed them in.

"Sleep, Ali," I whispered, brushing her hair away from her face.

Before I pulled away, her eyes closed.

"I love you too, trouble," I said, unable to keep it in.

And I stayed by her side, even as the others walked in, worry clear in their gazes. I wanted to tell them what she'd said and prod about that curious comment that suddenly seemed so large. But now wasn't the time, and if the ache in my chest told me anything, it was that I hoped it'd never be the time.

They didn't say anything, just watched with me. Listening as her heartbeat finally leveled out, and her breathing became even.

We stayed that way, watching over her until the last second possible. Even then, I didn't want to wake her. So I didn't. I pulled her into my arms and walked us out to the car. Her in my arms was a dream, and I held her tight.

This feeling, this love, it would destroy me one day. I knew it would.

Death came for everyone, after all.

So Xander had better have a fucking answer for this. Because I had no idea what I'd do if he didn't.

CHAPTER 29

AALIYAH

Fallon's fingers were cold on my sleep-flushed skin. The soft kiss of his lips soon followed, and I opened my eyes to meet his, still in my sleepy daze. My headache was gone for now, and I breathed in his smoky, earthy scent. He smelled like warmth and cinnamon cookies, and I burrowed a little deeper into his lap trying to chase the pleasant aroma. His smoldering green eyes bore down on me, and his lips turned up in a small, barely noticeable smirk.

"Time to wake up, Ali." His words, soft and melodic, settled on me, and I sighed.

Adrian and Fallon never strayed further than soft kisses and some stray touches, and it was something that I'd been taking full advantage of. I'd never much liked touch, and until six months ago, the thought of it only meant that I'd be strapped to that silver table again, but now, I craved it all the time. The way their hands would brush against me, the kisses they'd sneak in whenever they were close enough. They'd been taking it slow, treating me with all the love I thought I'd never get again.

It was addicting.

I looked around, only now realizing we were in a car, and sighed. My head was currently laid across Fallon's legs. Adrian was to my other side, his thumb rubbing absentminded circles on my hip. Until I remembered why we'd be driving somewhere.

It was time to meet this Xander that everyone was upset about.

I looked up, glancing out the window as the scenery passed by. All the trees had lost their leaves, and the street looked dead and barren as we cruised down it. Though, I was surprised to still see buildings around as we drove deeper and deeper into town. The winding roads of Oakridge were narrow and old, with Osiris hitting bumps and holes the entire way, grumbling about them to himself. It wasn't long before he stopped in front of an unassuming black building. There were no real markers about it. In fact, if they hadn't all been glaring at it, I would have assumed we were going somewhere else.

No one moved for a second, just watching out the window with me. It was when Fallon sighed, sinking his fingers into my hair again, that the others finally moved.

"Better not keep him waiting, then." Fallon's eyes lost their softness nearly instantly.

His face settled into a jarring scowl, one that I hadn't seen since my first night home. Home. *My home.* He looked ready for war, bloodlust eating his eyes. I wanted to settle his rage, to bring the smile back to his face.

"Is this guy that bad?" I asked, bringing my hand up to Fallon's face. I skimmed my fingers across his smooth jaw, and he leaned into the contact. Never closing his eyes.

"More like devious." Eirik's harsh words drew my gaze from Fallon. He was tense, his broad arms exposed, his scars shining along his skin.

"How so?" A breath of a question in the air.

"Xander has been alive for a long time. He grows bored and likes to entertain himself with deals. With tricking people." Osiris's voice was distant. I bit my bottom lip. "He is good at what he does, but he's also dangerous."

Dangerous. Wasn't everything dangerous at this point? I was getting really tired of things trying to kill us, or maim us, or make *a bad deal.* He was just another person that I'd have to worry about, and lucky him he just added himself to the bottom of that exceedingly long list.

"Well, let's get this over with, then," I said, practically crawling over Fallon to reach the door.

Their auras bit at my skin, snaking over me in harsh waves. They were nervous, and it was drawing panic from my bones. I was tired of being dragged around by my fear. Everything in me wanted to know what I was, to learn it, to use it to fix the mess that was my soul. To learn how to control it because I *refused* to lose myself to it.

"Aaliyah, wait." Osiris's desperate words rooted me to the spot, hand on the handle, hovering over a shaking Fallon.

Who was currently digging his hand into the seat of the car? Well, it was better than the suffocating anxiety that held him before.

"You must not make a deal with him under *any* circumstance." Osiris's words held a tone of command and fear. I swallowed harshly, steadying myself. "I already bought his information on your race. But that doesn't mean he won't try to push for another. Listen carefully to his words."

He was pleading with me. I hated hearing the terror in his voice. It made my blood boil. I had to bite back a growl. I wouldn't fail him.

My feet landed on the hard ground as I exited the door. The building loomed over us, no windows lit, even as night fully descended. It was ominous, and suddenly I couldn't walk closer. It wasn't like Audric's, the inviting exterior making me want to go forward—no.

All I wanted to do was turn around and *run*. That thought continued until Osiris stepped in front of me, blocking the building from my gaze, and I now realized that my men had boxed me in. Adrian to my left, Fallon to my right. Eirik an unmovable wall behind me.

The harsh glare of the moon illuminated the stone of the building, and with them by my side, it suddenly didn't feel so daunting.

We walked through the front door, with Osiris not bothering to knock, but the door wasn't locked either. The room that met us was small, much smaller than the outside had led me to believe, and was painted a mellow blue with geometric pieces of furniture lining the space for seemingly no reason. A staircase led to an upper level, blocked behind a black door, and to the left was a counter that stretched along most of the wall with various odds and ends situated atop it. Tea sets, herbs, and ... bones?

I took a step toward them on instinct, separating myself from my circle of protection. The relics of a life lived and lost pulsed a swirl of long-dead emotions, calling to me. The bones wanted me to see them, to touch them. As most dead things did, I supposed.

I hovered my hand over the top, completely lost to the room, to Fallon's hand on my shoulder, and to the sharp intake of breath as a door opened. The bones appeared firm and immovable. Like they were resisting death, even though they were obviously *bones*.

"Direwolf," an unfamiliar voice suddenly called, stopping my wandering hand. It was a deep rumble with a rasping tone that made the hairs on my arms stand, one that jolted down my spine and had me freezing like an animal stuck in fight or flight.

I turned my head slowly, only now realizing how tense my entourage was. Each of the men around me were like harsh walls of unrelenting sturdiness.

The man standing in the only other doorway at the end of the room didn't flinch at their show of power as a smirk flitted across his lips. His eyes stood defiantly against his deep brown skin, a forest green glowing almost unnaturally. He was dressed in a vibrant white suit that was the definition of immaculate, and he reminded me of Osiris in the way he carried himself. Like he was dangerous. Because he *was* dangerous.

This mystery man, no doubt Xander, continued his sentence as if he weren't being glared down with the intensity of the sun. "They're often used for vitality potions, though they can also persuade someone into loyalty."

I pulled my hands away from the bones, keeping my eyes locked on this man.

"They called to me." The words tumbled from my lips, trembling like the rest of my body. I straightened my shoulders, and the smirk on Xander's face expanded. Like he was pleased that I had a spine.

"They are quite striking. I procured them several years ago from a close friend of mine, a Chronomancer. Would you like them?" The question in his voice had me freezing in my tracks. Osiris's words were hard in my ears, resounding through me.

Don't make a deal.

"I'd rather we talked about why we're here," I said, as I dragged my hand into Adrian's.

His hand tightened immediately around my own, centering me. Xander quirked an eyebrow at the action, the smirk still firmly planted on his lips. He stepped away from the door frame, gesturing us inside with a flare of his hand.

"By all means, my lady, let's get more comfortable." He bowed as a delightful host would, but I didn't miss how his words sounded like a threat, like barely concealed energy.

We walked to the room he'd ushered us into, each checking the space as we moved. It was unnaturally warm, like we'd stepped into an entirely different building. I leaned into Eirik, who took the spot to my left. His arm fell around me, pulling me close.

The earthy smell of old books and alcohol flooded my nose, and I had to reach up to cover it as my eyes watered. The room, an office of sorts, had a single desk by the back wall, placed in front of a steadily burning fireplace. In front of it was a single couch, the red leather squeaking as we all sank down into it. The intensity in the air only increased as Xander moved, running his hand behind our heads.

"First matter, where is my payment?" Xander sat behind the tall desk, staring as if we were being judged and already found guilty of a crime we didn't commit.

Xander's gaze bore into my skin as Osiris pulled a small vial from his suit jacket, the contents a sickening red. He tossed it to Xander, the man easily catching it from the air. It was the same one he'd shown at dinner tonight, and I knew immediately that it was blood. *Powerful* blood. Xander looked at the vial with barely contained glee. The lid came off with a sickening pop, and he dipped his pinky into the foul-looking liquid.

When it settled on his tongue, I had to resist the urge to gag. It screamed dangerous. *Tainted.* Xander's eyes lit up, a mix of fury and amusement.

"This is old, *very old*." The words were so fierce they could have burned the hair off of my arms.

"Unfortunately, that's not my problem." Osiris's deep voice echoed, carefully leveled.

I barely picked up the hitch in it from his place next to me. I hadn't noticed that he had taken the spot to my right until now. It was like I was drowning for an entirely different reason now. I should be worried about Xander, so why did this seem so much more important? I shook my head, tensing when Osiris leaned farther into me.

It was an anxious few seconds as we stared at Xander, and he stared right back at us, his eyes searching and probing before his face split into a deep grin. My heart skipped as he capped the blood and settled it on his desk.

"You clever, old *vrykólakas.*" I half expected him to jump over the table and strangle one of us, but he kept smiling, his gaze less harsh. "You know, I typically expected dinner and a bit of wooing before I let someone *fuck* me."

But all the more calculating.

"It's been a while since a deal was turned on me. Bravo. Now, I would guess that the person in question from our last conversation is this lovely lady?"

Osiris nodded his head, his hand tightening almost painfully around mine.

"Well then, *a deal is a deal*." I flinched at the calculated force in his eyes. The words were narrowed and pointed. "I suppose an introduction is in order. I am Axandre. But you may call me Xander. So, dear *Aaliyah*, what can you tell me about you?"

Chapter 30

Unknown

It was a subtle thrumming of pain that woke me, a consistent ache that wouldn't give way. But as my senses came to me, and I slowly became more self-aware, that ache turned into an itch, then into a *burn* that extended over every inch of my skin, like it was peeling back, flesh ripping away from the bone.

Fear like nothing I could imagine made me shake and cry out, which only made me hurt that much more.

Where was I?

Who was I?

Only darkness greeted my silent question, enveloping me like it might hold the answer if I only screamed loud enough. But it didn't, and the endless umbra continued to taunt me as I lay there.

I tried to lift my right arm, shocked at how difficult it was, and was met with a wall, then another to my other side, and a file barrier above me. I was confined, the air stale and bitter, and suddenly that was worse than the pain. *No.* My body strained under the stress of my arm lifting, and I shook with the effort to keep it up. It fell, landing on my chest with a soft thud. The sound echoed, confirming both my suspicion and fear.

I was in a box.

Caged. A creeping sort of panic built in my lungs, coming out like a broken cry. Was I scared of small spaces? I couldn't seem to remember, but with how I shook at the thought, I would imagine that I was.

Was I going to die here? Completely lost, unable to so much as move. What would get me first, hunger? Thirst? Or would I run out of air?

Air.

I paused for a second, my nails gripping the surface beneath me. It was cold against my fingers, the sensation like running my hand against sandpaper. The revelation hit me hard, and as though my sanity wasn't already taking a hit, I realized...

I wasn't breathing.

I pulled in a breath, as I'd done when I'd woken up. The second one since I woke. How strange. Weren't you supposed to breathe? I would have sworn you *died* if you didn't breathe.

What the fuck was I?

But I had no idea. I couldn't remember how I'd gotten here or the means of my confinement. I couldn't remember what I looked like or even my *name*. Were there people looking for me?

A pressure settled over me, coming on so suddenly it made me sick. It pounded at my skull, seeming to thrum as though it was alive. It got increasingly more insistent, like it was waiting for something. Like it *knew* something I didn't. I tried to move again, forcing my arms up, fighting the agony with gritted teeth. When my hands met the obstruction above me, I shivered, the material cooling my scorching skin. It seemed almost less now, the pain far less gnawing, less all-consuming. Now, it was more like a dull ache, and as it faded, strength bled into my limbs.

I pushed hard against the roof above me, and my muscles screamed in protest. When was the last time they had been used? How long had I been here? It couldn't have been that long?

Right?

It seemed like I'd been fighting its weight forever, but eventually, a light appeared before me. The ceiling above me gave way, and the slab lifted. It slid off of the other portion of my prison before hitting the ground with a resounding crash. The sound echoed in the room, bouncing off of the walls before finding its way back to me. A black ceiling greeted me, and several small peeks of moonlight filtered into the damp room. There was moisture in the air that meshed with dust and age.

It gave me a reprieve from pitch-black, one that almost seemed *wrong*. This place ... I shouldn't be here. I knew that so deep in my soul that it seemed ingrained.

If not here, then where? Where did I belong?

The pressure in my skull hit a precipice, and without warning, I was *torn* out of the small container I was lying in.

No. Not *me*.

I glanced down, my transparent hands staring back at me. I was standing now, looking at the unfamiliar room. The room itself was gray, like the color had long since washed out of it. In fact, *everything* was gray. Panic ate at me. I hadn't stood; I knew I didn't. My eyes landed on it, what had confined me.

It was a *coffin*.

The material beneath my body was old, corroded, and the body in it was *mutilated*. The skin was a charred black that seemed to peel off the muscles, exposing flesh underneath. My head was pulled back, my eyes closed. It was like I was *dead*.

That body was *me*. For some godforsaken reason, that much I knew.

My eyes dropped to my hands, still transparent, and I realized dead was precisely what I was. This was wrong—all wrong. I was missing something. No, I was missing *everything*.

I was missing *her*.

Just beyond my current consciousness, I saw her, a woman. It was like she was right there, right beyond my reach. Why did she matter? Who was she to me?

Everything.

That was right. Wherever I was, whoever I was, it was all for her. I longed to remember her face, her laugh, anything. If I never learned my name or remembered nothing else besides her, then everything would be okay.

Another pull startled me, snapping me out of my thoughts. As quickly as I was jerked out of myself, I was thrown back. My soul hitting my body was possibly the worst pain imaginable. I shot up, my charred hands grabbing the sides of my coffin, and the pain hit so sharply I couldn't even scream.

I ignored the pain of movement as I hauled myself over the lip. I emptied whatever was in my stomach over the edge. It was a charred black substance, much like my skin. It was like razors were scratching at my insides, ripping me apart. Digging into my soul.

You okay, Prince?

A voice, tender and loving, washed over me. The razor's edge dulled, and the pain ebbed as my eyes slid closed. I tried to hold on to the feeling that her voice gave me.

Prince. Was that my name? It sounded right, in a way. If it was what she called me, this mysterious woman who was haunting me, then I would claim it. I needed to see her face and craved her closeness in my soul. So why was I here? In this coffin?

I pulled myself the rest of the way out, falling less than gracefully to the ground. The vile stench of scorched flesh and rot met my nose as I pulled in an unintentional breath.

Besides my vomit, the room was virtually spotless. There wasn't a speck of dust out of place. It was immaculate, almost surgically clean, and it left a strange eeriness with it. An aching feeling settled in my mouth, clinging to my gums, the tingling sensation making my mouth water.

Was someone else here?

The cold of the ground seemed to seep into me. The frigid feeling all but forced tremors from me as I stood. I used my coffin as an anchor as I lifted myself up, my legs shaking from the effort. Just to stay standing was a task, one that was becoming increasingly difficult.

Then the pressure again, that same gnawing, haunting pressure. I took a step toward what I hoped was a door.

I had to get out of here. Maybe if I got outside, it would stop. Maybe *she* was waiting for me. Then I wouldn't have to think of her face. I wouldn't have to deal with this alone. She had to be right outside because I wasn't sure what I would do if she wasn't.

Another step.

It didn't stop the pressure. If anything, it seemed to be amplified. The sweet, melodic voice lifted to my subconscious once again, and that angelic tone drowned out all other thoughts.

I can help you, Prince.

But *how* could she help me? Why wasn't she here now? Desperation clawed its way up my throat, and a strangled cry fell from my lips as I took my next step. Pain shot its way up my leg, and agony erupted.

You don't have to stay here with me. Let me help you, Prince.

But I *wanted* to stay. I knew that. Whatever she was trying to do to get rid of me, I couldn't let her. I *had* to be with her, didn't she realize that? This girl whose face I couldn't recall.

The next step was the final straw. The pressure erupted, and pain split my skull. It was worse than before since I knew it was coming. Rather than being wrenched backward, my eyes rolled back, and my body slumped forward as I fell to the ground. I wanted to roar, to rage.

I barely felt myself land, the sound lost to me. Memories that had been forgotten and love that had been lost soothed me, and ever so slowly, something *consumed* me.

Her.

This facility was a disgrace. Why had I wandered here again? Something was pulling me before, I was sure of it ... but hell, maybe I was bored, or just tired of watching everything go on around me and my brain played some tricks on me. Either way, I hadn't expected to end up here. *This place was haunting, even by my standards, and I'd seen some shit. I floated through the narrow halls, the stark white walls giving the building a distinctly sterile feeling.*

If I hadn't seen their 'Experimental Laboratory,' I would have just assumed this was a doctor's office. But the blood that coated that room was extensive, beyond any procedure or even gutting I'd ever seen. It was on every surface, but they made no effort to remove it, instead letting it all drain down the little opening in the floor.

Maybe the posh bastards didn't want to get their hands dirty. So they had no issues torturing people, but cleaning up after themselves was out of the question?

Fucking degenerates.

I needed to get out of here and go back home, where I could brood in silence. I was far too dead for this shit.

I took the last turn, intent on finding my way through the nearest wall when I heard it—the sound of laughing, the kind that ate at your insides. The laugh of someone who knew the one in their sights couldn't fight back.

Acid ate at me, and memories of my father attacked my subconscious. I had to at least see the poor fool who was trapped here. I had come all this way.

I turned and moved toward the laughing, each step lighter than the last. Like I was walking toward my destiny. Which was a load of bullshit. My fate was to be dead, as shown by my miraculously transparent body.

Death's a bitch.

"Bet you like all this, huh? You little freak." The words were harsh, and if I were alive, the man who had spoken them wouldn't have been allowed the privilege of living any longer.

Freak. What a shitty word.

I clasped my hands into fists, stopping at the corner of the hall. This man and whoever he was goading were just around it. This wasn't my problem, and it wasn't like I could fix it.

So why the fuck couldn't I leave? Why were my legs refusing to listen to me?

Bastards.

There was a sound, like someone falling, followed by the softest 'oof' I'd ever heard. Like the noise was being repressed. My hands trembled.

I needed to see ...

No, I didn't have to do anything. I could do whatever I damn well pleased, and this wasn't it. I had other things to do, like bothering my brothers and making some paper flutter or some shit.

I turned, intending on leaving, regardless of my body's protests.

Until I heard her.

"Please, Doctor Castillion."

The singsong tone of her voice seemed to calm every nerve in my body. What was this peace? Guilt made me feel like an utter piece of shit because I was in absolute heaven from hearing her voice while she was pleading with this man.

A man who should be dead.

"Please what? You should be happy that I can't do anything else to you." Castillion, one of the doctors in charge of this fucked-up place if I recalled correctly, laughed. His voice grated at my already shot nerves.

He was a wiry little shit, barely standing chest-high to me. It made sense that someone like him would take out his frustration on someone else. Someone who couldn't fight back. And those eyes. He had the coldest fucking green eyes I'd ever seen, and I'd fought Fallon on a bad day. This Castillion was the exact type of man I hated. I wanted to tear out his throat, then bathe in his blood. String him up so he'd have a front-row seat as I destroyed him and everything he loved.

Or better yet, fight him for his life and watch as he realized he was outmatched. That I was toying with him and that his death was inevitable.

Instead, I was fucking useless.

I'd never been useless in my life, not even as a boy had I been brought to my knees. Yet here I was, dead as those that I sent here before me. Fucking pathetic.

A whimper was the only response Castillion's target gave. Barely audible under Castillion's scoff.

"See you tomorrow, Glass. Get excited. Natalia has big plans for you." They should have been the last words he ever spoke. How dare he talk to them like that?

Why did it bother me so much?

I was all for the underdog. Hell, I'd been one myself at one point. Not for long, but long enough to gain backing. Recalling the days before, the days of fighting were all that settled me now.

I waited for what seemed like an eternity before I turned the corner. I would see this girl, and then I would leave. That would satiate my curiosity so I could leave this place behind me.

This wasn't my problem.

The cage I came upon was small, barely large enough for an animal and nowhere near comfortable enough for a human. My breath caught in my throat as my eyes landed on the bed that occupied it. The glass walls made it easy to make out the figure.

Her back was to me, her hair as white as snow against the gray of her bedding. There was a moment just as she came into view when I would have sworn my heart beat. I walked toward her. It was instinctual, and all too soon, I was standing by her bed.

She seemed to pulse, her body calling to me. Everything in me wanted to reach out, to brush the hair away from her face, but something stopped me, something unseen.

Like something terrible would happen if I touched her.

She shifted under my unrelenting gaze, but I was too fucking selfish to leave. It wasn't like she could see me, anyway. As she turned, her eyes landed right on mine. Their brilliant violet hue almost glowed in the dim lighting of the cell. They were breathtaking and exotic, and they were staring right at me. Her eyes were wide with wonder, almost hope.

But as soon as it appeared, it faded. She sat up, her gaze staying steady on my own as she stretched her hand out to me. I flinched away from her, avoiding the touch at all costs.

"Let me help you." Her voice was gentle, calling to me. I wanted to lean into her, to do as she said. And she was still looking at me.

Could she see me, really see me? The way she traced where I stood told me she might.

Panic, fear, and hope flared in my chest. How was this possible? Who was she?

What *was she?*

Curiosity spread through me. I had to know her, this girl who had attracted my attention, who saw me. For the first time in decades ... I wasn't alone. I felt tied to her, like something deep inside held me to her side and I didn't dare move.

The frown that adorned her face was melancholic, so I did the only thing

I could. I shot her a grin, waving from a safe distance away. The girl, maybe in her early twenties, managed one of her own. I leaned against the wall, turning to face her while keeping a fair bit of distance between us. When her own lips split into a smile, a small one that wobbled at the edges, but a smile nonetheless, I relaxed. It was the kind that you knew was real, that showed a peek of white teeth.

I pointed to myself before gesturing back to her. Her eyes seemed to gloss over before she leaned in close. Her voice was so quiet that I struggled to hear her words, but I would never forget them. Never.

"My name is Aaliyah."

The memory ended, and as though some cruel God had snapped his fingers, I was back in my broken body. I once again found myself on the floor, clutching myself to throw off the pain that barely even phased me as euphoria raced across my body.

Aaliyah.

I remembered her. God, how had I fucking forgotten? I didn't need any more memories to know that I needed to find her. I needed *her*.

But with the joy came the reality of the memory, what it meant, and the compound that housed her.

Rage licked at my neck, and every fiber of my being seemed to spark into action. I was powerless to help her then, but I could now. *Nothing* would stop me. I would level them, and make sure they could never touch her again. I was fuzzy on a few details, and I still wasn't sure how I got there or how I eventually left. Or anything in between. Let alone how I ended up here.

Regardless, I had something to work with now. Hopefully, the rest of my memories would follow, and then I would find Aaliyah. My Aaliyah, my *everything*. My empress.

My queen.

I would get to hold her, to feel her skin against mine if I ever fucking healed. And that was what drove me to stand again. The room appeared sharper now, everything clear and perfectly lit. Even though I knew in my bones it was still dark out. Everything felt enhanced, a fact that was only proven when the sound of a door closing flooded into the small space that had been my grave. My crypt. The whistle of an unfamiliar tune hit my ears.

Then the aroma, one that tickled at my nose, and the tingling in my gums came back in full force. Then a heartbeat, one that was steady and even. I crouched without thinking, sliding to the far wall to hide like a predator stalking prey. Fangs came forward, and I knew just what to do with them.

A boy, who couldn't be older than seventeen, walked into the room. He didn't even look around as his head bobbed to a soft beat that sounded like it was coming from his ears.

Odd.

He didn't notice me, not until it was too late. I was on him in a flash, fangs sunk deep into pale flesh, the movement primal and unavoidable. His words came out garbled as my hand fell over his mouth. He struggled, but I was stronger than him by miles now.

I fell into it like a lost friend, the bright red blood sliding over my lips, down my throat, coating me with ecstasy and a bare hint of ash on my tongue. It rejuvenated me enough, though, and within moments, I no longer felt the pain of my injuries. When I finally pulled away, I doubted there was any blood left in his body.

I pushed down any guilt as his corpse hit the floor.

It was only now that I noticed that my skin, once charred black, was a light olive. It was like I'd never been hurt to begin with. I clenched my hand into a fist and walked surely toward the exit of the building. I'd deal with the aftermath of this later.

For now, I had to find my queen.

Chapter 31

Aaliyah

The room was filled with the eerie crackle of a roaring fire. Xander continued to watch us, his sharp eyes unyielding as he waited for me to speak. But I was too distracted by everything going on, by the harsh contrast of the colors in the room, the rich mahogany desk against the maroon walls. Xander had poured himself a drink, sipping it leisurely as he watched us squirm.

"What do you want to know?" I asked, hands gripping the harsh leather beneath me, unsure where to start or what I even wanted this Xander to know.

He was dangerous, and not in the way my guys were. It was like he already knew the answer to my question. Like he was just waiting for me to confirm it. His knowledge was a weapon, and he wielded it well.

"Why don't you tell me what you can do, sweet Aaliyah?" He leaned back in his chair, watching me with those snake-like eyes. "How well do you heal?"

"Faster than most." The first words slid from my lips.

I choked on the reason, and like he knew, Osiris squeezed my hand. I accepted the comfort, unable to turn him or it away. Xander hummed, tapping his finger on the desk. His lips twisted into a smirk as he glanced between Osiris and me.

"And tell me, what *else* can you do?" His continued smirk made me swallow hard.

I couldn't find the answer, too caught up in the predatory gleam in his eyes.

Danger, *danger.*

"You can do something that no one else can, can't you?" He stood slowly, his hand still tapping at the deep oak desk. "No one else knew what you could be. No one else has been *alive* long enough."

How did he know that? Sweat broke across my skin, and Eirik tensed next to me.

"Tell me, sweet one." Giddy excitement swallowed his words.

"I—" I sank further into the couch as something cold caught my attention. Like a sliver of ice had buried its way into my mind.

"Now, don't be shy," Xander tsked.

Too small, the room was *too small.*

Eirik growled next to me, his entire body shaking.

"Xander," Osiris hissed, a warning, "enough."

Like the spell had been broken, the surrounding fog lifted. Finally, I could breathe, and that sliver of cold receded.

"Sorry, my dear." Xander shook his head. "Today has been rather taxing, losing a deal and all."

Cold eyes trailed between us all. So, it had been payback. The room was tense, and I struggled to keep from standing. Instead, I clenched Eirik's hand hard, gritting my teeth. Payback, *fine.* If he wanted to play rough, he would get rough.

"I can see ghosts. They actually seek me out." I bit my lip as his eyebrow raised. Curiosity sparked in his eyes as he leaned forward.

"Fascinating indeed." He walked around until he was standing in front of his desk. Eirik released a growl from beside me. One Xander returned with a quirked eyebrow. "Tell me, dear, can you talk to them? These spirits?"

He looked like a child in a candy store. It sent a fresh wave of trembles through me. He was looking at me like those at Ascension Rising had. Like I was an anomaly.

Like I was his next experiment.

"Ghosts can't speak, but they sing in a way. Through their emotions, their feelings. I help them move on." If that was even what I did.

Maybe I'd been eating them? My heart dropped as my thoughts wandered to Prince.

Xander's head tipped back, and a deep, rumbling laugh tumbled from his lips. He looked deranged. Crazy. Everything in me screamed he was.

"Oh, my dear, do you have anything else for me?" He was leaning forward now, his eyes raking down my skin.

That push again, the blistering cold at the back of my neck, right above my spine. The glow of the green of his eyes deepened, and I realized whatever he could do ... he was doing it now.

"I pulled the spirit from a man," I whispered, and in a flash the frigidness disappeared.

The corner of Xander's lips arched down just slightly, his eyes narrowing.

"I killed him." I hated saying it, hated hearing it.

But now it was out in the open, and in an instant, the smile dropped entirely from Xander's face. All of his excitement fell, his eyes going wide as his complexion dulled. Suddenly he wasn't so intent to speak, his Adam's apple bobbing as he swallowed.

"Are you sure?" he asked.

I only nodded. I was sure I had held Crustava's soul in my hand. I could have *crushed* him.

"This is interesting." Xander ran a hand across his shaved head. He shook off his shock, replacing it with an expression of barely contained curiosity.

"Well?" Adrian's voice cut the air. "Do you know what she is or not?"

Irritation was heavy in his words, poisoning his usually cheery voice.

"Oh, I do have an idea. But if I'm right ..." Xander settled his hand on his face, tapping at his lips.

He didn't finish his sentence. His voice was smooth, holding none of its previous curiosity.

But his hands were trembling.

This was the moment I'd been waiting on for months. What all of my efforts led to. Yet at the thought of his answer, I nearly puked.

"What am I?" I asked. My skin was ignited with goosebumps, and suddenly I didn't even want to know. I was terrified of his answer.

Death.

My body screamed the word at me, the murderous intent of it destroying me.

Death.

It was like an anvil on my shoulders, louder, more prominent. The voice from the hot spring chanted it.

Death.

A curse this time, and I already knew Xander's answer. It was clear in his eyes and the cruel twist of his lips.

"Death, my dear."

I froze in my seat. My hand shot out, and I clenched so tightly onto Osiris's that my fingers went numb. My soul purred at his words as if happy to be pulling in his fear. As if relishing it.

"If I am correct, which I usually am, you're a Reaper. A hybrid, by my guess." He paused, tapping his chin. "It was what I guessed the moment you walked through my door. The white hair, the striking violet eyes," Xander mused, shrugging his shoulders. "You *are* a Reaper. Your other gifts prove it. Reapers can see souls. In fact, they were the only ones that hear the *mortui carmen,* the Song of the Dead. It's how they help poor lost souls pass on to the afterlife, much like you said."

The anvil, the weight, was too much. Death, I was *death.*

"But can they pull souls from bodies?" Osiris asked, and Xander froze before he slowly nodded.

His face twisted, confusion muddling his stance as he leaned forward to analyze Osiris.

"Yes, but ... only once," he said, tapping his chin. "There isn't a lot on it, but it wasn't the same as a normal Call. It was a power they rarely used, and only those with potent blood could do it. It tore out both the soul of the Reaper and their victim. It ripped them both apart and destroyed the souls so neither could be reincarnated."

My breath caught in my throat, and I flinched as though someone had slapped me, gasping as I jolted into the harsh leather of the couch.

A tremor shot through Xander's body as he watched me. His forest-green eyes narrowed on me, the pupils expanding, covering his eyes in a sheen of black. Something like fog slid across the ground, and the room suddenly smelled like a forest, rich and earthy.

"You really did it, didn't you?" he asked, shaking his head when I didn't deny it. I was frozen to the spot. Xander walked back around his desk once, stopping at the shelves that were behind it. "You shouldn't be standing right now, dear Aaliyah. The other half of your blood must be *powerful.*"

He pulled a pristine glass bottle out. It had an intricate design etched onto the side like a dragon huddling over its pile of gold. It was a quarter full of a chestnut brown liquor. He grabbed a single quartz cup and filled it half full.

He downed it in one go.

"I don't understand. Reapers are a myth." It was Osiris who spoke, a dazed look in his eyes.

"Of course you'd think that. You're too young to remember a time with them." Xander's words were bleak, his tone indignant. He poured another drink, throwing it back again before whispering something. As though *mourning*.

"Osiris, too young for something?" Fallon's scoff was unexpected.

"Too young for the start of the Natural War? Yes."

Natural War? That didn't ring any bells. I hadn't known there was a war, and from the sound of it, and the way Eirik and Osiris tensed next to me, I didn't want to.

"Real nasty fight, that was. Lead to the Eternals, and order for us *savages*. But do you know why it started? Why it ended? *Why* the Reapers were hunted without mercy?" Xander's head dropped from my gaze. *Hunted?* His lips twisted, and he shook his head. "There's a reason the Reapers aren't remembered, you know."

"Why would people want us dead?" I asked, the words barely more than a whisper. Eirik's arms tightened over my shoulder.

"Because your blood is powerful; it carries your gift of death." He downed his glass again.

No.

"They drained your kind dry, using your blood to coat weapons, to kill the unkillable. It can drop a Vampire faster than the sun." Xander's eyes flicked to Osiris, but I didn't pay attention, *couldn't*. I was too lost in my memories of Ascension Rising and how all they needed was my blood. They were allowed to do *anything* else with me, as long as they got it. "Witches would rain it down on the battlefield. It would settle like acid on people's skin, eating them from the inside out. Even the Hallowed Three feared it."

No.

I was fully trembling when Osiris's growl met my ears.

"You have said enough about the war." He clenched my hand, and I couldn't even find the words to thank him for the comfort.

"You said hybrid. What's Aaliyah's other half?" Fallon's voice, callous and precise, cut through me.

"I don't know for certain, but it would have to be a powerful Natural. Reapers weren't particularly known for their healing. Besides their ability to send spirits on, they were no more than human. With the exception that as long as they weren't brought to earthly death, they were effectively immortal. Reapers can reproduce with every race, to my knowledge. The child born would be a Reaper but would frequently inherit abilities from the other parent. Increased strength from shifters, gills from sea folk. But it didn't happen often. Reapers were known for their difficulties conceiving. With a different species, it was even harder. It was why it was so easy to hunt them to extinction." He glanced at me. "Or near extinction, I suppose."

He tapped at his desk, leaning against it. Some papers he had strewn about the top fluttered to the ground. "But I have a guess. Tell me, my dear. Have you ever craved blood before?"

I breathed out, shaking my head with a certainty that I knew wasn't flawless. "Blood? No."

"Are you sure? Think hard. It doesn't have to be a big moment," he asked.

And I knew I didn't have a sure answer for him, not one with a clear conscience. In the last six months since I woke, I'd not craved blood. But the years before it? I had *no* idea.

"Where are you going with this, Xander?" Fallon asked. His suit was creased along his midsection, where he leaned forward. He glared at Xander, his hand reaching over Eirik toward me as if he was acting as a shield.

"Curious," Xander mused, standing fully again. He walked toward us until he was standing right in front of us. He reached out, only stopping when Eirik's growl sharpened, his face shifting when the Dryad got a little too close. "May I?"

"Back up," Eirik snapped, gnashing his teeth. The arm that had been around my shoulders tightened, pulling me to his side.

Xander rolled his eyes but didn't touch me. And I was glad for it, as I flinched away when he pulled back.

"Oh, come now, Eirik. You know if I wanted to hurt her I could have already, and then you would have killed me and this whole thing would have been for nothing. I don't have any ill intent." He waved his hand nonchalantly. "I just want to prove my theory."

"It's okay," I said, steeling my gaze. I moved, pulling Eirik's hand away so I could bring it to my front. I slid our fingers together, holding him tightly until the growling stopped. "What do you need me to do?"

Xander smiled, the action not screaming hostility for the first time since we started talking. There was an air of respect around him as he leaned forward again, and his touch connected with my chin, tilting my head back.

I still flinched but didn't push him away. There was no spark of heat, nor a desire to seek his touch.

"Open your mouth. I'm going to see if I can find some fangs hiding in there," he said.

I ran my tongue along the roof of my mouth, curiously searching and prodding. I couldn't have fangs. It wouldn't make any sense. But it didn't hurt to rule it out. In fact, it was needed. The second half of my blood was something I wanted to know.

I needed to know.

"Fangs? She isn't a Vampire, Xander. They have to be turned," Osiris said, but Xander just shook his head.

I opened my mouth as he asked. His pointer finger drew up to press behind my canine. There was pressure, slightly, before my mouth watered and I panicked. And then the pressure dropped, snapping away as the canine fell. Xander grinned triumphantly, letting go so Osiris could turn me to look at him. His eyes went wide, and I fought a quick breath.

"Did you forget what I just said? You're right, she's not a Vampire. But one of her parents was. A strong one at that. How your family stayed hidden, I can't even fathom. Tell me, do you remember your parents' names?" he asked, like he hadn't just thrown my entire life into shambles.

A Vampire. One of my parents was a Vampire. A Vampire and *Reaper*.

I'd remembered so few things about them, hints of my mother's soft kisses and the way my father used to read me bedtime stories. I held all of those memories close to me, no matter how few I had. But I couldn't recall anything like that ... until it came to me.

My father holding me in the kitchen after my mother had danced with me ... it was a memory I'd gotten recently. One that I hadn't dug deeper into. Like the icy touch of my father's hands.

Or the way he never smiled with his teeth.

I choked on my words as I tried to fight down the tears. It was like everything that I feared came roaring to the surface. I was a monster.

"My, my mother's name was Iris," I said, trying to think of my last name. It slid over my tongue like the softness of silk. My mother had kept her last name. She used to tell me about it, of what it represented. I still heard it in her bright songs, from the memory of her death.

"Iris Imperial."

The glass shattered in Xander's hand. His blood was like thick bog water, an earthy green that dripped to his table.

"You are telling me that not only did a Reaper survive the culling, but an *Imperial* did?" A tortured laugh fell from Xander's lips as he leaned back, his eyes lighting up with curiosity once again.

"Who were the Imperials?" The grumble of Eirik's voice had me leaning into him, his *Úlfhéðinn* soaking up the attention as a soft growl rumbled against me. It calmed me, as it always did.

Osiris was deathly still, and his face was a pane of white. The tremble in his jaw was barely noticeable.

"They were the royal family. Had been for centuries." Xander glanced at Osiris with a sneer. "Better not tell Sebek about her. He'd be furious he missed one."

The name rang across my ears, and like fire on my skin, it burned me. Just as quickly, pressure built in my head behind my eyes, *demanding* an answer. A memory. A scoff rang in the air.

"Why would *he* care about Aaliyah?" Fallon's voice was violent, exposed. Scared. Like the mere idea of me meeting Sebek was a death sentence.

Sebek.

"They don't call him *Death's Butcher* for nothing, darling." Xander didn't say anything else, his head dropping like he was devastated at the loss of my people. I liked him a bit more with that visage. "Their Maker more than earned that title. The rampage he went on after his brother died in battle was talked about for centuries."

That name was so familiar, so strange. So raw. It was nostalgic, unreal. Where had I heard that name before? It seemed trapped in my subconscious. I flinched as the pressure grew violent.

Now, my sweet ab. A familiar sentence, from the lips of my father. I didn't know what it meant exactly—*ab*—but I knew how it felt, like home and the safety I found in his embrace.

Osiris and Eirik shifted at my sides, saying something I couldn't hear. Osiris's story came back to me, the one he'd told me in the library about the princes ... and the princess they saved, and I could *hear* it. Hear it in my father's voice, hear as the tale came to life.

"What about your father? Do you remember his name?"

Panic ate at me. Of course I knew my father's name, just as I knew my mother's—it was the same name he used in *all* of his stories. *And then brothers Arvand and Sebek Ra saved the princess, Iris. Arvand and Iris fell in love, and together they lived happily.*

It couldn't be the same man. Cold hands cupped my cheeks.

Eventually, they had a child, a little girl that they loved with all of their souls. They called her Aaliyah.

Sebek was the second character in my father's stories. He always had been. Sebek was the name of the brother my father had lost before I was born. Only, they weren't stories, were they? The pressure finally pulled away enough for me to hear past the ringing in my ears as Adrian crouched in front of me. I slipped forward into his arms.

I bit my lip, my father's red eyes coming to mind. His *cold* skin.

A tremble shook through me, and my lip quivered. There was no way. *No way.* I opened my mouth to speak, but the words jumped their way into the walls of my throat, choking me. He *couldn't* be.

The soft hum of his foreign melodies sang across my skin.

Ready to hear another story, my ab?

"His name was Arvand," Osiris said, breaking the silence. An air of sheer bewilderment took over him, followed by a sharp recognition.

My father's name had slipped past his lips.

"Her father was *Arvand Ra.*"

CHAPTER 32

OSIRIS

Arvand Ra.

It had been centuries since I had heard that name uttered like a *curse* on my Maker's lips.

Arvand Ra, twin to Sebek. My Maker's blood brother, a twin in life and Vampire Crypt in death. Arvand had died long before I was turned, a story I'd never fully learned. But from what I'd heard of it, that death was the catalyst that drove Sebek mad. Losing his brother led him to turn me.

To turn us all.

Then how, *how* had this happened? What made Arvand fake his death? How had he kept it hidden for so long?

I hated that the answer was so blindingly obvious. My eyes settled on Aaliyah. She was trembling, her skin a ghostly white as she stared at me. She looked like she had pieced it together as she realized at least *what* her father was.

"Arvand *fucking* Ra." I'd never seen Xander this blown away. "Leave it to you to find the daughter of your Maker's long-lost brother."

This was truly and utterly confusing. I didn't blame him. She had that effect on people.

"That would explain the healing, and with blood as powerful as his, her pulling souls at will isn't a stretch." He was trembling from excitement or terror. I didn't know which. Possibly both. "If she truly can *control* death, then she is a force against nature. She shouldn't be possible."

He was staring at her like he wanted to tear her apart. Like he wanted to uncover her secrets.

"She didn't do it without help," I argued, reaching out and grabbing Aaliyah's hand, a show of support that made my palm warm in hers. She looked at me with masked anticipation, like she was waiting for me to pull away.

"She nearly died. We had to use a blood transfer to save her." At that, Xander brushed me off.

"Her material body needed help. However, her *soul* is perfectly intact." He glanced at Aaliyah. "I think."

I ignored his words, pushing past the want to maim the man in his own home. Was this what the people who held her were looking for? How had they even found out what she was? They had to have a source, an *ancient* source backing them and pulling strings. I ground my teeth. This was becoming an enormous problem. Fast.

"If I could get a sample of your blood, my dear—" Xander's words were wistful, hopeful.

And drowned out by the overwhelming sound of Eirik's furious growl. He nearly shifted on the spot. Xander raised his hands in defeat, his lips falling into a pout.

"No need to get so upset about it." His eyes never left Aaliyah's, and I hated it.

"We have been having other problems, problems which we assume are related to what she is." For the first time since her revelation, Xander drew his eyes away from Aaliyah. "She's sick, has been for about six months, after she woke up in a grave."

"Grave? Did she die then?" Xander asked, tapping his fingers against the wood of his desk. The sound echoed in the room, and Aaliyah became rigid beside me.

"She did," I responded, and Xander hummed.

"I see. So something brought her back, and now her soul isn't taking that very well, is it?" he pushed. "What else?"

"When I woke up, I couldn't even remember who I was. Every time I remember something, I die. These *Rends* recently stopped, but in their place, I've started to get sick. Headaches, nosebleeds." She shuffled, flinching as she rubbed at her temples. "We were hoping knowing what I was would help us understand how to fix it."

"And the Vivas Crypt, or being around them, was that what stopped your Rends?"

She hesitated before nodding. "I think so."

"You're quite the puzzle, sweet thing," Xander crooned, making Eirik snarl all over again. The Dryad rolled his eyes. "Oh calm down, I don't want your little Reaper, but I can respect the fire in her eyes. And the way she carries herself, even with all those marks on her."

His lips curled into a twisted grin as I nodded.

"*But* a deal is a deal. So what do I get for giving you more information? I agreed to answer questions about her race. We didn't agree to deal with any problem." His words were smug, no doubt happy to be paying me back for my earlier slight against him.

Fuck.

"What do you want?" I snapped, and his eyes sparkled.

He looked back at Aaliyah, my sweet *lux mea* flinching as though his gaze struck her. I snarled before I could stop it.

"I think you already know—" Xander was cut off by Eirik, who was already out of his seat, his growl holding his barely contained rage.

"No." Eirik may be younger than Xander and I, but he was no less powerful. His *Úlfhéðinn* blood flooded him with power, with a ferocious river of bloodlust. Xander frowned, but to my surprise, he didn't back down.

"That is my deal. If you don't wish to take it, then don't. But you had best muzzle your *mutt* before I make you regret it." Xander's words were hissed, and Eirik looked ready to explode.

Until Aaliyah's smooth voice hit our ears, with a wickedly frigid edge to it. Silencing the room.

I knew that tone.

"Threaten him again." She stood, ripping her hand from mine as she did. There was a snarl on her lips as her eyes bore into Xander's soul, and the poor man flinched. Like he was terrified of her. And if his words were anything to go by, he should be.

Black smog crept from the shadows. No ... the shadows themselves became near sentient, morphing like fire around her. The sharpening of her face, the twist of horns on her head. She moved to stand in front of Eirik like she was trying to hide him. It was *not* working, but the effect was there.

"I dare you." She released a furious growl, slamming her hands on his table in a swift motion.

The Dryad was on his feet and against the wall before we could blink. Her aura swirled around her, and the shadows licked at her skin. I felt nothing but admiration, and I didn't stray away from her touch nor the power that swirled around the room. In fact, I wanted it all over me. It sang across my skin like it belonged there. I wanted her blood on my tongue, despite Xander's cautionary words.

Xander looked at a loss, his mouth gaping open. He didn't move. I doubted he even breathed until a grin split across his lips.

"Marvelous." His word was a whisper. He made no move toward Aaliyah, though I could see the want to in his gaze. Instead, he drank her in, his eyes raking over her with a curiosity that infuriated me.

Eirik was looking at her like she had grown another head. He didn't hesitate as he wrapped an arm around her, pulling her snuggly toward him. Slowly, her flames died down as she melded into his embrace. The shadows cooled, returning to their expected places on the floor. She glanced at him with a confused look as the haze cleared.

"I'll be honest with you, sweet Aaliyah. I'm unsure exactly why you're sick, and there's likely no one on this planet that will know if not me." Xander shook his head, once again walking over to his bookshelf. "But I might have something of use."

The tomes seemed to morph as his hand reached for them. He eventually pulled down a leatherbound book. It was marbled in its age and the colors faded more where Xander's fingers pressed. Listed on the front, in old Latin, was a familiar phrase.

From the light born to the darkness bred. The Hallen.

The formation of a Maker bond?

"Vampires are particular in terms of the Natural community. You aren't born. You're made, as Osiris said." If he noticed he was giving away information, he didn't mention it. "Except for you, Aaliyah."

As he looked at her, there was a spark of respect in his eyes. Maybe he wanted to be on her good side.

"This connection allows a Maker to bring a new Vampire into the world. They take their chosen's blood, all of it, and replace it with their own. Then, as long as their body does not reject the trade, they will wake the next night as a Vampire. It's why a Maker can always find those turned. This transfer found in blood makes you reliant on it and makes you crave it. But there have been cases in the past where pairs of Vampires became reliant on each other rather than humans. Normally between those that have formed deep emotional connections. They lose the need to feed on mortals, and instead must feed on each other to live." He paused, flipping to what appeared to be a random page. "Mind you, this has *never* been between more than two people."

Xander set the book on the table, showing us the page he had flipped to. Scripts were explaining the affliction, as well as the telling sign for it. A mark in common, binding the vampires.

"The mark will confirm my suspicion. I don't think your current sickness is because of your *Rends*. I think it's because you've become Hallen Bound." Xander looked at us expectantly. I read the pages again.

And again.

"It says that the mark appears after blood consumption," I said.

Xander narrowed his eyes, checking the page, then glancing at Aaliyah's bare neck. "Have you not shared blood?"

"We weren't aware she needed it, and we would not feed from her without expressed consent," Fallon filled in for me, his words like ice.

"Hm, then I suppose that's all I have to say." Xander tapped his chin. "If I am correct in my assumption, you need a frequent blood exchange." His eyes darted across the room. "You all do. You haven't been feeling well either, have you? I've never seen any of you look as haggard as you do today. Achy, sick, unable to handle the taste of anything else."

It couldn't be that simple; there was no way. Our blood issues had been going on for years. But as I looked at Adrian, noting his wide eyes and sunken cheeks, I forced myself to wonder. It was like he was *starving*. Even Fallon and Eirik after Valen's. The blood that hadn't been tainted yet fell him anyway.

"Our feeding problem can't be Ali ... it's been going on for years, *decades*," Fallon said.

But he didn't seem sure either.

"Don't know what to tell you. There is always the chance I'm wrong," Xander replied, straightening his tie with a shrug.

"Didn't you say that her blood is the epitome of death?" Adrian chimed in, correct as much as I hated to admit it.

"To everyone else, yes. But if you are Hallen Bound, it shouldn't be an issue for you." He paused. "In theory, anyway."

He fiddled with some papers on his desk, never losing my gaze.

"What happens if we drink her blood, and you're wrong?" There wasn't an ounce of hesitation in Xander's voice as he responded to my quip.

"Then you'll die. With as strong as she is, she can bring down even you with less than a drop."

Aaliyah's gasp caught my attention. Her face was no longer a mask of rage, as terror took over. Her lip was bitten hard between her teeth, and any hint of her gifts fully faded away.

"They have to drink it?" Aaliyah's voice was back down to its mellow tone. She trembled in Eirik's arms, his purr sparking up in response to it. And I would have sworn that was pain in Xander's eyes.

"Unfortunately, yes. If they don't, then they will eventually wither into a state of comatose. As will you if you don't have a regular intake of theirs. A drop per night should do it." His words were surprisingly soft. Comforting.

I wanted to thank him and tear his throat out all in one motion.

No one spoke. No one moved as we all took in what had been said.

This was a cluster fuck.

"I'm not one to gift advice ... but you need to take care, Osiris," Xander changed the subject, his expression serious. "The Eternium is on the horizon, and Sebek's carnage has already been noted in the States. If he finds out about her—"

Osiris's response was curt, "We'll take care of it."

"Good. Now, if you have no more questions for me." Xander stood straight, though he never took his eyes off of Aaliyah. "I'll consider that information given out of the kindness of my heart since I'd love the chance to talk with sweet Aaliyah again." He paused, a vicious demeanor replacing his laxity. "But I won't be so kind a second time, Osiris."

The threat was obvious, one that I was coherent enough to understand, regardless of my anger at him. I didn't want to lose him as an information source. He was too valuable.

"We appreciate your kindness, Xander." I was on my feet before I finished the sentence.

I sought Aaliyah's touch on instinct, and her hand fell into mine seamlessly. She looked lost. Her eyes clouded over as she searched the room for nothing in particular.

"Do come back sometime. I would love to pick your mind, dear Aaliyah." I hated the sweetness in his voice, the admiration. "Oh, and Osiris, I'd back you at the Eternium, should you seek to remove Sebek. Challenge. Or *otherwise*."

I nodded, the motion swift as we turned to leave. Information on my mind and a world of questions threatening to drown me.

CHAPTER 33

AALIYAH

I was used to the cold. After all, it came whenever ghosts were around. It was familiar, but it had never been like this: frigid, unyielding ...

I couldn't feel my hands, and no matter how much I pressed them together, there was *nothing*. I struggled to level my breaths, to get anything past the wall of ice that had found a home in my throat.

All I could think about, the only thing I could see, was *Prince* and the day he faded away under my touch. Reaper, I was a Reaper. I took souls and sent them on. Like I did to him. Like I did to Crustava. I finally knew what I was, and rather than joy or a sense of victory, I only felt cold. Broken.

Like a monster.

The cold didn't fade as we walked inside or as we sat in the living area. Nor as the heat from the fireplace sank into my skin.

"Aaliyah." I wasn't sure whose voice slid across my subconscious.

A hand on my cheek, barely drawing me to move.

Why was I so cold?

"Adrian, do something." Another growled voice. Gravely words on top of what should be soundless whispers.

"I'm trying. She's having a panic attack." Cold hands cupped my cheeks, and trembles shook my body—*panic attack*.

I tried to focus on those words, tried to take a breath but found myself unable to. A hint of what that meant popped into my mind, and Eliza's face came as a reminder; her hands on my cheeks, the inability to breathe. My chest was heaving and straining. I was involuntarily sucking in quick gasps, unable to take any more than that.

I hadn't noticed. The cold had been all-consuming.

I tried to focus, to draw on anything. I found the hands that were still pressed to my cheeks. They were freezing, like the rest of me, so I pushed my own hands up, holding them against the foreign ones. I forced a hard breath.

"There you go, little love." A thumb ran across my cheek. Adrian's soothing words made it easier to think. "Deep breaths. Come back to us."

Each breath I took seemed to ground me. My eyes focused first. Adrian kneeled in front of me. His eyes were on my face, searching.

His lips had a small, forlorn grin.

"There you are." He was close. So close, I could see the creases on his lips as he talked. The small freckles that lined his cheeks. The subtle hint of almonds and fall leaves in his warm autumn scent. It was cozy and distinctly warm.

"Adrian?"

His grin stretched, crinkling at the corners of his mouth and reaching into his amber eyes.

"We lost you there for a little while. Do you remember what happened, Aaliyah?" It was kind of strange to hear my name on Adrian's lips. I'd grown so accustomed to his term of endearment that I'd stopped expecting to hear my name.

"Not. Not really." I paused. "The last thing I really remember was sitting on the couch at Xander's."

I closed my eyes, trying to sort through my thoughts. The hand that I was holding clenched tighter. Drawing my attention, Osiris was there, his eyes lingering over our connected hands. When he realized my gaze was on him, he looked up, the relief in his eyes palpable. His hand squeezed again, though he didn't speak. He didn't need to, not to express what was so clear.

He was worried.

"Do you remember anything else?" Adrian's gentle tone hinted that I was missing something, something important.

I flexed my free hand, bringing it to my chest as I fought to come up with an answer. That familiar chill crawled up my spine as I recalled the conversations we had. I remembered Xander and his prodding nature and grandeur smiles. When he *insulted* Eirik.

When he mentioned someone.

My breath caught, and it came rushing back in a wave.

Sebek. We talked about Sebek Ra. The same Sebek that my father used to speak of when I was a child. The man who always accompanied my father on his grand adventures. Adventures that were most likely far *more* than mere children's stories.

My uncle. The Maker of these men I held so dearly. And *me*. We talked about me.

I fought the cold down, trying to stay level-headed as I pushed out my following sentence. "I'm a Reaper."

I wasn't sure I believed that or anything that Xander had said. I didn't want to think that I was everything I feared. That the compound was trying to harvest death from my blood. But ... that wasn't even the worst part, wasn't what still caused the snakes to crawl up my throat, strangling me with a startling revelation and sheer terror. These men who had saved me had shown me there was more to the world than just fear.

Required that same blood to live.

If that was a *wrong* assumption, then they would die for it, and I would be the one responsible for the deaths of a few of the people in the world who mattered to me. Another crack in my shattered soul.

"Stay with us, Aaliyah. We have you." I think it was Fallon who spoke.

His steady voice washed over me. The same voice that struck fear into any who dared to harm his family calmed me in a way I didn't understand.

"I remember." That was all I could manage.

I couldn't get anything else past my lips.

They could die if they didn't have my blood. They could die if they did.

I risked killing them like I did Prince. Or *worse*, having to see them the same as I had Prince. For them to be dead, spirits. Would I be able to send them on after I had already held their hands in mine? After I had seen their beautiful eyes, and heard their hypnotic voices.

"Take a deep breath, Ali." Fallon's voice once again slid over my skin.

He took up the spot to my left, grabbing my hand in his own. He pulled my hand close, setting my palm over his chest. The steady thrum of his heartbeat under my skin rang like a slow melody. Stealing my thoughts forced me to think about only one thing.

Him.

"I know you're scared." Fallon's eyes slid closed. I watched as his lips trembled. "But you can't let it consume you."

His eyes slid open again, the steely green flaming as he leaned forward. His forehead settled on my own. I leaned into his slight contact, taking in his calming breaths and soft scents, like freshly washed sheets and mint.

"Push forward, Ali. You've overcome so much. You're the strongest person I know." His voice was more emotional than I had ever heard it. It forced my attention. Forced my heart to speed up in anticipation of his words.

"Far stronger than any of us. Which is why we need to do this."

His thumb ran across my cheek, and he took another shuddering breath.

"I can't, Fallon. I can't," I whispered, standing.

Panic wasn't new to me; I had spent years mastering it. But right now, it overwhelmed me. Silence swallowed the air, choking the breath right from my lungs. Then Fallon sighed, pressing his forehead to mine like he was scared I might fade away. He raised his hand, setting it on my cheek with such kind regard that I almost sank back down.

"Ali ..." It seemed like the room stilled, and even the fire's insistent roaring seemed to cease as Fallon spoke.

"No, I *can't*. I can't kill you too." I ripped myself away from him, my lungs constricting so tightly I gasped.

I looked between them, *all of them*, as sick understanding sank into my skin. Tears flooded my eyes. I tried to come up with my own words, with something. *Fallon's eyes faded, losing the glimmer that made him whole, his ghost sliding out of his body.* And he would try to tell me it was okay.

But no sound would come out. Nothing ever would again.

Because the *dead couldn't speak*.

I barely choked out a sob as I pulled away, and Fallon clutched my trembling arms tightly. I wished Prince was here. That he could tell me that everything was going to be alright. That Xander was right, and this would all be okay.

But he wasn't here.

I pulled fully away, wrapping my arms around myself. I knew I had to face this, that eventually, this was our only option. But I couldn't compel myself to, not right now, not with the bile rising up my throat.

I didn't give them a chance to say anything else, as I turned and ran up the stairs. I slid into my room, closing the door behind me. Quietly, *too quiet*.

Never make noise.

I wanted to scream.

Ice spread down my spine, and Red's comforting presence helped me rein in the absolute flood of emotions I was feeling. His energy bounced around, and the cloth in my pocket soothed me, warming where it was.

His emotions jumped from joy to eagerness, to silly. They were forced, but it did exactly what he was hoping. Exactly what Prince used to do.

It distracted me, and I leaned my head back, setting it on the door behind me.

"Thanks, Red," I whispered, leaning my head onto my knees.

I wasn't in the most comfortable position, but I was too drawn into my thoughts to move. I was used to being tucked in small spaces, and right now, my mind was in lockdown. It didn't register the bed, the warmth of the sheets, only the cool of the ground and the alternate heat from my skin.

A knock rang against the door just as tears slid down my cheek. The irony of it didn't slip past me, and I wondered if it was Fallon, holding a piece of his chocolate, with his green eyes showing far more than he realized.

"*Elskan?*" Eirik asked, blowing away the memory, and I sighed, curling tighter around myself.

I wasn't ready for this, to see him and have him convince me of what I already knew. That we didn't have a choice in the matter, and that if we didn't try to exchange blood, it was only a matter of time before one of us got sick again. Adrian still had those bags under his eyes, even if he smiled like he didn't. Eirik was still sick from Valen's, hiding it in the sheer amount of blood wine he drank to try to fix it. It was only a matter of time before one of us died.

"Please," I said, cupping my throat. "Please don't make me do this."

I swallowed another cry, the tears still falling.

"Move away from the door, *Elskan*," he grumbled, more beast than man as the doorknob jangled. "We won't speak of it again tonight, so let me in."

His words were insistent, if not flooded with worry, and I smiled softly against my knees despite my tears. I stood on shaky legs, taking a step away. Before my foot fully touched the ground, the door behind me was opened, and I was encased in warm arms.

Eirik's chest vibrated, the thick purr enough to make me sag into his arms. I reached up, brushing my hand against his bare chest.

I risked a glance down, noting the boxers he wore as he huffed and *flitted* me to the bed. He laid me down in the center before sliding in himself, covering us both with the thick comforter. His warmth helped to scare away the rest of the chill that had claimed me downstairs.

"Please—" I started, and he cut me off as he nuzzled his face into my neck, his arms tightening around me.

"I said won't ask, not today. But we have to face it soon," he said, as unrelenting as he was soft.

I pressed my hands onto his chest, taking in the heat as I nodded.

"I know," I whispered, but it didn't make it any easier to digest.

So I didn't. I just closed my eyes and pressed my nose to his chest. Breathing in the subtle scents of the sea and old oak.

Eirik's lips brushed the top of my head, and he pulled me ever tighter.

"Sleep, my brave *Valkyrie*. We will deal with this tomorrow."

CHAPTER 34

PRINCE

As it turned out, walking through the streets of an unknown city in the dead of night, while naked and covered in someone else's blood, wasn't exactly my *best* idea.

Shocking, really.

Still not sure who had it worse, the ancient-looking woman who was out sitting on the curb, smoking a cigarette. Or me, the crazed freak who'd only just woken up from what seemed to be the world's longest power nap. She'd screamed like a banshee, and my newly found sensitive ears revolted at the sound.

Me telling her not to worry, as the blood was, in fact, *not mine*, didn't help. I was led to believe I made it worse, as following her rather grand screeching, she promptly passed out.

I really shouldn't have laughed, but what else was I supposed to do? The absurdity of it all was reason enough. Despite that, like the gentleman I was, I held it in as her eyes rolled back, keeping as straight a face as I was able.

But when she hit the pavement?

Gold.

That brought me to now. Me, standing in the middle of what I hoped was the crazy bats' house, trying to avoid getting blood on the carpet. Still naked.

The woman? *Still passed out.*

My memory? *Still shit.*

Overall, I would say it had been a productive few hours. So, the question was, what to do now? My options were abysmal, and until I gained some more sense back, I was stranded in shark-infested waters, so to speak.

Who was I? Who were my enemies? Were they why I couldn't remember anything? Where was Aaliyah, and how did I get to her? She had to be as desperate to see me as I was to see her. Even now, I couldn't get her out of my mind. Her face was like a beacon of light, driving me forward.

A pain settled in my chest, and I reached up to soothe the ache on instinct. Instead, I was once again reminded that I was, in fact, covered in blood.

Blood that was now on the carpet.

Well, fuck me.

I glanced around, and the tiny home met me with little but a hideous blue couch in the center of the room that was placed in front of a small box of some sort. The walls were a sickly yellow, most likely from years of cigarette smoke clouding the air. The entire space was open to what I assumed was the kitchen. That room didn't appear to hold any more value than the one I was standing in.

Would she have a bathing room?

I stalked through the empty halls, leaving the old woman sprawled out on the couch. Hopefully, she would stay sleeping long enough for me to clean off and get out of there. Dealing with the fallout of my little show on the street sounded like a nightmare.

I walked through the small living area, doing my best to at least try to keep the blood fall to a minimum.

I, of course, failed miserably.

The bathing room that I found matched the rest of the house, and I had to fight a groan at the sight of it. The shower was narrow, the entire space less than three square feet.

Let us not forget that the height of the faucet only reached about my neck. Nevertheless, I tried to be optimistic as I struggled to get the water flowing.

At least I would finally be clean.

I hoped.

Chapter 35

Adrian

Aaliyah sat cross-legged on the floor. Sweat clung to her brow, and she took a steady breath. We'd been at this for hours. Hell, it was the fifth time today she'd tried to find the Void in that silver room again. Tried to get in touch with what made her a *Reaper*. Tried to get her mind off of what I knew was plaguing her.

She was terrified of giving us her blood, and honestly, I wasn't feeling much better about it. I trusted her—*that* much was undeniable—but I feared Xander would be wrong.

Feared that we'd die, and she'd be left with nothing but our souls for company.

We'd have to face it soon, likely far sooner than she was ready for, but we had a few days to spare for her. I was more than happy to help her in other ways, like this, I could do. I'd never been particularly good at meditating, but I could watch her for hours. Though, I imagined that the sound of Eirik's heavy boots against the training room floor were doing exactly the opposite.

"You're not helping, Eri," I finally said as Eirik let out another soft curse, turning my attention away from Aaliyah, whose eyes slid open slowly.

A snarl was Eirik's second response. It had become almost commonplace to have Eirik's wolf so close to the front of his mind. It settled in the

285

air like the *Flame* or a *Charm*. He huffed, and his growl teetered off into a low rumble.

"If it's bothering you so much, I can do this myself. It's just meditation, you know?" Aaliyah's words echoed in the room, and I took a second to take in her tired expression.

She wiped her eyes, clearing them as she leaned over her crossed legs.

"Absolutely not," Eirik said sharply. "Not after what happened last time."

But the question was, was he talking about death one, almost-death two, or *Rend* pre-almost-death two? Maybe hot spring death?

So hard to keep track.

"Then sit down, Eirik. I focus better when you're near me and not walking a hole into the floor." Aaliyah's soothing voice nearly had *me* sitting. What I wouldn't do to crawl into her arms. I'd sleep right here if she would let me hold her for a while.

But her eyes wavered, and the tension in her shoulders told me she needed something else right now. So I took a step forward, crouching down to her level. I reached out, pressing a palm to her cheek. The spark that always lit up my nerves when I touched her shivered down my spine, and her lavender eyes focused on mine.

"I have a better plan," I said, standing slowly, taking her with me. "We've been going at this for hours, love. You need a break."

She shook her head but didn't move away from me. Her skin was hot, exertion showing in the shake of her legs.

"A break isn't going to help us right now, Adrian. I need to do this." That determination was charming, if not slightly frustrating.

Adorable. I stood, pulling her the rest of the way into my arms. I couldn't help but sneak a quick peck on her lips.

"And you will. Because you are as determined as Osiris, *stubborn* as Eirik." She huffed but didn't protest. "Proud as Fallon, and loveable as me."

She laughed against me, pulling back just enough to gaze up into my eyes. Her head was against my chest, love in those vibrant violet irises. I moved closer, planting a kiss on her forehead.

"But you *need* to rest. So, what do you say to some ice cream?" I asked, and she sighed as she pulled away.

She rotated her stiff shoulders, glancing over my shoulder at Eirik. "We have that?" she finally said, looking back at me.

"Damn right we do. Want some?" I asked. She bit her lip, shuffling on her feet as I looked over my shoulder. "What do you say, Eri? Up for some fun?"

He huffed, his shoulders flexing before he turned and walked out.

"Guess that means yes," I said with a laugh.

"He's rather grumpy today, isn't he?" she sighed, shaking her head.

"Just worried, love. His wolf's got him a tad more protective these days. Ice cream will surely help him, too." She nodded, reaching out and taking my hand. "If not, then we leave him there and go on our merry way."

I had just turned toward the fridge, my free hand already reaching for the handle, when a soft knock rang against the door. I knew it was silly, the way I shivered at the sound and the way my ears trained on it.

If it had been Kali, she would have just appeared again. But it still shook me enough to question if the person who was interrupting our night was *her*.

"Adrian?" a shaky voice whispered on the other side, and Eirik was immediately up in arms, flipping around with a snarl.

But I knew that voice, and as I ushered Aaliyah behind me, Eirik swung open the door. I was not expecting to see the Basilisk Eternal tonight, shivering in the cold. His eyes were sunken, and he looked like someone had just torn his heart out of his chest with the way he hunched over himself. He had piercing green eyes, ones with slitted pupils that were dulled and panicked. His brown hair, normally flowy and well-maintained in a tall ponytail, was haggard behind him, knotted. Even his clothes were a mess, his suit covered in rain and mud, some smears telling me he likely fell, and he was shaking so badly that I nearly gave him my coat.

"God, *Avedal*? What the bloody hell happened to you?" I exclaimed, watching as Avedal looked over his shoulder in a jerky motion. "Come in, come in."

This couldn't be good.

"You're alive, good. That means he hasn't gotten to you yet," Avedal rambled under his breath.

The familiar stench of old magic permeated the air. Avedal pulled out a small sheet of paper from the breast pocket of his suit and whispered a few words that sounded like gibberish. The effect was immediate as the spell blanketed the area, so no one would hear us as the sheet sizzled and turned to ash.

A mute spell.

"I was worried I would be too late. Where are the others? Actually, it doesn't matter. You can tell them," Avedal said, his hands flinching as he again glanced over his shoulder at the door he had just walked through. He was cold-blooded, and this lower temp was probably not helping that. Whatever he had to say, it was important.

"Avedal," I said, reaching out to the panicked Eternal. He jerked away and bared his teeth. "*Calm* down. What do you mean?"

He didn't let me touch him, instead flinching away with an anxious noise. His mouth opened and closed, his hands getting increasingly shaky as he tried to find the words.

The room grew frustratingly silent, besides Avedal's panicked breaths. I reached forward to try again when a warm hand settled on my arm.

I looked at Aaliyah, her worried eyes trained on Avedal. A spark of jealousy that didn't belong bloomed in my chest as she took a hesitant step forward, hands raised in front of her in a way that I had seen before, between her and Eirik. And Osiris.

"You're okay," she said, not reaching out to touch him, merely offering him the comfort of her presence. "You're safe here. Come sit."

She pulled out a chair before stepping away from it, giving him room to choose. It took a few moments, with Avedal still looking over his shoulder like he expected a dagger in his back before he let out an uneasy sigh. He offered Aaliyah a thankful nod as he hobbled forward and sank into the seat before he turned his head toward me. His black hair bobbed, and his eyes glowed in the low light of the night.

"Two more Eternals have been found dead, Adrian. Fae and Dragonkin." I tensed, and Aaliyah reached out, gripping my hand tightly. "There's reason to believe that Fae Eternal Frileti was targeted by your Maker, based on how she was found." His eyes fell closed, and he shuddered. "She was torn apart."

He'd seen the body of the Fae Eternal then. Sebek wasn't known for his mercy, but why was he doing this? What did he gain from killing the Eternals? If anything, it seemed like he was just playing more into our hands, giving the others more reasons to get rid of him. But that didn't *sound* right. Sebek was cold and calculating at his core. He was a monster, but he was a strategic one.

"I don't know what happened, but he has been on a warpath since he got back to the States. Hillam and I had to come home early to do damage control," Avedal choked, rubbing his arms as he glanced behind him again.

Hillam, his mate. I nodded sharply, sympathizing with the shaking Eternal, something that I'd never expected to happen. Avedal was nearing eight hundred years old and would easily take me in a fight, maybe even Eirik if he got the jump on us first. Seeing him so *terrified* had me on edge.

"Where was he last seen?" I asked, noting the way Avedal covered his mouth like he was going to be sick.

"Washington state, heading this way."

My jaw clenched, and I nodded. That gave us two weeks—maybe.

"What about Teviticus?" Eirik asked from next to me, a complete lack of sympathy for the Dragonkin present in his tone.

Not that I blamed him; he was a terrible Eternal and an even worse man. Curtis, the bastard that had sold *our* girl, had taken after him, and it got his heart ripped out before his first quarter century.

Honestly, he got off easy. Osiris didn't savor the kill. Had it been Fallon, or even worse, Nero ...

Curtis got off *easy*.

"Not Sebek," Avedal said, and Aaliyah flinched next to me. I held her hand that much tighter. "Drakon."

That got my attention. Drakon Halsen was a quickly rising star in the light of the Natural world, for all the right reasons. He'd been talking about reform and pushing for a more diplomatic election process. *And* he'd killed every assassin that had been sent after him. He'd be an excellent ally to have.

Assuming he didn't go power crazy like his father, that is.

"His eldest?" Eirik asked, his eyebrows raising, likely thinking the same thing I was.

"Teviticus killed Drakon's unborn child and the Pearl of his clutch. Drakon is the stand-in Dragonkin Eternal, and now he has an even bigger target on his back. He's always been opposed to how the Eternals run things." Avedal's words hung heavy on the room, broken only by Aaliyah's gasp. Her face grew ashen, and she made no other sounds. It was like that was the moment that Avedal even truly realized she was still there, his curious gaze on her. "Look, I'm telling you this because we can't allow it to continue. These deaths need to end. Sebek *needs* to be stopped, Adrian."

He shook his head and looked away. I wished I had an answer to give him, something that would be of use, or some way to describe why Sebek did what he did. But he'd never been a predictable man, and now more than ever, he was like a beast let out of his cage.

And we were all going to suffer for it.

Avedal shuffled, nervously glancing back at the door again, before he spoke lowly, "Naturals can't continue to survive his wrath. Even now, the humans are suspicious. Please, *please* tell Osiris that I will back his claim at the Eternium. I'll vote on Exilium, but until then, I need to not be seen."

Bile rose in my throat at even the thought of how I knew Osiris would react. This didn't bode well for us.

"Stay safe, Avedal," I told him.

"You all, as well," he said back, and then he was gone.

And we were left to pick up the pieces.

CHAPTER 36

AALIYAH

The door closed, and the room was again silent. Eirik's growl grew, morphing until it echoed against the walls. But it was Adrian who brought us all back.

"I'll go get the others. We need to speak of this," Eirik rumbled, and my mind blanked as I continued to stare at the door where Avedal had just left.

Breathing became a struggle, and my chest throbbed and seized. Why couldn't something go right? *Anything*? I just wanted one day when we didn't have to worry about dying or volatile Makers or crazed people who wanted to buy me.

Just *one*.

"Now hold your horses, Eirik. That can wait a few more minutes." Adrian hummed, and the lulling sound of his voice was enough to get me to turn my head. The way he looked at me told me he understood how I was feeling. And when he stepped forward, wrapping his arms around me in a tight embrace, I sank into him.

"I know that look, love. Take a deep breath," he breathed against the top of my head, his hand making easy circles on my back.

I nodded, pressing so tightly against him that his heartbeat sounded in my ear. When he pulled back, that signature smile now present on his face, I had to admit that it calmed me down. I took another breath, as he instructed.

"Come on, we still need to grab that ice cream. Then we get the others,"

Adrian said, moving toward the fridge again. He shook off the visit with a Cheshire grin and an ease that helped to settle my own nerves. "What do you fancy, love? We have a few options to pick from."

I was still in shock, and in terms of overload, I was at my limit. I couldn't handle any more stress, any more threats on our lives for the day.

So, I didn't. I blocked it out, biting my lip as I thought about it. What ice cream did I want?

"I haven't had ice cream since I was a kid ... but I think I liked vanilla. Do you have any recommendations?" I asked, sliding into the seat next to me.

Eirik moved just as quickly, stepping behind me, his hands finding their way into my hair. The rough pads of his fingers gently played over the strands as I tipped my head back to glance at him. He raised an eyebrow, grunting when I laughed at the sight of him being so careful. The worry lines between his eyebrows softened.

"I love the caramel swirl," Adrian replied, his voice muffled by the inside of the freezer. I tipped my head toward him, catching his wink.

"Then I'll try that. What about you, Eirik?" I asked.

"Hm." He huffed, looking at me with a raised eyebrow. "No preference."

Adrian took that as whatever we were having, and he filled three bowls. They were placed in front of us before I knew it, and I settled into the icy treat.

Keeping my mind occupied, Eirik continued to fiddle with my hair, his own bowl completely disregarded. Not wanting him to be left out, I scooped a spoonful of ice cream just for him.

And, dutifully, he leaned forward and ate it.

"Ice cream?" a voice asked from the staircase.

Fallon and Osiris stepped in, both tensing as they took in the three of us.

"Yes, come get some. Ice cream makes everything better, Fal. It'll be better to have this talk with it. Avedal just left," Adrian hummed, taking another bite as Osiris's eyes went wide.

"He was here?" he exclaimed, his shoulders going taut.

"Yes. He placed a mute spell so we wouldn't be interrupted. To save the anticipation, Sebek's in the States, and he's left some bodies in his wake."

Osiris's jaw ticked, and he gripped his left hand. "Where was he spotted?"

I took another spoonful, my mind numb to the conversation even as it flooded my thoughts with the sight of a man in soft black sweats, with vibrant red eyes that crinkled at the corners and a gentle smile that I *knew* I'd gotten from him. My father. I wished I knew more about him, wished I could remember the way he'd laugh or how tall I used to be when sitting on his shoulders like I was at the top of the world. Those were the things I *wanted* to remember, but it had never been when I actually remembered.

My chest clenched as I wondered how similar they would look. Would they have the same smile that I used to beg myself to remember? Would they have the same laugh or the same kind eyes?

Would looking at him feel like home?

I had tried not to think much about my parents. Not in the last six months, anyway. They were something like a myth in a way, and as much as it hurt, I really didn't *remember* them much. Just a few stray memories telling me they were there. That they loved me and *died* for me.

"Washington state," Adrian confirmed.

Osiris clicked his tongue, crossing his arms before he gripped his wrist tightly. "Casualties?"

"Humans? No idea, but Avedal said he returned early for damage control, so I'd guess enough. We already knew he'd targeted the Gargoyle and Titan Eternals from before our trip to *The Devil's Details*, but we can add Fae Eternal Frileti to that list as well," Adrian said, counting each one. "All supporters of Sebek's removal. But there's been another death among the Eternals as well."

Osiris cocked his head with another clench of his teeth, another shudder. "Who else did he kill?"

Who *hadn't* he killed? That's three Eternals in under a month that had died to him if Avedal was right. Eliza had told me once that Eternals were long-lasting and that the last to die like this was over two hundred years ago. That's how uncommon it was, but at least one wasn't his doing.

"Wasn't Sebek this time, Osi. Teviticus was found dead in his court."

Osiris's eyes opened, surprise sneaking into his gaze. "The Dragonkin Eternal?"

"Yes. I don't know the specifics, but I believe he killed his daughter-in-law, the Pearl of his Eldest's Clutch, and his young grandchild. His son, Drakon, killed him for it. Taking the title of Eternal until the Ball can decide on a new one."

So much death, and what good did it do?

"Drakon is a good man, always has been," Osiris mused. "He reminds me of Carter, Eliza's mate. They have the same fire. If he goes for the title, I will support him. And if worse comes to worst, and we aren't able to convince Magelav and the others to vote for Exilium, then I'll Challenge Sebek myself."

That declaration, like the one of war that Eirik had mentioned, hammered down on us. But Osiris didn't crumble, and I'd never seen such determination in his eyes. Eirik was right, if nothing else, I trusted Osiris with this.

With what I knew was going to be a fight for our lives.

"Avedal backs your claim to Exilium, but he won't be showing himself until the Ball. So we at least have him," Adrian said.

The pieces were all falling into place, and for a second, hope bloomed. One ally here, and another, and another. I took another bite of my ice cream, the last one.

At the same time, Osiris moved. Pulling a short glass out, and a bottle of something other than blood wine from one of the cabinets. He poured himself a glass and took a sip. "And I've penned my letter to Magelav. I can only hope they'll respond. Get me the information on Drakon. I'll send him my regards for his Clutches Pearl and see what his plans are."

"Another ally?" Adrian asked.

Osiris's eyes darkened, and a spark of his power skittered across my skin. It had been coming out more lately, slipping past his defenses. "Or another enemy."

Would I ever stop aching?

I rubbed my temples, curling tighter into my blanket as I tried to stave off the chill. I shivered, my hands rubbing up and down my arms as I attempted to get the blood flow moving again.

The door to the library creaked open, and I looked up just in time to see Osiris stride in, a cup of steaming tea in hand. He was wearing his typical pinstripe suit, the deep blue undershirt pristine. He looked put-together and calm, something that this house had been sorely missing since Sorceri Eternal Kali's visit.

He closed the door, soundless this time.

"Good morning," I whispered as he walked toward me.

"Good morning, *lux mea*. How are you feeling?" he asked, approaching the couch I sat on slowly, before setting the tea on a coaster on the table. Worry twisted its way onto his features as he looked at me, and he schooled his expression as I sighed.

"I'm alright," I said instinctually. I laughed dryly when Osiris gave me a bland stare. "That bad, huh?"

There was something he wanted to say that I knew was on his mind as much as it was the others. His eyes traced my neck, flashing red for only a moment before they flipped back, and he shook his head.

"You should get more rest."

"I will soon." My hand went to the cloth that I always kept on me. The movement drew Osiris's gaze, and he was by my side in a blink, eyeing the red fabric.

"What's that?" he asked, his head tilting as though trying to recall where he'd seen it. I waited for Red to give me a hint that he knew something, but no sign of recognition mixed in with the array of emotions. He was just as curious as Osiris was about the red cloth.

"Red, the ghost from the cellar. Well ... what Red's attached to," I whispered his name, happy for the change of conversation. "I've been meaning to ask if you knew what it was. I found it down there a few days ago."

Osiris studied it for a minute before holding out his hand. A sudden flash of worry made the pressure in my head burn brighter, the hint of memory bleeding past my defenses. Something about the loss of an item. I'd never been given much, and I couldn't even guess what it had been, but it had been taken all the same.

I shook my head, pushing past the worry as I handed Osiris the cloth. Red's energy brushed against me carefully, showing assurance as Osiris carefully flipped it between his hands.

"If I recall, I found it while traversing China. I'd heard of a man who had roasted in the sun and turned to ashes. This was the last piece of him," Osiris said, his thumb rubbing against the fraying edges. "It was before I'd found Nero, and I'd discovered a kindred spirit in the cloth. Seems you have, too."

Osiris handed it back to me before reaching down to grab the tea again. He blew softly on the top, dutifully cooling it off in a way that looked extremely out of place.

"Yeah. He's been a big help," I said, using the words to hide my amusement.

Osiris hummed, reaching out with the cup and holding it to my lips so I could take a drink without coming out from my bundle of blankets. The tea was perfectly warm, with hints of vanilla and lavender sweetening it. When I pulled back, so did Osiris. He set the cup on the table.

His hands flexed by his sides before whatever he was considering finally settled in his mind. He reached out, in a way he hadn't in weeks, his hand settling on my cheek. The touch was enough to blow away everything else. It washed away the pressure from my skull, the freeze from my bones, and I sighed into it.

"I don't like to see you hurting," he murmured.

We'd done a lot of that recently, seen hurt.

"I don't like to see you hurting either, Osiris," I said, not wanting to push when I knew he was still building back up. He'd made progress, fantastic progress, but I would wait as long as he needed before truly asking how he felt.

But for now, I just needed him close to me, if he could manage it.

"I'll be alright, just ... sit with me a while?" I asked, curling in tighter, worried about rejection.

But Osiris shuffled in. I opened my blanket, and he wrapped us both in it on the couch. I leaned into his side, my eyes already drifting closed before he had us fully settled.

"Always, *lux mea*," he promised, as sleep claimed me.

CHAPTER 37

PRINCE

Clean, as it turned out, was a relative statement.

Even with the blood washed off, my skin felt grimy. Like there was filth that would take more than just a shower to remove. Maybe it was guilt? Having had a moment to step back, I realized that was exactly what I was. *Guilty.* I'd killed tonight without care. I wasn't so upset with the act, however, as I was worried. What would this mean for me?

Or, more precisely, what would Aaliyah think?

I was terrified of her reaction to finding out what I did. Or did she already know that I was a monster in hiding?

A familiar dull ache settled inside of me, traveling up my body before ending in my head. It seemed like my entire being pulsed to a rhythm that was unknown to me, like I was trapped in a soundless symphony. I clenched my jaw, curling back my lips as I struggled to find a place to sit before the inevitable pull dragged me under.

This ended up being on the floor.

The rather tight pants I had commandeered from the lovely home strained in protest, the already uncomfortable fit becoming nearly unbearable.

Pressure swelled in my head to where I thought it would burst. Then the tear, the pull. This part was the worst, the feeling like knives against my insides. There was no preemptive moment. I was just gone.

Ripped out of my body in a single swift movement.

Unlike the last time, it didn't take long for my soul to snap back, as though it was as disgruntled with the situation as I was. Then, just as quickly, I was dragged into a memory that didn't feel real.

The wind was blistering against my skin, penetrating as I stared into the dawn horizon. My hands trembled, though not from the cold. How could I let this happen? This wasn't supposed to end this way. This should have been in and out.

I'd told him this was a bad idea.

I could see a soft light peeking just over the mountains beyond me. I knew it meant I didn't have much longer.

Hope those fuckers in the compound were ready for a show. How had I been so careless as to let them catch me? Even with an Entromancer on their team, this should have been easy.

But it wasn't, because just like I'd expected, this mission was riddled with flaws. I'd been too cocky to fight against it more than once, my pride over-riding my survival sense.

Now, look where that got me.

I flexed my hands, the silver in the cuffs burning my skin, the searing leaving a foul smell in the air. The pain was irrelevant. I barely felt it over the panic.

The light was crawling toward me. I had about a foot before the rays would be upon me. I tried to prepare for it. Tried to take a deep breath. Maybe I could get out of this? Maybe my brothers were waiting to pull me out until the last second?

Those fucks.

I drew my trembling gaze off of the light, looking around the clearing as I pulled harshly against the restraints. There was no give, just like the last time and the time before that.

The light was inches away now, and the heat was sinking into my skin, ready to brand me. I could already feel the blisters forming, the dark lines of sun death sowing on my ankles. This couldn't be how I went out. There was so much that I still had to do, and I couldn't abandon them, my family—the only ones I had.

I sucked in a hard breath as the cold Russian air bit at my lungs, burning in a whole different way.

The light crawled up my skin, and the pain was instant. Harsh. I fought the screams for as long as I could, unwilling to give those bastards hiding away in their building anything. But eventually, even I couldn't take it, and I screamed until there was no more air left to give.

Until I was staring at my own charred body in disbelief.

Until I realized I was dead.

Before I could stop myself, I leaned over and let go of what was left in my stomach. Blood mixed with what looked like ash painted the floor as phantom pain licked at my limbs.

The sun had killed me.

The sun had fucking killed me.

Guess that went along with the whole 'needing to eat people' thing.

I fought back the panic as I settled myself. The only thing I learned from that was that the sun *hurt*. It was like I took a step backward—no closer to understanding why I was here.

I stumbled to my feet, doing my best to keep from getting my mess on me.

Didn't want to ruin these nice new clothes.

Sparks shot up and down my arms before ending at my fingertips. The tingle left my fingers numb. Glancing around the room, it looked as though nothing had changed.

How long had I been out?

I sauntered back out toward the living area, crossing the small threshold between it and the kitchen. I expected to see the woman still passed out on the couch I had placed her on. Or perhaps even up, stumbling around in a daze. I doubted anyone ever expected a hit to the face, especially with what I could only assume was a skillet.

Cast iron, perhaps?

The strike hit true, unfortunately, and my teeth rattled so viciously that I wondered if my skull split. I stumbled backward, barely staying standing.

"What the fuck—" was all I got out before my train of thought was interrupted.

"Take that, you damned fang." It was a shaky voice that reached my ears, the sound harsh. Her accent was pronounced, and it nearly swallowed her words.

It was familiar, so familiar that I almost forgot where I was.

That I had been struck by a *skillet*.

"You think to come to my territory all hostile? Tell me, boy, who did you kill?"

I understood less than half of that, and the ringing in my ears made it even harder to piece through what the old hag was saying.

"D'ya hear me, boy?" the impatient voice asked with a sneer.

"Unfortunately, yes. I hear you, hag." I pressed my hand against my forehead as blood slid down my face, settling in my eyes. "Not that I understood a fucking word of what you said."

I pulled my hand back in disgust before settling my gaze on the old woman. Her hands were clenched tightly around the handle of a medium-sized cast-iron skillet, as initially expected. She glared right back at me, her wrinkled face scrunched up at my declaration.

"Not hag. Mags. *Just* Mags," they snapped, and I raised a brow but nodded.

"Fine, just Mags. Can you *please* put the cast iron down now?" I asked, grumbling as I rubbed the rapidly growing bump on my head.

Mags watched me cautiously but didn't go to strike again. Thank fuck.

"What's your name, boy?" Mags lowered their weapon. Just enough for me to relax, at least for a moment.

Didn't want them going psycho on me again.

"I don't know. Prince, I think."

I didn't get the response I was expecting, as their face twisted into a scowl, before dropping the pan the rest of the way. Their arms shook from the weight of it.

"You're early, boy," Mags mumbled as they hobbled past me into the kitchen, not even giving me time to deduce what that could mean.

By the disgruntled noise they made, I'd guess they'd found my little mess.

"Ya can't even clean up after yourself? What am I to do with ya?" Mags's shuffling made me turn toward them again, my eyes meeting theirs just as they pulled out a small mop and bucket. "Well, Prince," Mags said my name like a mock, and I had to hold my tongue at the sound. The indignation made me angry, even if that wasn't my actual name. That was what she called me, Aaliyah. "Where did ya come from?"

The squeak of a mop against the floor made me want to puke again. It was a harsh reminder of my pain from the last flashback.

"I'm not sure." I ran a hand through my hair.

Would Mags even understand? They seemed to know what I was, at the very least. With reluctance, I sat at the table, the old chair creaking in protest at my weight. I brushed the blood out of my eyes once more before I spoke again.

"I woke in what I can only assume was a tomb." I rubbed the back of my neck. "I don't know how I got there, but I was in terrible shape. I only know that I shouldn't be here."

My explanation was broken, but it was all I had. No memories to rely on, no one I could ask.

She wasn't here.

"What a bother," they said, shaking their head and clicking their tongue. "Can't do anything right."

Then Mags turned to face me again, their old, wrinkled, and aged hand coming up to brush a thumb across my forehead. Their hand came back, thumb covered in blood. Mags shuffled around before coming back with what looked to be a towel. I was too stunned to move as they reached up and brushed the blood off my face like a mother would do to a child after a day of play.

"That doesn't explain the blood, young man," Mags said, their tone scolding.

Like this was a disciplinary action, and I was nothing but a child. Surprisingly, I wasn't offended. Something about this crazed bat told me they were much more than their ragged appearance let on.

"I think the boy was there to clean the room. I was on him before I knew what I was doing." I left it at that, and by their nod, I figured they knew the rest.

Mags watched me for a second, their eyes suddenly glowing gold. Power like nothing I'd ever felt stole my breath. Then Mags grinned, showing a mouthful of black teeth. "Don't worry too much about it now, boy. Mags will help however they can," they said, then hobbled away from me once again, rambling aimlessly about mirrors.

Well, that went better than expected.

Chapter 38

Osiris

I tugged the coat over my shoulders, unable to deny Aaliyah this request as she stood worried by the doorway.

Vampires didn't feel cold, not in the way humans did. But it had begun to snow, and Aaliyah was worried. So, there I was, wearing a coat over my second favorite suit.

"Be careful," she urged, biting her lip, a habit of hers.

I wanted to reach forward, to pull out the abused flesh. But it wasn't my place. That was the action of a lover, a companion.

And I couldn't be that for her yet.

"I will be," I said, regardless.

She pressed into Eirik, who stood by her side, sparing one more glance at me before turning fully to him. She leaned into him, wrapping her arms around his shoulders. He looked massive, engulfing her as she whispered the same things to him.

Be careful.

She made sure his coat was in order as well, pulling a chuckle out of Eirik. A rumbling purr started in his chest, and he leaned down, brushing a kiss to her forehead. I was enraptured by it, by the blush of her cheeks and the dazed way she beamed at him. Unfounded jealousy shot up, and I had to look away.

Can't be jealous about something you chose not to go after.

"Please, they're the ones who need to be careful. Think they're mad about Curtis?" Eirik asked, glancing at me with a raised eyebrow.

"I think Drakon was more than happy that we removed his kin from the equation," I replied flatly, catching Aaliyah's glance. "Curtis was a cancer, one that didn't suffer enough for what he did."

She didn't flinch when I reminded her of what I did. Again, she surprised me when concern once more sparked in her vibrant eyes.

"Are you sure you don't want me to come? I don't like this," she said, looking between us.

Eirik squeezed her hand, and Fallon swept to her side, pulling her into his arms.

It was odd, so odd that I had to watch and make sure it really was Fallon who moved. He smiled at her, kindly, something that I hadn't seen in *decades*. The only times he expressed joy were when he was in a fight. Aaliyah grinned back, taken by his kiss.

"We need to keep you off the radar. We can't risk news of you getting back to Sebek," he said, and she frowned. "Until we're sure Drakon is on our side, I don't want him seeing you."

But nodded.

"Right," she grumbled. "But that doesn't mean I like it."

"Wasn't asking you to, Ali. Just asking that you trust them. They're strong bastards."

She leaned into his embrace, and I stiffened when he looked at us.

"Adrian, Fallon," I said, making sure they caught my gaze. I didn't need to ask, not anymore.

They would protect her with their lives.

"Always," they said in unison.

"Come on, love, what do you say to another movie? I'll make popcorn." Adrian's soft question had her smiling again.

She glanced at Eirik and I one last time, apprehension not fully draining. Then they were gone, upstairs toward Adrian's room, where they had installed a TV a few days ago.

Eirik snapped at me, marching toward the door with his hands shoved into his suit pants pockets. The harsh black suit strained against him, and he looked furious under the light of the moon.

"God, what happened to the man who pulled me out of Brazen's cage? You've never been the one to hide from something, Osiris." Eirik's disgruntled words didn't bounce as they should have. "Why are you starting now?"

They sank into my skin, and all I could think of was how Aaliyah would feel pressed against me.

"I can't, Eirik. Not with this." We slid into the car, and I started it, letting the roar of the engine drown out the ache in my chest.

"I'm not going to push you, not like Fallon means to, and trust me when I say he *means to*. But I will say my peace to you." Eirik turned to me, the expression of old on his face. The Viking came to the surface as he snarled. His wolf prowled behind his eyes, and I settled my breath. "You're hurting her, and my wolf can only handle so much. So either get down on your knees and tell her you want her."

She was *all* I wanted.

"Or let her go."

I just needed to find the strength to do it. For me, for *her*. Because she deserved better than the person I was now.

"When are they supposed to be here?" Eirik sipped his drink, the heady aroma of brandy making my stomach roll.

It wasn't ash, but I had never been one for brandy. Even whisky didn't hold any appeal when Aaliyah was constantly on my mind.

"They already are. They've been scoping out the situation for the last few minutes." I could hear them now, heavy boots and the acidic whiff of heat and stone.

We were in a closed room in a small restaurant, one that was run by an old friend of ours. Another Dragonkin, one that had been opposed to Teviticus. It was locked away from the other occupants, so we wouldn't have to worry about our conversation getting out. While it was small, it had just enough life to not be claustrophobic. There were plants in two corners and a tapestry of the sea over one of the walls, imitating windows since there weren't any. The floor, covered in a shag carpet, helped to liven up the space, and even the smell of food helped to draw you in.

I added, "They'll be in shortly."

Eirik huffed, his beast lurking in his eyes. He shrugged his shoulders, rolling them after he flinched. He looked better, but not perfect. The sight of it scared me more than I could voice.

If Aaliyah's blood didn't work, then we were dead. And every time I saw Eirik, the Viking warrior who'd fell entire armies by himself, flinch, I wondered how much longer we had to mull over the transfer.

It was only a few short minutes later when the door slammed open and the eldest of Teviticus, the old Dragonkin Eternal, stormed into the room.

Drakon looked every bit like his father's son, a fact I was sure that he despised. I could empathize with hatred for one's Maker. Narrowed brown eyes with specks of fire lurking in them, blond hair, and a sharp face. A deep trauma in his eyes.

Features I always noted, because he was the exact man you would expect Sebek to turn. If he were human, I'd have worried about him. I still might, considering Eirik's predicament. Being a wolf hadn't stopped Sebek from trying then.

"Drakon," I said with a nod, and he rolled his eyes as he strolled into the room.

I didn't know the man behind him. Black hair against deep black eyes and ivory skin. It only took a breath to tell he was Dragonkin as well. His scent was marked by spice and tea.

"Osiris," Drakon started, taking one of the spare seats, the other man sliding in beside him. "Surprised you called me like this. You aren't exactly one for greetings."

There was hesitancy in his words, though he didn't back down from my gaze. A trait of their family, it seemed. Carter had been much the same.

Curtis had not.

"Rest assured, the surprise is not ill toward you," I said carefully, and Drakon relaxed, sinking into his seat. "We only wished to speak."

Drakon grunted but looked between us, then back to his guest.

"This is Aldric, my second. He wouldn't let me go alone after you asked to meet." He crossed his arms, and Aldric's glare turned to stone. It was an attitude I knew well, one that reminded me of Fallon. I nearly laughed at it. The man had a few hundred years before he reached the ice in Fallon's gaze. "Now, why don't you tell me why the fuck I'm here?"

"I told you, we wanted to talk," I said simply.

Drakon slammed his hand onto the table, a rolling growl on his lips. Much like Eirik, his eyes shifted, diamond slits taking up his pupil as his dragon came forward. Eirik didn't flinch, his own low snarl coming up.

"That's bullshit. You don't *talk*. Had you wanted a discussion, you would have sent the Collector. This is about Teviticus, isn't it?" He dragged a hand through his hair, a thick puff of gray smoke coming from his nose as he exhaled. Sulfur filled the air. "If you want to avenge him, you're going to realize really quick that I'm not as easy to cull as my brother was."

I took a deep breath, quelling the need to force charm into my words as the *Flame* crawled in my blood. He could likely feel it, the residual heat, the burning stench of cinders in the air.

"We've not come here for a fight, Drakon," I reminded him, leveling him with a glare. The air dropped a degree, then another my power spread throughout the room. "But you'd best find your tongue and watch it. I'm not in the best mood."

It wasn't much, but he flinched, his jaw clenching tight.

"I'm here to give my condolences." Drakon dropped his gaze, his entire face falling. "And to back your claim for the spot of Dragonkin Eternal *if* you'll back an Exilium against Sebek."

Silence met the room.

Then Drakon laughed, the booming sound echoing, even the table rocking as he smacked his hand over the top of it.

"You plan to pose Exilium, an *Honored Death*, for *Sebek*? You know how many votes you need for that, right?" he asked, incredulously confused. Of course, I did. You needed a three-fourths vote, which was why it happened so seldom. Why it had *never* happened. "Gotta say, I wasn't expecting that."

He shook his head, catching eyes with Eirik, who still hadn't stopped his rumbling snarl.

"What's in it for us?" Aldric asked, grabbing the table's attention.

"The backing of the Vampire Eternal and not having to deal with *Death's Butcher* at your door," I said, and Drakon nodded, his eyes closing. "I'm telling you that you have to deal with me or him. It's up to you to decide which evil better suits you."

Another moment of silence passed before Drakon crossed his arms and nodded toward me. There was command in his stance, in the way he sat. He would make a good Eternal.

"You have a plan?" he asked.

"We do," I answered, crisp.

"How many others have you convinced?"

"Enough."

He laughed, his head tipping back in disbelief as he looked at Aldric. Those cold eyes of his hadn't left us yet, but slowly, he nodded.

Like he was watching for something.

"God, you're almost worse than I expected," Drakon said, rubbing the back of his neck. "When I heard that *the* Osiris Vivas wanted an audience, I nearly died laughing. The Natural world hasn't heard from your Crypt in a century, and then you show up all pleasantries in your fancy tailored suits. Fucking hilarious."

Thick bands of black traced his exposed arms, the windings of Dragonkin tattoos.

"This is him talkative," Eirik said, taking another sip of his drink, eyes centered on Aldric.

"Look, I'm all for removing the old bastard from his seat. I'll jump for joy with you when it happens." Drakon's eyes sharpened, the diamond pupil in them narrowing as his eyes glowed. Dragons were truth seekers and could read people like open books. Living lie detectors. The press of that gift brushed over me, searching for my truths. "But I need more than your word. I need a show of faith that you won't be just as fucked up as him. Because based on recent news, I'm not sure which of you to trust. After all, twenty-three lives fell to you really fucking recently, didn't they?"

I bit my tongue, my hand gripping my wrist as the *Flame* flared in my throat. I wanted to lash out for the disrespect, but I knew it was earned. Knew that I had to play this right if I wanted the allies. If we were to get this done without bloodshed.

"Death's well earned, after their pack master tried to rape our ward," I seethed, watching carefully as Drakon tensed in his seat. "If that answer satisfies you, then what do you have in mind?"

Smoke fell from his nose, clouding the room in the rancid scent of ash. I wondered if he might stand and leave us sitting here. But there was a desperation in his eyes he couldn't quite hide behind all that fire.

"I want someone dead." I didn't miss the murderous intent in his eyes, nor the way his hands flexed as he spoke. This was personal, something that meant a lot to him. *We could use that.*

"You're the Dragonkin Eternal now. Anyone you want dead is as good as dead. So long as you can kill them yourself, and it seems like you can," Eirik butted in, his own expression turning savage. "Too chickenshit?"

Drakon snarled as he shot to his feet, his hands slamming on the table. His second, Aldric, stood as well, trying to stop the raging Dragonkin from reaching over the table. Eirik's own beast prowled, staring down Drakon's Dragon with a twisting smirk on his lips. Drakon snapped back, baring his teeth in the face of our Viking.

"I'd kill him in a heartbeat if I knew I wouldn't face Retaliation myself," he snarled, painting the picture clearer with each breath.

Retaliation meant he wanted to kill someone powerful. Someone with allies that would want revenge.

"An Eternal then," I said, and he clenched his teeth.

He wasn't expecting us to get it so quickly, likely hoping we'd accept before he got to the grittier details of his request. He thought us to be desperate since we'd called this meeting. But he didn't know us, nothing more than rumors. And I'd always made sure they did us more disservice than justice. It was better that way, easier to keep those that'd wish you harm out of the loop. He played a dangerous game, and it insulted me that he thought it would work.

"One with allies, ones that would seek retribution for their death." I continued, each word growing louder, more pronounced as a spark lit across my skin, ending behind my eyes. He looked at them, holding my gaze. "Ask something else. We won't clean up your mess."

He rolled his eyes, desperation building in his posture. The switch I knew was coming, the preserved predator becoming prey. It was the folly of a weak man, and I expected him to bow his head ... so I was viciously intrigued when he stood his ground instead.

Seemed Drakon was worth more than I thought.

"They'd look for revenge with *me*. But you? You're the turned of the Sebek Ra. *Death's Butcher*. They wouldn't dare. And by the time they'd even consider it, the numbers would be on our side at the Eternium. That's our offer, Vivas. Take it or leave it."

Even Eirik looked proud, his lips tilting. I caught his eyes, the bloodlust that had started to swirl. It was enough to at least see who Drakon wanted dead.

"You have a lot of faith in yourself and your allies. Who else would join our side?" I asked.

There was silence before Drakon tipped his head to Aldric. The lither of the two Dragonkin reached into his suit coat and pulled out a crisp piece of paper. He handed it to me, snatching his hand back as if I might bite him.

"We've been tallying our connections ever since Drakon took the mantle. With as many brothers as he has, we worried one might try to Challenge, and we wanted to know who would back us," Audric explained as I opened the note.

On it was a list of Eternals, each with markings next to their names, dictating where they stood. Even I had to admit I was shocked that they'd found so many allies ... though there were other names as well. Names of those that intended to Challenge.

"I know it's hard for you lot, but you'd have to trust me. The people on this list want change," Drakon grunted.

This was exactly what we needed, but it also depended on Drakon's party winning their challenges. I knew most of them and had kept tabs through Adrian. It wasn't impossible, but risky, nonetheless.

"Who is it you want dead?" I asked.

Drakon paused again, further worrying me.

"If you *do* decide to take me up on the offer, a little birdy told me that the one you're looking for is hosting an art gala soon. Your window is short, so you'd have to make it count. I even have a contact that can get you legit tickets, though that won't be a cakewalk, either."

He continued to stall, and Eirik snapped, "A *name*, Drakon."

The Dragonkin let out a breath, shaking his head like he already knew our reaction. He tapped the table, his frustration growing as claws formed where his nails had been. The click of them against the hardwood echoed.

"Demon Eternal Kri'Valta Veltum," Drakon seethed, his jaw going taut as his claws bit into the table.

I couldn't stop the dread that came, nor the tremor that worked its way down my spine. Kri'Valta was the last person—short of Sebek—I would want to fight. He'd been around for *eons*, and his power was just as well-known as Sebek's. But at least he didn't go around killing Eternals.

And allies, he had many. Eternals, Naturals, even mortals.

"The horror of the depths, the Demon Eternal himself. He's been around for as long as Sebek," I said, and Drakon nodded. "You do realize what you're asking, right?"

It was near suicide. And we'd have to put more than just the weight of Sebek's wrath onto us. Kri'Valta's allies would seek vengeance. We'd face Retaliation no matter what Drakon promised, I'd guarantee it.

"Do this for me and have our backing, Osiris. Me and all of my allies. We've wanted change for *decades*. This might just be the chance to get it," Drakon said, reaching over the table. "Since you're so graciously doing the same."

Admirable. He would make a good Eternal. That made me even more inclined to consider this now-crazed proposition. Killing Kri'Valta was a risk, but this was a deal we might not be able to pass up, although there may be a way around it as well. It was something to discuss. At least now we had options.

But there was a fire in Drakon's eyes, one of madness and sorrow. Kri'-

Valta had done something to deserve this, and I could only guess what it was.

"What did Kri'Valta do to you?" I asked, folding the note back up and placing it in my pocket.

It was a prod, and I willingly pushed where I knew I'd find open wounds. I wanted to see how he'd react, how he'd buckle under our pressure.

But Drakon snarled again. "None of your fucking business."

"This is exactly my business, son of *Teviticus*. You want us to kill him? I want to know why."

We deserved at least that much.

"He helped with the murder of our Pearl. Led Teviticus right to her," Aldric finally whispered, his head tipping away as anguish wiped away his neutral expression. "Then made sure there were barely more than bones left to bury."

So, this was more than just petty revenge. It was a statement; one I could get behind. Kri'Valta had taken their family. I considered my own reaction, should someone ever take Ali from me again.

I recalled the bodies that likely still littered the forest grounds.

I'd level the earth and cut down any who so much as dared to *look* at her. Drakon's reaction was tame compared to what I would do, so I merely nodded.

"My condolences for your mate and child," I replied.

Drakon flinched back, and Aldric turned away for the first time. Shielding his eyes from us.

"Twins," Aldric said, his clenched fists telling us that the feeling was still raw. As I expected it to be, just weeks after it happened. "Our Pearl and our twins."

My heart, unbeating as it was, went out to them. I could see the pain in them. They carried it well, better than I could.

Far better than I carried it now.

"We'll discuss it with the others," I said with a nod.

"If you choose to, the contact for the tickets can be found at *The Altar*. The Collector will know who to talk to." Drakon dipped his head, his eyes still far away yet always lit with that underlying flame. "The clock is ticking, Osiris. I hope you're ready for a party."

CHAPTER 39

AALIYAH

I paced my way across the library, strangled by the worry I couldn't keep down. My stomach twisted, and even though it was irrational, I couldn't stop thinking about everything that could go wrong with the meeting.

They said Drakon was a good man, like Carter ... but it was hard to trust that. Curtis had been a brother of Carter's too, and look where that had gotten him.

I jolted as arms gently circled me, pulling me out of my thoughts and manic pacing.

"You're driving yourself crazy, love," Adrian whispered, kissing me softly on the head. Like always, butterflies spread in my stomach. "They're going to be okay, I promise."

I hummed, looking up at him, then across the room to where Fallon sat, looking tense as well. Though he wasn't worried about Eirik and Osiris, his eyes never left me.

"I know ... I know," I said. "But that doesn't mean I'm not worried about them. Eirik still doesn't feel the best, and Osiris is finally looking better after everything that happened. I don't want them pushing themselves."

Adrian nodded, his arms tightening around me. "They're very lucky men to have you thinking about them, love," he mused before his lips broke into a grin. "But I think you could use a distraction."

He had me there, that I could use.

"Like what?" I asked.

Maybe we'd dance in the library again and see if we could entice Fallon into joining in. Or maybe we could make some sweets for when the others got back, so we'd have something nice to share. Or a picnic under the stars. Whatever he had planned, I knew it would be worth it.

"We've been run ragged the last few weeks, and I think we could use a break. An actual one." Adrian tipped his head toward Fallon, grinning from ear to ear. "What do you say, Fally? Fancy a night on the town?"

Town? My back went rigid, breaths coming out sharply, and I panted at the thought. I reached up, rubbing my arms to get some sense of reality back. The heat from my hands bled into my skin, and I took a deep breath, pulling in the scent of coffee grounds, whiskey, and old books.

Going to town sounded terrifying, but it was the glow in Adrian's eyes that had me pausing and not immediately saying no. The effortless way he leaned back, still keeping his hands on my shoulders, rubbing gentle circles with his thumbs.

"Didn't you hear Osiris? It's not a good idea to be going out right now. We should stay in," Fallon insisted, the voice of reason. And I nodded in return. "And when the others get back, talk about the blood transfer."

Because he wasn't wrong. With my uncle, Sebek, in the States, and Ascension Rising still out there as well, we really shouldn't risk it ... but I couldn't deny that I wanted to. That I wanted to spend some time away before the Eternium stole all of it.

"Spoilsport. He said it's not a good idea for her to meet *Drakon* right now. I'm not suggesting we go parading ourselves, but we *need* to get out. It's not good for the mind to be stuck like this for so long," Adrian protested, shaking his head. "And you realize that conversation is going to happen only when they get back, not sooner. We can get out without causing a fuss. We'll be back before Eirik and Osiris. Then we can have your talk, and all will be well."

Fallon weighed the words, his eyes landing on me. I shuffled on my feet, unable to keep my curious excitement at bay.

There was a crack in his façade, one that slid away as he shook his head, his lip raising at the corner. It flashed just enough of his white teeth, and something I rarely saw in him shone through. Mischief.

"Well, what do you have in mind?" he asked, and Adrian grinned.

He gave me one last squeeze, planting another kiss at my temple before he pulled away. "Hm. What about that little plaza? The one in Aspenway?"

I'd only heard of Aspenway a few times. It was small, smaller than even Oakridge. Eliza often went there to get spices and produce you couldn't get as easily in Oakridge.

"What's there to do there?" I asked, curiously.

"Not sure. I haven't really spent much time here. Let's just explore and see something new while staying out of the spotlight. It's perfect."

I hummed and looked at Fallon again. He watched me curiously before he walked up to me. When he was standing just inches away, he lifted his hand and cupped my cheek.

"What do you think, Ali?" he asked.

Just one day, always just one day. Hunting for time with the people I loved before it ran out. It was risky, it was bold, and it was probably a bad idea. No, *definitely* a bad idea. Fallon was right, we should stay in and talk about the last thing I wanted to talk about ...

But I didn't want to think about it right now. Not their deaths, not mine. I just wanted to live for one night, with them by my side.

"It would be nice, I think," I said anyway.

I waited for the denial and was already preparing myself for that answer when Fallon nodded and slid his hand down to take mine in his.

"It's settled then. Come on, love," Adrian said with a clap, coming up to my other side. His beaming smile was contagious. "We're taking you on a date!"

"You don't have a plan," Fallon muttered, rubbing the space between his eyes while glaring at the small complex of bustling buildings around us.

Though, bustling might not be the right word. It was quiet, quaint. A few couples were wandering around much like us, looking at the Christmas lights and admiring the stores. Though things weren't lit up like some grand festival, there was a definite air of work and pride, with everything exactly in place to give off a feeling that I could only describe as homey. It made me want to curl up on one of the benches that lined the square in front of one of the little fire pits just to watch the snowfall.

"Of course not. This was spontaneous. We're having fun exploring together! Where's your sense of adventure, Fallon?" Adrian laughed, though his eyes continually scanned the area.

He still grinned, now and then turning to watch me, but he stayed alert in a way that told me he was taking this much more seriously than he seemed to. His hand never left mine, the gloved fingers tightening as he hummed.

Adrian glanced at me. "What do you think, love? Are you having fun?"

"Yes," I murmured, ducking my head when Fallon squeezed my other hand. Sandwiched between them, I nearly melted. "The lights are beautiful."

Adrian looked away, scanning the lights as I did. Even sticking his tongue out to catch a stray snowflake on his tongue. "The humans put on a really splendid show every year with their Christmas parade. Maybe we can go see it before we depart for the Eternium?"

It was a dream at best, but I let myself think about it for a moment. The shining lights, Adrian, Fallon, Eirik, and Osiris, all by my side. We'd stay out until it got too cold to bear, then drink hot chocolate until sunrise.

It was a small dream, a simple, normal dream.

"I'd like that," I said, humming along to the tune in the air.

One day, we'd have that. A life where we weren't always looking behind us. A life that Prince would be proud of. That *I* would be proud of.

I shook it off and looked around again. The buildings were dusted in a layer of snow, and the shimmering lights glowed in varying colors. Unlike Oakridge, everything here was newer, the buildings filled with life and lacking the aged crumble. While every shop looked enticing if only for the warmth inside them, one particular building caught my eye, the flashing lights and upbeat music enough to stop me in my tracks.

It was marvelous, lit so brightly that I almost couldn't look away. Colors so vibrant it was overwhelming, the sounds slipping past the cracked open door exciting.

A shiver shot down my spine, and I rubbed my arms. Glancing around, a muddied feeling almost made it feel like I was being watched. But no one was around us, and the chill grew even more pointed as Red settled near us.

"What are you looking at, Ali?" Fallon asked suddenly, and I jolted, turning to peek up at him.

I bit my lip, glancing at the building again. We probably *shouldn't*. It was dangerous enough for us to be out here at all, and this little walk was more than I could have asked for. It was probably time to head home.

"Nothing," I said, right before my hand was pulled from Adrian's and I was hoisted into a pair of powerful arms. I squealed, seeing Fallon's white suit flash across my vision, and then I was looking down at him.

His eyes deepened, just as his arms tightened like bands around my waist. Fallon looked at me with a raised eyebrow, and I was too shocked to react to the sudden move, even as my cheeks heated and I glanced around to see if anyone noticed the scene.

"Now, now, love! This is a date. So tell us what you see, and our lady shall have it!" Adrian chimed from our side.

I mulled it over again, unable not to stare at the glowing palace that had caught my attention. I reached up, my hands looking for something to idle on, and they found Fallon's hair, toying with the strands while still leaving it mostly intact. I brush it away from his face, gently directing it back into the pushed-back style he preferred.

"It's getting late," I reasoned. "Shouldn't we be getting home?"

Adrian clicked his tongue, shaking his head just as Fallon grunted. "Tell us what you want to do, Ali. This is a date, remember?"

Hearing Fallon confirm that was enough to set me on fire, my cheeks flushing so red that I grew dizzy, becoming a mess in his arms as he grinned indulgently at me. My hands stalled in his hair.

I glanced again, and Adrian snickered next to us.

"Home can wait a bit longer, love. So, the arcade?" Adrian asked, following my gaze to the energetic building. I hesitated just a second before nodding. "Never been to one. What about you, Fally?" Fallon said nothing, and Adrian sighed loudly before walking ahead of us a few steps. "Right, not sure why I asked. So *boring*. Come on, then!"

And so Fallon was following Adrian, still bracing me in his arms, grumbling the entire way as we watched Adrian skip and gasp in exaggerated awe as we walked. Before I knew it, I was being set down inside.

"Well, this is shiny!" Adrian exclaimed, his hands on his hips as he scanned the room.

And it was. It was even more lively than the outside led me to believe. The rich colors that I'd been so drawn to covered the entire space, from floor to ceiling, with unique figures and toys placed everywhere. There were games strewn all about, most of them void of people. It smelled like metal and the overcooked hotdogs that Grigen used to beg Eliza for.

"Very shiny," I said in awe.

"And loud," Fallon scoffed, eyeing the space wearily.

I reached out, taking his hand again. His gaze flashed down to me, and all the stress drained from his expression.

"Oh! Let's try this one!" Adrian said before dashing off.

Fallon rolled his eyes, shaking his head as we followed. We passed several games and a couple eating a pizza that looked greasy, cheesy, and to die for. But we passed them all as Adrian came to a stop in front of a gigantic machine with a plastic seat at a rather odd-shaped steering wheel. It flashed brightly, showing cars on the screen.

"It's a racing game, see? And you can win these tickets to get prizes! Don't worry, sweetheart. I'm going to win you the best prize." Adrian winked as he spoke, fiddling with his pocket before pulling out a quarter.

The machine beeped and screamed when he put it in, and he sank into the plastic seat with a cheeky grin.

Then the game started.

And just as quickly *finished* as Adrian crashed his car directly into the wall. He grunted, pulling out another quarter, this one taking longer to find. To his credit, he made it farther this time, swerving around another car, his cheeky grin growing broad.

Before he crashed again.

This was the cycle, with Fallon shooting prodding comments when Adrian crashed and me giving encouraging words as he came in second to last. By the time he was out of quarters, he was a mumbling mess, and I was stifling my laughs in Fallon's side. Even Fallon chuckled, and Adrian shot him a withering glower.

"Dammit ... this wasn't supposed to be this hard. Fallon, fetch me another quarter, will you?" he asked, and Fallon shook his head.

"Move over," he said, shocking both Adrian and I as he unbuttoned his suit coat. To say I lingered on the dexterity of his fingers as he shrugged off the coat and rolled the sleeves of his white dress shirt up his arms was an understatement.

Adrian's eyebrows shot up, but he obliged, sliding out of the seat so Fallon could take his place.

"You're going to play? Oh, this is going to be good," Adrian snickered before walking over to me. "About time someone else got to sit in the laughing seat."

He wrapped his arm loosely around my shoulder, leaning in to kiss my forehead. That blooming heat from the press of his lips had me blushing, and I looked around the room to find a few of the patrons inside staring at us. There was a mixture of confusion, disgust, and curiosity in their eyes. I sank further into Adrian's side at the sight.

"People are staring," I said.

Adrian tipped in close, so his mouth was next to my ear as he whispered, "Good. They're jealous that we've snagged the most gorgeous woman in the room."

His breath, cool against my cheek, made me shiver as heat flooded my core. His hand, which had been sitting softly on my shoulder, tightened protectively, and this time, when he leaned in, it was with an intentional flare. His lips skimmed mine, teasing me before he dove in, claiming them in a possessive way I hadn't been expecting. His grip was tight, his claim almost terrifying.

But I leaned into it, soul almost bursting at the attention, at the way he showed so proudly that I was by his side. When he pulled back, I was breathing heavily, my eyes only on him.

"The most gorgeous woman who also gets to pick out a prize," Fallon chimed in, standing. I turned to him, shivering at his thick, heated gaze. His nose flared, and his pupils nearly dwarfed the green of his eyes. Sure enough, the game that was now behind him was flashing 'winner' in big red lights.

And spitting out tickets all over the floor.

Adrian made a noise caught between surprise and astonishment, his mouth wide open.

"You *cheated*," he hissed, looking between Fallon and the explosion of tickets that only continued to get worse.

A laugh fought its way up my throat again, and I covered my mouth with my hand.

"Of course I didn't. You're just bad," Fallon joked. *Joked.*

It always shocked me to hear him say anything with that cynical sarcasm, and right now, it was exactly what I needed.

"The audacity! You rigged the machine!" Adrian protested, and Fallon rolled his eyes as he tugged his suit coat back on. He stepped over his mound of tickets to get to me, reached up, and pulled a chocolate from his breast pocket.

"Here," he said, placing it in my hand like he always did.

"What's this for?" I asked, unable to stop my grin.

"Your prize. I won it for you," he said, and I laughed.

Adrian, who had been continuing his rant, fell silent. Fallon urged me to open it, scowling when I went to tuck it away. I caved and happily ate the sweet treat.

"You didn't win the chocolate," I mused, licking my fingers, and Fallon shook his head.

"No, but it got me you. It's more valuable than gold." I blushed at his words and the wolfish grin on his face. "Come on, why don't you try it?"

He reached out, and I took his hand with my free one. He walked me over to the machine, and I sat in the seat. It was cold, and I hissed at the feeling before sinking in. I looked at him in confusion, placing my hand on the steering wheel.

"What do I do?" I asked, and he pointed out the different gears and buttons, then inserted a quarter.

I barely did better than Adrian, managing only to get around the first bend before slamming into the back of another car. I jolted at the impact, blushing when 'restart?' flashed brightly on the screen. But Fallon didn't scold me or make fun, just shook his head indulgently before adding another quarter. I gripped the wheel and tried again.

And again, and again. I got lost in the silly game, making a play out of it when I'd crash, gasping loudly. Adrian stood to one side, Fallon to the other.

It wasn't long before Fallon ran out of quarters as well. He mumbled something, frowning before looking between me and the machine.

"I'll be right back," he said, quickly stalking off.

"What do you say we go get something to drink while he grabs some more quarters? We could hunt down another game as well." I nodded, my lips tired from how hard I was smiling.

I stood and followed Adrian to the drink kiosk, the mass of tickets bundled in his arms. There was a bit of a line, with several people in front of us, and just one poor worker who looked halfway dead to the world. His eyes were practically rolling out of his skull as the woman at the front of the line whispered something haughtily that I couldn't quite make out.

This was going to take a second.

"I'm going to pee really quick," I said, and Adrian tipped his head at me before looking across the way to the shining sign that read restrooms.

"Okay, let me get these and we can go," he said, and I shook my head.

I looked around the little arcade, shivering as I searched the empty games. The slight apprehension about being alone crept up, and I bit my lip. It wasn't the same pressing panic I'd felt the night when Curtis had found me on the street, on my way to Archons. That seemed like a lifetime ago, hoping that Archon would know what was wrong with me.

Now I was just tense, like I was searching the shadows for a bogeyman that wasn't there. My nerves had to be getting to me, and I refused to let them ruin the evening.

"No, it'll be fine. It's just right there. I won't be long," I assured Adrian, sliding away from his side.

He hesitated, eyeing the bathrooms again before nodding. "Okay, love. I'll meet you over there."

I nodded and turned away. I walked carefully, avoiding all the people I could, especially the ones who stared a little too long at what little skin I had exposed and the scars that lined it. But the bathroom was close enough, and I snuck in, went to the restroom, and was washing my hands when the door opened again. I tensed instinctually but didn't look up.

It was silly, being scared of someone else going to the bathroom. I admonished myself, making light of the situation as best I could.

Then the door clicked closed ... like the sound of a lock. That got me moving, my hands freezing under the water, and when I lifted my eyes, a nightmare was standing in the mirror.

"Glass?" a stentorian voice tinged with an accent hissed. It made pressure flare in my mind and made my blood freeze as my lungs contracted. My hands shook under the water, and I struggled to breathe as I came face to face with *Nilus*.

My nose flooded with the scent of iron, and the room dimmed as I flipped around, stumbling away from him.

He looked exactly like he had in all of my memories. His broad, unruly frame, with shoulders nearly the width of the doorframe behind him. Shaggy black hair hung around his shoulders in a formless mass, and his deep blue eyes were bubbling, snarling clouds of rage and pain. He was wearing what had to be rags, the clothes worn and dirty.

"N—" I couldn't even say his name, choking on it as tears flooded my eyes and my mantra started.

Never make noise.

"I *finally* found you," he sneered, the veins on his neck popping as he took a step forward. "Do you know what you did?"

A word, a denial, was lodged in my throat as I took a maddening step back. I couldn't speak, my voice as trapped as I was. I couldn't begin to understand what he meant, what he wanted.

They get more violent when I make noise.

I jolted my gaze around the room and on the flex of the shadows around me. The iron in my nose exploded, sliding over my lip. Blood painted my tongue as my fangs, the ones I hadn't known about, pressed against my gums. Why did this have to happen now?

Why *now*?

I balled my hands into tight fists, my head spinning as the room further fell into darkness and a sickening twist of rage started in my stomach.

"You died. I saw it. And they killed everyone because of it. Doctor C,

Donavan, *everyone* because of it. Because of a dirty little freak!" he roared, and each word made his accent more pronounced.

The words he'd said, what they meant, shocked me nearly as much as seeing him. Dead? Were they really all dead?

He took another step. "One who didn't even have the courtesy to stay dead."

"What are you doing here?" I whimpered as I curled in on myself.

"Been looking for you, Glass. Searching after your grave was found empty. Never lost your scent, disgusting like *death*," he snarled, feral. His entire face grew red, and then I saw it, something I hadn't recognized. His face shifted and morphed, feline in the way his cheekbones turned up and his eyes slitted. He was a *shifter*. "You will pay for the lives that were lost because of you."

"I didn't kill them! Please," I pleaded, the pressure in my head growing as quickly as the blood slipped over my lips. Nilus didn't notice, too furious with his own emotions.

"You didn't, but your *blood* did. It was in Donavan's veins," he hissed, stepping forward until my back was to the wall, and he was directly in front of me.

Donovan's face flashed across my vision like a specter, with sky-blue eyes and shaggy brown hair. He wasn't overtly cruel, but like any in Ascension, he wasn't kind either. He had *buried* me with Nilus at his side, covering me in dirt and leaving me in the cold ground.

"None of this would have happened had you not *died*. Had you lived and rotted in your cage." Then he reached out, jolting me against the wall as his hands grabbed my shoulders so harshly I gasped.

"Let me go!" I screamed, the pressure popping like a balloon, the shadows condensing and hitting Nilus in the chest. "Please, LET ME GO!"

He jolted at the shock, getting flung away from me. He only stopped when he hit the wall, his body bouncing off the door that opened only a fraction later. It slammed into Nilus's already prone body, and Fallon just pushed harder until he forced his way inside.

And when he saw Nilus on the ground, his eyes went that furious blood-red.

He had Nilus to his feet in an instant, slamming the giant man against the bathroom stall like he weighed nothing at all. Nilus had a couple of inches on Fallon, but he looked so small next to the furious man that held him. Fallon's fangs extended, and Nilus choked on the scream that couldn't slide past Fallon's grip on his neck.

"Who the fuck are you?" Fallon demanded, the quiet of his tone betraying the violent shake of his hands.

"*Nilus*," I filled in, rubbing my shoulder, numbness making it easy to move as I stepped toward them. "His name is Nilus."

Fallon looked at me, his eyes widening before Nilus choked again as Fallon tightened his grip.

"Nilus. I know that name," Fallon said, his head tilting as recognition suddenly burst in his eyes, followed by a rage so deep the red of his eyes nearly grew like molten lava. Nilus sputtered, his bravado suddenly failing him as he grew pallid. "*You* were at Ascension Rising."

Then Fallon said something, something so venomous that I didn't even need to understand the language to know what it meant.

Death was coming.

I should have feared that, should have felt *something*. But my mind blocked it out, and the part that made me ... *me,* that made me a Reaper, purred.

Ready for slaughter.

I shivered, equal parts disgusted with my thoughts as I was curious.

Adrian came flying through the door, grabbing Fallon's arm in a bruising grip. At first, I wanted to protest and almost did. Nilus deserved whatever was coming, right? But Adrian didn't have the look of someone that was here to save.

"Fal, not here. Home," Adrian urged, turning a pointed, seething glare on Nilus. "I've cleared the way. We have to move now."

"I'm not going anywhere with you," the big brute choked out, only for Fallon to slam him into the stalls again.

The metal groaned, and Fallon seethed something under his breath.

"You don't have a choice," Adrian sneered, grinning coldly before he turned to me.

The change was instant, as he moved toward me and pulled me swiftly into his arms. He trembled as he kissed my forehead, checking me over, his eyes landing on the bruises that peeked out from under my shirt. That malicious anger settled once more in his eyes, but he didn't set me down.

"Come on, love. Time to go home."

Chapter 40

Fallon

Why did this Shifter have to *scream* so much?

He'd been squealing like a pig for miles, groaning and crying at every bump and stick he slid over. Like he had a right to plead for his life.

Like he deserved a painless death.

My hand tightened in his hair, the black strands snapping and tearing, before he screamed again. Fuck, he was weak.

"Please, I'll do whatever you want. Just let me go!" His words were broken and disjointed by his heavy accent. Tears bubbled over his cheeks, his eyes swollen and red.

I ignored him. We were close now.

It had taken everything in me not to snap his neck at the arcade. Not to drain him dry and parade his body through the streets. The only thing that was keeping me sane was knowing that he wouldn't make it out of tonight alive.

Not after what he did to Ali.

Just the thought of it, of him being one of the ones who stood outside her cell and watched them hurt her, made me snarl and scream myself.

The man, *Nilus*, whimpered.

"It's not worth it. You must listen," he cried, his words falling on deaf ears. His accent made it hard to understand him, but his pleas for life would get him nowhere. "It is a *monster*."

I froze, stopping in the middle of the trees. There was a brisk wind that came with winter, biting into my just like his words.

It's not worth it. He wasn't talking about taking him home and interrogating him.

He was talking about *Ali.*

I tore him to his feet, taking pleasure in the pop that echoed from his shoulder as I slammed him against the nearest tree. The leaves above us shook, the few that had remained on the frosted branches floating down around us. He dangled by his hair, his hands gripping and tearing at my arm.

"Monster? No. The only monsters here are you and me. And the only thing keeping you alive right now is that your death isn't only mine. But if you say *one more* fucking word about Ali." I barely said her name before the man's eyes sickened with disgust.

I'm in control.

"Then I'll spend every second between now and sunrise making sure your screams haunt your ancestors, and even the ground will remember the taste of your blood." That was enough to silence the screams, and his mouth opened in horror. "You're not surviving this, Nilus. So, by all means, *keep screaming.* Let's see how long you last."

I dropped the weight of his body, dragging him along again. His screams continued until he lost his voice, and the only thing he could manage was harsh, garbled words and pleas of mercy he wouldn't receive. But he never spoke of her again.

Guess he had some sense of self-preservation after all.

By the time I slid through the door to our home, he was nearly catatonic. I pulled him into the kitchen, strapping him to a kitchen chair with the materials already gathered by Adrian, who was next to the island, preparing two cups of tea.

"Ouch, now that looks like it hurts. You should put some ice on that," he said, sipping from the steaming mug as he looked at Nilus. "You know, funny how life works. I spent weeks looking for any hint of the little organization you work for. I couldn't find any of it, not even a trace. Yet here you are, stumbling right into our laps. Why is that?"

The man trembled, his head shaking.

"The rest are dead. I am the last," he said, coughing up a lungful of blood. "They were disposed of after it died."

It. My hand curled into a fist so tight blood pooled under my nails. And it was no lie. The way he spoke, the horrified twist to his words. They were dead, and I was fucking *furious*. I had wanted to be the one to end them. But at least this meant they wouldn't be around to haunt Aaliyah anymore.

Nevertheless, a question remained: Who killed them?

"Where's Ali?" I asked, and Adrian tipped his head toward the stairs.

"Upstairs. I'll get her," he said, setting down his drink.

I shook my head and looked at the filth that stained our home.

"No," I said vehemently.

I'd seen her eyes as I'd held this man by his throat, the echo of her past that had come kicking and screaming until it was all she could think about. She didn't need to see this. Not him, not his death.

And not the pleasure I was going to take in it.

But Adrian scoffed, and both my eyebrows went up at his denial.

"I need to. She asked to be here, for whatever we do," he said.

She wanted to see this? It wasn't going to be pleasant or clean. I wanted to protect her from it, and needed to gain some control over the situation.

"She can't—" I started, but Adrian cut me off.

"We don't have any right to tell her what she can and can't do. If she can't handle it, she'll tell us. But until then, we *won't* take her choice away." His words hit me dead in the chest, killing any argument I had. Dulling some of the furious panic.

I took a breath and nodded. Slowly, I unbuttoned my jacket one button at a time. I hated blood on my suits.

"Why don't you settle our guest in?" Adrian asked before he *flitted* away.

Adrian and Ali joined me downstairs just as I finished my preparations, with Nilus still staring firmly at the ground. I stole a glance at her before I walked her way. I wasn't the touchy type, or I hadn't been before her. I leaned in, pulling her into my arms and pressing a kiss to the top of her head.

She held me just as tightly, tilting away just enough to look into my eyes. I searched them for any trace of doubt or regret, but there was only conviction and a need to see this through. I nodded once and held her by my side as I turned us to face Nilus. She startled when she saw him, and I had to take another leveling breath.

Or risk tearing him apart where he sat.

And if I couldn't shelter her from this moment, then I would be her knight to lean on.

Nilus glanced up, his eyes landing on Ali for only a second before his head was violently pulled away. Adrian was in his view, his grip bruising on the man's jaw.

"You don't look at her. You look at me," he said in a sharply pleasant tone.

Nilus didn't respond, but when Adrian let go, his eyes didn't waver again.

The door clicked open then, and I turned to face Eirik and Osiris as they walked in. Dread bubbled up, and I had a feeling this was about to go even further south. They were covered in a fine layer of snow and reeked of fresh soot. They glanced between us and the man in our kitchen.

"Adrian, Fallon," Osiris said, shrugging off his coat, curiously assessing Nilus. "Want to explain why there's a gentleman strapped to our kitchen chair?"

"Mostly because I didn't have time to get one of the foldy ones," Adrian mused, and Eirik shook his head with a huff.

"Did he sneak onto the property? I didn't feel a disturbance in the wards," Osiris asked, and it was Ali who shook her head.

"No. We ran into him in Aspenway. At the arcade," she confessed, and Osiris and Eirik went rigid.

Eirik's growl started low, before growing so loud it nearly shook the room. "You left the house with her? Knowing Sebek could be out there, *anywhere*?" he snarled.

"She was worried about you both. She needed a distraction," Adrian replied with a shrug.

We'd known this was a potential outcome, and honestly, a few hours ago, I had been thinking the same thing ... but they hadn't seen how Ali glowed there. Didn't get to see her without all the stress that had been piled onto her shoulders.

Even with Nilus, the arcade had been worth it to see her let go like that.

"Then distract her here. You put her in danger!" Eirik protested.

Ali tapped my arm and pulled away, walking toward Eirik, who continued to rant and posture about our failures. Ali reached him in three strides, her hand reaching up to cup his cheek. He paused and lowered so she could, stopping his sentence dead in its tracks.

"It's not his fault." She spoke with confidence, even as Eirik's eyes flashed a deep-sea blue. "I recommended the arcade, so *don't* yell at Adrian, please."

Eirik's jaw clenched, and it took nearly ten seconds before he nodded.

He reached his hand up to cup hers against his cheek, kissing her wrist harshly. "I'm glad you're safe, *Elskan.*"

It took her by surprise and made jealousy sear through me, more than a little. At least it did until he pulled back and she relaxed. He leaned in and whispered something in her ear I didn't quite catch but sounded like 'trouble.'

"Well, who is he?" Eirik asked, but it was Osiris who stepped toward the man.

He'd been silent since they first walked in, and it was now that I realized his human façade had dropped entirely. He stalked in front of Nilus and leaned down to look him in the eyes, before he turned his head to check on Ali. His eyes lingered on the bruises on her arms that Eirik hadn't noticed yet.

I quickly filled them in on what I knew, finishing with what he'd said earlier. Eirik looked just as displeased as I felt, knowing his blood would be the only one we'd get.

"He's Nilus. He was one of my guards," Aaliyah said, and that was all it took before Osiris struck.

His hand shot to Nilus's throat with such force that the chair slid back and struck the table. Adrian jolted forward, trying to urge Osiris away without touching him. Osiris's eyes bled red, and the spark of his power touched the air.

The lights flickered, and even my blood stung as his lips curled back from his teeth in a snarl.

"No killing, not yet. We need him to *talk* first," Adrian assured, still not touching him, the pleading part of his voice breaking through. "Seriously, you lot are *terrible* about killing our leads."

Osiris's eyes were nothing but wells of hatred, and the restraint he held onto nearly snapped when Nilus looked up at him. But Osiris tipped his head in a shallow nod. He let go of Nilus's throat, the purple ring of bruising booming where his hand had been. Osiris didn't take his eyes off of him, Nilus now sputtering coughs, his gaze planted back on the ground.

Then Osiris unbuttoned his suit coat like I had, shrugging it off and placing it on the counter. Next, he undid the buttons at his wrists, rolling his blue dress shirt up to his elbows, exposing his arms. Osiris liked his coverings, and the only time he ever went without them was when he was planning on getting bloody. *Very* bloody.

"Are you sure you want to be here for this, *lux mea*?" he asked, gripping his wrist as he tipped his head to look at her.

She swallowed hard, seeing the predator in his eyes, the one that lacked human breath. Osiris was ancient, and his power bled into the air if he didn't actively pull it in. Right now, it soaked into the wood of our home and sucked the air right out of Nilus's lungs. But had I ever thought Ali wasn't the one for us? That was shattered when she stepped forward.

She reached her hand out, palm up, and Osiris took it without a moment's hesitation. He searched her eyes before nodding.

"I can see it in your eyes, your compassion, even for *them*. So today, I'll be your monster. He won't leave this building with his heart beating, Ali. But you control what you see," he vowed with care and kindness as Nilus trembled behind him.

Ali closed her eyes, taking a deep breath before she nodded.

"I want to stay. I-I *need* to stay," she said finally, looking at Nilus fully for the first time tonight.

She flinched, her jaw tense as it snapped closed. She didn't say anything else, and I knew her mantra was ringing in her head.

We'd destroy one of her demons today.

"Ascension Rising, who runs it?" Osiris asked, not hesitating as he turned around.

He ushered Ali back toward me, and I pulled her into my arms. Encasing her like a shield, but still allowing her to see as she wanted.

Nilus didn't respond, his gaze on the ground as his body began to shake.

"I'll ask again," Osiris said, dipping down to Nilus's level.

He didn't touch him, didn't need to, as the gift of the *Flame* started on Nilus's arm. The controlled burn singed his skin until he was screaming and writhing. Ali flinched again, sinking further into my embrace, but she didn't turn away.

"I don't know! I don't know, I never saw him," Nilus cried out, his screams growing louder as the simmering flames sank below his skin.

"Not good enough. Try again," Osiris pushed, snarling now as he leaned forward.

"He was never there! And when he was, I wasn't allowed to see him. Fuck! I don't know his name! Doctor Marcus Castillion hired me. I worked under him and Nox, that's all I know!" he cried, then seized, his eyes rolling back before Osiris forced them open with blood magic.

The impact of it in the air made the hairs on my arm stand on end.

"His *name*," Osiris pushed, one last time, forcing his *Charm* into it.

Nilus shuddered, his eyes hazing over as the blazing *Flame* crawled up his neck.

"I don't know," he cried, and Osiris pulled back.

"Then you're of no use to me." He lifted his hand to end it when Ali pulled away from my arms.

"Wait!" she screamed, and everyone stood still.

"Ali—" I started, but she shook her head.

"I need to ask him something. Please, Osiris," she pleaded, and Osiris could only nod.

He lowered his hand, and the Flame that had been eating Nilus's skin faded away. The man sagged, sobbing and heaving.

Osiris turned back to him, snapping to gain his attention.

"You'll behave," he demanded, and Nilus didn't respond beyond a horrified whimper.

Ali took another step forward, crossing her arms, her fingers digging into her skin as she swallowed hard enough to hear. She was silent for a moment, shuffling her feet.

"Why did you work at Ascension Rising?" Ali asked, her voice low.

Nilus shrugged, cringing as his skin pulled.

"Just another job, needed the money," he said, his words harsh from the strain on his vocal cords.

"You knew what they did there?" Her voice was hollow, and I gritted my teeth as he nodded.

"Of course I knew, had to deal with your fucking screams all hours of the day. *Annoying*." He coughed again, and Eirik stepped forward with a menacing growl. Nilus just laughed, his eyes shooting up to stare Ali in the face. Adrian moved to turn him away, but Ali put her hand up. "Don't search for pity from me, Glass. You won't find any. You were a job, a loud one, one I wasn't allowed to fuck. One that got my friends killed."

"That was how you saw my life? My torture? An annoyance?" There wasn't any accusation in her eyes, or her tone, just resignment.

"Can't exactly feel bad for an *it*, can I? Castillion and Nox were doing good work, getting rid of monsters like you and your little men. *Fangs*. A stain on the Natural world."

There was silence again before she nodded.

"Will he look for me? The man who was in charge at Ascension?"

"I don't know. But if the bodies are anything to guess, I'd say yes."

She took a shallow breath, but when she turned around to me, she smiled. Far brighter than someone who'd just witnessed torture should be able to. But I was glad to see it, more than happy to see some of her strain leave her.

"Goodbye, Nilus," she said, continuing to watch me.

That was all the prompting needed before Osiris removed Nilus's head from his body.

Blood sprayed everywhere, though Osiris took the brunt of it. Adrian cursed as Ali stumbled toward me.

"Fuck! You got blood all over the goddamned floor!" he chided, and Osiris nodded, tossing the head onto the ground.

He hummed, rubbing his face to clear the blood but only managing to smear it.

"Get rid of his body," he said, ignoring Adrian's sputtering. "Castillion, you've already searched for him, correct?"

Adrian groaned but nodded. That name, even spoken by Osiris, made Ali flinch so badly that I had to keep my hand on her to make sure she didn't slip on the blood now all over the floor.

"Yeah. Dead end, like the rest. We really should have got the location out of him," Adrian mused.

"Didn't need him staining the room with his thoughts anymore," Osiris said, dismissing the body and walking toward the sink. Like that would help the fucking disaster that was the blood all over him. "At least we know most of them are already rotting. Now we just have to deal with the leader."

Ali sighed and pulled away again, this time looking up at me with worry in her eyes. For as stone-faced as she'd been about this, I was surprised to see it now.

"You alright, love?" Adrian asked, seeing it too.

She nodded before she looked over her shoulder, shivering at the dead body. Or rather, the space above it.

Fuck. Me.

"We should have taken him outside," I hissed, and Osiris froze, realizing his mistake too late. Ali pulled away, stepping toward the body. No one stopped her as she reached out, sending Nilus away. Forever. Her hands stayed lifted until they shook, and when she pulled them back to herself, she let out a breath that ended with a stilted cry.

I walked behind her, encasing her again, and she continued to tremble as cries wracked her body.

"We're here for you," I said, and she nodded.

She stepped away, minding the blood on the floor, before she wobbled slightly. I caught her, pulling her against my chest just in time to see blood pool on her upper lip. Her eyes hazed, and pain showed in how she tensed.

Her hand came to rest on her head.

"Are you alright?" I asked, and Ali nodded.

But she wobbled again, whimpering and flinching when I cupped her cheeks.

"I'm okay. Just tired," she said but didn't protest when I shook my head. "Sending Nilus on must have been too much."

Too much, it was all too much. She was still sick; we were still sick. This was a conversation that had been coming since Xander's, and it needed to happen now. Even if it was only her taking ours, then at least one of us could sleep tonight without discomfort. I knew she had worries about giving us hers, that she'd end up in a situation like Prince all over again. And I couldn't fault that, but we were running out of time for her to decide for herself.

"Ali, we can't push off the blood exchange anymore," I said, and she grimaced. Her eyes wavered, and the lavender that always glowed with strength closed. "We could start with you, give you the blood you need to keep going."

But she shook her head, stubborn to the bone.

"I just need a few more days. Please, I can't do this tonight," she begged.

Eirik moved around the muck, setting his chin on top of her head, his eyes pointed, his face sharp as his beast slid forward. "It's time, my *smár Valkyrja*," Eirik whispered, his growl soothing.

Another pause and her hands clenched at her sides. The options weighed in her mind, and her face twisted as she shook her head again.

"I can't. I *can't*," she finally said, breaking her silence as her arms wrapped around her body. Eirik's arms circled her as the purr deepened in his chest. "I'm a *monster*. I can't risk you dying because of me, not tonight."

The purr skipped, and Adrian sucked in a hard breath.

Monster wasn't a word that had any place by Ali, and that sick, rotting corpse had only further burrowed it in her mind. I took one step forward, and another, until I was in front of her. Trapping her between Eirik and I.

"You're *not* a monster, Ali. You were never a monster," I said, rage blaring when her lip trembled and she looked around the empty room. "The monster is the one that watched you get picked apart day in, day out, and still have the fucking gall to say it didn't mean anything. The monster is the one that took you from your home and strapped you to a table for your blood. You couldn't be a monster. Not even if you tried. That's why you have us, Ali. *We'll* be your monsters, so you don't have to. You are my soul. And I know you wouldn't hurt us. Not willingly. Not unwillingly."

"I'm scared." The words came out garbled, broken as she choked on a sob.

"Then let's start here, like this. At least let us see if our blood helps you. *Please*, Ali, let me help you."

Denial was again firm in her eyes. The notion of all or nothing showing so clearly I nearly backed off. But I couldn't, not this time. Not when she wobbled on her feet, only being supported because Eirik was at her back.

I pulled my arm to my mouth before she could protest, sinking fangs into the skin of my wrist.

She was going to say no, and I couldn't let that happen. It was a cruel move, and part of me already regretted it, but I'd always put her safety above all else. Over the way she normally looked at me like I was something she could love, and over the way her eyes went wide in horror.

I pulled in a mouthful, not swallowing. My blood flowed from the open wound, blocking out the sick scent of Nilus. It took one glance at Eirik to see he was on the same page as me, as I took another step, only a breath away from her now.

"Fallon—" she started, as her eyes widened, and she tried to back up as Eirik's arms tightened around her. Her eyes went wide in surprise.

Sorry, trouble. I leaned in, sealing our mouths together and in her shock, her mouth opened.

She made another cry as my blood flowed from my mouth to hers, and I kept my eyes open, always on hers. They clouded with a haze of blood induced lust as she swallowed, my blood sliding down her throat. I licked her lips as I pulled back. The tinge of fear I'd felt at giving her my blood faded when she sighed into Eirik's arms.

She heaved a few heavy breaths, tears still trailing down her cheeks. But the change in her appearance was immediate. Her skin gained a dash of color, and the support she'd been getting from Eirik was no longer needed as she stood straight.

"Better?" I asked, and she frowned at me.

The look in her eyes was biting, but I stood in the face of it anyway. It was a tense minute, where she just stared at me. I waited for the gavel, for her to scream or rage. I'd have deserved it for taking the choice away from her. But she just sighed, and that almost felt worse.

I never wanted to take her choices from her, but in this one case, I didn't see another way.

"Yes, I feel better," she whispered. Her glare was steady but less intense than I'd been expecting. I moved toward her again, testing her boundary. "But that was dirty, Fallon. You too, Eirik."

"I know," I breathed, pulling her from Eirik's arms into my own. But if I hadn't done it, she would have fought it to the end, and we would never have known that it was what helped her. "I'm sorry."

She shook her head, searching my eyes before she sighed again. She reached up, brushing her lips, her tongue moving to taste my blood that was still against them.

"You'd do it again?" she asked.

I nodded before she even finished speaking. "In a heartbeat. Your health means everything to me, Ali. I will keep you safe, even from yourself."

Her posture softened, and she rubbed her face, wiping her tired eyes and the tears that still left trails on her cheeks, doing her best to avoid spreading any blood. While there was more color to her skin now, the fatigue hadn't completely waned as she now leaned into me for support.

"Guess I deserved that. I've been putting it off. I don't know if I ever would have agreed myself," she admitted. "Just ... give me one day? And we can do this for real?"

There was silence before each of us nodded.

One more day, and we'd see how true Xander's predictions were. Either we'd live, or we'd die. There wasn't any middle ground.

"Come on, sweetheart, you look exhausted," Adrian soothed, his own expression tight, even as he smiled, walking over and pulling Ali out from between Eirik and I. He brushed her hair back, leaning in to kiss her forehead. "Someone really made a mess of you. Dirty boys my brothers are. Why don't you go shower, and I'll make us some dinner, yeah?"

That got a laugh out of her, her lips tilting as she shook her head at his antics. Then she closed her eyes and took a breath. Before she nodded.

Progress.

Chapter 41

Aaliyah

"Now would be a great time for your advice, Prince," I confessed into the empty evening air, but like normal, there was only a quiet breeze to greet me.

I'd spent most of the day here, on the porch, just watching as the hours passed by, the sun beating down onto the ground until it slowly disappeared over the horizon. How was I supposed to sleep when I knew what was coming?

There was a push of indignant mocking in the air, as Red prodded at my voiced thought. I grinned and shook my head and sank further into the step I was sitting on.

"Sorry, sorry. You're right, I should have asked you instead. What would *you* do, Red?" I asked, more than a little sarcastically, knowing that he couldn't answer.

But his emotions played in the air anyway, sparking across my skin with a tale of happiness and a pinch of what I *thought* was lust? It made me blush, and that only pushed Red to go further with his antics. A distraction, a pleasant one.

I'd been so preoccupied with the light feeling of ease that when the pop of power rumbled in my skull, it took me by surprise. It was like a bolt of lightning had hit behind my eyes, my vision going white as I gasped.

Bog.

That word, so pointed, echoed in my head. Another push, another prod from Magelav. It was so frustrating I nearly screamed.

What else could they want? What else could they *need*?

We were working on the Eternium, with Adrian spending most nights gathering intel. From what I understood, things were going well. I just wished I could have a bigger role to play, that I could help more. I wondered what it would be like to go just a day without one of these headaches. To see the others perk up and feel better.

I waited for a more incessant push, but there was nothing else, just that prod to remind me of them. I stumbled to my feet, needing a reprieve, needing to move. I had spent so long trapped in a box barely large enough to take five steps in, and right now, I needed to feel something.

I shivered, my limbs stiff after hours of sitting in the cold, lacking a lot of what I should have been wearing. Frigid didn't really cut it. It wasn't cold in a stinging way, but more of a creep. I walked down the porch steps and rubbed my frozen arms. I definitely should have brought a coat.

The door opened behind me, and it was only a second later when the smell of heavy oak and saltwater encompassed me. A jacket was draped over my shoulders, and I turned to smile softly at Eirik.

He huffed, walking over and standing so close that our legs brushed against each other. We didn't speak, didn't need to.

Today, everything changed. And as I glanced at Eirik, his sharp features accented by the soft glow of a new night, I hoped it was for the better.

We could use a little luck today.

CHAPTER 42

EIRIK

Her doubts were grave in the air, haunting the night with a slogging feeling of dread. Her fear of our deaths on her hands. That was why I was here, why I'd been awake for hours, listening to her pace and mutter and come to terms with what was to come.

She was worried, but I didn't.

No matter what tonight held, she was mine, and I was hers. If my death by her hand was my fate, then I'd take it smiling.

But death wasn't an option, not for all of us, not yet. That was why the current tactics weren't going to work, not when she risked losing *all* of us. We needed to narrow in if she was to agree.

Give her a more pointed choice.

I hated to see the tension in her shoulders, the way she bit her lip so hard I worried it'd bleed. She curled into my jacket, the same one I'd slept in to keep warm, intent on giving it to her. Though, I hadn't expected to find her outside, clothed only in thin sweatpants, a t-shirt—one of Osiris's—and thick wool socks that Adrian had found for her a few days back. They had small pumpkins on them, with those fancy carvings that I often found around All Hallows' Eve.

My beast huffed and prodded, like always telling me to fix the problem and see her warm. The dried tears on her cheeks burned me, made my wolf writhe and my skin tremble as a partial shift stole my breath. They were like a personal affront, and I had to swallow my growl.

335

I reached out my hand to her.

She looked at me curiously, wiping her eyes. But she didn't hesitate, fear so far from her mind that it wasn't even a thought as she set her hand in mine. I forgot how small they were, *tiny* and delicate. I ran my thumb over the back of her hand, and the spark off of her skin was perfect, warming me and building heat deep in my chest. She sighed into the touch like she was exactly where she needed to be. It only took a tug for her to meld to me, a sigh on her lips as she accepted my warmth.

One day soon, I would claim her fully, *wholly*. Because this wouldn't be my end, and if I died following what was going to happen tonight, then so be it. I'd die a lucky man. I'd die knowing she was mine.

Mine, my beast echoed, though I didn't miss the melancholy in his voice, knowing that we wouldn't have a gift for her tonight.

Her head settled just below my heart. I drew my nose along her forehead, taking in the subtle scent of lavender that she always carried.

"Elskan." The word was like a prayer on my lips. I hoped it expressed everything I couldn't with words. "Run with me? Let me show you something."

It was a question, not a demand, unlike how I would have spoken to anyone else. Aaliyah's laugh bounced over the moss yard, mirth swimming in her eyes.

"I don't run, Eirik."

"No? You should. Good for the soul. Builds character."

She just shook her head, brushing her hair back and exposing the skin of her shoulders as the fabric slid down. I reached out, tightening my jacket around her shoulders, fussing with it until it covered her entirely.

Pushy wasn't in my nature, but my beast? He wanted time with her, craved it.

"But if you insist on not running, we can walk for a while," I mused, raising my eyebrows with mirth as she rolled her eyes and jokingly crossed her arms. "And if you're not opposed, my *beast* will run."

Her eyes lit up at that, and my beast preened at the joy in her eyes as she bounced on the balls of her feet. She bit her lip, and I reached up, soothing the flesh.

"I'll get to meet him properly? He stayed with me for a while after—" She shook her head, trying to voice the aftermath of Prince's second death, but was unable to. "But I didn't really get a chance to actually meet him." She shuffled again, this time more anxiously. "He wants to, as well?"

I barked a laugh, her eyebrows shooting up, and even I knew it was uncharacteristic. But she didn't have to hear the way said beast howled and screeched at the idea of being in her arms again. He preened, purring so deeply that it found its way out through my chest.

"More than anything," I said, the rumble unending.

"Then a walk it is. But you have to put on your coat too," she said sternly before realizing she was wearing it. Her cheeks flushed a pretty pink as she mumbled, "Well, another coat."

Never in my life had I been scolded and been so happy to hear it. So I nodded, watching as she moved gracefully around me, stepping back inside to go searching in the closet to grab my own shabby jacket.

"You know I don't need it, right?" I asked, and she just frowned.

The slip of joy slid away as she examined me from head to toe.

"Eirik, you're still not fully recovered. Just put it on, for my sanity's sake," she said.

I couldn't say I felt my best, but I did my best to fake it for her. My entire body ached, and breathing was more of a chore than I'd like to admit. The incident at Valen's had done more damage than I'd led on, and with blood no longer helping to heal me, I knew it was only so long before I'd start to shut down.

Days, maybe. A week if I was lucky.

Aaliyah held the shabby fabric out to me, and I raised my hands in defeat, shrugging it on. I'd lose it soon enough to the shift, but at least for now, she'd be sated with it.

"We should tell the others we're heading out," she said, but I shook my head.

"No need. We won't be going far," I replied, a pleased growl rumbling when she nodded. "And they'll know if something happens. The bond will tell them."

That seemed to be enough, as she looped her arm through mine, brushing her hair out of her eyes as her spare hand landed on her pocket. I grumbled, making sure she was adequately bundled. My beast was so close to the surface that I felt the subtle shift of the bones in my face, but even he paused to make sure she was warm before we walked out the door.

It was the soft crunch of snow that conversed for us, our attention on the way we walked, mine on the steady beat of her heart. I listened to it closely, checking that it never wavered as we moved.

We'd only walked for a couple of minutes, our eyes on the gray sky, when Aaliyah sighed, pouting beside me.

"Can't see the stars today. I was hoping you'd be able to point more out," she said, with melancholy.

I wanted to tell her about all of them, just like the last time we'd walked. That moment had quickly become one of my favorites. I wrapped around her shoulders, encasing her completely. She leaned into the touch as her hand reached up, hesitantly pressing to my lower back. She hummed, her face flushing a deeper red.

"Next time. I'll always be here to tell you about the stars," I promised.

I'd be there to tell her of the stars, to speak to her when she needed an ear. To hold her close and protect her from the world.

To make her come on our tongue, my beast supplied, sending a shiver of arousal down my spine. My arm tightened, and my face further shifted as I hardened in my pants.

Damned bastard.

A growl started in my chest; one I couldn't control. She shivered next to me, eyeing me with wide eyes and blown pupils. I pulled in a breath, trapped by the heat-scented lavender.

"Eirik. I like you," Aaliyah confessed beside me, sending my need from partial to full-blown. The press of fangs made my mouth water. Even more, the thought of *hers* did something to me. Made me crave the feeling of her own fangs digging into me, claiming me. "I mean, of course I like you, but I just really wanted you to know that, just in case—"

She always caught me off-guard. Even as she trembled, she didn't look away from me.

"*Elskan,*" I growled, shaking my head as my lust made me want to turn.

To press her against the nearest tree to see how loud I could make her scream. I *craved* it, craved her with everything I was to where it should scare me.

The others cared for her, *loved* her, but I couldn't even find words to describe the obsession I felt. I blamed a lot on my beast, on the part of me that wasn't a man. But deep down, I knew it was me. Knew I wanted her to run, wanted to chase and claim her just as badly as he did. And I would, one day when she was ready for the monster I was.

And she had my gift in her hands.

"You don't have to answer, Eirik. I'd understand if you didn't feel that way. I just wanted to tell you. I didn't want to keep it bottled up anymore." Her words were enough to center me, to stop that teasing pleasure. "I'm scared, *so* scared ... and I didn't want to give you my blood without you knowing."

One day, one day *soon*, she would be mine. As soon as Valen finished my gift, I could lay myself at her feet and confess the same. Confess far more than that. She would wear my mark, wield my steel, and I would show her what it meant to love a beast. Until then, I would wait, because she deserved the best of me. Deserved to be courted and loved, wooed and charmed. *Then* fucked until the only word she could manage was my name.

I turned, fully staying calm even as the sight of her flushed face and the brush of her warm breath against my palm drove me. I cupped her face in my hands, thumbs running across her cheekbones as she leaned into the touch.

"*Elskan*, my sweet *Valkyrja*. I'm still finishing the preparations to ask you properly to be mine," I said, the haze of lust making my words sharp. "But I won't allow you to think I don't care for you. Every piece of me is yours, should you want it. I'll be your sword if you don't want to cut, and your shield against all those who wish to hurt you. Which is why I want to do this right. *Need* to show you what you mean to me. So I ask you to wait a while longer. Because we will survive this, have faith in that."

She didn't take her eyes off me, and I devoured her attention. There was something equal parts calming and igniting about her eyes, the way they never strayed from my face.

"Run with me," I asked, leaning in to press our foreheads together. "Meet my beast and run with me. It will help you clear your mind."

My skin shifted, and my beast pushed for control.

"Okay," she whispered, and I was already pulling away from her.

The jacket came first, hitting the snow with little regard. Aaliyah protested, but it barely lasted, the noise dying as I pulled my shirt over my head. As much as my beast pushed and begged to keep going, I let my hands linger. Aaliyah's breath caught, and I grinned, more than pleased as my thumbs slid to the waist of my pants. I undid the button, pushing them down as I turned so she could see my back.

I was half tempted to let her see me as I was. To get a glance at my hardened cock, so she could prepare. So I could feel her heated gaze linger, even as her breath caught. I wasn't small by any means. I shouldn't be the first man she sees, and I *knew* I wouldn't be the first inside of her. The last thing I wanted to do was hurt her or scare her away when she was so close.

So I stayed with my back to her, a purr starting in my chest when that soft breath of lavender became tantalizingly teased with heat.

I rolled my boxers off next, another hit of that delicious scent making my eyes roll back. There was no more space to wait, as my beast shifted for me, his eager press to come forward jolting me as he took over.

My senses sharpened, and her scent became encompassing. I nearly sank to the ground, wanting to be covered in it. My beast all but presented his stomach to her, strutting in front of her as if to show off, and I nearly rolled my eyes. It wasn't like I wasn't there anymore, control still enough in my grip that I could pull back if needed, but my thoughts were almost a haze, and it was like looking through gray-tinted glass.

But I would give my beast this moment, his time with Aaliyah.

She stood with her hands clasped in front of her face, her giddy awe making my beast preen again. He flexed and stepped toward her, careful about his size as he approached her. I was about eye level with her, maybe even an inch taller, as she had tipped her head back to look at us.

"Wow," she breathed, her hands lifting in the air before they paused. My beast tilted our head, exposing our chest and throat. "Hello. Sorry, I don't know if I can touch you—"

We huffed, shoving our head against hers, marveling as her laugh sparked in the air. Her arms circled our neck, holding us close. She rubbed and brushed, and we soaked in every bit of her scent we could. Greedy for it, desperate for the mark of her claim.

Mine.

"You're beautiful, Eirik," she gushed, and we huffed again with no other way to speak, grumbling as we pulled back. "What?" she asked, just before our nose brushed her neck and she jolted. "Hey! Your nose is cold."

It startled another laugh out of her, and she rubbed the spot warm again.

There was a pinch in my ribs, the pained ache leaving as a huffed breath, but I shook it off as we leaned down again, motioning for her to come closer. She frowned, stepping back in a way that made my beast whine.

"You want me to get on? I don't want to hurt you," she whispered, biting her lip. "You can run. I'll wait here."

Like we were going to take no for an answer. My beast stepped forward again, tapping her stomach with his nose before pushing against her more insistently. Teasingly maneuvering her toward our back.

"Okay, okay!" She paused a second more, finally caving as we laid down for her and only getting on when we nudged her again. "Don't push yourself. And please don't let me fall."

Her fingers dug in, and she sank close to us as we stood fully again.

Never, I wanted to whisper. She would never fall, not with me.

When I was sure she was stable, I took off. We bolted through the woods, dashing around fallen trees and lingering in places that I knew she would enjoy. We traced the trees, moving in a way that was ingrained in us.

I soaked in every gasp, tense, and cry like they were treasures. I hoarded them, even as that pinch in my ribs spread. My beast seemed to take notice as well, but I pushed it away again.

It was only a few minutes later when we came just a few meters from what I was searching for. I stopped us, Aaliyah lifting her head from my fur to peek around. My beast purred, crouching so she could get off. She slid down, stabilizing herself against us, as the shift took me again. Shifting always hurt, my bones rearranging and shrinking to fit a human form. Everything ached, and with the extra pulse in my head, it was even worse.

I pulled away, moving toward the trees, where a stash of my clothes was. That heat mixed with lavender again, and I smirked as I tugged on my pants and shirt, before turning to face Aaliyah again. I stalked toward her, opening my arms for her to step into. Her head pressed against my chest seconds later, her warm breaths further heating my skin. Even and steady as she continued to take comfort in my embrace.

"Now that was fun," she beamed, panting softly. "We have to do that again sometime. Maybe in the spring, when everything is in bloom."

I lifted her face to mine, cradling her chin. Her eyes glittered, and swirling in their depths was the fear she wanted to let out. I took another deep breath, allowing her scent to calm me.

"Nothing would make me happier. But this adventure isn't over, *Elskan.*"

I purred for her as her nose scrunched up, and she looked around the seemingly random woods.

"Close your eyes." The rumbled words were more assertive now, and Aaliyah's eyes slid closed. It warmed my chest. Her trust in me. I *flitted* us the rest of the way, stopping in the middle of my claim on our territory. The place I called mine. I rubbed my thumb across her chin again, huffing as her eyes fluttered open.

She looked around the small clearing, her eyes going wide.

This place, this field of flowers, made me call this plot of land home. The white blooms, glowing in the low light of the moon, swayed around us, dusting the ground like freshly fallen snow. They were everywhere, well-maintained and spelled to never die.

Curiosity burned in her gaze, covered only by her joy. The sight of her so happy at my little piece of heaven, the way she looked at the flowers like they were gold ... made me fall for her all over again. I didn't say it, but this place was hers now as much as mine.

I'd give her anything to make her smile like that again.

"Moonflowers," I said, as the vibrant lavender of her eyes met mine. "They were my sister Tove's favorite. Whenever Father would return from the sea, he would always bring them back with him."

She leaned down, running her fingertips against one of the soft white petals. She didn't pull it from the ground, just admired it with a gentle touch and a dreamy sigh.

"They're beautiful." Her words were a breathy whisper, and I leaned down to her, taking in her soft, thoughtful expression.

I grabbed one flower, cutting it off at the stem. I placed it in her hair, brushing the white strands away from her face. The white perfectly matched her hair, the lavender of her eyes sparkling as she beamed at me. The defiant tilt to her nose that I always lingered on led me to reach out, running my thumb along the bridge, over her cheek, until I was cupping her chin.

She tilted her head, showing her neck in a move of submission that made my beast purr.

Yes, smár Valkyrja. You're mine.

"Yes," I said as I traced her face, eyes lingering on one of the few scars on her face. "They are."

Just as much as I am yours.

A blush lit up her skin, and she glanced away from me. Her hands ran across the flower in her hair, her eyes searching the forest, glancing between the blank spaces.

"Tell me something?" Her words confused me, coming out of nowhere.

I hadn't expected her to speak, and I froze when I recognized what she meant, but she shook her head when she noticed, understanding now crossing her face.

"Something good," she added, a knowing glint in her eyes. "Something bright."

"I had five sisters." She gave me an incredulous look, and the tilt of her nose had me laughing. "I was the youngest. My oldest sister, Yrsa, was nearly twenty years my senior. But that was typical of my pack. My parents were still in their prime when they had me." I pressed my hand to her cheek, unable to keep myself from touching her.

My nose twitched, the ache from the woods rearing its head as it pressed at my lungs, my next breath a wheeze so quiet she didn't hear it.

"One day, Yrsa took me out hunting against Father's orders. I was about eight summers, if I recall correctly. I'd begged her to. She was the best hunter in our village, dead-eyed with her bow, and I'd wanted nothing more than to learn from her. We didn't encounter any game on our hunt, but on our way back, we stumbled across another group." I took a deep breath. "Men not of our clan, who were intent on an ambush."

Her attention caused the hairs to raise on my arm, and my gaze drew to her mouth as she bit her lip.

"That was the first time I ever fought side by side with Yrsa. Her with a bow, and me with a small bone dagger she'd gifted me a few days before." I had locked that same dagger away in a vault in my room, the bone now aged and cracked. "It was how I got this." I pointed to the scar on my face, the only one worth earning.

"Getting that scar is a happy memory?"

I nodded, pride swelling as she reached her hand up, pressing her fingers against the ink around my eye.

The dragon had been her suggestion, one that had made my father scoff. We were wolves, and if I wanted to show my pride, it should have been a wolf, he'd said. But I'd never forget the way Yrsa had stood up to him.

Wolves are what we are, but Eirik was always meant to fly above the rest of us. Toward danger like a magnet.

"This one is, yes. Because I got it by protecting someone that I loved. I added the surrounding tattoo on my fiftieth year." *Just before I was taken.* "To symbolize my willingness to sacrifice for my family, for my fellow men."

For jumping in front of the blade meant for Yrsa.

"Not all scars need to be a reminder of your pain." She didn't seem convinced, her free hand roaming over her shoulder. Which old wound was there, hidden just below the fabric?

"What happened to Yrsa?" Aaliyah asked, and Yrsa's vibrant blue eyes cut across my thoughts.

She'd been a spitfire that could make a sailor blush. A wicked tongue I'd hoped to one day fight with again. "Last I checked, she lived on the coast of Sweden with her mate. She bore four sons, a fact that mother had always been happy to point out." The reminder of the sight made me laugh. "They'd been just like her, stubborn to the bone."

And I'd missed all of them, their lives and their younger days. I'd missed the chance to see them grow and to know them. One day, I hoped I might get the chance to.

"You miss her?" The softness of the question belied its painful nature.

"I miss all of them. I wish I could have talked with them again after my turn, but it just wasn't possible." Fear of Sebek finding them had driven me to stay hidden. "Maybe soon I can speak with them again. They'd love you, *Elskan*."

If we got Sebek out of the way, then nothing would stand between me and them anymore. I liked the thought of introducing them to Ali, of sharing stories. Of dancing around a roaring fire ... but it had been decades, centuries since they last saw me.

Would it even be worth the pain to show up after all this time?

"What does it mean?" she asked softly, sinking into my arms. "You always call me that, but I don't even know what it means."

Her body was warm, and I rubbed slow circles on her back, as I had seen Osiris do. Elation flooded me when she sighed, content. At the same time, the pinch in my chest grew and grew, and I knew I'd no longer be able to fight it. The pain took my breath away, and I could no longer hide the grunt of pain as I pressed my forehead to hers.

"Eirik?" The same pain that came from feeding at Valen's swallowed me. "Eirik, what's wrong?"

She shook her head, trying to pull away. I gave her enough to move but didn't release her. I trailed down, kissing her skin until I was at her neck, savoring the taste of her skin.

"It's a Norse term of endearment." I held her as closely as I was able, marveling at the way she held me just as tightly. Her breath caught, and her hands shook. "Darling, it's how one would express their love for someone."

"You love me?"

My chest warmed to the point of agony, and for a second, I didn't know what to say.

"Vikings hold onto the things they find valuable." Her lips parted, and I leaned in again. "Love you, Aaliyah? You're the most priceless treasure in the world to me." Just the thought made me feel whole. Of course, I loved her. How could I not? "The thought of living without you scares me more than the risk of dying. I would do anything to stay by your side, *Elskan*."

Tears flooded her eyes, and I wiped them away, holding her gaze through them all.

"You're scaring me." Her thundering pulse echoed in my ears. And the only fear in her voice was *for* me, not of me. She trembled under my touch. "And you're *bleeding*!"

I heard the words; I tried to listen to them as I forced myself onto unsteady feet. Aaliyah, my sweet *Valkyrja*, immediately moved to my side. Her arms wrapped around my torso, and I snarled at myself when my leg gave out and my weight sank onto her before I could stop it.

She grunted, steadying us both even as she shook. I forced my eyes open even as red clouded my vision, and Aaliyah's panic-stricken face came into view. My beast whined as I glanced at the tenebrous sky.

I hadn't wanted it this way, the choice so heavy on her shoulders. But we were out of time.

I didn't have a day or a week. I felt the rot in my bloodstream, tearing me apart. If her blood didn't fix me, I wouldn't be surviving this. *I* was out of time.

CHAPTER 43

AALIYAH

I struggled to keep us standing.

Eirik wasn't quite dead weight, but his legs shook, and his hand came up to cover his mouth as he coughed. The scent of iron was in the air.

Blood in the air.

"We have to move," I urged as gently as I could, and Eirik grunted.

His jaw was clenched, his eyes swirling between a stormy ocean blue and the light sky that I knew.

"What happened?" I asked.

Eirik didn't immediately answer, and that was enough to settle in how bad this situation was.

"Don't know," he whispered, wiping away the red streaks around his mouth. "Never felt anything like this."

My heart thundered, and I leaned back into his side, pressed in closer, the heat of his skin searing me where we touched like his body was in over-drive trying to fight whatever this was. We took a step. It was just one, and I clenched my teeth as I bore Eirik's weight. Eirik hissed next to me, coughing again.

We had to get back home.

"How do we fix it?" I pressed carefully, trying to keep my composure as what had been a wonderful moment crumbled.

He didn't have to say it. There was only one thing that might fix it. I

346

knew that was going to be his answer, felt it in my bones. He needed blood, *mine* if Xander was right. And if not ...

Then he was dead anyway.

I tried to push us into another move, but he held firm. Then gently uncoiled himself from around me. I cried out as he did, trying to stop him from hitting the ground. He grunted, staying in the sitting position that he landed in. I moved, immediately trying to pull him back to his feet. We had to *move*. So I could *fix* this.

I ground my teeth, having to hold in a cry as I really realized what I'd done. They'd been suffering for months, *years,* and I'd been too cowardly to try for a cure. To fix them, like Fallon did me last night.

Like last time, everything felt new. I could walk without aching, and my head hadn't hurt all day. But I just let them suffer, and that fact came slamming down on my back, as my legs gave out as well, and I came to kneel in front of him.

"My *Elskan.* My sweet *smár Valkyrja,*" he began, coughing, blood coating his hand. "You are not weak; you've never been weak. You're the strongest person I know."

His words, the final ones he spoke before his eyes rolled back again, were broken and disjointed.

Eirik isn't moving.

That was the only thing on my mind. It didn't matter that I could see the rise and fall of his chest, no matter how ragged his breathing was. Eirik wasn't moving.

And I had never been more terrified to keep my eyes open. To see a soul as it left someone's body. But I stood, what seemed like hours passing as I barely breathed. This wasn't a bad dream or something I would wake up from. This was *bad*. This was up-shit-creek-without-a-paddle bad. My breathing spiraled, and as I watched Eirik tremble on the ground, blood sliding from his lips.

A light snow fell, the added briskness in the air showing as my breath fogged in front of me. It covered Eirik's skin, melting on impact, then freezing. With each small move he made, the tauter he became, before he seized, his eyes rolling back in his head unnaturally.

When he opened them again, they were filled with a painful resolve.

And I knew what I needed to do.

I took a deep breath, looking up at the gray skies and praying that this would work. That I wasn't about to kill someone else, that I wasn't going to watch another man that I loved die. I looked back at Eirik, to where he was slumped against the ground. He trembled like the cold was already affecting him, but when my fingers brushed the skin of his cheek, he was boiling.

So when a chill hit me in the chest, I shivered.

"You have impeccable timing," I whimpered as the air filled with a questioning probing sensation that made me turn to Eirik again. "No more running," I whimpered, and Red poked again, this time settling over Eirik.

I pulled away, reaching into my mouth and pressing against the roof. Like at Xander's, a numbing feeling built, and I shook as my canines fell. Sharp fangs brushed my lip and against my wrist as I brought it to my open mouth.

But I still hesitated, watching Eirik's body struggle to pull in air as I trembled so hard I thought I might pass out next to him. Fear sank deep into my stomach, and I closed my eyes as a feeling of faith soothed me enough to breathe.

When the flower that had been tucked in my hair fluttered to the ground. The thought of it being the last one he'd ever give me pushed me to move. I bit into my wrist, and blood flooded my mouth. The burn from the wound grounded me as blood poured down my chin and splattered against the ground.

And then I waited, watching Eirik's chest rise and fall, until the wound began to close, and I choked on the sob that shot through my chest, trembling so hard it chattered my teeth. And I *waited* until pressure swelled in the air, and I sucked in a hard breath.

Now? *Now?* I couldn't *Rend* now, I wouldn't survive. *Eirik* wouldn't survive.

Pressure bled into my skin, into bones and blood. It was such a force that it stole my breath, searing even my lungs. I took another as my vision became shadowed with black fog. A strength I knew I didn't have bled into me, giving me the energy to keep moving, to reach out. The pressure pushed, ached, and sang.

But I didn't *Rend*.

Whatever this was, was just ... me. And it was telling me to move.

"Please," I begged, looking at the sky again. The black sheen didn't fade, and the slip of power that I'd felt at the hot spring became my voice. My hope. "Please let this work."

I pressed my torn wrist to Eirik's mouth.

"Fucking—*Aaliyah*?" Fallon barked, stumbling back as Eirik barged through the door with me in his arms. The spark of his skin on my own wasn't enough to drive away the cold. "Where the fuck have you guys been?" he demanded, the words so close together I could barely make them out.

I tried to speak, but my body revolted. I shivered into Eirik's arms, and he snarled so hard it shook me. We were in the living room in a blink, with Fallon screaming behind us for the others.

Eirik paid no attention to him as he *flitted* off, returning just seconds later with arms full of blankets. He surrounded me with them, making a fort for me in front of the living room fireplace. He reached out, cupping my hands in his, so I couldn't feel them.

"We need to get you warm," he said, blowing warm breaths over them.

But he wasn't panicked like Fallon was, nor Adrian and Osiris as they came barreling into the living room. There was a gentle curve to his lips, and his eyes were warm as he traced the black mark along my wrist.

And the lavender one along his.

Before he went back to my hands, assessing the damage with a disgruntled grimace on his face. He flipped them, checking each finger before blowing warm air onto them.

"Are you alright, *Elskan*?" he asked softly, guilt in his words.

"I'm fine. It's you I'm worried about, Eirik," I admitted.

After I'd given him the blood, it had been nearly a full minute before anything happened. I'd waited, breaking down as each second passed with his haggard breaths. When he opened his eyes again, it was the most relieved I'd ever been.

For the first time in days looking healthy, looking like he had that first night I'd seen him. The angular twist to his jaw, the flex of Nordic tattoos along his exposed arms, and the tilt to his pink lips. Such handsome viciousness. Eirik, my proud Norseman, flashed me a roguish grin as if hearing that thought, making butterflies flutter in my stomach. "Me? I've never been better."

They were quiet for a moment before Adrian's soft voice filled the air, and he crouched next to my makeshift fort. "So, you going to tell the class what happened?" He cupped my cheek, brushing his hand against the still dried blood on my mouth.

"It worked," Eirik grunted, lifting his hand so he could show them the new mark along his wrist.

It was nothing intricate or flashy. Just a single lavender line that wrapped itself around his wrist, maybe an inch wide, covering the end of the ink that had been there before. I doubted I'd ever seen him smile that widely as he reached up to touch it.

"We just went on a walk," I added, pulling my knees to my chest, further sinking into my blankets. "Then he got sick."

Eirik grunted, the rumbling purr beginning in his chest again as he crawled onto the ground, joining me in the blankets. His hand rose, running over my hair as his heart beat under my ear.

"Told you it'd be fine," he said, his nose warm against my neck as I sank into him. "I'm not going anywhere, *Elskan.*"

That filled me with warmth, comforting me as I curled into his arms. The others spoke quietly between themselves, their words filling the air, but I brushed them off, the adrenaline from the night crashing. And then I fell asleep, wrapped in Eirik's arms.

CHAPTER 44

AALIYAH

I didn't like the tension in the living room today, and as I stared down at the glasses on the table, five of them in line, I could only worry more.

Eirik was fine after our transfer. Better than fine, really. I stared at my proud Viking, admiring his soft grin as he ran a finger over the mark on his wrist. It was wrapped around it, like a rich lavender band. I looked down, and much like his, I had a black tattoo around my wrist, a twisting detail inside of it that almost looked like the ink that covered Eirik's body.

It hadn't been there before, and as much as I didn't like it, I believed Xander was right.

Hallen Bound.

I looked at the glasses again, five in total. One for each of the guys, and one for me. Each of theirs had a single drop of my blood, and mine had theirs. I bit my lip, glancing at those at the table.

Adrian, as though sensing my tension, walked around to me. He pulled me into his arms, and I sank against him.

"It's going to be fine, love," he whispered against the top of my head, the brush of his lips sending a shiver down my spine. "I promise."

"You can't promise, though," I mumbled back.

There were so many things that could go wrong. What if I wasn't bound to all of them? What if there was a limit?

What if? What if? What if?

"I can sure as hell try." He chuckled. "Trust us, love," he said reverently, pulling me away from his chest. His cool fingers ran across my jaw, sending a spark down my spine as he leaned in, brushing his lips against mine. It was a quick kiss, one that had me leaning toward him as he pulled back.

"I do," I said, hiding the tremble in my lips behind a smile as he pulled back, moving to sit.

I glanced around the room, as I did sometimes. Still looking for Prince and his reassuring grin, and just like every time, it left a hollow feeling in my chest when I didn't find him.

Would I ever get used to not seeing him?

"All at once?" Fallon asked from the end of the table. His eyes bore into me, calmer and more focused than I'd ever seen them, and that reassurance settled the rest of my nerves.

I reached out and grabbed my drink. They each gave me another encouraging nod before each one tipped their glasses back, and we drank.

The blend was surprisingly sweet with the dry wine they had paired it with. Almost like a medley of fruit and spice. I almost immediately felt better, and the headache that I had been dealing with for the last few days faded completely.

I sighed, opening my eyes and focusing on the looks of wonderment that lit up the others' eyes.

"Damn, this is a *rush,*" Adrian said, flexing his hands as he stood.

Sure enough, he looked better. The gloomy circles that had become commonplace under his eyes had faded, and that Cheshire grin of his lifted the weight that had been on my chest.

Fallon grunted at the end of the table, his eyes narrowing at the tan skin around his wrist. Then, slowly, a lavender band twisted around it, much like Eirik's.

One by one, each of the guys gained a band, and I let out a breath of relief. I looked at my own and found four markings stretching around my arm. Unlike the guys, mine weren't solid bands, each a cool black with differing intricate details inside of them I knew I'd be admiring for hours.

"Thank God," I muttered, bringing my hands to my face and rubbing away the strain that this had brought to me.

Just as before, Adrian pulled me into his arms, feeling less cold than normal as I sank into his embrace. "Told you it would be okay," he whispered against my hair.

I nodded, unable to pull away as I thanked whatever god would listen that they were alright.

"Come on, you've had a stressful few days, love," he said against my hair, pulling back and sliding his hand into mine. "Want to watch a movie? Or get some dinner?"

Fallon appeared at my other side, taking my free hand and pulling it up to place a chaste kiss on the exposed skin.

"What would we have?" I asked, more than happy to sink into their good mood.

Adrian considered it for a moment before his face lit up with an excited expression.

"Hey Osi, you still know that Banshee? Ah, what was her name? Little thing. Japanese, I believe." Adrian glanced at Osiris for an answer.

But Osiris's eyes were on me, on the hand that held Adrian and Fallon. My chest ached as his eyes narrowed, and he looked away.

"Aya?" he asked, a coarseness to his voice that only made that ache worse.

He reached out, covering the marking that he had gotten with his hand, squeezing until the surrounding skin lost its color, going white. I flinched at the sight. It was just above the tattoo around his wrist, part of it covering the ink.

"That's the one. She still runs that little noodle shop in Treten?" Adrian asked, his eyes also on Osiris.

"She does," Osiris replied. He released his death grip, his now shaking hand crossing over his chest. "I'm sure she wouldn't mind bringing us some, so we can eat in."

I was at a loss on how to respond, a burning ache in my chest when I tried to speak. I wasn't sure if I would get words or tears out.

"Best noodles in town, swear on my heart," Adrian responded. He ran his thumb over the top of my hand.

I nodded. "Sure. I could go for some noodles."

<hr>

The Banshee, as Adrian had said, differed from what I was expecting. The woman, no taller than four feet, beamed as she stepped into the Vivas household.

Solid black eyes that matched her ink-black hair swayed as her hands moved rapidly. She didn't speak. At least, not verbally. Her hands flew at speeds I couldn't catch, but it was familiar. She was signing. Not quite like Prince and I had, since we made up our gestures, but actual sign language. To my surprise, Osiris did the same back, his hands moving in fluid motions. It was almost artful how he moved.

"She says it's a pleasure to come by, and that she has missed our visits," Osiris relayed, and Fallon raised an eyebrow. "Fallon, she wants to know when you'll be back to discuss the *Hokusai* painting you spoke of last time."

"After the Eternium, if that works?" he replied.

He had his arm snuggly around my shoulders. The protectiveness extended to Eirik, who was at my other side, gripping my hand in his.

Osiris was again animated in his movements, even cracking a smile at something Aya said when she glanced at me, mirth in her deep black eyes. She reached down, grabbed the bag she'd brought and handed it to Osiris, bowing low. Colorful displays of cherry blossoms and dragons covered every inch of the paper material. She then looked back at me, making a few smaller signs, and Osiris's face blanched.

"Yes. Of course," Osiris started, now using one hand to sign with much slower movements. "Aya, this is Aaliyah."

She stepped forward, reaching out so I could take her hand as she extended it to me.

"What is she saying?" I asked.

"She said to ring her if we ever gave you trouble. She'd be happy to show you around sometime," Osiris translated, and Adrian broke into a fit of uncontrollable laughter, just as Eirik growled.

I blushed, pulling my hand away as she winked. There was no malice in her eyes, and from the way she wiggled her eyebrows, I'd assume she had Adrian's sense of humor.

"She seems sweet," I said, as she continued to sign to Osiris.

He made a few more himself, not translating, before she bowed again. She waved, leaving back through the door and closing it with a click.

"Oh, Aya is a doll. Osiris, Eirik, and Nero helped her and her family escape Japan during the Feudal Revolts," Adrian supplied, quickly taking the spot at my side, leaving Fallon and Eirik to fight over who got the other.

"Why was there a revolt?" I hadn't heard of them, at least not from Eliza.

"They happened pretty frequently in the first two thousand years after the Natural War." Adrian's tone turned melancholy. "Nero, Osi, and Eri all dealt with plenty. Aya wasn't the only one that they saved. They have a few friends all over the world, which helped to combat Sebek's reputation. Avedal is another."

"More war is likely coming," Eirik chimed in from next to me, having beaten Fallon to the spot. "Several are tired of the Eternals, how they run things and how they let their greed govern their choices. And then there's Sebek." Eirik shook his head, and Osiris looked at him with a raised eyebrow.

"Not wrong there, Eri," Adrian fired back. "I've heard talk that some are planning on protesting at the Ball. It could be a disaster, especially if Sebek is there. Might actually bring the Hallowed Three out of hiding."

Eirik seemed to like that idea, his smile turning roguish. But I had no idea who he was talking about this time.

"Eliza mentioned the Hallowed Three once, and so did Xander ... Liz said they were a myth. Do you believe in them?" I asked, gazing at Adrian inquisitively.

He took my hand. "Definitely not a myth, but unfortunately, that's *all* that I know. They haven't made a public appearance since they crafted the idea of the Eternals some four thousand years ago. Not even Osiris has seen them."

Eirik huffed at Adrian's words, but Osiris didn't deny it.

"They must be old," I said. "*Really* old."

"That's the thought. Would be a treat to actually see them in person." Adrian said, sighing. "With *him* causing so much trouble, I might just get that wish."

Him.

There was obvious tension as Adrian said it. A man they feared so much that even his name seldom came up.

"Sebek ... He doesn't sound like a stable man," I said, shaking my head as I tried to imagine my father's face twisted with cruelty.

I couldn't even imagine it, couldn't see those red eyes as anything but kind. How was I going to face him, *Sebek*?

"Understatement of the century," Adrian muttered, releasing my hand to clap his together. "Now, we've done our damn conversing over this. I'm damn well starving. What about you, love?"

"I am, too. Though I've never had this. Is it soup?" I asked.

Adrian looked surprised before he busted out laughing. The deep sound echoed around the room. "No, it's far, far better than soup. I'm going to introduce you to ramen," he said, unstacking the carefully prepared bowls Aya had made for us, as a calm conversation began.

We bantered and joked, laughing as we ate, and before I knew it, I was in Adrian's arms.

"You look better," I whispered, running a hand over his cheeks.

I reached up, trailing his jaw and the soft underside of his eyes. He leaned in, his lips branding me with a soft kiss. "So do you."

Chapter 45

Prince

A burning, seizing ache woke me from yet another memory. It scorched me like hellfire, and I fought a strangled gasp for air I didn't need as again pressure built in my skull.

Another pull, another memory, more ripping, and vicious agony as my soul tried so desperately to tear me apart.

Aaliyah's face. The compound. Shrouded figures that feel more familiar than I do.

How does one person have this many memories?

"Take a breath, boy," Mags insisted from beside me as I descended out of yet another episode, their voice sounding cracked and far away.

I forced an eye open, the remnants of the last memory still clear in my mind as the sickening feeling of pressure again built in my skull. It had been like this for days, relentless. I hadn't slept, hadn't eaten.

Only remembered.

When we played a makeshift Tic Tac Toe, using the dust on the floor of her cell.

"Never seen nothing like this." Mags dabbed a wet cloth across my clammy skin, and I shivered.

The water they used was cool and smelled distinctly like sulfur. Their frail hands, wrinkled and with age, were gentle as they tended to me like they had for days.

Nilus stared at her through the glass door, the sick want on his face turning my stomach. I wanted to scream at him, to tell him to leave her alone. Or gut the spineless coward where he stood.

"If I knew, I'd tell you," I groaned, forcing the words out. It was like my body killing itself for sport. "God, please make it stop."

The throbbing in my head became unbearable again, as it had been for nearly four days. How many times had I gone through this? How many memories? And why did it feel like I was barely scratching the surface?

The door opened, and Aaliyah froze. The tremble of her lips broke me, but I kept a strong face for her when she looked at me. She smiled then, trying to convince me it was fine. She did it to comfort me.

"I think I'm going to puke," I said through clenched teeth as Aaliyah's face flashed in my mind, and the feeling of uselessness brought tears to my eyes.

It was never the pain that did it; it didn't hurt enough to cry over. It was always her, her pain, *her* cries. The things that I couldn't stop then haunted me now, and even my skin screamed at me to move.

To find her.

I couldn't follow her to the lab, not when I knew what they'd do. I screamed for hours, begging every god I could think to ask that someone would hear me. No one did. They never *did.*

Because the only one who could see me was strapped to a table, flayed open for the amusement of fucked-up doctors. Her screams would forever haunt my nightmares.

"Not on my floor! Already cleaned up one of your messes," Mags chided, but I could see the flash of fear in their eyes. "Can't have this continue, can't keep anything down," Mags babbled, placing their hand against my forehead. "Wait here."

I clenched my teeth as they stood, leaving me laying in the thin single bed that they'd crafted in the living room.

"As opposed to what? Maybe I'll go for a pleasant stroll through the city streets. Oh, wait ... it's daytime, Mags. And I think I prefer my skin unroasted," I said through the push of the memory, trying to fight it. I tried to get more out, to do anything to keep my mind off of *this*.

But I couldn't respond, not as agony swallowed my words.

Because the only screams I could hear were hers, *reminding me exactly how useless I was.*

The pressure peaked, and I was torn out of my body. Just like every time, I was caught staring at myself, splayed across the ground like a corpse.

The black and gray of the world sank in around me, telling me that this was where I was supposed to be.

I was dead. I *should* be dead. But I wasn't, and I still had no fucking idea why.

Mags slowly hobbled back into the room. There was a small vial in their hand and a glass in the other. I couldn't tell what either of them were. Time seemed to move differently here, the motions dragging like Mags was shifting through water. They leaned over me, wispy white hair frazzled, their eyes sunken. I wasn't sure why they were helping me after all that had happened, but I was thankful for it. Thankful for a friend in these times.

A friend that knew spells and potions, at that.

Just as quickly, I snapped back. The dragging ache of my body returned as the mostly living flesh took my soul back. I wasn't sure how long it had been, each time getting longer.

I shivered, forcing back the memory that dragged its way out of my subconscious. But like always, I couldn't stop it. And like *always*, Aaliyah's tormentors came to haunt me.

Reminding me I had done nothing to stop them.

Ghosts can't get sick, but fuck if my stomach wasn't trying to right about now.

Aaliyah smiled at me from her spot on the threadbare mattress in her cell. It was crooked, the swelling on the right side of her face making it impossible for that side of her mouth to lift.

Still, she tried. And I couldn't even manage one back.

"I'll be okay, Prince," she promised.

It was hoarse and cracked because of her bruised vocal cords. She didn't normally scream, and they normally didn't go this far.

Every day, these fuckers found another way to make my blood boil.

Electric shock was their method of choice today. The sick black lines that covered her skin like branching tree arms told me that. She was still dealing with the aftershocks, shaking even now.

And I couldn't do anything to help.

"We'll get out of here one day, right?" Her question was almost incoherent, and as I looked at her again, I realized her eyes were dropping. "Just you and me. We can go somewhere. Maybe see the ocean that Nilus is always talking about."

It sent a bolt of panic down my spine, and I was by her side in an instant.

That lavender of her eyes I'd grown so fond of clouded over, and she clenched her teeth, a wheezing breath coming from her lips.

It froze me to the ground, and for a moment, I was stuck with the dreaded question: Had they finally gone too far? Was she unable to heal from this?

Was I about to watch the person I loved most in this sick world die?

The desire to reach out, to finally pass through her like the others had, to join her in death nearly brought me to my knees. I couldn't do this without her, not again. I had spent decades alone, decades without her, and hundreds more before that, not realizing what I was missing. I couldn't do it again. So I reached out, that comforting draw to her taking my metaphorical breath away. Then her eyes opened, and the resignation in them had me snapping back.

What was I thinking? I couldn't leave her with these monsters, let alone leave her to die, so I gave her a shaky grin, trying to push my forgiveness into it.

And Aaliyah, my Aaliyah, with the strength to hold up the world, smiled. She raised her hand, pressing it to her chest, ring finger and pinky down. She tensed, obviously pained by the movement, but she didn't lose my gaze.

The motion was so starkly familiar, the same one my bastard brother had used so many times before, for an entirely different reason.

"I understand," she started, tears covering the pain in her eyes. "If you want to go, Prince, then I won't stop you. I want you to be happy, above all else."

She looked away then, and I couldn't avert my gaze from the tears in her eyes.

"You're my forever, Prince." Choked words, ones that burned me.

I sank to the ground in shame, wrapping my arms around myself, hoping for warmth. I did the same as she had, pressing my hand against my chest, ring and pinky finger down. Funny how things worked. Our newest symbol, one that meant so much more than words could ever describe. Something that held more weight than I could ever tell her.

And now it meant forever.

My hand was against my chest, its weight crushing with the symbolism of the way I had it sat. Exactly like the memory, my pinky and ring finger tucked under my hand, right over my heart that raced with the memory. I couldn't feel the pain, barely even registering it.

You're my forever, Prince.

Fucking hell.

"Drink this," Mags said, snapping me out of my thoughts so abruptly that I flinched.

The cool trail of tears stuck to my skin as I turned to glare at them, but they only raised an eyebrow in response. In their hand was a stained glass, one that held a viscous liquid shimmering with a metallic glow.

That would be a *no*.

"You're not supposed to take drinks from strangers, Mags. Especially not ones that look like they have ground up bones in them," I retorted flatly, leaning back as the pressure built again. "So I think I'm going to pass."

"Quit your drama. This will help keep you stable." Mags forced the drink into my hand with more force than I thought possible, and I stared at it in distaste.

"What is it?" I asked.

But I should have known better than to expect a detailed, understandable response. Instead, Mags just grunted, "Potion."

Because of course that was their answer.

"Very telling. Still going to go with no." I tried to hand it back, and Mags shrugged.

"Fine, suit yourself. Good luck finding your girl like this." I had told Mags a little of what I remembered about Aaliyah. Of the compound. Of the home I knew she was at now, the one full of men with shrouded faces, like my mind wasn't ready to remember them.

And I knew Mags had me there.

"Dammit," I grumbled, staring at the solution that moved like spoiled milk. "Bottoms up." I tipped the glass, downing it in one go. Of course, as expected, it was nothing pleasant. "God, why does it taste like socks?" I sputtered, wiping my mouth as I waited for something to happen.

After a few seconds, nothing changed, and I looked at Mags with a glare.

"So glad I drank your vile concoction for nothing to happen. Please, remind me to do it again—" I didn't finish, couldn't as the metallic bite of iron flooded my mouth, and I couldn't choke the words past.

Blood spilled from my nose. Clouded my eyes with red. The last thing I saw before I fell back was Mags's eyes, shining with worry and curiosity.

Fucking. Rude.

Chapter 46

Osiris

"Kill an Eternal outside of the Ball. Have you gone *mental*, Osiris?" Adrian asked, looking at me like I had somehow insulted his entire being.

I'd given them a day to settle after the blood exchange with Aaliyah. We needed a day to come to terms, but I couldn't give them any more than that.

We were out of time, and we needed to figure out a plan.

"It's this, or we risk not having the numbers needed for an Exilium vote. Most of the others on your list are already covered by Drakon. If we can pull it off, we can win this without further bloodshed," I explained, and Adrian rubbed his temples.

Everyone was gathered around the island in the kitchen, with equal looks of worry. Fallon was behind Aaliyah, his arm around her shoulder, stroking her arm as she looked between us. She looked better, her eyes clearer, and even her skin held more color. But there was still unease in her eyes, twinges of pain that she couldn't hide. I'd have to give her more blood.

"And if we don't?" Fallon asked, pulling my attention.

"Sebek is in the States, coming this way. It's only a matter of time before he makes it to us," I said carefully.

In the States and completely off-grid. He could still be on the west coast, *or* he could be in Oakridge. There was no way to know for sure, so the faster we could get ahead of him, the better.

"What exactly would we be walking into?" Eirik asked, his eyes focused and primed.

He was the least stressed, his shoulders tight but not strained. The tactical portion of him was at play, and I only hoped it would stay that way.

"Kri'Valta is old, older than Sebek, and just as volatile. I won't lie and say it will be easy," I replied, and Eirik huffed.

"And what can we exploit?" he pressed. Ever the tactician, Eirik rubbed his jaw, thinking over his own question.

"He's a Demon. If we take out his core, we take out him. But getting to it, getting him to expose it? I don't know. We won't have any idea until we fight him," I said.

It wasn't the best plan, but it was all we had for such a fleeting period to decide. We needed to move because even a wrong choice here would be better than the alternative.

Would be better than sitting like ducks for *Death's Butcher* to find us.

"That's assuming we agree to this stupid fucking plan," Fallon grumbled, kissing Aaliyah on her head before he pulled away.

He walked around her, toward Adrian. Eirik didn't leave her standing alone for long as he moved behind her, wrapping his arms around her to hold her close. It was a fluid move, and she smiled softly at him as he purred. Her eyes fluttered shut, and she sighed.

Another tweak, pain flashing for just a second.

"Adrian, what are our other options?" I asked.

"Honestly? I don't know. This is our best chance at securing allies. Well, assuming Drakon keeps true to his word," Adrian replied, shrugging his shoulders as he raised an eyebrow at Fallon.

Fallon just walked past him, toward the fridge. Adrian turned, looking with the same curiosity as Fallon shuffled through the stuff in it.

"He will. He had the air of a fighter, a warrior. Didn't reek of lies," Eirik continued, his focus solely on me. "I trust him."

Trust was the fickle word that worried me here. We'd be placing a lot of trust in Drakon and his moral ground. Everyone thought they were good until faced with true terror. Would he and his faction still stand with us when faced with the finality of Sebek's wrath?

"With Drakon's additions, we'd barely be brushing the three-fourths majority needed for Exilium," I said, crossing my arms and reaching for my wrist. "It's risky to place all our bets on him, but I'm not sure we can do it without it. Not without further bloodshed."

I looked down, glancing at the lavender band that now sat on my wrist.

It was above my brand, and every time I looked at it, I was forced to see that as well. It filled me with equal parts joy and sorrow. This mark tied me to Aaliyah, irrevocably binding souls, and seeing it so close to my torment made me sick.

"Will there be backlash for killing this man?" Aaliyah suddenly asked, and I glanced up.

She was looking right at me, always so observant. I let out my breath and lowered my hand.

"Yes. But we're hopeful that it won't hit until after Sebek has been dealt with and I take his place. It's harder for them to deal with an Eternal, even outside the Eternium. But there is always a chance for Retaliation," I said, shoving down the lie that had built instinctively.

I didn't want to tell her that there was a risk this high, but I refused to lie anymore. We were open now, and everyone needed to know what we were getting into. There was always a chance for Retaliation, the means of the common Natural, to take revenge for the death of an ally. And I worried that was exactly what was going to be waiting for us.

But I could take a fight with anyone else. I'd end them before they could move and it would stop any other resistance on the spot. Sebek *had* to go down with Exilium.

And for that, we needed allies. Ones that wanted Kri'Valta dead.

"Seems like a lot of ifs, Osiris," Adrian said, now munching on some brownies that he and Aaliyah had made a few days back.

Fallon was to his right, doing the same, and Ali had one in her hands as well. It softened the room and further solidified the thought in my mind. Yes, I would fight anyone to achieve this. I'd kill Kri'Valta; I'd destroy his entire court if it'd help us. Because Aaliyah's safety depended on it.

"How do you even plan on getting close to him? It's two weeks from the Eternium. He's going to be more protected than the pope," Adrian reminded, finishing his brownie and going for another in the pan, only for Fallon to smack his hand. They glowered at each other.

"Drakon gave us a contact that can get us tickets. Said you would know the place, Adrian. It's called *The Altar*," I said, and Adrian nodded.

"Yeah, I know it. The Alderi Horde and I have been on good terms for years now. Not surprised that's where we have to go. But they're *Demons* too, Osiris. Getting those tickets isn't going to be as easy as you're hoping, even if Drakon requested them," he warned.

I knew that all too well. Drakon's request was a box of snakes, and this was just the first pick of it. He hadn't lied. He had a way for us to get into the gala, but he'd never said it was going to be easy. That much became clear when he gave me the code tonight, the one that would get us an audience with the leader of the Alderi Horde.

It was clear when he'd wished me luck.

"That's why I'm asking if you can do it," I said.

It wasn't a demand, simply a request. I knew he could. He'd proven himself many times over the years. But I rarely asked if he could do it. Or if he wanted to. He deserved that courtesy, something that I'd begun to realize. They wanted me to include them in my thoughts and plans.

So I asked him, instead of telling him, waiting for his thoughts if he had any suggestions to add.

"Yeah, I can get it done," Adrian said slowly.

I nodded, and Adrian never took his eyes off me. "I'll go with, assuming we agree, to make sure nothing goes awry."

Adrian barked a laugh, shaking his head. "You'll go *with* me?"

"I won't risk your safety right now, and I won't get in your way. But yes, I'll be going with you," I said, leaving no room for argument, and Adrian shrugged. "Now. I call a vote."

Silence broached the room before Eirik grunted and stated, "I'll place the first vote. Aye. Let's kill us a Demon. Been a while since I've had the pleasure of fighting one."

That got the rest going, with Adrian shrugging as he shook his head in minor disbelief. "I don't see another way. Guess that's my vote."

I looked at Fallon, who sighed, pinching the bridge of his nose. "This is going to come back to bite us. But I don't see another way out of it, fine."

That left just one.

Aaliyah was frozen in Eirik's arms, her eyes staring straight ahead.

"Ali?" Fallon asked, and she blinked slowly.

When she looked up, her conflicted gaze bounced between us before searching the empty air around us.

"There's no other way?" she asked softly.

I almost stepped toward her then. So tender, she was, after everything that had befallen her, still so soft. The kindness in her eyes was only shadowed by her will.

"Not that we know," I said, and she nodded sharply.

Eirik's arms tightened around her, his purr growing as she finally nodded. "Alright. I vote yes."

I let out a breath and fixed the cuffs of my undershirt. This was a plan, the best we had. Now we just had to make it count. Two weeks, and we'd be at the Eternium. Then, before we knew it, we'd be home.

All of us.

I looked at Aaliyah again, the mark on my wrist heating. The craving, gnawing feeling to be close to her was always there, and I wanted it. Wanted to be near her, to hold her how Eirik was. I wasn't a perfect man; I never would be. But I could be her shield, her sword. The executioner for her demons and any that would come to harm her. I would always be hers, however she would have me.

But I needed to be my own first, needed to fix the cracks in my soul so she wouldn't cut herself on them. She deserved the best of me, not the broken bits. I was working on it, would continue to, and hopefully soon I would be comfortable enough to ask her to stand by my side like she did the others.

I looked away, resolved, strengthened, and for the first time, the mark on my wrist didn't mean desolation. The one above it showed a hope I'd thought I'd lost.

"We leave first thing tomorrow evening to acquire the tickets. The art gala is in three days," I said, and each nodded. "This should keep us on the move. From the gala, we go directly to the Eternium. Once on the grounds, Sebek won't be able to retaliate."

"Why?" Aaliyah asked, and I was taken aback before remembering how little she knew of our world.

That needed to change as soon as we could.

"Because only fights of Challenge or Retaliation are allowed, and they are official fights done before the Eternals. It's the rule the Hallowed Three placed," I explained.

And they were unbreakable. Once you walked onto the grounds, you couldn't raise a hand, even if you wanted to. The spell ran ground deep. A Challenge for the place of Eternal.

And Retaliation, for the vengeance of those who have lost.

"So he can't hurt us there?" Aaliyah asked, and it was Eirik who nodded against the top of her head.

"Not without going through the official methods," he said, and she visibly relaxed.

Adrian stretched before clapping his hands. He had a way of dispersing tension, and it bled from the room as he walked back over to Ali. He didn't wait or hesitate before cupping her face and sealing his lips to hers. It was an enticing sight, watching her cheeks flush as she tensed in Eirik's arms, caught between two immovable forces.

Adrian pulled back a moment later, grinning like a madman as he tipped his head back to me. "Alright. I'll go do a little digging. I need to make sure I know what we're getting into," he said, winking before turning away and walking toward the stairs, quickly disappearing up them.

Fallon was the next to move, doing the same as Adrian had and stealing Aaliyah's lips until she was a flustered mess. Fallon grinned, the joking tilt to his lips catching her eye.

"This has me too amped up to sleep. Eirik, down for a spar?" he asked, looking over Aaliyah's head.

Eirik nodded, coiling around her tighter, holding her close for just a moment longer.

"Read my fucking mind," he said, tilting Ali's head to catch her eyes. "Want to join us, *smár Valkyrja*?"

It was strange seeing this from the outside. But jealousy wasn't exactly what I encountered. I was glad to see the joy in their eyes, to see them alive again. It pushed me to do the same, to conquer her lips as I had countless kingdoms. I wanted to feel the soft intake of breath as I grew close, wanted to hold her hands above her head so she couldn't move and steal everything she'd give me so I could hoard it away.

"I think I'm going to relax in the library if that's alright," Aaliyah said, panting between Fallon and Eirik.

Both of them stayed close to her for a while longer before pulling back.

"Course it is. Come find us if you need us," Fallon said, and she flushed even brighter than before when he leaned in, pressing a kiss to her ear and whispering, "Love you, trouble."

Then he was gone, Eirik quickly following after. She stood frazzled in the middle of the kitchen, looking dazed as she touched a hand to her lips.

"Might I join you in the library? I'm just about finished with the trans-lation for your next read," I asked, lip tilting up when she jumped and looked my way.

Aaliyah grinned, sheepish, before nodding and whispering, "Always."

She walked up to me, humming softly. I reached out my hand on instinct, and she took it in stride, sliding hers into mine.

I was broken ... but I was *hers*. And one day at a time, I became worthy of her. One day at a time, I gained what I needed to truly ask her to be mine.

And I knew that time just drew one day closer.

"So, which book did you pick this time?" Aaliyah asked as we walked through the large oak doorway that led to the library.

Thoth's ever-watchful eyes followed us in, and I snapped my fingers, lighting the fireplace in an instant as the *Flame* coursed through my veins. I hummed, walking over to the couch and the small side table that held my latest translation.

"One I know you'll enjoy," I said, and she raised an eyebrow.

Her hand tightened on mine, and we both sat.

"Knights?" she asked, and I shook my head. She pinched her face in concentration. "Princes?" I shook my head again. "Dragons?"

"No, no dragons," I said, and she giggled as I lifted the original copy of the book. The flash of emotion on her face was instant before it slid away to a neutral position. "Gladiators."

She reached out, running her hand over the scrawling ornate script on the cover of one of Nero's novels. He'd written it just shortly after being turned to remember his time in the Colosseum.

Fabula Fortium. A Tale of the Brave.

"Nero dabbled in writing. This was one of his accounts in the Colosseum. Though, he added some flair for dramatics," I said.

Meaning, he added all kinds of mythical beasts and champions. Fairly sure he also fought Ares in it. It would be a splendid read for her because it *was* a splendid read. Even if it hurt to look at. I glanced at Aaliyah, having been lost in my thoughts, and she looked at the book with the same sorrow I always had. It covered her eyes in a haze and drowned out the excitement.

"Is everything alright?" I asked, and she turned to me with a fragile gaze.

Something was on the tip of her tongue, a breath away, before she shook her head. Her eyes closed off familiarly, the shunning of a thought.

"Do you mind translating these for me? I know it takes a lot of time," she said, covering her confusing emotions with a question I wasn't expecting.

I waited a moment before responding, threading our fingers to show my support for whatever had just grabbed her. I didn't want to push, not when whatever it was sat so heavy on her, but I wanted her to know I was there, regardless.

To show her she wasn't alone.

She took a few breaths, her gaze falling to the book again.

"I quite enjoy it, actually. I haven't read many of these books in lifetimes," I said, and her eyes brightened a bit. "I fell in love with learning languages in my early years and found it a good way to pass the time. It's nice to keep my skills sharp after so many decades of them dulling."

"How many do you know?" she asked without waiting, her attention fully on me again.

"Too many to count, I'm afraid. Though, many are no longer fluent. Latin has always been one that stuck."

She paused again, this time reaching out and gently taking the book from my hands. She opened the first cover like she'd seen the book before, her eyes landing on the scrawling signature that stained the inside cover.

"Because of Nero?" she asked, quietly pressing her fingers to his name.

She set her palm against it like she might learn something about my closest friend. My confidant and my brother. Seeing her so emotional about it made it easier to talk about.

Made it easier to breathe.

"Yes. He preferred it to all others, being his native language," I said, setting my hand over hers. "Perhaps we could read this together after Adrian and I return from our task."

She bit her lip but didn't pull away from me.

"Are you sure? I don't want to make you uncomfortable," she said.

I smiled. Fully, happily. She always knew how to ground me to her, to keep me level. Because she knew me so well, so thoroughly. But I needed this as much as she did, needed to hear his words.

"Yes. I think I'd like to remember him. He deserves to have legends told about him. He'd have it no other way," I said truthfully.

Aaliyah softened, and any previous doubt or worry faded from her eyes. Whatever had clouded her memory lifted, and she leaned onto my shoulder with her hand still pressed to Nero's signature.

"I think you're right," she sighed. "He ... he'd be proud of you, Osiris. I'm proud of you."

I choked up at her words, having to turn away as tears flooded my eyes. As always, Aaliyah knew before I did how to help. She turned her hand, lacing our fingers again. The heat of her palm, the way she held me captive, was enough to drown out even the loudest of demons.

"Will you show me how you do this? I obviously don't know Latin, but maybe I can learn?" she asked, and I nodded.

"If you want to learn, I'll teach you. Anything you want, *lux mea*, you'll have it."

Because I would do whatever she needed to be happy. Anything.

And always.

CHAPTER 47

ADRIAN

"You know, Osiris, it's really hard to seem approachable and personable when you're trying to glare your way into the building. Maybe tone down the murder vibes a bit?" I joked, smirking when Osiris tipped his head back, whispering something to give him strength as we walked up to the shining, vibrant building that housed *The Altar*.

Only the hottest luxury voyeur club on this side of the Atlantic.

"You be personable. I'll make sure no one gets too close," Osiris said, standing straighter as the distinctive sound of conversation became apparent.

"Ah, Osi, what a lovely way to show that you care. I knew bringing you was the right choice. Fallon would have just grumbled and tried to fight me. Not to mention we don't get to spend much time together, Osiris! This is a lovely bonding moment," I said, grinning as I shoved my hands in my pocket, taking a moment to admire the grandeur in front of us.

The name shone above the door, the sparkling font equal parts decadent and trailing the line of erotic. A line of people extended out the door, wrapping into the alleyway, but I didn't pay much attention as I walked up to Alderi'Theodious. He was always running bouncer, and being a Demon of Wrath, it fit him nicely.

He was dressed in a finely pressed black suit, his hair a deep ocean blue, matching his eyes as he looked at me over his sunglasses.

I snorted, delighted by his appearance. It seemed to change every time I came here. Sometimes he'd be dressed to the nines, other times in rags, but most of the time he'd be wearing some strange amalgamation of colors and patterns that was an insult to the eye.

But the typical 'bodyguard' style was really the cherry on top.

He didn't say anything, merely nodded at me and Osiris as he let us in, grinning viciously as the crowd at the door protested weakly. He *wanted* a fight, and no one there was brave enough to give him one as they dropped silent.

We slid in the door, blasted by the scent of sex and the heady pulse of the music. I scrunched my nose and nodded back to Theo, uttering a quick thank you. It always took a moment to acclimate to *The Altar's* upbeat and sensual mood, so I wasn't surprised when I looked back to find Osiris as stiff as a board. One person got a little too close, and Osiris's eyes flashed red as he shoved them, a human, away.

They stumbled, their mouth open to spew some expletives before their eyes grew wide at the sight of my eldest brother. I snickered as the man's face went pale and he jerked away, disappearing into the crowd.

The Altar was lit up in a delicate blend of red and black, and everything about it was dipped in sin as you would expect from a joint run by Demons. The steady beat thumbed even through the floor, and there was plenty to focus on, from dancers swinging from the ceiling, showing as much skin as possible, to the swirl of smoke that lingered across the ground, the scent like that of glitter and gold, meant to entice and muddle the brain. A gift of a Lust Demon, one I likely knew, and the owner of this fine establishment.

I wished I knew more about them, the Demons, where they came from, and how close to biblically accurate they were. They were Naturals, of course, born from the blood of the Hallowed of Death, like the Vampire. But that was all I knew. That was really all anyone knew.

Damn, I'd really love to pick one of those Hallowed brains one day, assuming they didn't pick mine, literally.

I dragged Osiris through the bodies, sliding us into a booth so we could get a full view of the floor.

"This is..." Osiris started, his thought falling off.

"Crazy, I know. But Amadeus runs a tight ship. Should have guessed that Drakon would send us here. The Alderi Horde is one of my primary sources of information," I said nonchalantly.

It was really an understatement. I got more from the Alderi than I had from anyone else. They were Demons, each an embodiment of sin, like most Demon Hordes. Though most of my interactions were with Theo and Amadeus, the owner of this lovely establishment of lust and sin.

I wondered which I'd see tonight.

I twitched, the surrounding bodies muddling together and the scent of them sparking an instinct that I always tried to push down. The touch of the *Call* pressed at my tongue, flooding my mouth with saliva and the need to feed. It always happened here, so fully surrounded by desperation.

But that didn't mean I didn't have to fight to keep my fangs in. I clenched my fists, looking around the room.

"You alright?" Osiris asked. He may be tense, but the focus in his eyes was unwavering as I turned to face him.

"Yeah, blood's just a bit on the fritz, I think. Nothing I can't handle for now. It's charged in here, isn't it? The magic is so thick you can taste it," I said with a grin.

It was strange, being here with one of my brothers. This was something that had always been my own, though I'm sure had I asked, one of them would have accompanied me. When I'd first taken it over, Nero had only been gone some three years, so I hadn't wanted to push for something they didn't have the energy to give.

"I'm sorry, Adrian," Osiris said suddenly, startling me out of my thoughts.

Sorry?

"For what?" I asked, genuinely confused about what he could be talking about.

Osiris wasn't someone who apologized often or with such sincerity. But he didn't look away, emotion driving out the numbness in his eyes.

"Not being present. I see now how much you've had to take on yourself, in my wallowing," he said, and I blinked.

Osiris had done a lot of things in my hundred years, but this ... this was growth. An understanding of his faults. *Voicing* them.

I smiled so widely that I felt the stretch in the corners of my mouth.

"Water under the bridge, Osi. It's what family does. It's why you're here tonight, and I'm not alone. It's why Eirik and Fallon are keeping Ali company, likely joking and *living*." I didn't say it, but he knew what I meant. "Which means we need to hurry this up so we can get back to her."

He knew we were functioning as a family again for the first time in decades. And I knew we had one person to thank for that. A lovely, beautiful soul that I suddenly couldn't wait to have in my arms again.

"We're Vivas. Bound by blood," Osiris started, his eyes far away, his thought likely the same as mine.

This family of ours finally felt whole again, and I'd risk everything to keep it that way.

"And brothers by choice," I chanted the next verse of our calling. "Glad to see you coming around, Osi. Now you just need to talk to Ali, and we'll be right as rain."

I bit my tongue, watching carefully as Osiris weighed my words before he nodded. Pure elation stole my breath, and I leaned back onto the heavy leather bench.

"Yes, I do," he acknowledged, *finally*. "I worry I'm not enough for her, Adrian."

I chuckled at that. With someone as resilient as she was, someone that bled life so thoroughly, it was hard not to think that way. I knew I did too, at times.

"Why don't you let her decide that, Osi? She'll surprise you," I said, and he shook his head.

But I didn't miss how hope had spread into his eyes in a way that made the opposing blues seem more open. He covered his wrist, looking at the two opposing inks there. The mark of his past, and what I knew was his future.

For once, he didn't cover it.

"She always does," he said, trailing the lavender band with the tip of his finger.

We fell into a comfortable silence. Well, as silent as it could get in a sex club. I shook my head, ready to get home, which meant I needed to get this show on the road.

"Now, why don't you sit here and have a good time, and I'll go do what I do best, yeah?" I asked.

Osiris nodded, sitting straight again, the emotion in his eyes bleeding away as the point of the evening again became our focus.

"I will keep an eye out. Be safe, Adrian." Then he turned away, scanning the room diligently.

I stood and walked my way through the dancing bodies, coming up to the bar. Sure enough, sitting on one of the stools was exactly who I was hoping to see: Alderi'Amadeus. I took the seat next to him, tapping on the counter to garner the attention of the bartender.

"I'd like a whiskey on the rocks, with a splash of amaretto," I said, not looking in her direction as Amadeus straightened.

It was the code he'd been waiting for. After we'd agreed to come here, Osiris had called Drakon for more information, so I wasn't surprised to hear it was a drink. It damn near appeared in front of me, and I chuckled when Amadeus tipped his head back, downing his drink with a dry laugh. I followed suit, needing the liquid courage before dealing with whatever this trial was going to be. Amadeus's eyes were a rich gold, matching the highlights in his summer brown hair. He breathed attraction, and even I shivered as a bolt of lust shot down my spine.

"Collector. Drakon didn't mention you'd be the one here. Of everyone I thought he'd try to get for this ... well, I guess overkill isn't such a bad thing," he said, nodding toward the counter as the barista walked by.

"So good to see you too, Amadeus. It's been ages. What do you say we find somewhere quiet to talk?" I asked, and he nodded.

We both stood, and he looked around the room, catching eyes with Theodious, who nodded toward us from the door.

"Follow me," he said, not allowing me time to respond before walking into the crowd.

I trailed him to the back of the room, past a set of guards I didn't know well enough to name. The room we stepped into was blissfully quiet and sat at the table was a man I'd never met. Dressed to the nines in a tailored suit, with a cigar held between two fingers as he pulled it away from his mouth. The smoke wafted up, brushing the ceiling and filling the room with a bitter sweetness.

And I thought Osiris screamed gangster.

"I'll leave you two to it. Go easy on him," Amadeus said, chuckling to himself. Whether he meant that for me or the man, I'd never know.

Then Amadeus was gone, the door clicking behind me. I quickly gauged the man in front of me. No tension held him hostage as he sat easily. He had piercing green eyes, a mark of Greed, with black hair against deep olive skin. He was built like a tank though, his physique screaming Wrath.

"All this for me? You shouldn't have," I said, crossing my arms as I stepped toward his desk. There were two chairs in front of it, and I took the one to his left.

The man smiled, not so much malice as amusement in his eyes.

"Alderi'Vidius. But please, call me Vidius," he said with a click of his tongue.

His words shocked me, and I did my best not to let that show as I relaxed in my seat. I'd never met the Alderi head before, but God did I know his name. It wasn't often you got to deal with a descendant of an original Sin, bred by the Hallowed of Death himself.

"Pleasure's all mine, Vidius. You know, I've been wanting to meet you for ages, but every time I've been around, you've been away," I said truthfully. "Say, your name is familiar. Son of Valtori, if I remember correctly, and descendant of none other than Mammon himself, no?"

I couldn't help the prod, putting some of my knowledge on the table to get some baseline on what he thought I knew. Mammon was one of the first Demons born of the Hallowed of Death, the original Demon of Green. And knowing that Vidius was a direct descendant showed I knew more than he gave. The Alderi clan was *notoriously* reserved. Vidius didn't react to this how I might have expected, as he simply smiled again. *That* was dangerous.

"I know your game, Adrian Vivas, *Collector* of the Crypt of Vivas. Yes, your information is correct. But before we start this, I'd like to ask you something," he said, and I nodded.

"Go ahead. You know, it's getting hard to keep track of all these things people want. I hope you're ready to make it worth my while. In fact, we really should get Osiris for this. I'm sure he'd love to join the party."

"No, *Challe* Vivas is being well entertained. Just your time will do. After all, I'd like to keep my head on my shoulders." A fair point, really. "It'll be worth your while, and another backing at the Eternium."

Now that was surprising. Of all those I knew to be hunting for the spot of Eternal, I never would have pegged one of the Alderi. They were already influential, even though they'd sprouted up only in the last few centuries, without all the prod and posture that came with being one. But a Greed would always be a Greed, I supposed.

"Oh? You plan to take poor old Kri'Valta's place, do you? You have a lot of competition," I said, and Vidius chuckled dryly.

He reached over the table, picking up the glass that had been in front of him. He lifted it, and I did the same, each of us taking a drink.

"I do. But that's not a concern," he said.

And he meant it. If he was in the running, then he already had the title. No one in their right mind would try to fight him for it.

"You know, from my intel, you never seemed like the sort to aim for Eternal status. Greed or not. What changed your mind?" I asked, and his eyes grew distant.

He set his drink down, tapping the table a few times with a finger before he answered, "A promise I made a long time ago."

He shook it off, smirking at me again as he leaned back, his façade cleanly back in place.

"Here's the deal, Collector. Play with me, humor my questions, and you'll get your chance at Kri'Valta. And the new Demon Eternal on your side, as well."

Straightforward enough, but also riskier than he was letting on. You didn't make deals with Demons.

You didn't barter with Greed.

"Let me guess, the catch is I have to win?" I asked, and Vidius nodded.

"Wouldn't be fun otherwise, would it?" he asked. "Don't worry, I won't ask for your soul should you lose. But you won't get your information or your tickets if you do. And we might have to reconsider our partnership in the future."

Fair enough.

"What's your game?" I asked, downing the rest of my drink as Vidius reached into his desk and pulled out some decrepit-looking dice.

They were battle-worn, aged by the rolling salt of the ocean based on the smell. The numbers on the sides had long since faded. Vidius tapped one of them, humming as he sat back.

"Liar's Dice. The perfect game to lead into the end of the *Horror of the Depths*. I'll even give you the honor of the first bid," Vidius said, and it was my turn to laugh.

Of course he had to pick Liar's Dice. I was horrendous at this stupid game. I could count on one hand the number of times I'd won it against Nero, and I'd spent *years* playing against him. Hell, on our trip to the States after I'd been turned, before we'd even started building our home, I'd won a single game against him.

One out of *thousands.*

"How do I know you haven't loaded the dice?" I asked, and Vidius shrugged.

"Have a little more faith than that, Collector. I'm a Demon, not a cheat. So, do you agree to my terms?" he asked, and I sighed, picking up my five dice and weathered cup.

"I never was much good at Liar's Dice. But as a show of good faith, sure, I'll play," I said, tossing my dice into the cup.

The rules of Liar's Dice were simple. Each player had five dice that were rolled each turn and kept hidden from your opponent. The goal was to guess the number of a certain face on the table, without going over the actual amount. The other player got the chance to guess as well if they thought there were more of that face. But if you guessed over the amount, and the other person playing called you on it, then you lost the round.

And were quite the liar.

"You know, I'm curious. Why now, of all times, to work toward Exilium?" Vidius asked, and I shrugged.

"Osiris is of age to Challenge, and we'd rather not deal with Sebek in one of his moods again," I said easily, looking at my set. My numbers were varied, but I had two sixes, which made it easy enough to pick my first guess. "I bet three sixes."

Vidius looked under his cup, humming.

"Osiris has been of Challenging age for decades. If you wanted to dethrone Sebek, you would have started years ago. Something changed recently. *Very* recently, didn't it?" he asked, looking up from his cup with a mocking smirk.

Cheeky bastard.

"How do you know we haven't been working toward this? We're a rather secretive bunch, Vidius. We like to keep things under wraps," I pushed, leaning forward. A touch of the *Flame* sparked along my arm, and the burn settled behind my eyes. "Make your bid."

"Right," Vidius responded, never taking his eyes off me. "So it wouldn't have anything to do with the lovely lady spotted with you in Aspenway. I heard you and Fallon caused quite a scene in her honor."

I froze, and Vidius's grin grew.

"I bet five sixes," he said, as my fangs dropped.

It was such an easy prod, not even a threat based on how easily he sat, but it was enough to make my blood boil. No one mentioned Ali, no one spoke of her, and if he said one more word, I'd tear out his throat.

I wasn't the violent type, but her safety meant more than pretense. More than my partnership with this Horde.

"You're overstepping, Vidius. We're barely friends, yet you ask me to talk about my love life. Shouldn't you at least treat me to a drink first?" I asked, the sharpness in my voice bleeding into my eyes as my vision tinted red. I took a deep breath and settled into my seat. "Don't worry, no offense taken. Even if you are a liar."

I picked up my cup, showing two sixes. He lifted his to show two as well. His bet was greater than four, so it was a win for me.

Vidius grinned and shook his head.

"Well played. I knew this would be entertaining," he hummed, picking his dice up to roll again. I did the same. "You've played this before, haven't you? I bet four fours."

I scoffed, shaking my head as I looked under my cup, spying two fours. He'd played a confident enough bet ... and my gut was telling me he had more than that.

"Nero was fond of games. I've learned more than the world remembers. Five fours," I bet, and Vidius shook his head.

"Liar," he prodded, lifting his cup to show *no* fours. I hadn't even seen a hint of a tick. This might be harder than I'd hoped. "What will you do if your Exilium fails?"

Die probably. Beg for our lives? Surely. But that wouldn't happen.

I wouldn't fucking let it.

"It won't. We have a solid plan, with or *without* you," I emphasized, only partially bluffing, looking under my cup. It was a mash of differing values, and I threw out, "Three fives."

Vidius paused for a moment, scrutinizing my expression before he grinned.

"*Four* fives."

"Not this time," I lifted my cup, breathing out a sigh as he lifted his cup. One five under mine, two under his, making a total of three fives on the table. Another win for me. "You know, it's quite the nice place you have here. Love what you've done with it," I mused. "How did you get the Sword of Goujian?"

We shook our cups again, and even though this was largely a game of luck, a distraction wouldn't hurt. Vidius raised an eyebrow but indulged me, nonetheless.

"Got it from an auction several years back. One of my favorite pieces," he said, an honest expression of joy on his face.

He reminded me of Fallon when he'd talk about his paintings.

"Don't suppose I can barter it off of you, then? Eirik would swoon," I joked, and Vidius laughed.

"No, I'm afraid not. I like to keep my things close," he said, shaking his dice before setting his cup down on the table.

"Shame. But what else could I expect?" I asked, setting my cup up again.

Vidius dipped his head, looking under his cup. "To be honest, I've never been the betting sort. Which is why I never spent much time around *The Devil's Details*. Before it shut down, of course."

I wasn't sure if he was playing my tactic against me or truly pushing to get information. I ground my teeth, shaking my dice again.

"Careful," I said, slamming the cup onto the table. It rattled the bits and odds scattered across the top. Vidius leaned in, the hint of his heritage showing as his glamor wavered, and thick twisting horns came into view on the top of his head. His skin rippled, morphing between a deep green, much like his eyes and his olive skin.

"I heard you and your Crypt had shown there just before Darius Verslini's departure. There are even records of a purchase—"

I stood, cutting him off. "So what if we had? The purchase was legitimate and protected by our right as Naturals."

Vidius lifted his hands, dipping his head. His glamor dropped back into place, and he leaned back. "No need to get so defensive. Simply curious," he mused, rolling a pointed nail across the top of his cup. I was flustered, red flashing in my eyes as my fangs pressed against the roof of my mouth. "Call your bet, Vivas."

But suddenly it was hard to talk, hard to breathe as that rage morphed in my stomach, eating at my insides as the *Call* took advantage of my weakness all over again.

Fuck me. *Now was not the fucking time.*

I sat reticently while straining to keep my eyes from shifting fully to that blood-red. Vidius had taken to watching me, blatant amusement replaced with sharp worry. I didn't even lift my cup as I threw out my bet, desperately hoping my fangs wouldn't drop as I spoke.

"Five twos."

Vidius appraised me with a careful eye, lifting his cup. No twos.

Fuck. *Fuck.*

"Liar, Adrian," he declared, and I shook my head. "Better be more careful next time."

Shit, I wouldn't survive another round like this. The *Call* poked at every nerve, and suddenly I could hear Vidius's heartbeat. This needed to end, *now.* Lifting my cup with a shaking hand, there sat five twos.

I let out a breath, not daring to suck one back in as the push of the *Call* continued to build in me, ripping me apart from the inside out.

"Wrong again, Vidius. Game over, no?" I asked, glad to have won a third round, winning me the game as well. I put the cup down and slid it to him.

He nodded, tilting his head away as he reached into his desk. The move exposed his throat, showing thickly corded muscle. I didn't mean to listen to the roll of the blood in his veins, had tried to ignore it, but it built in the air like ever-growing music. I jolted, nearly going toward him as he faced me again.

He eyed me warily, eyes squinted as he slid an envelope toward me.

"You win your tickets, Adrian Vivas. Be sure Osiris is there. Kri'Valta would be displeased if he weren't," he said briskly. "And you may wish to pull the reins on the people of your district. Word has gotten out about *The Devil's Details* being shut down again, and Darius Verslini has been seen in Oakridge as recently as a few days ago. And I'd guess by the look on your face that he's not supposed to be here. Don't worry, that little slip of information was just a show of good faith."

He didn't give me time to process what he'd said, not that I'd been able to. He stood, buttoning his suit coat as he did.

"It's been a pleasure, *Collector*," he said, nodding in my direction before gesturing toward the door.

I stood, having to force myself to turn away from him. The pull of the *Call* rode on every nerve I had, and I took stilted breaths.

"Thank you for your company, Vidius," I managed, and he nodded once.

His face shifted, glamor falling again as he waved. "See you soon, Adrian."

I was already moving when he spoke again, opening the door to a pool of sweaty bodies and overwhelming scents. Everything prodded and poked, making the press of bloodlust burn brighter. My eyes flashed red, and I stumbled into a human trying to get through it all.

He nearly fell, eyes wide as he turned to face me. He was close. It would be easy to just—

"Adrian, *stop*," a voice commanded. Just my name was enough to pull me back, but the brush of a *Charm* took the edge off of the *Call*. But it would be back.

It always came back.

"Home," I grunted, leaning into Osiris as he came to my side.

He flinched, nearly jolting away before his arm went around me to hold me up. I'd feel bad about it later when I could breathe without the thought of making another bloodbath.

"The *Call*?" Osiris asked, wearily looking around the room.

I could only nod as Osiris guided us through the room. People kept their distance, the press of his magic in the air warding them off. It helped me breathe a little easier. We passed through the front door, with Theo giving me a strange look.

I had no idea how long we walked, but the further we got from the bustle of *The Altar*, the more my mind cleared. I gripped the envelope clutched in my hand tightly. The *Call* hadn't hit me that hard since I'd been turned. I nearly lost a deal because of it.

That thought destroyed me, and I stumbled.

"Sit," Osiris said, suddenly planting me on the side of the road. There was a mess of mulch surrounding us, the filth of the city sinking into my clothes. "What do I do?"

I took another breath, gripping my arms. Fallon was normally here to help me through this. There wasn't a cure for it, but Fallon always knew what to say, how to coach me into pulling away from the dragging feeling.

"Nothing, just—" I started, my fangs aching so hard I had to take another breath. "Just stay here for a minute."

Osiris was frozen for a moment before he crouched in front of me. It was the oddest thing, seeing him take a large, exaggerated breath in. But he did, before letting it out slowly. He did this a few more times, and I eventually fell in sync with him. His breaths were soothing.

He didn't speak, didn't touch me, just breathed.

And suddenly I wasn't looking through a sheen of red.

"That ... that actually worked," I blurted out, laughing as my head fell into my hands. "Thanks, Osi."

He nodded, standing and brushing off his pants. He paused again before reaching his hand out to me. I stared at it, confused for a moment.

"Come. We must go home."

I nodded, reaching out and carefully taking his hand. He flinched, and I knew he would.

But he still helped me to my feet. Made sure I was good to stay standing.

"Yeah," I said, flashing my envelope, trying to understand the switch that I was seeing in our eldest. "We have a gala to prepare for."

Chapter 48

Aaliyah

Adrian and Osiris had been gone for a few hours now, and the silence in the house was something I was no longer used to. The quiet was something I'd known in my memories, and I hated it. I missed Adrian's humming as he moved about the kitchen and the way he'd tap at the cabinet doors.

I hoped they were okay.

I sighed, walking down the creaking steps that lead to the ground floor, hand trailing along the gray walls. That silence followed me here, to an empty kitchen. I hadn't expected to find anything, not considering that Eirik had also left a few minutes ago to check the wards around the land.

A thud sounded in the air, catching my attention as my spine shot straight and I went on the defensive. But there was nothing else around, and I wasn't filled with dread at the sound. The surprise wore off quickly, as another one echoed louder this time. I shook my head and walked toward the training room.

I opened the door, being careful not to disturb Fallon as he rained hit after hit against a hanging punching bag in the middle of the room. The fluidity of his movements blended with the speed of his hits, and I could barely see them connect before he was throwing another.

Sweat glistened along his tanned skin, defining all the intricately toned muscles that hid under his suits. Fallon *wasn't* small. Every time he moved, they flexed and bunched, showing exactly how much power he kept locked in. His calf and thigh flexed, and he tipped his head toward me as his next hit connected, his entire leg flexing against the bag in a way that made my own thighs clench. His hair, normally so perfect, was brushed back haphazardly, strands falling over his face in blond waves.

There was something startlingly sexy about a man with this much strength, and knowing how gently he'd hold me with those same ripped arms.

"Ali, enjoying the show?" he asked, completely ripping me out of my fantasy.

He smirked at me, wiping the sweat from his brow as he turned away from the bag. He walked to me slowly, giving me ample time to trace every inch of him. He only wore a pair of boxer-type shorts that clung to his hips, showing the defined 'V' there that led below his waistline. My fingers twitched, and I had to fight the urge to reach out and touch it.

He lifted his hand, his knuckles bruised and bloodied, and brushed a piece of hair behind my ear. The gentle caress of his thumb against my cheek made me flush so hard that I grew dizzy.

"I was," I mumbled, and Fallon cracked a smile, shaking his head. "But I think I like having you closer, anyway."

Fallon's face softened, his eyes gaining that light that only really showed when he thought no one was watching. He brushed my cheek again.

"What brought you here?" he asked, and honestly, I didn't have an answer. The need to be close to him was enough, but as I looked around the room, a thought came to me.

I'd never been much of a fighter, preferred not to be in fights at all. But that wasn't an idea I could entertain, knowing what we were going into. I didn't want to use my magic, not how I'd done at the hot spring ... and that made me useless in a lot of ways. I didn't want to be a hindrance to them, something that could only be protected.

I wanted to protect them, or at the very least, not be some damsel waiting to be saved.

Fallon knew how to fight, and if anyone could teach me how to protect myself, even a little? Well, he was at the top of the list.

"Can you teach me?" I said suddenly, and Fallon's eyes went from heated and lustful to curious.

"Teach you what?" he asked.

"How to protect myself."

Fallon paused for a moment, pulling his hands back to cross his arms over his chest. He glanced over at the bag behind him.

"Protecting yourself isn't something that's learned in a day, Ali," he said, dashing my hopes. "But I understand, and we can *start* today. I'll make sure you can take care of yourself when we can't get there immediately."

Leave it to Fallon to break the news in a way that sounded like rejection. I grinned so wide my cheeks hurt and threw myself into his arms. He was sweaty and smelled like heat and man, but it was electric. I held on tighter, even as he set me on my feet and walked me to the bag.

"Thank you," I whispered, and Fallon's head dipped to my ear, a low, sinful chuckle making me shiver.

"Oh, don't thank me yet, trouble," he chuckled, grabbing my arms to move me into a position meant to start swinging. His body immediately tensed behind me, and when I glanced up, any hint of my Fallon was gone, and in his place was someone ready for a fight.

I might be in a bit over my head.

"Again," Fallon chided as I threw yet another punch at his swinging punching bag.

My arm shook, and every single muscle I had screamed at me to sit. But I couldn't; I'd already asked once.

I tried not to get frustrated with Fallon's brutal teaching methods, but when he said he'd show me how to protect myself, I wasn't expecting *this*.

I'd meditated with Adrian and Eirik to try to hone my gifts, and I expected something of the same, some kind of soft way to introduce me to it. I thought this was going to be some cute distraction or a way to keep my mind occupied without leaving the house ... though I really shouldn't have. Fallon was a brawler. He *loved* to fight. I should have known that this would have been how his teaching would go as well.

So, my arms trembling, my breathing hard, and my legs threatening to give out, I turned to him.

"You know, this isn't what I expected when I asked you to teach me to defend myself," I groaned, leaning against the bag and taking in the acidic scent of sweat. Fallon huffed something like a laugh behind me. "I was thinking more Rocky montage, you know? It takes on the end of thirty seconds, and then I can bench press a car or something?"

I tipped my head back, watching as Fallon's lips curved into that sinful grin, and he walked up to me. He pulled me away from the bag enough to move me to face him as he slid his hand to the back of my head, tilting it up to look at him.

"I told you training your muscles to do what you want doesn't happen overnight, Ali." His words spoke of experience, and the leisurely perusal of the tight muscles of his arms showed it was experience well-learned. "It takes patience and hard work. I'm not about to baby you when it comes to your safety."

I sighed but nodded. As much as my muscles protested it, I was glad that he was taking this seriously, that he wasn't treating me like glass. I caught his gaze, prideful and caring.

"Yeah, I'm sure I'll be glad in the future, but my legs want to commit murder right about now," I groaned, and he ran a thumb across my cheek as if to say, 'I'm happy to do the murdering for you'. "Are you sure this is going to work?"

I tipped my head down, turning and pressing my head back into the bag. I hadn't meant to say it, to voice the concern that built in my skull every time my head hurt. I felt weak, like none of this was going to make any difference.

I don't want to die. Now more than ever.

"Look at me," Fallon instructed from my side as he placed a steady hand on my bare arm. He was freezing, like normal, but he almost seemed hot with the intensity that he stared at me.

I jerked my head down, unable to hold his gaze. But Fallon wasn't one to take that standing still, and his hand slid under my chin, tilting my head with a persistent pull.

"Look. At. Me," he said, louder this time.

He was close, and I shivered, allowing my head to move to catch his gaze again. Those vibrant green eyes stole every word I had.

"It takes time, Ali. It may not seem like it now, but you will get this. In a few months, you'll look back and wonder how you let this get to you at all." He pressed his forehead to mine, the ice of his skin mixing with the spark of contact, and suddenly I wasn't shaking from exertion but from the bloom of heat between my legs. "But while you're learning, trust us to keep you safe. Hell, I'd appreciate it if you trusted us after, too."

Husky words and darkening eyes were signs I was learning to catch. Ones I now understood as arousal.

At least I wasn't the only one.

"It's okay to be scared, but don't let it cloud your judgment. Especially in a fight." He leaned in, so close I could feel his breath. He was close, so close ...

"Now, again." Then he was back, arms crossed over his chest, with a trickster mirth in his eyes that I'd only ever seen from Adrian.

I scowled.

"Fallon, I can't," I groaned, wiping the sweat from my forehead with a shaking hand.

"You can, just one more," he assured, his lips tilting. That heat didn't leave his eyes. If anything, it grew as his hands flexed against the firm muscles of his arms. I gave in, a shiver inching down my spine as I turned towards the bag again.

I threw one hit, my arm shaking again.

"No. Keep your legs separated, but comfortable. You don't want them taking them out from under you, and you can throw a better hit if you have a sound foundation." He breathed the words like a whisper in my ear. Then, his arms settled on mine slowly, giving me time to pull away if I wanted. His front to my back, he surrounded me. "Arms close. Keep them in line with you."

He pulled my arms in, pressing his lips to my jaw. I jolted, head tipping back.

"Now," he encouraged, stepping away, again leaving me in my frustration.

So I did. I hit that stupid bag, and sure enough, it *gave*. Well, it swung anyway. I took a deep breath, watching as it moved more than I'd seen it all night, and I flipped back to show Fallon just as he pulled me into his arms.

His lips hit mine. There was a clash of teeth and lips, and all the sexual tension that had been sizzling finally came to the surface. He pulled back with a breathless sigh, pressing a kiss to my forehead.

"You have a mean right hand, Ali," he growled into my ear as he lifted me up.

I jolted, gasping as my legs went around his hips. It pressed me against him, against the strain in his pants. I held him closer, shivering as he groaned. The sound skated sinfully across my skin.

"Fallon?" I asked as he walked.

He didn't hurry, instead taking his time as he moved with purpose. His hands clenched my thighs, and his lips pressed against the curve of my neck, each step molding us tighter together.

"Yes?" The deep timbre of his voice, normally so controlled, sounded desperate.

All too soon, we were against the windows. He slid me down to my feet, flipping me so I faced them, my palms against the cool glass. The soft glow of the moon and the slow drop of snow met my gaze. I shivered, sinking into the feeling of frost beneath my fingers as Fallon leaned over me. He kissed my neck again, worshiping the skin, dragging me against him.

"What are you doing?" I whimpered, trying to find purchase on the window, my legs shaking in an effort to keep me standing.

Fallon must have noticed, as he reached one hand around, setting it over my chest near my neck to hold me up. The other pressed into my hip before sliding up over my stomach, toying with the string of my yoga pants.

"Rewarding you," he whispered, tapping at the bare skin of my stomach. "Do you want a reward, Ali?"

His words shot to my core, and I groaned as I pressed back against him. He chuckled above me, the deep, husky sound making my core clench as he continued to trail that line above my pants. But he didn't stray further, merely held himself there, waiting for me to pull away or give the go-ahead.

I sighed breathlessly, relaxing into his hold completely.

"Yes," I pleaded, the sound turning to a sharp gasp as Fallon's hand dipped below the waistband of my pants. Two fingers circled my clit, and he tightened the hold of his other hand, molding me to him, again groaning in my ear.

"You're wet for me." The harsh pull of an accent came through his words, emotion thick in them. "God, trouble, you've been driving me fucking crazy."

I nodded, pressing my cheek into the glass as my legs trembled. His secure grip kept me standing, and the hard press of him against my back had another gasp choking past my lips.

"Watching you like this, having to teach you while staying so close but knowing I couldn't touch? Has been torture."

Cool breath slid over my ear, and I jolted as dull teeth bit down on the sensitive skin. It was a sharp pain, one that dulled and left me hyper-aware of the slow strum of Fallon's cool fingers against my clit. For the frantic press of his body against mine, and the grip that he held me with, he lingered. It was almost maddening, and my breath came out in pants as the hand that was holding me up slid down and under my shirt.

Fallon's fingers found my nipples already hard. The cool press of his palm against my skin had me leaning further into the glass. I jolted and groaned, again met with a sinful chuckle in my ear.

"I've thought of this before," Fallon breathed, pinching my nipple sharply before sliding his hand up to my chin. He pulled my gaze until I could see his reflection. I pressed back into his hand, another wave of heat making my legs shake at the burning lust in his eyes. He looked feral, his green eyes so focused on me that I nearly fell apart right there. His hand sped up, just enough to notice the change. I whimpered. "You pressed against these windows."

His fingers stopped their maddening movements, and I cried out as the sharp edge of pleasure faded.

"Though you were falling apart on my cock, not my hand."

I moaned at his coarse words, my eyes falling closed as I tensed. His hand slid up again, lifting my head softly but surely.

"Eyes on me, Ali." They fluttered open, once again focusing on his face in the glass.

I was rewarded with the brush of his fingers again, pushing me closer and closer. I kept my eyes open through it all, focusing on Fallon as the soft pants of his breath skittered across my skin, his lips pressing to my neck as his fingers worked me into a frenzy again.

I jolted, pushing back against him with a cry, the hard press of his dick flexing as I did so. He growled into my ear, his eyes sliding red as his fangs fell. I heard it, his mouth next to my ear, when it happened. I shivered in his hold, tilting my head to the side, showing my throat.

Fallon cursed behind me, groaning as his weight laid the rest of the way onto me, dousing me in pleasure until he was all I could feel.

"You sure?" he asked, his breath fanning across the back of my neck, goosebumps rising on the skin there.

I could only nod as I rocked back against him. The press of his hot length at my back, his sure fingers strumming my clit, and the delicious pressure of him on top of me. The mark on my wrist began to burn, the ache shooting to my core. It was too much, and it was never enough.

But he still didn't move, his hesitancy bleeding into how he kissed my neck, his lips shaking.

"Use your words, Ali. Tell me what you want," he growled into my throat.

"Please, Fallon," I begged, and that was all it took. "Bite me."

He cursed, his hands tightening to the point where I was sure it'd bruise, shaking as he pressed one more kiss to my neck before his fangs sank deep. His wrist shot to my lips, the brush of his skin there making my own drop. It was a startling feeling, but then I heard the rush of his blood under his skin. I followed his lead, unable to keep this need at bay, and I sank my own fangs into his wrist.

He jolted, moaning into my throat as he took another mouthful of my blood. His bite set off my climax, shooting throughout my entire body, stringing me up on a live wire and setting my nerves aflame. He was every-where, everything. We were connected in a way that made me writhe, sobbing as I let go of his wrist and crumbled in his arms.

I wasn't sure when he stopped, or when I stopped coming. He held me up as I panted, still working through the last effects of the orgasm. He shifted behind me, and I was sure he was going to pull away and whisk me off somewhere to cuddle. When his hand dipped lower, two fingers sliding deftly inside of me, I jolted forward, heaving a strangled gasp. I was wet enough that I barely felt the stretch, only the intense burst of pleasure as he touched a spot inside me that made my legs give out the rest of the way. Still he held me steady, and I caught his eyes in the mirror, still flushed red as he panted behind me.

"Fal—" I couldn't even finish, his name dying on a moan as he gave a teasing thrust against that spot again.

I was tapped out, dried blood on my mouth and my legs shaking so badly I knew the only reason I was standing was because of him. But his moving again sparked something in me, the smoldering feeling of a climax building. He eased me up, making me squirm in his arms all over again, turning me into a whining mess as my body tried to figure out what was happening.

"Can you come again for me, Ali?" he asked, pulling his hand back, softly pressing against my over sensitive clit, making me cry out. "Just one more. Let me feel you fall apart one more time."

Like I'd be able to tell him no with the desperate way he spoke. There was something about the way he said my nickname, like he was *begging*, that made me want to give him another even as my body tried to convince me there was nothing left to give. I groaned, the sound hoarse from my screaming. He gave slow circles, dipping down to toy with my entrance and slide a finger in, before going back to that little bundle of nerves. It was everything and too much, all at the same time.

"I don't know if I can," I whimpered, pushing into the glass and onto the tips of my toes, all while Fallon continued his steady rhythm. He surrounded me, his sandalwood scent warm and comforting, absorbing all the way to my lungs.

"You can do it, trouble," he breathed. He sped up, and my spent body protested as a jolt of pleasure made my eyes roll back. I would have jumped right out of his arms if not for the steady way he held me. "Just one more."

I didn't have time to object, not that I would have, as the hand that had settled at my chest moved to my nipple again, toying with the stiff peak. All while the fingers between my legs drove me to the brink of insanity. I didn't think I could come again, but Fallon proved me wrong as he shoved me over the edge with startling precision.

It differed from the last one, more pointed and bordering the edge of pain in a way that made my heart flutter. I felt his breath along my neck as I came this time, his tongue trailing the recently healed bite. I nearly blacked out as I sobbed into the glass that was now fogged and wet with my sweat. Through it all, Fallon didn't pull away, his soothing, sinful voice guiding me as I finally came back down. All I knew was we ended up on the ground, with Fallon at my back, holding me close to him. He peppered kisses along my neck, whispering words I couldn't understand. They were soft and filled with love.

"You okay?" he asked, brushing my hair back out of my face, enough to catch my eyes.

My cheeks flamed, and I nodded. I half expected him to grumble out 'Use your words.' But he just chuckled, holding me firmly to his defined chest.

We were silent for a moment, with just the sound of our slowly leveling breaths keeping us company. For once, the silence didn't bother me, Fallon's arms speaking to me in a way that I knew he struggled with words.

I never wanted to lose this.

Cool lips against my forehead woke me, and I blinked a few times as my eyes opened. Adrian's soft expression came into view, his eyes lit with mirth and joy. Confusion swallowed me for a moment.

Before I remembered where I was, and that I was still pressed onto the training room floor, Fallon's bare, muscular arm wrapped around me. I blushed, sputtering for something to say when Adrian leaned in, kissing me so fiercely that I jumped.

"Missed you, love," he whispered, crawling onto the floor next to us.

He took my front, encasing me in his arms. His heart thundered in his chest, and I did my best to hold him close while Fallon still held onto me from behind.

"You get them?" Fallon asked, and Adrian nodded against the top of my head.

"Yeah, we got 'em," Adrian said, and Fallon grunted.

"Good, then shut up," Fallon bit out, and I jerked to peek at him, noting his cheeky grin even as his eyes stayed closed. "We were taking a nap."

Chapter 49

Aaliyah

Things had been quiet since Adrian and Osiris returned last night, like everyone was taking a moment to breathe. I wasn't an exception, as I trailed one row in the library. This spot in the house was my safe place, and it was where I always seemed to go when I needed a moment to think. The books weren't placed in any particular order. At least, not one that I was privy to. It was chaotic, and thrillingly random, as I worked my way down the shelf in front of me.

This one's in Latin. The next was written in 1604. The one after that was copyrighted in 1893 ...

I picked up a book that wasn't in a language I recognized, though that was the case with many of the novels that lined the walls. I opened it to the first page. The curling script was beautiful, ornate, and distinctly familiar. I traced it as I walked back toward the couch, the vibrant red fabric coarse under my hand as I sat. I reached out and tapped at the rim of my wine glass, the soft bubbly white wine popping at the agitation.

"What could you be?" I asked out loud, mostly out of habit, my eyes scanning the room for Prince.

He wasn't there, but I took comfort in talking like he was. It'd been an adjustment so far, a painful one, getting used to not seeing him around. One I still struggled with, one I doubted I would ever truly grasp. Not seeing him, his smile, and his carefree antics left a hole in my chest, one that ached and burned all hours of the day.

The guys helped as much as they could, distracting me or holding me when I needed it. But there were some things I just couldn't get away from.

Seeing the guys healthy and thriving again helped. It soothed my worries like nothing else ever could. Adrian didn't have those rings under his eyes anymore. He breathed easily and laughed easier. Fallon and Eirik had more spring, and Eirik no longer had to hide his aches from the incident at Valen's. They could even drink the blood wine again, even had a glass of it with dinner last night, a drop of my blood in each cup.

Just like I had a drink with a drop of each of theirs.

But *I* still hurt to move and still struggled with bouts of pressure and unease. *I* wasn't getting better like they were, and I had no idea how to tell them that. I traced the lettering again, sorting through the feeling with a deep breath.

"What am I supposed to do, Prince?" I asked, tears burning my eyes.

"Everything alright?" a voice whispered, one that had me jolting on the couch.

In typical Osiris fashion, he appeared practically out of thin air, and I choked down my scream.

The sting of tears was still clear in my eyes, and I flipped my head at his sudden appearance. He was dressed in one of his usual suits, the flaring pinstripe a deep blue that clung to his body, a black undershirt bringing out the highlights of his eyes. He held the book he translated the other day, *Fabula Fortium,* in his hands.

I let out a breath, tipping my head back to rub my temples. "I was until you snuck up on me."

Osiris's lips dipped into a scowl at my pout, and he walked around the couch to stand in front of me. He set the book on the end table as he leaned forward and gripped my chin gently, cool hands lighting a spark along my skin. The ever-mismatched blue studied me intensely, making me squirm.

"You look wan. You need more blood," he mused.

His fangs dropped the next instant, and I jolted at the quickness of it. I half expected him to tear into his wrist as Fallon had, but he just lifted his hand, pricking a finger on one of the deadly points. He brought it to my lips and waited.

My face heated, and I looked between him and the welling bead of blood. He wasn't going to let me back away. There was something far too controlling about Osiris for that, so I simply sighed and opened my mouth.

A thick heat flooded his eyes as he moved his hand the rest of the way forward, brushing his finger against my lip before pulling away. I licked off the blood, immediately flooded with a brief burst of energy. It was enough that Osiris seemed pleased as he picked up the book again, this time handing it to me before taking a seat.

I pulled the thick tome to my chest, hugging the steady weight as I sank into the warmth of the couch. Just as quickly as his blood had helped, the feeling faded, and my head started a slow ache.

"You finished it?" I asked curiously, flicking through the pages of perfectly marked English.

"Not quite. I came to see if you were still interested in learning some Latin," he said, and most days I would have jumped on the chance.

But the ache built, and as I tried to focus on the words, they blurred together.

"Do you think you could tell me a story about Nero instead?" I asked, buying myself some time to settle and clear my head.

Osiris's eyes dulled a moment before he nodded softly.

"Of course, I have plenty. Where to begin?" he mused, picking up the original copy of Nero's book and tracing the intricate symbols with his eyes.

"What was he like? What did he like to do?" I suggested.

His lips slanted up at the corners, and I barely breathed, hoping to not startle it away.

"That's a perfect question. Nero liked to travel, and we spent many early years before finding Eirik traversing the old continent. One specific place we visited often was China. It was a beautiful land, with amazingly generous people. Nero liked it because they had remarkably similar tastes in entertainment. And for this specific trip, we were there because of rumors about a new game that had been developed there. One you've played," Osiris supplied, and I knew instantly what he was talking about.

"Bones?" I asked.

Osiris's lip twitched, and I knew I was right.

"Yes. A very crude, early version of it, and *somehow*, we ended up in the emperor's company. Nero could talk his way into making a nun sin, so I was not too surprised." I laughed at that, unable not to. "The emperor, Hui of Jin, if I recall correctly, was an ... interesting man."

Osiris's eyes dulled a bit, his hand tightening on the book.

"We played, and of course, Nero won. And Hui decided it was best to throw us in prison for our indiscretion."

I gasped, mouth agape.

"So what happened?" I asked, leaning in.

Osiris surprised me again, shrugging his shoulders.

"We made a *bet,* of course. If Nero could win again, Hui would let us go free," Osiris continued.

I could imagine this story going several ways and the way Osiris's eyes lit up as he spoke enraptured me.

"So you won then?" I asked.

"No, but we didn't lose either. Hui had an unfortunate accident during the game. He became quite ill and died at the table."

"What?"

"Nightshade can be quite a nasty plant," Osiris said nonchalantly before his eyes widened.

I knew what he was thinking, that he was worried about how I would react, and had this been a month ago, it would have been exactly as he was expecting. But this was now, and the man in front of me was one of the few I trusted above all else. Osiris could be brutal; he could rip out hearts and scare gods.

But he also was gentle, and in this way, huddled in the library with a fire roaring and snow falling outside, he felt like mine.

"Osiris? Did you ...?" I asked as he turned to me with a startled expression on his face.

He sighed, almost exasperated, as he shook his head. Then, slowly, his own lips curved up. It lit his face and made him appear almost mischievous.

"Technically, yes. He was a rather rude man, and he offended me during my more vindictive years," he finally said when I didn't go running out the door, screaming for a merciful death. Osiris shook his head like he was remembering the day.

The sight made me laugh, and I pressed further into Osiris's side.

"You are not angry," he said, watching me skeptically.

"No, Osiris," I said, wiping my eyes. I reached out, holding my hand above his on instinct. He flinched, soft like I might change my mind and turn away before he settled his hand into the hold. "That was something that you did in your past, mind you, several *hundred* years ago. The Osiris from then is not the one that's here with me now. And it sounded like Hui had it coming."

Osiris didn't make a sound, just held my hand tighter. I looked up, catching his gaze. Heat pooled in his blue eyes, and I caught a gasp as it worked its way up my throat.

"I quite like the Osiris you are," I murmured. Osiris's throat bobbed, and his spare hand reached up, cupping my cheek. "You saved me."

From the auction, from Crustava, from myself. I didn't have a better way to put it. I hadn't thought of it because I didn't want to think of it. I'd tried to get it out on several other occasions but hadn't been able to.

Another push of pain and I flinched, my hand going to my head. Osiris moved instantly, startling me as he cupped my face in his hands. I should have guessed this would be the outcome after our talk with Xander.

I'd hoped for better, for a cure. But I had never been able to outrun death, and it was silly for me to think that could start now.

"You don't feel well, do you?" he asked softly.

The fear in his eyes screamed of desperation, begging me to contradict him. But I couldn't lie, not to him. Never to him.

"No, I don't," I said, reaching up to grab his hands. "I'm not sure why. The blood is helping, but something is still wrong. I don't know ... maybe I just need to remember."

It was a thought that both haunted and plagued me. *Rends* had become nothing more than a faint nuisance since being here. The idea of going through them again scared me more than even the thought of Castillion.

I didn't want to remember. I didn't want to see them again.

Didn't want to see Prince and know I'd never get to truly see him again.

"What if the *Rends* need to happen? What if there isn't any other way out of this?" I asked, and Osiris's expression grew numb.

His eyes became cold, and a calculating look stole the human from his façade. He stopped breathing, his body straightening in a way that made instincts scream at me to run. It was like looking into the eyes of a predator for a moment.

"Your *Rends* have to be a side-effect of your gifts. If we can control them, maybe you can control the memories," he said, standing. He brushed his coat and turned to walk toward the door, leaving me starstruck on the couch. "But it's dangerous, trying to force something that is so closely tied to your life."

"I know," I said, but I didn't back down. This was important, and doing everything I could to fix myself was something I still needed to do. "But I can't keep sitting stagnant, Osiris. We found out what I was, and that wasn't the miracle cure I'd been hoping for. I'm still dying, I can feel it."

Jaw clenched tightly, Osiris didn't have anything to say.

"I can't help you like this. I'm not an asset going into the Eternium. I'm a hindrance—"

Osiris cut me off. "*Never.* You are no hindrance, Aaliyah. Don't even speak it."

The authority in his voice made me shiver, but I stood. "I want to move without feeling sick, without worrying that this day might be the last I see. I want to be able to help, but to do that, I need to heal first."

That struck a chord, Osiris's hands going slack, losing the tense flex they'd held. A spark brushed along his skin, and suddenly the room tasted of power.

"Will you help me?" I asked.

In an instant, Osiris breathed. There was always an intensity in his eyes, the kind that grounded me and made me wonder what he was thinking. He nodded once.

"Always, *lux mea*. I will help you always," he promised, opening the door now and motioning for me to follow him. "Come."

But I couldn't move. Osiris's voice *commanded* my presence, but not in the way he was expecting. I tried to follow him, I did, but I couldn't stop the instant spike fear if I tried. Not of him, never of him again. But of what he was looking to do. Of the pure chaos and power I knew he held in him. I was scared he had an idea to bring my gifts forward as much as I wanted him to.

And even worse, I was scared he'd do it. That he'd push me to the Void, and I'd remember.

"You're afraid?" Osiris asked, suddenly frozen by the door to the library.

He gripped the wooden frame, his eyes so focused on me, I nearly jolted back. His body relaxed slightly, and he took a jarring breath. But his façade didn't fall back into place.

"No, Osiris. I'm not afraid of you," I said, clearing the air, my tension lessening when Osiris's shoulders dropped. "But the Void? It *terrifies* me. Whatever this is, it doesn't feel like me. It feels rotten. It feels—"

I couldn't find the words, but luckily, I didn't need to. Osiris *flitted* back to me, leaning forward until he was so close, I could see the lines and delicate patterns of his clothing. His suit, that familiar pinstripe tinted with a deep blue, creased as he moved.

"Dangerous?" he asked.

"Yes," I replied as I took a deep breath, greedily accepting the scent of mint that came from him, the mark on my arm pulsing. I waited for Osiris to move, to reach forward and brush his fingers across my skin.

"You are aware I studied as an Echomancer in my human years, yes?" Osiris reminded me.

How could I forget something like that? I eyed the marks on his wrist, the ones that were now slightly obscured by a lavender band.

"Of course," I said.

"Did you know that magic comes to humans young, normally no later than fifteen summers past their birth? I developed my gifts at twenty-three, rather late for that kind of power," Osiris started, flexing his hand before he lifted it.

I watched the way he flexed, his fingers moving as a *spark* traveled along the hand, cresting at the tip of his finger before it disappeared. Then he closed his hand, that brand on his wrist exposed.

"I killed someone with it the day my magic came to me. An acquaintance of a man that I knew. He tried to take something I wasn't willing to give." I choked on a startled gasp, not needing to ask more when Osiris's eyes closed. "I boiled him alive using his own blood. Because of that, I was jailed and put on trial. That was where Kali found me, and that was when I was—"

He didn't finish, didn't need to; the pain told enough. I still recalled the numbness in his eyes, after Kali had left, and at that moment, I'd thought it was just her appearance that had startled him. But ...

"That was the same thing that Kali did to Fallon and Adrian. And you, Osiris," I said. "She did it on purpose, didn't she?"

Osiris solemnly nodded.

"I worried at the time that I was a monster. Stressed for years over the death of a man who was worth barely more than the dirt he was buried in. I feared the magic that had been my own because of it. But I've realized something about magic since then. Do you know what that is?"

I shook my head, and he reached his hand out. I placed my own in his, like always, and he cradled it.

"Magic is cruel, dangerous, and *savage*. It takes, and it takes, and it *takes*. But above that, your magic is *yours*. It is dangerous to your *enemies*. It is savage to those that would hurt you. And it holds you above all else," he insisted, lifting his hand to show my own.

The breath of power that he had subtly flowed into me sat in my hand, swirling and flowing before it dissipated.

It didn't feel like it had at the hot spring. It didn't burn me from the inside out or seek to destroy Osiris. It just flowed.

"Your magic is yours, *lux mea*. It chose you, and you need to stop fighting and choose it as well."

But how did I choose something so volatile? Something that took Prince from me?

"I don't want to hurt people, Osiris," I said softly, clenching my hands.

There was a chill in the air, one that told me Red was close. I shivered, and just as quickly, Osiris reached up, his hands beginning to glow with a subtle heat. He hovered them over the skin of my arms, warming them slightly.

It was the *Flame*, their gift of fire. And it was warming me.

"Why do you assume your gift is to hurt?" he asked, continuing to move his hands up and down my arms, keeping them from touching the skin.

"I'm a Reaper. What else could it mean?"

He paused at that, pulling back just enough to show his hand before it was engulfed in flames. The startling heat sizzled in the air, sparking and bouncing, such a chaotic difference from what it had been. "There are two sides to everything. Maybe you just haven't found the other side yet."

The flames died down, leaving just Osiris and I in our thoughts.

"Osiris, do you think whatever you have planned will work?"

"It is worth trying."

Was it? I didn't really have a choice. Either I figured this out, or I was a liability. And I refused to be the reason they were in danger again.

My brows furrowed. "What do I need to do?"

"Come, let's take this outside. It's better to be connected to nature for something like this," Osiris said, taking my hand and leading me out of the library.

His presence calmed me enough not to panic as we stepped through the door. He walked us a way into the woods, to a small clearing that was barely large enough to fit us both. Osiris hummed, loosening his tie as he took in the surrounding air. It was cold, the winter months now firmly setting in as snow fell slowly around us, coating the already frostbitten ground.

"This should do. Now, breathe deeply," he said, that rolling tone to his voice making me shiver. "Focus on yourself, on me, and the surrounding air. Let it ground you."

I did as he instructed, falling into a kind of meditative trance like I'd learned from Eirik. I breathed in the soft scents around me, accepted the weight of the world, and prepared myself the best I could.

"I'm going to use my magic to try to call yours. Are you ready?" Osiris asked, his voice sounding far away, and I nodded.

"Yes," I managed, just as power flared in the air.

It felt like Osiris, the touch of it ancient yet sure, and goosebumps lined my skin as it poked and prodded. I tried to let it past my defenses, to let it do what it needed, but something stopped me, and made it impossible to let go.

I took another breath, and the magic bared down, pressing in until I swore I could feel it in my blood. I opened my eyes, gaze landing on Osiris across the field now, his hand pointed toward me.

With his ring and pinky finger tucked down.

The sight startled me, and that was all his magic needed as it surged, finally pushing past the mental barrier, and it *burned.*

I choked on my scream, watching as Osiris's eyes went wide, and his power faded from the air instantly, but the roaring, burning rage of my gift as it tore through me anyway, landing on my skin. I pulsed, trying to keep it in. There was no pressure, no pain.

Only power.

Another pulse and Osiris was speaking. I tried to scream for him to get away, but the words stayed trapped in my throat. I gasped as the power flooded my mouth, tasting like soot and steel. The surrounding ground rocked, and the world grayed like I'd *Rended.* The bold flavor of metal only grew, and when a hand touched my shoulder, the power flooded out of me.

It was like a dam that had cracked and corroded over time and had finally fallen to the weight of the water behind it, and I gasped as everything released and everything went black.

I wasn't sure how long I sat there, staring at the recently disturbed dirt of my grave—my unmarked *grave—trying to come to grips with my fate, but by the time I pulled myself out of my mind and back to the present, it was nighttime. The moonlight gave an unnaturally static feel to the world around me, coating the forest in an ethereal glow. My body hadn't moved, not that I expected it to. It hurt, knowing it never would again.*

I let my hand hover over the top of the mound, never touching the dirt. Knowing Nilus and Donavan buried me beneath it did little good for my fractured nerves.

It was strange, being cognitive and aware of my surroundings while knowing that I wasn't really there. Not in a way that mattered. I still had thoughts. I could move, though no feeling followed. I could see, but no one would ever see me.

I hadn't taken the time to think about how ghosts perceived their demise, but I realized now that they must have been so confused. Like they were watching their lives go on without them, trapped behind a glass wall with no hopes of reaching anyone. Trapped in an endless cycle, forced to wander around the mortal plane.

No wonder spirits tried so hard to get to me. Like they could feel the pull, could sense the Void just beyond my skin.

I would if I had the same opportunity.

I ran my fingers over the dirt again, this time letting them dip into the earth. Then, as if karma itself had heard me cursing it, or maybe because my luck couldn't get any worse, I felt it.

I shuddered at the familiar yet foreign touch that shattered over my skin, and even in this form, a shiver shot its way through me. I wasn't cold, per se. Not like I was used to. But it was like pins were sinking into my skin. No pain followed them, but I could tell that they were there. Incessantly prodding me along to do my work, as though I was slacking on my job.

Whoever had joined me, it wasn't Prince. His chill was comforting, and I knew it better than I knew my own soul.

I wished it would have been him.

I'd often dreamed of a noble prince coming to save me from my nightmare. The aptly named Prince showing up was a godsend. I wouldn't have survived Ascension without him.

That same guilty feeling that sometimes crawled from the woodwork of my mind came at me with a vengeance. It ate at me, as it always had. It was the same feeling that came up whenever I thought of Prince's situation.

That I was glad he stayed, that he didn't want that peace from the Void. I had selfishly held onto him, and I had slowly grown terrified of the day he would finally leave. Would I be able to let him go if he asked? Would I be able to forgive myself if I didn't grant him that wish?

If I ever got to see him again, that is.

I forced my eyes closed, pulling my thoughts from Prince. It hurt to think of him, and I needed anything but that pain.

A shockwave raced down my spine, not quite like a touch but more like concentrated energy. I could feel the pressure in the air, the singe of power calling to the cursed part of my soul. It was a battle-cry, a beckon, one I was intimately familiar with yet couldn't place, and I scrunched my eyebrows at the feeling of it. I stood, taking a moment to settle myself, my eyes dropping closed instinctively.

Something about opening them scared me. It always had. You never knew who could be waiting, or whose cruel face would be there to meet you.

Though I wasn't worried it was Castillion behind me; they were a ghost, that much I could tell. Ghosts couldn't speak, not in a literal sense. They had a unique way of conveying their thoughts. Their emotions would often sing across my skin, letting me know what they were feeling, giving me an insight into what led them to that moment.

What had led to their inevitable deaths?

With the ones behind me? I could feel their indecision, their worry. I could feel everything, their emotions—most stiflingly, their pain.

And the steady pulse of the Void as it grew stronger, more insistent.

And not from me.

Anxiety started its slow crawl up my throat, and a pulse echoed in the air, skimming over my skin like an old friend, and the familiar pull of the Void sifted its way through me, echoing from the ghosts that had joined me. It was like ...

Like the Void was coming from them.

"Aaliyah," a voice whispered, disembodied like it echoed from inside me.

I tried to shake it off as the forest warped; this was strange, wrong. I'd never met someone like me, someone who could see the dead. I glanced over my shoulder, glimpsing two people standing only feet away, their faces shrouded from me.

It was strange when the pull wasn't originating from me. It was like I was an onlooker in a game that I'd made like someone was changing the rules I'd set.

When they finally came into view, it wasn't them I saw, as I was ripped away from the forest, the call of my name bringing me back to the real world.

"Aaliyah."

CHAPTER 50

PRINCE

"Aaliyah," I whispered as the last memory faded. Everything ached and seized as my eyes opened.

The memory was still clear. Aaliyah, at the site of her grave. She was dead, her spirit hovering over a shallow patch of dirt. Aaliyah *died*, and I hadn't been there to stop it.

But I had been there for when her hand had shot up from the broken earth. I'd been the first that she'd seen, the first that she'd *forgotten*.

The first that she remembered.

"Why do I feel like I've been trampled?" I asked, my voice croaking like I'd just spent the last century screaming. I looked over, spotting Mags at my side, stirring something that appeared equal parts horrendous and jarring. It looked like they'd put a frog in a blender with charcoal and just hoped for the best. "Am I in hell? It would only make sense, considering I'm stuck staring at your ugly mug."

Mags passed me said glass. I sent them a deadpan glance until the scent of it hit me. Blood. I took it from their hands and sipped at it. It tasted much like ash, and though it did little for my thirst, it made the burn less pointed.

"You've been out for three days," Mags said, standing and stretching. Their old bones creaked and popped.

"What the fuck did you do to me, Mags?" I asked, finishing the drink and laying back.

"Don't use that language with me, boy. How do you feel?"

I rolled my eyes but didn't contradict them.

And taking a moment, I realized I felt surprisingly good. Besides the waning pain and the relentless hunger.

"Less like a corpse," I said, rolling my neck and waiting for the pressure to start again.

Only it didn't, and I could have kissed the crazed Chronomancer had I not been so busy marveling at the peace that their sock potion had brought.

"I didn't stop them, but you should be more stable now. Tied you to the earth," Mags said, walking toward the kitchen and away from me. "You remember little beyond your time as the dead. This may change that."

Their voice was muffled, and the usual sounds of things crashing echoed in the small room. Quickly, the savory aroma of cooking meat filtered into the space. It was almost nice before Mags burned whatever poor beast they'd put on the fire to nothing but ashes.

"You know, Mags, I just may believe that this time," I mumbled, tilting my head just enough to see them mashing the bone dust in a mortar and pestle.

"I know well, boy. Things are going as they go," Mags said, cryptic as always. "Fate plays its strings, and they sing for us today."

They tapped the mortar softly before grabbing a piece of paper. Then they dipped their hands into the dust, writing something I couldn't see.

"You're crazy," I said, loud enough for them to hear.

Mags chuckled, walking back over to me with blackened hands still covered in soot.

"No, I'm Mags. And you better be thankful for that, otherwise you'd be a dead one."

Hard to dispute that, as much as I wanted to. I sighed and rubbed my head, waiting for the stupid pressure to come back. But Mags's trick worked, and there was nothing.

"Thanks, Mags," I said, honestly.

Mags watched me for a moment before grinning deeply.

"Now, you rest. And rest *well*. Beasts await us, and I have to send a letter. It's time for the ones that live to understand death's consequences," Mags replied, continuing with their unintelligible banter.

And I did as they said: rested. Because today, there was sleep. And tomorrow, there was Aaliyah.

Chapter 51

Osiris

The feral brush of power scorched my skin, promising death and destruction as it flooded over me. I *should* have died there, should be as lifeless as every plant and animal that had been in range.

But instead, I just caught her.

Aaliyah dropped, her eyes rolling back as the last of her gift seeped out. She was ice-cold to the touch, and I held a broken breath until I heard her heart beating.

And the intake of air into her lungs.

I let it all out, falling to my knees with her body still in my arms, listening intently for changes in that steady rhythm. She wasn't hurt, not outwardly as she had been at the hot spring, but I did scent blood, likely in her mouth.

I reached up, cupping her cheek to get a better look. As always, her skin beckoned rather than disgusted, and I took a selfish second to admire the touch of her skin.

"Aaliyah," I whispered, my hand beginning to shake.

There was no standard to weigh this against, no guide to show us the way. I could only hope that this was right, that she was okay.

I looked around the field again, most of it lacking any color at all, the life of it pulled out at the very seams of their cells. Her power still stuck to the ground, tapping at my skin as if looking for more to steal.

Was this the power of a Reaper? Or was this just my sweet *lux mea*?

"What the *fuck* was that?" A rough voice, the cold drawl of Fallon, pulled my attention. It wasn't a surprise that the others had come running, and I dropped my hand from her soft skin just as his eyes landed on us. "Ali!"

But it wasn't Fallon who rushed forward, but a wolf. A feral *Úlfhéðinn* hell-bent on getting me away from what he saw as his. I barely had time to set her down before Eirik snapped at me, barely missing my arm as I jumped back.

Even so soon after, I missed the touch.

"Let go of her, you crazed fucking beast!" Fallon snarled, getting far too close for the beast's comfort.

It'd been so long since Eirik's more volatile days that it was strange to see the animalistic drive in his eyes. But today, that drive wasn't to kill.

It was to protect.

Eirik, or the beast, snapped at Fallon, sending the brawler back a few steps as he cursed and his eyes flooded red. I half expected to need to break up a fight when Adrian stepped into the clearing, appearing winded.

"Holy shit," he breathed, looking around, noting the dead vegetation and how the gray clung to everything. "Are you guys seeing this?"

That got Fallon and Eirik's attention, as they finally seemed to realize the change in the earth around us as well.

That power, cruel and infinitely deadly, swelled again at the feeling of fresh blood coming toward it, and Ali stirred.

"That blast was from her?" Fallon asked, shaking his head, stepping back sharply as he felt it brush against him. "There's no way this is a regular Reaper thing, right? Because this just seems..."

"Crazy," I supplied, quoting his own reference to her gifts.

And it *was* crazy. This was the power that people went to war for. That got races wiped out and the Reapers killed.

"Powerful," I said, taking a step toward her, even as Eirik began snarling at me.

People would kill for her, and from the sound of it, some already had. I couldn't let them have her. Her protection was paramount now. With the Eternium so close ...

"*Dangerous,*" I finished, moving until I was kneeling next to her. Eirik continued to growl. But my own gifts were close to the surface, the pulse of human magic enough to get the beast to leave me be.

"Do you think maybe this is what Ascension Rising was looking for?" Adrian asked, awe taking over his features. "The power to kill *anyone*?"

No one had any more chance to say anything, as another spark of power built and flashed in the air. It tasted bitter and smelled like swamp and rotten leaves.

I clenched my teeth just as a single piece of paper materialized in front of us. The paper itself was aged, the marks of harsh ink and an unsteady hand staining the surface. I reached out and grabbed it, the unfamiliar script reacting to my touch, moving until the message on it became clear. I read it once, then twice, before as quickly as it had appeared, it turned to ash in my hands.

"Well damn, I didn't realize it was mail day," Adrian joked, walking toward me to examine the ashes that now sat in my hand.

I clenched my fingers into a tight fist, eyeing the mark on my wrist.

It had been a bane since my turn, since my life as a human, and now it dared to muddle the mark of Aaliyah. The crossing spiral of her mark etched into the mark of Darius, the magics of both clashing, neither refusing to give in.

"It's Magelav," I said, letting my hand fall.

"Well, what did they say?" he asked.

"They'll back us at the Eternium."

"Really? Well, thank *fuck* for that. That does it, doesn't it? All we have to do is take out Kri'Valta, and Sebek is as good as gone."

My lips curled back in a grimace, but I nodded. Because the letter had been everything we could have hoped for. It was war, it was power.

"There's more. They won't just show their support. They're planning on taking the title from Kali," I said, shuddering at even the name, and nearly the moment the last syllable left my lips, Aaliyah gasped.

I breathed, willfully, with a purpose as she sat up, her eyes wide as she glanced around the clearing.

"What happened?" she asked, squinting as she took in the desolation around us. "What—"

Eirik huffed next to her, placing his enormous head on her lap, startling her enough to jump. When she recognized the beast for who he was, she calmed, gently pressing her hands into his fur coat. But she didn't stop looking at the clearing, hollow-eyed and haggard.

No one spoke as she took in the devastation around us.

"Did I do this?" she asked, her voice cracking.

I wished she hadn't, that I could tell her a lie. But I promised her long ago that I wouldn't do that. She deserved the truth, and so I nodded.

Fallon was by her side before she could say anything else, baring his fangs at Eirik when the beast snarled.

"Are you okay, Ali?" Fallon asked, cupping her cheek.

"Yes," she said hesitantly, beginning to shiver.

Fallon noticed, shrugging his suit coat off before I could offer, pulling it around her shoulders. The bottom threading touched the ground, muddied by the snow-covered earth.

Fallon didn't even notice, never taking his eyes away from Aaliyah's.

"What were you guys doing out here?" he asked, and Aaliyah's mouth trembled.

"We were trying to work on my gifts." She shook her head, looking around the clearing, confusion lighting up her face.

"Did you *Rend* then?" he asked.

"No, she never stopped breathing," I chimed in, and Fallon looked at me.

There was still mistrust in his gaze, mistrust I deserved, mistrust I wasn't sure would ever go away.

"No, I remembered something," she whispered.

She curled a little tighter on herself, glancing around the clearing again.

"What did you remember, love?" Adrian asked, not feeling as brave as Fallon, sticking by the tree line.

Aaliyah shivered, pulling Fallon's suit coat closer.

"I think ... I think it was how I got brought back. After I died at Ascension," she whispered.

And the clearing fell silent.

Every time it came up, it made my soul ache. And every time, she surprised me with her silence, as she looked up at Fallon with sure eyes, lifting her hand to cup his cheek as his face twisted into a glower.

"What do you mean?" he asked, bloodlust so clear in his voice, even his eyes tinged red.

"I mean, *I* didn't bring me back from the grave," she said, biting her lip, looking unsure of her next words. "Another Reaper did."

Aaliyah

"Come on, love, pick one!" Adrian mused, showing me the spread he had just wheeled into my room.

After the incident yesterday, the guys had been in overdrive. They rarely left my side beyond going to get something for us to do to keep us all from falling into complete boredom. They worried and fussed like mother hens, and honestly, I soaked it up. Their attention was a balm to my soul, and after yesterday, even my head was better.

There was no pressure, and the aches that had been growing had slid away. Whatever Osiris did had bought us some time.

And me a new memory.

"Love?" Adrian suddenly asked, next to the bed.

In one hand, he held some puff pastry. It made my mouth water, and I knew that this wonderful concoction was what I'd been smelling for the majority of the last few hours. On the other was a plate with the leftover cake we'd made prior.

My two kryptonite.

"Why should she have to choose at all? Just let her have both," Eirik said from his spot behind me. He played with my hair, braiding it and unbraiding it, his fingers working magic on my tension.

"Of course she'll get both, but she has to pick which one she wants first," Adrian retorted, and I looked between the two delicious morsels.

And came up blank.

"Here, let me see that," Fallon said, stealing the pastry from Adrian's waiting hand.

Adrian, of course, protested this. He reached for the treat, with Fallon evading every move.

"That's for little love! You can't have that, Fallon!" Adrian protested, stuck on one side of the bed while Fallon was on the other.

"Why don't you close your eyes, Aaliyah?" Osiris chimed in, standing from his spot across the room. He'd dragged in a chair and one of the end tables from the library, so he had a place to work on his translation without having to leave the room.

I tilted my head curiously, though I did as he said with an amused grin. There was more shuffling around me, mostly just the sound of Adrian grumbling before each side of the bed dipped. The cool press of metal set against my lip, and I jolted back into Eirik's chest before realizing what it was.

I opened and accepted the spoonful of cake, humming softly as it melted in my mouth. Just as quickly, there was another press, and I nibbled the offered pastry.

Pure bliss.

I opened my eyes, only for one more thing to touch my lips. My eyes widened in surprise as strawberry chocolate flooded my senses, and Fallon's lips split into a devastating grin.

"That's cheating," Adrian mumbled, the cake in his hands, though he didn't look upset at the fact.

"How are you feeling, love?" he asked.

"Like I said before, I'm fine. I feel better than ever, I promise," I assured him, and he hummed noncommittally.

"Well, you still look a little pale," Adrian said, hiding his worry behind a Cheshire grin as he lifted the plate of cake once again. "What do you think about some more cake to make it better?"

Hard to say no to that. I was taking a bite just as Fallon stood, throwing Eirik a glance I couldn't decipher.

"Where are you guys going?" I asked, and Fallon wasted no time in reaching my side and kissing me senseless.

From the slant of his lips over mine to the teasing way his tongue traced them. The best part, though, was when he pulled back, his hand still threaded through my hair. His expression softened, and I got to see the true Fallon for a second. The one he hid behind the mask.

God, I'd never tire of that.

"It's rumored that Darius is back in the state. We're going to go check it out," he said.

Darius ... I shivered at the name. I now knew of two of them, but the one they spoke of now was the one I'd met. The one who'd sold me, hoping to make a quick buck. His greedy brown eyes, and the way he'd looked at me when Curtis had pinned me to the wall.

Right before Osiris had ripped his heart out, of course.

Fallon noticed, his eyes narrowing into thin green slits.

"Don't worry, Ali. You're safe," he promised, standing straight again.

"But he isn't. Not when we find him," Eirik growled.

He maneuvered himself out from behind me, tucking me into the soft blankets and placing one more kiss on my forehead.

"We won't be gone long. Just rest," Fallon said, giving one last look before he and Eirik disappeared through the doorway.

I sighed, rubbing my temples.

"I'll take that cake now," I said, and Adrian laughed as he crawled up, sitting next to me.

Then dutifully fed me another spoonful of cake.

Chapter 53

Eirik

"That fuck better hope this was a false sighting, because if we find Darius out here, I'm going to kill him," Fallon seethed, even more disgruntled than normal, his entire jaw grinding as we walked through the shallow marshes.

It smelled of sulfur and muck, and I wasn't in a much better state. My wolf paced behind my eyes, and I was fighting the turn even now.

"Only if you get to him first," I said, eyes narrowing on the small hut that slowly came into view. A weak barrier spell brushed against my skin, trying and failing to keep us out. "But I doubt it's him. Darius is a slimy bastard with only self-preservation on his mind. He wouldn't have gone against Osiris's demand."

When Adrian first told us about Vidius's tip, I really wanted to believe it wasn't true. But Adrian did some digging and quickly found that the sighting had been called by a Kelpie, a water spirit. I doubted they were expecting their findings to get back to us.

Adrian was good at his sleuthing. I'd give him that.

The old hut was decrepit, falling apart at the seams and tilting slightly to the side. The stench of sulfur grew, and I covered my nose as I knocked on the door. There was silence, then shuffling and cursing behind it, telling me they weren't expecting company.

We waited, and there was no answer.

Fallon's patience hit its end next to me, as he reached up and knocked on the wood again.

"Unless you want to have ash in the place of your home, I'd suggest you open the door." A jolt on the other side of the door followed Fallon's bitter voice.

I listened closely as the Kelpie's heartrate skyrocketed. More shuffling, more cursing, before the door crept open. The man was small, even smaller than Aaliyah, with wide blue eyes and kelp-green hair that had enough slime and mold growing on it that I could barely see the strands. Unluckily for us, that was the only thing on him.

Disgusting.

"Fangs?" he hissed, showing his long, pointed teeth. "Didn't want any more fangs."

I rolled my eyes and leaned down, coming at eye-level with him.

"We're looking for someone," I said, and the Kelpie sneered.

My hands clenched into fists, and my wolf nearly shot out at the disrespect.

"Always looking, always watching ... here to kill me, too." The Kelpie's sporadic mumblings were followed by him rubbing his hands together. They were stained black with what looked and smelled like charcoal. "Got nothing for you. Nothing for a fang."

Then he slammed the fucking door in our faces.

Fallon rolled his head to the side, taking a deep breath as he lifted his hands, cracking his knuckles. We'd partially expected this. Most didn't treat Vampires with much more than fear, and I honestly couldn't blame the Kelpie much. If we were anyone else, he'd already be dead.

"I'm considering it," Fallon said, deathly quiet as he started unbuttoning his suit coat, something he did so he could avoid staining the white fabric. "Do you know who you're insulting?"

A huff sounded before there was a crash. "Another fang, another death. What does it matter?" The man's voice was muted by the wood.

"It matters when our Crypt is the head of the Pennsylvania territory." Harsh indignation buried the worry that clung to Fallon's words. Worry that Darius was here, that he'd already reported back to Sebek. "It *matters* when the man we're looking for has been exiled, and his last spotting was here. In your decrepit little neck of the woods."

He'd been in a fit since we heard of Darius's reappearance, worried that he would come back for Aaliyah. That Sebek was using him to spy on us.

He'd all but dove at the door to hunt down the fuck.

"Damned *Vivas*," he said our name like a curse, and the door flew open. He was partially shifted, his face long, eyes aglow with a green light. "Knew I shouldn't have talked about it. I've nothing more to say to you!"

He tried to close the door again, but Fallon pressed his hand to it, holding it open as he glowered.

"I'm not one for games, Kelpie," I finally said, and the man turned to me. "Darius Verslini. You see him or not?"

There was a pause, the Kelpie's face further shifting.

"Fuck," he swore, letting go of the door to run his hands through his hair, flecks of slime and mud hitting the ground. "Just follow me."

It was enough of an invitation for us to slink inside. The Kelpie's home was full of plants and varying bottles of liquid. There was no furniture, only a mat on the ground that he likely slept on. The same mold that took over his head was pressed against all the walls, and I recoiled at the stench that only grew worse as we were led toward the back of the room. The scent of death and decay became overwhelming.

"Jesus Christ," Fallon hissed, covering his nose as he looked down at the familiar body marked with crude black lines. The last time we'd seen Darius Verslini had been at the auction, the same one he'd sold Aaliyah at. Seeing him like this was almost a disappointment because it meant he got off far too easily for what he'd done. "Did he meet the sun?"

"Don't know, found him like this. Gasping for breath in the swamp. All I got out of him was his name before death took him home." The Kelpie hummed, tapping Darius's body with his foot. Darius's eyes were open, and dried blood caked down his face like tears. "Take the body and go. I've no use for a corpse." The Kelpie paused for a second, a look of contemplation on his face. "Least not an old one."

I ignored his words. This could mean trouble. I shook my head, heading toward the door, leaving the body behind, even as the Kelpie screeched behind us about bad manners or some shit like that.

"You really think he met the sun?" Fallon asked as we closed the door behind us.

"No. Smelled wrong," I said, still breathing in that peculiar scent of death. It was acidic, sweet ... familiar. "Less like heat, and more like ..."

"Aaliyah?" Fallon asked, his jaw tensing.

I nodded, shaking my head. If that was true, then we had more problems to deal with than just Darius's death.

"We need to talk to Osiris about this. Sebek had been using Darius to monitor us, and while he might have let us sending him away slide, he's not going to take kindly to learning of his death," Fallon said, sighing.

"We can't catch a fucking break," I growled, anxious as even my beast stilled. All that came to mind for getting rid of that tension was violet eyes and a soft touch. "There's nothing else to do here. Let's go."

***

I knocked on Valen's door with increasing agitation.

And the damned bastard was ignoring me. I even heard him laugh a few times, scuttling around his home. I'd reached the very end of my patience when the door finally slammed open and Valen popped his head out.

"Oh Eirik, back already! You truly outdid yourself this time, not barking down my door halfway through the process. Hell, you're only,"— he paused, looking at his empty wrist as though he was reading the time —"forty-three minutes early."

And then he promptly slammed the door in my face.

Yep. I was going to fucking kill him.

I slammed my fist on the door again, my lips pulling back to expose teeth as my face shifted and sharpened under the ire of my beast. "Do you have it or not, Valen?"

More shuffling, and the sound of Valen grunting as something crashed to the floor. I chuckled as his muffled voice echoed.

"Depends. Do you have a new pinky for me?" he asked, and I rolled my eyes, shaking my head as I considered breaking the door down. Luckily, I didn't have to. The door flew open again only a moment later. Valen gave me a distasteful grunt, raising an eyebrow when I didn't respond. "Didn't think so. I am, again, *disappointed*. I thought we were friends."

What was the downside to killing him again? Ah yes, no steel.

Valen's lips split into a cheeky grin, and he shrugged his shoulders. "Nothing? Tough crowd. Yes, your sword's done, you thick bastard. Come inside, and I'll fetch it for you."

He backed away from the door then, leaving it open so I could walk in. Luckily, the smell of blood had faded from the air, and there was only the heated scent of steel and fire. Though beneath that, there was the press of power, of a spell engrained in metal.

"It reeks of magic in here," I commented, and Valen snickered as he shuffled around the forge.

"Wow. Shocker. It's almost like I can *use* magic," he grunted, rolling his eyes.

And grumbling again as he knocked his horns against the ceiling. A chip fell off from the tip, hitting the fire and sparking like dry wood. Valen, when seeing this, decided the best course of action was to reach in and grab it.

His magic sparked, and the fire erupted around him, singing his clothes and making him yelp as he jumped back. Karma really was just a bitch.

"Valen, the magic uses you," I added, snorting a laugh when he glowered and patted down his clothes until they stopped smoldering.

"And man, does it know I like it rough," he said, making a sound of revelation before finally coming back to the living room. He cradled a blade in his hands, and my beast purred at the sight of it. "Here, here."

I took it from his hands as he extended it out to me. The weight was steady and balanced in my hand while remaining light enough to be easy for my *Valkyrja* to wield. It was perfect, exactly like I knew it would be.

Valen was the best bladesmith I'd ever known, and I knew better than to doubt him.

"Well, come on, take it out of the sheath. Let that baby shine," Valen pushed, his eyes full of glee.

I did as he said, unveiling the blade. My jaw dropped at the sight of it.

"Holy fuck, Valen," I blurted out, thumbing the blade that glowed and shimmered under the firelight.

"Alvredan steel pulled directly from the Dragonkin mountains, the lightest metal I had that still held strong. I dug into my purest stock. Traces of Molybdenum and Nickel for strength. And just enough Tungsten to keep it sharp for centuries," Valen explained, hovering his hand over the blade. It reacted to his presence, the surface warping like a wave had washed over it. "I don't think I've ever made a finer blade. A good one to quit on."

I didn't have words, too absorbed to give it the praise it deserved.

"It's beautiful," I finally managed, and Valen scoffed.

"I spill my guts on the floor and spend two weeks by a blisteringly hot forge and I get two words? At *least* grace me with three," Valen joked but pulled his hand back, regardless.

He looked haggard, and it was hard not to notice he was missing even more pieces than last time. Another finger was gone now, and his tail was missing its thin tip. Blood, sweat, and tears had gone into this blade for me, and I couldn't ever thank him enough for it.

I reached a hand out, and Valen grabbed it like always, his hand against my forearm in a show of respect.

"Truly, Valen. This is your finest blade," I said, and Valen's eyes brightened as he grinned sheepishly. "Guess you might be worth the price after all."

Valen pulled back, flexing his hands as he crossed his arms.

"That's more like it. You're going to make me blush. Now, you'd best get that beauty to your lovely lady," he said, shooing me toward the door with his hands.

I didn't protest, sheathing the blade and attaching it to my hip for easier transport.

"What's your plan now? You mentioned leaving?" I asked as I reached the door.

Valen hummed noncommittally but glanced back at his home with a longing look.

"That's right. Getting out of dodge while I can," he said before turning to face me fully. A serious expression came over his face, no longer holding the joking prance he usually did. "But I'll give you some advice first if you'll take it."

I nodded, my beast sharpening behind my eyes, coming to the surface to hear what Valen had to say as well. "Always."

Valen grunted and looked around us like he was checking for more uninvited guests. His form filled out, growing in size as the full weight of his Sentinel side slid forward.

"Zercara Vestig, the Gargoyle Eternal, was one of the recent deaths, though I'm sure you know that," he said, and I nodded once. "He has two sons fighting for his place. If you have any sense, you'll make sure that *Axius* wins. His brother, Hyland, is as wretched as a snake with a silver tongue just as sharp. He'd be a dangerous enemy to have and an even worse ally."

"I'll make sure this gets passed along," I said gravely. Valen nodded, softening his stance again as he grinned. "Stay in touch?"

"Yeah, yeah, I'll make sure you get an invitation to the funeral. Make sure you bring that pinky? I'll even take one of your own," Valen joked, and I took a deep breath.

I hoped this wasn't the last time I'd see him, but I tried to come to terms with it, regardless. I reached out again, shaking his hand one more time, before yanking him into a hug.

"Not even in your dreams. Though, I'll consider one of Adrian's," I replied, and he laughed deeply before pulling back.

He tipped his head, his wings bumping the door frame. "Stay safe, my friend."

"I'll see you again, Valen. In this life or the next."

"You'd like that, wouldn't you? I knew you loved me, you old dog." I grinned and turned away, waving over my back, as Valen called after. "Until we meet again, Eirik."

CHAPTER 54

FALLON

"You're sure, Adrian?" Heavy silence met my question, and I choked on the feeling of pressure coming from Osiris. "Archon is on Sebek's side?"

We sat around the table, with Osiris looking out over the snow-covered moss. I didn't like it, this uncontrolled power that he held in shaking hands. Each day I saw more cracks appear, and each day I wondered if he'd tip.

We'd made it through the hell that was Kali, but I didn't know how much more he could handle without breaking entirely. And the world would suffer for it.

"Yes. It was confirmed by the old bagman of *The Devil's Details*." Adrian tapped at his chin, a worried expression on his face. He stood by the stove, a bubbling soup on the burner. "Archon and Darius apparently have both been at his call, likely for months, if not years. Sounds like Curtis only just joined a few months ago."

Osiris, hands flexing and rage painting his face, seethed as he stood. He began pacing directly over the scorched spot on the ground. The lights above us flickered.

"The filthy swine got what he deserved," he said, malice lacing his tone.

"Well, you'll be happy to know that there's only one more to deal with," I chimed in, both of them turning to look at me. I'd been dreading this revelation. "Darius faced death shortly after the auction."

The ticking of the clock above the table broke the silence before Adrian cursed.

"Our doing?" Osiris asked, turning that troubled gaze at me.

"No, the marks assume death by sun."

This was problematic, at the very least. Sebek wasn't going to be happy, and we couldn't risk him showing up before the Eternium.

If he found out about Ali ...

I couldn't let that happen. I refused to even risk what happened at my turn coming to light again. I'd kill him if I had to.

"And what do you think?" Osiris asked, pulling me out of the thought.

I recalled Darius, his body molted and covered in the lines of the sun, the malodor of rot ... and lavender.

"His body was veined, the burn sinking as deep as his blood," I said, scrunching my nose, still unable to get the stench out. "Whatever killed him, I think it was internal."

Adrian scoffed, brushing his hair out of his face.

"Vampires can't catch mortal ailments," Adrian said, only half confident as he grabbed the mark at his wrist.

Osiris did the same, for an entirely different reason, as he hid the ink from his past.

"We'll keep an eye on it. Don't want something like that getting back to us," he said, finally stopping his pacing. "Adrian, get me a list of all who were at the auction, and record any sickness they have had following it."

"I'll get right on it," Adrian said with a sigh before walking toward the stairway. "And remember, I get to be there when Eirik rips Archon in half."

Then it was just Osiris and I.

Osiris gave a wary sigh, standing and walking toward the cupboard himself. He pulled out a few glasses and one of the whiskies I knew he'd hidden down here some years ago. He poured an amount for us both and handed me a cup.

"I have a theory," I started, raising my glass and downing my drink.

It was a bitter taste, one that made me cringe. I never had liked the taste, and I really couldn't see what Osiris liked about it.

"Oh?" Osiris asked, eyebrow tipping as he sipped his own.

"You said Curtis was already at death's door when you found him," I said.

Osiris nodded in confirmation.

"Well, he was in direct contact with Aaliyah's blood. It must have gotten into his neck wound after she smashed the vial on his head," I said.

Osiris nodded, likely having come to the same conclusion.

"That would explain Curtis's rapid decline. But Darius distinctly lacked the evidence of a feed," Osiris said, shaking his head, looking skeptical.

Hell, I was too. It sounded crazy. It *had* to be crazy.

"What if he didn't taste her? What if he touched her, came into contact with her blood inadvertently?" I asked, and Osiris's eyes narrowed again as he sighed.

"What led you to this?" he asked, and I looked away.

I couldn't get the sick stench of his blood out of my mind, the way it lingered in my nose.

"He *smelled* like her," I bit the words out, hating them. "Like lavender."

"Would such a small amount of blood, on the skin and not ingested, be able to cause death?" Osiris asked.

"I don't know, but I'd guess that wouldn't be far off," I supplied, listening as that same woman laughed at something that Adrian said. The soft lilt of her voice made my chest ache. "She killed Crustava without even wounding him, Osiris."

"But that wasn't her blood," he said, a curious fire in his eyes.

"I know, but it matches the timeline and what Xander said about her. She's the daughter of a Ra and an Imperial. To ignore that would be a grievous mistake," I said, just as the taste in my mouth soured. "Ascension Rising must have known. They *had* to. Otherwise, why would they know to take her?"

The thought still made me sick, and my hand tensed as she laughed in the other room.

"They were after her blood, Osiris. What if they *knew* this already? What if they were trying to make a weapon? Not that they'd have to try hard. Just keeping enough of it bottled would be threatening enough."

Osiris's jaw tensed, but he didn't appear too surprised. Resigned to the facts of everything, he sighed.

"A weapon, but what for?" he asked, pressing me. Likely to see if I'd come to the same conclusion as him. "It's already strong as is. What else could they possibly do with it?"

That was the correct question, one I dreaded the answer to.

"What if we're not the only ones planning an uprising at this Eternium?"

Osiris froze at my words, narrowing his eyes.

"There would be more chatter. Something would have come up. Not even Audric knew of a group by the name of Ascension Rising. But if you're right, and I have a feeling you're on the right track, they might be useful to us."

The last part of his sentence died out just as his face contorted into a scowl. The lights flickered again.

"You'd work with them?" I asked, already knowing his answer.

"Never," he snarled. "But we may use them as leverage before we gut them. Nilus showed enough potential in that regard."

And that had been the play all along. I saw it now. I huffed, almost laughing.

Rex interfectorem.

"Is that all?" I pushed.

"I expect we'll hear other news soon. We've made a lot of noise in terms of plays recently. Eternals are bound to take notice. Keep an eye out," Osiris ordered. I nodded as I stood, straightening my tie. "That's all for now."

Ascension Rising was quickly becoming more than just Aaliyah's captors. Nilus, the man who still stained our hardwood floor, had mentioned something. He said the rest of his friends were dead.

So maybe this problem had dealt with itself, and I wouldn't have to worry about it anymore.

A pipedream, at best.

The even stroke of the brush against canvas shone dimly in the soft lights of my room, and I marveled at it. It was too bad that Osiris hadn't caved when I said I wanted windows here; it would have looked even better under the glow of the moon. The smell of paint and the give of the bristles was strange. In fact, I couldn't remember the last time I'd pulled out my set and painted. My paint had been dried, brushes fragile and breaking ... but I felt the need to express myself. For the first time since my turn, it was natural to pick up a brush.

I brought another stroke down, taking care that the neutral colors came together, meshing with what I had in my mind. It was close, almost where I wanted it. Just a touch more ...

The creak of the door had me looking up, and in walked the muse that had led me to paint again to begin with.

"Ali," I whispered breathlessly.

That shimmering glow of her eyes was calming, and it was like having her in my sight again settled every nerve that I had.

"Am I interrupting?" she asked, looking around my room and pulling me out of my head.

It was tidy, with the king-sized bed in the middle with satin black sheets and two nightstands. But there was almost no space between the paintings I'd strung up. Picasso, Gogh, Rembrandt.

Aislinn's.

"No, I'm finished now," I said, wetting my brush and cleaning off the paint as I took a second to marvel at the piece.

I didn't have time to guess if Aaliyah would like my mind's rendition of her, as she walked up toward me, glancing at the canvas. I bit back my need to ask her what she thought as her eyes traced the vivid colors, the twist of a curious smile.

She reached out, her delicate fingers hovering over the surface of the still wet painting. Her lip slid between her teeth, and I fought the need to take their place. To claim her lips with my own, like my blood screamed for me to do. It was much like a need to fight, the roaring in my ears like the drums of war.

"Is this me?" she asked, her eyes wide.

"Yes," I said with a nod, trying to gauge how she felt about it. "Do you like it?"

"It's beautiful." She reached out again, not touching, but hovering over the paint like it was something rare to behold. "I thought you just collected paintings?"

I shook my head, raising an eyebrow as she laughed, and I couldn't help but reach out, running a thumb over her flushed cheek. The way her eyes lit up, and she leaned into the touch, sparked that fire under my skin from an ember into an inferno. She grabbed my hand, keeping it pinned against her, as she let out a wispy sigh.

"I do," I said, unable to stop my gaze from tracing her thin lips and the soft curve of her shoulders. "Though, sometimes I like to indulge in the art as well."

A blush was on her cheeks, spreading down into her shirt. She wasn't wearing our clothes today; instead, she was dressed in a pair of faded jeans and an oversized black t-shirt. Some of the things that she had brought home from Eliza's. I found I missed it, the sight of her in my clothes.

"You should do it more. You could make a killing," she said breathlessly. "Be like the people on your walls."

"I wanted to, for a while. But it would be too easy for humans to trace.

Don't want to risk it," I supplied, shaking my head and pulling my hand away.

But she didn't let me off that easily, snagging my hand back in hers.

"Fallon. You and I both know that something like this would be easy enough to fake. Look at Eliza. She runs a business that caters to both humans and Naturals," she said easily. "It's okay if you don't want to paint for others, but don't lie. Whatever you're feeling, it matters to me."

Aaliyah leaned forward, wrapping her arms around me, likely smearing paint all over her nice clothes. I shook my head, holding her close. She could read me like a damn book. Had been able to for weeks. It was strange how easily she did it, and saw the things that even my brothers missed.

"Painting was Aislinn's hobby, ever since we were small. She taught me."

I pulled back, just enough to get a glimpse of her eyes. Sincerity and compassion blended with heat. I leaned in and kissed her temple.

The warmth of her skin sank into my lips. A spark shot down my spine and even with such a bare touch, I craved more. She shivered, the kind that shook your soul, whispering my name in question. I wanted to kiss her again.

See how well she squirmed with my tongue on her. I still hadn't tasted her, and fuck me if I didn't want to see her splayed across my sheets again. I'd keep her there forever if she'd let me.

"She would be glad to know that you're still doing it. Because it looks like it's yours now, too," she said, in a whisper. She watched me intensely, like she was searching for something. That soft smile of hers teased the corners of her lips.

"I suppose you're right," I said, dragging her closer. "Would you like to paint with me, Ali?" I asked, brushing her white hair out of her face.

She pulled away, taking that spark of heat with her. "I'd love to. Though fair warning, I've never been much good with crafts." She looked over at my easel again and raised her brows in question.

"You don't have to be good at something to have fun with it." Aislinn's motto rolled off my tongue, and Aaliyah's face split into a stunning grin.

"Wise words, Fal," she said, looking around curiously.

I had a spare easel and two fresh canvases out before she could blink, and she laughed again.

It didn't take long for us to fall into the swing of painting, and I once again got lost in it. This time, Nero came to mind, the unruly wave of his hair hidden behind his gladiatorial helmet, steadfast silver eyes daring me to fight him. I painted it as I remembered it, the roguish whip of the wind, his devil-may-care grin.

All too soon, Aaliyah was biting her lip again, looking at me with apprehension.

"Done?" I asked, and she balked.

She fidgeted where she stood, her hand rubbing her arm, blots of green paint covering her hands. Even a splash of blue on her face. I didn't like the uncertainty in her eyes.

"You can't laugh," she said finally, setting her brush in the water and cleaning it with care.

I walked over to her, pulling her to me before she could protest it. I had never been the affectionate sort, even with Aislinn, but I found I couldn't get enough of Aaliyah in my arms.

She sagged against me and looked at her canvas with woeful eyes. I wasn't sure what she would paint.

But I wasn't expecting me.

I'd say it was like looking in a mirror, but I had never seen myself as soft as she had portrayed me. It was rough, the lines bolder than they needed to be, the colors off, but it was me. A grin on my lips, the kind that only she had seen, and my *eyes*.

I huffed a breath, and she pulled on my shirt.

"I said you can't laugh!" She blushed crimson, looking away from me, trying to pull out of my arms. I didn't let her get far, grabbing her chin softly. "It's your eyes, isn't it? They're so ... full."

They were stunning, showing so much more than I thought a painting could. They were warm, and compassionate.

Was that how I looked at her?

"You have the most expressive eyes out of anyone I've ever met, Fallon," she confessed like she was trying to justify how she saw me.

Like she thought I didn't like it. But I did. It was raw, beautiful. A gift to prove to myself that I wasn't as cold as my chest seemed to make me think.

"Can I keep this?" I asked, and her eyebrows shot up.

She squirmed against my chest.

"Well, I made it for you. Of course you can have it." Her flushed red skin was my breaking point, the way she glanced away, so bashful.

I reached up, palms against the sides of her face, watching as her eyes widened and her breath hitched. The first brush of her lips broke me, and I moved. One hand going to her hair, the other at her back to pull her closer. Her hands gripped my shirt like she couldn't get close enough.

I pulled back, watching with rapt attention as she breathed in quick gasps. Her eyes were a haze of pleasure.

"It's beautiful, Aaliyah. Thank you."

I leaned back in, lips on hers again. Slowly this time, memorizing every curve, committing them to my soul forever.

"You're welcome, Fallon." That whisper of my name.

Fuck me.

What have I gotten myself into?

CHAPTER 55

PRINCE

The brisk air sent a shiver down my spine, and I almost felt wrong taking a step outside of the small shack that had been home for the last few weeks.

"Will be good for ya, boy," Mags said, pulling a coat around their shoulders. "Got some errands to run, and you need to get out of that damn house."

"Right, right. Where *are* we going, Mags?" I asked, and they paused for a moment before walking away from me.

I sighed, but followed. The roads were dimly lit by streetlights, and I walked them aimlessly, occasionally holding a bag or wares that Mags tossed my way.

Nothing like errands to get the blood pumping.

It wasn't until we'd turned down a narrow street, with flickering lights and a rain-covered walkway, that I saw it. In the distance, there was a building. The massive structure stuck out like a sore thumb.

Pressure built in my skull as I stood, narrowing my gaze at the towering monument. My hands trembled.

"That building? What's that building?" I couldn't force the fear out of my voice. The sound of it caused Mags to raise an eyebrow at me as they looked where I pointed. Like the booming of cannons in my ears, I listened to my heartbeat.

"That?" Mags turned to me like I'd lost my fucking mind, and for the first time, I turned my attention back to them. It felt like my throat was closing as the fire spread through my limbs. "It's the Colosseum."

My breath caught in my throat, that word snapping into place in my mind like the puzzle piece I hadn't known was missing.

"You know, the Roman Colosseum. You're in Rome, my boy." Mags shook their head like it was apparent. I didn't respond, couldn't find the words as I turned back to the *Colosseum*.

The Roman fucking Colosseum. The pressure was at its peak now, and it was only a question of *when* the next memory would hit. It hurt worse than normal and sank further than skin-deep as Mags's concoction fought to stop the rip before it happened. But it didn't work, and I pressed my hands to my head, trying to stop the tremble in my limbs as I sucked in a harsh breath.

The rip hit like a bomb going off. The snapback had me trembling, and when my memory took over, I embraced it like an old friend.

Pain shredded me as I opened my eyes. Every part of me screamed like it was on fire, like I had just been tossed to the lions. I took a deep breath, drawing in fresh air. It burned with the rancidity of iron, of spilled blood in the gallons.

When my eyes finally focused on my hands, I found them to be doused in blood. The familiar red substance coated most of my body. On my skin, in my hair.

My tongue shot out, trailing over my bloodied lips.

Blood was nothing new to me. It took a lot to be a gladiator, and it took even more to be one as distinguished as I was. All to see the look on my father's face as I removed my helmet. That had been last night, had it not?

Or was it?

I had been his champion, his prized gladiator until I removed my mask for him and all to see—the forgotten bastard son. My head thrummed angrily as I looked around. What happened? That was the last thing that I remembered. The moment he realized who he was looking at.

No...

No, there was something else.

The thugs he'd sent after me when I'd left the ring. Eight of them. But I beat them, didn't I? I was the one standing, after all. My memory was hazy, like I was missing days.

I took a step forward, the squelch of liquid beneath my foot surprising me as I glimpsed red. Ice soared through my body at the sight that met me.

Bodies. Bodies everywhere. Most missing limbs, their eyes still open in shock.

I stumbled back, falling directly into a puddle of what I could only assume was more blood.

"What the fuck is happening?"

Silence greeted me. I think I needed to hear something. To prove to myself that this wasn't some sick nightmare.

"This is the effect of your turn." A deep voice washed over the blood, the sound melodic, almost commanding in its presence.

I looked around, desperately looking for the source. By the time I heard footsteps towards me, I was already on my feet.

I moved faster than I thought I could. Too fast.

"What the fuck is happening?" The growl in my voice sounded broken. Weak.

I wasn't weak.

I pulled my hands into fists, raising them as I had thousands of times before.

"The Hallen Bond has been formed. That's what you're feeling right now. Don't worry, the haze will fade. The first few days are typically the worst." I saw the shadow shift this time as a figure stepped into the light, his tall stature screaming power. I fought to keep my hands raised at the sight of him.

"The what?" I tried to keep a level head as the unknown figure stepped closer, his shoe-covered feet causing the blood to splash up. He was so close. Just a few more steps and he would be bathed in moonlight.

"The Hallen Bond. A gift from our Maker." He was just out of reach now. I kept my arms up, ready to fight if he came at me. "You're a Vampire, a turned of Sebek Ra, and I am here to clean up the mess. Make sure that you survive, though the worst is already over."

I froze at his words. Vampire, I had heard that term before. They were a myth—a legend.

"You're a crazy son of a bitch." I bit out the curse with a choked breath. He had to be crazy. It was the only explanation, the only reason that made sense.

This wasn't happening.

And then he was in front of me. He moved so fast that I didn't even see it. His face was pristine, the only hint of something out of place being the specks of blood covering his shirt. His eyes shined like gems in the night.

Distinctly different shades of blue.

"My name is Osiris Vivas, and this conversation would be much easier to have somewhere else. The sun rises soon, and there is a lot you need to know."

He paused, his eyes going to the horizon. I was frozen in place, unable to move, to even think.

He was crazy. He had to be crazy.

"What is your name?" The question almost flew right over me, and I was nearly too stunned to answer. With a stutter unbecoming of an emperor's champion, I got the word out.

"Nero."

Osiris's smirk was cryptic as he extended a gloved hand out to me, and I stretched my hand out without thinking, setting it in his.

"Well. Welcome to the Vivas family, Nero."

I fell onto the ground hard, the screams of Mags echoing into my ringing ears. I struggled to regain my balance.

My name was Nero Vivas. I was *Nero Vivas*, and I knew what that meant. In my soul, I did. It was my name, my *true* name.

And this Osiris was my brother.

That wasn't what I clung to though, no... It was another name that had only been danced over in my previous memories. A name that I now understood.

Sebek.

Panic shot through every part of me as I stumbled backward. I had to get to her, get to Aaliyah. They didn't know what was coming, *none* of them.

"You okay, boy? That's the first one you've had in days." Mags was snapping in front of me. Their wrinkled hand was just inches from my face.

"Nero," I said, and Mags paused at my words, their eyes scrunching at me.

"What—"

"My name is Nero Vivas," I said, and in an instant, understanding took over.

I half expected joy that they'd finally had a name to call me that wasn't Prince. But Mag's expression darkened, something like worry making them antsy as they looked around.

"So soon ... too soon," Mags mumbled the words like a curse.

"What? What are you going on about now, Mags?" I paused for only a moment to look at them. "Do you know what this means? Do you know where I can find Osiris?"

"Knew this day would come. I did, just didn't think it'd be so soon. The future, so finicky... Vivas..." Mags shook their head again.

"*Mags*," I pressed, grabbing their shoulders when they continued to ramble. "Can you find Osiris or not? Aaliyah needs me *right now.*"

For just a moment, their eyes cleared, no longer a clouded haze over them, before their head bobbed.

"Follow me, boy. We'll get you to Osiris," Mags said, a grave warning in their voice as they held up their hands. "But heed this. Not all paths lead to redemption."

Always with the riddles, but I didn't have time to sort through their confused rambles.

"I don't have time for this. Let's go," I huffed, grabbing Mags's arm and leading us back through the patterned walkways.

I had to get there in time. I wouldn't fail her again. Not when I was given this chance, not when she was finally in my grasp.

I just had to get to her in time.

Chapter 56

Aaliyah

"Eirik, when I said you should show her your steel, I didn't mean literally," Adrian prodded, as I inspected the blade that Eirik set gently in my hands.

It was impeccable, and even searching for flaws, I found nothing. The blade was a deep blend of grays and blacks, and the hilt was a hardy redwood that breathed magic, the pull of it singing in the air as I ran my hands over it.

"Shut it, Adrian," Eirik bit out, shuffling in front of me as he searched my face.

Adrian made another joke behind us, but I didn't pay much attention to it, too lost in the gift Eirik had set in my hands. Adrian sighed before I heard him walking away and saying something about playing safe.

"You got this for me?" I asked, looking up at Eirik.

Adrian and I had been in the middle of preparing dinner when he'd all but stormed into the house, beelining straight for me. He was a man on a mission, and by the look in his eyes, this was exactly what he wanted. They were devoured by the deep blue of his beast and hinting at feral, making me shiver. Eirik crossed his arms and huffed.

"Courting gift, as I promised," he said, running his thumb along the blade carefully. "Handcrafted by Valen. Alvredan steel, and a handle made from red oak."

He took the blade back, gently turning it so I could see the intricate woodwork. I was scared to touch it, like it was a work of art that deserved to be framed and showcased.

"Our hair is braided into it. See here," Eirik said, and I noted the white and blond strands that had been tied in with the lavender twine.

"It's beautiful," I whispered, at a loss for words.

Eirik made a noise deep in his chest and lifted his hand to my cheek.

"A gift made for a *Valkyrie*. You deserve nothing less," he said, the smoldering heat in his eyes suddenly raging hot. "You're *mine* now, Aaliyah."

There was a possessive hint to his words, one that should have made me afraid, but it was the gentle way he held me that told me I possessed him just as much as he possessed me. I would burn for his touch, and I was so happy to have him so close.

"So does this mean we're together now, too? Like Fallon and Adrian?" I asked, and Eirik nodded without hesitation.

I shuffled a little closer, careful of the blade he still held.

"Then ... will you kiss me, Eirik?" I asked, and Eirik set the sword down, pulling me into his arms before I could register.

His lips landed hard on mine, and the way he kissed was much the way I imagined he fought. He battled for every inch of my mouth, biting and nipping, the harsh noises that spilled from him making me tremble. I savored every second of it and I was near begging by the time he pulled back, the press of his hot length against my core mind-numbing.

"Please," I pleaded, and Eirik hissed out a curse.

His room was around us in the next instant, my back to the bed as Eirik hovered over me.

He looked like a beast, the savage way he traced where I lay like he wanted to imprint the image of me there. He crawled in with me, pulling me into his arms so I straddled his waist. That vicious heat in my core pulled tight, and I whimpered as he hauled me close again, grinding me against him in an age-old rhythm.

"You don't have to beg with this one," Eirik said, the tone of his voice such a deep timbre, I knew his beast had come to the surface. **"You're *ours* now."**

Chapter 57

Eirik

I gripped Aaliyah's thighs, keeping her pinned against my length as my body reacted to her closeness, straining not to hold her too hard while fighting the press of my beast to mark her with us. The heady smell of lavender in the air, spiced with arousal. I couldn't take it anymore, and I reached up, hand at the back of her head so I could pull her down to eye level. She shivered, and it took everything I had to pause.

I let out a breath, my teeth chattering in a growl, as I asked, "This okay?"

She pressed her nose against mine, her trembling hands still on my shoulder. Her soft breath against my lips had me straining to get her closer to me than she already was.

"Yes," she whispered, her violet eyes on mine before they darted to my lips. Always one to fight her fears. She looked back up at me and smiled. "Kiss me again, Eirik."

I growled, the beast behind my eyes swallowing her claim, hoarding it in our mind like a Dragonkin does gold as I dragged her the rest of the way to me. Her lips met mine in a fiery dance, passion radiating down my spine, engulfing me until I was nothing but ashes. I couldn't get enough as I held her close, trying to meld her into my skin, into my soul. She seemed to do the same, the tightening of her legs frenzied.

That scent of arousal spiked, and I gripped her hips so tightly that I worried I might bruise them, and I nearly pulled back before she cried out, trembling as she arched, grinding against me.

And when she moaned again, it was *my* name on her lips, and I committed each syllable to memory as I tipped us forward, holding her head before letting her settle against the plush sheets of my bed. Our scents mixed, blending in a way that I'd treasure. I kneeled between her thin legs; the smooth ivory of her stomach exposed to me.

My hair must have come undone, or she'd been grabbing it and I hadn't noticed. The long length spilled out around us, with Aaliyah entranced as she reached up to touch the strands as I'd done with hers.

"Eirik?" The question clung to my name on her lips, another breath of slight fear in the air, and I tried to focus, to show her it was alright.

Her face came into view, her trembling lips. I reached for her, cupping her chin and covering her, hiding her from anything that might hurt her. My forehead brushed hers as I leaned forward to tease her with a tender kiss. "Let me love you, *Elsken*."

She sucked in a breath that ended in a startled groan as she tipped her head back. It was a tense few seconds before she looked at me with hesitant eyes. I had no idea how far she'd been, how slow to take this, but I was happy to have any bit of her I could. I needed to touch her, feel her against me to soothe the chaotic mess inside of me. Every scarred piece of me, every bit that made me a broken man. She looked at me, *saw* me.

And she nodded anyway.

"Just ... just touching?" she asked, fidgeting under my gaze.

There was still fear in her eyes, still a worry I couldn't process, but I knew what she meant. We needed to take this slow, and she wasn't ready for sex yet.

But I'd heard what she'd done with Adrian and Fallon and had to choke my lust at the smell of the training room the other day. I could do slow.

But that didn't mean I couldn't make her come.

I leaned over her, kissing the skin behind her ear, reveling in the way she trembled. "Touching," I growled, moving down her neck, tasting the sweetness of her flesh. "Licking."

She groaned, her eyes falling closed as she hummed. Hesitant fingers trailed my back. When I reached her shoulder, I nipped slightly. The slight burst of pain had her eyes opening, mouth wide on a strangled gasp as I pressed my hips against her at the same time, giving her nowhere to go, and no option but to feel as pleasure and pain blended. "Biting."

She dipped her head back, giggling breathlessly. I leaned down, pressing my lips to hers again, gently, savoring the delicate slide of her tongue against mine. When I pulled back, she tried to follow, and I smirked at the groan she gave.

I slid her shirt up, exposing a plain black bra and the bare ivory of her skin. She took a deep breath, turning her head away when I finally slid back to look at her.

I couldn't stop admiring every piece of her, every inch that told the story of her life, of her strength. She couldn't see that in her scars, the power she held, just like I could only see the damage in mine.

When I leaned in again, I pressed a kiss to her nose, where a single raised scar sat. She froze, her lavender eyes wide. I did the same with the scar on her lip, as well as each scar I could reach on my way down her body, loving her in every way I could express. She watched me, each kiss, each scar until tears brimmed in her eyes. The sight made me shake, and my beast snapped at me for making her cry, even if they weren't sad tears.

"I love you, Eirik," she whispered, and a shiver rocked down my entire spine.

I'd known love in my life. The love of a mother, of a father. The love of my sisters and my Crypt. But I'd never known love like what I felt for Aaliyah. It sat bone-deep in a way that would forever be a part of me. I'd do anything for her, kill anyone who tried to harm her and love her whenever she needed me.

Mine was my beast's decree, as he used my eyes to trace our mate.

I watched her eyes for hesitation as I leaned down, pressing a kiss to the waistband of her pants, and when I found none, I dove. I ran my tongue across the slip of skin there, savoring her unique flavor and the way she shivered. I took my time, never wanting this moment to end.

"Please." A whisper, one that had my eyes rolling in the back of my head as my claws dug into the comforter beneath us.

She didn't have to ask twice. I pulled her pants and panties down her legs in one motion, sinking between them. I barely caught her alarmed face as I slid my nose between her wet folds.

"Eirik!" she choked, her body straining as her legs tightened around my head, trapping me between her thighs as if I even considered backing away.

The scent of her so close had me salivating, a growl starting low in my chest that I couldn't contain. I leaned back just enough to reach her thigh. I pressed a heavy kiss to it, running my fangs along her skin. She threw her head back in a moan, her fingers suddenly digging into the bed. I huffed at the sight, reaching up enough for her to grab my hand, so she could dig her claws into me instead.

"What are you doing?" she asked, gasping when I nipped at the tender flesh of her inner thigh.

My fangs ached, and the need to bite suddenly made me dizzy with desire. My fangs sank into my lip, and I had to hold back as my wolf stirred.

Claim, my beast snarled, rattling the cage of my mind.

"I'm going to make you come, *Elskan,*" I growled, the words only half mine, and she shivered again.

She let out a tumbling breath, her body so tense that she continued to shake. But there was no fear clouding her scent, only the sweet hint of lavender marked by the heat of arousal. I leaned back in, taking a long lick from her opening to her clit, gripping her legs as she jumped, keeping her pinned to me.

"Oh," she whimpered, blushing down to her breasts, her one free hand clenching the sheets, the other sinking into me.

I didn't let her say anything else, only went back in, tongue against her clit, then down to her opening, thrusting into her, pressing as deeply as I could, trying to lick every inch. She made small noises in the back of her throat, covering her mouth.

Trying to stay quiet.

I couldn't help the swell of pride and the challenge that she gave me. Accidental or not.

She's going to scream for me.

I trapped her legs over my shoulders, grounding her to me as I devoured her. I trailed my hands along her legs, moving to tease her clit with my tongue as my fingers found her entrance.

Her breathing hitched when I pressed there, circling the small hole, teasing and testing at the same time. I paused for just long enough to wet the finger before diving back in. When I slid the first finger in, her strangled cry slipped past her fingers mixed with my groan. Fuck me, she was tight. *Too tight.*

She was going to need a lot of prep to fit me, and as much as it pissed me off ... one of the others would need to go first. Or I'd risk hurting her.

My beast thrashed, some ancient notion of being the first to claim sending him into a frenzy. My dick strained in my pants, jumping at the thought. Even the idea of her wrapped around me drove me insane.

Mate.

I started moving, beginning with slow, steady thrusts with one finger, my tongue strumming her clit in maddening circles. Licking and biting until she was squirming and delirious. It wasn't until I arched my finger, finding that spot inside of her that made her toes curl, her heels digging brutally into my back, that her hand fell from her mouth, and she cried out, choking on the moan.

I kept that same, devastating pace, memorizing the way she moved against me, the sounds she made, and the gasping way she said my name before I added another finger to the fray.

She tensed, and I paused, waiting for her to adjust to the feeling as I kissed her inner thighs, nipping the flesh and meeting her gaze. When she saw my eyes, she moaned again, her core fluttering. I took that as my cue, my tongue finding her clit to distract her from any lingering discomfort. The way she shuddered, her eyes flooded with lust, cheeks lit with a cherry blush ... it was mesmerizing.

And I couldn't get enough of it.

I alternated between slow and fast, driving her closer and closer until she was straining in my arms.

She clenched around my fingers again, a strangled cry on her lips as her hips bucked. Her hand had found its way to my hair and now pulled until it hurt in the best way. Her head flipped to the side, the tension in her skin, tears in her eyes.

The overwhelming vision that she was nearly had my eyes rolling back. But it wasn't enough, I wanted the words, wanted her to *scream my fucking name.*

"Please, Eirik!" she gave me my wish, my fingers stilling as I grinned at her.

Her eyes clouded with pleasure, the sight making me shiver in every way it shouldn't, but enough to satisfy the urge of my beast. I made sure I held her gaze as I pressed my tongue against her clit, hard. My fingers curled into her, in even thrusts.

One. Two. And she was coming.

She choked out a breath, my name tumbling from her lips with a mix of praises and curses. She was beautiful with her flushed face and the hazed pleasure in her eyes. I pulled my fingers out, replacing them with my tongue, devouring her as she fell, the sweetness of her release nearly making me come in my pants like a pup. The scent that followed her was only accented, lit with spice on my tongue in a flavor that I would forever hunt for. I wanted to live here endlessly between her thighs.

She trembled, gasping when my tongue slid over her clit again, the sensitive bud still straining and sensitive. I took one last lick before I pulled back slightly, her legs still on my shoulders. She looked at me with dazed wonder, breathing hard. My beast purred at the sight.

Again, make her come again.

She was splayed over my bed, looking well-satisfied and happy. I reached out, pulling her into my arms once more.

Mine. Claim, my beast repeated, over and over.

The gentle press of her hands, tentative against my chest, soothed me.

Until they dipped lower, sliding along the hard press of my abdomen, reaching the waistband of my underwear. My mind jolted, flooded with everything I wanted her to do. The thought of her small hands on me, or her mouth spread wide to take me in.

But I wasn't small. I *wasn't* the one that should introduce her to this. I didn't want to scare her away.

"What are you doing?" I asked, probably too gruffly as I grabbed her wrist.

Her fingers flexed at my grip, gently pressing over the muscle above my waist. I trembled at her touch, head falling back as I tried to keep my beast from shooting forward. He rattled and roared, so intent on her touch that he nearly snapped my mind in two.

"I-I wanted to touch you too," she said, and an excuse was on the tip of my tongue. "Please?"

Any fight left my body as I let out a breath. I couldn't tell her no. I looked down at her, trying to gauge her intent as I let go of her hand.

"You sure?" I asked, groaning through clenched teeth as she trailed a finger under the thin elastic band.

She nodded, and all was lost. I let out a low groan and fell back with my hands buried in the sheets.

She was about to fucking kill me.

Chapter 58

Aaliyah

"You don't have to," Eirik pressed again, as I took a moment to study him.

He was drawn taut, his entire body tense as I explored the planes of his waist. I snuck a glance at the bulge in his pants, the one I'd been so shamelessly grinding against.

He was big, bigger than I ever thought someone could be, and I wasn't even really seeing him yet. But I *wanted* to. I wanted him as needy as he made me feel, wanted to hear the groans that came from deep in his chest. I wanted him to feel good.

I wanted to give back to him, so I could give back to all of them. So I could get used to seeing their bodies, and maybe get to where I could think about sex with them without breaking out into a cold sweat.

"But I want to. I-I want to make you feel good, too. If you're comfortable with that," I confessed, feeling suddenly insecure.

Did he not want this? I pulled my hand back a bit, worried that I'd overstepped. But his own hand shot out, grabbing mine as a rich purr started in his chest. His expression shifted, his face sharpening as he pressed my hand back to the band at his waist. Before he trailed it lower, over taut abs that were trailed with winding tattoos that accented every bump and curve. Then lower, past the waistband of his boxers and over the coarse fabric. By the time it reached the destination, I was a blushing mess.

"Oh, we want you all over, sweet *Elskan*. In my pores, in my bones, buried so deep no one would dare step too close. **So *play*, claim this one,**" he purred, distinctively feral as he reached up and cupped my cheek. "**We won't bite, *much*.**"

I shivered again, whimpering as I took in his words. Eirik shot me a savage grin before he reached down, letting my hand slide away as he rid himself of the last of his clothes.

My eyes went wide as they landed on the thick length between his thighs. I knew it was big, had felt it ... but *seeing* it was a different story. It jolted as I stared at it, my core clenching so tightly I whimpered again, equal parts curiosity and fear.

While today was just for exploring, I wanted to go farther with Eirik one day, wanted to know how he would feel buried deep inside me. I'd thought about it before and knew it would happen one day when we were ready for that step.

But as I stared at the tree between his legs, I couldn't help but wonder ... what if it didn't fit? His length was the size of my arm, from my elbow to my wrist, and he was *thick*. I was almost scared to reach out and touch it. Eirik's eyes twisted, and he whined beneath me, sitting up in an instant. He cupped my cheeks again, looking into my eyes.

"What is wrong? **Tell us.**" he demanded, and my words stuck in my throat as I glanced back down at the monster he'd hidden so well.

Eirik's face deflated, and he pulled back. Watching as his hand shot up to his neck, before trailing along his sharpened face. He looked down, then away, showing his entire neck to me.

"**We scare you. This one *scares* you**," the beast said, the whine in his chest growing.

"No, Eirik—" I struggled to speak as my face flamed so hot I worried I might pass out. "I mean ... *you* don't. You're just very—"

I cringed, suddenly needing to hide as Eirik's head tipped to the side, his eyes dulling slightly before bouncing back.

"**Big? He mentions this. You fear our size? We would never harm you, *Elskan*. When we take you, you will be prepared,**" the beast assured, purring again. I clenched my thighs on instinct. His hands came out, passing soothing caresses over my skin, building my own desire again as fingertips skimmed my ribs. "**You will love it, the press of our flesh. *Scream* for it.**"

The beast continued to purr, petting my sides as I fell into an even deeper mess. Stuttering too hard to even come up with a reply for that, I glanced down again, watching how the hard length throbbed when I swallowed.

"He wishes to soothe. He is what you need now," the beast said, still soothingly petting my arms when I looked up. **"Trust us. We'd not harm you."**

Eirik's eyes shifted, the deep ocean blue turning light. Eirik jerked his face away, his cheeks flushing red.

"This is why I said we should wait," he grumbled, worry still stark in his words. He shifted, and when I glanced down, eyeing the beast again, I swallowed.

I set my hand on his hip, following the ink there as Eirik took in a sharp breath.

"I'm not going to say it's not intimidating. But I still want to try," I said, inching closer to the throbbing length. Eirik growled, his teeth bared as I gently wrapped my hand around the base, swallowing hard when my fingers didn't reach all the way around. "T-tell me what to do?"

But he didn't move. His eyes stuck on where my hand was, the veins in his neck popping as he sucked in a breath. Yes, this was exactly what I wanted.

I made a slow, measured stroke, keeping my eye on Eirik as he twitched, his hands digging into the sheets beneath him, ripping them to shreds as claws tore through his fingertips. His growl fell deeper, digging into me as my core flooded with my arousal.

"You don't have to do that, *Elskan*. We—" he started, but I was already leaning forward.

Licking the tip of the angry length in my hand.

Eirik's back bowed slightly, his hips snapping as he let out a snarled curse that ended with a groan that rocked the room.

"That sounded like a good sign," I whispered, and did it again, loving the way he struggled to stay still.

It was so freeing to see this powerful man holding himself back for me. Making sure he didn't move or jerk too hard so I could take this at my pace. His eyes flashed open, going red as his fangs dropped.

"Yes." His voice was a decadent mix of feral and Eirik, him and the beast watching as one. "You're doing so good, *Elskan*."

I hummed, getting comfortable between his legs as I leaned back in, this time pulling him into my mouth experimentally. I could barely get my mouth around the tip and only a few inches in before I gagged. I wrapped my hands around the base, my fingers not touching.

Eirik's fingers threaded through my hair, and he put just enough pressure on the back of my head to make me whimper. When I looked up at him, his face was sharpened again. Lips were stretched thin over white teeth, cheekbones more pronounced, and his eyes a molten sea.

"So beautiful, **taking our cock like that**," Eirik growled, his beast's words slipping through in a gravelly tone that made me whimper. I pulled back before sucking him back in, tears coming to my eyes at the stretch. "You like it, don't you? **You'll like it just as much when this one takes you.**"

His words, so hoarse and rugged, pushed me to move, and I fell into a rhythm as I bobbed up and down on him. His growls motivated me and drove me to insanity as I savored his salty taste. His hand didn't press down again, just settled in the strands, shaking as he jolted under me.

"Just like that," Eirik praised, moving to run his thumb over my stretched bottom lip. "Don't strain yourself ... *Fuck.* You're going to make me come, *Elskan*," Eirik's voice shifted, a desperate touch to it urging me on. I took him to the back of my throat, humming when he grunted, his thick thighs straining. He panted beneath me, his next words a savage growl. "**Do you want that?**"

I could only nod, continuing to move as Eirik's body grew taut, his climax hitting as he threw his head back and roared. I swallowed it as best I could, unable to stop it from sliding out.

Eirik looked down at me. His eyes locked on my hand as I wiped my lip and chin, licking off the rest of him in pure bliss. He reached down and pulled me to his chest. The purr began again, and he wrapped us in blankets, cocooning us in before he kissed me.

His tongue traced my lips, diving into my mouth without care, and I sank into him, warm and sated.

"*Ég elska þig,* Aaliyah," he whispered as he pulled back, keeping me protectively tucked against him.

"What does that mean?" I asked.

"I love you, my *smár Valkyrja.* You lay claim to my heart, to my soul. Everything I am, I share with you. May I always walk by your side."

I sank into his embrace, mapping the patterns of his tattoos on his side absentmindedly. I pressed my nose against his chest.

"I love you too, Eirik."

The purr grew, and my eyes slid closed. I wasn't sure how long we lay like that, but by the time they opened, Eirik was pressing a kiss to my forehead. His arms were still wrapped around me, and I was comfortably warm as I slipped into sleep.

CHAPTER 59

ADRIAN

It was so funny how such a simple mark could make such a change in my life.

I ran my fingers over the rich lavender ink on my wrist, toying with it like it might fade away. The dense line almost seemed to move as though alive under my touch. It filled me with unending contentment, and I smiled, beside myself as I sat at the table.

My dreams had been saturated with the breathy cries of Aaliyah that had gone on well into the morning, stirring me awake and leading me downstairs. Hearing her like that would never get old, and fuck me if I hadn't been hard since Eirik stole her away last night. But I couldn't fault him. He needed his time with her too, especially after waiting so damned long to finally ask her to be his.

But damn, had I wanted to join in on the fun.

But my early rising meant I had been the one to discover our little gift, a letter that had been at the door when I woke. The envelope itself wasn't that extraordinary, just white with the Vivas name scrawled on the front. It was the seal on its back that worried me. I knew it well, as was my job to know. It was a rich green, the swirling marks of a smoke cloud painted gold. The wax gave off an aroma similar to gold.

Archon's marker.

"A summons?" Osiris asked, scaring me right out of my thoughts.

I jolted and tilted my head to watch as he walked down the steps. He was well put together today, finally looking himself even if that meant he was again wearing that dreaded pinstripe suit.

Always that fucking suit.

"Looks to be Archon's," I said, toying with the seal before handing the entire thing to Osiris. He opened it with a slash and pulled out the letter inside.

"It is," Osiris confirmed, though he lacked the surprise I anticipated.

"You were expecting this?" I asked, and Osiris nodded once.

"We've been making waves. I wasn't sure who would request an audience, but I knew we'd likely get one before the Eternium," Osiris said, and I shook my head.

"Remember, sharing is caring, Osiris. Let me in on it next time," I chastised, half expecting him to scowl at me and walk away.

But he merely paused and nodded to himself. It was a fucking miracle.

"Right, I will. I wasn't sure it would even happen, just a hunch. I'll be sure I'm more clear next time."

Progress was progress, and with Osiris, who hadn't changed in centuries, this felt like a big step. Slowly but surely, he was opening up, learning to trust us to take some of the burden, and that was more than I could have ever asked for a month ago.

"So, what do you think we'll get out of this?" I asked.

There was no hesitation in Osiris's answer, as he set the letter down on the table. "He is looking into us on Sebek's command, a fact that benefits us. This could be our last chance to get information from Archon about Sebek and his motives," Osiris reasoned.

A crash interrupted the conversation as a door upstairs slammed closed. Only seconds later, Fallon was flitting down the steps, my sweet little love and Eirik right in tow. Perfect, that made a happy family.

"What's with all this noise so early? You're making my head spin," Fallon grumbled, but I paid him no mind, sliding past him and directly into Ali's surprised arms.

"Love!" I laughed, lifting her easily, her startled yelp falling into a soft laugh as I spun her around. God, I'd never grow tired of that sound. "I was hoping you'd wake up soon. I missed my morning kiss!"

She blushed but didn't hesitate to cup my cheeks and give me a soft kiss. So timid, exploratory. She hummed as she pulled back, staring up at me shyly. "Good morning, Adrian."

I could make it an even better morning. Make her come so many times her head spun and then see if I could get a couple more. She was just too damn cute, and as I set her on the ground, I considered stealing her away for just that.

"The best morning, now that you're here." I leaned in then, brushing her hair away, entranced by the blush that stuck to her skin. "Though, I'd have loved to be with you last night. Sounded like you had a lot of fun."

She made another choked noise, and Eirik smirked, walking up behind her to pull her away from me. Though he placed a chaste kiss on the side of her head, his eyes were as heated as mine were.

Lucky bastard.

"Can we stay focused here?" Fallon asked, acting exactly like the spoiled brat I knew he was.

If he couldn't make Ali laugh, then he sure as hell was going to ruin my fun.

"Spoilsport," I murmured but didn't get the chance to do much else, as Fallon pushed me out of the way and pulled Ali into his arms.

This was twisted into a game of Don't Touch the Lava, but the only one that was playing was Ali, and she didn't know she was in the game. I snickered, mocking a glare as Fallon said his own good mornings.

And if I thought she blushed at what I said, I wished I could have heard what Fallon whispered. Her cheeks flamed, and Fallon smirked like he couldn't get enough of it.

"Hey! That's cheating. I put her down. You can't pick her back up!" I protested, more than happy to poke some fun to clear up the tense energy.

"Seems like I just did," Fallon said, walking over to the table and taking a seat. Aaliyah stayed on his lap, happily wrapping his arms around her. Though, the nice joking air couldn't last long, as Fallon turned his stony gaze to Osiris. "So, Archon?"

I scoffed. "You heard that?"

"We did."

"It would be the best chance to dig into what Archon knows about Sebek and his plans. As much as I'd like to ignore him, we can't reject a summons. It would be a poor play so close to the Eternium," Osiris said, glancing between us all. "So, who wishes to go?"

Fallon was the first to speak, his arms tightening around Ali protectively. A fire raged in his eyes, and he glowered. "Bastard could use a few scars. I volunteer."

Eirik was next, his jaw tightening as his beast came forward as well. "Aye. I'll go too."

That just left me, and I *had* to go. Osiris would just have to deal with it and stay here for a while with the little love.

Oh, what a task it would be! I felt *so* bad for him.

If he doesn't pull his constipated feelings out of his ass while we're gone, then I guess I'll just lose faith in Vampiremanity.

"And I need to go, to get him talking. Which leaves you here, Osiris. Are you alright with that?" I asked, and he nodded.

Though his eyes weren't on me, but rather on Aaliyah. She watched him with the same calm expression, and I knew that if he didn't bring it up, she sure as hell was going to. She was straightforward like that, and I loved her for it.

"Yes, I'll keep watch," he finally said, and I shrugged a bit.

I took a step toward him, stretching high. "That was a lot easier than expected. You don't want to tear him limb from limb? Got something else on your mind?"

Wink, wink.

He shook his head, his lip tilting in a minuscule grin. Before his eyes went cold. Devious, sinful rage bled so deeply I wondered if Archon sensed it from here.

"I will be, just not tomorrow. And neither will you," Osiris said, and Fallon made a disappointed noise. "You can't kill him, not now. There's too much at play to kill another Eternal beyond Kri'Valta. But there will come a time in the future when he *will* pay for what he did."

Point taken. Osiris rolled up his sleeves, exposing his tattooed arm, and that explosive expression only grew.

Yeah, Archon was a dead Djinn walking. Almost felt bad for him. At least, until I remembered what he did to my girl. Then I wondered if I should bring some popcorn and maybe some marshmallows to roast over his corpse after Osiris went inferno on him.

"Should have guessed as much, bastard," I said with a smirk. Then I turned to Ali, catching her eyes. She knew the drill by now, and I noticed how lost in thought she was as she stared off into space. She rubbed the red cloth she kept in her pocket. Red, as she called him, though her eyes kept searching for Prince. "Love? You're the last vote."

She looked at me slowly, pulling her pouty bottom lip between her teeth. Fallon quickly pressed his thumb there, soothing the abused flesh.

"I'm ... I'm worried," she said, fiddling with her fingers.

"What has you worried, *Elskan*?" Eirik asked, walking over to her.

He was a big man, huge. Honestly, I wondered if his mother fucked a giant. But he kneeled next to her and Fallon, coming at eye level with her, so he didn't intrude on her space.

"Something's wrong. It's just a feeling I get sometimes. Like before Curtis got me and Eliza. And before Prince at the hot spring. Or you at Valen's," she explained, eyeing us like we might call her crazy.

But she would never get that from us, never. If she was worried, then we were worried. And we could use that kind of skepticism right now. With everything so close, we needed to be careful. This had to go perfectly.

Archon. Kri'Valta. Eternium. Avoid Sebek at all costs.

"Okay, what can we do to minimize risk here? Osiris, can you up the wards before we leave?" I asked, and he nodded instantly.

"Of course," he said like he hadn't already been out there every day, pushing as much of his power into those little wooden wards as he could. He reached into his suit pocket, pulling out several thin chains sporting small emblems. "Now would also be a good time to give you all these."

They were barely quarter-sized, each one an unpolished gemstone encased in metal. They glowed, shimmering and molting under the moonlight. They even smelled like magic.

"Protection charms?" I asked carefully.

Osiris nodded, walking to each of us and handing them out. "Should negate most minor magic. It's too little too late—"

"They're perfect," I cut him off, and they were.

They breathed power, and every part of me grew charged under the unbridled press of Osiris's magic. I forgot how strong he was, the weight of his age. It happened living so long with him, and after seeing how Kali affected him. But it wasn't a question.

Osiris was a force to be reckoned with, and that thought had me standing a little taller.

"Thank you," Fallon said as well, with Eirik grunting his affirmation, still kneeling next to Ali, her hands now in his hair.

"I don't like leaving for so long. It could lead to trouble," he mumbled, his wolf beginning to purr.

"It's just a few hours. And if we don't appear for an official Eternal Summons, then there will be questions. We leave for Kri'Valta's gala tomorrow. So don't stall too much," Osiris pressed, and Eirik grunted an affirmation.

It would have to do.

I stole a glance at Ali and watched the way her eyes still narrowed in.

"Better, love?" I asked.

She hesitated a moment before nodding. "I still don't like it. But I trust you," she said, catching my eye. Like always, the stunning strength that emanated from that shook me to my core, stealing my breath. "I'll see you guys soon."

Eirik was up the next second, stealing her lips in a kiss that looked *feral*. Fallon soon after, obviously not happy with being second, as he held her captive until she was panting.

And I wasn't about to be left behind.

I walked up to her, snagging her into my arms. I kissed her until her legs shook, and she gasped out little breathless sounds. I wanted to give her something to look forward to, something to think about.

Because fuck if I wasn't going to be thinking about her every second of this.

Archon. Kri'Valta's. Eternium.

"Be safe," she said, pulling back and rubbing her arms as she shifted from foot to foot.

"Always love," I replied, tapping her nose. "Why don't you and Osiris get settled, and we'll get started on setting up the tree when we get back? I know we won't get to enjoy it for Christmas—" I rambled, and Aaliyah leaned up, kissing me silently.

She hummed again, and I melted at her initiative.

"I'd love that, Adrian," she said, waving as Fallon and Eirik walked toward the door. I followed them, against my better judgment.

"Be back soon!"

Archon. Kri'Valta's. Eternium.

Oh, and definitely make her come. That was at the top of the fucking list.

Chapter 60

Fallon

Fellow Manor was lit unpleasantly under the crisp full moon. Everything about it screamed occult magic, from the long twisting spires to the crumbled scent of graveyard dirt.

I still didn't know what Aaliyah was thinking, trying to go to Archon Sewire for help. The Djinn Eternal was nothing but a parasite that stole the title from its rightful holder. Elania had been a good Djinn if you could call any Djinn good. She didn't use the petty lies that most of their kind followed, and when she died, all the Natural community wept for it.

Murdered ... When she was *murdered.* Only for Archon to be there to conveniently take her spot.

"It's a good thing Osiris already got rid of Curtis," I vaguely heard Eirik growl from his place next to Adrian.

They stood frozen, eyes narrowed on a barren piece of ground in an empty alleyway.

Aaliyah's scent was nearly washed away now. However, her blood still lingered in the air, and it was enough to send an already volatile Eirik into a frenzy.

"She's safe, and we don't have time to linger here." Eirik turned his glare to me as I spoke, his eyes narrowing with a scowl.

"She'll be safer when we're all back home," Eirik growled out.

"Careful, your overprotectiveness is showing, Eri," Adrian said, his head tipping back in nervous laughter, as though we weren't feeling the same.

We all wanted to be home, but we wanted to give Osiris a chance to reach the same understanding that we had.

That Aaliyah was ours.

Besides, this summons gave us a chance to pay dear Eternal Archon a visit. He had to pay for his actions, for selling Ali. It made my blood boil just as much as it made it sing. Had Archon not given up Aaliyah to Curtis, then she wouldn't have been at the auction that night, and we never would have found her.

She never would have invaded our lives, never would have made Adrian laugh to the point of tears, never would have made Eirik sing again.

Never would have helped me find my way back to the world that I'd left behind.

"Osiris has had enough time to serenade her. We should be home." Eirik was losing his cool, his head flipping away from Fellow Manor. "Fuck Archon. You and I both know this summons is bullshit, and the only thing he's going to tell us about Sebek is how good his boots taste."

"You're willing to give up a fight? Where is my Eri, and what have you done to him?" Adrian placed his hand over his forehead, feigning surprise. However, his Cheshire grin told me he knew exactly what beast he was prodding.

"And Osiris won't be the one doing the serenading. We aren't waiting for her to fall for him. We're waiting for him to understand that he's a fucking idiot," I paused. "She feels for him, as she does us. I know it; you know it. The only bastard who doesn't is him."

"He doesn't think he deserves her," Eirik chimed in, his shoulders rolling.

His beast hovered behind his eyes, tracking Adrian's and my movements. There was a cunning feeling to Eirik tonight, the kind that showed he wasn't in control. Eirik may be the one speaking, but if Archon stepped out of line, the *Úlfhéðinn* wouldn't hesitate to kill him.

That could bode poorly for us. Killing an Eternal outside of the Eternium Ball could quickly lead to a death sentence. We didn't need the threat of Retaliation on our plate, not when we were already going to be taking out one Eternal. What startled me further was that I would do it, too. I wanted to make Archon scream for what he did. What would Aaliyah think if she knew I tore out his heart?

"And he's probably fucking right. None of us do," I said after a pause, my words tinged with the bitterness of my thoughts. "That's why we need to work toward becoming men who are worthy, and that has to start somewhere."

"Well, Fallon, I never expected you to be the one giving the love speech." Adrian stretched his hands above him as he spoke, cracking his neck.

He was right, of course. Eirik wasn't the only one out of his element. I had shut this part of me off the day Aislinn died, and I didn't expect it to ever come forth again. Then I felt the ache in my chest, the need to bring a smile to Aaliyah's lips. It was new, and it made me feel weak in the best ways.

I may not be a good man, but I would be the best I could be for her.

"She changed my mind," I said.

"Oh, I'm aware. I was there, remember?" Adrian's blissful words blended with Eirik's jealous growl.

"The feel of her soft skin, the surprise in her eyes when she realized what you were doing." I stiffened, my nose flaring. The scent of blood in the air worked against me as the memory of that day came back to me. "Or was it the sound of your name on her delectable lips?" Fangs popped from my gums, and Adrian beamed like he knew exactly what he was doing.

The bastard even winked.

I wasn't the only one affected as Eirik flipped Adrian around, leveling our youngest brother with a steadfast glare.

"Adrian," Eirik growled. A warning.

"You are far too easy to prod, Eri," Adrian said, laughing. "I care for her all the same. I would do anything for her."

Adrian bowed his head, conviction showing in the way he moved. He may joke and prod, but I didn't doubt that statement. It was why he was here, why he had told her about his turn.

"Besides, we know you had some fun without us, you sly dog. So don't pretend that you didn't." Then, right back to teasing, Adrian shoved against Eirik's shoulder, winking at the agitated giant.

I was slowly getting more used to this Eirik, the one that was ready to tear into people for even looking at Aaliyah wrong. The bond of a wolf's soul, he said. His beast knew before he did that Aaliyah was theirs, and now that they were on the same page, nothing would keep them apart.

"Can we get back on topic here?" I asked, just as Eirik returned Adrian's push, shoving our brother, who continued his boisterous laughter.

We were getting off track.

"Oh, right? I call making her come next." The darkening of his eyes was my breaking point. I was already straining to continue to Archon's. "You two got your own time. *I'm* next."

I would be *damned* if Adrian got to her first. I could still feel the heat of her skin, the sight of her eyes in the glass. She had been a picture of perfection, and even now that sight was burned into my memory. I wanted to see it again, to *hear* it again. So the next time Aaliyah came, all sweet and breathless, it would be with me between her legs.

I bit down, straining so hard that my teeth cracked against each other.

"Adrian, I swear," I bit out, and he ignored me as he took a step in my direction.

"Together again, then?" Adrian asked, effectively breaking what little patience I had left.

We had to talk to Archon. Aaliyah's safety was in question, and I would not lose focus on our goal.

I turned, ramming my fist into Adrian's shoulder, which threw the smug bastard off his feet.

"No need to hit so hard, Fallon," Adrian protested, once again glancing away from Fellow Manor.

Then it all clicked.

"You're stalling," I said.

Adrian sighed, as if knowing his ruse was up. Then, just as quickly as it appeared, his cavalier attitude faded, replaced by a stony equivalent.

It wasn't an expression that Adrian often sported, the harsh frown unfamiliar on his face.

"Unfortunately, I want to be home just as much as you lot. And whenever I try to think of anything, it always goes back to her. I'm just trying to give Osiris some time before I barge in and steal her away. And I *really* don't want to deal with Archon tonight."

I rolled my eyes but agreed. Because he needed time, and I was tired of waiting.

"Let's get this over with," I said, sighing when the other two finally nodded.

The rest of the walk to the manor was done in relative silence, our thoughts on two things.

Murder and Aaliyah.

At least, mine were.

We walked our way up the long stretch of steps, past the ornate gate, and approached the door. It swung open before we even had the chance to knock. The air from inside Fellow Manor was rigid and held the particular scent of old spells, making my skin crawl. Just as quickly, Archon's face came into view.

I'd forgotten how small he was, standing barely chest height. His brown hair fell in a middle part, long enough to reach his shoulders, and his eyes, like brandished gold, took us in warily. As he should.

He didn't know we had Ali yet, at least I hoped not, nor that we'd heard all about what he'd done. That he'd sold her and Eliza out for money I damned well knew he didn't need. The thought of it made my blood sear, and I had to bite my tongue to stop my fangs from dropping.

"You're late. And you're missing a member." I barely kept a straight face at his audacity. I took another breath, forcing calmness as I tried to remember why we were here, that this was an official summons. And a dead Eternal on our hands was the last thing we needed, knowing that Kri'Valta was already going to be a test of our plan. "When an Eternal summons, you're all supposed to follow the call. Didn't Sebek teach you any better?"

Bastard. He'd purposely used Sebek's name for sway. He knew who we were, and he could out us to Sebek if anything here went less than favorable to him.

"Sorry, Osiris was rather tied up," Adrian placated. "He sent us all in his place. I hope you understand, so close to Eternium."

Archon's eyes danced between us as he opened the large doors of his home to us. "Fine. Come in. Though, I hope you're not expecting tea. It's already cold."

We didn't say anything as we followed him through the twisting entryway and into a sitting room. His house was as grand as it seemed from the outside, though showing its age as the sprawling marble cracked under a moving foundation. And it stunk like age, a mold having found its way into those cracks, something even the heaviest of cleaners wouldn't be able to get out.

Some pieces we passed—sculptures, paintings, and works that deserved to be shown in museums across the world—were covered in dust, some even hidden away, stacked on top of each other. Pieces that others would kill for, that he was hoarding for the sake of hoarding.

Leave it to the Djinn to be so blatantly egotistical.

We were led to a sitting room that seemed on the surface freshly cleaned. He motioned for us all to sit, and I quickly traced the exits around us and the guards that now manned them. The room was silent, dead silent. There wasn't a bustle of workers like you'd expect, with a house of this size, and that lack of life put me on edge.

We sank down, the old sofa and chairs releasing dust as we did.

"I have a question for you, Archon, if I might," Adrian said before anyone else could speak.

Surprise lit up Archon's eyes, and he narrowed them before nodding once.

"You may recognize the name, Eliza Barlow," he clarified, giving him no room to play off the words. "Do you know who that is?"

Archon contemplated for a second, tapping at his chin with a long black fingernail. Slight traces of blood were in the air, and I could clearly see that it was coming from under his nails.

Gold eyes trailed my face, and I struggled to stay steady under the gaze of the ancient.

I fucking hate Djinn.

"Ah, the young granddaughter of Ilenia. Yes, I know of her," Archon said hastily, with a wave of his hand, like it was merely a game. "Why are you so curious about them, Vivas?"

The guards shuffled around the room, their hands falling to their weapons in innocuous ways, making it seem like they were adjusting. But I knew what it looked like for someone to be ready to fight. Had seen Nero do it more times than I could count.

"She and her friend went missing in our territory some weeks back, which could prove problematic if the human enforcement gets involved," Adrian said smoothly as he watched the guards, his jaw tensing.

"Ah, well, I don't believe you need to worry about that, gentleman." He bowed low like that solved everything.

Like he hadn't fucking sold her.

"It would still benefit us to know." Adrian pushed, smile slipping as rage flooded his auburn eyes.

"Sorry, I have nothing else to share," Archon retorted, eyes narrowed. "In fact, you're being quite audacious, Vivas. This was my summons, yet why do I feel like I'm the one being questioned?"

Something old filled the room, a power that smelled like gold and cigarette smoke. Archon's eyes glowed, and he flashed his teeth like a wild animal. But it didn't have the effect he was hoping for as he went on guard, looking like prey. Eirik shot to his feet, baring his own teeth as his beast pushed forward.

"You lying, egregious bastard," he hissed, eyes so pointed that it looked like they could draw blood. Any chance of us keeping our real thoughts subtle flew out the window like Adrian's sanity, as he rubbed his hands along his face. "You *sold* her to Curtis."

"Now, I'm not the only one telling half-truths, am I?" Archon looked indignant as he spoke, eyes narrowed. He sipped his lukewarm tea as Eirik continued to snarl, his eyes flashing red. The guards around us were on edge, tension lining them as they watched the beast unravel. "Curtis never got Eliza. So you must mean the little thing Eliza wanted me to help. Well, if you already knew that, why did you feel the need to ask? It's not illegal in the Natural community. I merely told the Dragonkin that there would be a pair of girls on Century side for a small fee."

Sold them for a quick buck. Even knowing the relationship he had with Ilenia, he sold them. I wasn't surprised, but it made me sick regardless.

"Why did you do it?" Adrian shook his head, words grim.

"Why *not*? This world isn't meant for the weak. If they had any sense, they wouldn't have tried to make a deal with me in the first place." Archon was getting irritated, his shoulders tense and jaw clenched tight.

Don't kill him. Just don't fucking kill him.

But that sentiment didn't transfer to Eirik as his eyes flashed red, his face snapping and cracking as his wolf drove him to the edge.

"**Your men are going to have to bury you in pieces,**" Eirik snarled the words, and every atom in my body knew he planned to make true on that statement.

The guards sprang into action at that, shooting forward with guns and knives drawn. Surrounding us.

God fucking damn it.

"You wouldn't dare!" Archon screamed, his glass suddenly hitting the ground, tea and porcelain exploding off the hardwood.

"Oh, I wouldn't push that button, mate. He's not been in the best mood tonight," Adrian said, no longer smiling.

Archon's face twisted into a sneer. "Your Maker is responsible for the deaths of thousands, if not more. Entire fucking races." I flinched, knowing the exact race he spoke of. "Yet you feel you may threaten me in my home. During a summons *I* called. You don't hold any power in this house. *I am* the Eternal!"

His teeth gnarled as his jaw went tight. Smoke swirled around him.

"Guards, contain them. This insult can't stand," he snapped, and the guards descended fully.

And I almost cheered.

Guess I'm getting that fight after all.

The guards closed in, the scent of their fear heavy as they tried to pick a point of attack. But we'd already moved as well, standing back-to-back so not a single spot was left open to them.

The first man shot forward, and he was dead before the others could think of intervening. Eirik's teeth were buried in his neck, and his maw mostly shifted. They all descended then, a mix of Naturals that didn't stand a chance. Even Archon's own power barely scratched me as his screams joined in the fray.

I turned to him, blood on my hands and covering my suit. His eyes flashed wide with fear, and I took a step forward. And another, my shoes splashing in the blood of his guards. I couldn't kill him, but I damned well could scare him a bit. My wrist began to ache, where my Hallen Mark with Aaliyah was, and I reached up to scratch it, agitated by the distraction. Until it burned ...

And the pain hit.

It started low, just below the skin. Slowly, it grew until the smoldering ember roared like hellfire, and the pain turned to agony.

"What in the bloody hell is that?" Adrian hissed, falling to his knees as he grasped his wrist. One guard took advantage, landing a blow across his head.

Adrian hit the ground.

The mark seared into an inferno; the pain was so intense my vision went black. Another body hit the ground, a pained whimper in Eirik's shifted voice.

Aaliyah.

"No..." It overwhelmed me, burned me, *destroyed me.* "Aaliyah."

It was the last word I got out, as the pain became overwhelming. I couldn't think, could barely breathe.

The last thing I saw as I fell to my knees, clutching my wrist, were crisp boots. The familiar scent of cured leather flooded my nose. Archon's sick gold eyes came into view, and unconsciousness slid over me as his words bit into my skin.

"Where's all that bravado now, Vivas?"

CHAPTER 61

OSIRIS

The dust-littered piano keys no longer held the answers to my questions, not like they did a hundred years ago. I longed to hear their sound, to have my brother next to me as we made serenades until the sun peeked over the mountains and called us to sleep.

For them to give me the strength to do what I was about to do.

The creak of the hallway door told me that Aaliyah was there, breaking up the thoughts that she had unknowingly started. I turned to her, taking in the tenderness in her eyes and the tentative smile on her lips. Such an innocent look, such openness and light directed at me. I wanted to pull her into my arms, to feel her lips, to understand this love that had taken my brothers.

A love that had already found a home in my chest.

I wasn't sure I could place the exact moment it happened, but wasn't that how love was? The trivial things, the building blocks of a relationship that slowly grew until you were standing in wonder, waiting for what would happen next.

"Aaliyah," I said, watching as she fidgeted by the door. "What can I do for you?"

Her cheeks flushed, and the sweet scent of her spread throughout the room. Her hair, that snow white, flowed softly over her shoulders and bare arms. She was wearing one of our shirts today and a pair of leggings that were cut off just above her ankles. My attention drew to the marks on her arm, the flowing black bands that represented us.

I wondered which one was mine.

"I—" She paused, then sighed with trepidation. "I wanted to spend some time with you."

I froze. My chest ached, and the phantom throbbing of my heart beating roared in my ears. This was what I wanted, exactly how I wanted this to go with the others gone.

So why did I struggle to speak?

"I'd understand if you don't want to. I just figured that since the others were out ..."

She was uncomfortable, something of my doing. I swallowed hard.

"Your company would be acceptable." The words slipped out, sounding cruel, and I knew that could I blush, I would have. She'd turned me into a stumbling, bumbling mess. But she didn't turn away as her face softened again. She walked over, her stride slow as she came up to the piano stool. She glanced at the open space, and I nodded toward her.

She sat and turned her attention to the same keys I still had my hands on. Was she asking them to bear their secrets like I was?

What would you do, Nero?

"Adrian mentioned you know how to play," she said, not knowing what her words did to me. "Would you show me a song?"

My first instinct was to tell her no. I hadn't played these keys since I'd buried Nero. But something made me move anyway, the same feeling that had stolen my voice the day we'd found her. The same one that made me want to touch her when everyone else on the planet made me sick. I reached up, holding out my hand to her.

And like always, she trusted me enough to set her palm in mine, humming quietly. My eyes caught on the markings on her wrist, closer now, the intricate black bands that wrapped around it. Suddenly, I knew exactly which one was mine. It had archaic swirls, some almost looking like an old font I could no longer recall but knew existed. It was beautiful, almost moving, and the sight of it had me struggling not to reach for my wrist.

"A piano is best played in a duet," I said, mirroring Nero's words, the same ones he'd told me whenever he'd sit down to play. "I could show you."

Aaliyah skimmed her gaze over the ivories, her excitement bleeding into her words. "I've never played."

"That's fine. I wouldn't overburden you."

Something coiled in my stomach as she let go of my hand, placing her fingers over the keys haphazardly, not yet pressing down. My heart skipped in my chest as I waited for her to press one, for the familiar sound to ring in the air.

"I'd be happy to learn, then." Her lavender eyes held me captive.

What would Nero do?

I took a shuddering breath and moved her left hand into position for a simple set.

"Here is C3." She followed my direction and carefully pressed her finger down, the note ringing in the air. It was haunting, soul-wrenching. I hadn't heard our piano's song in a millennium.

I'd forgotten how beautiful it was, even out of tune.

"Then to G3." She followed my fingers, eyes focused. "To C4."

She did it a few times, getting the hang of it and moving a little more confidently each time.

"Then, G3. To E4." Each note was a mark on my soul, each second digging deeper and deeper. I waited for the ache, for the ruin of memories to flood me and send me running. I waited to see Nero's eyes flashing in my mind or for his damnation. But each press made my shoulders drop and had me leaning into Aaliyah's warm side. Even through my suit, I felt her heat. "Then finally, G3 back to C3."

Each note was more aching than the last. More freeing, more exhilarating. I caught Aaliyah's gaze again, the one that had been haunting me every waking second. The one I didn't deserve to have on me. And I savored it, selfishly watching the way her cheeks flushed red, and her lips curled at the corners. I questioned what they would feel like, if only for a moment.

"Like this?" she asked, unaware of the struggle I had.

She pressed the notes, stumbling only a few times before she fell into it. I nodded, and I moved instinctually, sinking my right hand over the keys.

And I played.

The notes came easily, my fingers knowing the pressing and pull of the old keys as I played a melody to her line. Aaliyah's laughter tinkered in the room. She leaned into me, still giggling as she watched the fluid motion of my hands in improvisation. I flew through several pieces, some I'd learned, some that simply came to me.

"Why did you learn to play?" she asked, eyes still glued to the movement of my fingers.

I realized she had stopped playing, and I'd taken up both positions. I took a heavy breath, seeing Nero next to me, my brother's brash grin.

"Nero wanted to learn," I whispered. "Said us Vivas should look the part of sophistication."

I tapped at the key again and remembered the first piano we had studied on. The dusty old oak, the off-key ivories. It had smelled heavily of whisky and fire, and half the notes were forever off-key. It had been in horrendous shape, but it had been ours.

"Of course, he'd been joking, but I had always wanted to learn. So, we did." I still recalled Nero's face, his raised eyebrows and his jolting laugh.

He hadn't expected me to agree, but he hadn't told me no either.

Sheesh, if you wanted to learn so badly, you should have said so, Osiris.

Aaliyah watched with rapt attention, her hand reaching up to grab my arm.

"He loved it more than he would say. He was much like Fallon, brash, a brawler. Didn't like people thinking he was soft because of his more artistic feats." Not that anyone would have. He would have leveled them before the words left their mouths. "I've only ever played with him."

The moment wasn't lost to me, baring my soul to someone I'd known for weeks, not years. Aaliyah had that effect on me and made me want more. Made me want to *say* more.

About me, about Nero. About the fact that I couldn't keep her off of my mind, and at this point, I didn't even want to. Waking up, knowing she'd be at the table for breakfast. Walking through our home and listening for her subtle heartbeat I knew I'd likely find in the library.

"Tell me about him?" Aaliyah murmured, still clinging to my arm.

I turned away, unsure why acid built in my throat, or why it hurt so badly to even try to speak. It wasn't the first time she'd asked me that, but sitting here with her at my side had me struggling to speak. Everything was right there, the way he'd grin to his unruly pranks. I wanted to share, because I wanted her to know, to show her I was trying.

We're family, Osiris, it's what we do.

"I don't know what to tell," I admitted, and she reached out, cupping my cheek.

I flinched, an action that she was all too familiar with. She didn't pull away this time, just held me comfortingly.

"You know everything, Osiris. You have him in your mind." She tapped my temple before moving to settle her hand over my heart. It sped up for her, and I leaned into the touch. "And in your heart, even if he's not here anymore."

She glanced around the room before reaching for her pocket. She'd been carrying around that red cloth, keeping it for comfort in moments like this. She was talking about Prince, I realized. Comforting me of a loss nearly a hundred years ago, when hers was still so fresh.

What would Nero do?

"He was tall, I'd say a few inches taller than I. He had the brightest silver eyes I'd ever seen and unruly brown hair with red highlights. Looked a lot like his father, a fact that he hated until the day that the old bastard died. He always wore a smile, not much different from Adrian's, I'm afraid. But brasher. Proud," I said.

Talking of Nero had been so difficult, so painful. But sharing it with Aaliyah, with the little light that had stolen a piece of me every day, every second she spent in our home. Everything seemed lighter, more open.

"We have a picture of him, if you would be inclined to see it?" I asked.

There was a pause as she glanced around the room again. She hesitated this time before something like steel took over her expression.

"I think I'd like that," she said. "I wish I could have met him. He sounds extraordinary."

I wished that more than anything else. He would have loved and cherished her in all the ways I wanted to.

"He was," I said, not looking away even as I stood, and walked around the grand piano until I was close enough to gaze into the open back. Tucked inside was a small, age-stained envelope.

I reached in, pulling it out with care. It held the only picture we had of Nero. I slid it out, taking a second to admire it and its frayed edges.

I hadn't looked at this portrait in decades, not since the funeral. Nero's defiant eyes told me everything and nothing. But I knew, if he were here now, he'd be asking me what the hell was wrong with me.

And why I'd denied something that made me so happy.

"Here," I said, as I slid it back into the envelope. "It's not in color, I'm afraid."

She reached out and grabbed it from my hand just as I cupped her cheek. My hand shook there, and my will battled with the words stuck in my throat. I wanted to feel her skin under my fingers, wanted to feel its heat. I'd wanted to work on myself, to make myself worthy of her, but I knew the moment she tipped her head to the side, leaning into my touch, that I couldn't do it away from her anymore.

What would Nero do?

"Aaliyah, I have a confession to make," I said suddenly. Aaliyah's hands froze, and she peeked up at me, her lavender eyes wide. "I know I've done wrong, know I'm not the man you should take into your arms. But I can't keep this in any longer, for my sanity's sake, if nothing else. I care for you, deeply. And I know I still have much work to do to become someone worthy of you, and I'll spend every day working toward that."

I paused, leaning in and slowly pressing my forehead to hers. Aaliyah waited so patiently as I worked through the words.

"Would you do me the honor of being mine?" I whispered, finally.

There wasn't any hesitation before she nodded, smiling as tears lined her eyes.

"I was already yours, Osiris. I was just waiting for you to see it."

I breathed, in and out, taking her in. I didn't lean in, didn't kiss her as I craved. This closeness was all I could handle for today, but I had hope for tomorrow. I lifted my hand, stealing hers, the one that held the black bands showing our bond. I lifted it, kissing the mark I knew in my soul to be mine. My own wrist, the one with the mark of my past, and the hope for my future came into view, and for once the sight of my skin didn't turn my stomach.

Because Aaliyah would also rise above those demons that haunted me, just like her symbol covered the ink that had been my brand of damnation.

Lost for words, I pulled back, not able to take my palm off her cheek as I released her hand. I just motioned to the envelope, and she opened it carefully. She pulled out the only photo we had of Nero, her eyes scanning the page. Watching them go wide as her face paled had my entire stomach twisting.

She set it on her lap, swallowing. Such fear had no place on her face, and the gravity of that look sank into my stomach. The joy that had come from being hers suddenly disappeared.

"Osiris," she started, hesitating, "I need to tell you something."

My gaze glued on her rapidly paling face, and the way she glanced at the picture she held so delicately in her hand. *No.*

But she didn't get to finish her thought, and I didn't have any more time to process what that look could mean as a knock chimed against the front door. I turned away from Aaliyah and focused on the lack of breath from whoever had come to our home.

There had been no trigger in the wards, no hint that someone had shown up. That was enough for me to stand and step in front of Aaliyah, keeping her at my back as I strained to hear anything else.

Just a steady heartbeat. My chest ached, and I looked at Aaliyah over my shoulder.

"Stay here, *lux mea,*" I stressed.

This didn't bode well.

I trudged toward the steps, but before I could register who it was or even make it to the door of the leisure room, there was a sickening crunch and searing pain down my spine. Whoever it was moved so fast I hadn't even seen their face before I felt nothing.

Pitch-black claimed my sight, and Ali's cry followed me into oblivion.

CHAPTER 62

AALIYAH

Osiris hit the ground, his body crumbling unnaturally, his head twisted fully around. Everything around me stood still, like I was forced into a *Rend* as I waited for him to move. To *breathe*. But he didn't, still like *death* against the cold oak floors.

"Osiris?" I asked, waiting ... always waiting to see a spirit. I took a step toward him, disjointed and off-center, just as his arm twitched.

Not dead. He was alive; *I* was alive. I knew by the thunderous beat of my heart and the breaths that fought their way out of my chest like rabid animals trying to tear me apart. *Alive,* and standing just beyond the threshold of the mosaic glass door of the game room.

My eyes traveled up from Osiris's body and settled on the figure that had dropped him like it was nothing. But my mind, as frayed as it was, refused to understand what I was seeing, *who* I was seeing. Because standing over Osiris's body, face twisted in a crazed grimace, was the one person I never thought I'd see again.

Or rather, his brother.

Sebek stood with his arms crossed over his suit-clad chest. Stripes of red-brown covered the material, the fraying edges of cuffs dipped red. His heavy posture contrasted with the laxity of the rest of his body. His face held a twisted glower, his red eyes crinkling at the corners, their red hue glowing in the low light of the room. His black hair was brushed back, not

467

a *strand* out of place. I recoiled on instinct, taking a step back, overwhelmed by fear.

He felt like torment.

Monster.

Sebek, realizing I was there, turned to me. Shock and a horrid possessiveness seared in his red eyes, and his volatile expression morphed into a rage-filled scream that shook the room. It was an expanding cry that bled aggression.

"*You* shouldn't be here," he seethed. His eyes, manic and crazed, shot up to me as I stepped back again, slamming directly into the door to the library. Thoth's carvings dug into my back, and the sneer he sent my way was enough to keep me frozen to the ground. "You shouldn't be here!"

Sebek Ra, my *uncle.*

"It wasn't supposed to be you with them, *never you*. Why are you *here?*"

He took a step forward, and my mind couldn't comprehend that this man was anything but my idol, but the man who used to sing me to sleep and share cookies when he thought Mom wasn't looking.

Another step and my breath dropped from my lungs.

"Do you know who I am?" I asked, choking when fury flooded his eyes. I looked at Osiris, suddenly throwing my entire attention at him and his still unmoving body. I needed to protect him, keep Sebek's eyes on me. His fists clenched so hard I heard bones crack, but I didn't stop, unable to keep myself from speaking as I looked at the man that was close to home. "Do you know *me*? My dad, Arvand—"

There was barely a breath between my father's name and when Sebek was in front of me, his hand in my hair. His fingers dug in, insistent but not painful, as he tipped my head to look at him.

"Wait—" I cried, gasping as his hand tightened.

He pulled until I was standing on my tiptoes, his face just inches from mine.

"Do not say his name," he snarled. The smell of blood and copper suddenly made my head spin, and I realized he was covered in it. "*Never* say his name."

Then we were moving as he dragged me across the floor, past Osiris's slumped body and the mosaic door, before heading down the stairs.

"Wait, please! Why are you doing this?" I screamed, trying to pull away. I wasn't sure what awaited me outside, but I didn't want to know. This wasn't my dad, this was Sebek. The Maker that made my men tremble and snapped Osiris's neck. "Please, you don't have to do this. I'm your niece. Please, *just talk to me.*"

It made my head burn and made the man that looked so much like my father snarl. There was no hope in his gaze for a conversation, just like there was no hope of finding the warmth I'd secretly hoped I'd find in his eyes.

He was just empty, a shell of anger and mania.

"Stop your struggling, *Glass*," he hissed, his grip tightening enough for sparks of pain to burst at the roots of my hair.

But any fight I had in me flooded away. The way he said it, the breath of a word that always found its way into my memories. It was jaded and cracked along the edges. There was a hint of madness that made the ending hiss off his lips.

Glass.

I *knew* that voice, my body telling me as much as I froze solid, unable to even breathe. I knew that voice like it was ingrained in my soul, and as if responding to it, my *mantra* started.

Never make noise.

Because they got more violent when I made noise.

Castillion used to fall into fits, where even an off breath would cause him to spiral and become unhinged with savage rage. Even now, with the scalding grip of Sebek's hand over my mouth, holding it closed so I couldn't scream. My mantra had been for *Castillion* because it was always better to stay silent, rather than deal with his reaction if it happened to be a day when *he* was in. The leader that had always brushed the corners of my mind, but I couldn't see. For sir *Amoun.*

He was a ghost, a man who never showed his face, but was always watching. A man whose *voice* still echoed in my brain, and the way he'd scold the doctors for straying from what he wanted. Strayed from getting my blood above all else.

And he used to hate *it when I screamed.*

Sebek, the Maker of the men I held so close, my blood uncle ...

Was the leader of Ascension Rising.

To be continued...

Need more to sink your teeth into?

Then come and join my newsletter! You'll get exclusive chapters about how the guys found and built their home. Along with this, you can expect to be the first to hear about all things book (and sometimes life) related. Including being the first to see cover reveals, exclusive commissioned art, and new ideas in the works!

You can find the sign on my website!: https://krrainbolt.com

Still craving more? Then stick around for a brief look at the third book in the Ascension Rising Series, **Of Ash and Blood**. See you all soon!

Of Ash and Blood

Book 3 of the Ascension Rising Series
Coming Soon!

What would you do to live?

The Eternium ball grows ever closer, and with it, comes old foes that threaten to shatter the already strained bond of the Vivas Crypt. Now, I'm left stumbling with a whole new set of problems, each more complex than the last.

Ascension Rising, the ones responsible for years of torture, is looking for me, and there's no telling what they'll do when they find me or how they'll punish me for escaping them.

My growing attraction to the Vampires who saved me, and the ever present reality that death is only one Rend away, drive us forward. We need to figure out what I am and find a way to survive the Eternium all in one breath. It will be a miracle if we all make it out alive.

And if I've learned anything ... ***it's that miracles don't happen to me.***

A Note For You, Dear Reader

If you've made it this far, then this is for you, dear reader. Thank you for jumping into this story and enjoying the twists and turns that Ali and the guys' adventure has taken so far. Book two was a wild ride to write, and I hope, for a while at least, I gave you someplace new and exciting to explore. I can't say how excited I am to continue this series and this experience with you.

Thank you for being you.

With that being said, it would mean the world to me if you could take a second to leave a review on this book's Amazon or Goodreads page. Reviews are like lifeblood for many indie authors, me included, and your support—with even just a sentence—would help me leaps and bounds.

Thank you so very much for your support. I couldn't do this without you guys!

Acknowledgments

First, to my readers. Your support means everything to me, and know that this book is only possible because of you. I've always wanted to share my stories, and I'll forever be thankful that you've taken a chance on me and picked up this book. From the bottom of my heart, *thank you.*

To my family and friends, thank you for shaping me into who I am. If you do end up reading this, let's just pretend you didn't read the sex scenes, okay? Thanks. Love you guys.

To my betas and alphas: Gisele Lærke, Amanda, Amy, Gitte, Maria, Rachel, Rebecca, Nicci, Alexis, and Phyllis. You guys gave me the confidence to keep moving forward. It was only because of your kind feedback, support, and friendships that this novel is what it is today. You guys truly are the best, and I can't even express how much you all mean to me. I'll forever be grateful to you!

To the ARC readers. If you made it this far, I hope you loved it. Thank you for giving this novel a read and for giving it a chance. I'll forever be grateful for that!

To *Artscandare Book Cover Design*. Thank you for giving me the cover of my dreams. It couldn't have turned out more perfect! Your endless kindness and willingness to work with me was so appreciated.

To Ashley Olivier, thank you for being the best editor I could have asked for. You were extraordinary, and I have you to thank for how this book shines. Thank you!

And of course, Dominic, the absolute love of my life. I've said it before, and I'll say it a million more times. Thank you for always believing in me. This book and this series are better because of you. I love you, handsome, ten trillion percent.

About the Author

Born and raised in the Wyoming Rocky Mountains, K. R. Rainbolt, or Kennady, is a lover of cakes and all things sweet. She also has a *minor* obsession with suits, but who doesn't love a nice, crisp waistcoat, right? She has been crafting stories for as long as she can remember, and nothing makes her happier than bringing a character to life. Now, as a first-time publisher, she's excited to share them with everyone else as well.

Kennady spends a lot of time writing, both for her novels and the occasional video game mod. When she's not immersed in one of her stories, she can be found spending time with the love of her life Dominic or playing with her fur baby Marlie.

Kennady loves to bowl, fish, play video games, and watch movies (the spookier, the better). Along with this, she is big on the world of science and research, and as a Chemical Engineer, she loves to include hints of her studies in her novels.

Lastly, a word of advice that her grandmother used to say: *Remember, live life.*

After all, you only have one, so you better spend it doing something you love!

Want to know more about Kennady? Then stalk her on social media! You can find her Official Facebook group, TikTok, Instagram and more on her Linktree: https://linktr.ee/k.r.rainboltauthor

Glossary

Latin

Vivas — To live
Lux mea — My light
Et in domum suam in solem — Home of the sun
Frater — Brother
Te desum — I miss you
Rex interfectorem — Kingslayer
Fabula Fortium — A Tale of the Brave
Mortui carmen — Song of the Dead

Icelandic/Norse

Elskan — Darling (term of endearment)
Fífl — Idiot or Fool
Úlfhéðinn (singular)/*Úlfhéðnar* (plural) — Wearers of the wolf skin, or Odin's special warriors
Smár Valkyrja — Small Valkyrie, or tiny warrior.
Muna langt fram — Remember from a long time back
Dreyrugr — Bloodstained
Lítár hana — Look at her
Ég elska þig — I love you

Aboriginal Australian

Mob — Family

Greek

Vrykólakas — Loosely translated to vampires

Coptic

Ab — My heart and soul

World Specific

Baba — Old Siren dialect meaning grandmother, or matriarch.
Charm — A Vampire ability.
Chronomancer — A Sorceri that can control the flow of time to a degree. They can often look

into the future a short distance and read someone's past with a touch. They can also slow and speed up time in an area.

Crypt — A grouping of Vampires, typically living together. A Crypt does not have to contain Vampires of only one Maker.

Echomancer — A Sorceri that can mimic the abilities of the other Sorceri classes to a degree. They are a jack of all trades but master of none.

Eternal — A leader of a Natural Race. Each defined Natural Race has an Eternal.

Flit — A Vampire ability that allows them to move at extremely fast speeds. Their physical form warps when flitting, making them appear as little more than a burst of ashes.

Forgemancer — A Sorceri with the ability to enchant or craft magical items. They specialize in charm and ward making.

Hemomancer — A Sorceri with the ability to manipulate blood cells, and in some cases, other cells as well.

Himal — A figure that most Waterborne Naturals consider to be their primary deity.

Maker's Call (often called The Call) — This is an undeniable pull that a Vampire Maker can place on his spawn. It is a Charm that they must follow. As time goes on, this pull can lessen, and they can resist it. It doesn't go away, unless the one who placed it dies.

Natural — The term for supernatural beings in this universe.

Rend — Aaliyah's affliction. The first part of a Rend is her soul leaving her body for a time. This time grows in length with each Rend she has. The second part of a Rend is the memory. Rends are often brought on by 'triggers' or events that remind her brain of something from the past.

Siren's Call — The Sirens' ability to muddle minds. This often makes people forget periods of time or do small things at the Sirens' behest.

Sorceri — They are human wielders of magic, though they are still considered Naturals.

Swell - A grouping of Waterborn Naturals (including but not limited to Sirens, Mermaids, Selkies, etc.).

The Flame — A gift passed down the Vivas bloodline from one of the original six Vampires, Ferrion.

PRINCE'S CODE

You okay? — Pointer finger to the nose while nodding.

Danger — Crossing arms over chest in an 'x' formation.

All clear — Pointer and middle finger pointed at the eyes.

Quiet — Pointer finger over lips in 'shush' motion.

Tell me? — Middle finger dragged from lips to left ear.

Sorry — Hands with interlaced fingers brought from chest to lips.

Forever — Hand settled over the heart, with the pinky and ring finger tucked underneath the hand.

Idiot — Swirling a finger around the ear.

Rend — Hands together, palms against one another, before they are pulled slowly apart.

www.ingramcontent.com/pod-product-compliance
Lightning Source LLC
Chambersburg PA
CBHW022253310726
48973CB00001B/55